and now for Julia, to whose Big Tiger I'll play Christian, or vice versa, at any time. With love, Susan

May 12, 1968

Big Tiger *and* Christian

By

FRITZ MÜHLENWEG

Illustrated by RAFAELLO BUSONI

PANTHEON BOOKS

NEW YORK

 Published in New York by Pantheon Books, a division of Random House, Inc., and in Toronto, Canada, by Random House of Canada, Limited. Manufactured in the United States of America.

Library of Congress catalog card number: 52-9672

Translated from the German
by Isabel and Florence McHugh
Original Edition: In Geheimer Mission durch die Wüste Gobi,
Verlag Herder, Freiburg

1st printing, September, 1952
2nd printing, February, 1955
3rd printing, November, 1957
4th printing, April, 1961
5th printing, August, 1963

CONTENTS

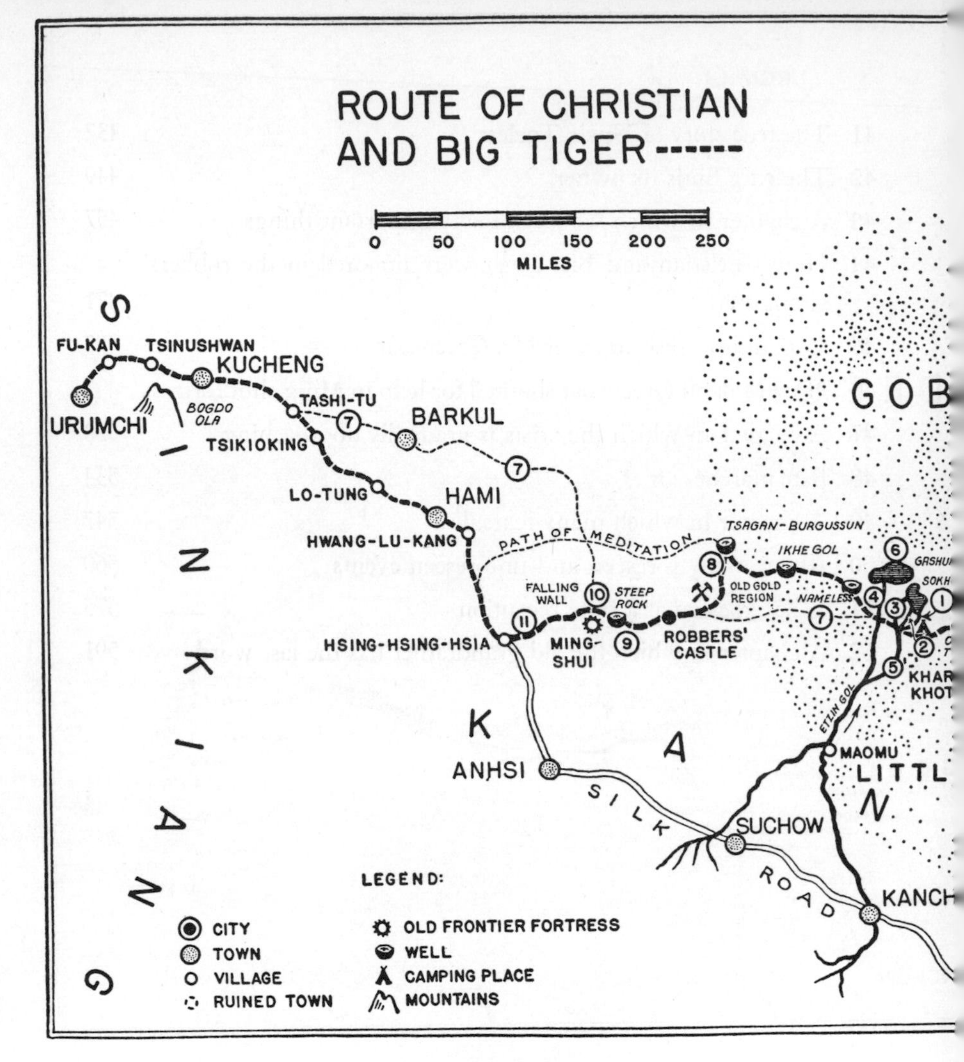

THE WESTERN SHEET

1 The Goitzin Gol, where the gasoline depot was
2 The Narin Gol, where Naidang and Sevenstars lived
3 The Dondur Gol
4 The Morin Gol, where Mr. Ping lived and traded
5 The Ikhe Gol, where the old märin lived
6 Here Moonlight lay when he got the sword wound
7 The route of Ma's caravan
8 The Hidden Well which Dampignak got dug
9 Here the meeting with Dambit took place
10 Stony Brook Valley, where the frontier captain, Kao-Cheng, lay in wait
11 Where Dambit met Greencoat

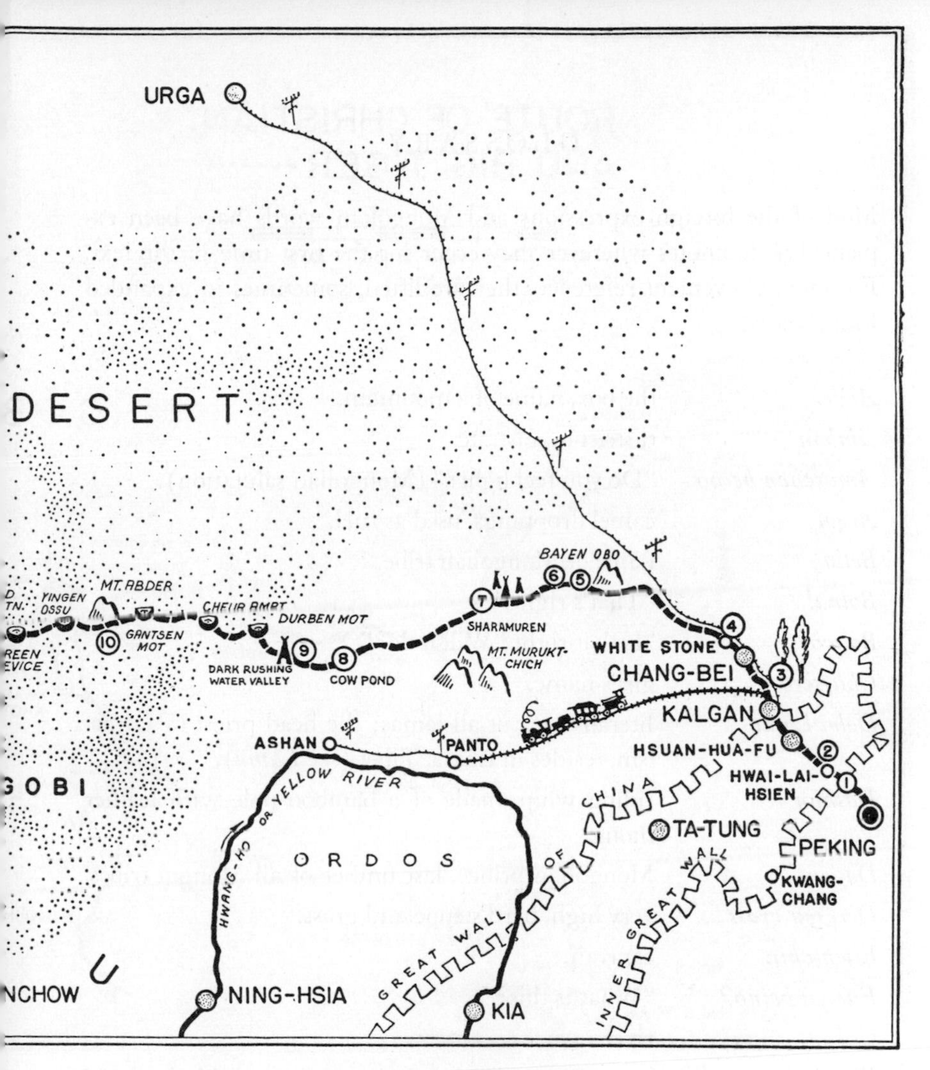

THE SOUTHERN SHEET

1 Ching-lung-giao, where the battle for the Nan-ku Pass was lost
2 Hwai-lai-hsien, where General Wu-Pei-Fu had his headquarters
3 The inn of the "Two Little Silver Dishes"
4 Here stood the inn "Joyous Prosperity"
5 Bayen Obo, at the foot of which the King of the Sunits camped
6 Orte Golen Sume, the monastery where Christian and Big Tiger met the King of the Sunit Mongols
7 The tents of the rich Mongol Pandiriktchi
8 Cow Pond, where Uncle Chen and Dragonstooth lived
9 The Valley of Dark Rushing Water, where Nowhere-at-all threw the leaf to the winds
10 The dangerous mountain, Abder, the Box

GLOSSARY

Most of the foreign expressions and Mongolian words have been explained in footnotes wherever they occur for the first time in the text. For more convenient reference, they are listed, sometimes in expanded form, below.

Abder	the box, name of a mountain.
Amban	district magistrate.
Amorchen beino	"Do you feel light?" (Mongolian salutation).
Argal	camel droppings, used as fuel.
Belin	name of Mongolian tribe.
Bolna!	"That's right."
Bolwo?	"Is that right? Will it do?"
Chussera	girl's name.
Dalai Lama	literally: sea of all lamas; the head priest of Lamaism, resides in Lhasa, Tibet (*see Lama*).
Dashior	riding whip, made of a bamboo pole with leather thong.
Dagan	Mongolian prince, last unifier of all Mongol tribes.
Deresen grass	very high, hard steppeland grass.
Eijen-chin	caravan.
Ene yu beino?	"What is this?"
Gol	river.
Five human relationships	sovereign and subject; parent and child; husband and wife; senior and junior; friend and friend—all lie at the heart of the moral code formulated by Confucius.
Genghis Khan	Mongolian conqueror, 1167-1227, one of the most famous, successful and destructive of Mongolian leaders.
Haddak	blue (rarely white) silk scarf always given with a present.

Hammagua	"Don't worry; it does not matter."
Hung-hu-tse	red beard, name for bandit.
Ishang	long jacket worn as overcoat.
Kang	Chinese bed that can be heated like a stove.
Kansu	Chinese province.
Khara-khoto	The Black City (present name of the ruins of the ancient town Etzina).
Khoshut	Mongolian tribe.
Koorultai	legislative assembly of Mongol princes.
kwai, kwai!	hurry!
Lai, lai!	come!
Lama	priest or monk of Lamaism, a form of Buddhism prevalent in Tibet and Mongolia.
Living Buddha	Lama who is regarded as Buddha reborn, and enjoys highest veneration.
Loess ravine	deep clefts caused by water, wind and drought.
Märin	chief herdsman.
Middle Kingdom	name given to the Chinese empire as occupying the center of the earth.
Mongol joss	the law of the Mongols.
Nine coins	throwing nine coins several times is a means of fortune telling.
Obo	a shrine or heap of stones; *obos* are the signposts of the desert.
Orte Golen Sume	monastery at the Long River.
Ossu	water.
Sarts	inhabitants of Eastern Turkestan, a part of the Chinese province of Sinkiang.
Shara-mot	yellow wood, an evergreen shrub.
Silk Road	the most important and romantic trade route in the world, which went westward over desert and steppe via Khotan to India, Persia and Europe, and eastward vie Tun-hwang and Suchow to China proper.

Sunit	Mongolian tribe.
Tinger metne	"Heaven only knows."
Torgut	Mongolian tribe.
Tungan	Chinese of Mohammedan faith.
Wang	Mongolian for king.
Yamen	government building, town hall.
Yurt	circular Mongolian felt tent.

ANCIENT CHINESE DIVISION OF DAY AND NIGHT INTO TWELVE DOUBLE HOURS

11 – 1 A.M.	Hour of the Rat
1 – 3 A.M.	Hour of the Ox
3 – 5 A.M.	Hour of the Tiger
5 – 7 A.M.	Hour of the Hare
7 – 9 A.M.	Hour of the Dragon
9 – 11 A.M.	Hour of the Snake
11 – 1 P.M.	Hour of the Horse
1 – 3 P.M.	Hour of the Sheep
3 – 5 P.M.	Hour of the Ape
5 – 7 P.M.	Hour of the Cock
7 – 9 P.M.	Hour of the Dog
9 – 11 P.M.	Hour of the Boar

BIG TIGER *and* CHRISTIAN

For those who want to know exactly:

In the Spring of 1922, General Wu-Pei-Fu took Peking. Those were the days of the civil wars or "generals' wars," of bandit chiefs who prospered, and of presidents of the Chinese Republic who were powerless. In those times one came across many splendid people, but also many not so creditable characters. They appear in this tale, good and bad, just as they really were. The author knew many of them personally, and he celebrated the New Year Festival of 1932/1933 in Naidang's *yurt*. It was from him and from Sevenstars that he learned most of his story, for which he owes them a debt of thanks.

THE AUTHOR

1 BIG TIGER AND COMPASS MOUNTAIN DECIDE TO GO KITE-FLYING

A BOY born in Peking must know a great deal. Christian was twelve years old and already knew all sorts of things. He could speak Chinese just as well as English, and besides he knew a whole lot about snaffles, stirrups and Mexican saddles, for he was often on the glacis, where you rode if you had a horse.

The great thing was to get away an hour's distance or so from home, but this was difficult, as the amah was always on the lookout. The old amah was the children's nurse. She had brought up Christian and therefore she treated him as if he were still a toddler, whereas he was a big boy already going to Junior High, and he knew his way about Peking well.

"My amah's crazy," said Christian to his friend Big Tiger, whom he met on the city wall. "She should be content with looking after my sister; *she's* still little."

Hu-Ta, the Big Tiger, nodded. "Try speaking to her more respectfully and calling her 'O Venerable Chariot!' " he said.

"Will that help?"

"Yes, you'll see it will."

Christian sat down on the stone steps which led from the high city wall to the Tower, still higher up, where the heavy black bronze instruments of the old observatory were.

Big Tiger sat down beside Christian. He was the same age but a little smaller, and he had black shiny hair. During the New Year festival he had worn a gray coat which reached to his toes and Christian had hardly known him he looked so dignified. Luckily the festival of the New Year lasted only three weeks, and now it was March.

The sun was shining warmly and pleasantly. Big Tiger was wearing ordinary padded trousers and a jacket with long sleeves.

"Have you got a string?" asked Christian.

"I have one four hundred paces long."

"Then we can fly the kite," said Christian. "Tomorrow is Wednesday and I've no school in the afternoon."

"No good to fly it here," said Big Tiger. "The wind is always from the south these days. We must try it at the Ha-ta-men Gate."

"That's no good, either," said Christian, "because the amah takes my sister along the wall at the Ha-ta-men Gate."

"Sorry," said Big Tiger. "I didn't think of that. Then it's best for us to go to Chi-chi-men Station. There's a big square there."

"I've never been there. Is it very far away?"

"We will set off early in the afternoon," suggested Big Tiger. "Then we'll be back by evening."

"I'll see what I can do."

"That's not enough. You must say 'yes.' "

"All right, yes!"

"Good," said Big Tiger, standing up.

"Why did I have to say 'yes'?" asked Christian.

Big Tiger hesitated. "You must be big-hearted," he said, looking at Christian in the way he always did when he was going to ask a friendly service.

Now he will call me by my first name, thought Christian, and he thought this great fun, because Chinese boys cannot pronounce "r" no matter how hard they try.

Not that Big Tiger had tried to for a long time past. He simply said "Kwi-Chan" because it sounded so like Christian, and was a splendid Chinese name which meant "Compass Mountain."

"Kwi-Chan," said Big Tiger, "you have no school tomorrow afternoon, but I have. So you must go to my teacher and say: 'Most venerable uncle! Hu-Ta, the Big Tiger, who lives two doors from me, cannot come to school and therefore I, his poor friend, come to you. Big Tiger regrets that he is not in good health today, but he will drink some tea and tomorrow he will come to school.' Have you got that right?"

"It's a long speech," said Christian, "but I'll remember it."

"Be here on the wall when the midday gun goes off."

"I'll be here," said Christian.

2 OF THE SPLENDID ASCENT OF THE KITE AND OF ITS LAMENTABLE END

Boom!

The midday gun resounded over Peking, and anyone whose watch was wrong could set it right. But most people in Peking have not got watches, and they do not need them. They do not even need the midday gun, for the sun rises and sets, and with a little practice anyone can see where the sun is and so know how late it is.

"Where are the guns they fire at midday?" asked Christian, as Big Tiger came along with his kite.

"I don't know and I don't care," said Big Tiger. "Have you spoken to my teacher?"

"I gave him your message, and he's very sorry for you."

"I don't believe that. Probably he's only polite to you because your father is a doctor who can do more than just say 'Put out your tongue.'"

"Indeed, no, Big Tiger, that's not so. Your teacher looked at me kindly and he actually sighed. 'Big Tiger,' he said, 'is a person for whom one must feel great pity.' "

"But don't you know that means that he'll spank me tomorrow?" cried Big Tiger.

"Oh, is that it?" said Christian. "*Now* I understand."

"It can't be helped," said Big Tiger indifferently. "Let's go to the station."

Christian took the reel with the thin silk cord, and Big Tiger carried the yellow paper kite which his father had given him on the feast known as "The Dragon raises his head." They walked along the city wall, at this time deserted and bright with sunlight. From here one could see over the roofs of the whole city of Peking. The great buildings, many stories high, and the imperial palace, towered over the low gray expanse of streets. The tiled roofs of the imperial city shone yellow; streamers and little flags fluttered over the shops and booths, and apricot trees bloomed in the gardens.

At Good Example Tower Big Tiger and Christian descended from the city wall. Now they had to look sharp. In the crowd of horse-drawn vehicles, pedestrians and rickshaws one could easily lose one's way. There were, as well, trucks full of soldiers which raised great clouds of dust. But Big Tiger knew the way. He was familiar with the quiet side lanes, and after half an hour's walk the north wall of the imperial city became visible.

In the streets were marching soldiers in gray uniforms going in the same direction as the boys. They were merry and laughing, and one of them said to Christian: "Little foreign devil, would you like to come to the war too?"

"I'm not a foreign devil," Christian said. "I was born in Peking and I can speak Chinese as well as you can. But I don't want to go to the war."

"Now, now, little brother," retorted the soldier, "don't be so cross! Where are you going?"

"We are going to Chi-chi-men Station," said Big Tiger. "There's a square where a good wind blows. Kites fly very high from there."

"I would like to see how your kite flies," said the soldier. And another soldier cried: "Just hold my rifle a minute; I've only to look at a kite to know if it will fly well or not."

Big Tiger gave the soldier the kite and took the gun. Soon many soldiers had handled the kite, and they all treated it with due respect and remarked how very well it was made.

At the Chi-chi-men Gate there was a tie-up. Many people were waiting to get through, but most of them turned back when they heard that only soldiers were being allowed through. The soldiers had to go to the war, and so the station was reserved for them.

"Stay with us," said the soldier whose rifle Big Tiger had carried. "We'll get you through."

"Most respectful thanks," replied Big Tiger and Christian.

But the sentries at the gate were on the lookout. "Halt!" shouted one of them, who looked at least a sergeant. "Where do you want to go, you little scoundrels? Back with you!"

"They're not scoundrels," said the soldier. "They're my young brothers."

The sergeant pointed to the blond Christian. "Is he also your young brother?" he asked.

"Yes," replied the soldier. "We're a big family." He passed through. And because the sergeant was busy watching the grown-ups, the boys slipped through the gate after him.

So here was Chi-chi-men Station. The tin roof shone in the sun, but it was still a long way off, and the big square, which was usually crowded with many boys and also grownups flying kites, was quite empty. It was almost uncanny.

"Come up to the station with us," said the soldier. "We want to be there when you let off the kite. It goes better in company."

On the track alongside the station building stood a long train. A lot of soldiers were entraining horses, cars and artillery.

"What are you doing with the guns?" asked Christian.

"We'll leave them behind us if the enemy comes. Then he'll have something to keep him busy."

"Is he really coming?" asked Christian.

"Yes, he'll be here soon," said the gunner. "We're going a bit of the way to meet him."

Christian would have liked to know who the enemy was, and if it would be bad if he came to Peking, but just at that moment Big Tiger laid the kite on the ground and straightened out the long paper tail. "Put a stone on the end, Kwi-Chan," he called out, and Christian did so. Then they both fastened the cord. Christian wetted his first finger, held it out in the air and said: "The wind is from the south."

Big Tiger nodded. Even without wetting his first finger he knew it was blowing from the south. Christian took the cord, and when he had walked about three hundred yards into the wind he began to run. Then Big Tiger ran a little too before letting off the kite. The kite was a really good one. Although there was very little wind it rose easily. The soldiers stood around in a semicircle, shading their eyes with their hands and calling: "Bravo!" and saying to each other:

"It's a fine specimen."

"It's first-class."

"It has a grand pull."

"There's not much wind, but its belly is full of it."

"Now it's becalmed! Oh, woe!"

"We'll whistle to the wind!"

"Yes," they all cried, and they began whistling to the wind. And the gunners came along too, and they helped to whistle and call out: *"Lai, lai, lai! Ni yao lai!"* which meant, "Come, come, come, come! O come along please!"

But the wind did not come. Instead the Captain came, a bamboo cane tucked under his arm, and began whistling with the soldiers. But that did not help either. The kite hovered in the air and would not go any higher.

"What are your names?" asked the Captain.

"He's Compass Mountain and I'm Big Tiger."

The Captain grinned and then he had a bright idea. "Mountain and Tiger," he said, "go well together. Are you friends?"

"Yes, we're friends," said Christian.

"We love one another," said Big Tiger.

"Then come with me to the rear car. We're starting at once and you can travel a bit with us. Then the kite will be drawn up into the sky."

"But we can only go a little way," said Christian.

"We have to go to school in the morning," said Big Tiger.

They both spoke at the same time, but the Captain only laughed and took the kite string himself. Apparently he knew something about flying a kite. He ran with skipping steps, drawing the kite back and letting it free again, until they got to the open freightcar at the end of the train. With one jump he was in. "Come on up and don't be afraid! Your teacher won't spank you until tomorrow!" And he called out to the soldiers: "Hurry up, boys! Hurry up, you lazy rascals! Jump in, you hundred sleepyheads!"

Then the soldiers came at the double and jumped on the train. The gunners sat on the guns, the Captain blew a whistle, the engine began puffing, and the train wound slowly out of the station. Instantly the cord tightened and the kite sailed nobly into the upper air, where the wind was strong. It was a splendid sight to see it following the train, rising ever higher and higher. The Captain paid out all the string.

"Now we must get off," said Christian.

"Please stop the train, Commander," said Big Tiger.

"My word," said the Captain, "I'd quite forgotten about you two! Kite-flying is such a fine sport." He tied the cord to a gun, took the whistle from his tunic pocket, and whistled as loudly as he could, three times, four times, ah, what am I saying?—ten, twenty times. But the train did not stop. It went even faster, and what with the pounding of the locomotive and the rattle of the wheels, it was quite impossible for the engineer to hear anything.

The kite was still following the train, but the cord was pulling very hard. Suddenly there was a jerk. The string had broken. The kite gave a leap, turned over in mid-air, glided downward, righted itself again, but then it lost its balance. Far away it fell into some fields where peasants in blue smocks were digging and hoeing. They did not see how the kite bored into the earth, how the smooth wooden framework broke up, the beautiful yellow tissue paper tore, and the long tail curled up.

Tears came into Christian's eyes, but he pulled himself together when he saw that his friend was smiling.

"It can't be helped," said Big Tiger.

"It can't be helped," said the Captain too, but he meant the train, which was going faster and faster and was at that very moment roaring through Ching-ho Station.

3 THE GREAT BATTLE OF THE NAN-KU PASS

"PERHAPS IT will stop in Chang-ping," said the Captain Then you can walk home along the track. But it will be night before you reach Peking."

"The city gates will be shut by then," said Big Tiger.

What will my amah say, thought Christian.

But the stationmaster of Chang-ping did not want soldiers in his station. So he set the signals for a clear-ahead, and when he had bowed to the train in accordance with the rules, he telephoned to his colleague at Nan-ku telling him to do the same with the signals there. So the train went through Nan-ku also without stopping, and evening came. Big Tiger and Christian looked at each other miserably, and Big Tiger said as calmly as he could: "It can't be helped."

"It can't be helped," said the Captain too. "Take two blankets and lie down to sleep."

But Christian and Big Tiger did not want to sleep. They hung the blankets round their shoulders and looked out at the high Hsingan Mountains, which they saw for the first time. The train was going slowly now, for the track was uphill. Soon they could see huts and fields, and the highway on which men on horseback and others leading loaded asses were going down to the valley. There were small squads of marching soldiers, too, who waved and called out something, but it was impossible to make out what it was. The Captain frowned but said nothing.

Soon it grew dark. The crescent moon showed over the western mountain peaks, and in the valley a dog was barking. Then silence fell. Only the pounding of the engine and the rattle of the wheels was to be heard.

Suddenly the train whistled and there was complete darkness. A great thick cloud of smoke rose up. Christian was terrified, and Big Tiger was frightened too.

"Don't be afraid," said the Captain. "We're in a tunnel. We shall arrive at Ching-lung-giao soon, and then we must all get out. If you're lucky you'll be able to travel back to Peking early in the morning in the empty cars."

"And if we're not lucky?" asked Christian.

"Well, then you're simply unlucky," said the Captain. "You'll just have to put up with it."

Scarcely had the Captain said this than the train drew into the station. Alongside the track there was a little station house, and a monument to the memory of the Chinese engineer who had built the railway. Every train had to stop here and reverse the engine.

"You can stay in the train and sleep," said the Captain. "We shall not be going on until morning, or else we shall unload here. It all depends."

"What do you mean by 'It all depends,' Commander?" asked Big Tiger.

"Are you brave?" asked the Captain by way of reply.

"It all depends, Commander," said Big Tiger.

The Captain laughed and said Big Tiger was a young rascal. He pointed to the black mouth of the tunnel through which they had just come, and to another some way off. "We have to get through there to reach the pass," he said. "But the enemy may be at the other end before us."

"Who are your enemy?" asked Christian.

"Our enemy are . . ." But the Captain stopped short, for suddenly something like lightning flashed from the mouth of the tunnel, and there was a great bang.

"Here they are already!" cried the Captain. "Out with you quickly! We've lost the battle!" Thereupon he hopped down as light as a feather from the train. The gunners jumped after him leaving their guns behind just as they had said they would. In a trice all had disappeared.

Christian would have liked to run away too, but he didn't know where to run to.

"Stay here!" cried Big Tiger. "We must lie flat. It can't be helped."

Ah, thought Christian, what will my amah say? But he lay down obediently beside Big Tiger on the floor of the freightcar, and their hearts beat very loudly. They did not dare to look out. If they had, they would only have seen the dark nozzles of the guns and the shimmering stars overhead.

For a full hour they lay like this. The silence all around was dreadful. The axles of the train, which had been red-hot from the journey, now crackled as they cooled. That was the only sound, so no wonder they were thoroughly frightened. Moreover, our two heroes were freezing with cold, but in spite of this they did not dare to lift their noses.

4 HOW IT FARES WITH ONE WHO IS NOT ON THE WINNING SIDE

Two SOLDIERS of the Third Division, called the Unconquerable, stood looking down for quite a while at the two survivors of the great battle. The soldiers were brave and gallant fellows.

They had been patrolling through the tunnel just at the moment that the train came into Ching-lung-giao Station. Precisely as the Captain said "Our enemy are . . ." they had raised their guns and had fired, and immediately fired again, and then again, so that the Captain should know who exactly the enemy were. Then they saw the Captain jump down from the train and the gunners jump down after him.

When they had all run away the two soldiers realized that with six blank cartridges they had captured a whole train, with horses, trucks and cannon. But they had not been able to take a single prisoner, since none had remained to be taken. Only when they came to the last freightcar had they any luck.

"But they're only little boys," said the first soldier gently.

"They must grow up," said the second soldier.

"But perhaps they're dead?"

"No. They're still alive; they're trembling."

"We're shivering because we're so cold," cried Big Tiger, raising his head.

"Stand up!" ordered the first soldier.

"Do you know what you are?" asked the second soldier.

"He's Compass Mountain and I'm Big Tiger."

"That's not what I mean," said the first soldier.

"You're prisoners of war," said the second soldier.

Christian hung his head and so did Big Tiger. It was dreadful suddenly to find oneself a prisoner of war.

"Do you understand anything about engines?" asked the first soldier.

"No," said Big Tiger and Christian. "We understand nothing about them."

"Then you're stupid into the bargain," said the second soldier. "Now come along with us!"

"May we take the blankets with us, Commander?" asked Big Tiger.

"Take them, but hurry up! We have only a few minutes."

The two soldiers took their guns under their arms and led Big Tiger and Christian down to the middle of the train. There there was one car with a little turret on top of it and an iron ladder up to it. When they had all climbed up the first soldier said: "Look at this wheel with a handle to it. You must both start turning it with all your might as soon as the train whistles. It's a brake, and you may stop only when it won't turn any more."

"We'll turn it without ceasing," said Big Tiger.

"We're going straight uphill to the pass," declared the second soldier. "We've captured you two rascals, and all the horses and guns. So you have to do what we want you to do. Perhaps it will succeed, perhaps it won't. It's dangerous—but that's war."

"It can't be helped," said Big Tiger.

The two soldiers laughed and went off. As they could not reverse the engine by themselves they merely threw the switch instead and then they climbed on to the engine.

The two soldiers belonged to a railway detachment and they knew their job. After a quarter of an hour a mighty shower of sparks rose from the funnel. "We're off!" shouted the soldiers. "Hold tight, you two in front!"

"We're holding tight!" cried Christian and Big Tiger. Nevertheless they fell back against the wall of the caboose when the locomotive started. The buffers of the cars struck violently one upon the other. Then the wheels began to turn obediently.

Immediately afterwards the train entered the tunnel from which the two soldiers had fired. Again there was a thundering roar, and smoke, but this time the smoke came from behind, because the locomotive was pushing the whole long train in front of it.

Christian and Big Tiger wished very much that the tunnel would come to an end. But the tunnel was long and remained dark. The train slowed down, and suddenly a shrill whistle rent the air. It was like a cry of terror.

Immediately Christian and Big Tiger started turning the wheel. At first it was easy but soon it became harder, and they found it all they could do to keep on. At the end of the train the locomotive could be heard panting, its wheels were revolving wildly, and there was a continuous glow of fire on the roof of the tunnel.

For some seconds the train stood still. Then suddenly it began to run backwards. Quite slowly and uncannily the whole train started gliding downhill.

Big Tiger was the first to realize that an accident was threatening. He pushed his shoulder firmly against the handle of the brake. "We've got to hold this wheel fast," he panted. "Our lives aren't worth much now."

Then Christian hung with both hands on to one of the spokes, and so they both remained, exerting all their strength. But the train continued gliding downhill.

At last one of the soldiers came running by. He swung a lantern and called out: "Don't let go, old warriors! Hold fast, noble sons of heroes! Nothing worse could happen to us than this!"

He ran from car to car, taking down the brake shoe which hung by each wheel, and ramming it quickly under. The wheels creaked, the backward slide slowed down, and finally the train stood still. Having reached the last car the soldier came back at a walk. He was happy again, and his lantern glowed cheerfully. "You can let go now," he said. "You've been real men!"

The second soldier climbed down from the locomotive. He was carrying a bag of sweet poppy-seed cakes. The symbols for riches, happiness and a long life were written on them in sugar icing. He shared out the cakes with the long life emblems first, "for we have had a wonderful escape," he said.

Christian and Big Tiger were terribly hungry. "We thank you," they said. "Please excuse us if we eat heartily."

"Eat away," said the soldiers.

When all the cakes had been eaten the first soldier said: "You are prisoners of war, but we trust you!"

"We have eaten your bread," said Big Tiger, "and we are no loafers."

"That's good," said the soldier. "We must stay here and guard the train, which won't move any more. You two must take courage and walk through to the end of the dark tunnel. Then stand and call out 'Gentle Wind.' As soon as someone says 'Brings Success' you can go on, but not before or you will be shot."

"We hear and obey," said Big Tiger and Christian.

"The tunnel sentries will ask: 'Where do you come from?' Answer: 'We are sent by Good Companion and Yellow Arrow.' Then they will ask: 'Where do you want to go?' and you shall say: 'To the great General Wu, for whom we have a message.' Don't let them question you. Be firm and don't chatter. Report what you know and what you have seen only to the General. Ask him to send us another locomotive so that we don't have to stick a hundred years in this tunnel. Do you understand all that?"

"Yes, we understand," said Christian.

"Farewell, elder brothers," said Big Tiger. "We shall go now."

They bowed three times to the soldiers.

"You are polite people," said Good Companion. "One can see that at once," said Yellow Arrow. "Farewell, and may you have many lucky stars!"

5 A CHAPTER IN WHICH WE MAKE THE HONORABLE ACQUAINTANCE OF GENERAL WU-PEI-FU

As LONG as the soldiers' lantern lighted them a little all went well. But they had only got to the last car when Big Tiger stumbled against a plank. It hurt him a lot. "We'll fall often on the stones or the iron rails," he said, feeling the painful spot.

"Wait," said Christian. "I've just thought of something." He climbed up into the last freightcar and crawled around in the dark until he found the bamboo cane which the Captain had left behind when he fled. "Now we needn't be afraid," declared Christian. "Give me your hand."

Big Tiger was surprised, but then he noticed that Christian was feeling his way along the railway line with the stick.

"Have you ever heard of this General Wu-Pei-Fu?" asked Big Tiger.

"Never," said Christian.

"Few know him, but all love him," said Big Tiger. "He's going to beat General Chang-Tso-ling and end the civil war, and then he'll make a happy peace."

They had been walking a full hour when they saw before them a semicircular opening. A few stars were visible and beneath them a nocturnal landscape with the railway lines shining in the middle.

Christian stopped. "Do you remember the password?" he asked. Is it 'Fresh Wind' or 'Pleasant Wind?' "

"It's 'Gentle Wind,' said Big Tiger. We learn at school that wood and wind are gentle. So it's 'Gentle Wind.' "

From now on they were careful not to make noise, and since they wore felt shoes this was possible. They stopped more than a hundred yards from the exit of the tunnel.

"It's best if you call out," said Christian.

Big Tiger raised his hands to his mouth but before he could shout even one word a sharp voice called out: "Who goes there?"

"We're here," said Big Tiger, confused.

"Gentle Wind!" cried Christian promptly.

"Brings Success!" answered the voice.

"May we go on now?" asked Big Tiger.

"Come on!" said the voice. "You seem queer birds."

"We're prisoners of war," said Christian.

"But we're unguarded because we are trusted," said Big Tiger.

They held hands again and walked on with beating hearts toward the mouth of the tunnel. Four soldiers were standing there, wearing fur cloaks and fur caps with ear flaps which left only the face free.

"Where do you come from?" one of them asked.

"Good Companion and Yellow Arrow have sent us."

"Indeed? And where do you want to go?"

"Take us to the great General Wu. We must give him a message."

"What? You?" cried the soldiers, and suddenly they began laughing uproariously, and when one of them stopped, another began. "Your Excellencies' names?" asked one of them, but he could hardly speak for laughing.

"This is Compass Mountain and I am Big Tiger."

The four soldiers clapped their hands gleefully.

"You really mean," cried one of them, "that one of you is Mountain of Charcoal and the other is Black Tiger?"

"Oh, mighty young princes," cried another, "where is your royal domain?"

"Were you born beyond the ocean where the sun makes men black?" asked the fourth.

At this Christian and Big Tiger realized that there was something queer about them. They looked at each other and in spite of the darkness they could see that their faces and hands were black and that their clothes too were covered with soot.

"We're not Negroes," said Christian.

"It will come off when we wash," Big Tiger assured them. "Is there water anywhere?" He looked around and saw a signalman's hut a little way off. Then he started, for a figure in a wide cloak emerged suddenly and stopped between them and the soldiers. No one had noticed the stranger coming. He was wearing a gray military cloak with narrow epaulettes on which were three stars.

"Why are you laughing so loudly?" asked the man severely. "Are you not on sentry duty?"

The soldiers shouldered their rifles in haste and stood to attention. "We beg Your Excellency's pardon," they said.

"You are fools," said the man, "to make a row like this when you should be quiet. You are bad soldiers."

"We admit it," said the soldiers penitently.

The stranger now turned to Big Tiger and Christian. "I have heard what you want. Give me your message. I am General Wu-Pei-Fu."

Big Tiger and Christian bowed very low three times, but they did not venture to say anything. They remained with bowed heads, their blankets around their shoulders, for they knew they were as black as hobgoblins.

"Speak!" said the General.

"We haven't washed yet," said Big Tiger.

"In war," said General Wu-Pei-Fu, amused, "it does not always matter whether one is clean or not. Say what you have to say."

"I'm Compass Mountain," said Christian, "and this is Big Tiger, and we're prisoners of war."

"Pray, how old are you?" asked the General. If it had not been dark they could have seen that he was smiling.

"We're both thirteen years old," said Big Tiger. "Of course Kwi-Chan is only twelve, but that's because his parents don't count the year of birth as mine do. Yesterday evening we let a kite off, and the string broke because the train was traveling too fast, and then we were suddenly at Ching-lung-giao, where the monument is."

"And there were shots," continued Christian, "and our soldiers jumped off the train."

"Were they so frightened, then?" asked the General.

"They said the battle was lost and it couldn't be helped."

General Wu-Pei-Fu gave a little laugh, and then he said that the soldiers of General Chang-Tso-ling didn't seem very keen on fighting.

"They just left the train there with a lot of horses and cars and guns in it," said Christian, "and Good Companion and Yellow Arrow conquered the lot and us as well. But now they're stuck in the tunnel because the engine won't go any more, and they've sent us—to tell you—we mean—to ask you if you would please—if General Wu would be so kind . . ."

"You should say 'If Your Excellency would care to'," whispered one of the soldiers.

"No," said the General, "you needn't say that. I'm to get another engine from Hwai-lai-tsien and send it to them in the tunnel? Isn't that it?"

"Yes, that's it," said Big Tiger.

"Then we'd better hurry. Come along!"

The soldiers were still standing there, shamefaced, but General Wu did not look at them again. He just walked off along by the railway line, and Christian and Big Tiger ran behind him. The automobile in which he had arrived was standing by the signalman's hut. A soldier was beside it. Seeing the General approaching, he saluted and opened the door.

"I'll drive myself," said the General.

"As Your Excellency wishes."

The soldier was about to get in at the other side. "Stop!" cried General Wu-Pei-Fu. "The boys are coming with us."

The soldier already had one foot in the car and was a bit discomfited at having to step off again. He looked rather grimly at the two soot-covered figures, but did not dare to say anything. He opened the back of the car, spread some canvas over the seat muttering to himself, and told Christian and Big Tiger to get in.

Despite the bad road the General drove quickly and without

lights. Only when going uphill along a series of hairpin bends did he switch on the headlights and slow down. A gigantic structure stood like a cliff across the valley.

Wu-Pei-Fu turned round. "That is the Great Wall," he said.

He drew up in front of a tunnellike entrance. Soldiers with fixed bayonets sprang up from dugouts at each side.

"Gentle Wind!" cried the General, stepping out of the car.

"Brings Success," answered the soldiers.

An officer stepped forward and saluted.

"Good morning," replied General Wu-Pei-Fu. "How are things?"

"The enemy forces have withdrawn and the fortifications are free, Sir."

"Good," said Wu-Pei-Fu. "Then we shall move forward."

Christian and Big Tiger huddled shyly together when they noticed that the General was going to sit with them.

"Drive on as fast as you can to Hwai-lai-hsien," he called out to Good Fortune.

"Yes, Sir," said the soldier, Good Fortune.

Wu-Pei-Fu pointed behind. Dawn was just breaking and one could see the Great Wall with its towers and fortifications. It ran over hill and dale, seemingly without end. "Children," said Wu-Pei-Fu. "It is easy to see that that is the Great Wall, but it is difficult to realize that it was built by the hand of man. There is a planet called Mars. Perhaps there are human beings on it. If there are, they would be able to see the Great Wall through strong telescopes. But it is the only work of human hands which could be seen from Mars."

Christian and Big Tiger were duly impressed, and Wu-Pei-Fu smiled.

But then the houses of Hwai-lai-hsien came in sight, and Good Fortune sounded the horn, waking up the inhabitants.

6 ALL GOES WELL WITH CHRISTIAN AND BIG TIGER

For the first time since we started to follow the fortunes of Christian and Big Tiger, we come on a difficulty, namely, that we really do not know what a *kang* is. But since our two heroes are lying on one apparently fast asleep, the *kang* would seem to be some sort of bed.

It is a kind of chest made of clay bricks, the height of an ordinary table but much bigger, and it generally occupies two-thirds of a room. There is space for several people on a *kang*. Inside it is hollow, so that it can be heated in winter. You lie on top of it, cover yourself up, and go to sleep.

When Big Tiger and Christian awoke the sun was shining into the room. It was a beautiful room and the walls were covered with white paper. The *kang* was covered with rugs, and on the rugs lay Big Tiger and Christian, a saddle and a leather portfolio.

"The General sleeps here," said Big Tiger.

"Do generals sleep with their heads on saddles?" asked Christian.

"Soldiers do," declared Big Tiger.

He stood up, slipped down from the *kang,* and crept over to the window which looked out on the yard. But the window was not a glass one. It was divided by a wooden lattice into many squares, which were pasted over with thin rice paper. And so, though light came into the room, one could not see out. One had to bore a hole in the paper with one's finger. This Big Tiger proceeded to do, because he wanted to know what was going on in the yard.

First he saw the tub in which they had had a warm bath immediately on arrival. Horses were being groomed, and soldiers were carrying pails of water and washing cars. One was the General's private car. Another was a truck with a high driver's cab.

"Kwi-Chan," cried Big Tiger. "Just look, Good Fortune has to wash down the truck."

"Serves him right," said Christian, and he also bored a hole in the paper window.

"Can you see everything?"

"Yes, I can see everything. Look, here comes Good Companion!"

"And there's Yellow Arrow coming behind him!"

"Don't shout so loud, or you'll frighten him and he'll drop the parcels. He's staggering along like a porter on New Year's Day."

"They're coming here. Let's pretend we're asleep. And when they say 'These poor children are quite exhausted,' we'll give a shout."

"Yes, we'll do that," said Christian, clambering quickly up on the *kang*. "But what shall we shout?"

"Anything that occurs to us," said Big Tiger. "It will be best if we shout 'Wu.'"

"'Wu' like a dog, or 'Wu' like a person?"

"'Wu' like a dog would be nicer," said Big Tiger. He threw a blanket over Christian and another over himself, and both shut their eyes.

Soon they heard footsteps stopping before their door. The entrance curtain was raised.

"They're asleep," said Yellow Arrow softly. "We'll lay the presents beside them."

"Yes, that's what we'll do," said Good Companion, creeping on tiptoe into the room.

"They can't stir yet," remarked Yellow Arrow. "They're pale and tired."

"The poor children are quite exhausted," said Good Companion.

"Wu! Wu!" cried Christian and Big Tiger, jumping up.

"Oh, what a fright!" cried Yellow Arrow, immediately dropping two of the parcels, which were tied up in red gift paper.

"Are you people or are you dogs?" asked Good Companion.

"Bow-Wow! We're dogs!" cried Christian.

"Please excuse us then. We've come to the wrong room."

"No, we're people!" cried Big Tiger.

The two soldiers laughed and asked Christian and Big Tiger to sit down on the *kang*.

"But dare we sit down in your presence?" asked Big Tiger.

"We ask you to do so," said Good Companion.

So Big Tiger and Christian sat down on the blankets and the two soldiers stood in front of them and bowed solemnly. They had already laid the parcels in front of them on the floor.

"You are our respected younger brothers," said Good Companion, "and we salute you in gratitude. You turned the wheel of the brake at the right time, and you held it firmly when we thought we were done for. You went through the dark tunnel for us, and you deserve the highest praise. We beg you not to despise the poor gifts which we offer you. Here are some noodles and eggs, with wishes for a long life. They are of poor flavor, and the cakes are not appetizing. But please accept them."

When Good Companion had spoken, Christian and Big Tiger jumped up and bowed. Taking the parcels Big Tiger said: "We are unworthy to receive such beautiful gifts from you," and Christian added: "We don't deserve such kindness."

Then they all sat down on the *kang,* and laughed and talked, and the soldiers told how a second engine had arrived in the early morning and brought them out. The General himself was at the station when the train drew in, and he had promoted them non-commissioned officers there and then.

"We wish you luck ten thousand times," said Christian and Big Tiger.

Then they opened the paper bags, and they all started eating the salted almonds and peanuts and cakes.

"Now we must go," said Yellow Arrow.

"We shall conquer Peking tomorrow or after," said Good Companion.

"May we come along?" asked Christian.

"I don't think so," replied Yellow Arrow, hesitantly. "The General says there'll be a lot of fighting. General Chang-Tso-ling's soldiers have got new silver money and have more courage now than they used to have."

"We live near the old observatory," said Big Tiger. "When you arrive in Peking will you please visit my home and say to my father: 'Your obedient son, Big Tiger, sends you reverent greetings and good wishes. He will soon come home.' "

"Please go to my father too," said Christian, "and say: 'Your son Christian is not naughty. He cannot help being far away. He only wanted to fly a kite. And the old amah couldn't help it either. Indeed no one could help it. It just happened."

"We will do as you wish," promised Good Companion. "You are good boys." And Yellow Arrow said: "Farewell, and may you have many lucky stars!"

7 CHRISTIAN AND BIG TIGER BECOME SECRET COURIERS

THE GENERAL was standing in the yard talking to Good Fortune. Christian and Big Tiger were sitting on the edge of the washtub under the projecting roof, eating poppy cakes and sweets.

"Do they taste good?" a rough voice asked suddenly, and when they looked round a man was standing behind the tub. He was wearing a round embroidered cap of a kind that even Big Tiger had never seen before.

"What are you two doing here?" asked the man, trying to look friendly. His dark eyes flitted restlessly from Christian to Big Tiger; he looked at Good Fortune and at the General, and finally he seemed to be only looking into space. He had a black moustache and beard which hung over the corners of his mouth and made him look rather sinister. And he was wearing a beautiful black silk coat. Again he asked: "What are you two doing here?"

"We're eating sweets," said Christian.

"Don't be stupid," growled the man, and spat into the tub.

"Now the tub is no longer clean," said Big Tiger.

"Impudent brat," retorted the man, looking angry. Then he pulled himself together and made another effort to look friendly. Furtively pointing in the direction of Wu-Pei-Fu he asked: "Is that the General?"

"Perhaps it is," said Christian.

"We're only here since yesterday," said Big Tiger.

"Yes, yes," growled the man. "Is there a truck here?"

"Yes, over there," said Christian.

"Yes, yes," muttered the man, slipping away silently as he had come. He turned round once, and Christian thought he detected him exchanging a wink with Good Fortune. But just at that moment Big Tiger whispered: "Here comes the General!"

Christian hurriedly swallowed his sweet as the General came up to them.

"Hello!" said the General.

"Hello!" replied Christian, but scarcely had he said it than he flushed, deeply embarrassed.

"Please excuse me . . . I shouldn't have said that . . . I didn't mean to."

Wu-Pei-Fu laughed. "It was just what I wanted to hear, otherwise I wouldn't have said 'Hello' myself. We Chinese don't say 'Hello.' "

"We don't either, except sometimes, and generally only boys," Christian assured him.

"And what about you?" the General asked Big Tiger, with a laugh. "Can you say 'Hello'?"

Big Tiger bowed. "The boy with the unworthy name Big Tiger learned it from Compass Mountain."

"Hello is a very useful word," said Wu-Pei-Fu. "When a fellow is downhearted he should say 'Hello' often to cheer himself up. Now come with me. I have something to tell you."

He walked along under the projecting roof, and entered a room with white walls, but with no *kang* in it. Instead there was a big table in the center, covered completely by a huge map. There were little red and blue flags stuck in the map and one could see that the blue flags represented Wu's soldiers and the red flags the enemy. Over Peking there was a big red flag representing General Chang-Tso-ling, who had his headquarters there, while General Wu's blue flag waved over Hwai-lai-hsien.

"Take a pencil," said Wu-Pei-Fu in a quiet tone of command, "and write down where you live, and when I get to Peking I shall tell your parents that you are safe and sound and where I have sent you. Can you write?"

"Yes, we can," said Big Tiger, and he painted the beautiful sign for Peking on the white paper, and under it the name of the street.

"I can't write quite so well," said Christian.

"That doesn't matter," said the General. "Give it to me."

He took the piece of paper and read it. "So you live near the old observatory, Big Tiger? I shall find your house. And I see, Compass Mountain, that your father is a doctor. Did he once live in Loyang?"

"Yes," said Christian.

"Then we're old acquaintances. Your father was the best doctor in the Province of Honan. I shall be very glad to meet him again."

"It will be a lucky day of the first order for my father," said Christian.

"I hope he will not be annoyed when I tell him that his son is on his way to the Province of Sinkiang. Do you know where that is?"

"I know," said Big Tiger. "You cross the Gobi Desert, and you're there."

"That's right," said Wu-Pei-Fu. "You've noticed that Good Fortune is cleaning a truck? Well, that will be the first automobile to cross the Gobi Desert. Tomorrow morning you leave here, for I cannot send you home by the ordinary route. The war is warming up. General Chang-Tso-ling's soldiers have entrenched themselves in the western mountains and are going to defend Peking. That is why you have to make this round-about journey. Do you want to make it?"

"Yes, we do," cried Christian and Big Tiger.

"But it's a very long, round-about way," continued Wu-Pei-Fu seriously, "and I'm giving you a task which will not be easy. Here is a sealed letter which you must not show to anyone. I trust you to keep it secret."

He drew from his pocket a letter written on thin rice paper. On the envelope were two vertical red lines, and between them, written in black Indian ink:

To His Excellency
Yang-Tseng-hsin
Marshal of China
Governor of the Province of Sinkiang
Tihwa-fu*

Bowing low, Big Tiger took the letter in both hands, saying: "No one but His Excellency Yang shall read this letter. Compass Mountain has a secret pocket in his jacket, and he'll keep it there."

"This is up to you. You are my secret couriers. Do as you think fit."

"We'll keep it absolutely secret," said Christian.

"Here is money for the journey," said Wu-Pei-Fu. "Probably you won't need it, as my old friend Yang will look after your needs. It is just for an emergency." And he gave twenty-five big silver pieces to Christian and the same to Big Tiger.

* Tihwa-fu: the Chinese name for Urumchi.

"Many thanks. We will only use the money in case of necessity."

"Oh, I don't mean that. The money is yours as a reward for brave conduct. Good Fortune is to know nothing about it. He knows nothing about the letter either. His only orders are to take you to Tihwa-fu. He may be a bit unfriendly at first because he would have preferred to come to Peking with me. But do not mind that. He's the only man who knows the way and I have nobody else to send. He's a native of Suchow and has been in Sinkiang several times."

"Is he a Tungan?" asked Big Tiger.*

"No, he's not. You needn't be frightened. He's as Chinese as you and I. He's a good-natured fellow, but I do not trust him absolutely, for he loves money more than a soldier should. That's why I'm glad to have you. Tomorrow you will drive to Kalgan, and then straight through the steppe and the desert to the Etzin Gol, which is a river. There is a place there called Ollon Torre where my ally, General Feng, has a gasoline depot. Good Fortune will be able to refill the empty drums there. As soon as you arrive at Tihwa-fu go straight to the Governor's *yamen.*** Give him my letter, and . . . well, that's all. Is everything quite clear to you?"

"Yes, we understand," said Christian.

"And we shall obey," said Big Tiger.

"And please ask my elder brother Yang to think kindly of me."

"We shall say it all."

"Well, good-by now," said Wu-Pei-Fu, standing up. "You will find a brief case in your room containing all you need for the journey. If all goes well you should be in Tihwa-fu in ten days."

Big Tiger and Christian bowed, saying: "We wish you many lucky stars!"

"Be silent, my children," said the General, "and leave talking to others."

"Who are the others?" asked Christian.

* *Tungan:* Mohammedan Chinese.

** *Yamen:* Chinese official building.

"All whom you meet," said Wu-Pei-Fu. And he bowed farewell to Christian and Big Tiger as if they were grown-up men. This made them feel very proud.

8 DESPITE BAD OMENS, THE JOURNEY BEGINS WELL

"Tut-tut-tut-tut" Good Fortune honked, and this meant "Hurry up!" Big Tiger and Christian hurried.

It was early morning and still cold and dark. Good Fortune ran round the truck with a storm lantern. He counted the gasoline drums, the tins, cans and oil bottles. After that he pressed the tires with his thumb, and then honked again.

Christian and Big Tiger came running with their things. They brought the brief case, the long noodles, and the last bag of poppy cakes. But they had to go back twice, for the two fur coats, two fur caps, two tarpaulins and two sleeping bags which the General had sent them by a soldier.

"You can't sit in front with me," said Good Fortune gruffly.

"We'll sit wherever our respected elder wishes," said Big Tiger.

"Come here," said Good Fortune, already sounding more friendly. He helped them up on the truck. The platform was very high off the ground. In the center there was just enough space for the two sleeping bags, which they spread out. Then they put on the fur coats and caps. The cans stood round like a fence, and behind their backs, against the driver's cab, iron drums were ranged. Standing on tiptoe they could just see the top of Good Fortune's cap through a little window.

"Are you ready now, or is there something else we need?" asked Good Fortune.

"We know of nothing lacking," said Big Tiger.

"I know what's lacking," said Good Fortune, "but it's something which can't be seen. Can you read?"

"Yes, we can read."

"Then read this." He threw a tattered yellow book into Big Tiger's lap. "You can give it back to me at Kalgan. Not another man but myself would travel one *li** today." And he got down to start up the engine.

The streets of Hwai-lai-hsien were empty; nevertheless Good Fortune kept on honking.

"Why is he doing that?" asked Christian.

"I don't know," said Big Tiger. "Perhaps he wants to wake the people up."

As the houses by the roadside grew fewer Good Fortune drove more slowly instead of faster, and suddenly the truck stopped. The honking ceased, but the engine continued to run. "So you've come at last," said a gruff voice. "You've taken your time."

"Get in," replied Good Fortune curtly.

Christian and Big Tiger heard the door of the driver's cab opening and a man climbing in. Good Fortune started up and the truck moved on.

"That's he!" whispered Big Tiger.

"Who?" asked Christian.

"The man who spat into the washtub. I know his voice."

"Oh, that's awful!" said Christian.

"It can't be helped," said Big Tiger.

Hwai-lai-hsien disappeared behind hills, and beyond these the Hsingan Mountains could be seen lining the horizon. The ground mist had dispersed and the sun rose radiant in the blue sky. They were driving along the old highway which followed the course of the Hwang-ho. Far below them they could see the yellow river; it looked hardly like water at all, it was so thick with sand and clay.

Not a single boat was in sight. The rushing waters glittered in the sun and wild duck rose when Good Fortune honked. The poplars which lined the banks were still leafless, but there were crows in the branches cawing and flapping their wings.

* *Li:* A Chinese mile, about one third of an English mile.

"Look!" said Big Tiger. "It's a good sign when the crows fly eastward. But if they fly westward it's a bad sign."

"But these crows aren't flying at all. They're only cawing and flapping their wings," said Christian.

"Then there's danger approaching," said Big Tiger, "and there's no escaping it. Now I'll read the calendar." He opened the yellow book which Good Fortune had thrown into his lap.

"This is the sixth day of the second month," said Christian.

"On the sixth day of the second moon," read Big Tiger, "it is wise to refrain from undertakings. One desires to go forward with energy, but hindrances come. On that day the spokes fall from car wheels. It is not a day for traveling. If you try to force fortune only ill-luck will result. Be content with results gained. Keep to preparatory work. Do not cut your hair. Do not marry. Perseverance brings success."

"Aha!" said Christian. "That's why Good Fortune is so frightened."

"It can't be helped," said Big Tiger, shutting the book.

Good Fortune was now driving slowly. The road fell steeply down to the river, the ground was soft and broken, and a cloud of yellow dust followed the car. Wherever the road left the riverbank they passed through scattered hamlets which seemed to be inhabited solely by old women and children who were collecting the dung of horses and asses. Behind the bamboo hedges scanty little gardens were turning green. A black pig stood in the middle of the road, and though Good Fortune honked furiously it would not move, so he had to get out of its way. The drums banged together and Christian was thrown down by the jolt. He fell on the carton containing the noodles for long life.

"There goes!" cried Big Tiger. "Now our bad luck is beginning!"

But nothing more happened, and after two hours' driving they arrived in Hsuan-hua-fu. *Fu* signifies provincial town of first rank, but this was not very evident here. In the poorer outlying streets there were many neglected and abandoned mud huts, and within the town itself many of the shops were shuttered. The run-down inns were the most striking thing. The big courtyards and stables stood empty and the signs hanging over the doors had not been painted for many a year.

"That's what the coming of the railway does," said Big Tiger. "Formerly the caravans bound for Peking stopped here, but now they no longer come."

Christian, who had been curious for quite some time, now inspected the brief case. It was divided into three compartments, which in itself was splendid. Inside were notebooks, pencils, a compass, a ruler and . . . "Cheers!" cried Christian. "Here are two penknives."

"Good!" said Big Tiger. "Please give me the one with the red handle."

"As you wish," said Christian, taking the black-handled one for himself.

Besides there was soap, a towel, a comb, and two maps, one marked "Mongolia—Southern Sheet," and the other "Mongolia—Western Sheet." With the maps they found a large magnifying glass. Christian unfolded the Southern Sheet and found Hsuan-hua-fu at once. "Here's where we are now," he said.

They were just then passing the *yamen,* in front of which a drowsy soldier was standing guard. He looked with amusement at Big Tiger and Christian as they passed. "Where are the gentlemen off to?" he shouted. "Into the mountains," Christian shouted back.

At this the soldier tapped his sword, grinned, and made a gesture of beheading.

"What's he doing that for?" asked Christian.

"He thinks you're going off to become a bandit," Big Tiger explained. "To 'go into the mountains' means to become a bandit."

"Are there bandits here?"

"There are none left here, but there are plenty beyond Kalgan."

"We shall soon be in Kalgan," said Christian, studying the map.

Big Tiger had never had a map in his hand before, but he pretended to know all about maps and remarked airily: "I can't read the names on this one because they're in English."

Christian realized he would have to show his friend how to read a map. "The top is north," he said. "The little circles are towns and villages. Blue means rivers and lakes. The thin lines are roads and the thick ones railways."

"There's nothing at all here," said Big Tiger, pointing to one of the many white patches.

"That means it's just desert," Christian explained. "You have to go into the desert to know what it looks like."

"Where's that funny place where General Wu said there's gasoline?" asked Big Tiger.

"You mean Ollon Torre?" said Christian, beginning to search. But he did not find Ollon Torre. Then he got out the magnifying glass and after a long time found the Etzin Gol. "Here's the river," he cried, pleased to have found something.

"It must be somewhere near the river," Big Tiger decided. "You must search more."

"Let's eat a poppy cake first," suggested Christian. And he folded the maps and put them away.

The truck was going slowly uphill all the time. As hardly any dust was rising now they had a magnificent view. Hsuan-hua-fu and the Hwang-ho were long ago lost to sight. They passed through many small villages and over many hills, and suddenly the railway line became visible again. They now ascended a steep mountain on the top of which stood a fortresslike building, but it was only a dwelling-house round which the owner had built a wall complete with loopholes and gun embrasures. From the mountain top they could look down on Kalgan and see the railway station with its many empty tracks on which not a single freightcar stood.

Good Fortune drew up on the station square. "Let's get out and have something to eat," he said. "Are you hungry?"

"We are, honored Sir!"

9 ABOUT THE MAN WHO SPAT INTO THE WASHTUB

"COME HERE, BOYS," said Good Fortune. "I want to introduce you to a gentleman to whom I am giving a lift, as people should help one another. This gentleman will be coming part of the way with us."

"We are honored," said Big Tiger, treading warningly on Christian's toe.

The stranger, who was sitting on the running board of the truck, did not stir. His black moustaches hung over the corners of his mouth, and his embroidered cap was pushed down over his forehead. He looked very glum. Instead of the beautiful black silk jacket he was now wearing a shabby green coat with a red sash.

"Come on!" said Good Fortune. "Introduce yourselves! You need not be so stiff."

"My unworthy name is Compass Mountain," began Christian, bowing.

"I hardly dare tell the gentleman my name. I am called Big Tiger."

"Yes, yes," growled the stranger, with a curt nod.

"Permit me to tell the boys that their elder is Mr. Greencoat," said Good Fortune.

The formalities would have ended here, but Big Tiger held Christian firmly by the tail of his jacket. Both bowed once more and Big Tiger spoke the beautiful compliment: "Our long yearning for the sight of you has at last been appeased."

At this the man called Greencoat laughed, but it was impossible to know whether he meant this politely or whether he laughed because such ceremonial speech from a boy struck him as absurd. He stood up, walked over to the station, and sat down in the sun with his back against the wall.

Not a single railwayman or anyone else was to be seen, and the station presented a sad sight. Plaster had fallen from the walls, and there were bullet holes everywhere. Most of the windows were smashed, and broken telegraph wires hung down from an iron pole.

"It can't be helped," said Big Tiger; and he thought of Peking, to which the war had now reached out.

Good Fortune was searching about in the driver's cab. He lifted the top off the seats and was looking through the stores. At last he emerged with a basket of bread, some dried figs, and bean cheese. They all sat down near Greencoat, and Christian and Big Tiger took off their fur coats as the sun was hot. It was not so bad to be traveling, seeing strange new towns, and enjoying good food at the same time.

Greencoat seemed to be known in Kalgan. A man who looked like a camel driver greeted him politely as he passed. Greencoat gave him a condescending nod, muttering into his beard something which sounded like "Old *Hung-hu-tse*".

I must ask Big Tiger afterwards what that word means, thought Christian. He was eating bean cheese and bread and surveying the station square. Three beggar boys had appeared a little distance off, but they did not venture to come nearer although they too would have liked something to eat.

"Vermin," snarled Greencoat, but then he beckoned the biggest of the boys, a pitiably starved looking ragamuffin who might have been fourteen, or a little more or less. His face was gray with dirt and dust, his clothes hung in rags, and as he came timidly near he whispered: "What is your command, big uncle?"

"Get us a can of boiling water for the tea," Greencoat ordered.

"But I have no can, big uncle."

"You have no can!" shouted Greencoat indignantly, jumping up and giving the boy a resounding slap. The boy tumbled over, but nimbly dodged the kick which followed and ran off without uttering the least whimper of pain. The others followed.

How awful to have to look on at such beastly cruelty, thought Christian. Suddenly the lovely journey seemed spoiled for him, he

did not want any more breakfast, and he looked over miserably at Big Tiger, wondering what he thought. But Big Tiger was sitting there quite unmoved, and it was only when he saw the angry tears in Christian's eyes that he gave a wink which meant: "Be quiet and pretend not to notice anything." This was very difficult for Christian. He hated Greencoat and would have liked to have beaten him up, if that had been possible. But he could think of nothing but the inevitable "It can't be helped."

"Did you say something?" asked Good Fortune.

"I was only thinking aloud," Christian replied, wiping away his tears.

Greencoat cast a malicious glance at him. "It's not polite to think aloud," he said. And from that moment it was plain that the two were sworn enemies.

Some minutes passed in silence, and Greencoat appeared to be waiting for someone. At last he stood up, walked away a few paces, and came back muttering "No one can be depended on" or something of the sort.

"Who does he mean?" whispered Christian.

"Apparently the boy he hit," answered Big Tiger.

A little time passed, then the boys reappeared carrying a steaming brass kettle.

"So you've come at last?" said Greencoat taking a coin from his purse. "Come here, I have something to say to you." He took the eldest boy aside and whispered to him. The boy nodded a few times, and then Greencoat came back with him. "Eat what's left; there's lots here," he said.

But there was only a little bit of bean cheese left, so Good Fortune went over to the truck, and took out a piece of bread for each boy and cups for tea.

"You're feeding up these scamps more than they deserve," remarked Greencoat. "They'll get fat bellies and then can't be sent out begging any more."

"Is that so?" asked Good Fortune.

"No, Sir, we're begging for ourselves. We have lost our parents and our home was destroyed in the war."

"Eat," said Good Fortune. "When the cock crows at midday the stomach is empty."

Greencoat drank his tea hurriedly and said to Good Fortune: "I've some business in the town for a few minutes, but I'll be back by the time you're ready."

"You'd better hurry," replied Good Fortune. "You yourself want us to spend the night at White Stone."

"Yes, yes," said Greencoat. "You needn't lay down the law to me."

He went off, and Good Fortune looked after him with an air of annoyance. But then he got busy with the truck.

10 WE LEARN WHAT LITTLE SNOWBIRD KNOWS

CHRISTIAN and Big Tiger looked at each other, and neither knew what to think. If the three strange boys had not been there Christian would have said, "There's something fishy going on," and Big Tiger would have nodded and answered, "It can't be helped." But they just sat in silence thinking hard. At last Christian had an idea. "You have no food, but we have some for you," he said to the boys.

They both ran to the truck. When they came back Big Tiger said: "Here are some noodles. The box is crushed, but please accept them."

The three poor boys stopped eating. They looked in silence at the box of noodles. Then the eldest bowed politely and said: "We are poor country boys, and we haven't any fine words. You are very kind to us." Then he sat down, and Christian and Big Tiger sat down beside him.

"My name is Little Snowbird," began the big boy, "and these are my brothers. We are from Chang-bei, which is beyond the northern gate. There were five huts there, and one of them was ours, but they're all burned down now."

"We're from Peking," said Big Tiger, "and we're going to Sinkiang."

"I know that," replied Little Snowbird. "Greencoat told me."

"Do you know him, then?" asked Christian.

"Everyone in our huts knew him. He often used to come our way when he had business in White Stone. There's very little farmland in our parts, and the steppe, where the Mongols live, begins there. Greencoat buys skins and wool from the Mongols, and sells them salt, flour, tea and cloth. He's always traveling and he's very rich. His caravans go through the desert to Sinkiang, but no one likes him because he's hard. My father owed him thirty silver pieces."

"Is that why he hit you?"

"Oh, no, he does that because he thinks no one can stand up to him."

"The low man abuses his power," remarked Big Tiger wisely.

"It can't be helped," added Christian.

"Oh, but it can be helped," said Little Snowbird. "He can be hindered. Only we must be united."

"We are united!" cried Christian. "Tell us what you know."

Little Snowbird looked around to see that the coast was clear. Then he said in a low voice: "I trust you and therefore I will tell you. You saw how Greencoat took me aside to speak to me. 'Here is a little silver coin for the can of water,' he said. 'You'll get a big coin if you find out why those two little scamps are going to Sinkiang. I'll go away for a while to give you time to find out.' "

"Why does he want to know?" asked Christian.

"He didn't tell me."

"We're going to Sinkiang," said Big Tiger, "because General Wu-Pei-Fu wants to help us to get home. We're traveling in his truck now, and afterwards we'll go by train, and be home in four weeks when the fighting is over."

"Shall I tell him that?" asked Little Snowbird.

"That's the truth," said Big Tiger. "But the truth is too simple for people like Greencoat. He won't believe it."

"We must invent something then," ventured Little Snowbird. "What about telling him you have a message to deliver in Sinkiang? He'd soak that up like almond oil."

"We have no message to deliver," cried Christian in alarm.

Little Snowbird was startled by the effect of his suggestion. Then he said quietly: "Well, we must think up something else."

"We must consider the matter from every side," said Christian. And they all put their heads together.

"I've got it," cried Big Tiger. "Here's an explanation which Greencoat will understand. General Wu said to us: 'This will be the first automobile to cross the Gobi Desert.' You can tell Greencoat the General is sending his truck to Tihwa-fu to impress Marshal Yang. A caravan takes ninety days. An automobile does it in ten days or less. Governor Yang will then buy many trucks, and trade with the coast will be much faster than with camel caravans. General Wu wants a thriving trade between the provinces. Do you understand all this?"

"Yes," said Little Snowbird, "and Greencoat will understand it too, as he's a trader. But tell me, what have *you* got to do with it?"

"We? Well, just what we said, and no more," said Christian.

"You must tell him," explained Big Tiger, "that another reason why we're being sent is that Kwi-Chan's father is a great doctor and an esteemed friend of the General."

"Many thanks. That's fine. I'll get my silver piece all right."

"But will Greencoat give it to you?"

"He won't want to, but I'll get it. Don't you worry!"

"You'll get one from me too," said Christian, handing Little Snowbird a silver batz.

"You are squandering your heart," said Little Snowbird.

Good Fortune sounded the horn and Greencoat reappeared instantly. Little Snowbird went up to him and said a few words, keeping at a safe distance.

"Cheeky brat!" cried Greencoat, looking as if he wanted to hit Little Snowbird again. He stepped forward, but Little Snowbird dodged him. Then Greencoat threw him a coin, whereupon Little Snowbird spoke for quite a while longer and Greencoat asked him more questions. But then Good Fortune honked again.

"You're in a mighty hurry," said Greencoat.

"We must get to the mountain early," Good Fortune replied dryly.

The truck started, and Christian and Big Tiger waved to Little Snowbird and his brothers. They stood on the square in the sun, the youngest carrying the box of noodles, and all crying: "We wish you a happy and comfortable journey!"

II ABOUT THE INN OF THE TWO LITTLE SILVER DISHES AND THE INNKEEPER WHO WAS A REDBEARD

THE MAIN STREET of Kalgan was wide, and full of shops with big gilded inscriptions over them. Lots of people were about, and if half of them had not been soldiers no one could have dreamed that machine guns had been firing in that same street only a week ago. Now children were playing in the street, the knife sharpener was blowing his long trumpet, the barber was beating his tuning-fork, a draper was calling out "Ten cents a foot, only ten cents," and through all this medley of sound the bells of a homing caravan could be heard.

Good Fortune had to drive quite slowly. Once he had actually to stop because a restive ass wanted to throw its rider.

"Look out, you!" shouted Good Fortune, leaning out of the truck window. "Don't you know what an automobile is?"

"I do," said the man, "but my ass doesn't. Be good enough to tell him."

"I'll teach the rascal something!" shouted Good Fortune, and he honked so loudly that the ass galloped off terrified.

Good Fortune laughed; but when the town gate came in sight the customs barrier was already down, and he had to stop again. He started scolding and the customs man scolded back.

"How dare you hold up a military car?" shouted Good Fortune. "You should be trembling in your shoes!"

The customs man grinned. "I do dare, and I'm not trembling," he shouted back.

"I'll break your bones!"

"Don't shout so loud. Have you anything to declare? A man on an ass just told me you have."

"He's a liar," shouted Good Fortune, "and his father and mother are liars, and his grandmother too. I'll put a bullet through your belly for believing him instead of me." Saying this, Good Fortune drew out his pistol. A brass ring adorned the handle and a silk tassel dangled from it. It looked magnificent.

At sight of the red-tasseled pistol the customs man hurriedly opened the barrier. "You scoundrel!" he shouted after Good Fortune as he passed through. "May the spokes fall from your wheels, you wicked fellow of evil ways!"

Outside the city gate there were only a few wretched mud huts.

A broad riverbed, strewn with stones, with only a thin trickle of water, came out of the side valley into which Good Fortune turned the truck.

Christian took out the map and tried to figure out the route. "Now we're here," he said to Big Tiger, with his finger on the Kalgan region, and a while later, "Now we're here," but he was not too sure.

"What's the name of the next place?" Big Tiger wanted to know.

The question took Christian by surprise. "I shall have to look with the magnifying glass," he said.

For Christian it was a question of not losing face, as they say in China. For even little boys have to take care they do not get their faces darkened or even lost altogether by bragging and bluffing. In his embarrassment he looked up from the map, and noticed a lot of thick-trunked trees with spreading crowns.

"Black poplars," Big Tiger declared.

Scarcely had Big Tiger said "black poplars" than Christian got a bright idea. It occurred to him that there is very little woodland in China, in fact hardly any in the northern provinces. Therefore this lot of poplars, which might almost be called a wood, should certainly be marked on the map. Sure enough there they were, right to the north of Kalgan. He found the road too, and behind the circles a little settlement of four or five houses was shown, with a name beside it.

"The next place is called Home in the Rocks," reported Christian. "As soon as the trees end we'll see the houses."

"That's a fine map," said Big Tiger. "It's useful to be able to look up beforehand the places we reach later." And he was even more impressed when the trees ceased and the houses of Home in the Rocks came into sight. They stood on a mountainside to the right of the highway, and each was surrounded by a wall. The big doors of rough-hewn planks were shut.

"That's on account of bandits," Big Tiger explained.

"Are there really bandits about here?" asked Christian.

"Perhaps it's written on the map," Big Tiger ventured. "Look and see."

"There's nothing here about robbers. But the road keeps going this way and that way, and then there's a village called Laketown, and on the way there's an inn called 'The Two Little Silver Dishes,' where the road begins to wind like a snake."

"Your map is wonderful," Big Tiger acknowledged once more. "In the end the inn will turn out to be a robber's house, only we won't know it."

The truck now jolted over big stones and boulders, the drums banged together, and Christian and Big Tiger were lifted up and flung heavily down. They were crossing the riverbed.

The valley became narrower, little islands overgrown with brushwood lay in the riverbed, and the mountains all around were now higher. White clouds drifted over their rocky crests and in the clouds an eagle hovered. And then the end of the valley came in sight. Not far off was a steep wall of rock toward which the road ran in a straight line. The distant roar of a waterfall could be heard.

The mountain walls grew ever closer together. This made the roar of the torrent louder, and the truck traveled along a stone dam high above the riverbed in the direction of the dark rocky wall.

"The Two Little Silver Dishes," said Christian, pointing to a wayside inn.

At that moment Good Fortune stopped the truck and began honking furiously, and the din of the horn, mingling with the roar of the waterfall, echoed down the mountains.

The host of The Two Little Silver Dishes appeared at his door, and Good Fortune shouted up to him: "Quick! Quick! Get us tea!"

"As Your Excellency commands!" the host called back, bowing low at the sight of the military uniform, and then disappearing quickly into the inn.

They all got out. Greencoat, looking very surly, sat by the roadside. "I thought you were in a hurry," he said to Good Fortune. "Why then are you stopping here?"

"It's plain you're no motorist," replied Good Fortune, opening the steaming radiator. "The steepest stretch of our journey begins here, and I've got to prepare for it. The motor has to be cooled. While I'm cooling it you must walk on ahead."

"We'll go on ahead too," said Christian.

"We shall observe the confusing variations of the road," said Big Tiger.

"No," said Good Fortune. "You must walk behind."

Along came the innkeeper, carrying a steaming tea kettle, and bowing and scraping to left and right, and . . . "Oh! Mr. Good Fortune," he cried. "Oh, Your Excellency, please forgive my old eyes. And good day to you also, young gentlemen! Do please look at the magnificent landscape. Great poets who have come here have written immortal words on the walls of my dining-room: 'The waterfall roars like thunder over the mountains' and 'It veils the valley in mist'. Beautiful poetical words, Sir. Drink your tea, Sir. That's the stuff to keep you sound and well!"

"Oh, shut up!" growled Greencoat, raising his head.

"Oh, what a joy!" cried the innkeeper. "So Mr. Greencoat is here too! Welcome, Sir! At your service, Sir! The tea is excellent and piping hot. A very special tea, Sir, a lucky tea, so to speak, with acacia blossoms in it."

"Be off with you!" said Greencoat.

The innkeeper poured out the tea. "I shall be off directly, Sir. Indeed I'm gone already. But what joy, what a pleasant surprise, what a happy reunion!"

"Old *Hung-hu-tse,*" growled Greencoat, and again Christian wondered what the word meant. After the second cup of tea Greencoat disappeared into the inn.

"There go two old *Hung-hu-tses* together now," said Good Fortune with a grin.

Christian picked up courage. "Please forgive my ignorance, honored Sir," he said. "I know that *Hung-hu-tse* means red beard, but neither of the gentlemen has got a red beard."

"Good heavens!" exclaimed Good Fortune. "I didn't think you were so innocent. You seem pretty well up in most things!"

"Well, that's one thing I don't know," said Christian.

"I'll explain it to you," said Good Fortune. "Those two worthy gentlemen haven't always been gentlemen. People say they were formerly redbeards, but nobody knows for certain, as that's a thing nobody speaks about. For a redbeard is a man who goes into the mountains."

"Aha!" said Christian. "So a redbeard is a bandit!"

"Hush!" said Good Fortune. "I didn't say that!"

"Why then does Mr. Greencoat call other people redbeards when he himself was once . . ."

"Hush!" said Good Fortune. "It's not known for certain."

"But it's impolite to call other people *Hung-hu-tse.*"

"He does that," said Good Fortune, "to keep people from thinking he may have been one himself."

"Let's see what they're up to," whispered Big Tiger to Christian. They then asked Good Fortune if they might fetch him a pail of water. Taking the pail they climbed the steps, passed through the garden, and entered the half-open door of the inn. The dining-room, in which—so the innkeeper asserted—great poets were inspired with high thoughts, was a soot-blackened room with a pot hanging over the fireplace. From the next room Greencoat could be heard speaking in a low voice. "What possessed you to let out that we're old acquaintances, you idiot?"

"But we are," the innkeeper countered. "And old friendships should not be broken!"

"I'll break your neck!" muttered Greencoat. "You reckless idiot, you're treading on the tiger's tail!"

"Beg pardon, Mr. Greencoat. I only meant, Sir, I only thought, Sir, of old times . . ."

"There you're at it again! It's safer not to think, I tell you! Is the road in order?"

"In first-class order."

"Take care you don't flood it!"

"Oh, how could I dream of doing such a thing? . . . Ssssh! Excuse me, Sir, I think I hear someone in the dining-room. Excuse me, Sir, I must go and see."

Big Tiger had thoughtlessly put down the pail, Christian had tipped it with his foot, and now they were both scared. They stepped back quickly two paces, and stood in the doorway as if they had just come in.

"Oh, so the two princes have come to imbibe the wisdom of the poets in my poor dwelling!" exclaimed the innkeeper with a smile.

"We came to fill our pail," said Big Tiger. "Is there a well here?"

"There's a splendid well just behind the house. May I show the young gentlemen round to it? No, not that way! Around the house, please."

The innkeeper went on ahead. Behind the house there were stables full of horses, and a bamboo hedge behind which a dog began barking fiercely. "Here's the well," remarked the innkeeper. "Now I'll let down the basket."

"But we've got a pail," said Big Tiger.

"Heaven preserve us from folly!" cried the innkeeper. "How could I trust a valuable pail to this old rope? No, it's best to draw up two basketfuls of water, and then the pail won't get scratched. Now, please, there, there! The first basket is down already." They could hear the willow basket splashing in the well shaft. "Up, quick!" cried the innkeeper, "that the good may become visible, as the poets say."

Chattering away, he pulled vigorously at the rope, which ran over a wooden pulley, and the basket reappeared. Big Tiger lifted it down and emptied it into the pail. "Half a blessing is not the whole," said the innkeeper starting the rope running again. "Completion follows upon increase."

"We thank you," said Big Tiger and Christian when the pail was full.

"Why such hurry?" asked the innkeeper. "Where are my younger brothers traveling to?"

"We are on our way to Sinkiang."

"Not for a carload of devils . . . I beg pardon . . . I only mean . . . this is a bad day for traveling. I didn't expect any guests today. But times are changing. No one heeds the calendar any more."

"Oh, yes, they do," said Big Tiger. "We've read that the spokes fall out of wheels today."

"Didn't I know it?" cried the innkeeper, delighted. "Didn't I know the young gentlemen were men of learning? Most certainly the spokes will fall out of the wheels! It may not happen right away, and it may not be exactly the spokes. You can't take the calendar by the letter, but all sorts of misfortunes can befall travelers—snowstorms, heatwaves, sandstorms, floods, thunder, lightning . . . Yes, indeed, and bandits too!"

"We haven't seen any yet," said Christian.

"That's a thing you can never know," said the innkeeper, looking serious. "You can't read off a man's face whether he's a bandit or not. The noble bandit fraternity go home to till their fields this time of year, but the really tough guys, the deserted soldiers—they don't go home, and they're up to every kind of devilment on all the roads. As I say, it may not happen today. It may be tomorrow or after. At any rate, I wish you young gentlemen a safe journey and prosperous business."

"We haven't any business," said Christian.

The innkeeper laughed as if to say: "Tell that to the marines!"

"Please excuse us," said Big Tiger. "We have to go. Good Fortune is waiting." As he walked on ahead the innkeeper tried once more to turn the conversation on to business, but Big Tiger said: "We have no experience of any sort of business."

"We are young and ignorant," Christian seconded him.

It was plain the innkeeper was irritated though blessings continued to flow from his lips. At last he turned back to his inn.

"He's an old gossip," said Good Fortune. "What's he been saying to you?"

"He thinks it's not lucky to travel today," said Big Tiger.

"I know that too. Haven't you read the calendar?"

"Yes, I've read the calendar, honored Sir."

"And what do you think of it?"

"I think it's nearly evening already, and nothing has happened to us yet."

"That's true. And nothing is going to happen. But if something does happen I'll shoot a hole through that talkative fellow's body."

"Oh, please don't do that," said Christian. "He can't help it if we meet with misfortune."

"That's all *you* know," replied Good Fortune, closing down the radiator and wiping his hands. "But I know these scoundrels as well as I know this region. He hasn't only got an inn. He's got a stable full of horses too."

"And he's also got a dog," said Christian.

"He hires out the horses to travelers who need fresh horses to reach the pass," continued Good Fortune. "If a traveler doesn't hire his horses, something happens. Do you see that little temple up there? Well, there's a young shepherd there, minding the innkeeper's sheep. As soon as the innkeeper gives a sign, the boy turns a lever which diverts the stream from the waterfall, and it runs over the road instead. The traveler's car gets stuck, and then he has to take a yoke of horses at double price. If he's late, he has to stop the night, and that costs a lot of money too. Moreover, his goods are stolen, and nobody can find them again because they're hidden in the kennels where no living mortal would venture. I can tell you that chattering fellow has cunning enough in him for ten scoundrels."

Saying this, Good Fortune got into the driver's cab, and though he saw Greencoat coming, he began to honk. And Greencoat, though he heard the honking, did not hurry. He walked solemnly past the truck, which was already slowly moving off.

12 A CHAPTER IN WHICH FRIGHTFUL THINGS HAPPEN

THERE ARE difficult mountain roads all over the world, but most of them are made for motor traffic. The road at the inn of the Two Little Silver Dishes, however, had never seen an automobile before. Two deep ruts, of the gauge of Chinese carts, led through the boulder-strewn riverbed. If Good Fortune could have driven fast he might have fared better. For the tires sank in the gravel and stones flew up to left and right, but the truck did not move forward. Good Fortune had foreseen such emergencies and had taken four strong planks, two shovels and a pickaxe with him. These were now unloaded, and Big Tiger and Christian helped to shovel the gravel aside, while Good Fortune pushed the planks under the wheels.

"This truck is no good," said Greencoat, who was looking on twiddling his thumbs and spitting occasionally to show his displeasure.

"It's a good car," retorted Good Fortune, "but the road is bad. Call the innkeeper. Now, boys, when I start up you must push behind to get the wheels up on the planks."

"Here I am," cried the innkeeper. "At a time like this it would be a crime to leave my guests to fend for themselves. No man is lost who has friends, and the strength of the insignificant keeps the world going."

"Hold your tongue and push behind," cried Good Fortune, who was already at the steering wheel. "One, two, three, push! *Lai, lai, lai,* come, come, come!" He started up, the tires gripped the planks, and the truck began to move. The planks had to be carried forward a few times, and then the riverbed ended and the steep mountain road began. Fortunately it was fairly wide, and the abyss was right up to the edge at only a few places.

"I shall go on ahead if I may," said the innkeeper.

"Go on," said Good Fortune. "You know this place well, old redbeard."

"Mr. Good Fortune likes his little joke."

"I like to use my pistol if things go wrong."

"Good heavens," cried the innkeeper, alarmed. "Nothing will go wrong and nothing will go crooked. I wish you a safe journey." He hurried on ahead and stopped when he got to the first turn of the road. Christian and Big Tiger came up behind. Each of them was carrying a heavy wooden skid shoe which Good Fortune had instructed them to push under the rear wheels if the truck should roll backward.

"A bit to the southwest," shouted the innkeeper. "A little more please! That's right . . . Stop! Not that way! The rocks won't make way for us. Reverse a bit and then turn eastward."

"Say right or left," shouted Good Fortune.

"Please don't be angry with me, Sir. I don't understand right and left."

"Then signal with your hands instead!"

"I can't signal with my hands," asserted the innkeeper, "because there may be people around here who might think I was signaling them."

"I trust there are no such people," said Good Fortune, menacingly.

"Oh, woe, woe," lamented the innkeeper. "It can't be helped! Perhaps one of the young gentlemen could go on ahead? There's a herd boy up there by the little temple minding my sheep. The young rascal must be told not to stir from there. . . . Otherwise he might think . . . You know, Sir, there's no accounting for what these lads can think."

"Perhaps he might think you're still the old scoundrel you used to be," said Good Fortune. "Get going, Big Tiger! Run up to him at once!"

"May Compass Mountain come with me?" asked Big Tiger.

"Must you two always stick together? Very well, you may both go. Greencoat will take the brake shoes. Off with you now!"

The two ran on in front. The road led in four turns up to the waterfall. When they reached the top they looked down into the treeless valley, at each side of which stood ranges of hills, their deep rifts looking like the folds of a garment.

When they saw the little temple up on the slope they began to run. A big boy was standing on the top step leaning against one of the wooden pillars which supported the projecting roof. He wore leather breeches and an open sheepskin smock. Under the smock he was naked, and one could see that he was a strong boy and somewhat older than Big Tiger and Christian. He held a hefty stick in one hand. With the other he shaded his eyes. He had a short shiny black pigtail.

The boy was looking neither at Big Tiger nor at Christian. He was gazing down the deep gorge to where the truck was still standing before the first turn of the road. Twenty paces ahead, just where the road circled round, the innkeeper was standing open-mouthed, looking up. Greencoat was not to be seen.

"Hello!" shouted Christian as loud as he could.

"Here we are!" cried Big Tiger.

At that moment the engine began to hum, they could hear the innkeeper shouting, and some stones tumbled down into the valley.

"What are you shouting for?" asked the shepherd boy roughly.

"We have come to tell you you're not to stir from here," said Big Tiger.

The shepherd boy looked contemptuously at Big Tiger. "Are you the provincial bailiff?" he asked. "Get out of my way! You're between me and the view." He pushed Big Tiger aside and made as if to knock him down, all the time keeping his gaze fixed on the road below where the innkeeper was guiding the truck with gestures, now to left, now to the right, and then to the left again, urging it forward and then bringing it to a halt.

"You needn't trouble about the truck," said Big Tiger.

The boy did not cease from watching. He only grinned and gripped his cudgel more firmly. Suddenly he started. "The sign!" he cried. "The sign!" He turned round like lightning, tore off his smock, and gave Big Tiger, who tried to bar his way, a push in the chest, flinging him backward into the dark recess, where his head struck against the altar of the temple. Then he sprang down the steps to where Christian was standing.

With a lightning swing of his cudgel he dealt Christian a powerful blow. But the same instant he himself lav stretched full length face downward on the terra-cotta tiles, for Christian had deftly put out a foot and tripped him. The cudgel fell from his hand. Christian pushed it aside and flung himself on the boy, who hit out with hands and feet, scratched like a cat, and even tried to bite. He writhed desperately in an effort to get Christian down, but Christian knelt on his shoulders, twisted his pigtail round his hand, and pressed his face down on the tiles.

The boy panted with rage. He was hurt by the fall, his knee was barked and bleeding, and his veins were nearly bursting from the pressure. With a desperate effort he freed himself, and leaping up flung Christian off in such a way that he fell head over heels backwards.

I mustn't let go, thought Christian desperately, but it was of no avail. The big boy now had his hands free, and he started right away to bash the prostrate Christian in the face. Christian had to let go of the pigtail in order to defend himself, but already the other was on top of him, scratching him in savage triumph with his finger nails. Christian yelled.

Suddenly a dark shadow flitted over the wrestling pair, something swished through the air, and the herd boy's cudgel came bang down on his own head. Now he too was down.

Big Tiger stood over him panting, while Christian struggled to his feet. All three were in a bad way, covered with bleeding cuts, scratches and bites. Even handfuls of hair were torn out. Big Tiger had a great weal across his forehead.

"Have you killed him altogether?" asked Christian anxiously.

"I'm not quite sure. There seems to be a bit of life in him still."

"Then let's tie his feet at once. If we don't, he'll jump up and get at the gadget and turn on the flood water."

"Have you got a piece of string?"

"No, the kite took it all."

"Look, he's got a leather belt on," cried Big Tiger.

"That would be unfair," said Christian.

"What does 'unfair' mean?" asked Big Tiger.

"Anything you really shouldn't do is unfair," said Christian.

"But we have to do it," Big Tiger decided. "If we don't, he'll kill us both with his cudgel. He's stronger than the two of us together, and as wild as ten wolves."

Without waiting to hear further objections Big Tiger bent over the boy and took off his leather belt. Christian dropped his scruples and together they bound the feet of their savage adversary. They had scarcely finished when the boy came to himself. He looked around him wildly and at once tried to jump up, but Big Tiger and Christian flung themselves on him and held him down. Then they each sat on an arm of their conquered enemy.

"You're cowards ten times over!" screamed the boy. "Let me up till I stamp you to pulp!"

"We'll take mighty good care never to let you free again," said Christian.

"We'd be very sorry to have to kill you," Big Tiger assured him. "You'd best remain lying there. You'll save us a lot of trouble."

"You talk a lot of high-sounding words instead of being ashamed of yourselves," said the boy. "I won't speak to you any more." And he shut his eyes to show he did not consider them even worth looking at.

Big Tiger said: "You'll soon talk again when the innkeeper comes and asks why you disobeyed his orders. And Greencoat will be very angry with you too. Perhaps you know him?"

"What's that you're saying?" cried the boy, opening his eyes instantly. "Is Greencoat here?"

"Yes, he's very near," Christian asserted.

"And he's in a very nasty temper," Big Tiger remarked.

"That's all the same to me," cried the boy. "There are worse things than that. Let me go!"

"It can't be done," said Big Tiger.

The shepherd boy now began to plead. "I'll be peaceful if you let me go. I have to get away. I have something important to do."

"We know what you want to do," said Big Tiger.

"You want to flood the road," said Christian.

"No, I don't," cried the boy, who was nearly crying. "I have to go somewhere. Let me go if you want to remain free of guilt."

"You will have to tell us what you want to do," Big Tiger stipulated.

"I could never do that," said the boy, beginning to cry. "I'm lost, and Bator's father is lost too," he wailed.

"Who's Bator?" asked Big Tiger.

"Bator is my friend."

"And who are you?" asked Christian.

"I'm Lo-Chang. But what's the good of telling you? It's no use, and Greencoat, the . . ."

"Scoundrel, you mean?"

"I didn't mean to say even half a word."

"Well, I'll tell you what we think of Greencoat," Christian declared. "This is Big Tiger, and I'm Compass Mountain. We both consider Greencoat a downright villain. It's true he's traveling with us, but that's because the soldier Good Fortune took him for a lift. But he's nothing to us. We despise him."

"Are you traveling by the horseless car?"

"Yes, we're traveling in that car."

"And Greencoat?" asked Lo-Chang, terrified. "Is he traveling with you?"

"Yes, we've told you he is," said Christian.

Lo-Chang began to sob again. "I knew it," he cried despairingly. "We're all lost!"

Christian exchanged a look with Big Tiger, then he said: "We'll let you free if you promise to leave us in peace."

"Promise it by your face," added Big Tiger.

"I promise it by my face," said Lo-Chang.

They untied his feet and gave him back his belt, and Lo-Chang, who just a moment before had been so wild and savage, sat meekly on the floor, weeping.

"Does your head hurt?" asked Big Tiger.

"That's not what's troubling me," said Lo-Chang, drying his eyes. "It's not on account of myself. It's on account of Bator's father, and his face, and the camels, and a whole lot of things you wouldn't understand."

"Perhaps we'd understand if you'd tell us," ventured Big Tiger.

"Speak!" urged Christian.

"Tell us while there's time," pleaded Big Tiger.

"I'm from White Stone," began Lo-Chang.

"That's where we're to spend the night," cried Christian.

"I thought so," said Lo-Chang, "as Greencoat is here. He always stops the night at White Stone, because he wants to take the camels from Bator's father."

"Can he do that?" asked Christian.

"Up to the present he hasn't been able to, because I've always warned Bator's father in time, and he's driven the camels away. But today Greencoat is traveling by the horseless car, and no horse could gallop quickly enough to get to White Stone before him. Bator's father is named Serat, but everyone calls him Dogolon, because he's lame."

"Go on, tell us quickly. Don't you hear how near they are?" Big Tiger urged.

"They're at the third bend of the road," said Lo-Chang, unmoved, "and it can't be helped."

"We could warn Dogolon," Christian suggested.

"You?" asked Lo-Chang, and the old scornful look came back. But suddenly he changed his mind and said quickly: "If that's so, I'll tell you:

"It was two years ago at this season. Greencoat arrived at White Stone with a caravan of three hundred camels from Sinkiang, laden with cotton. On the way through the desert he had lost some camels. He went to Dogolon. 'Sell me ten camels,' he said. 'I'm going over the pass down to Kalgan, and I can't do it without spreading the loads over more camels. Will you accept sixty batz?' Dogolon had never before made such a good deal, and he sold his ten best camels at sixty batz apiece. He still had twelve camels left. The next day Greencoat went on and camped at Laketown. The day after that he was to cross the pass when the caravan would be rested. But a snowstorm came in the night, and half of Greencoat's camels died of cold because they were weakened from the journey and hadn't enough felt covers. When Greencoat reached Kalgan he went straight to the *yamen* and lodged a complaint against Dogolon for having sold him ten bad camels, saying that otherwise they wouldn't have died of cold. But Dogolon viewed all the dead camels at Laketown, and not one of his was among them. But the *amban** in Kalgan was unjust. He sent armed men . . ."

"They're coming!" cried Christian, jumping up.

"It can't be helped," said Lo-Chang.

All three looked down to the road where the truck was rounding the last bend. The innkeeper was running ahead, beaming with pleasure, hopping from one foot to the other, and waving his arms. When he caught sight of Christian and Big Tiger he called out: "We have overcome the insurmountable. The abyss yawned, the boulders rolled down on us, but we kept bravely pressing on, and now, behold, we're up! Nothing can stop the wheels any more."

Lo-Chang stood by as if waiting for a word from the innkeeper, but the latter only shrugged his shoulders and "No lamb this time" was all he said. Then Lo-Chang went up to the temple to fetch his sheepskin jacket.

"I hope he made no difficulties for the young gentlemen?" inquired the innkeeper.

"Not the least," said Big Tiger.

"We had a most interesting talk with him," Christian asserted.

"There's nothing in the world better than a good talk," declared the innkeeper. "Isn't that so?" he continued turning to Good For-

* *Amban:* District Magistrate.

tune, who had stopped the truck at the temple steps and got out.

"Be off!" growled Greencoat, who had come up panting behind the truck and flung down the brake shoes.

"Have you been fighting?" asked Good Fortune, seeing Christian's scratched face.

"I've been clumsy and fallen," said Christian.

"And *you've* bashed yourself against a rock, it seems?"

"It was not rock, it was wood, honored Sir," Big Tiger replied.

Good Fortune laughed, and was going to say something about the perils of mountain-climbing, but at that moment the innkeeper called up from the road: "Must I then part from Your Excellencies and the young princes in this unceremonious fashion? I regret you will not avail yourselves any longer of the hospitality of my poor hut. But do please honor me another time."

"Yes, certainly, another time, old redbeard!" Good Fortune called back.

"A thousand thanks!" cried Christian and Big Tiger.

Greencoat said nothing. He did not even look around. The innkeeper walked down the road, looking back again and again, and even after he was lost to view his voice still resounded from the valley, calling: "May you have many lucky days!"

Good Fortune thrust a stick into the tank, to see how much gasoline was left. "We shall have to fill up at Chang-bei," he said, "and we must hurry, otherwise darkness will overtake us."

"There's a bit of a moon," remarked Christian.

"It doesn't shine for long, and it won't give any light at all tonight," said Lo-Chang suddenly. He had been standing aside and now he came nearer. Saluting Good Fortune with a hurried, "I wish you good rest, Sir," he pointed to the scurrying clouds which had rolled up from the direction of the wind. They were driving over the mountains, at times hiding the crumbling watchtowers which crowned the summits.

"That's bad," said Good Fortune anxiously. "But are you sure?"

"Lo-Chang speaks the truth," said Christian.

"Old shepherds are the surest weather prophets," cried Good Fortune. "Come on! Quick! Quick!"

"Good luck to you," whispered Lo-Chang. "And when you reach White Stone inquire for Dogolon."

"Yes, we'll warn him against Greencoat," Christian assured him. "Does he speak Chinese?"

"He'll understand you, but you must be very cautious for it will snow soon."

Christian wondered what the snow had to do with the caution they were to observe in their mission.

Up till now there had been valleys and hills, gorges, cliffs, and many boulders. But now all of a sudden there was nothing but a high tableland over which Good Fortune was able to drive quickly. For a time the old watchtowers punctuated the route. There were some remnants of the Little Wall which belonged to the chain of towers. But the Little Wall had never been an imposing structure like the Great Wall. It was more in the nature of an outwork which the Ming emperors had built for their soldiers lest they should be too frightened by the sight of the uninterrupted steppe.

They reached Laketown in ten minutes. It was not a town at all, and Good Fortune drove at top speed past the few poor houses. No lake was to be seen anywhere.

"That's funny," said Christian, searching the map diligently with the magnifying glass.

"No, it's not funny. It's just a name like yours or mine. I'm called Big Tiger, though in reality I'm small, and a tiger looks quite different. What's the name of the next place?"

"Pole Home," announced Christian.

"Pole Home is just a designation," said Big Tiger loftily. "It's sure to be quite a new place, and there'll probably be only one or two houses there, inhabited by the people who look after the telegraph line."

"The line is in a bad way all the same," Christian remarked,

glancing up at the telegraph poles with their torn dangling wires.

"It can't be helped," said Big Tiger. "The line is destroyed."

Pole Home, which they reached in half an hour, turned out to consist in fact of only two houses. But both were in ruins. The surrounding walls were broken, the wells were silted up, and when Good Fortune sounded the horn no one appeared. Two half-burned trees, which the former inhabitants had planted in a garden outside the enclosure, were visible for a time. Their charred branches stretched helplessly into the evening air. Otherwise there was nothing either living or dead to be seen—nothing but the bare plateau.

Good Fortune drove on the grass bank between the road and the telegraph poles. There was less dust this way. The wind had dropped. To the north and west a brown bank of cloud edged the horizon. It boded ill for the night. The sun was yellow, and stood a hand's breadth over the horizon. As it sank into the bank of cloud as if into a soft bed, Good Fortune honked, and suddenly there were more houses, a town hall, and a gate through which the truck thundered noisily.

"Here we are in Chang-bei," said Big Tiger.

A broad street led straight through the town from the south gate to the north one. Even before they reached the north gate the houses ceased, and there was an immense open space. Good Fortune drove right into the middle of it, stopped with a jolt, and, jumping out, cried: "Now, honorable gentlemen, we're in a great hurry!"

"So you're aware of that at last?" growled Greencoat. He got out, looked at the sky, then at the pale moon, the cloud bank, and the town gate, and shook his head. But Good Fortune refused to be depressed. It seemed indeed that the more ill-humored Greencoat grew, the more cheerful Good Fortune became.

"Kwi-Chan, you hold the funnel, and Big Tiger, hand me the gasoline. Hurry up, young princes!"

"We hear and obey," Christian said.

When they had finished, Good Fortune switched on the headlights; the engine was humming, and the horn honking.

"Look out!" shouted an old watchman. "Those roaring motor cars kill more people than they leave alive."

13 A CHAPTER IN WHICH IT IS NIGHT, AND THEREFORE NOT ALL THAT IS HAPPENING CAN BE SEEN

NIGHT HAD fallen suddenly and completely. The crescent moon was giving all the light it could, and the stars were shining. Big Tiger and Christian had never before seen such a starry sky.

"There are a lot more stars here than in Peking," said Christian.

"Let's look for the pole star," Big Tiger suggested. "My teacher says it stays in its place and all the other stars move round it."

Christian agreed eagerly. "We must stand up, then," he said. "The pole star is somewhere in front of us. We can't see it from here."

Both stood up, leaned their arms on the metal drums and scanned the sky for the pole star, but it was impossible to find it as the glare from the headlights dazzled them, and beyond this glare the sky was black as ink. The telegraph poles, some straight and some bent, flew past them on the right. To the left, wheel tracks stretched along the road like flowing ribbons.

Suddenly the moon became obscured and dark orange-colored. It seemed veiled by floating gray clouds, then all of a sudden it disappeared behind the cloud bank to the west. At the same time the fair-wind rose.

"I don't understand what's happening," said Big Tiger.

"It's snowing!" cried Christian.

In a trice everything was blotted out by whirling snowflakes. Big Tiger pointed to the little window through which they could see the rim of Good Fortune's cap, and his hands on the steering wheel. His right hand now reached for the hand brake. With his left hand he tried to keep the steering straight, but this was impossible; the truck skidded and there was a crash—it had run into a telegraph pole. One of the headlights went out. The other still glowed quietly, lighting up the damaged telegraph pole which hung slantwise over the truck, held only by its wires.

"It can't be helped," said Good Fortune coolly. "It's an unlucky day for traveling; it says so in the calendar."

"What do you mean by 'It can't be helped?' You promised me we'd reach White Stone today. How is it to be done?"

"Only heaven and this telegraph pole know that."

And that was that, for the time being, as far as Good Fortune was concerned. He climbed out and went in front to survey the damage. "It's not so bad," he said, when he came back. "The bumper is bent and one of the lights is smashed. We'll sleep for an hour or two. Do you hear me, you two up there?"

"We hear you, honored Sir," answered Big Tiger and Christian.

Good Fortune got in again; he turned out the remaining light, and then they heard him settling down.

Christian and Big Tiger spread out the sleeping bags. Over them they spread their coats, with a tarpaulin to hold them down. Then they slipped off their shoes and wriggled into the warm bags, pulled their fur caps over their faces, and fell asleep.

It had become dark in the driver's cab. The wind had blown snow over the windshield, and Greencoat could not see out. This irritated him still more. True, he could hear the wind whistling and the telegraph wires humming as if current were still passing through them; but he did not notice that the snow had eased off. When at last it occurred to him, after half an hour, to open the window, only a few stray flakes blew in.

"Hey!" he shouted, shaking Good Fortune's arm. "Wake up! It's stopped snowing."

Good Fortune was tired. He would have preferred to turn back to Chang-bei, but Greencoat gave him no peace. He shouted so loudly that Christian woke up too: "You promised to drive me to White Stone, and you know I've got business there. The gate of Chang-bei is shut long ago."

"Leave me alone!" cried Good Fortune crossly. "Your business at White Stone is nothing to me."

"That's true enough," said Greencoat scornfully, "but it *is* your business to drive more carefully. This truck may easily lose in value."

"What do you mean? Do you . . .?" began Good Fortune loudly and indignantly. But then he thought better of it and lowered his voice, and Christian could catch nothing more. This went on for two or three minutes. Then Good Fortune got out to start up the motor. Greencoat also made himself busy and the quarrel seemed to have died down for the time. Greencoat swept the snow from the hood, wiped the windshield and held back the broken telegraph pole to allow the truck to reverse.

Christian lifted his fur cap slightly, nudged Big Tiger and said: "Listen, Big Tiger, they've been quarreling. Greencoat said the truck would lose in value if Good Fortune didn't drive more carefully."

"Is that all?"

"Yes, that's all, and we're snowed in. But I'll stay where I am."

"So shall I," said Big Tiger.

And so they remained snug in their sleeping bags and slept most of the time. They became wide awake only when Good Fortune sounded the horn and the truck began to pursue an erratic course for what seemed an interminable time. The drums banged together, and someone shouted: "A little to the southwest. . . . Stop. . . . Move on just a little."

Christian thought it was the host of the Two Little Silver Dishes who was shouting, and Big Tiger dreamed he was walking up to the pass and there at the top was Lo-Chang with a stick as thick as a tree. He opened his eyes quickly, and when he saw nothing but darkness and felt the warm fur tickling his face, he threw back his fur cap. He was glad then that Christian was lying beside him, and Christian was glad to see Big Tiger. Above them they saw the dark threatening night sky, across which ragged clouds were scurrying. A man with a paper lantern was running in front of the truck, and when Good Fortune switched off the headlight they could see the lantern swaying like a stray star. The truck stopped and the man came nearer. It was the host of the inn Joyous Prosperity at White Stone. When he turned his lantern on the faces of the nocturnal guests, Greencoat shouted angrily: "Hey, you clown! Lower that lantern at once! Understand no one is to know I'm here!"

"Sorry, Sir, very sorry!" stammered the innkeeper in alarm. "I didn't know . . . how was I to guess . . . that you would be favoring my poor wretched inn with a visit so early in the year. And in a horseless car too! It's easy to see . . ."

"Shut your mouth," Greencoat interrupted, "and show us to our room!"

"If you'll excuse me, Sir . . . but the room you mean, the onc with the warmed *kang* . . ."

"Yes, of course, that's the one!" cried Greencoat. "I wouldn't have any other!"

"But that little room, Your Excellency," lamented the innkeeper, "that lovely warm room is occupied."

"Throw out whoever is in it!" commanded Greencoat.

"I daren't do that. Five or six little barbarians—a whole crowd of Mongols—are sleeping in it!"

"We'll throw them out," said Good Fortune, tapping his pistol. "Go on ahead and light us!"

"On my knees I beg for mercy! They're my good guests!"

"You mean they pay you?"

"I beg your generous forgiveness. No, these guests don't pay—but as for turning them out! You might as well expect an ant to shift a mountain!"

"Pray who, then, are these mighty gentlemen?" asked Greencoat contemptuously.

"Are they armed?" asked Good Fortune.

The innkeeper assumed a solemn and important air. "No, none of the gentlemen is armed," he said in a low voice, "and they didn't intend to put up here—I am far too unworthy of that—but the snowstorm forced them to stop here."

"Speak up!" urged Greencoat.

"It is Yolros Lama who has come—the abbot, the Living Buddha,* of the Belin Sume Monastery. And there's a real prince with him, and his suite—all high Mongolian lamas! I simply can't help it, Your Excellency!"

"That's true!" muttered Greencoat, stopping to reflect. "Let it be," he said then, turning to Good Fortune. "There's nothing we can do. My business might suffer, you understand, if I made any unpleasantness."

"The devil take your business," said Good Fortune crossly. "I want to go to bed."

"Show us into the other room," Greencoat ordered the innkeeper. "You should have got the *kang* there walled in long ago. Let's hope you've at least got blankets and fur covers."

"I'd give Your Excellency the clothes off my back," the host

* "Living Buddhas" or Gegens: Abbots in Tibet and Mongolia who are venerated as reincarnations of their predecessors.

assured him. He raised his lantern and led them through the courtyard which was crammed with snow-covered baggage and bales. On reaching the low front of the house, which enclosed the courtyard to the north, they walked along under the projecting eaves until they reached the last door.

"I'm dying to know what's happening," said Christian. And he crawled out of his sleeping bag and knelt behind the barrier of drums. At first he could distinguish nothing but the dimly lit doorway through which Greencoat and Good Fortune were disappearing like shadows. Then the door closed. Everything sank into inky darkness, and suddenly Christian noticed that Big Tiger was kneeling beside him.

"Kwi-Chan," he whispered, "I'm curious too. Isn't it awful?"

"We'll be all right. Can you see anything?"

"I can see very little. There are a lot of bales lying about, and there's some round thing; I don't know what it is. And there must be camels somewhere, but I can only hear them."

"They're lying in the south corner," said Christian. "I can hear them too. They're making a noise like the grinding of corn."

"All night they keep chewing over again the food they've eaten in the day," explained Big Tiger.

"Cows do that too," said Christian, "but not so loudly."

"What are we to do now, Kwi-Chan?" asked Big Tiger, anxiously.

"I'm thinking of that the whole time," said Christian. "We're in a desperate fix, and it's so dark."

"And it's snowing again. How on earth are we to find Dogolon now?"

"Keep quiet!" said Big Tiger in alarm, grabbing Christian's arm. "The round thing down there is stirring!"

"It's a barrel," said Christian, "and barrels can't move about."

"They can, perhaps, if there's someone inside them," suggested Big Tiger.

"It's shaking itself!" cried Christian, horrified. "It's an animal!"

They both remained kneeling, looking down at the thing in the courtyard below, which was shaking itself and throwing off the snow. They were frightened—they were clearly aware of that, for they felt their spines going hot and cold. It was good that they were perched high up and that the thing down below in the yard was a fair distance away and apparently couldn't fly. When it stopped shaking itself it fell over slowly on to its side, and while it lay there, not stirring any more, something wriggled out from under it.

It ran along on all fours and disappeared quickly behind the nearest bale. Then it raised its head cautiously, peered around and, thinking it was unobserved, ran quickly to the next bale, where it stopped again. Just as Christian was about to say with relief, "It's a dog!" it stood upright. It was a human being. It ran straight as a dart toward their truck, and disappeared under it.

Christian and Big Tiger could no longer see it, but they could hear it panting, and scratching round by the numberplate. Apparently it was looking for a foothold by which to clamber up on the truck. "Should I shout?" whispered Christian, but Big Tiger put a hand over his mouth.

Two hands appeared on the edge of the truck, then a fur cap, and after that two eyes which fastened themselves on Christian and Big Tiger. Their gaze seemed peaceable, but it was hard to know for certain, as it was so dark and snow was falling again. All was silent. Only the wind blew, and the camels' jaws continued grinding. It was far more terrifying than the night they walked through the railway tunnel.

"It can't be helped," murmured Big Tiger, pressing more closely to Christian, and they both gazed as if bewitched at the uncanny face which was slowly propelling itself upwards. When the chin reached the edge of the truck a fresh boyish voice said: *"Hammagua!"**

It seemed to wait for an answer, for the owner of the face did

* *Hammagua:* "Do not worry" or "It doesn't matter."

not move up any further. Christian nudged Big Tiger, and then they both said together, as if by mutual agreement: *"Pu-tchi-tso!* We don't understand you!"

"You Chinese or what?" asked the voice, in broken Chinese.

"We're from Peking," answered Christian.

"That good. I say first, no frighten."

"Come up to us," said Big Tiger bravely.

With one spring the hitherto invisible figure leaped almost noiselessly into the truck. Big Tiger and Christian were astounded. "Are you an acrobat?" asked Christian.

"No. I Mongol of Tchachar tribe. Bator my unworthy name. Easy and safe be your road!"

"So you're Bator?" cried Christian. "Oh, that's fine. Lo Chang sends you greetings and a message. This is Big Tiger and I'm Compass Mountain. Won't you sit down?"

They bowed to each other, Bator murmuring a salutation which Big Tiger and Christian could not understand.

Then Big Tiger went straight to the point. "Greencoat has arrived," he said.

"Me see bad man already. Me have great fear," said Bator.

"Lo-Chang says you must hurry on account of the camels, and you must be careful in the snow."

"Me understand," said Bator. "Me understand all. Perhaps forgive; great hurry. Me come again soon."

When he stood up Christian noticed that his feet were bare, but his long fur coat almost covered them.

"Have you got no shoes?"

"Hammagua," said Bator. "Boots under car. No snow tread there. I back here soon." Like an expert rider leaping on his horse Bator leaped over the side of the truck. His coat fluttered like a flag and his leap was almost inaudible.

Christian and Big Tiger watched him as he glided swiftly across the yard, cleverly using everything in his path as cover. He had soon reached the south corner where the camels lay in the darkness, and one could not see what went on. For a while all was silent. Then they heard the angry roar of a camel. Immediately afterwards a figure in a fluttering coat manipulating a rope appeared on the wall of the courtyard, but only for a moment. Then Bator disappeared, and all was as before. The camels continued chewing the cud, the wind blew over the roof of the inn Joyous Prosperity, and the snow fluttered down in little flakes.

"He's a fine athlete," said Christian approvingly.

"What's that?" asked Big Tiger.

"I mean that Bator is good at getting over walls."

"He can't fly over walls because he's not a cock. Did you hear the camel roaring?"

"Yes."

"Well, it roared because it was annoyed, and it was annoyed because it had to stand up."

"You mean that Bator had frightened it?"

"I know how things like that are done, and when I don't know, I think something up," Big Tiger explained.

"My father calls that making a diagnosis," said Christian. "It's often right and it's often wrong."

"Good," said Big Tiger. "I make a diagnosis that the camels are lying very near the wall. There's a rope there, fastened firmly in the ground. The men tie the camels to this rope with a short halter, so that they can lie there and can sleep if they're tired. But sometimes someone wants to get away quickly in the night when the gate is shut, without awakening the innkeeper to let him out. So he just goes to a camel lying near the wall, and loosens the

halter. The camel looks on wondering what's doing. He then gets up on the camel and drums on its belly with his feet. The camel knows it can't be helped, it must stand up, and as it's night it roars. Perhaps someone comes to see what's wrong, but if there's a wind blowing and it's snowing no one comes. Naturally that's much better than if someone comes and makes a row as if the stars were falling from heaven, when it's only someone wanting to get away quietly without waking people up."

"Yes, that's much better, but what then?"

"When the camel stands up, he leaps nimbly from its back on to the wall, and that's all. He can then jump down the other side."

"But if he wants to get back?" asked Christian.

"Then he must take a rope with him, which he has first fastened to a post, or a car wheel, or something that's lying round. He throws the rope over the wall, and in this way can get back easily and doesn't have to say 'Thanks ten thousand times' to anyone."

"And you think that Bator did that and will soon be back?"

"That's what I think," said Big Tiger.

"Then let's get back into our sleeping bags."

Their sleeping bags were still warm, but the fur caps, which they had forgotten to cover, were full of snow.

"Ooh!" said Big Tiger. "We must rig up some shelter from the snow—some kind of a roof or something like that."

"That won't be necessary," Christian surmised. "We're soon getting into the desert, and it doesn't snow there. It's hot in the desert."

"It's not always hot in the Gobi Desert," Big Tiger maintained.

"Let's ask Bator when he comes back. I'm for it's being hot in the desert."

"I'm for and against," said Big Tiger.

"Can you be both?" asked Christian, astonished.

Big Tiger reflected for a moment. "It often seems wise to be for both," he said.

"Shall we sleep for a while?" asked Christian.

"I'm for it," said Big Tiger.

"I am too; do we agree?"

"We always agree."

"Even if it's hot in the desert?"

"Of course, since we're friends," said Big Tiger.

They slept very soundly and did not notice that it had stopped snowing and the wind had dropped. The last clouds drifted away, and the stars appeared one after the other. The pole star was there too, and the night was getting colder.

Bator did not return for a long time. He had had a lot to do. Indeed never before had he got through so much work in so short a time. When at last he climbed up on the courtyard wall by the rope he looked up at the stars and noticed it was already nearly three.

It's the hour of the tiger,* thought Bator, and when it is past Yolros Lama will set out. I haven't much time. He looked into the courtyard where the camel had lain down again with the others. He could not jump on to its back, so he slid along the wall looking for a convenient place from which to jump down.

The truck was standing just near the entrance. The wheel marks and footsteps of the evening before had been snowed over. New footprints would be visible. But Bator consoled himself with the reflection that when the lama would be setting out a lot of people and camels would be walking about the courtyard, even before daylight. The only tracks left to betray his nocturnal wanderings would be on the short stretch of wall where he had swept off the snow when sliding along. *Hammagua,* thought Bator.

He swung down on to the truck. Only the tips of the two sleepers' noses were visible. The rest of their faces was hidden in the fur caps. Bator did not know how he should awaken them. He would have liked to tweak their noses, but he didn't know them well enough for that. So he decided to say aloud *"Sa untavo?"*

* In the old Chinese division of the day into twelve double hours 3-5 A.M. is the hour of the tiger.

which means "Have you slept well?" and knowing this, we already know more Mongolian than Christian and Big Tiger, who didn't yet know a word. Despite this they awoke all right, and Big Tiger said: "Good morning, Bator. How are you, and how are things at home?"

"We house broken up. All packed, camels take away soon," answered Bator.

Christian sat up perplexed. "Your house?" he asked. "How can you break up your house and pack it away?"

Bator was now perplexed, and Big Tiger explained. "He means they have packed up their tent."

Bator shook his head. "Tent not there. You and you must learn Mongolian. Our houses *girrs*. We make of felt and staves round as sun and warm, and quick to pack."

"We call your houses *yurts,*" said Christian.

"To all foreigners our *girrs yurts,*" said Bator. "We Mongols . . ."

"That's enough," said Big Tiger. "Kwi-Chan and I want to learn Mongolian later, but there isn't time now. Tell us your news."

Bator scratched his head, looked up at the stars, and said: "Could say much, but soon hour of hare.* And Bator have very cold feet, Bator shiver."

"Sit near me," said Christian, holding his sleeping bag open. "It's warm in here, stick in your feet. There's room for both of us."

"Thousand times thousand thanks," said Bator. "I tell story easy now."

* 5-7 A.M.

14 BATOR'S STORY, WHICH FIRST HAD TO BE PUT INTO CORRECT CHINESE, AND THEN INTO ENGLISH

"I AM sixteen years old, but I know nothing of my first year of life, as I was not yet in the world. My father's name is Serat, and my grandfather, who is dead, was called Gombo. He was a much-traveled man, and one of the old kind who wore pigtails, and he had friends everywhere. Grandfather Gombo made a pilgrimage to Kumbum* where the miraculous tree grows which has prayers written on its leaves. He traveled to Uliassutai, where there are many traders. He knew Urga, the city of the gods, and when anyone asked him 'Where have you not been to yet, Gombo?' he used to answer, 'Nowhere at all.' Soon my grandfather was no longer called Gombo, but 'Nowhere-at-all.'

"When my father was eight years old, grandfather Nowhere-at-all came home from a journey he had made to the Etzin Gol. There he had found a new friend called Naidang, and as Nowhere-at-all liked doing extraordinary things, he had scarcely got down from his horse when he said to my father: 'My son, I have found a bride for you.' That in itself was all right, because among us Mongols children are betrothed when they reach seven or eight years. So my father rejoiced, as a dutiful son should, and said: 'I am unworthy of your kindness.'

"But my grandmother was not pleased. 'A Mongol of the Tchachar tribe,' she said, 'takes a Tchachar girl to wife, not a stranger. What kind of people are those at the Etzin Gol?'

" 'They are of the Torgut tribe,' said Nowhere-at-all.

" 'That's just it!' cried grandmother. 'The Torgut Mongols are tramps. A few hundred years ago they were in Russia, and a few hundred years later they came back. They have no feeling for tradition, and you have been so long with them that you too no

* The Sacred Tree of Kumbum is an ancient white sandalwood tree, believed to have sprung up from the hairs of Tsong-k'apa (b. about 1306 A.D.), founder of the Yellow Lamas.

longer know what is right.' She said this because while grandfather was away she had been looking around for a suitable daughter-in-law. But Nowhere-at-all kept firmly to his decision and so, when my father was eighteen years old, he married a Torgut girl. My good grandmother had a lot of trouble with grandfather. Instead of bringing the bride home here to White Stone, he took father off with him to the Etzin Gol when the time came for him to marry. And there, as grandmother kept saying for the rest of her life, they celebrated the wedding with little formality. She said this because she was not there, and because Nowhere-at-all remained a whole year at the Etzin Gol.

"When at last he returned home he said: 'It was a perfectly correct wedding in every way, for the celebrations lasted a whole year.'

"Grandmother did not like such jokes, but she was pleased that my mother brought her home a grandchild. It was I. My name is Bator. One of the descendants of the Genghis Khan was called Bator. I was born in the desert near a well which gives only bad salty water. It is called the Box Spring because near it there is a mountain which is called Abder, the box, because it looks like one, and it is generally considered a dangerous mountain. I have never been there, but I would like to go there, for it is sad not to know one's birthplace, even if it is dangerous.

"Since I was born our *yurt* has stood a thousand paces from here at the foot of the hill White Stone. An hour ago we broke it up.

"A stone's throw from our tent is the well called White Stone. The water is good and never dries up. To make sure that it would always remain clear Nowhere-at-all did something wonderful. From far and wide he brought willow rods, both thick and thin, and with these he plaited a water-tight basket work around the shaft of the well right down to where the water begins. Since then no crumb of earth has ever fallen into the well. When Nowhere-at-all had finished his task, he called my father and spoke very seriously to him, and commanded him to pass on his words to his son

—that's me—and that he—that's me again—should save them up for his sons, and so on to the end of all time.

"Later I learned from my father what my grandfather had said. 'My son,' he had said. 'Look at this well hole which I have encircled firmly with a thousand times a thousand willow rods. No more earth can ever fall into it, and no stone can come loose. It was a frightful task. Your mother is happy and proud that we now have a well such as no one far or wide has got. But your mother is an unwise woman. I have gone down into the well so often and clambered up again by the rope that I realize I have lost face thereby. It was a work unworthy of a free Mongol. If I had known at the beginning what I know now, I would never have begun it. Your mother is an unwise woman. But she was right when she said once that the Torgut Mongols know nothing of good custom. I saw a well like this at the Etzin Gol, and I wanted to have one like it. And so I have let myself be tempted to do base work. The Torguts are good people, but they have no sense of honor. They must have lost it through living so long at the Volga. I shall leave you now for several years, for how could I ever look at a free Tchachar Mongol without blushing for shame? When I come back I hope the matter will be forgotten. Forget not, my son, what your father is saying to you. Herd horses, and kill the wolf when you meet it, breed camels, and ride if you will to the edge of the world. But do not soil your hands with base labor!'

"Those were the words of my grandfather, who was called Nowhere-at-all. Away he rode, and he died on his wanderings in the Valley of Dark Rushing Water, and as I was small then I can hardly remember him. Not long after we heard he was dead Grandmother died too. 'What have I to live for now?' she said. 'I have spent all my days waiting for Nowhere-at-all to come back to me. I need do so no longer.'

"About this time our ill-luck began. A Chinaman came from Kalgan. No one knew him, he never said where he came from, and as we had no longer a prince to forbid him, he camped here where the inn Joyous Prosperity now stands. He bought our skins and wool and gave us flour, salt and tea instead. As he wore a green coat we called him Greencoat, and so he is still called. He did not stay long at White Stone. Nobody wanted to trade with him as he was a deceiver. The flour he sold was bad and his weights were wrong.

"One day he brought another Chinaman who gave him a great deal of money for the land which Greencoat said belonged to him. Greencoat disappeared and we heard he had joined the redbeards. The other man began to plow up our pastures. He sowed millet and built a hut. My father said it would be a good thing to strike him dead, but we are under the strict *amban* of Kalgan, and so the stranger was left alive. What his real name is I do not know. We called him Hailstone because he used often to stand looking up at the sky for something we don't have here. Grandfather Nowhere-at-all told us there were such things as hailstones and that he had seen them, but that they were very rare.

"Hailstone is a peaceable man. All the same he took more and more of our pasture land, which he called his own because he had given Greencoat money for it. After his arrival three more Chinese families came from Shensi, and they live beyond in the hills. And so our sheep had not enough to eat. We used to have two hundred, but by the time Hailstone had built his inn we had only forty. He opened his inn on a New Year's Day and a man came from Kalgan and painted the words 'Joyous Prosperity' on a black shield. Hailstone pasted lucky red paper strips on the door of the inn and said he was a good neighbor. At the opening ceremony he invited my father Serat to drink three glasses of wine with him. 'I don't mind' my father said.

"It is a custom of ours to visit relatives and friends on New Year's Day. We ride at a gallop from tent to tent, drink wine made of mare's milk, and are merry. The man who rides the farthest in the shortest time has a 'big face' for the whole year, and people say that his horse is a grandson of Bosafabo. Bosafabo was the great

Khan's stallion, and even the little children sing songs about him.

"My father was one of the most renowned horse herds of the Tchachar tribe, and he had a nut-brown horse with a white star on its forehead like Bosafabo. On New Year's Day he rode as far afield as the country of the Sunit Mongols, and by the time he arrived back at White Stone he had left all the other riders and horses far behind him. He drank the three glasses for friendship with Hailstone, and set out in the night to return to his herd, for he was a *märin,* that is a man who has charge of three hundred and sixty horses. He had himself lashed fast to the saddle, for he had been obliged to drink a great deal; and as he rode off he sang songs about Bosafabo, the stallion of Genghis Khan. It was snowing and blowing a gale, but the horse knew the road, and it went at a gallop, because no horse dare walk on New Year's Day. On the way it stumbled into a hole which was covered with a snowdrift, and my father's song had a sudden end. The horse broke a leg and died of exhaustion in the night. My father also broke a leg, and when they found him he was lying half frozen under the dead horse. The leg remained stiff and after that he was no longer called Serat and he could not be a märin any more. He was given the shameful name of Dogolon, the lame one. And as he could no longer herd horses he sold the twelve that belonged to him and bought camels instead.

"As we had lost most of our pasture land to the Chinamen, it was all the same whether we grazed the camels one day's journey distant or ten. From that time onward my father stayed away during the summer months. He used to take the camels out to where the steppe ceases and the desert begins. In the steppe there is green grass and weeds, and when the camels came into the desert they ate deresen grass and *shara-mot*. They gnawed the tamarisks* and grew fat and strong. Traders came and bought them, we had enough to eat, and my father had some silver shoes** in the chest. He had begun with ten camels, and we possessed twenty-two when Greencoat came to us two years ago. Greencoat had meantime become a rich merchant, but there were people who wondered how that came about, and who shook their heads and said 'Aha' and 'We know how he did it.'

"Our camels were still on their winter pastures a few hours from here, and Lo-Chang and I were herding them. Lo-Chang is the eldest son of one of the three families from Shensi, and as he was poor my father gave him two silver batz a month to herd the camels in the winter with me, and the sheep in the summer, and we were friends. We hunted the wolves, and we knew the steppe and all the good wells around.

"The evening my father made the regrettable deal with Greencoat, the two of them came out to us. They picked the ten best camels, and Greencoat asked Lo-Chang 'Who are you?' Lo-Chang said who he was and where he came from. Greencoat seemed astonished and said: 'Come over here, I have something to say to you.' He took Lo-Chang aside. 'You must be a poor dog indeed,' he said to him, 'to be in service with a Mongol. I know a better job for you. A friend of mine will give you four silver batz a month and good food. If you're clever you'll earn all sorts of extras, but you must keep your mouth shut.'

"Lo-Chang reflected that he owed it to his parents to earn more, and he said: 'I am at the disposal of your friend.' The next morn-

* Deresen grass: steppeland grass; *shara-mot:* an evergreen shrub; tamarisk: a small evergreen tree.

** Silver shoes: Lump silver is still a form of currency in China and Mongolia. It is melted down by the silversmith into "shoes" or bars of various weights from which the money-changer chips off pieces, giving silver or copper coinage in exchange.

ing he went away with Greencoat, and my father said: '*Hammagua!* That's what the Chinese are like. For money they forsake their friends.'

"But that was not so. Lo-Chang did what he had to do as a dutiful son, but he didn't forget us. The very next day he sent us news of the disastrous death of Greencoat's camels in the snowstorm. We learned that the camels we sold were alive, and my father rode to Laketown to see the dead ones with his own eyes. Later when Greencoat went to the *amban* at Kalgan and when he sent armed police again and again from the *yamen* to take the camels, Lo-Chang always came and warned us the night before. We gave him a present of a lamb each time, and Lo-Chang brought it to his employer the innkeeper, who had lent him a horse to come to us.

"We were always able to drive away the camels, and my mother remained alone at White Stone. She gave the men from the *yamen* a few silver batz to report that they had looked everywhere but had found none of us. And so each time all went well, but now it can't go on like that. How it will go now, heaven only knows. I realized that when I looked at the sun yesterday evening, and saw it was yellow. I noticed the brown cloud bank and my camels noticed the sun and the cloud bank too. They came to me without being called and tried to make me understand their fear.

"I saddled a swift camel, and reached home by sundown. My father praised my foresight, and I praised the camels. While we were tying them for the night a long procession of distinguished people passed by in great haste. A standard bearer rode in front, then came a man with a big umbrella though the sun was no longer shining. Behind rode men with red fringes on their hats. They were officers of the Belin *Wang,* who is a king. Then came high lamas, and a young man on a white horse. They were escorting a magnificent carriage drawn by a camel, and were seeking refuge from the coming snowstorm, and Hailstone came out and invited them to stay with him.

"I begged my father to let me stay behind at the inn for a while to see everything. He allowed me to do so, so I spoke to the camel man. He told me that the Living Buddha of the Belin Sume Monastery had come and that his name is Yolros Lama. He rides in the beautiful carriage and the eldest son of the Belin *Wang* rides beside him on a white horse.

"Yesterday evening the Living Buddha and the Prince remained in the beautiful room on the warmed *kang*. But as I wanted to make my *kowtow** to Yolros Lama and to receive his blessing, I stayed in the courtyard until the gate was shut. Then it began to snow, and I crept under the big umbrella which is carried in front of kings and holy men even when the sun is not shining. I was asleep when you came, and I was frightened at first by the terrible noise of the car.

"I had never seen a horseless car before, and I gave thanks to heaven for permitting me to see so many new things all at once. I quickly made a little hole in the umbrella. Then I saw the car, and the strange soldier with the pistol, and Hailstone who was frightened, and Greencoat who was angry. When they went away I noticed that there was still someone in the car. I looked and looked, and then I saw your heads over the edge, and I heard you talking about some misfortune. One of you said: 'But how shall we find Dogolon?' O joy, I thought, here are friends and I must greet them. So I ran quickly across the courtyard and took off my boots so that I could climb up on the car. Now I'm with you, and that's all."

"Tell us," said Big Tiger, "why you broke up the *yurt* which had stood at White Stone for such a long time, and what your father intends to do."

"When I left you I ran home, and my father said: 'You're late!' I reported all I knew. My father said *'Hammagua!'* and then he awoke my mother. When she had heard everything she said: 'You will break up the *yurt* at once and pack it.'

* *Kowtow:* The Chinese custom of kneeling and touching the ground with the forehead as a mark of deep respect.

"My father was horrified, and I was still more horrified, but we did not let mother see it. '*Bolna,*'* said Dogolon.

" 'Bator will saddle the camels,' mother continued, 'and I will go to the Shensi people behind the hill and barter a sheep for flour. It will be a bad exchange, but we can't take the sheep with us as we're going to the Etzin Gol. When everything is ready packed,' mother continued, 'we will delay loading up until the Living Buddha and his suite set out. We will then ask permission to go part of the way with them. Our tracks will then be covered up by theirs and Greencoat will not find out where we are. Neither will he dare interfere with us while we are traveling in the company of the holy man. For a long time past I have ceased to be happy at White Stone, and so we will go to a place where the land is free and where there is no *amban* to give unjust verdicts. My father Naidang will welcome us at the Etzin Gol. He has the ear of the Torgut *Wang,*** and we shall have better pastures for the camels than we have here.'

"My father was overwhelmed on hearing these words. He knelt down before my mother and said: 'It has all happened for the best, and it is heaven's decree.'

"We then packed and tied up our belongings. We worked until the hour of the tiger. When we were finished, I said: 'I must go now and say two words to my friends, who are waiting for me.'

" 'Go,' said my mother, 'and when the holy man is stepping into his carriage, kneel down before him, beg his blessing, and ask his gracious permission for us to travel part of the way with him.'

" 'I will do what you tell me,' I replied, and went away. Then I climbed over the wall, and now I am here with you."

* *Bolna:* "Agreed."

** Torgut *Wang:* King of the Torgut Mongols.

15 ABOUT THE RING WHICH IS SEEKING ITS OWNER

BATOR's story had saddened Christian and Big Tiger. They had never heard of the Tchachar Mongols who had been driven from their pastures by the Chinese and obliged to withdraw to the barren steppe right out on the edge of the desert. A few times Christian and Big Tiger had seen a Mongol in the streets of Peking gaping with wonder at the unfamiliar treasures in the shop windows. He wore a rich colorful robe, and held a prayer chaplet in his hands, and when he swung along in his heavy riding boots they had looked furtively after him, and the grownups had smiled and shrugged their shoulders, saying: "There goes a barbarian!"

"You have made our hearts heavy," said Big Tiger.

"*Hammagua!*" cried Bator. "We Tchachar Mongols have little pasture now, but lots desert. And everywhere we merry as larks."

"But it's hot in the desert," said Christian, giving Big Tiger a friendly nudge.

"Big heat not there," declared Bator. "Now great cold in desert and friendly sun weak. My father says we walk two moons to Etzin Gol, and only then will it be lovely and warm. But now good time for traveling. The moon of the hare is cold, the moon of the dragon is cool. Camels walk well then and don't get tired."

Big Tiger gave Christian a return nudge which meant: "Do you hear that?" Aloud he said: "We're going to the Etzin Gol too, and we'll be there earlier, if the spokes don't fall from the wheels."

"Nothing real fear," Bator asserted. "Today and tomorrow very lucky days for traveling. How many days travel you?"

"We'll be there in five or six days, Good Fortune says."

"This Good Fortune soldier with small gun?"

"Yes," said Christian. "He's a soldier of General Wu, and he's driving the horseless car, and he has a pistol in his belt."

"Good or bad man?" asked Bator.

"Half and half," said Big Tiger.

"And Greencoat traveling with you too?"

"We don't know," Christian admitted. "Good Fortune says he's coming part of ways with us. He has not said when this part of ways ends."

"Very important find out. Must begin at once."

Christian was astonished, and Big Tiger said: "It can't be helped. We wouldn't dare ask."

"To ask not good," declared Bator. "Better much learn without asking. People say truth easily in sleep."

Christian and Big Tiger looked at each other puzzled. They didn't know what Bator was getting at. But Bator sat there grinning, and said: "When sun rises know we already what we want to know." As he said this, things began to liven up in the courtyard. A man with a storm lantern went over to the camels. A few of them stood up, and when some of them didn't want to lie down again, he called "zook, zook" to them. Then they lay down, and he hung feeding bags around their necks.

"What's the man calling?" asked Christian.

"When says zook, zook many times, camels know must lie down," Bator explained.

"Do they get something to eat?"

"Yes, they get soft beans, because the Prince of the Belins and the Living Buddha want travel quickly. That very good if people have money for it. We Tchachar Mongols no have silver for beans. Our camels eat what find, become cunning as foxes and cost nothing. Now I pray graciously excuse. Must go."

"May we go with you?" asked Big Tiger.

"Bolna," said Bator. "Great reverence show holy man Yolros Lama. Always wise do that."

Big Tiger looked at Christian and Christian asked: "What shall we say?"

"Say nothing you. I very good words speak for all, you only kneel down very nice like camel."

"Bolna," said Christian; and Big Tiger said: "We will *kowtow* and wish 'ten thousand times luck'."

Thereupon Big Tiger and Christian pulled on their felt shoes, and Bator murmured approvingly: "For work in hand those kind shoes very splendid—much better than mine."

Then all three climbed down from the truck. Under it stood a pair of high black riding boots, curved upwards at the toes like little boats. The legs were decorated with brown and green leather. Bator slipped them on.

"You and you," ordered Bator, "wait near Abbot's carriage. I speak two words with camel man, then I come too."

A light glowed in one of the rooms under the projecting roof. The flickering reflection of a fire ran up and down the ricepaper window pane. It was the kitchen. They could hear voices, but the voices were speaking Mongolian, and it was only when Hailstone said something in Chinese that the reply came in that language. Christian and Big Tiger stood still.

"Here's the tea for the Excellencies," they heard Hailstone saying. "And here are the cups for our most honored guests."

"We do not need your cups," the answer came. "The Abbot and the Prince have their own silver bowls with them."

"Please forgive my forgetfulness. Of course princes must have silver or gold drinking vessels. But what about one or two leaves of saffron for long life?"

"You may put them on a plate. Now open the door."

Christian and Big Tiger felt that it was time for them to decamp. They hurried along under the roof, and after having passed two doors they stumbled over the long shafts of a carriage which stretched into a roofed-over doorway.

"The carriage of the Living Buddha," whispered Christian.

"Let's climb into it," said Big Tiger resolutely. "There's nothing else to do." He climbed in nimbly, and Christian followed him with a beating heart, for he feared the carriage would tip over at any moment.

"No fear," Big Tiger whispered; "I've looked, and there's a prop behind it."

The carriage was firmly and squarely built, and had two big high wheels. Instead of the usual sides it had a superstructure like a little house, open at the front. To the right and the left were miniature windows hung with dark curtains. Inside was a heap of cushions, on which Christian and Big Tiger sat down. They would have been very comfortable had they not felt sure that sooner or later someone would come and make a great row at finding them in the holy man's carriage. And they would not even be able to run away.

"There's no way of escape," said Big Tiger. "We're like crickets in a cage."

"Hush!" said Christian. "There's someone coming."

They heard the slouching sound of Mongolian riding boots, and suddenly they noticed with a shock that there was a door right opposite them. Scarcely three paces separated them from the bedroom of Yolros Lama and the Prince. Before there was time to think along came two men wearing long robes and fox fur hats. One was carrying a steaming kettle and the other a tray with various little dishes. They walked straight into the room and shut the door. Christian and Big Tiger heard salutations. They also saw a light being lit, and when they were just wondering whether they should seek another hiding place, the two men came out again. They would have passed by if Hailstone had not come running up to ask them: "How do their Excellencies feel? Have they slept well? And the tea—what do they say to my fine Pekoe tips?"

"They say nothing. The Prince is only now getting up, and His Holiness has been saying his prayers for the last hour."

"Perhaps he will say a little prayer for me too?"

"He prays for the welfare of every living creature."

"I think," said Hailstone, "that he might make some slight exceptions."

"There are no exceptions," said one of the men severely. He wore the red robe of a lama.*

* Lama: A priest or monk in Tibet and Mongolia.

"I only meant," Hailstone excused himself, "that there are people, for instance . . ."

"Be silent!" said the lama. He turned away and signed to his companion, and they both walked off toward the kitchen.

Hailstone looked after them and when their footsteps had died away he shrugged his shoulders contemptuously and came up to the carriage. Obviously he wanted to do something unlawful, for he looked around him furtively to make sure no one was looking. Then he took a step forward, then another, and as he was about to stretch his inquisitive head into the carriage something round and black flew out in his face. Though it was soft and did not hurt, it gave him a terrible fright, and he fell down with a yell. At the same moment there was a skirmishing sound and two dark forms emerged from the carriage. In their desperate hurry Christian and Big Tiger took no notice of the prostrate form which lay between the shafts. One of them stepped on Hailstone's chest, the other on his face, and Hailstone thought he was done for. He shut his eyes and remained lying there.

At Hailstone's yell the door opposite opened and the young Mongolian Prince emerged. People came running from the kitchen too, asking "What's wrong?" But as it was still pitch-dark no one noticed Hailstone, who was lying half under the carriage.

"We don't know what's happened," said the people from the kitchen.

"We see nobody about," said the Prince.

"But someone yelled," said the stern lama.

The camel man now came along with his lantern, followed by Bator. "The man who yelled is lying here," cried Bator.

"It's Hailstone," said the camel man, swinging his lantern. "Come here, men!"

"Stand up!" the Prince ordered. "What's wrong with you?"

"I'm dead," said Hailstone faintly.

"You're wrong," the Prince assured him. "You have not yet left the world."

"I'm nine-tenths dead," asserted Hailstone obstinately, heaving a groan.

The compassionate camel man knelt down beside him. "Test your limbs one by one," he advised him. "If you can move them all it's not so bad."

"It can't be helped," whined the innkeeper. All the same he tried to sit up. Then he stretched his feet and stood up. "I'm alive," he said, relieved, "but it was frightful."

"What was frightful?" asked the Prince.

"The nine-tailed fox was here," reported Hailstone. "He attacked me as I stood between the shafts counting the stars. He threw a great big stone at my head and I lost consciousness and fell down like a sack. Then the fox stamped on my face and I've been dead to the world until now. Thanks ten thousand times for saving my life."

"Here's the stone," cried Bator, lifting up the cushion which was lying in the snow.

Everyone laughed, but Bator soon regretted his thoughtless words, for the Prince ordered silence and demanded sternly: "Who has been in the carriage of His Holiness?"

Bator was terrified. He could figure out well who had been in there. And the people from the kitchen said: "We must look and see where the fellow is hiding."

"He must be found at once," the lama ordered sternly.

"No," cried Bator, treading on the camel man's foot as if by accident. "You needn't look for him, because it was me."

"You?" asked the camel man, astounded. But Bator trod on his foot again and he fell silent.

"You?" asked the Prince, looking at Bator and then at Hailstone. When he had looked well at them he burst out laughing. "So you're the nine-tailed fox that stamps on people's faces?"

"I trod on him by accident," said Bator dejectedly, "and I beg for leniency, because it was so dark."

"No pardon is possible," cried the lama. "It is improper for anyone to enter the carriage of His Holiness. The criminal who did it must be flogged."

Bator was frightened. He looked up at the Prince, but the Prince was no longer laughing, and indeed it looked as if a ruthless trial would be held.

Then Big Tiger, who had been hiding behind a pillar, ran forward, followed by Christian, who had been hiding behind another pillar, and both *kowtowed* before the Prince and cried with one voice: "We beg for justice!"

"Who are you?" asked the Prince.

"He's Compass Mountain and I'm Big Tiger, and we crept into the carriage because . . ."

"Because it was so cold," said Christian.

"And because we wanted to *kowtow* to the Living Buddha," said Big Tiger.

"But you need not have hidden for that reason," the Prince remarked.

"Certain people," Big Tiger explained, "need not know that we're awake and running around. For we should be asleep."

"This seems a difficult matter," said the Prince. "Stand up!"

"We do not dare," Big Tiger objected.

"Stand up all the same," the Prince commanded. "You are polite, and that makes amends for a great deal."

"But not for this," cried the lama, indignantly flinging his red robe across his shoulder.

"Nothing has been decided yet," declared the Prince. "We do not know who has been in the carriage—whether one, or two, or three, or anyone at all. But we are going to solve the mystery. The rest of you, go to your work. Come, you three!"

"We hear and obey," said Big Tiger and Christian.

"Bolna," murmured Bator to himself. "There's certainly going to be trouble."

"Were you saying something?" the Prince asked, and as he spoke Mongolian, Bator knew that he was being addressed.

"I said I'm thankful to Your Highness."

"We think you're a young rascal," said the Prince.

He opened the door of the guest room and went in, followed by Big Tiger, Christian and Bator. It was warm in the room, a tallow candle was burning faintly, and when the Prince stepped aside, Christian and Big Tiger saw a *kang*. Bator's eyes were cast down, and so he saw only a bit of faintly lit floor. The *kang* was covered with beautiful rugs, and on the rugs, upright and motionless, sat a very old man in the red robe of a lama. His bald head was bent slightly forward, and the beads of a prayer chaplet were gliding through his fingers.

"He's like the Nephrite Emperor in Peking," whispered Big Tiger.

"Only not so fat," said Christian under his breath.

Bator, who up till now had remained in the background, pressed forward and threw himself on his knees before the venerable man. Then Christian and Big Tiger also knelt down reverently. Yolros Lama interrupted his silent prayer. The beads ceased to glide between his fingers. There was complete silence.

"Here are three boys," said the Prince, "who come to beg your blessing on a long journey before them." He spoke Chinese in order to indicate to the Living Buddha that Christian and Big Tiger did not know Mongolian.

Yolros Lama stood up. He was tall, thin and very solemn, and his eyes were black. When he had laid his hand in benediction on the tousled heads of the three boys, he said: "Stand up, my children!"

It sounded like a command, and Christian and Big Tiger obeyed at once, murmuring only a hasty "We do not dare."

"And you," said the Abbot in Mongolian to Bator, "do you not hear my words?"

"I hear them," said Bator, without looking up.

"Then do as I bid you. We are alone, and you need not fear my warden."

"It is contrary to all custom," Bator excused himself, standing up. But he kept his head bowed, his eyes shut, and his hands crossed reverently on his breast.

"Bolna," said Yolros Lama smiling. "I do not rebuke your obstinacy." Then he reflected for a moment and said: "We shall speak Chinese so that we all understand each other. Do you also understand this language?"

"Speak Central Chinese very very good," said Bator.

The Prince of the Belins suppressed a laugh, and Yolros Lama sat down again on the *kang*.

"We have three young culprits here," said the Prince, "but we do not know which of them really did the deed."

"It is those two," said the Abbot.

Big Tiger and Christian were startled, for they had often heard that eminent and venerable lamas know more than other mortals.

The Abbot smiled. "The matter is simple," he said. "I heard you two boys come running along. You tripped over the carriage shafts in front of my door, and one of you said: 'This is the Abbot's carriage.' "

"That was me," said Christian.

" 'Let's climb in,' the other whispered. 'There's nothing else to do.' "

"That was me," Big Tiger admitted.

"I know even more," said Yolros Lama. "The Prince asked your names, and so I learned them. My warden has told me what he heard from the innkeeper, and so I know quite a lot about your journey with the soldier Good Fortune, without having to ask you anything. But there's one thing which I do not know, and perhaps you will tell me."

"We'll tell you everything," declared Big Tiger.

"With the exception of one thing," Christian let slip.

"Probably that's just the one thing I want to know," said Yolros Lama amiably. "Where are you going in General Wu's horseless car?"

Christian breathed a sigh of relief, and Big Tiger said: "We are traveling through the desert to Urumchi."

"That is a long way, my children," said Yolros Lama. "And you must be careful, for you have with you a man of evil reputation."

"That Greencoat very bad man," Bator confirmed.

"Be silent!" cried the Prince of the Belins. "And speak when you're spoken to."

Bator lapsed into penitent silence and bowed his head still lower, but the Abbot said: "Let him be, Prince. I see he has something on his heart. He will tell it to me presently, but I wish to question each of them in turn. Big Tiger has replied, and now I ask his friend, Compass Mountain. Come here to me, my child, and whisper to me if you do not wish to say it aloud, why General Wu is sending you with the soldier Good Fortune to Urumchi."

Once more Christian was frightened, and he searched his mind in consternation for an answer. He would have found it quite impossible to lie to the Abbot, and the Abbot, he knew, would have spotted any untruthfulness. Christian would have preferred to remain silent with bowed head like Bator.

"General Wu-Pei-Fu is sending us home by a round-about way," he stammered at last. "We are from Peking, but there's a big battle going on there, and as it's dangerous for boys, we have to go by Urumchi."

The Living Buddha smiled benignly. "You have spoken the truth, Compass Mountain, but not the whole truth. You are hiding something from me."

"General Wu," said Christian, "does not permit me to speak about that."

"Then it can't be helped," said the Abbot. "Keep your secret, but keep it better than you have kept it from me. If someone asks you again why General Wu is sending you to Urumchi, do not become confused. Answer without hesitation so that you will be believed. Your secret is known to me, and apparently I know more about it than you do, for General Wu is my friend and his thoughts are not hidden from me. Therefore I will lend you and Big Tiger my poor help. I have a ring which I have worn for twenty years although it does not belong to me. I now perceive that the time has come: the ring seeks its owner. Take it from me and give it to him who desires it with a great desire. He will help you if you are in need." Saying this, Yolros Lama slipped a silver ring from his finger and handed it to Christian, who bowed deeply. "It will go on your right thumb," said the Abbot. Christian tried and found it was so.

"But how is the ring to find its owner," asked Christian, perplexed, "when I don't know what the owner looks like? In the end someone will say 'Give it to me,' and it will be the wrong person."

"Sit down beside me," said Yolros Lama. "I must speak to you under my breath, for walls have ears."

Christian and Big Tiger climbed up on the *kang*. Christian sat on the left and Big Tiger on the right of the Abbot.

"There is still a place left," said Yolros Lama to Bator. "Sit opposite me, my son, and tell me who you are."

"My humble name Bator, son of Dogolon, and son's son of Nowhere-at-all. That all like breath of wind which blows away, not worthy speak."

While Bator was saying this, Yolros Lama seemed to glance at him with surprise for a moment, but when he spoke it was as calmly as before: "Look at me, son of the son of Nowhere-at-all. Here is the place where you must sit."

"Great awe say no, heart say yes," replied Bator, raising his eyes timidly. Then he sat down in the place indicated.

"Prince," said Yolros Lama, "I thank you for having brought these three culprits to me. Harken you also, and learn how events separated by long years become linked together in this hour."

The Prince of the Belin Mongols bowed slightly and said in a low voice: "We listen with reverence to your words."

"Twenty years ago," said Yolros Lama, "I was traveling to Urga for the Festival of the Seven States. Joyful people in silk robes and mounted on their best horses were riding thence by every road. On the fourth day I rested with my suite by the Well of the Yellow Ravine. There I met a young man who was sorrowful, and his eyes were full of gloom, for he had sworn a terrible oath to kill many men as retribution for what had befallen him. He came into my tent, and I said to him: 'You darken the light; no noble man lives thus.' But the man was silent. I said: 'Haughty dragon will have to repent.'

"Then the man threw himself on the ground, drew a ring from his finger, and said: 'Pray take this ring of anger by which, with twenty others, I have vowed a vow of vengeance. But ask nothing more of me.'

"I looked at the ring, and it was a silver snake which wound itself around the finger in a double coil. 'The snake,' I said, 'is not only the emblem of anger. The snake is also a despised creature because it creeps along the ground, hence it is also an emblem of humility. I will wear your ring to remind me to be humble.' At this the man wept, and I knew he would have liked to have the ring back for the sake of its new significance. He became gentle as the wind, and in that moment his life lay before me like an open book. 'I will give you back the ring,' I said, 'when my days are numbered. In the hour when you hold the humble snake in your hands again, think of me as of one who has departed from the world!' "

Yolros Lama was silent, and so were they all.

Christian looked furtively at the ring which was a snake, and it did not please him nearly as well as before. The Prince put his hands up to his face, and wept, and lamented in Mongolian; and Bator told later that he had said: "With you the light shall disappear from the earth. How shall we go on living?"

Yolros Lama made no reply to the Prince's lament. He simply said: "This is the story of the ring. But it is not yet finished. The man thanked me, and wished to ride on, but I said to him: 'Wait for one hour. You have given me a ring. I do not wish to let you depart without a return gift, but as I possess nothing you must wait until someone comes the way and gives me a gift.' We sat down and drank tea, and after an hour along came a merry fellow riding a camel. He sang as he rode, and when he saw my tent and learned who I was, he dismounted and begged me for the travelers' blessing. I gave it willingly, and I asked the merry fellow his name. 'I am Nowhere-at-all,' said he, 'and I thank you for your powerful blessing, in which I shall always rejoice.'

" 'Nowhere-at-all,' I asked, 'have you brought me something?' 'Forgive my great forgetfulness,' cried Nowhere-at-all, taking a little book from his belt. In the book were three dried sandalwood leaves. He gave them to me, saying he had plucked them from the Sacred Tree of Kumbum, and though it was only permitted to take one, he had got three, and did not know how it had happened. I took the leaves, and handing one to the man who was sad, I said: 'Take this leaf to remind you that there are people who are joyous and without guile.' The second leaf I returned to Nowhere-at-all, saying: 'You, my droll fellow, require no such advice. Keep the leaf until you come one day to the Valley of Dark Rushing Water. Then throw it to the winds.' He did not understand what I meant, and I was glad of that. I kept the third leaf for myself. This morning it fell from my hand, and when I tried to pick it up, I trod on it by accident. Then suddenly all that had happened long years ago at the Well of the Yellow Ravine stood before my eyes, and that is why I tell it to you now. Another will complete the tale."

"But if some wrong person wants to have the ring," asked Christian again, "what shall I do?"

Yolros Lama smiled. "You have a sufficient burden to bear with one mission," he said. "It was unwise of me to load you with another."

Christian got red and embarrassed, and the Living Buddha ordered: "Give the ring to your friend Big Tiger. He has a much too splendid name, and will benefit by the humbling influence of the snake."

Christian then passed the ring to Big Tiger, who bowed and said: "Thanks ten thousand times for your esteemed confidence."

"He to whom the ring belongs," said the Abbot, "will get a great shock when he sees it on your finger. Thus you shall recognize the rightful owner."

Yolros Lama was silent. Then he looked at Bator. "What have you got to ask me, Bator?" he said.

"From my father Dogolon message great reverence, great request. We intend journey. Camels wait. Dogolon wait too, and ask: May he travel two days with honorable caravan of holy Abbot Yolros Lama?"

"Dogolon may travel with us as long as he wishes," said the Abbot. "There is nothing to prevent him." Saying this, he dropped his eyelids. Christian and Big Tiger realized that they were dismissed, and Bator too stood up. Before leaving the room they *kowtowed* once more. But the eyes of Yolros Lama were closed. The beads were gliding once more between his fingers, and the Prince signed them that they should go very quietly.

One after another they went out into the courtyard, over which the cold morning star was twinkling.

16 ABOUT THE KANG WHICH WAS NOT WALLED IN

"WHAT are you doing there?" asked Bator's mother, who had been visiting the Shensi people behind the Hill of the Well, and had bartered the sheep to them. "Are those your friends?"

"Yes," said Bator, "these are my friends, and we are resting a little. You must speak Chinese to them, else they won't understand you."

"What are your names, children?" asked the mother.

Big Tiger and Christian told her.

"You can call me *etch*. *Etch* means mother, and as you have no mother here, I'll look after you. Otherwise you'll do silly things."

"These very grown-up people. No silly things do," Bator explained.

"Bator," called Dogolon. "Hi! Where are you hiding?"

"I'm here, but I'm coming," answered Bator.

"And we?" Christian offered. "May we help to load?"

"Come with us," said the mother, and then they all went to Dogolon who had already saddled the lead camel and tied the others together. Dogolon took the reins of the lead camel. It stood up and the others also stood up. Dogolon then lead them skillfully one after the other through the lane of packs, and when the lead camel stood between the two sacks of flour which it was to carry, the other eight stood each in its proper place, at the correct interval between the bales and the tied-up wooden poles of the felt tent. "Zook, zook," cried Dogolon, giving two short pulls to the halter of the lead camel. It knelt down obediently and the other eight did likewise.

"Take this stake and stick it through each of the ropes," said Dogolon to Christian.

"Bolna," said Christian, and Dogolon praised him, saying he already spoke Mongolian quite fluently.

The loading then began. Dogolon and Bator worked together. At each side a pack was placed upright, laid against the knee, then raised a little, and soon, to right and left, each at the same time, a pack was secured to the camels' backs. Christian grasped the slip ropes, pushed them in between the humps and ran the stake through them. The load then lay fast, Big Tiger meanwhile holding the camel by the halter to prevent it from standing up. In ten minutes the little caravan was ready for the road.

"We're off!" said Dogolon. "May your way be easy and good."

"Good-by, children," said the mother. "I'm sorry I cannot look after you, but don't do anything silly all the same. Come, Bator!"

"Dear Mother," whispered Bator.

"Little Son," said the mother. "I see you want something."

"I want," answered Bator—and then he spoke very quickly in his own language, pointing appealingly to Christian and Big Tiger. When Bator had finished speaking, Dogolon looked at his wife, and she looked at Dogolon, who stood there unable to decide whether to say yes or no. At last the mother said: *"Bolna,* he may stay behind a while."

"But only until daylight," said Dogolon, mounting the lead camel and riding slowly forward. The others followed, and the mother rode behind. "Do not forget your promise," she warned her son.

Bator took one of the camels by the halter and went with Christian and Big Tiger behind a snowdrift. There they could not be seen, but could watch the inn. Before long two horsemen emerged. One was carrying the umbrella and the other the banner, unfurled, and it looked impressive although it was dark and one could not read the words on it. The two horsemen were followed by five others. Then they heard the Living Buddha's carriage rolling through the gateway. Dogolon dismounted and *kowtowed,* and the Prince, who was riding his white horse beside the carriage, gave a friendly nod. The train of pack camels followed, and when they had passed, Dogolon and his wife joined on with their train. The caravan disappeared in the darkness, they could hear the creak of the gate, and Big Tiger said anxiously: "The servant is pushing the bars in front of it."

"How shall we get in again?" asked Christian.

"*Hammagua,*" replied Bator. "Need no worry at all." He took a thin, firmly plaited rope of goats' hair, of which many were hanging on his saddle, made the camel kneel down, and wound the rope three or four times round its left knee. "Sit there quietly," he said, scratching the camel behind the ears. "Don't try to stand up, we're not going yet." Then he turned to Christian and Big Tiger. "Present time splendid begin intended work. You and you no more word lose, no smallest sound make. Our work hurries," he explained, pointing to the morning star. "Better act quickly than words say."

Hiding his hands in his sleeves he walked boldly up toward the inn. Christian and Big Tiger followed, though they had no idea what he was up to. The camel raised its head and looked after them. "Very good camel know well something going on," whispered Bator.

Christian whispered back that he did not know what was going on, but Bator did not enlighten him.

When they arrived at the wall which Bator had climbed up before, they turned round to the next corner instead of going on. Here the wall merged into the back wall of the inn premises. There were three square holes in this wall a few feet from the ground. Two of them were smoke-stained, and in front of these lay a heap of snowed-over firewood and brushwood for warming the *kang* inside.

Bator now walked very cautiously, making signs that they should be frightfully careful. When he reached the first hole where there was no firewood and no smoke-stained edge, he stopped, signed, then pulled off his fur coat and laid it on the ground half inside the hole, to smother any sound.

"The room with the *kang* which has not been walled up is over this hole," whispered Christian, and Big Tiger nodded.

Bator, who had already knelt down, put his finger to his lips warningly. One after the other they crept on all fours into the dark hole, which widened into a little cave in which they could with difficulty sit bent down. Round poles and cross rafters formed the roof. In between them straw had been stuck and plastered with clay, but the work had been badly done, and the chamber would never have heated the *kang*. Bator angled in his fur coat and laid it over his shoulders. Then they all waited for a sign of life. They were quiet as mice, and nothing could be heard but the breathing of two sleepers—Good Fortune and Greencoat. Once one of them turned in his sleep, and there was a dull thud. Evidently that was Good Fortune, who did not take off his pistol holster even at night. Then all was quiet again until a soft sound of groping fingers began. It was frightfully exciting, because something might happen any moment.

But nothing happened. Now and then Bator bent forward and looked out to see if it was nearing daylight. Just when one might think that the sky was not quite so black, and the snow not quite so gray, and that the stars were getting a little paler and the night nearing an end, the door of the room above opened, and someone stepped in cautiously. Instantly the fingers ceased their groping. They all heard this, and none of the three dared to breathe, so great was the silence and so loudly did their hearts beat.

"I wish Your Excellencies rest and comfort," said Hailstone.

For a moment all was silent as before. Then they heard Good Fortune saying irritably: "It's still the middle of the night. Why are you disturbing us?"

"Be off with you!" snarled Greencoat. But one could know by his voice that he had been awake already.

"He who goes out the door and the gate will have reason to lament," remarked Hailstone, meekly.

"What do you mean?" cried Greencoat, and one could observe that he had sat up, because little bits of clay fell from the roof on to Christian's and Big Tiger's necks.

"Get out!" shouted Good Fortune. "Have you never heard that the sleep of man is sacred?"

"I will come again when the cock crows," said Hailstone. He went off affronted.

"That old clown always comes at the wrong time, but he wanted to say something," remarked Greencoat.

"Something wise, no doubt," said Good Fortune, contemptuously.

"Quiet there! Perhaps it was something important, and you stopped him with your roaring from coming out with it."

"You roared like a bull yourself," said Good Fortune.

"Are you trying to quarrel?" inquired Greencoat.

Good Fortune turned the conversation into another channel. "No," he said. "I don't want to quarrel with you. I'm out for something else. You promised me a payment on account as soon as we'd reach White Stone. We're here. What about it?"

"Aha!" said Greencoat. "So you want money, do you?"

"I want two hundred silver batz."

"Everything must be done in the correct order," said Greencoat, admonishingly. "As soon as it's daylight I'll go and find Dogolon. He's a scoundrel who lives here and owes me ten camels. Being a sly fellow, he's always cleared out when it came to paying up, but Hailstone told me last night that he's here all right. So I'll catch him this time, and the fellow may count himself lucky if I agree to settle for cash instead of taking the camels. Then you'll get your due."

"But what if this Dogolon has no money?"

"He has got money. Be sure of that. These Mongols are misers. Every one of them has got a heap of silver, on which he sits tight."

"If that's the way," replied Good Fortune, "he won't give you any money."

"He'll have to. I have a warrant for his arrest in my pocket from the *amban* in Kalgan."

Good Fortune laughed. "This Dogolon will have a good laugh at you when he sees the warrant. For who's to arrest him in White Stone, eh?"

"Why, you, of course. You wear a uniform and you've got a pistol. So you'll arrest him."

"No, I won't. I'm a soldier, not a policeman, and I don't meddle in other people's affairs."

"But you'll just come with me to frighten the fellow?"

"Very well, I'll go with you," said Good Fortune, after a moment's reflection. "And you'll give me the two hundred batz immediately afterwards."

"I'll give you the two hundred silver batz," said Greencoat very slowly and emphatically, "even if the car has greatly lost in value."

"It seems to me," said Good Fortune, "that it's you who are trying to quarrel with me now."

"That's because you no longer seem to know what we agreed. Our agreement was that the truck should be in the condition it was in when I saw it in Hwai-lai-hsien. Since then it has changed."

"It has one headlight less, that's all. You can buy a new one anywhere."

"Not here."

Good Fortune growled an answer which sounded like "Go to the devil," and all was quiet again.

Bator grinned with satisfaction; but Christian was freezing and would have liked to be in his warm sleeping bag. He looked out to see if it would soon be day. But then Greencoat began to talk again, and Christian quickly forgot his cold feet. He even got warm and his face got red from sheer excitement when Greencoat said: "There's something else I must speak to you about."

"Out with it," said Good Fortune. "I wonder what your 'something else' is."

"Those two impudent kids," began Greencoat. "They sit in the truck as if they belonged there—but they don't belong there, and you must throw them out somewhere. The Gobi Desert is big."

"How is it," asked Good Fortune, "that you're suddenly taking such a friendly interest in the boys?"

"I'll tell you why. We've agreed that you give me the truck in Hsing-hsing-hsia . . ."

"We have agreed," Good Fortune interrupted him, "that the truck is to be stolen in the night at the inn in Hsing-hsing-hsia, and I'm to know nothing about it, and that you then quietly give me a thousand silver batz. That's our agreement, and there's no 'something else' over and above that."

"Listen to me," said Greencoat.

"There's no 'listen to me' either," Good Fortune interrupted him roughly.

"Very well," said Greencoat maliciously. "I'll tell you what there is. There's an *amban* in Kalgan, and there's a judge in Maomu, and besides there's the army court martial. All three will be pleased to make the acquaintance of a former member of the Red Mountain robber band."

"When you take that line with me," cried Good Fortune, his voice trembling with anger, "you don't notice, you old turnip face, how ridiculous you make yourself."

"It ill becomes you to speak like that," replied Greencoat coldly.

"A lot could be said there," said Good Fortune scornfully. "Two words from me, and we'd both be in the same boat."

"You could say as much as you'd like, but no one would believe you. We'll assume, shall we, that there's a certain honorable trader, who, believing he's dealing with honorable gentlemen like himself, bought goods a few times from you crooked bandits of the Red Mountain. Such things happen, but they're not crimes by a long shot. The good man was simply deceived. But if later on he meets one of the lawbreakers of those days, then he does a public service in denouncing him. I believe the honorable merchant would actually receive a reward. Don't you think so?"

Christian and Big Tiger, who had been taking in every word, began to tremble. And it was not only the cold which was making them tremble. It was because their hearts were in their mouths and because they expected that at any moment Good Fortune would jump up, fall on Greencoat, and murder him.

But nothing of the kind happened. True, Good Fortune gnashed his teeth and muttered "Dog," "Traitor," "Black-faced rascal"—until suddenly, with a laugh of relief, he slapped his pistol holster. "Here's the reward for the honorable merchant," he cried, "and he can have it at any time!"

Greencoat did not seem to be alarmed, for he laughed too, and his laugh had a contemptuous ring. And just as he was beginning to say he was not afraid of a pistol, a cock crowed in the courtyard. He coughed a few times and then said placatingly: "That sheep-faced fellow will come in again at any moment. Be reasonable, Good Fortune, and I'll explain to you another time why we must get rid of those impudent lads."

"Your speech is long and full of error," retorted Good Fortune.

"You'll agree later on that I'm right," said Greencoat. Then they heard Hailstone coming along the corridor, and as the cock crowed a second time, he walked in. Greencoat pretended to be annoyed. "Is that you again?" he asked, yawning loudly.

"I have come to ask whether I shall saddle the horse Han-Kan for the honorable gentleman. I also wish Your Excellencies a successful morning's business."

"What's this jabber about the horse Han-Kan?" asked Greencoat.

"He's the fastest horse in my stables. Perhaps he could overtake Dogolon."

"What's that you're saying?" cried Greencoat, jumping up. "Do you mean to say that Dogolon is gone?"

"That's just what I have to say," declared Hailstone.

"The scoundrel!" shouted Greencoat. "They're all scoundrels. And you're another. But Dogolon isn't going to slip through my fingers like that. I'll get the money from his wife."

"Dogolon has taken his wife with him," reported Hailstone calmly, "and the *yurt* and all the camels. The chest was packed up too, so he didn't leave his silver behind, even though he was in a hurry. His leave-taking was without ceremony."

"Oh, you accursed blockhead!" cried Greencoat. "Why didn't you tell us this sooner?"

"Keep your shirt on!" Good Fortune interjected. "We'll soon catch up on Dogolon with our car."

"I didn't think of that," said Greencoat. "That's all right, Hailstone. You may go."

"I may go, but duty bids me say two words more to Your Excellency."

"Don't talk nonsense. I know enough."

"It's easy to let the goat escape," lamented Hailstone. "But it's better to put up with the loss when powerful force is about. For Dogolon is not traveling alone."

"We know Dogolon has his wife with him," Greencoat interrupted, "and he's got a young scamp of a son named Bator. Of course he's not traveling alone."

"You misunderstand me. For your sake I stayed up all night, and by doing so found out all you should know."

"Speak up," said Good Fortune. "But not more than two words."

"I shone the lantern into Dogolon's face," began Hailstone, "and I said: 'Do you want to leave us?' 'Yes,' he replied. 'This is a good opportunity.' 'No doubt you want to travel with the Prince of the Belins and the Living Buddha?' I asked. 'Yes,' replied the wretch. 'I'm traveling under their protection.' Then they all set out by the light of the stars, and the Prince rode beside Dogolon as if he were his friend, but I didn't see Bator. . . . Yet, as Your Excellencies do not wish me to say more than two words . . ."

Hailstone was silent, and Greencoat also remained silent, but they could hear him panting. And Christian, who got more sand down his neck, noted that Greencoat had sat down on the *kang*.

"I don't understand all this fuss about Dogolon traveling in company," said Good Fortune.

"Of course you don't," snarled Greencoat. "But it can't be helped. My business would suffer."

"You're at that again!" scoffed Good Fortune. "I do understand that you cannot risk friction with the Living Buddha, but I also understand that I'll get no money and that I'm hungry. Hurry up, Hailstone, and get a breakfast for four grown-up men."

"At your service, Sir. I'll hurry, I'll run. The fire is lighting, and the millet is . . ."

"Millet?" shouted Good Fortune. "You dare to set millet before us? Get us rice, or . . ."

Christian and Big Tiger could hear no more, for Bator made them an urgent sign to get out of the hole. One after the other they emerged silently out of the darkness, shook themselves and straightened up. In the east there was clear daylight over the snow-clad hill of White Stone. A rose-pink aurora surrounded the hill-top, making the cold snow look warm.

"If blessed camel only does not roar," said Bator anxiously when they reached the corner, and looked around cautiously to see if the coast was clear.

"He's coming!" said Christian. "I hear him."

"He open mighty gate," said Bator.

"If only he doesn't shut it again," whispered Big Tiger.

"Men," said Bator. "We take now sorrowful leave in haste. I ride away to my father, you go quickly back through gate."

"Good-by," said Christian, bowing.

"I wish you good luck," said Big Tiger. He said no more, for he saw how much it was hurting Christian to lose their new friend.

"May your way be peaceful!" cried Bator. After two paces he turned back. "You make heart joyful if you write letter very long, about ring, and Greencoat whom you must kill soon, and car with one eye. Write all exact to Bator, Torgut Tribe, Etzin Gol, with Grandfather Naidang."

"*Bolna!*" cried Christian and Big Tiger, and together they ran to the gate of the inn Joyous Prosperity, which fortunately was ajar. They slipped in, climbed unobserved into the truck, pulled off their felt shoes, and slipped into their sleeping bags. They sat up again when they saw over the courtyard wall the head of a rider wearing a fur cap. The head bobbed up several times and disappeared again.

"May your way be peaceful!" shouted Bator.

Then all was silent, and the first rays of the morning sun spread in broad streaks over the silent desert.

"Are you frightened?" asked Christian solemnly.

"I'm frightened, Kwi-Chan, but that will pass over. In front and behind us there's an abyss. We know it, but no one must see that we know."

"Are you very frightened, or only a little?" Christian inquired.

"Not very much and not very little," said Big Tiger. "We must be brave like the old men of the mountain. It can't be helped."

"It's hard to be brave," said Christian.

"Not when you have to," said Big Tiger. "You'll see. And anyway there are two of us."

17 ABOUT THE SECRET OF THE LITTLE STONES

"GET UP, you scoundrels! Breakfast is ready!" cried Good Fortune, who had climbed up on the truck.

"Oh, our revered elder!" said Big Tiger, rubbing his eyes.

"You needn't pretend to me," remarked Good Fortune. "A man learns many things in his sleep. For instance, there are boys who should sleep at night, but they run around making trouble. Hailstone is right mad over it. He says one of you stamped on his face, and the other trampled in his ribs. When he wanted to punish you, you had disappeared."

"We can't disappear like smoke," Christian pointed out.

"We're not invisible like the nine-tailed fox," said Big Tiger ambiguously.

"Beware of Hailstone. He wants to spank you," warned Good Fortune.

"We beg the protection of our revered elder," pleaded Big Tiger.

"We are very innocent," added Christian.

Good Fortune laughed. "I know that," he said. "Are you ready?"

Christian and Big Tiger walked along behind Good Fortune to the kitchen. When Good Fortune opened the door he was hit in the face by a cloud of steam and smoke. A sickly fire was flickering in the bricked-up fireplace, which was streaming smoke from every crack.

"The sun is shining on the hearth," declared Hailstone, raking out the cinders.

"It's shining into your face," cried Good Fortune. He pushed the door open, and when the smoke had cleared a bit they could see a row of black saucepans hanging on the wall. Under them stood a black table on the firmly trodden clay floor. Greencoat was sitting on a bench beside it, with a big dish of rice in front of him.

"Put the dish on the table," said Good Fortune. "We want to eat, too."

"Certainly," growled Greencoat, and went on chewing. "I don't grudge it to you. Fill your bellies!"

"Good morning, Mr. Greencoat," said Christian.

"I wish you rest and comfort," said Big Tiger politely.

Greencoat made no reply. He put the dish on the table and shouted: "Hailstone, bring dishes! The young gentlemen want to eat. Now set to," he continued, laughing. "As I said before, fill your bellies full. We've still got something to eat today. Tomorrow we shall be in the desert. The sea of sand is big, gentlemen. Eat so you don't fall off the truck. Ha! Ha! Ha!"

Big Tiger and Christian felt frightened hearing him talk that way, but they had resolved to be brave. All the same Christian turned pale. Big Tiger noticed this, but tried to be unconcerned. "We'll eat because we're hungry," he said, casually.

"Of course," Greencoat nodded eagerly, turning round to Hailstone. "You simpleton," he scolded. "You wanted to set us down to a breakfast of tea and millet, just as if we were camel drivers!"

"Rice is a costly food," Hailstone pointed out.

"Not for people of our kind," said Greencoat insolently. "Where are the new-laid eggs?"

"But the gentlemen didn't order any."

"Eggs are a necessary part of breakfast. Be off, and don't come back without half a dozen."

Hailstone was astonished, but there was no help for it. Good Fortune was astonished too, but as it was none of his business he sat down to the table, and they all ate the good rice. When Hailstone brought the eggs, there were only five instead of six. Then suddenly Greencoat decided he didn't want any, and Good Fortune swore that one was quite enough for him so Christian and Big Tiger had two eggs each.

"I seemed to hear you shouting in the night," said Good Fortune to Hailstone. "Isn't that so?"

"I remember that, too," remarked Greencoat. "You bellowed like a dragon in the dark. I believe you woke me up."

Hailstone sighed, took the poker and stirred the fire. "It's better to be silent," he said at last, "lest I bring shame on anyone."

"Speak up," cried Greencoat, "and tell us why you frighten your guests with your yells when they want to sleep."

Hailstone pretended to be scarcely able to remember. "It happened," he drawled, "when I heard that Dogolon was leaving. I cried out with fright thinking of Your Excellency's loss, and of the camels which by right belong to you."

"It would have been better if you had awakened me," declared Greencoat. He had finished eating and was sitting playing idly with some little stones or marbles in his pocket, and looking triumphantly at Good Fortune, who was eating heartily and was in just as good a humor as he.

"How could I have awakened you?" asked Hailstone plaintively. "I got such a fright that I fell down flat like a bottle gourd. As I lay like a dying man someone came and stamped on my face and trod my ribs into many pieces."

"We beg for forgiveness," said Christian quietly, continuing to eat heartily.

Big Tiger laid down his chopsticks, stood up and bowed. "It happened through unintentional haste," he said. "We beg for leniency."

At that moment one of the little stones with which Greencoat was playing fell, and Big Tiger quickly put his foot on it.

"You see, Hailstone, these boys are polite people," said Good Fortune. "How can they help it if you fall over and your body lies about in the dark? It's easy to stumble over something like that."

"Respect for elders is disappearing," replied Hailstone. "That's all I have to say."

When they had all finished, Good Fortune asked for hot water. Christian stood up quickly to help him to carry it, and Big Tiger, in his haste, let his chopsticks fall. When bending down to pick them up he reached for the little stone under his foot. It was no stone, however, but a cylindrical thing made of brass with a rounded point. Big Tiger hid it away.

"What's the name of the place we're going to today?" asked Christian.

"It's not called anything," replied Good Fortune. "We just go on until sundown, and no longer."

"But there are places which have names, and wells which are not just called wells, and perhaps there are mountains which are not just called mountains."

"Yes, there are lots of them," said Good Fortune. "But I only remember the names when I see where I am. There's a well called Amun Ossu, but we shan't see it because we turn off before it. And then there's the Bayin *Obo,** which we shall see because it's on a mountain. But it's better not to speak of it or the spokes will fall from the wheels, or something else will happen. But why are you asking?"

"Because I have a map," Christian confessed. "The General gave me one as a present."

"Maps are no good," asserted Good Fortune. "You'd best throw it away. You look for a well, for instance, and there it is in big letters on the paper. But you don't find the well—it no longer exists, because it has filled up with sand. There you are in the desert with no water, all because of the map which was no good. If you see on the map 'Encampment of a Mongol Prince,' he's moved away by the time you get there."

"But the mountains don't change," Christian objected.

"The mountains collapse and the hills are easily moved. These Mongol magicians do that every day at breakfast. You must be very careful."

"Greencoat has also told us we must be very careful," Big Tiger interjected, coolly, "or we may fall off the truck."

* *Obo:* A shrine erected in the open by Tibetans or by Mongols.

"Greencoat is an ass," said Good Fortune, startled. "So long as I'm driving you need have no fear. I drive carefully and no one can fall off." He got into the driver's cab and sounded the horn. Immediately Greencoat came running. Good Fortune paid Hailstone for the night's lodging, and then drove out into the sunny winter landscape.

Christian and Big Tiger had settled down comfortably. They took off their shoes, stuck their feet into the sleeping bags, and sat in their fur coats, their backs against the drums. Big Tiger put his hand in his pocket and took out the thing which Greencoat had lost. "What's this?" he asked casually.

"A cartridge!" cried Christian. "A real cartridge! Where did you get it?"

"It was lying under the table," Big Tiger reported. "And Greencoat lost it. He must have a lot more, because he was playing with them." And he told how it all had happened.

Christian took the cartridge in his hand and said it belonged to a pistol. "I'm quite sure of that," he said. "I saw cartridges once in my father's drawer, and he caught me. I wanted to know if one would be missed if it disappeared. There were twenty-four of them. But afterwards they were gone, and I don't know where my father put them. 'Those are not things for boys,' he said."

Big Tiger said that that was the way fathers talked, and grown-ups would put on great airs if they had cartridges, but soldiers didn't. They were so used to them they treated them quite casually. "I have it!" he cried suddenly. "Oh, Kwi-Chan, I've discovered a secret."

"Tell it to me," asked Christian.

"You must know it already," Big Tiger whispered. "When we were sitting with Bator under the *kang,* waiting for something to happen, and it was so frightfully silent, didn't you hear something? I mean just a tiny little sound?"

"Yes, like fingers groping or a mouse scratching," cried Christian.

"Well, that was Greencoat stealing the cartridges out of Good Fortune's holster. That was the noise like a mouse. And he was very pleased with himself afterwards, because he thought now Good Fortune could do nothing to him if they quarreled."

"It can't be helped," said Christian. "You're right."

Suddenly the truck went more slowly, and Christian heard Good Fortune opening the window and crying "Here!" Big Tiger, who had fallen asleep, brightened up again, and they both saw wheel tracks which branched off southward, and near them were many hoof prints of camels and some of horses.

"There go my two hundred batz," said Good Fortune.

"Drive on," cried Greencoat irritably. "Nothing can be done."

Good Fortune shut the window and accelerated.

"Now they're quarreling again," said Christian.

But Big Tiger was in no mood for talking. He pulled off his coat and slipped into his sleeping bag. Christian did the same, and in a few minutes both were fast asleep. An hour passed by, and another, and Good Fortune continued to drive northward. The last Chinese huts disappeared in a valley behind some steep slopes of crumbling earth. Greencoat had wished Good Fortune to stop, for he didn't feel well. He wanted to drink a whisky, he said, while there was still one to be had. But Good Fortune said he felt even worse because he had not got his payment on account. At this Greencoat was silent, and Good Fortune drove past the huts, honking furiously. A few ragged children ran out screeching, the grownups stood on their doorsteps open-mouthed, and the dogs bristled and barked from a safe distance.

Another hour passed. Then there were no more valleys, only the flat steppe with its yellow grass of last year. The snow was melting under the rising sun, and a pair of eagles were hovering overhead. Good Fortune became cheerful in spite of Greencoat, who was glumly indifferent to the beauty of God's good morning. When the first Mongol *yurt* appeared Good Fortune could not resist honking loudly, but no one emerged. The *yurts* were far away and the horses which stood beside them turned their heads and swished their tails. An automobile attracted no particular attention here. The indicator showed that the car had covered almost a hundred miles since they had left the inn. When a low ridge of hills appeared in the west, Good Fortune began to take note of every height until they reached an artificially terraced mound of stone. Here he turned off from the telegraph lines, and drove into the open steppe.

"Why are you not driving to Amun Ossu?" asked Greencoat. "The cart road goes by there."

"I'm not a caravan," answered Good Fortune haughtily. "I'm an automobile."

"Nevertheless you should keep to safe roads."

"I keep to what I know," retorted Good Fortune, pointing to the hill with the mound of stones. "Don't you see the *obo?*"

"I see the *obo* but I don't know it."

"You've a lot to learn yet," said Good Fortune. "The best thing you can do is to hold your tongue, for I must bear due west now, and it's no easy matter."

18 ABOUT MR. MOONLIGHT AND HIS SCAR

CHRISTIAN and Big Tiger were fast asleep. They didn't even notice that the truck had stopped and the sun was shining on their faces. Only when Good Fortune shouted "Up, you lazy scamps!" did Christian awake.

"What does the honored Mr. Good Fortune want?" asked Big Tiger, rubbing his eyes.

"I want all sorts of things. Perhaps the young princes want something too?" Good Fortune was holding a basket. "I have to tell you several things," he announced. "Just look around you."

"The snow is gone!" cried Christian, astonished.

"It's past midday," Good Fortune explained, "and we are in Mongolia. The sun is shining, the snow is gone, and we shall eat."

"Yes," cried Christian, "that's what we want!"

"For that we need a fire," continued Good Fortune, "and for the fire we need *argal*."

"What's that, honored Sir?" asked Big Tiger.

"*Argal* is dried dung, and you must go and look for some. But only pick up camel dung; it burns best. Here's a sample," he said, pointing to the basket. "In ten minutes the basket must be full."

Christian and Big Tiger took the basket, in which there were some nice round little balls, quite light and dry.

"You'll find most around the well!" Good Fortune called after them. Neither of them could see any well, but as they were now desert travelers they set out bravely to look for it.

The truck was standing in a flat, basinlike hollow. All around were low hills covered with dry steppe grass, but not a single tree. In the west the round dome of a mountain showed over the shimmering horizon. Several riding tracks ran down from it through the yellow grass, and converged at a bare space in the middle of the great depression.

"I'm sure the well is in that bare space where there's no grass," said Christian. They set out for it, and when they found camel droppings on the way they picked them up and tested if they were dry.

As they approached the spot a man on a camel followed by another camel carrying a water cask on each side came over the ridge of hills in the west. He caught up with Christian and Big Tiger just as they had located the well.

"There's another over there," said the man, pointing with his whip to a water hole a little distance off beside which stood a long wooden trough.

The man alighted. He was wearing a blue coat which reached to the top of his riding boots. Instead of a belt he wore a dark-red silk sash, from which hung an embroidered pouch and a dagger with a silver handle. His pointed silk hat, which was also dark red, was almost completely hidden by a circle of fox fur, under which the copper-brown Mongolian face grinned amiably.

Christian and Big Tiger bowed in silence.

"*Amorchen beino?*"* greeted the stranger.

"*Bolna,*" answered Christian.

The Mongol laughed. "I notice that one must speak to you in Chinese," he said.

"It would be better," Big Tiger admitted.

"You're lucky to have met me," said the Mongol. "For very few around here speak Chinese. You must learn Mongolian."

"We would very much like to," said Big Tiger.

"But we don't know how to begin," said Christian.

"That's quite simple," the man declared. "You must ask: '*Ene yu beino?*' Then everyone will know what you want."

"What does '*Ene yu beino*' mean?" asked Christian.

" '*Ene yu beino*' means 'What is this?' "

"Aha!" said Big Tiger and Christian; then, pointing to the well, Big Tiger asked: "*Ene yu beino?*"

"*Hutuk,*" replied the man.

"*Hutuk,*" repeated Christian and Big Tiger, and the Mongol nodded approvingly. Suddenly he grasped Christian under the armpits and lifted him on to the camel. Then, pointing with his whip in the direction from which he had come, he said several times: "*Wang!* Sunit *Wang!*"

"Lift me up too, please," pleaded Big Tiger. The Mongol lifted

* *Amorchen beino:* "Do you feel light?"—a Mongolian greeting.

him up beside Christian on the saddle, and from there they could see over the edge of the hills the yellow glazed tile roofs of a few houses.

"*Wang!*" repeated the Mongol, and then, pointing again to the well hole, he said: "*Wang-ne hutuk!*"

Christian got an inspiration. "*Wang* is the name of the man who lives over there?"

"*Wang* means king," the Mongol explained proudly.

"And this is the Well of the King," said Big Tiger, also beginning to grasp things.

The Mongol nodded, and Christian and Big Tiger jumped down from the camel's back. Then they stood chatting pleasantly with the Mongol. While they talked they filled the water casks, and when they had finished the Mongol pointed out a lot of camel dung at the next well, where the animals were watered. As they had helped him to draw the water, he helped them to collect the dung, and the basket was soon full.

"Where do you come from and where are you going?" asked the Mongol.

"We come from there, and we're going off there," said Big Tiger, who had decided they must be more discreet. And he pointed to the east and then to the west.

The Mongol gave a start, and Big Tiger thought his evasive answer had given offense. But it was not that. "You speak like one who has been in the grassland before," said the Mongol, warily. And then he looked down. "I must make a request of you," he said. "Show me the ring on your thumb."

Big Tiger was frightened, and his hand trembled as he laid it in the Mongol's.

"That's it," murmured the man. A deep flush suddenly suffused his copper-colored face. He pushed his fox-fur hat off his forehead, and Big Tiger and Christian saw, just under the hairline, a big, long, still imperfectly healed scar. It ran like a fiery red ribbon from one temple to the other, and looked so frightful that Christian and Big Tiger wondered if they now had really got something to be afraid of.

"Where did you get the ring?" asked the Mongol in tense excitement, and the scar on his forehead changed from red to blue.

"It doesn't belong to me," replied Big Tiger evasively.

"I know that," replied the Mongol. "I cannot ask you again. Therefore tell me here and now how the ring came to be on your hand."

"A holy man gave it to me, saying: 'This ring seeks its owner.' For this reason I wear it on my thumb."

"Let us sit down somewhere," the Mongol suggested. From the leg of his boot he took a thin-stemmed pipe with a nephrite mouthpiece, filled the miniature silver bowl with tobacco, and began to smoke.

"There are people waiting for us," said Christian.

"We're in a hurry," pleaded Big Tiger.

"There's nothing to hurry for," the Mongol retorted coolly. "You needn't be frightened. I don't want to know who your holy man was."

Then Christian and Big Tiger squatted beside the Mongol as if they were quite used to that posture. They waited for him to speak, but he went on puffing blue, stinking clouds of smoke into the air.

"My name is Moonlight," he began at last. "I'm one of the twenty men who knows the ring that is on your thumb."

"We have heard of the twenty men," said Big Tiger.

"The holy man said they had sworn an oath," added Christian uneasily.

Moonlight's face darkened. "Do you know more than that?" he asked. "Do you know the name of the man to whom the ring belongs?"

"We do not know it," said Christian and Big Tiger together.

"Then it's not for me to tell you his name. But if you meet him, tell him: 'Moonlight is alive. In the eleventh month of last year he lay as one dead by the shores of the Gashun Nor.'* The Gashun Nor is as big as the sea. The wolves might have eaten me as I lay there, for I was more dead than alive, as you can well imagine."

"Yes, we can," Christian admitted, glancing at the scar.

"Things like that happen," said Moonlight. "It's not very pretty, is it? A man could bleed to death. Luckily four men of the Western Sunit tribe, who were returning from a pilgrimage, came my way. They took me with them and looked after me. When I had recovered they invited me to remain with them. I said: 'I shall remain four moons with you, and then I shall return to the desert.' The men understood what I wanted to do for them, and they said: 'We want no thanks.' But I begged them to consent. I said: 'You have made a long journey and need a rest. Allow me therefore to do your yearly service with the *Wang* instead of you.' They did not wish to accept, but I insisted, and I went to the *Wang*, who lives over there behind the hill. The *Wang* allowed me to do their service, and I am therefore serving him a month for each of my four rescuers. I shall be free again the first day of the fifth month, and shall then return to the man who owns the ring."

Moonlight knocked the ash out of his pipe and stuck it carefully back in his boot-leg.

"We have heard all, respected elder," said Big Tiger, reaching for the basket.

"We shall forget nothing," Christian assured him, standing up.

"Don't be in such a hurry," said Moonlight. "I shall go back with you. You need fresh water for cooking. I can give it to you. Then you needn't go back again to the well."

"Many thanks," said Christian. "That is more than we dared expect."

"It's nothing at all," replied Moonlight. "I want to see the people with whom you are traveling."

"Good Fortune is the name of one of them," said Big Tiger. "And he's a soldier of General Wu."

* Gashun Nor: "Bitter Lake," a salt lake in the Gobi Desert.

"Indeed," said Moonlight. But his face did not betray what he thought of soldiers in general or of Good Fortune in particular. He led the two camels one after the other by the reins with an air of assumed indifference. "And the other man," he asked casually. "Isn't there another?"

"There's another man," said Christian, stealing a glance at Big Tiger.

"Yes, there's a second man," Big Tiger said. They stood a moment, as if they found the basket heavy, and together they watched to see what kind of face Moonlight would make when they would tell him who the other man was.

"He says he's a merchant," began Christian.

"And people call him Greencoat," Big Tiger burst out.

"I'm very glad to hear that," said Moonlight, without batting an eyelid. "I'm very glad indeed. I've been wanting for a long time to meet that gentleman. But listen—it's best not to tell him my name. The soldier Good Fortune need not hear it either. Can you keep it to yourselves?"

"We're very experienced in keeping names secret," asserted Christian.

"I've noticed that," said Moonlight laughing. "You're bright lads, and seem born for the steppes. Now remember: Neither of you knows my name."

"We've forgotten already," declared Big Tiger.

"No one is to know anything," repeated Moonlight emphatically.

"Nobody," affirmed Christian and Big Tiger.

They reached the truck, where Good Fortune had made a small fire. He had been getting impatient, but was pleased when he saw the Mongol bringing water. Moonlight pushed his hat down on his forehead and greeted Good Fortune and Greencoat with: "Have you had a good journey?"

Good Fortune said it was tolerable up till now, and he had lost only one headlight.

"Much can be seen with one eye," said Moonlight.

Greencoat remained silent, and apart from a muttered greeting, behaved as if the Mongol were not present.

"I learn with pleasure that you are the celebrated merchant, Mr. Greencoat," said Moonlight, turning to him.

"So I am. What do you want of me?"

"Oh, nothing at all. I would not have thought it was you. No, indeed, I really want nothing of you."

"Nonsense," cried Greencoat indignantly. "Why, then, are you talking to me?"

"Your fame resounds to the skies," asserted Moonlight. "Therefore I greatly desired the honor of exchanging two words of greeting with you."

"To be sure," snapped Greencoat, looking up at the sky as if he expected rain.

Moonlight wrinkled up his face and grinned. "Your Mr. Greencoat is a gentleman of few words," he said aside to Good Fortune. Then he made the camel with the water casks kneel down, and when Good Fortune had filled two pails, he climbed into the saddle.

"Farewell," he cried. "I wish you comfort at every hour."

"Good-by," cried Big Tiger and Christian.

As he rode away Good Fortune looked after him for a long time. Lost in thought, he scratched his head and pushed his cap back. But then suddenly he got busy, put the pot on the iron tripod over the fire, and shouted: "Fetch the kneading board, Compass Mountain! Fetch the rolling pin, Big Tiger!" While they ran to the truck, he began to mix the flour, and Greencoat looked on.

"I'd swear I've seen that fellow somewhere before," said Good Fortune.

"I haven't," replied Greencoat brusquely, looking up again at the sky.

But the sky was blue, the sun was shining, and the water was beginning to boil.

19 STRANGE INFORMATION ABOUT MOONLIGHT, AND AN AUDIENCE WITH THE KING OF THE SUNITS

"Well, how do you like Mongolia?" asked Good Fortune, as they sat around the pot fishing long noodles out of the salty water.

"We like it, honored Sir," said Big Tiger.

"The noodles are good," added Christian.

Good Fortune was pleased to hear that, for he was in fact a gifted cook. When he made a fire of camel dung it burned well from the start. When he rolled the dough it became thin as rice-paper. The rolling pin was only a thick round stick, and the knife with which he cut the strips was just an ordinary knife, but you would think they had been measured with a ruler. To the expert eye that meant much.

Greencoat took no notice of all this. He just ate up the good noodles as quickly as he ate up anything, laid his chopsticks aside and sat there looking peeved.

"Mongolia," said Good Fortune, "is like the sea. A man's heart is low when he's away from it and swells with joy abounding when he sees the steppe and the stony desert again."

Christian and Big Tiger stared at him and he got red as if he had let out something he would have preferred to keep to himself.

"You should say 'the red mountains' of the desert," remarked Greencoat sarcastically, and Good Fortune became still more disconcerted.

"Do you know what nonsense you're talking?" jeered Greencoat.

"It's not nonsense," said Big Tiger bravely. "Mr. Good Fortune has spoken very beautiful words about the steppe and the desert."

"You impudent young puppy!" shouted Greencoat. "How dare you interrupt my conversation, which you do not understand. I should punish you as you deserve."

"Do no such thing," warned Good Fortune, angrily.

"I see already on whose side you are," retorted Greencoat, looking very sinister. "Just think for a bit, and you'll remember perhaps where you met that Mongol before." Having said this, Greencoat stood up, stroked his black moustache, and went off toward the truck, where he sat down on a stone in the sun.

Good Fortune was grimly silent. He had been merry, but that was now over, for he had to think hard. "Listen, boys," he said, "weren't you chatting with that Mongol just now? Did he tell you his name?"

"If you mean the man who came over with us," began Big Tiger cautiously, "he has a big scar right across his forehead. It looks like a sword cut."

"Indeed!" said Good Fortune, startled. "I never noticed that."

"You can't see the scar right away," Christian explained. "You can see it only if he scratches his head or pushes back his hat."

"Then it can't be he," said Good Fortune. "Still I wish I knew his name."

"Have Mongols got names as we have?" inquired Big Tiger politely.

"No, they haven't got family names as we have," Good Fortune explained. "They only have a name which they get soon after they're born. But it's not much good to them, for most Mongols get a nickname. In the end a fellow hardly knows himself what his real name is. He only knows his nickname."

"Aha," said Christian. "That means every Mongol has two names, his right one and another."

"Nearly all of them, or at least a good many," Good Fortune agreed. "I knew a fellow once called Moonlight. He was proud of his name, and he told everyone who wanted to know it or didn't, that his name was Moonlight. But it was no good. Everyone called him Little Paw."

"And doesn't Mr. Moonlight like that? I only mean . . . I'd like to know why he's called Little Paw."

"It's a silly story," answered Good Fortune. "This fellow Moonlight likes a joke, as all Mongols do. And when something happens to him which makes him appear ridiculous, he turns it into something to his credit. A few winters ago Moonlight was traveling at night with some camels. As his feet were freezing he got out of the saddle for a while and walked behind. There was a halt, and the whole line came to a standstill. Only Moonlight, who was half asleep, kept on walking until he walked bang into the hindquarters of the last camel, which at once let fly at him, knocking him senseless. Two other Mongols came along and brought him around. 'What's wrong?' asked Moonlight. 'Why am I lying here looking up at the moon?' 'The camel kicked you,' they said. 'Ah, yes, I remember,' said Moonlight. 'The good creature wanted to give me its little paw.' So ever since Moonlight has been called Little Paw, but he doesn't like it. And altogether he's a man it's better not to meet."

"Why?" asked Christian.

"Was it he, then?" asked Good Fortune, fixing Christian sharply.

"Who?" asked Big Tiger, feigning surprise. "Do you mean the Mongol with the scar?"

"Oh, of course!" Good Fortune said. "I had forgotten the scar. Only for the scar I'd think that fellow was Moonlight. But it's easy to make a mistake."

"Yes, it's very easy," Big Tiger agreed.

"You're sensible lads," said Good Fortune. "A fellow can talk reasonably to you. So I'll tell you—and it's no secret at all—that this Moonlight is an out-and-out bandit."

"Perhaps our respected elder would tell us a bit more about him?" Christian asked.

"Yes, but not now," said Good Fortune. "Up with you now. We must pack for the road again! When we come to the Etzin Gol remind me. We'll be resting for a day there and I'll tell you about Moonlight."

The journey continued. Greencoat delayed getting in until the last minute. Long after Christian and Big Tiger were in their places he remained sitting in the same spot, sunk in thought and as aloof as a stranger. At last, when Good Fortune was starting up, he got in. Not a word was spoken, and Christian and Big Tiger also said nothing. When the cans and the drums were rattling and knocking together, Christian asked Big Tiger whether it would not have been better to have told Good Fortune that the man with the scar was Moonlight.

"No," said Big Tiger decisively. "We promised Moonlight we would be silent."

"But if he's a bandit?"

"Banditry is an honorable calling," said Big Tiger, "and one must keep one's word to honorable men. Besides, Good Fortune has secrets from us. Why should we not have secrets from him? Let's wait and see. There's safety in waiting."

"Does your teacher say that?"

"No, my grandfather says it. He also often says: 'Youthful folly is rash and brings confusion.' "

"My amah used to say something quite different," Christian countered. "She often looked at me and shook her head, saying: 'Youthful folly brings success.' "

"All that is long past," Big Tiger dissented gravely. "We're men now and must act as men should."

"Does that mean we should kill Greencoat?"

"Perhaps. Bator thought it would be necessary."

"But I can't do it."

"I can't either," Big Tiger admitted frankly.

"Then we must let Greencoat live," sighed Christian.

Meanwhile Good Fortune had driven round the hill on which stood the King's houses with their roofs of yellow glazed tiles. The roofs glistened in the sun. But that was all one could see for they were a long way off, and the heat haze was quivering as on a hot summer day.

The dome-shaped mountain top in the west came nearer, and

seemed no longer so high. That was because the steppe was slowly getting higher. Soon it descended equally gradually into a broad valley. Then the mountain became big once more, and Christian and Big Tiger, whose eyes had been fixed on it for a long time, noticed the stone shrine on its summit, from which a light-colored pennant fluttered.

"That's the Bayin Obo," said Christian, studying the Southern Sheet. "But now the map is white and there's nothing more with a name for a long time."

"It seems Good Fortune is right—a map like that isn't much use," said Big Tiger.

"The General wouldn't have given us the map if it was not useful," Christian objected.

Big Tiger had no answer to this, but Good Fortune's prejudice had definitely undermined his trust in the map. "Why is there nothing but white when there's a riverbed here? Of course there's no water in it—nothing but stones. But there are green bushes around it and probably there are wild animals here."

"Yes, there are," cried Christian excitedly, pointing to a herd of startled antelopes which at that moment bounded out of the shara-mot thicket. They did not run away, however, but sprang in long bounds like practiced racers alongside the truck. Good Fortune put up a furious spurt of speed, but from the outset it was a hopeless race for the lumbering truck. The antelopes outraced it with ease, then, leaping high in the air, changed to the other side, where they quietly began to graze. The flight was at an end. The car had been overtaken. Obviously it was not a dangerous adversary.

"You see," said Big Tiger, "there are wild animals here, but you can't read that on the map."

"There aren't animals on maps," Christian defended himself. "Do you know what those animals are?"

"They're antelopes. I know them from pictures," said Big Tiger. "Wherever there are antelopes there are also wolves."

"I'd love to see a wolf," said Christian. "It would be nice to be sitting up in a tree and see one going by underneath."

"But there are no trees to go under," said Big Tiger. "Since Home in the Rocks we haven't seen a single tree."

While Christian and Big Tiger were discussing these important subjects Good Fortune was driving silently through the steppe watching the sun for his westerly direction and the ground for the holes made by foxes and marmots. But there were not many holes, and as evening fell there were none at all and Good Fortune observed that they were not far from a monastery called Orte Golen Sume.

"Why are you suddenly driving so quickly?" asked Greencoat.

"Because it will soon be dark."

Greencoat was about to reply angrily that he was aware of that, but instead he asked quite civilly whether Good Fortune knew where he was and what the neighborhood was like.

"There's a monastery hereabouts," replied Good Fortune, flattered. "We'll get to it in ten minutes. It's only a small one, but it has two good wells, a Living Buddha who is still a child, and friendly monks."

"Indeed," muttered Greencoat approvingly, again suppressing what he wanted to say, namely that since Good Fortune was an old redbeard it was no wonder that he knew his way about Mongolia better than others, and that that was nothing to boast of. But as he was hatching out a new plot, he held his peace.

"Take off that silly grin," said the unsuspecting Good Fortune. "You'll see at once that I'm right." Greencoat replied he did not doubt it and was only admiring Good Fortune's knowledge.

In the west the sun was hanging over the jagged peaks of distant mountains. It was big and red like a fiery ball rolling over a half-finished world. All around were undulations and low hills which looked as if they might easily be somewhere else tomorrow. The ground was deeply fissured and the scanty grass seemed a futile attempt to bring life into a region which tolerated none. Apparently it would be withered next day, and one would wake up between boulders of primeval stone and drifts of rippling sand—if indeed one ever woke up.

Happily Good Fortune saw things otherwise. For him the earth was reliably solid, and the steppe was a race course over which to speed. He sounded the horn triumphantly, meaning: "Wasn't I right? We've arrived!"

Christian and Big Tiger stood up eagerly and peered ahead through the little window. They saw a gray mountain slope and half way up to it ten or twelve white buildings with flat roofs and red gables. The houses were single-storied with the exception of one in the center which towered above the others. Up in that wilderness it looked like a lead camel surrounded by a lot of frightened white sheep.

"There are tents there too!" cried Christian.

"And a whole lot of horses near the tents," said Big Tiger. "And they're swishing their tails."

Scarcely had Big Tiger spoken than Good Fortune ceased to hoot. He too had seen the blue tents and the horses beside them, and he didn't know what to think of them. So he no longer drove quickly, and the truck lumbered hesitantly and more and more slowly over the great expanse of gravelly ground.

The monastery was no more than five hundred yards distant. But Good Fortune had suddenly lost all desire to stop the night with the friendly monks. He was silently counting the blue tents, and when he had counted sixteen, he made a rapid calculation: Sixteen small tents must shelter one hundred and fifty men, even allowing for a Prince and two or three nobles, who would have tents to themselves. Good Fortune was sure they were Sunit Mongols—people with whom he had never had any contact. But this fellow with the copper-brown face who had come over at midday—what if he were Little Paw? And if so, what was he doing here at Sunit?

Good Fortune looked out the window. To the left and in front stretched the gray gravelly plain. Then came the mountainside with the monastery on it, and a little distance off the tents and the horses. A few men could be seen walking and standing about. Evidently they had seen the truck. To the right there was a gentle height covered with long grass, and up on it Good Fortune noticed a *yurt*. He immediately turned the steering wheel, and Christian and Big Tiger almost fell, so sharply did he turn. Then the truck drove quickly up the hill and stopped.

Christian and Big Tiger jumped down and stood by the door. But Good Fortune still sat in the driver's cab with his left arm hanging half out of the window, staring at the setting sun.

"Is there anything to worry about, honored Sir?" asked Big Tiger timidly.

"There's lots to worry about," replied Good Fortune. "But in Mongolia it's no use planning ahead. Things happen as they must. Fetch some water."

"Yes," said Christian. "Has this place a name?"

"It's not a place," replied Good Fortune. "It's a monastery called Orte Golen Sume."

"And all the tents?"

"The tents belong to Mongols," Greencoat suddenly chimed in. "And the Mongols have come here because there's a festival at the monastery. I know that."

"You don't know that," said Good Fortune, "or you don't know it properly. If there were a festival at the monastery the tents would be much finer tents, and there would be a few *yurts* here too. There's no monastery festival at this time."

"Very well," muttered Greencoat. "You know what you're talking about, no doubt. But what do you think is going on up there . . . you being an old . . . I mean, have you any idea?"

"I should think," said Good Fortune, "that there's going to be just an ordinary wolf hunt tomorrow."

"Bolna!" shouted Christian, gleefully.

Good Fortune turned round astonished. "I hear you speaking Mongolian. Do you know that language?"

"We want to learn it," said Big Tiger, "but it's not easy."

"Fine!" said Good Fortune. "Now take the two pails, and if you meet a king up there at the tents he will be the Barun Sunit *Wang*. You must make a nice *kowtow* to him, and then you can speak to him just as you would to me."

Big Tiger got down the pails while Christian climbed quickly back on the truck and fetched his notebook. Then he went to Good Fortune and asked him to explain the words.

"Barun means western," said Good Fortune, "and *Sunit* is the name of the tribe. So *Barun Sunit Wang* means 'King of the Western Sunits.' "

Christian wrote the words neatly in his book, put it away, and then said: "Now we're going to the King of the Western Sunits to fetch water."

"Take a good stout stick," Good Fortune warned him. "For there'll very likely be dogs there. And the Mongolian dogs are nearly as dangerous as wolves." He went to the driver's cab, lifted the seat, and took out a bamboo stick with a leather thong at the end of it. "Take this," he said. "It's a riding whip. The Mongols call it a *dashior*."

On the way they discussed serious matters, and wondered why Good Fortune, who seemed to know Mongolian, had kept it to himself up till then. "He spoke only Chinese with Moonlight," said Christian. "I took note of that."

"He did that," Big Tiger explained, "because he didn't know for sure whether Moonlight was really Moonlight, and because he thought Moonlight wasn't sure either whether he was Good Fortune or another man. You see, they both distrust each other and are afraid of each other."

"Moonlight isn't afraid at all," said Christian. "He doesn't look as if he was."

"Then it's Good Fortune who's afraid," said Big Tiger.

"He doesn't look afraid either," said Christian.

They went down the slope, and the nearer they got to the valley, the less grass there was. Finally the ground was as bare as a threshing floor, and the two wells which Good Fortune had mentioned stood out as dark, circular spots. Not far off, on the mountainside, were the Mongols' tents. In front of the white monastery buildings the horses stood in long rows. They were tied by their halters to cords stretched on poles like washing lines.

The last light of day was fading, the stars were coming out one after another, and the moon was up too by the time Christian and Big Tiger reached the wells. They were much the same as the Well of the King. Near the first well stood a hollowed-out tree trunk, from which a Mongol was taking water. Two other men were coming down the mountainside with several horses. There was no one at the other well, and Christian let down the first pail by a chain which was lying there. The Mongols looked on, nudged each other, and laughed. Christian did not know why, but he soon

perceived that the chain clanged at the bottom, and when he pulled the bucket up, it was empty.

*"Nash-jirr!"** cried one of the Mongols, signing to Christian and Big Tiger to join him. He then let down a long rod with a canvas bag at the end of it. When he drew it up he poured the water into their pails.

"They're full and we thank you," said Big Tiger politely.

"Bolna," cried Christian merrily.

This time the word was exactly in place, for it means "That's right." The Mongols were delighted. One after the other they put long and elaborate questions to Christian, but he answered not a word. At this they patted him on the back saying no doubt he was shy. When he still remained silent they realized he really could not speak Mongolian. The conversation would have petered out if it had not occurred to Christian that he had learned a new word. Picking up courage he said distinctly: *"Barun Sunit Wang."*

This had a startling effect, but whether a good or a bad one it was difficult to see at once. The Mongols clustered together and talked excitedly. At last the man who had drawn the water came and took Christian and Big Tiger each in a friendly way by an ear, and said as before: *"Nash-jirr!"* Christian answered *"Bolna."* Then they followed the Mongol up to the encampment. He took their heavy water pails, and Big Tiger, who had been getting nervous, felt his courage return. He looked up at the moon, that mighty comforter of souls, and it seemed to him that they lacked some special word and if they could find it all would be well.

"Kwi-Chan," he whispered, "it can't be helped."

At this Christian too cheered up. And now they were already in front of the first of the sixteen blue tents, which looked in the pale moonlight like a collection of black moths which had settled with outspread wings on the light-colored gravelly ground to spend the night there.

The Mongol put down the water pails, signed to Christian and

* *Nash-jirr:* "Come over here!"

Big Tiger to wait, and then entered the tent. After a little while he came out again, grinning amiably, and saying something which sounded like an invitation.

Christian and Big Tiger took hands and entered the tent. It was small, but bright and friendly, and lined inside with white. In the center a fire was burning in a round iron grate, and a tea kettle was boiling. There were carpets laid to right and left. In the background sat two men wearing fur hats like Moonlight's, only more splendid.

Christian and Big Tiger *kowtowed,* murmuring in a low voice: "We wish ten thousand times luck."

Then they looked up at the two men, and Christian thought that the older one must be the King, he looked so dignified. But the older man's face suddenly clouded over, and Christian began to hope that the younger man was the King, for he smiled roguishly and even winked ever so slightly, but said not a word. That made it seem certain that the cross old man was the King, and this seemed specially bad for Christian, at whom he kept looking angrily. This went on for quite a while, until the old man, beside himself with anger, shouted: "Get out, both of you!"

"No," said the younger man in beautiful Peking Chinese. "These are innocent boys; they are only inexperienced. I think they are good people." Then he turned to Christian and asked his name. When told it, he said Compass Mountain was a very unusual and beautiful name.

"This is Big Tiger," said Christian. "He's my friend."

"Ah!" said the younger of the two men. "Now I know you both. I am the Sunit *Wang* and this gentleman is my old cousin. He is angry with Compass Mountain for bringing a whip into the tent. That must not be done."

"I did it through ignorance and on account of the dogs," Christian excused himself, throwing the whip out the door.

"There is nothing to fear," said the King. "We have no dogs with us as we are going wolf-hunting tomorrow."

"Don't you need dogs for that?" asked Big Tiger, astonished.

"We Mongols hunt the wolf without dogs," the King explained. "Sit down and drink a bowl of tea with us."

"We do not dare," murmured Big Tiger and Christian. But then they sat down, as was correct, on the right-hand side of the tent, near the exit.

Their polite behavior made the King's old cousin friendly again. He said one could not always expect the best of manners from foreigners, but fortunately there were exceptions. Then he stood up and led Big Tiger and Christian to the seat of honor on the left-hand side of the King. He himself sat down on the right.

The King and his cousin were drinking tea from wooden bowls, lined with silver. When they noticed that Christian and Big Tiger had no drinking vessels with them, the old cousin sent for two bowls. Then they talked about the boys' journey to Sinkiang and desired Christian to tell them about life in America. But Christian knew no more about it than the King himself, and much less than the old cousin, who had studied in Peking and was very clever.

"We were both born in Peking," Big Tiger explained, "and we have never yet seen the big ocean. We know little of the world."

"We traveled in a train for the first time four days ago," Christian confessed. "And it ended badly."

"No, it ended well," said the King. "For now you have a chance of seeing the steppe and the desert. Nowhere in the world is life so beautiful as here."

"Good Fortune thinks that too," said Big Tiger. "He says Mongolia is like the sea, and that a man is always homesick for it."

"Who is Good Fortune," asked the King, "and where does he come from?"

Big Tiger and Christian told all they knew. The King listened attentively and wanted to know everything, and when something did not seem quite clear to him, he asked for further explanation.

"There are millions of men in China called Good Fortune," the old cousin commented. "I see no real cause for fear."

But the King was not satisfied. "Does this man speak Mongolian?" he asked.

"I believe he does," answered Christian.

"Then I shall ask Moonlight about him," said the King to his cousin. "He's coming tomorrow morning before the hunt begins."

"We must go now," said Big Tiger, "and we thank you for your hospitality, which we do not deserve."

"My child," said the old cousin, "in the steppes hospitality is something which need not be mentioned. My tent is your tent, and my food is your food. That is the way among us. But before you go show me the ring on your hand."

"It's only a snake," said Big Tiger, casually. "I wear the ring to counteract the splendor of my name."

"Who advised you to do that?" asked the old cousin, examining the ring which Big Tiger passed to him.

"A holy man," said Big Tiger.

The old cousin bent forward, the better to see the ring in the firelight. As he did so his face grew sad, and when he passed the ring to the King so that he might look at it too, there were tears in his eyes.

"I believe that ring is a bad ring," said Big Tiger, depressed.

"No *thing* is bad," said the old man. "It is man alone who gives things their meaning and their message. Have you time to hear two words?"

"We're in no hurry," Christian assured him.

"It's good to hear the experience of the aged," said Big Tiger.

"Twenty years ago," began the old cousin slowly and solemnly, "I traveled to Urga for the Feast of the Seven States. There I met Yolros Lama, the Living Buddha of the Belin Sume Monastery. We were old friends, and we spent happy days together. As I took leave of him I asked him to let us meet again. 'Only four days' travel to the southwest separates us,' answered Yolros Lama. 'Why then do you ask that?' I excused myself on the plea of urgent business which called me to Peking. He smiled and said: 'Short distances are the greatest hindrances for friends who desire each other's company. If we are to grow old apart, I will give you a sign. Look at this ring!' He lifted his hand, and I saw the ring which you, Big Tiger, are now wearing on your thumb. 'The ring does not belong to me,' said Yolros Lama. 'One day I must give it back. But before it finds its owner you shall see it, and then you shall know that I am calling you because I shall be leaving the world a few days later. Thus we shall see each other again before it is too late!' "

The old cousin stopped speaking and wiped away his tears with his sleeve, but they came back again and again. The King returned the ring to Big Tiger. Then he laid his hands on the knees of his old cousin, saying: "We shall ride in an hour. I shall ask the Duke of Hanta to lead the hunt for me. In two days and two nights we shall be in Belin Sume with Yolros Lama."

The old cousin nodded, and Big Tiger and Christian stood up to go.

"I must ask you for your generous forgiveness," said the old cousin. "I was unfriendly to you. You, Big Tiger, are the messenger of the holy man Yolros Lama. Accept this bowl as a souvenir of your aged friend, the Duke of Sunit."

Saying this, he drew from under his sash a strip of sky-blue silk, laid it over his two palms, placed on it the silver bowl out of which he had drunk his tea, and with bowed head offered it to Big Tiger.

"You must take it," whispered the King of the Sunits, and Big Tiger took it, murmuring: "Thanks ten thousand times!"

"The *haddak* goes with it," whispered the King, whereupon Big Tiger accepted the strip of blue silk too.

"Compass Mountain," said the King, "I see you also have no bowl. We Mongols always carry one with us so that we can be served with food and drink in any tent. Take my bowl for your use and as a souvenir." And he handed it to Christian, as the old cousin had handed his to Big Tiger, on a strip of blue silk.

"Ene yu beino?" asked Christian.

A swift smile passed over the King's face, and the old cousin too smiled sadly. "The strip of silk is a *haddak,*" the King explained, "and without it no Mongol may either give or receive a gift. The bowl is called an *eich.* May you use it during many years of health."

Then Big Tiger and Christian thanked them again with a *kowtow* and were about to go. But the old cousin and the King were quicker than they. Both stood up and hurried out of the tent before Christian and Big Tiger. Only when outside did they bid farewell with blessings.

20 ABOUT THE MAGIC WORD *"YABONAH"* AND A WOLF HUNT AT WHICH NOT A SINGLE SHOT WAS FIRED

WHEN the King of the Sunits and his old cousin had gone back to the tent, Christian and Big Tiger stuffed the silver bowls and the *haddaks* into their pockets. But their pockets were too small and the bowls were too big, and they stuck out.

Christian picked up the whip. Then they took the water pails and set out to return to the truck. It was a slow journey, however, for they had to put down the heavy pails often to rest. When they were half way, Good Fortune came toward them with a Mongol boy who was driving a herd of goats.

"You're late," scolded Good Fortune. "Greencoat is raging for his food."

"Oh, woe!" cried Christian.

"It can't be helped," said Good Fortune. "Give me the pails. What's that you've got in your pockets?"

"We've each got a present," said Big Tiger.

"Because we're friends of the King of the Sunits and his old cousin," Christian explained.

"You're what?" asked Good Fortune, astonished.

"At first we were not friends," Big Tiger admitted, "but now we are." He showed the silver bowl and Christian showed his. Good Fortune was so astonished that he could only mumble "That beats all." The Mongol boy stood by, silent and awestruck.

"That's very wonderful," said Good Fortune, "but now I'll take back the pails. You boys go with this lad who lives in the *yurt* nearby. Help him to drive the goats up to the monastery, because there's a wolf hunt here tomorrow morning, and they have to be put in safety. Hurry up, we're having noodles!"

Christian and Big Tiger said: "We hear and obey." Then one of them went to each side of the herd of goats and the Mongol boy walked in the center. Unfortunately there was no conversation.

There wasn't a speck of light in the monastery, but the boy knew his way well. Right next to the first little house there was a large courtyard into which they drove the goats. On their way back they met the Mongol who had conducted them to the King's tent. He was holding six saddled horses, and he gave Christian and Big Tiger a friendly greeting. The boy tried to speak to him, but the man did not answer. He only said "*Yabonah.*" It seemed to be a word full of significance, for the boy repeated it several times on the way, as if he found joy and delight in it. All the same, no real conversation got going. True, Christian knew quite a lot of Mon-

golian words, but nothing near a hundred yet. I must ask Good Fortune what *Yabonah* means, he thought. It seems to be a magic word.

When they reached the hill on which the truck stood all was dark and silent. There was no Good Fortune and no Greencoat, no fire, no pot cooking, and therefore nothing to eat. Christian and Big Tiger looked around in dismay, but the Mongol boy laughed and signaled them to follow him to a *yurt* which looked like a gigantic molehill in the darkness, with the moon shining on it. When they reached it the boy bent down and raised the entrance curtain. Christian quickly laid aside his whip.

"Orr! Orr!" cried a deep male voice from inside.

That means "Come in" thought Christian and Big Tiger. Though they were small they had to bend down, for the timber frame of the entrance was low.

"Don't stumble!" Good Fortune shouted to them. "It's an unlucky sign if you do."

Christian and Big Tiger stepped carefully and found themselves in a round felt tent. In the center a fire was burning in the same kind of portable iron grate as in the King's tent. All around it the earth was stamped firm. Polished beams joined to form a square. All the rest of the floor was covered with rugs, and under the rugs were soft felts. Altogether it was a pleasant dwelling.

Opposite the entrance sat the Mongol who had called out: *"Orr!*

Orr!" To the left, in the seats of honor, sat Good Fortune and Greencoat. The seats to the right had been left for Christian and Big Tiger. They bowed and were about to say: "How is the respected elder gentleman?" but Good Fortune interrupted them before they had properly begun.

"Men who are on terms of friendship with Mongol princes must say: 'Do you sit lightly and well?'" he told them. "That is a Mongol greeting. And now sit down, but *not* with your feet toward the fire."

"Is that forbidden?" asked Christian.

"In Mongolia nothing is forbidden," said Good Fortune, "but certain things are not allowed, because they are impolite."

"We are very sorry," said Christian.

"Please excuse our slow understanding," said Big Tiger.

"Fire is a god," Good Fortune explained. "If you stretch your feet toward it, it is offended, and the master of the house and the whole family are offended. Moreover, it shows that a person has no knowledge of correct etiquette, and such a person loses face, and no one thinks anything of him any longer. This evening you two have acquired a big face, and it's now being told in all the tents that the King gave you a handsome gift betokening friendship. You must therefore be particularly well-behaved."

"We wish to be faultless in our behavior," Big Tiger assured him.

"We shall be very polite from today on," Christian agreed.

The Mongol now joined in the conversation. He pointed to the pot on the fire, spoke polite words, and urged them to eat. Christian and Big Tiger drew the silver bowls from their pockets. This made Greencoat stare. His jaw jutted forward and he tugged at his beard. Good Fortune filled the bowls with the noodle soup. There were pieces of meat floating about in the pot, and the host fished out the biggest ones and put them on top of the noodles.

"Eat now," said Good Fortune.

"I do not dare," replied Christian timidly, looking over at the entrance near which he had just noticed a woman and a little girl sitting.

"Don't mind them," said Good Fortune. "Eat!"

"One mustn't notice the women," whispered Big Tiger.

Then they started eating, and the boy Odburring also got his share. In the course of time it transpired that the father's name was Sertchi, and Good Fortune said that was a magnificent Tibetan name meaning Golden Armor.

"Stop showing off your knowledge," said Greencoat crossly.

"My despised knowledge has procured you a good meat dinner," answered Good Fortune.

"That's true," growled Greencoat, and suddenly he nodded amiably because he remembered his new plan. He stroked his beard and tried to make a pleasant face. "I hear the young gentlemen are frequenting the company of reigning princes," he said.

"We couldn't help it," Christian explained apologetically. "We were conducted to a tent and the King was sitting there with his old cousin beside him. Then we said who we were."

"And when we got to know each other better," Big Tiger continued the tale, "we were given these silver bowls as souvenirs."

"Show them to me," said Greencoat.

Big Tiger and Christian, who had finished eating, wiped the bowls clean and handed them to Greencoat. They were beautifully turned and finely polished and ornamented around the rim with silver leaves. One could see the knots in the wood, and then again a silver garland. The bottom was particularly beautifully worked, with leaping antelopes, deer, trees and birds, all in shining silver.

"Well, well," said Greencoat, visibly impressed. "So that's what you get from a king for saying who you are."

"We had a little talk too," Christian hinted, "but not much."

Greencoat gave back the bowls with a friendly grin. He would have liked to shout: "You infernal little liars," or "You needn't show me a louse with a saddle and say 'That's a horse,' " but that might have been detrimental to his plot. "Watch out that you don't let the bowls drop," he said amiably. "It would be a terrible shame. That's a splendid ring you've got, Big Tiger."

"I've just noticed it too," said Good Fortune. "You haven't been wearing it long."

"I've only been wearing it since today," said Big Tiger casually.

"Is it another present?" asked Greencoat.

"No one gave me a present of this ring."

"But where did you get it from, little son?"

"Well, I just have it," said Big Tiger hesitantly. He really wanted to say nothing more, but when they all kept silently looking at the strange ring, he felt he had to tell a lie. "My grandfather," he said bravely, "gave me this ring to counteract the splendor of my name."

"Your grandfather is a remarkable man," said Greencoat.

"He says 'Self-abasement and perfect truthfulness are good for the soul.' "

"Bravo!" cried Greencoat. "Your worthy grandfather is a sage of the highest rank."

"Why have you been wearing the ring only since today?" asked Good Fortune.

"Because I wear it only when the moon is in its first quarter," Big Tiger explained, "or when it's past it. Sometimes I wear it when the moon is waxing, or when it's round as a silver batz. It's all a troublesome secret."

"I know that," cried Greencoat. "It's a lucky ring."

"I don't speak of it," said Big Tiger modestly.

"You're right," said Greencoat. "One must be careful."

"It's unwise to penetrate into the secret workshop of nature," said Christian, trying to change the subject. "There are lucky rings which no one understands. There are also magic words, and I heard one of them on the way."

At another time Greencoat would have snarled "Nonsense," but now he asked with a great show of interest: "What's the magic word?"

"*Yabonah*," said Christian.

Up till then Sertchi had remained silent, for he understood scarcely a word of Chinese. But now he became animated, slapped his thighs and cried "*Yabonah!*" Then he asked Good Fortune all sorts of questions, and Odburring too joined in.

"Get out your notebook again and write *Yabonah*," said Good Fortune to Christian. "*Yabonah* really means only 'Go,' naturally not on foot, for nobody goes on foot in Mongolia as long as he can ride. It means 'Let's start!' or 'We're off!' and as there's nothing more delightful than traveling, everyone rejoices when *Yabonah* is heard."

Sertchi now told that the hunt was to begin an hour before sunrise. The wolf would be encircled within a wide radius of the monastery of Orte Golen Sume. In the afternoon they would hunt at Yellow Hill Gap, and in the evening somewhere else. This was necessary in order to kill the many wolves that had come down from the north during the winter.

By the time Good Fortune had translated Sertchi's tale the fire had burned down, and Sertchi pulled a string which closed the smoke vent in the roof of the *yurt*.

"Now it will remain nice and warm and we shall sleep, so fetch your blankets and sleeping bags," said Good Fortune.

Christian and Big Tiger went out to the truck. Big Tiger had just climbed up to hand down the sleeping bags, when the most frightful howling filled the air. It sounded as if the whole endless misery of the world was finding voice in a wolf's throat. When the wolf stopped for breath it was as if a pipe was playing, and when he started again, the howling seemed to come from just behind the *yurt*. One almost expected his green, glaring eyes, the cloud of his breath, and his bushy tail to appear at any moment.

Big Tiger and Christian jumped with fright, and Christian was about to climb on to the truck, but Big Tiger said: "He's a long way off. There's nothing to be afraid of."

"Why then is he howling like that?" asked Christian.

"He's got a sick stomach," said Big Tiger glibly. He jumped down from the truck without waiting for further questions, and they both returned to the *yurt*. They walked a bit faster than usual, for the night had turned cold, the stars were twinkling, and the wolf had stopped howling. It was probably prowling up for a closer look at the truck, or perhaps it was attracted by the smell of the goats.

In the *yurt* Sertchi pressed on his guests the best places, and when they wanted to lie at the edge, he said: "I'm responsible for your safety. Many people freeze to death if they lie at the edge. But I must go out to the hunt early in the morning, and I won't have time to look after dead people."

Saying this, he distributed felt covers and furs, and as each one chose his sleeping place, he said: "Sleep soundly and well!"

And so they did, for they were all very tired. Christian lay awake for a while listening lest the wolf should be prowling around, but his eyes soon closed. Outside the night passed quietly, the moon disappeared, and the stones of the desert did not stir.

Toward morning Sertchi rose quietly and awakened Odburring, and before long a horse was heard stopping before the *yurt*. Sertchi and Odburring went out, and then a rough voice said: *"Yabonah!"* Thereupon Sertchi and Odburring rode away with the strange man who had brought the horses.

"Who was the man who said *Yabonah?*" asked Christian.

"It was Little Paw," whispered Big Tiger.

"I think it was Moonlight," said Christian.

After another hour Good Fortune got stirring. Usually he slept eight hours non-stop. Then, when he awoke, he did not waste much time yawning. He just looked round, noted where he was, jumped up and got busy lighting the fire, fetching water, filling the tank with gasoline, and being generally industrious.

But Sertchi's wife would allow none of this. "Lie quiet and rest," she said.

"I don't want to lie quiet," Good Fortune objected.

"You have to," said the Mongol woman, laughing. And without more ado she seated herself on him as if he were a bench. "You're our honored guest and you have to obey."

She emptied the ashes and revived the few glowing embers. Then she filled the pot with water, threw a few pieces of brick tea into it and a good pinch of salt, opened the smoke vent and busied herself with cleaning until the tea boiled.

Christian, who was following the woman's movements, saw that it was still dark outside. So one could remain lying down and talk for a bit, as the ancient Romans used to do. Why, they even ate and drank lying down, and no one came and told them to "Sit up!" But just as Christian had thought of a suitable question to start a conversation about the hunt, Good Fortune said: "Get up, men! Roll up your sleeping bags. We're starting."

"But it's still dark," said Christian, pointing to the smoke vent, through which pale stars were shining.

"We must get away," said Good Fortune. "Otherwise we'll disturb the hunters and get held up."

"I'd love to see a wolf, or even two," Christian admitted.

Good Fortune had no such desire. He said the hunt would begin at sunrise and they must be on the road by then. For he wanted to drive as far as Cow Pond today, and that was at least seven hundred *li*.

So Christian and Big Tiger got up, and Greencoat greeted them amiably with: "Good morning, young princes!"

The housewife filled their bowls with tea, into which she shook a handful of yellow millet.

"What do we do with this?" asked Christian under his breath.

"I don't know," whispered Big Tiger. "I'm not a cock."

"Set to!" cried Good Fortune encouragingly. "This is a breakfast for eating and drinking." He raised his bowl, took a gulp of tea, and then chewed the millet that had swum into his mouth with it.

"I know that," said Greencoat. "It's Mongolian."
"We didn't know it," said Big Tiger, "but now we know it too, and it tastes good."
When Good Fortune stood up to go out the woman and the girl hastened out before him, and Good Fortune said that was the custom here, and that it belonged to the Mongol *joss*.
"Ene yu beino?" asked Christian.
The Mongol *joss* is the law of the steppe," Good Fortune explained. "It comes down from the time of Genghis Khan, and every man of honor must live in accordance with it."
They went over to the truck, and Good Fortune poured hot water into the radiator, as he had done the previous morning at White Stone. But the motor wouldn't start. "Hand me the little can with the red stripe," he cried.
Christian handed it down from the truck, and watched Good Fortune take a little squirt, fill it from the can, and inject some of the liquid into each cylinder.
"Now," said Good Fortune, satisfied, "the car will bound forward like an antelope!" He handed back the can and went in front again.
"What's the name of the stuff in that can?" asked Big Tiger.
"I'll look and see," said Christian, opening the screw cap and sticking in his nose. But he recoiled in haste. "It's ether," he said coughing. "My father uses this stuff when he cuts people's stomachs open."
"Does he do that often?" Big Tiger inquired.
"Almost every day," said Christian," "but of course only when someone wants him to."
"Look out!" shouted Good Fortune at that moment. "The lord of the steppe is coming! Stay up there!" He leaped into the driver's cab and slammed the door.
"What's up?" asked Christian, letting the screw cap drop.
"Good Fortune means the wolf," said Big Tiger calmly.
Christian jumped up. Dawn was breaking in all its glory over

the hills. The sun was rising slowly and above the valleys strips of mist floated, thin as a breath. Here and there galloping riders were emerging out of the mist. More and more of them appeared, and they were shouting and swinging lassoes fastened to sticks. In a few moments hell had broken loose round the height.

"The hunters are coming!" cried Christian, but Big Tiger shook his head.

"You think the wolf would come up here just on his own?" asked Christian.

"Yes," Big Tiger asserted. "They always make for hills and mountains when they're pursued."

"He's coming!" cried Christian. "No, they're coming! There are two of them!"

Big Tiger looked eagerly over the rampart of drums. Up the mountainside where they had driven the goats to the monastery last evening, came two wolves in full flight, pursued by a horseman. With his left hand he was whipping his horse to the utmost speed, while in the right he held his lasso aloft, ready to throw. The wolves were running for their lives. Then the man stood up in the stirrups and the horse galloped all out. It was almost flying. But the wolves were going all out too, until at last one of them became exhausted and was caught in the lasso. There was a mighty tug and the cord pulled taut, lifting the wolf high off the ground. He fell on his back and the hunter and his horse, both possessed with the same fury, galloped downhill dragging the wolf behind them. He turned several somersaults, then rolled over dead.

The other wolf had reached the height. He stopped exhausted not ten paces from the truck, his flanks rising and falling, and looked around at his enemies, who were now pressing uphill, their reins hanging. The wolf wanted to break away again, but he couldn't, for riders had suddenly appeared from behind the *yurt* too. Then, seeing he was hemmed in, the wolf crouched on the ground, his back arched and his fore legs straight, gnashed his teeth, snarled hoarsely with his jaws open, then snapped them shut with a crack.

Big Tiger felt his spine going hot and cold, and Christian was no longer so keen on seeing a wolf near. Both gazed as if bewitched, as he crouched lower and lower, at the same time creeping backwards. By the time the first hunter galloped by with his lasso aloft the wolf had disappeared.

"He's sitting under the truck!" whispered Christian.

"It can't be helped!" said Big Tiger calmly.

The circle of hunters had closed in. The horses snorted, foam dropped from their mouths, they pawed the ground, and the riders shouted a kind of "tally-ho" at the top of their voices. Some of them tried to poke their poles under the truck, but the wolf refused to be dislodged. In spite of all the noise they could hear the whistling of his breath and the snapping of his jaws.

Good Fortune opened the little window at the back of his cab. "What's up?" he asked.

"The wolf is sitting under the truck," Big Tiger reported coolly.

Greencoat grinned. He was safe and sound, and it was easy for him to be complacent.

"Drive on," he said to Good Fortune. "It's high time."

"Certainly, if you get out and start up."

"You know I don't know how to do that," replied Greencoat, abashed.

"I'll show you how," said Good Fortune affably, half opening the door.

"Help!" shouted Greencoat. "He wants to set the wolf on me!"

"Don't shout like that," said Good Fortune, laughing and shutting the door.

At this juncture a rider in a blue coat and with a fur-trimmed hat pulled well down over his forehead detached himself from the crowd of hunters. He seemed to be the only one who did not have a lasso. Instead, slung around the right wrist, he had a leather strap to which was attached a leather bag, apparently full of some heavy stuff, for it hung straight down and hardly swung at all.

"Moonlight!" whispered Christian.

"It can't be helped," murmured Big Tiger. "It's Little Paw."

The rider urged his unwilling horse right up against the truck door and tapped sharply at the window.

"It is me!" he cried half aloud in Chinese. "Open!"

Good Fortune turned pale, but he obeyed mechanically. Hardly had he opened the window than Moonlight said in a tone which brooked no opposition: "Remember your promise!"

"I remember it," Good Fortune answered.

"Then get out and start the car! Quick!"

Without waiting for a reply Moonlight moved off, but pulled up again a few yards behind the truck.

Christian and Big Tiger felt desperately frightened. They looked first at Good Fortune and then at Moonlight, who was staring with lowered eyes between the wheels of the truck, swinging the leather strap with its weighted bag.

Good Fortune got out pale but completely composed. Almost as if in a trance he walked to the front, bent down and turned the crank. The motor began to hum, the truck trembled gently, and Good Fortune walked back to his seat as if there were no Moonlight and no wolf. He shut the little window at the back, released the brakes and started up. The car gave a few jerks, the drums banged together, and the tally-ho of the horde of hunters rent the air. Christian and Big Tiger watched Moonlight's horse rear as a gray shadow shot from under the truck and hung for a moment on to the reins of the terrified animal. They also saw Moonlight's raised arm, and heard the swish of the leather strap with its lead-filled bag. But the bag missed its mark. The wolf, in his blind assault, had bitten through the horse's reins. His paws, which were seeking the hunter's hands, did not reach high enough, and clawed the chest of the rearing horse instead, leaving a bleeding gash. The wolf fell, rolled on the ground, jumped up again, and suddenly there he was hanging by his forepaws on to the side of the truck.

In their terror Christian and Big Tiger nearly stopped breathing, for simultaneously with the paws the head appeared, with bared fangs and flashing, desperate eyes. With his last ounce of strength the wolf was trying to pull up his hindquarters, and Big Tiger and Christian saw with horror that he was about to succeed. Up rose the head, then the shoulder blades; and the pointed muzzle pushed forward between them. Without stopping to think, Christian grabbed the can with the red stripe, and poured a good dose of the contents down the wolf's throat. Then he shut his eyes, and when he opened them again the wolf had disappeared. Moonlight's strange weapon swished through the air. There was a short, solid bang, and a cry of jubilation rose from a hundred throats.

Good Fortune, who had not yet stirred from his place, let go with the horn and wanted to make his way out through the surge of riders, but it was impossible. While he was thinking how to make a fast get-away, Moonlight tapped on the window again. "Get out," he said gravely.

Good Fortune opened the door obediently, and Moonlight dismounted. Odburring came forward, took the wounded horse, and saddled a fresh one for Moonlight. Most of the hunters dismounted to have a close look at the dead wolf.

"He has crushed his skull," said Big Tiger, who had remained in the truck with Christian, because from up there they had the best view of everything that was going on.

"Come over here," said Christian, plucking Big Tiger by the sleeve. He pointed furtively at Moonlight and Good Fortune. The two appeared to have something important to say to each other, for they moved away out of earshot. Big Tiger and Christian stood behind the drums and looked on. Greencoat too bent forward inquisitively, and believing himself unobserved, noiselessly opened the window on his side. But all the same he could not hear what Good Fortune and Moonlight were saying. Moonlight was apparently trying to talk Good Fortune into something. Then he stepped back, bowed, put his hand into his belt pouch and drew something out which he offered to Good Fortune with both hands, and which Good Fortune took with a reverential air, held to his nose and then handed back. They bowed again, and then turned and rejoined the others, laughing and talking, and suddenly the best of friends. Greencoat closed the window again.

"Hi, boys!" cried Good Fortune merrily. "Where are you hiding?"

"We're here," said Big Tiger and Christian, emerging from behind the drums.

"Come down!" cried Moonlight. "You must be mighty proud of yourselves!"

"The young do not wish to put themselves forward," replied Big Tiger politely.

Good Fortune snuffled and blew his nose as he came toward the truck. "Have you spilled the can with the red stripe?" he asked.

"Some of it has been spilled," Christian admitted.

"But only a little," said Big Tiger. Then he described their adventure with the wolf which Christian had anesthetized and Moonlight said to Good Fortune: "Your two younger brothers are heroes and sons of heroes. Let us speak two words of homage to them."

"Do as you like," said Good Fortune. "But they've thrown away enough ether to knock out ten wolves." He climbed into the truck to see if there was some left in the can, and Moonlight lifted Christian and Big Tiger down. He led them through the throng of riders up to the man who in the beginning had pursued the two wolves alone, and killed the first one with his lasso.

They bowed and Big Tiger said: "We salute the Duke of Hanta, and we wish him riches, good luck and a long life."

"How do you know who I am, my sons?" asked the Duke.

"The King of the Sunits said: 'I shall ask the Duke of Hanta to lead the hunt,' " said Christian. "Since you opened it you must be the Duke."

"Heaven knows what kind of boys you are!" cried the Duke, astonished. "Will you ride with me?"

"I've never been on a horse yet," said Big Tiger meekly.

"We beg you graciously to excuse us," said Christian. "We have to drive to Cow Pond today."

"To Cow Pond?" cried the Duke, displeased. "What do you want there?"

"Perhaps there's a tent there in which we can sleep," said Big Tiger.

Moonlight remarked that there was a tent there, and when the Duke looked at him inquiringly, he added: "The merchant Greencoat is also traveling in the horseless car, as he intends to spend the night with his agent at Cow Pond."

"Look out!" warned the Duke. "You're in no good company!"

"We know that," said Christian, sadly.

"We are sitting in distress under a leafless tree," said Big Tiger.

"Stay with me, then," the Duke proposed. "You will be safe in my tent. Each of you shall have a horse, and I shall teach you to hunt the wolf with a lasso."

"We thank you for your immeasurable kindness," said Big Tiger.

"But we must go home," said Christian. "My father and mother are waiting for me; and my old amah is waiting too. If I don't go home people will say: 'This amah is guilty of letting Compass Mountain get lost.' She will be dismissed, and she will lose face."

"In that case," the Duke agreed, "you must certainly get home quickly. The King told me you're going to Sinkiang?"

"Yes, we're going that road," said Christian.

"The honorable commander in Urumchi is to help us," said Big Tiger.

"It's a long way to Urumchi," said the Duke anxiously, and turning to Moonlight he asked: "How is the road?"

"*Hammagua!* There's nothing to fear."

"Is that really true? You know what I mean, Little Paw."

"Beyond the Etzin Gol all beneath the heavens is in safe hands," Moonlight replied; and he added a few words in Mongolian. The Duke was reassured, and he called Odburring, who at his order brought two small bags. "Here is a worthless gift," he said, taking from his belt a sky-blue *haddak*. Presenting it ceremoniously he continued: "Please be gracious enough to accept my poor gift."

Christian and Big Tiger bowed low. As they murmured "Thanks ten thousand times" Christian suddenly remembered the Sunit *Wang* saying that it was not permissible in Mongolia either to accept or present a gift without a *haddak*. He quickly put his hand in his pocket, and while Big Tiger took the sky-blue silk cloth from the Duke's hands, Christian offered as return gift the *haddak* which he had received from the Sunit *Wang*. The Duke of Hanta accepted it with thanks and put it away in his belt. Moonlight stood behind the Duke smiling. He raised his right thumb several times, and that meant: Well done, Compass Mountain.

Christian and Big Tiger then bade farewell. Moonlight accompanied them back to the truck, and as he lifted them in Good Fortune sounded the horn. The truck moved off slowly and the Mongols fell back raising their lasso poles aloft like spears with a great cry.

"*Yabonah!*" they bellowed in chorus. "*Sä Yabonah!*" The cry rolled like thunder over the gravelly plain, and the echoing hills answered.

In the midst of the riders and horses stood Moonlight, and because he had no lasso he pulled off his fur hat and waved it aloft, and the red scar across his forehead turned crimson and almost blue, so loudly and heartily did he cry: "*Yabonah! Sä Yabonah!*"

21 CONCERNING THE WILD LAMA THUNDERBOLT AND UNHAPPILY ALSO A LIE WHICH WAS TOLD

The riders on the height became smaller and smaller, and as the truck drove by the Well of Orte Golen Sume the sun was rising over the distant grassy hills in the east, bringing with it the certainty of warmth and light, and of the joy of travel.

"Do you feel light and well, Kwi-Chan?"

"Yes, I feel light and well, Big Tiger."

"That's the way Mongols greet each other," said Big Tiger. "Odburring told me so."

At that moment a slow, swelling, droning sound began to fill the valley. It was like the howling of wolves, and the blast of trumpets, and one could not know straight away what to think of it, or whether it was horrible or beautiful.

"Is that something to be afraid of?" asked Big Tiger disconcerted.

"I believe it's nothing bad," said Christian, for he noticed that Good Fortune was calmly driving on.

The white walls of the monastery gleamed in the sunshine; in their midst stood the monks' little houses looking like dice. The Mongols' tents lay folded together in rows. Two old men were loading them on to camels which sat there and stretched out their necks when the swelling, booming sound began. The two old men looked up the mountain slope. When Big Tiger and Christian looked up too they saw four Mongols standing up there, dressed in the red robes of lamas. The young monks had clean-shaven heads which were red from exertion, for they were blowing huge horns. And when one of them got out of breath, another began.

"These horns groan and howl," said Big Tiger. "Why do they do that?"

"They groan," Christian explained, "because they're being blown, and they're being blown because the sun is rising."

Soon they were both merry again. The monastery of Orte Golen Sume disappeared and the boom of the horns died away. They were now driving across a wide plateau where there was little grass but a lot of gravel as evenly strewn as on the path of the imperial garden in Peking.

"Perhaps there's something to eat in the bags," said Christian, opening his one.

"In my bag," cried Big Tiger, "there are round white slabs with fluted edges, and a flower printed on top of them; or perhaps it's a symbol."

"Probably it's a secret sign," Christian surmised.

"These signs," said Big Tiger, "are round as the noon sun and divided in the middle, so they must be lucky signs."

"And I've got little brown squares in my bag," Christian remarked, "and they smell of honey."

They settled down comfortably, and as they looked out at the endless plain where there were no animals or anything but stones, they chewed the little squares which tasted sweetly of wild honey. Big Tiger began to nibble one of the white, deckle-edged disks. "This stone doesn't taste very nice," he said.

Christian tapped at the little window of the driver's cab, and when Good Fortune opened it, he passed him out a disk, asking: *"Ene yu beino?"*

"Sheep cheese," said Good Fortune. "Where did you get it?"

"We got it as a present," said Big Tiger.

"That's because we're on friendly terms with the Duke of Hanta," said Christian casually.

"My respects!" cried Greencoat. "Just what I'd expect of the young gentlemen."

"Mongolian sheep cheese," said Good Fortune, "is a wonderful food. You bite off a little bit, let it soften in your mouth, swallow it, and you're well fed for half a day."

"May we offer our esteemed elder a little?" asked Big Tiger.

"Yes, pass it," said Good Fortune, and bit off a piece. "Sheep cheese is as good as bread, and better."

"None for me, thanks," said Greencoat coolly. "I know it."

After two hours' driving the landscape became more interesting. Though the plateau still remained almost as high as ever, there was grass and *shara-mot*. Good Fortune had to drive slowly, for the ground was no longer firm. Red mounds of loose crumbling earth —the so-called *loess** hills—formed an amphitheater in the distance, from which there was only a small outlet to the west. Toward this gap Good Fortune steered his course, and by midday two *yurts* appeared just before they reached the defile. The *shara-mot* thicket grew higher, there were bushes of it, and sometimes it looked actually like little trees, of which the grazing camels had left only the naked branches. Little camel foals were on the pastures with their mothers. They wore felt coats and caps, and when Good Fortune sounded the horn they leaped in the air, all fours together. Dogs came running from the *yurts* showing their teeth, and so much out of breath that they could hardly bark.

Good Fortune stopped beside the first *yurt* and got out. He took the whip to keep the dogs at bay, but it was not necessary—a young Mongol came out of the *yurt* and called them back, but they began to snarl again when Greencoat got out.

* *Loess:* A word introduced by German geologists to describe the crumbling reddish soil made of desert sand and earth which forms the high jagged peaks and cliffs and the low chains of hills characteristic of North China and Mongolia.

"Come down, boys," cried Good Fortune. "The dogs won't touch you."

"*Hammagua!*" cried the Mongol. "There's nothing to fear."

"Do you feel light and well?" asked Good Fortune affably.

"I feel light and well," answered the young man, "and have you had an easy and good journey?"

Good Fortune took out his snuff bottle, which had a silver stopper. The Mongol also took a snuff bottle from his belt, but his was made of pure chased silver, and the stopper, with its thin wooden spoon attached, was decorated with coral.

Good Fortune and the Mongol stood at the correct distance apart. They bowed like dignitaries and with outstretched hands exchanged snuff bottles. But neither took a pinch, as Christian thought they would. Each only smelled the other's bottle and solemnly handed it back, murmuring a benediction or a secret formula as he did so. After this they smiled at each other like friends. When they had put back their snuff bottles Big Tiger whispered to Christian: "Now they've clinched a friendship."

"Like Good Fortune and Moonlight after the wolf hunt," whispered Christian.

"Come on!" cried Good Fortune. "Now it's Compass Mountain's turn. Here! I'll lend you my snuff bottle."

Christian took it, and suddenly remembering what he had

learned the evening before in Sertchi's tent, he said in fluent Mongolian: "Do you feel light and well?"

"Yes," the Mongol replied. "Have you had a good and easy journey?"

"Good," Christian answered. But then he knew no more and looked appealingly for help to Good Fortune, who stood proudly by. He then showed Christian the correct way to take the snuff bottle in his hands and taught him to say: "Are you well in health? Are all your livestock well?"

While Christian repeated the words the Mongol exchanged his snuff bottle with him. Christian held it to his nose, and when he had given it back, and got back that of Good Fortune, the salutation was at an end.

It was then Big Tiger's turn, and after that Good Fortune said: "Now you know more or less how to behave. Anyone who exchanges this salutation with a Mongol is sure of his friendship."

"And what about Greencoat?" asked Christian.

"He thinks himself too superior to observe Mongolian customs," answered Good Fortune.

"But isn't that impolite?" asked Big Tiger.

"It's downright stupid," Good Fortune replied. But he said it in a low voice, for Greencoat came along just then and asked whether there would be something to eat, as he was hungry.

"I'll just see," said Good Fortune, and leaving the whip outside, he entered the *yurt*. Christian and Big Tiger followed, and Greencoat tramped in behind them.

The young Mongol was the last to enter. "I'm a herdsman," he said to Good Fortune. "Therefore all I can offer you is some meat. My brothers and two others of our family herd the horses and camels of the rich Pandiriktchi, to whom these two *yurts* belong."

"Pandiriktchi?" asked Greencoat, knitting his brows.

"Wait two minutes," answered Good Fortune irritably.

They all sat down in the *yurt,* the floor of which was covered with brown felt made from goat's and camel's hair. In place of cushions, as in the King's *yurt,* there were saddle covers.

"My name is Dasha," said the young Mongol, "and I think I know the gentleman who did not greet me."

"He's the merchant Greencoat, and I beg your forgiveness for his impolite demeanor."

"The arrogant dragon will have cause to repent," said Dasha, lifting the wooden cover of an iron pot, under which a low fire was burning. "I have cooked enough meat for two days. Please start eating." He took a fork and put a big piece of boiled mutton in each person's bowl, saying with an embarrassed smile: "I beg you to excuse me, but we are bad people."

"What do you mean?" asked Good Fortune. "You are treating us to a generous feast. Where does the badness come in?"

"We Mongols," explained Dasha, "are not supposed to slaughter beasts until the fourth moon. But after all we're no lamas, we're lawbreakers and don't keep strictly to the rules."

Good Fortune laughed. "Three cheers for the lawbreakers!" he said. "Last evening, too, we had the good luck to eat in the *yurt* of one of them."

"I know I'm not the only one," Dasha admitted, "but it's not right all the same. In the monasteries the lamas are fasting at this time, and many of them get the sickness that makes the head and legs thick."

"Where's Pandiriktchi?" interrupted Greencoat.

"You seem to have a bad conscience about Pandiriktchi," Good Fortune retorted, munching. "Let me alone about him."

"I must know," said Greencoat, obstinately.

"A man who has a clear conscience," Good Fortune admonished, "keeps a calm heart if there's a knock at the door at midnight."

Suddenly the dogs outside began barking, and soon afterwards the short trot of a Mongolian horse became audible. They could hear the rider cursing, and the horse kicking, and then one of the dogs began to whine. Apparently the horse had kicked it. Then they heard the rider dismounting, and the heavy tread of boots.

"I don't know that man," said Dasha, listening. He was about to stand up when the felt entrance curtain was thrown back, and the massive form of a wild-looking man filled the doorway. He wore a sheepskin coat with the wool inside and the skin outside. The skin had once been white, but now it was black from the smoke of many a campfire. Around his waist he wore a yellow sash which likewise was no longer pure yellow. From it hung a tobacco pouch, a dagger, and a crescent-shaped flint for kindling fire. Even by Mongolian standards his attire was shabby. But when you looked at the man's hat you forgot about the burst seams and the missing buttons, for the hat was a most magnificent one, made of yellow silk and silver fox fur.

"Do you sit lightly and well?" asked the man in a rolling bass, and his glance flitted from one to the other of the strangely assorted company around the fireplace. When it reached Good Fortune and saw the uniform it stopped, and the stranger's face suddenly became hostile. The sharp lines between the eyes deepened, and the black moustache trembled in the gust of his breath. "Chinaman," asked the man brusquely, "does the horseless car belong to you?"

"The horseless car belongs to the great General Wu," Good Fortune replied, undaunted, "and my name is not Chinaman."

"This warrior has exchanged the greeting of friendship with me," Dasha said appeasingly.

"Hm!" growled the stranger. "So that's the way." He sat down, put his hand in his sash bag, and exchanged snuff bottles with Dasha.

"Eat," Dasha bade him. "I see you've come a long way."

The stranger looked down at his dusty boots, drew his eating bowl from under his coat, and filled it with meat broth.

"That's enough," he said. "I eat no meat."

Then for a while everything was very quiet. Only the crackling of the fire and the gentle simmering of the pot could be heard, and Christian and Big Tiger began to feel uneasy.

"Why doesn't he eat?" Christian whispered to Good Fortune.

"He's a lama," Good Fortune whispered back. "He must not eat any meat at this time."

Christian wondered, and became more uneasy than ever. He thought of Yolros Lama, who was as kind as a father, and he thought also of the King's old cousin, who was riding day and night without stopping in order to see his old friend once more. Where might this rough boor, who was also a lama, be riding to?

"Please excuse me," said Christian, who had got a sudden brain wave. "I'll be back at once."

He put down his silver bowl and left the tent. First he glanced toward the dogs, but they were lying lazily in the sun, panting, with their tongues hanging out. All the same he fetched Good Fortune's whip, which was leaning against the *yurt*. Beside it was another, thick as a cudgel, and beside this cudgel stood a rifle, a modern cavalry carbine. The polished shaft shone in the sun, and from the barrel hung a tuft of horse hair, dyed red. Christian glanced at it timidly, took Good Fortune's whip, and crossed over to the truck.

The warlike monk's horse was tied to the door of the truck. It was a piebald, short, wild, and vigorous like its master. A fringe of white hair surrounded the fetlocks and hung over the hoofs, making them look like paws. Ribbons were plaited into its mane, and its tail swept the ground. Christian prudently decided to give it a wide berth as he climbed into the truck.

He took three pieces of sheep cheese from one bag and a handful of honey cakes from the other, and then went back to the *yurt*. He found the same dismal silence as before. They were all solemnly chewing mutton, and the lama was blowing his soup to cool it.

Christian sat down and whispered to Big Tiger: "I'm going to do something splendid. Give me a *haddak*."

Big Tiger put his hand in his pocket and took out the piece of sky-blue silk which he had received from the Duke of Hanta. Christian spread it out, laid the sheep cheese and honey cakes on it, and then, taking the silk at each end, he bowed politely to the wild lama. He wanted to find a few suitable words in Mongolian, but finding none, he said in faultless Peking Chinese: "I beg the great old father not to reject my poor gift."

While Christian was speaking these beautiful words, the word he was looking for suddenly occurred to him, and he ended his little speech beaming, with an expressive: *"Bolna!"*

"You should have said *Bolvo,"** whispered Good Fortune.

The lama stopped blowing his soup. He put down his bowl, looked at the *haddak,* then at Christian, and as he did so his expression softened. Finally he grinned from ear to ear. "I to have?" he asked, and one could see that his Chinese was even worse than Bator's.

"My gift is a poor one, Your Excellency," said Christian. "I therefore beg for forgiveness. *Bolvo?"*

The lama snorted, put his hand into his sash and pulled out a faded *haddak,* which he handed to Christian with a solemn bow. Then he accepted the gift. "Little son," he asked, and his voice had a friendly boom, "you friend Sunit *Wang?"* And he pointed to the embossed sign on the sheep cheese which Big Tiger had taken for a lucky symbol.

"The Sunit *Wang* is our esteemed friend," said Christian.

"And his old cousin too," Big Tiger added, letting the wild man see the silver bowl.

"Great respect say!" cried the lama, bowing, whether to Big Tiger, or to the silver bowl, or to both they did not know. Christian was sorry his bowl was not empty, but the lama noticed nevertheless where it had come from. He became quite genial and began asking questions in a mixture of Chinese and Mongolian until Good Fortune thawed and explained to him in Mongolian where

* *Bolvo:* "Is this right?" or "Will this pass?"

they came from, where they were going, and how they had fared at the wolf hunt.

"Where is the Sunit *Wang* now?" the lama inquired.

Good Fortune shrugged his shoulders and said he did not know.

The lama cursed between his teeth, then he boomed in a tragic bass which filled the whole *yurt:* "Heaven and earth come together, but the water on the mountainside cannot be found! I have ridden ten horses almost to death that my eyes might behold the Sunit *Wang* and now he is I know not where."

"Why is he roaring so sorrowfully?" asked Big Tiger.

"Because he doesn't know where to find the King of the Sunits," Good Fortune explained.

Christian looked at Big Tiger, and Big Tiger took it he should speak up if he thought fit. "Yesterday," he began slowly, "we thought it was a secret, but perhaps it's not a secret, and it can be told."

"Yes, it can be told," Christian agreed.

"What are you two talking about?" asked Good Fortune, who again could not follow.

"We're talking about a secret that isn't a secret, and that we can therefore tell," Christian explained.

"Rubbish!" cried Greencoat irritably. But he quickly checked himself and smiled benignly.

"You there," asked the lama, pointing toward him with his forefinger, "what kind of man you?"

Greencoat pretended not to understand, and Big Tiger said: "Yesterday evening the King of the Western Sunits set out with his cousin to ride to the monastery of Belin Sume to visit the holy Abbot Yolros Lama."

"How do you know that?" Good Fortune was just asking, but the lama would not let him finish. "You say Sunit *Wang* in Belin Sume?" he asked excitedly. "That truth quite sure?"

"My friend Big Tiger has never yet told a lie," said Christian convincingly.

"You little foreigner," cried the lama, pointing to him with his forefinger, "what name you?"

"My name is Compass Mountain."

"That good. All now know Dorchi." And he pointed to himself with a friendly grin.

"Ene yu beino?" asked Big Tiger.

The lama was more astonished than ever. "Why did you not say at once that you speak Mongolian like ten Mongols?" he boomed in his own language. "My name is *Dorchi,* or as such I am known. It is a Tibetan name and means Thunderbolt. But you should be sincere with Thunderbolt, who is your friend."

"Pardon, Dorchi Lama," intervened Good Fortune, "this young person can only say *'ene yu beino'* and nothing more."

"If that's the case," boomed Thunderbolt, "I take back what I said." He pushed the three pieces of sheep cheese under his sash, ate a few of the honey cakes, and prepared to stand up. In order to make complete amends he turned once more to Big Tiger and boomed: "You say *ene yu beino* splendidly. Who taught it to you?"

"A man," said Big Tiger.

"Moonlight," Christian burst out.

"Ha, little man from beyond the seas," bellowed Thunderbolt, overjoyed. "You kindle great light in me. You also now my friend. Where is Moonlight?"

"Moonlight is with the Duke of Hanta and the men of Sunit wolf-hunting," said Good Fortune. "Yesterday morning they were around the monastery of Orte Golen Sume, but now they're hunting at Yellow Hill Gap and beyond."

"It is wonderful that I met you," cried Thunderbolt. "I want to know one thing more: Is Moonlight whole and sound, or does he lack a part—an arm or a hand, or anything that way?"

"Moonlight is whole and sound," said Good Fortune. "His temples were split in two, but they were patched up."

"Thanks be to heaven! All has turned out for the best," said Thunderbolt with emotion. "My Moonlight, my Little Paw, I shall see you again!"

He stood up, clenched his fists so hard in salutation that the fingers cracked, and bellowed: *"Yabonah!"*

"Yabonah!" cried Good Fortune, also standing up.

Dasha hastened to be first outside. While the others left the *yurt* one after the other, Christian held Big Tiger back. "Why did you take the ring off your finger?" he whispered.

Big Tiger hesitated to answer. "It seemed to me likely," he said at last, "that this lama Thunderbolt would know the ring."

"I thought that too," Christian admitted. "But what if the ring belongs to him?"

Big Tiger shrugged his shoulders. "Then it just can't be helped," he said dejectedly, and went out after the others.

Christian understood quite well why Big Tiger had hidden the ring. If the lama Thunderbolt had recognized the ring he would have bellowed it out and Good Fortune and Greencoat would have noticed something. They would have said: "Big Tiger has told a lie, and his grandfather is also a liar. They have both lost their face. It has got quite black, and there will be no regard for the family any more, it has fallen so low."

Even out in the sunshine the matter did not take on a happier aspect. The dogs wagged their tails at sight of Dasha, but they growled at the strange men. The lama Thunderbolt picked up his gun as if it were the usual thing for him to go around heavily armed. Even Good Fortune did not handle firearms so casually. And Greencoat looked up at the sky as if he expected rain.

"I'm off!" cried the lama Thunderbolt, slapping his boot with his whip. Then the dogs began to bark, but kept a respectful distance. It was only when the wild lama mounted and trotted off that they ran after him, trying to bite the piebald, which kicked out left and right. The lama's carbine glistened in the sun, the red horse hair shot out of its barrel like a non-stop fire, and he bellowed: *"Yabonah! Sä Yabonah!"* Then, giving the piebald a mighty wallop, he galloped off.

Good Fortune walked behind for a little way carefully noting the hoofmarks, and Christian looked on and asked: "Why is Thunderbolt riding back the way he came?"

"You notice everything, too," said Good Fortune. "But it's not quite as you think. The lama had a long journey behind him. He said so himself. He came from the west, and he's going back to the west. We're also traveling westwards. Do you see the red *loess* cliffs?"

"Yes, I see them," said Christian.

"Where they close in," continued Good Fortune, "and where it gets so narrow that a car can hardly pass through, a new world begins, with lots of beautiful grass and gentle hills. You can see a long way from there, almost to where the steppe ceases, and the region is called the Sharamuren Valley. If you watch out well you'll soon see where friend Thunderbolt has ridden to."

"To the north or to the south?" asked Christian.

"To the south of course," answered Good Fortune. "For he's going to Belin Sume to the King of the Sunits. I shall sound the horn when we come to the spot."

"And what about Cow Pond—is it far?" asked Christian.

"Do you want a good dinner?"

"We want it very much," Christian answered, giving Big Tiger a nudge to back him up.

"It can't be helped," said Big Tiger, who hadn't been listening, because his mind was still on the ring.

"Oh, yes, it can," cried Good Fortune. "We'll be in Cow Pond for our evening meal. I'll drive as quickly as Thunderbolt rides."

22 ABOUT MOUNT MURUKTCHICH AND ABOUT THUNDERBOLT, WHO RODE AWAY

"ANY NEWS of Pandiriktchi?" asked Greencoat obstinately, before getting in. Good Fortune, who was pouring gasoline into the tank, said: "Oh, yes. Just wait a minute," and he beckoned to Dasha.

"We're off now," he said to him, "and we thank you for your good meal."

"I cannot bear such words," replied Dasha modestly.

"Then pass them on to your master, Pandiriktchi."

"Pandiriktchi won't be back for two or three days," said Dasha, winking significantly. "He's ridden to Kwei-hwa to see the *amban*."

"On his account?" asked Good Fortune, glancing toward Greencoat.

Dasha nodded and put his finger to his lips.

"Hammagua," said Good Fortune. "There's nothing to fear." "Hey, Greencoat!" he shouted. "Come over here! Pandiriktchi has ridden to Kwei-hwa to see the *amban* about a certain matter."

"I know that," said Greencoat amicably. "Tell the fellow his master needn't trouble any more. I withdraw my charge. My agent in Cow Pond will come and settle the business as Pandiriktchi wishes." He sighed as if he had given away a kingdom and went back full of dignity to his seat.

Good Fortune repeated Greencoat's words to the astonished Dasha, who was very pleased to have good news for his master. "Why has Greencoat turned so peaceable?" he asked.

"I don't know," said Good Fortune. "What's the dispute about?"

"It's about four camels, and if you would like to know . . ."

"Yes," said Good Fortune, "I would. I think I left something behind in the *yurt*."

"We'll go and look," said Dasha.

They both turned back to the *yurt,* and Dasha told the story:

"Three years ago in the third moon Greencoat came to Pandiriktchi and said: 'I hear you wish to get your daughter married; then you need money.' 'I don't need your money,' said Pandiriktchi. 'You could sell me some camel foals,' Greencoat suggested. 'I pay cash, and you won't lose a single batz if one of them dies.' Pandiriktchi was surprised, for what does a merchant want with camel foals? A merchant needs pack camels three or four years old, and then they cost sixty or seventy batz each. But Greencoat wanted camel foals, and that was that. He offered thirty batz apiece. So Pandiriktchi sold twenty foals and pocketed the money, which he needed though he had said he didn't.

" 'I can't take the foals with me now,' said Greencoat. 'Put them out to pasture, and I'll fetch them in the autumn.' Pandiriktchi agreed, and by the autumn the foals had become fine young animals. Greencoat came and branded his mark on their cheeks. 'I can't take them with me now,' he said. 'I'll take them in the spring. Herd them well, and don't let the wolves get them.' Again Pandiriktchi agreed."

"Aha!" said Good Fortune.

"Why do you say 'Aha'?" asked Dasha.

"Because I know exactly what's coming."

"You can't know it."

"Yes, I do," said Good Fortune. "It's easy enough. The following spring Greencoat came back, and in the autumn he came again, and each time he said: 'I can't take the camels.' "

"It was just as you say," cried Dasha astonished. "How can you know what you didn't hear and didn't see?"

"The thoughts of a bad man are easier to guess than the thoughts of a good one. Go on, tell me more."

"The last time Greencoat was here," Dasha continued, "Pandiriktchi said to him: 'It is only right that you should pay some small compensation.' 'You want to cheat me, do you?' shouted Greencoat. 'For three years you have had the hair of my camels, and their food costs you nothing. There can be no question of money.' 'Then give me four of the twenty camels as compensation,' said Pandiriktchi. 'My people have herded and reared them for three years, and when it was cold we covered them with felts.' 'There can be no question of that either!' shouted Greencoat, enraged. And he went off and brought a charge against my master with the *amban* in Kwei-hwa."

"Aha!" said Good Fortune.

"Why do you say 'Aha'?" asked Dasha.

"Because that's what Greencoat does always," said Good Fortune, "but it's the first time he has taken back a charge. I'm wondering what's behind it. Good-by, Dasha, and I wish you a good and easy time."

"May your road be easy and safe!" Dasha replied.

Good Fortune would have liked to drive off at a high speed to show what a magnificent car he had, but the ground was too soft. The red *loess* cliffs were getting nearer. At their feet the sand was blown into drifts, and soon they turned into the narrow gully between the cliffs. There were only a few inches to spare at each side, yet he never let the truck rub against the walls of *loess,* and the cliffs remained untouched.

As they emerged from the gully what Good Fortune had called a new world opened before them. A gentle slope glided down to a broad valley, in which a great herd of horses was grazing—probably about four hundred. Three mounted herdsmen were minding them. The sun shone on the yellow winter grass, and the countless distant hills were also yellow and glittering. Only on their north sides were they cold and dark, and streaked with the snow of the day before. In the south, edging this incredibly vast landscape, lay mountain chains showing a confusing jumble of peaks and jagged teeth. They glistened in the sun, and when one tried to look at them steadily, they seemed to hop up and down.

So this was Sharamuren Valley. For a valley in the real sense it was much too vast, because it embraced all that the eye could see far and wide. But there was no river, not even a little brook in it. No smallest trickle of water was to be seen, nothing but the empty, stony riverbed. True, to the north between the hills a blue, mobile stripe which looked like water appeared now and then, but anyone knowing Mongolia and the Gobi Desert would know at once that this was a mirage. The Arabs call it a *Fata Morgana,* but the Mongols don't waste a word on it.

Right in the middle of Sharamuren lay a broad, dark mass not at all high, but deeply clefted and strangely out of keeping with the gentle hills around. Emerging from the high *loess* cliffs Christian could see into the clefts as into a labyrinth which had opened up. This great massif was made of greenish-black stone, and its name matched its appearance in strange wildness: it was called Muruktchich.

We hear on the one hand that the mountain has this beautiful but wild name. On the other hand we hear that it is not so called. Big Tiger and Christian did not know this, but Good Fortune explained it to them later, saying: "The mountains have names, but their names must not be spoken when you are near them. Only if they're far away and can't be seen may you safely speak of them. But when they're beside you, such as this terrible Muruktchich now, it is a different matter . . . For on all mountains, particularly the wild and high ones, dwell demons, who do not wish their dwelling places to be called by name. Therefore they are given some harmless neutral name. Muruktchich for instance is called by a word which means the clefted region. If the demons hear this they don't suspect you are talking of their mountain. Whereas if you spoke its right name you would be sure to meet with some great misfortune."

But now they looked with astonishment at the vast expanse and jumped when Good Fortune sounded the horn, "Tut-tut." The horses grazing nearby bounded away, and the boys looked to see what was there. They knew at once what Good Fortune meant. A narrow path branched southward, and looking at it closely they could see the fresh hoof prints of a horse. A long way ahead they saw the lama Thunderbolt, who was hastening to the King of the Sunits.

The journey passed merrily. Good Fortune was able to drive as fast as he liked, and in the gaiety of his heart he trilled a song. After two hours a well-trodden camel path emerged from the south. Good Fortune opened the little window, and Christian and Big Tiger stood up to hear him.

"This is the great caravan road from Kwei-hwa to Hami. Is it on your map, Kwi-Chan?"

"I shall look and see, honored Sir."

"Do we still drive to Cow Pond by this road?" asked Greencoat.

"Yes," Good Fortune replied, "and we shall go by it to Sinkiang. True, there are deviations . . ."

"At Four Trees, for instance," said Greencoat.

"I see you know the route well," said Good Fortune.

"Yes," said Greencoat complacently. "From now onwards I know my way. Will you therefore please stop and we shall change places."

"What?" cried Good Fortune. "Do I understand you rightly or wrongly?"

"But we've spoken of this before," Greencoat replied in a low voice, closing the rear window.

Soon the truck stopped and they changed places. After a slightly bumpy start Greencoat got into his stride and drove like an experienced driver, following the camel track as straight as a line.

Christian and Big Tiger sat quietly in their places. Though it was not cold they drew their coats closer around them, and pulled the fur collars up on their necks.

"It can't be helped," said Big Tiger, gloomily.

"It can't be helped," agreed Christian.

"What?" said Big Tiger. "You say 'It can't be helped' too? You mustn't. You must say something else."

"I can't think of anything else."

"Kwi-Chan," entreated Big Tiger. "Think of something else! The two of us can't be without courage."

"Then we must make an agreement," said Christian. "Only one of us at a time can be desperate and say 'It can't be helped.' "

"Agreed!" declared Big Tiger. "I'll begin: It can't be helped." He looked at Christian and they both burst out laughing.

Christian opened the brief case. "I'll have a look at the map," he said, "to see how we're situated."

"Can you read that on the map?"

"We can read it together. Look, here's Sharamuren where we are now. And there's the caravan road which Good Fortune spoke of. It's all green round about. But after that it's white or brown and there's no more green until the Etzin Gol, where there's a narrow streak of green. So the desert begins right behind Cow Pond. And it looks bad for us."

"How does that make it look bad for us?" asked Big Tiger.

"Remember what Greencoat said at White Stone," Christian reminded him. "Besides, he's been so friendly in the last few days, that's the worst sign of all."

"It's a bad sign for Good Fortune, too," Big Tiger suggested. "Greencoat doesn't say a cross word to him any more."

"Perhaps it is," said Christian thoughtfully, "or perhaps it's something else." Then both fell silent.

"What about showing Good Fortune the cartridge," suggested Big Tiger. "He'll ask where I got it, and I'll say I found it and perhaps it fits his pistol. Then he'll try it, and when it fits he'll notice all the rest are gone too, and he'll kick up a fearful row. Then I'll say: We don't know who stole it, but Greencoat has a whole lot like that one in his trousers' pocket."

"I'm afraid," said Christian, "it's not a very good plan."

"It is good," Big Tiger insisted. "Just leave it to me."

"But Greencoat must be far away when you come out with it."

"He must be away somewhere for at least half an hour. The best way is for you to go for a walk with him until I have talked to Good Fortune."

"Perhaps he wouldn't go for a walk with me."

"He must," said Big Tiger. "There's no way out."

Christian made no further reply. He only reflected how unpleasant it would be to go for a walk with Greencoat, and wondered whether they'd talk about the weather or the antelopes. It would certainly be frightening to be as long as half an hour alone with him. But he would not admit it. So he just looked silently at the black cliffs of Muruktchich, which were coming nearer.

As evening fell they came to the end of the valley of Sharamuren. Christian pointed to the map, saying: "It's not far now to Cow Pond."

An hour later two *yurts* popped up on the right-hand edge of the valley. The pale moon rose in the clear sky over Mount Muruktchich, and no one seeing it could remain depressed.

23 ABOUT THE BRAYING OF AN ASS, AND DRAGONS' TEETH, AND AN IMPORTANT DISCOVERY

ONE OF THEM was called Chen and the other Chin.

Big Chen bowed and said: "We salute the esteemed Mr. Greencoat."

Little Chin said: "Great and honorable old father," and he clucked when he said it, for he was not very well brought up.

"Thanks, thanks," said Greencoat condescendingly. He sat at the wheel greatly enjoying the astonishment of his employees, who continued bowing, so great was the respect inspired by the sight of the car and of their employer, who was able to drive such a monster.

Good Fortune got out. "Get down from your throne," he said.

Greencoat was nettled but made no reply. Later, however, when

Chen and Chin were admiring the truck he remarked audibly: "Unfortunately this car has lost its fine appearance. The soldier Good Fortune, whom you must salute, very carelessly ran into a telegraph pole."

Chen and Chin bowed to him. "How is your precious health?" they asked politely.

"All right," Good Fortune answered, turning away, and one could see that he was enraged with Greencoat.

"These princely young gentlemen have come with me," Greencoat continued calmly. "Their names are Compass Mountain and Big Tiger."

Chen and Chin bowed once more, and Big Tiger and Christian did the same. "We wish you luck ten thousand times," they said.

Chen was a square-built, robust man in a worn black coat. He had a slight stutter and it was hard to understand him. Chin had come as an apprentice to Cow Pond at thirteen years of age. He was now fourteen, and his uncle called him Dragonstooth, for dragons' teeth* were an important article of commerce at Cow Pond.

"Go and prepare the meal, Dragonstooth!" cried Uncle Chen.

"What's there to eat, little monkey?" asked Greencoat amiably.

"Shall I make meat dumplings?" asked Dragonstooth.

"Yes, do," cried Good Fortune, "and spice them well."

"We have swordfish sauce with sun root," said Dragonstooth, "and we've also got sliced chilblains."

"Cheeky pup!" scolded Uncle Chen, picking up a stone. But Dragonstooth had already disappeared into the *yurt*. "I'm sorry," said Uncle Chen with a stutter. "My ill-bred nephew deserves scolding and chastisement."

"Yes," grunted Greencoat. He took Chen aside. "Not a word of business," he said, "before those three rascals who have hung themselves around my neck."

* "Dragons' teeth" or fossil molars, and also antlers' horns, ground to fine powder, are much used as medicine by the Chinese.

"I understand," whispered Chen. "I'm sorry indeed, honored Sir, to see you in the company of worthless persons."

They went into the *yurt,* while Christian and Big Tiger helped Good Fortune to attend to the truck. "We must prepare for the desert," said Good Fortune, covering the hood with felt rugs, "and from now on we have to carry water." Christian filled three cans.

It was night by the time all these things were done. The moon was bright, the north star was twinkling, and Mount Muruktchich lay black and silent between the gentle hills. The air was still. A barn owl was screeching in the distance.

"Listen to me, boys," said Good Fortune. "I take it you can hold your tongues."

"The honorable gentleman always assumes what is correct," said Big Tiger.

"We excel in keeping our mouths shut," Christian assured him.

"There's something which doesn't please me," began Good Fortune.

"It doesn't please us either," said Christian.

"What do you mean?" asked Good Fortune, flabbergasted.

"I mean," said Christian airily, "that it might be, for instance, what Mr. Greencoat is now hatching out with Mr. Chen."

"If we don't like it perhaps the honored Mr. Good Fortune doesn't like it either," Big Tiger added meekly.

"You're a pair of young champions!" cried Good Fortune. "Yes, it's as you say. Where there's rotten fish, there's a stink. Keep on your toes, find out what you can, and if you notice anything, tell me."

"*Bolna!*" said Christian.

"Will the honored gentleman keep on our side?" asked Big Tiger, warily.

"I won't leave you in the lurch," Good Fortune promised.

In the *yurt* they found Greencoat sitting on the seat of honor. Chen was next to him, talking, but stopped short when Good Fortune came in. Christian, who followed, stumbled over the axle

beam which Chin, who was crouched near the entrance, pushed between his legs, and he would have fallen if Big Tiger had not held him tight. Big Tiger would have liked to thrash Chin, but that would be a breach of manners, so he just trod hard on Chin's toes, saying: "Excuse me, I stumbled; there must be a bit of dough or something there."

"Sit down," Chen bade them. "There'll be something to eat presently. Are you hungry?"

"The young gentlemen are always hungry," Greencoat remarked, benevolently. Then he talked about the weather, saying it was still cold, and Chen said the camels had a very thick coat this year.

"Let me see the wool stocks," Greencoat ordered. "Have you got much?"

"A fair amount," said Chen. But then he said that unfortunately he had no lantern, only an ordinary oil lamp.

Good Fortune stood up and said: "Wait a second." In no time he was back with a beautiful storm lantern which he had brought with him from Hwai-lai-hsien. "I'll light you," he said, and before Greencoat could make any objection he was already outside. "Let it be," Greencoat whispered to Chen. "I'll say what I have to say afterwards." They stood up and followed Good Fortune, who was waiting outside the second *yurt* in which Chen kept the merchandise that the Mongols brought him.

Meanwhile Chin was busily kneading the dough for the meat dumplings. His thin shoulders rose and fell, and Christian and Big Tiger could hear the regular clap-clap as he turned the dough.

"Shall we thrash you now?" asked Big Tiger amicably.

Chin turned round with a contemptuous grin. "You might spoil your good meal," he said, "and that would be a pity. Besides, it would be cowardly as you're two to one."

"Just wipe your hands and come out with me, then," Big Tiger proposed. "Compass Mountain will stay in here."

"It seems you can't take a joke," said Chin.

"We can take lots of jokes," said Big Tiger, "but that wasn't one."

"It might have been a joke," Chin excused himself, "but you spoiled it. If Compass Mountain had stumbled a bit better, he would have knocked over the pot. Then Uncle Chen would have got a wetting, and he couldn't have beaten me. That would have been a lot of fun!"

"Does he beat you?" asked Christian.

Chin sighed. "You have no idea what it's like here," he said gloomily. "But what's the good of telling you?" He made a ball of dough and then took the rolling pin. "You can cut the meat," he said to Big Tiger, "but you must cut the pieces small, or I'll catch it afterwards."

"Leave it to me," said Big Tiger. "I know how it's done."

Chin passed him a board, a knife, and a fine lump of fat mutton. While Big Tiger took off his coat and got to work Chin said: "This is a lucky day for me. While you're here he can't get drunk."

"Do you mean your uncle?" asked Christian.

"Who else?" cried Chin. "Didn't you notice the way he speaks?"

"That's right," said Big Tiger. "He's got a stutter."

"When he's drunk," declared Chin, "you can't understand anything he says. Then he gets cross and beats me."

"I'd run away from him," said Christian.

Chin shook his head vehemently. "You don't know what you're saying," he said. "How could I bring shame on my family?"

"Chin is right," Big Tiger admitted. "The heart may desire what it will, but it must keep patient."

"A change often comes in the twinkling of an eye," said Christian, trying to be comforting.

"Good luck doesn't come twofold," asserted Chin. "It's luck enough for me that you've come and that I'll be away the whole day tomorrow on account of the lightning letter."

"On account of what?" asked Big Tiger.

"But there's no telegraph line here," said Christian.

"There is in Ashan," explained Chin. He rubbed the dough from his fingers and reached for the pocket of his coat, which hung on the tent frame.

"Can you read?" he asked, in a low voice.

"Yes, we can read and write even the most difficult words," said Big Tiger.

"Then tell me quickly what's written here. But you must be quick!"

"Don't be afraid," said Christian. "We'll hear them coming back."

"But only if the donkey isn't braying," said Chin miserably. "Read it quickly!"

"To Li-Yuan-Pei in Hami," began Big Tiger.

"That's right," said Chin, satisfied. "Li is Greencoat's agent. Read on!"

"Send forty can gasoline to Hsing-hsing-hsia at once. Shong-Ma," continued Big Tiger.

"Is that all?" asked Chin, disappointed.

"There's nothing more," said Big Tiger, giving back the piece of paper to Chin. "Who is this Shong-Ma?"

"Shong-Ma," said Chin, "you don't know who Shong-Ma is? There was a man here yesterday asking for him, but Uncle Chen told him he knew nobody of that name."

"Was it a man with a gun and a yellow hat?" asked Big Tiger.

"How do you know that?" asked Chin, startled.

"We know almost everything," Christian explained, and then added boldly, "and we also know that Shong-Ma is Greencoat."

"Why do you ask me," complained Chin, "when you know his real name?"

"People do that," Big Tiger explained, "to make an entertaining conversation."

"Don't mention it to him!" pleaded Chin. "He doesn't want anyone to know his real name. Everyone calls him Greencoat, and nobody is to know more."

"Don't worry," said Christian reassuringly. "We're used to keeping our mouths shut."

"I was hoping," said Chin, "there would be something different in the lightning letter—perhaps that we were to leave here. But I see everything is to go on as it is."

"Well, you've a journey tomorrow, anyway," Big Tiger consoled him. "Is it very far to Ashan?"

Chin laughed. "It's two days' ride with a good horse. I've only got a donkey."

"I see," said Big Tiger, trying to figure out where Ashan might be, "that it can't be done on the donkey. How then do you do it? Where do you take the telegram to?"

"I ride over to Muruktchich," Chin explained. "The Dondur *Wang* has been living there for the past month. His soldiers are glad to earn a bit extra. I give the lightning letter to one of them and he rides to Ashan, and when he comes back in four days with the receipt from the post office, Uncle Chen gives him a good tip. Generally they both get drunk."

"And what do you do?" asked Christian.

"Hush! They're coming!" whispered Chin.

There was a brief silence, and Christian wondered how Chin had heard footsteps despite the fact that Good Fortune, Greencoat and Chen wore felt-soled shoes.

"Put out the lantern," they heard Greencoat saying to Good Fortune, "and save the oil."

"It's my lantern and my oil," Good Fortune replied gruffly.

"Aha!" cried Uncle Chen as they entered. "Two pairs of hands are better than one!"

"And three are better than two," said Good Fortune, as he put down the lantern, pulled up his sleeves, and took off his cap. "Dragonstooth!" he cried. "You must make a better fire than that. Come, let me take your place. I have a passion for cooking."

They all looked on as he cut the dough into perfect squares. Then he flavored the meat with turtle sauce and garlic, blew some finely ground ginger over it, rolled it into small balls, and laid it on the dough squares. "I'd give anything for a pinch of sugar," he lamented, and he beat the meat balls with a broad knife to flatten them. It was all done like magic, and Big Tiger counted the dumplings as they were thrown into the boiling water.

When they all sat down to eat little Dragonstooth quite forgot that he was really unhappy. Good Fortune kept putting more and more dumplings into his wooden bowl, and when they had all eaten enough Uncle Chen hiccoughed loudly in order to show Good Fortune how much he had enjoyed the meal, and how greatly he appreciated his cooking. "What about a little drink?" he asked then, squinting toward a brass can which stood on a chest behind him. "I mean of course only for health's sake . . ."

"Of course," said Greencoat, "only for health's sake."

"In my poor hut there's unfortunately only some watery wine," bewailed Uncle Chen. "It's really a sh-shame."

"Let's have it!" said Good Fortune curtly.

Uncle Chen raked out the fire and stood the can on a trivet over the glowing embers. "When wine is wa-warmed," he said, "it's best for health." He handed around small glasses, filled one for himself, drank it off and announced: "The wine is too cold. I've tried it for you . . ." Here he was interrupted by a long piercing braying.

Greencoat shuddered. "The braying of donkeys gets on my nerves," he said.

"It's enough to turn a man's stomach," Uncle Chen agreed.

The donkey continued braying. Chin grinned stealthily, and Uncle Chen got annoyed. "You're laughing at me, you mean little devil! Go out at once and stop the donkey from braying."

Chin stood up obediently. "The last time he kicked me," he whined.

"I'll go with you," said Good Fortune, taking the lantern, "then nothing can happen to you."

"May we come too?" asked Christian.

"Come along the lot of you," said Good Fortune. "There's plenty to learn."

They left the *yurt*. The lantern shone brightly, but the moon also was shining its best. The stars were out and the night was cold.

"Where's the donkey?" asked Good Fortune.

He was answered by a long-drawn-out bray from behind the storage *yurt*.

"Please be careful, honored Sir," Chin warned him. "In the daytime he's tame and good, but at night he's wild and kicks."

"No fear," said Good Fortune. "This isn't the first donkey that I've tied to a stone by its tail."

"Why is that done?" asked Christian.

"When a donkey brays," Good Fortune informed him, "he raises his tail. When he can't raise his tail he doesn't bray. That's all, but it's useful to know."

Chin, who had run on in front, stopped. "There he is," he said.

"Hold the lantern, Compass Mountain," Good Fortune ordered; "and you, Chin, give me the stone."

Chin bent down and lifted a big stone which had a rope tied crosswise over it. When the donkey saw these preparations he cocked his ears, pulled on his chain and leaped backwards.

"This won't do," said Good Fortune. "It's much too heavy and would pull off the donkey's tail. Look for another stone. When you've got it I'll be back." And he went off toward the *yurt,* but for all anyone knew he might have gone to fetch something from the truck.

"Perhaps this stone is right?" asked Christian, louder than was necessary.

"It mustn't be round," Chin objected, "or it won't hold the rope."

"Aha," said Christian, making a sign to Big Tiger. "We must look for a suitable stone." He took the lantern and went off a little way toward the caravan road, saying: "It's not easy to find the right stone for tying to an ass." Now and then he picked up one which he knew Chin would reject, and Big Tiger did the same. By the time Chin himself had found a suitable stone several minutes had elapsed. It took several more minutes to tie the cord around it, and as they returned to the donkey he raised his tail and started braying again.

"Did you find a stone?" asked Good Fortune, stepping out of the darkness.

"Yes, we've found the right stone and the rope is already around it," said Big Tiger.

Good Fortune took the donkey by the halter, stroked him between the ears, talked to him and patted his neck. The obstreperous donkey tried to kick out but Good Fortune stood well aside, got hold of his tail and tied the stone to it firmly. The donkey looked back dejectedly toward his hindquarters, then stood still and shook himself. "Now we can go to sleep," said Good Fortune.

Chin, who was cold, hurried back to the *yurt.* Big Tiger and Christian went to the truck, and Good Fortune helped them to get their sleeping bags and blankets.

"Have you found out anything?" he asked.

"Yes, we have," said Christian eagerly.

"But we know only half," Big Tiger interjected. "We must ask Chin to tell us the other half. It's a telegram," he whispered solemnly. "Chin says if we give him a silver batz he'll let us see it."

"Here's the silver batz," said Good Fortune, putting his hand in his pocket. "Take good note of what's in the telegram and to whom it's addressed."

"I know that already," said Big Tiger shrewdly. "The man is called Li-Yuan-Pei and lives in Hami."

"Aha!" said Good Fortune. And he sat down on Christian's sleeping bag, gasping.

"Does that mean anything in particular?" Big Tiger inquired.

"Ah," sighed Good Fortune. "Not very much, and actually it's what I expected, for it's quite in order. But I'm thoroughly sick of trying to cope with these swindlers."

"Is this Li the same kind of man as Greencoat?" asked Christian.

"Much the same," declared Good Fortune, "only a little less rough and more sly."

"Has our esteemed elder also found out something?" asked Big Tiger straight out.

"I listened outside the *yurt* just now. It seems Greencoat is giving up this Cow Pond branch."

"Chin will be glad, I should think," said Christian.

"Say nothing to him about it. He'll know soon enough."

"Why won't Greencoat carry on his business here any more?" asked Big Tiger.

"I don't know," said Good Fortune. "Perhaps the place is getting too hot for him. Someone must have been here inquiring for him."

"We'll find that out," Christian promised. He took his sleeping bag under his arm, and Big Tiger took his. They walked the few steps to the *yurt* in silence.

"Oh, there you are!" cried Uncle Chen. "I was afraid you we . . . we . . . were lost."

"We were admiring the shadowy power of the moon," said Big Tiger. "It's waxing."

"We've brought our bedding," said Christian.

"Time enough for that," cried Uncle Chen, taking the brass can out of the embers. Good Fortune drank a glass, then shuddered and said "Phew!" "One leg isn't much good to a man," urged Chen, but Good Fortune replied that now was no time to drink such strong stuff.

"He's right," said Greencoat, taking the can from Chen.

"As the honorable gentleman wishes," said Chen submissively. "Temperance leads heavenwards, but the drink was only for my health."

He then apportioned the sleeping places, giving Greencoat the best spot and the biggest share of pillows and blankets. Christian and Big Tiger crept into their sleeping bags, taking Chin in between them to have another little talk before falling asleep.

"What are you whispering about there?" asked Greencoat sternly.

"I asked what's a dragon's tooth," said Christian apologetically, "as I've never seen one."

Uncle Chen laughed. He was only a little drunk and in a good humor. "We have no dragons' teeth," he said, "except the one that's lying beside you chattering. Ha! Ha! Dragons' teeth are very scarce now and, alas, there are only poor specimens to be had. They cost four silver batz apiece. It's a shame."

"Be quiet!" growled Greencoat. "How can anyone sleep while you're chattering?"

The last glowing embers went out and when all was in darkness Big Tiger stealthily pressed the silver batz into Chin's hand and whispered into his ear that he should stay awake for another hour and when the rest were asleep have two words with him.

"Good," whispered Chin, beginning to breathe regularly and loudly like a tired sleeper. He did not have to wait even an hour, for Good Fortune dropped off at once, Uncle Chen did the same, and once Greencoat began to snore there was no longer any danger of a whispered word being heard.

"You're to leave Cow Pond," Big Tiger began. "Are you glad?"

"I'm glad," said Chin. "But how do you know that already?"

"We just know it," said Christian. "But you must speak more quietly."

"We speak like the old kings in the bowels of the earth," said Big Tiger.

"There's nothing to fear," whispered Chin. "Uncle Chen sleeps like a dragon on Mount Muruktchich."

"Why are you leaving Cow Pond?" asked Big Tiger.

"Greencoat intends moving his business into the Province of Kansu," said Chin. "He's planned doing that for a long time past, but when he heard the man with the gun had been here, he suddenly decided to pack up. When I've seen to the lightning letter we're to fetch sixteen camels that the Mongol Pandiriktchi owes us, and then we're going on to Suchow. That's a town between Lanchow and the place mentioned in the lightning letter."

"Hsing-hsing-hsia," said Christian.

"Yes," whispered Chin. "That's the place. It's on the Silk Road. Greencoat says there's better business there, and not only in wool and dragons' bones."

"Perhaps," said Big Tiger casually, "he wants to travel by horseless car. They can drive on the Silk Road."

"Uncle Chen also thinks that will be possible," said Chin eagerly. "I'm glad because I'll have a chance of going in them."

"It will certainly be possible," Christian assured him. "But why doesn't Greencoat call himself Shong-Ma since that's his name? I find Greencoat a silly name."

"Many people have two names," Chin explained. "If one isn't good any more they take another. Perhaps the name Shong-Ma isn't good any more."

"Does the silver batz belong to me?" asked Chin excitedly.

"Yes, it's yours," said Big Tiger.

"Why are you giving it to me?" asked Chin. "I can't give you anything for it."

"For friendship and as a pleasant surprise," said Big Tiger. "And anyway you'll soon have a birthday."

"I don't know when my birthday is," replied Chin.

"That's all the better, for then it's today."

"I believe," said Chin, "that it must be today, it's such a fine, happy day. I've never had such a day before." And he swallowed hard and even got red, so great was his joy; but they could not see that as the *yurt* was dark. "What a beautiful happy day this is," murmured Chin once more, and then he fell asleep.

24 WHICH TELLS OF THE MEETING WITH MATEH AND WITH THE CARAVAN LEADER

GOOD FORTUNE was a great believer in early rising, so they were all sitting at their morning tea while it was still dark and cold. Uncle Chen, whose habits were quite different, sat huddled over the fire, cold and miserable, but tried to look pleasant and said solemnly: "I wish the gentlemen an agreeable journey." Then he looked sharply at Chin, who was stirring a yellowish mixture of roasted barley, and adding tea and butter to it.

"That's just right," Good Fortune announced. "It can now be eaten as it is, or thinned with tea. And it can be eaten politely or impolitely, just as a fellow likes."

"Is it a Mongolian dish?" asked Christian.

"No," replied Good Fortune. "It's a Tibetan dish called *zamba*. Set to! *Zamba* is just the right food for old caravan men!"

At first Christian and Big Tiger poked around in the thick mush with their chopsticks, but then they decided to follow Chin, who had put the bowl to his mouth and was pushing the mush in with his chopsticks.

If my amah saw this! thought Christian. But he didn't get time to imagine what her words of reproach for such bad table manners would be, for Good Fortune said: "The best way with *zamba* is to let it run into your mouth."

They all followed this simple advice, and Christian and Big Tiger found that *zamba* tasted fine.

"I've given you the best kind, with sugar in it," said Uncle Chen patronizingly. "It's a first-class luxury, a real feast!"

There was no more conversation, for indeed it was impossible to talk while eating *zamba*.

Then Good Fortune lit the lantern and Uncle Chen went out before him and Greencoat to the storage tent, behind which the ass had lain down. "You won't plague me much longer, you old bawler," said Chen.

"Hold your tongue!" snarled Greencoat, giving him a nudge.

"I only meant," said Chen apologetically, "that next time he'll have two stones on his tail—really that's all I meant!"

On the eastern horizon the sky was brightening, the stars were growing pale, and one could already see how black the cliffs of Muruktchich were and how light the surrounding hills, and also that it would be a beautiful day. This made Good Fortune very cheerful. "Heaven is kind to us," he cried. "Take your seats, men! The light is rising over the earth."

Christian hurriedly gave Chin a handful of honey cakes. Then Good Fortune sounded the horn, and the motor started humming. Chen and Chin stood bowing for a long time by the side of the caravan road. Only when the *yurts* had grown small in the distance did the travelers see Chen turning back and Chin skipping off.

"Now he'll take the stone off the ass's tail," said Big Tiger.

"And then he'll go with the telegram," said Christian anxiously.

"It's a miserable business," sighed Big Tiger, in deep gloom.

Christian buried his head in his fur coat, and thought unhappily of the perplexing nature of many things. Why had Big Tiger not let him speak up yesterday evening, and why had he lied again to Good Fortune, saying he knew only half the contents of the telegram? Christian didn't understand why Big Tiger was coming out with so many lies these days.

Big Tiger was meditating too. "You must be broad-minded, Kwi-Chan!" he said. "You and I know a lot of things, but we must not let anyone know about them."

"Especially Greencoat," said Christian.

"No; especially Good Fortune," Big Tiger disagreed.

"Why so?" asked Christian, wondering why exactly Good Fortune should not know anything.

"To open your mouth is dangerous," Big Tiger declared. "To keep it shut is safe. Good Fortune must never guess that we know anything about his bargain with Greencoat."

"Aha!" said Christian. "But why?"

"Because Good Fortune would lose face. That mustn't happen, and we must manage things so that he always appears to be a man of honor. In this way we'll keep him as our friend. That's why I . . . do you understand?"

"I understand now," said Christian.

"Anyone who lies once has to lie many times," said Big Tiger sadly. "Don't be shocked, Kwi-Chan, if you hear me coming out with lies."

"I won't be surprised any more," promised Christian.

"We mustn't say anything to Good Fortune about the gasoline or about Hsing-hsing-hsia. So I must now think up what I'm to say when he asks me: 'What was written in the telegram?' "

"I'll think too," said Christian, "and in the end I'll get an idea. You mustn't have to tell all the lies."

He tucked himself deeper into his coat and drew the fur cap over his ears, and Big Tiger did the same. They looked out for the little pink clouds in the east, but they had become pale and thin, and when the sun rose majestically in the clear sky, they disappeared altogether.

An hour later there was no more grass to be seen. There were more and more stones, and there was a low, flat mountain ridge which pushed its spurs from the north into the valley like the fingers of an outstretched hand. The first spur promised an easy ascent, and the caravan road could be seen going up the gentle slope. Despite this, Good Fortune left the road at this point and turned southward into a somewhat uninviting, boulder-strewn slope. The truck clattered for a while over rough stones, until it reached a broad basin which, however, only prepared the way to a second stony slope.

These alternations were repeated several times, until a valley opened up, sharply cut through by a water course, which broke the monotony of the landscape. Bastions of *loess* ten to fourteen feet high bordered the riverbed, indicating the force of the water which had made a way through. But the riverbed was full of stones instead of water, and it was only when the valley broadened out that clumps of reeds could be seen, with a pool here and there among them. The mountain ridge in the north curved backward in a perfect semicircle, and then flattened out. From this semicircle the caravan road emerged through a rocky gorge into the low flat country, and it was easy now to see why Good Fortune had diverged from it. On the edge of the fields of reeds stood a *yurt,* sheep were grazing on the mountain slope, and the heads of camels appeared above the reeds. It was nearing midday when Good Fortune halted by the *yurt*.

"Get out!" he cried. "We are in the Valley of Dark Rushing Water, and this is probably the last *yurt* we shall see before we reach the Etzin Gol."

"*Bolna!*" said Christian, slipping out of his fur coat.

"Have you got any ideas?" whispered Big Tiger.

"I know what we've got to say. Let me speak if Good Fortune questions us."

"Have you considered everything?" asked Big Tiger anxiously. "It must be a good lie."

"It's a very good lie because it's quite simple," Christian replied confidently.

They got down. An old man was standing there and he greeted them like long-awaited friends. His wife shooed off two terrifying, tooth-gnashing dogs which were as big and fierce as dogs must be which have to fight wolves on their own. They were brown and white and had thick ruffs round their necks like young lions.

After the salutations, which Christian and Big Tiger got through almost without faltering, the old man invited them in. Instead of a curtain the *yurt* had a little two-winged door which stood open, revealing a home of modest comfort. Good Fortune and Greencoat entered first, then came Big Tiger and Christian, and finally the master of the house. When they were seated in order of rank the woman also came in, brightened up the fire and put on water for tea. Christian and Big Tiger noticed that the *yurt* was quite different from Sertchi's poor tent or Uncle Chen's smoke-blackened *yurt,* and far more magnificent.

"I'd like to stay here," whispered Christian.

"Happiness dwells in this worthy palace," said Big Tiger calmly.

The felt walls were new and white, and trimmed with blue. They shimmered through the black framework on which a board hung, near the door, covered with rows of shining copper vessels. There was a carpet on the floor, and piles of red cushions. In the background stood an ancient carved chest, covered with a blue damask *haddak*. Two lighted butter lamps stood on it, and behind them several silk-bound books. On a raised throne sat a bronze Buddha with the big ears of perfect wisdom. There was a faint perfume of incense and an atmosphere of peace.

After an interval of perfect silence the old Mongol began to speak in a deep voice which neither rose nor fell. Turning to Christian, he said: "Have you been long in the land of the Mongols?"

Good Fortune felt impelled to come to Christian's rescue. "The poor foreigner has only known the grassland four days," he said.

"I am indeed sorry for him," replied the old man.

"How sad it must be," said the woman, "not to be born a Mongol!"

"It is certainly a misfortune," agreed the old man. "But what luck he has had to have found the way to us!"

When the tea was ready they were given millet and fresh cream cheese, and the old man began to speak again. "My name is Mateh," he said, "and every spring I come to the Valley of Dark Rushing Water. I have been here four days. The water is good. The camels and sheep find enough to eat. I need no more."

"What about the wolves?" asked Good Fortune. "I see your sheep grazing on the mountainside and nobody with them."

"The wolf seldom comes here because there are no antelopes. Hares are also rare, but the big wild sheep live in the mountains. They have horns which the wolf fears, and they are as nimble as the Four-not-alike."

"The Four-not-alike?" asked Greencoat eagerly. He understood the strange word, for it was one of the few he had troubled to pick up. "What is the Four-not-alike?"

"The Four-not-alike," Match explained, "was a deer, and yet he wasn't a deer, though he had antlers. He had feet like an ox, fur like a mole, and the tail of an ass. That is why he was called the Four-not-alike, and he lived in the woods of the north, where Mongolia ends. I never saw him, but seven years ago a widely traveled man, who knew everything there is in the world, visited me. He had seen the Four-not-alike, and he said he was a terrifying beast with sad eyes."

"He probably guessed he would die out," said Good Fortune, and he translated Mateh's story into Chinese. Then Christian got a bright idea and cried: "The widely traveled man was Nowhere-at-all." He noticed at once that he had said something indiscreet, but it was too late. He had forgotten Big Tiger's warning that it was dangerous to open one's mouth.

"Nowhere-at-all?" cried old Mateh. "My child, what do you know of that worthy man?"

"And how do you know about him?" asked Good Fortune.

"We have heard this name," Big Tiger hastened to explain, "because Nowhere-at-all was a celebrated man who is always being spoken of. He is said to have died in the Valley of Dark Rushing Water. More than that we do not know."

Mateh listened attentively. "Yes, it is as you say," he cried, "and Nowhere-at-all is a man to remember with reverence."

For some minutes there was complete silence. They could hear the fire crackling, and the camels treading through the near-by field of reeds, and one of the dogs began to growl.

*"Eijen-chin!"** said Mateh's wife quietly, and then the silence became if possible more complete. A thin distant clanging sound became audible, and each time the clang came nearer, the dogs growled more loudly.

"A trader's caravan," said Greencoat, making a move to stand up.

Mateh rose at once, and was standing outside the door with his wife before Greencoat had time to stand up.

"Where are your manners?" asked Good Fortune angrily; but Greencoat put on an insolent expression, and went out without replying. "It can't be helped," sighed Good Fortune. "One must suffer the uncouth with patience."

"Where does he want to go to?" asked Christian.

* *Eijen-chin:* "Caravan."

"He's an inquisitive person," said Good Fortune contemptuously, "and he's not ashamed to show it. Did you hear the bells? There are two of them—no, three. That means it's a big caravan. It's coming down through the ravine and Greencoat wants to know where it is coming from, what it is carrying, and where it is going."

"Take the whip with you!" they heard Mateh saying, and Greencoat's muttered: "Yes, yes!" Mateh called back the dogs and then he came in with his wife. "Is your worthy companion a merchant?" he asked.

"He carries on that low profession," said Good Fortune.

"Traders," said the wife tolerantly, "have to pursue what is petty in order to gain what is great." She filled three bowls of milk, and Mateh took three white *haddaks* out of the chest. Then on his knees he offered the milk to the guests one after the other, with the *haddak*.

"You are honoring us too greatly," said Good Fortune.

"We are unworthy," said Big Tiger and Christian.

They drank a little of the milk and watched Good Fortune raising the *haddak* to his forehead and then putting it away. Then they did the same, and Good Fortune said: "We do not deserve this honor. We are only wretched travelers."

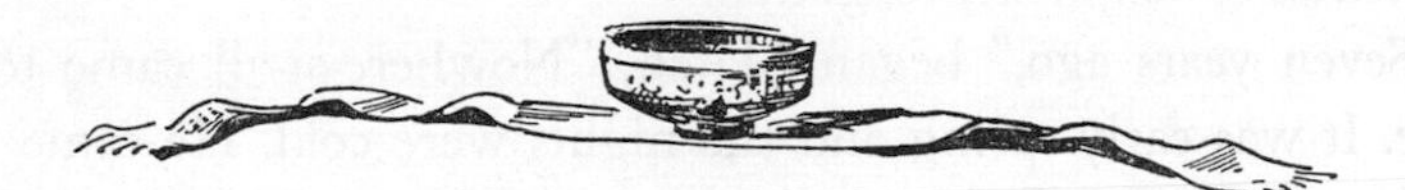

Mateh would not let that pass. They were already close friends, he asserted. Then in eloquent and poetical language which even Good Fortune could not understand completely, he spoke of the glory which they had brought to his *yurt*. "Anyone who knows my true friend Nowhere-at-all," he said, "is very near to my heart."

"That's you," said Good Fortune, giving Christian a nudge.

"But I don't know him," protested Christian unhappily. "He's dead long ago."

"We beg our esteemed elder not to betray us," said Big Tiger. "It would not be good if Greencoat were to learn of our friendship with the son and grandson of Nowhere-at-all. The one is called Dogolon, the other Bator."

"Aha!" said Good Fortune. "You seem to have made some choice friends. I have indeed heard something of Dogolon."

"But he's not a bad man," cried Christian.

Good Fortune raised his eyebrows and gave Big Tiger and Christian a searching look. He said nothing further, but began to explain to Mateh, who was awaiting an explanation, that Dogolon was the son of Nowhere-at-all, and Bator the son of Dogolon.

"I know that," the unsuspecting Mateh replied. "How is Dogolon and does he still live at the White Stone?"

"He left there three days ago," said Good Fortune irritably.

"He's on the way to the Etzin Gol," Big Tiger announced. "Naidang, who is Bator's grandfather, lives there, and we're to visit him if we find him."

"The past thrusts forward into the present, as the tree comes forth from the earth," said Mateh. "Have you two minutes to spare?"

"We have," said Good Fortune irritably; but then he added politely: "We've lots of time," and smiled, for he wanted his impoliteness to be quickly forgotten.

"Seven years ago," began Mateh, "Nowhere-at-all came to us here. It was early spring and the nights were cold. He came late in the evening, and after we had become acquainted, we went to bed. The next morning he wanted to ride on but we begged him to remain, and he told us about all the things there are in the world. We had mutual friends of whom we talked, and as evening fell again the conversation turned on Yolros Lama."

"We saw the Living Buddha in White Stone," said Christian.

"He is like a father and mother," said Big Tiger.

"He is kind to man and beast," Mateh agreed. "Nowhere-at-all had a leaf of the Sacred Tree of Kumbum, which Yolros Lama had bidden him to cast to the winds in the Valley of Dark Rushing Water. But there was no wind. On the evening of the fourth day Nowhere-at-all drew a slender little book out of his belt. In it lay the leaf, and many pages of the book were written on. 'I am a bad, inquisitive man,' said Nowhere-at-all. 'Can you read?' 'That is an art I do not understand,' I told him. 'But you have got many books,' he replied. 'Why do you keep them?' 'They belong to my first-born son, who is a lama in the monastery of Orte Golen Sume.' "

"We were there also," said Good Fortune, "but we did not stop."

"That's a pity," said Mateh. "In Orte Golen Sume dwell the flower of the wise men of Ordos and Sunit."

"The Sunit *Wang* was there," remarked Big Tiger. "And his old cousin too. He is very clever."

"The old cousin is a perfect wise man," said Mateh. "Nowhere-at-all had visited him too, and the learned man had written many things in the little book, which Naidang was to read to him as soon as he reached the Etzin Gol. A storm had arisen and the wind was blowing through the Valley of Dark Rushing Water. 'I want to obey the command of the holy man,' said Nowhere-at-all, 'and I beg you to be my witness.' We went out in front of the tent, where the dog was lying sheltering from the wind. Nowhere-at-all took out the little book, and threw to the winds the leaf of the Sacred Tree. It flew away and with it a leaf of the little book. I grasped for it, but it had been whirled away in the storm of the night. '*Hammagua!*' cried Nowhere-at-all. 'It is not right to run after the written word.' We went back to the *yurt,* and I slept until I awoke. But Nowhere-at-all did not awake. He was already stone cold when I went to call him, so suddenly had he died. When we had mourned him we bade a lama come, and he decided the place in the mountains where Nowhere-at-all was to be laid."

"Is he buried far from here?" asked Christian.

"We would like to pay our respects at his grave," said Big Tiger.

Good Fortune shook his head. "You can't do that," he declared, "because there's no grave."

Mateh, who understood the gist of the conversation, said: "We Mongols do not bury our dead. We lay them in a place far away shown us by the lama, and then we wait three days and pray that their wandering soul may be well received on the other side. Their bodies serve as food for the wolves and the eagles. Only the bones of Nowhere-at-all were left when we went back on the third day. He was a good man, otherwise more of him would have been left."

"What is done then?" asked Big Tiger, horrified.

"Nothing is done," said Mateh. "The bones are left where they are."

"But what about the relatives?" asked Big Tiger.

"I sent them word," answered Mateh, "and I gave the messenger the camel and everything else belonging to Nowhere-at-all. But Dogolon sent them all back to me as a gift. And so I got the camel mare which Nowhere-at-all rode, and she became the ancestress of our little herd. Good luck came to us and since then we have not lost a single sheep by the wolf, and though we withdraw to other pastures in the winter, we come back each spring to the Valley of Dark Rushing Water."

"It's well for us that you do," said Good Fortune. "Otherwise we wouldn't have met you and heard your words of wisdom."

Having paid this compliment Good Fortune finished his bowl of milk, and this was the sign for departure.

"Forgive me," said Mateh, "if I trouble you with a request."

"There is no question of trouble," said Good Fortune.

"I would like the young gentleman to take the book to the Etzin Gol," said Mateh, "so that Naidang may learn the two words written by the *Wang*'s old cousin. Perhaps Naidang needs this news urgently."

Mateh took the little book out of the chest, and Christian received it reverently with both hands. "We shall pass on your greetings," he said.

"Whereabouts does this Naidang live?" asked Good Fortune.

"I'm told he lives by the Narin Gol," said Mateh. "More than that I do not know."

"We shall find Naidang," Good Fortune assured him. "I know where the Narin Gol flows. May you dwell in peace." He started up the motor, and Christian and Big Tiger were surprised that he intended leaving without Greencoat.

"You needn't be afraid," said Good Fortune. "We shall meet him on the road. He won't be far off. Get in in front; you can change places later."

Good Fortune drove off quite slowly though the ground was smooth enough. As the caravan road came into sight, and they could have heard the bells only for the noise of the truck, he suddenly asked: "What about that telegram? Did you manage to see it?"

"Yes, we've seen it," said Big Tiger.

"What did it say?" asked Good Fortune.

"I believe there were only six words in it," said Christian. "One of them was Suchow."

"And what were the others?" asked Good Fortune impatiently.

"They were: 'No more Cow Pond, but Suchow. Greencoat.'" said Christian.

"Was that all?" asked Good Fortune, disappointed. "And was there no other name?"

"Where?" asked Big Tiger innocently.

"At the end where 'Greencoat' was, I mean."

"No," said Christian. "There was nothing but 'Greencoat.'"

"Has Greencoat got two names, then?" Big Tiger probed.

"I didn't mean that," replied Good Fortune. "I just thought that it was rather brief—only six words."

"They mean that Chen is going to Suchow," Christian explained proudly. "We found that out."

"That wasn't much," growled Good Fortune, beginning to drive faster.

"Where is Suchow, honored Sir?" asked Big Tiger.

"It's on the Silk Road," replied Good Fortune. "But haven't you got a map?"

Christian was about to reply that they would look it up, but the car suddenly dipped down, for they were crossing the riverbed of the Valley of Dark Rushing Water. Christian and Big Tiger had to hold on tight to prevent their heads from hitting against the windshield, and then they fell back when the car began to climb up the steep bank at the other side. Good Fortune had to change gear several times. "That was a near thing!" he said as they got up again.

In front of them they saw the caravan, and the last camel was carrying a heavy copper bell which gave a melancholy boom at each step. Behind was a man guiding a horse by the bridle, and beside him walked Greencoat. When they saw the truck coming Greencoat stood still, and his companion leapt quickly to his saddle and rode toward the truck, waving at Good Fortune to stop.

"Now, now! Keep your shirt on!" muttered Good Fortune, continuing to drive. Then he slowed down.

The man on the horse was quite out of breath. "Can't you hear," he shouted angrily, "and can't you see?"

"I hear and see that you're a lout," said Good Fortune calmly. "Those who say that one should not converse with such people are right. Therefore I shall drive on."

"Excellency," cried the man, "I ask forgiveness and clemency."

"Under these circumstances," said Good Fortune, "I shall listen to you if you wish. But make it short!"

"I beg you not to ruin me," pleaded the man. "Our camels are carrying heavy loads, but they will take fright and throw them off if they see Your Excellency's car and hear its noise. Therefore I beg you to turn a little aside and let us pass on in peace."

"My eyes are dim," Good Fortune asserted, "and my ears have grown weak from your bawling. Have you got any remedy for this illness?"

"We have various remedies," said the man sadly.

"Very well, go fetch me a twenty-pound bag of rice, but honest weight, mind!"

"It will be yours at once," replied the man in a tone of relief, and he galloped off.

Good Fortune followed slowly with the truck. When he reached Greencoat he stopped. "You've taken a fine long walk," he said. "Did you have an interesting conversation?"

"Yes," answered Greencoat. "And those who say a man should only have intercourse with his own kind are right."

"Are you referring to the lout on the horse?" asked Good Fortune good-humoredly.

"He's the leader of this great caravan, and a virtuous man. How can you call him a lout?"

"Has he given you a gift?" asked Good Fortune.

"It is not customary to make gifts on the road," said Greencoat sternly.

"That's out-of-date," Good Fortune enlightened him. "You will see presently what is customary nowadays." And he sat down near Greencoat beside the camel track.

Christian and Big Tiger got out too. When they saw the rider coming back they climbed quickly up on the truck again, and then they heard the horse stopping and the man saying: "I have hastened back to you before you overtake us, honored Sir. Please accept my poor gift."

"You may put it in the truck," said Good Fortune graciously.

Christian and Big Tiger got ready to help the man. He tried to heave the sack over the side of the car, but his horse was restive and frightened by the humming of the engine. At last he got it near enough, and then Christian took hold of one end and Big Tiger the other. "Thanks ten thousand times!" they said, but it was of little avail. The man was in a rage, his eyes gleamed with hatred; he muttered "little scoundrels" between his teeth, gave his horse a blow of the whip, and galloped off.

Good Fortune winked complacently and tapped Greencoat on the shoulder. "Do you see now," he said, "what is customary when people meet on the road?"

"Old *Hung-hu-tse!*" muttered Greencoat; and then he asked if he might drive.

"No," said Good Fortune. "From here to Durben Mot the road is much too difficult for beginners."

Greencoat put on a forced smile. "I quite agree with you," he said. "Please forgive me."

At first Good Fortune drove straight on and then he turned out to the left. Be it said to his credit that he made a very wide detour around the caravan, so that none of the camels could be the least frightened. Thus they could survey the whole caravan from end to end. There were definitely more than three hundred camels in it, and Christian tried to count them; but each time he got to twenty-four or thirty he became uncertain, and started again from the beginning.

"Just count the drivers," Big Tiger advised.

"There are twenty-five including the one who goes right out in front," Christian announced.

"Then," said Big Tiger—and he paused for a moment—"then there are three hundred and twenty-five camels, or a few more."

Christian was astonished, but as most Chinese boys are expert at figures, he only asked casually: "How do you make that out?"

"By taking thirteen as the number to reckon," Big Tiger explained. "Thirteen or at most fifteen camels are tied together one behind the other by their nose ropes, and one man guides the lot. So you have only to multiply twenty-five men by thirteen and you know how many camels there are."

"So that's it!" said Christian. "But what about the man on the horse?"

"He's the leader of the caravan—you don't count him, and I hope we'll never meet him again. He was terribly angry."

"We shouldn't have said: 'Thanks ten thousand times.' He took that badly."

"We shouldn't have helped him to put the sack in the truck," declared Big Tiger. "Now he takes us for apprentice redbeards. Did you see his eyes?"

"They were like fiery coals."

"And his hair bristled so much that it lifted up his hat," said Big Tiger.

"Let's not bother about him," said Christian cheerily. "He's far away."

They looked back once more at the caravan, and it seemed like a writhing centipede left far behind. Good Fortune then took to the caravan road again, and before long the smooth plateau changed to rough terrain. The path wound through endless low dome-shaped hillocks, and often the truck slid over into the sand when the track was not wide enough. At the foot of the little hills lay sand drifts which made progress still more difficult. Good Fortune breathed a sigh of relief when the ground rose higher and the maze of low hills ceased.

The road led imperceptibly into a basin-like depression. There was a well there surrounded by a spacious camping place. But suddenly the view became obstructed on all sides. True, the road, which turned sharply northward, could still be seen; but that was about all. Now it vanished behind jutting crags, now it appeared in defiles, but on the whole it seemed to be the only negotiable track in all that maze. Good Fortune ignored it, nevertheless, and steered resolutely toward an upper slope which proved to be not so steep as it appeared. All the same it took all his skill during an arduous hour to reach the foot of a mountain ridge which led to the west. To the south was sheer desert.

"Sand!" cried Christian in dismay. "Where can so much sand come from all at once?"

He took out the map and magnifying glass. Then he noticed

the small, closely placed dots near a nameless chain of hills. Not far from this there was a blue semicircle indicating a well, and beside it the words: Durben Mot.

"Now we are really in the desert," said Christian apprehensively.

"The sea of sand is terrifying only to the timid," Big Tiger remarked. But he himself did not sound very happy. "What surprises me . . ." he continued, slowly and wonderingly, "is how Good Fortune can find his way about here," Christian completed the sentence.

Big Tiger nodded and both gazed out on the long waves of dunes which broke against the slope. The sand dazzled their eyes. It was only late afternoon, and Good Fortune was driving as if it were a matter of life and death. But he had to be very careful, for the car was all the time tilted slightly against the slope.

Later the sand receded a little, the dunes got flatter, and at last they came to a dilapidated group of trees. That was Durben Mot, the place of the "Four Trees," and the well was also there.

Good Fortune now drove more slowly, for he knew that he was coming to a gravel-filled basin. When he reached it he halted. "Enough for today," he said.

"There's nobody here," remarked Greencoat. "Where shall I sleep tonight? You should have brought a tent."

"Peculiar young fellow," said Good Fortune, and left Greencoat standing there. This was a very offensive thing to say, and Good Fortune made it worse by following it with a laugh. Then he set to work to pour water into the radiator and cover the hood up. "You must fetch fresh water," he said. "The well is just beside the trees. But take a rope as there's no hoist."

The trees were black poplars, bent over by the wind. Only one stood upright. It was impossible to imagine how they had managed to take root and become trees here in gravel and sand with hardly any earth, and how the branches continued to put forth leaves again and again, even when the crowns lay on the ground smothered in sand drifts.

The poplars grew at the other side of the gravelly basin, just where it narrowed and firm ground began again. A stone's throw away the sand dunes drifted in waves from the south against the slope. From the north came the stream of boulders. It rose gradually out from the broad bed, and then suddenly climbed steeply half way up the mountain wall. There it disappeared in a ravine, from which the caravan road wound in spirals down to the valley.

Good Fortune came running after them over the field of gravel, carrying a shovel. "Stop!" he shouted. "We have to clean up a bit first." The well was covered with boards from which he carefully removed the sand. Then he shoveled the gravel aside. "If everyone did this," he declared, "there wouldn't be so many choked up wells."

When he pushed the boards aside the mirror of water could be seen glittering scarcely ten feet down. It was so clear that every little stone could be seen distinctly at the bottom, and when Christian let down the pail, it came up almost half empty, so he had to draw several times before he got a bucketful.

"Most caravans go an hour's journey further," said Good Fortune. "There's another well there which has lots of water, but there's soda in it and it gives you stomach ache."

"Then we'd rather stop here," said Christian.

"But where will Greencoat sleep?" asked Big Tiger mischievously. "He says he needs a tent."

"We haven't got a tent," said Good Fortune, "and we don't need one. Just look around you . . . could you find a better place?"

"It's a splendid place," agreed Christian without conviction.

"I've seldom seen so fine a place," chimed in Big Tiger.

"I mean for camping," said Good Fortune. "We have everything here."

"Oh, yes," said Christian. "For camping, of course." He looked around, but could not see what Good Fortune alluded to, so he picked up the pail.

"Leave that there," Good Fortune ordered. "We're remaining on this bank. The truck must stand further away this time," he continued, "as we've got wood to burn. That's why we don't need a tent. Greencoat doesn't understand that. How could he? He's always done his traveling in comfort, with tents and everything, just nicely on the fringe of the desert, and always on the go. He's a cowardly fellow, and as lazy as sin. Look at him sitting there, just as if he was painted on the rock. Enough to make a man quit! Phew!"

"Shall I get Greencoat away?" asked Christian, as he happened to step on Big Tiger's toe.

"Perhaps for half an hour?" suggested Big Tiger.

Good Fortune laughed. "You'll never be able to do it," he said.

"We're ready to tackle anything," declared Christian eagerly.

"We undertake the most difficult commissions," asserted Big Tiger. "I only ask our esteemed elder to state his wishes."

"Very well," said Good Fortune, amused. "See if you can get him away for half an hour, or anyhow until the rice is cooked."

"Compass Mountain will see to that," said Big Tiger.

"Bolna," said Christian, carrying the pails to a level spot which looked suitable for making a fire.

"What are you going to do?" asked Big Tiger quietly.

"You'll see," said Christian, and he walked across the boulder-strewn region toward the ravine, as if he wanted to examine the neighborhood. Big Tiger looked after him, and Greencoat, who had heard the crunching of the gravel and the clatter of the stones, looked too.

"Hello!" shouted Christian suddenly. Though he was a good way off the words were audible. "There's something queer here."

"What is it?" Big Tiger shouted back.

"You won't believe me, but I'll show them to you later."

"What will you show me?"

"Silver batzes! They're lying about here. It's very queer. I won't come back till the meal is ready."

"I'll call you."

"Better shout," called Christian. "I'm going a bit up the mountain."

"I'll sound the horn. Can you hear that?" Big Tiger jumped into the driver's cab, and when he sounded "Tut-tut-tut" Greencoat stood up slowly. "You're making an awful noise," he complained. "It's outrageous!"

At this Big Tiger honked again. Greencoat put his hands to his ears and said: "I can't stand this din." He walked off, sometimes slipping but with dignity for all that, over the gravelly basin toward the slope, where Christian stood beckoning him excitedly. He even ran part of ways to meet him.

"Mr. Greencoat," said Christian, "could you please tell me in what year this silver batz was minted?"

"In the third year of the Yuan Shih Kai government," Greencoat declared. "That's when they minted the best silver."

"I've heard that before," said Christian. "They don't make good coins any more. They put too much copper in them, the rogues."

"Where did you get the batz?" asked Greencoat.

"Two paces from the caravan road, at the entrance to the ravine. You should look around a bit. Perhaps someone walked up here with a hole in his pocket."

"That's right," said Greencoat, and both climbed to the edge of the ravine and looked around right and left.

"There's nothing here," said Greencoat.

Christian remained a few paces behind, dipped into his pocket and took out three silver pieces. Then he bent down quickly and shouted: "Here are three together!"

He showed them to Greencoat, who smiled sourly, murmuring: "Congratulations on unexpected wealth!"

Christian then went on ahead into the ravine, where the evening shadows were falling on the rocks, making his search more difficult. "You have to bend down," he advised Greencoat. "Then you'll still be able to see quite well."

Greencoat bent down, and if there was a silver batz there, he would certainly have found it. But there were none, until Christian went on a bit ahead. He had put the silver coins back in his pocket with the exception of one which he held in his hand. When he went around the next bend and Greencoat could no longer see him, he ran quickly up the slope.

"You shouldn't run so far ahead," cried Greencoat from below. "You could fall and break your bones!"

"I didn't think of that," Christian called back. He quickly laid a batz in the loose gravel in a place where it could not fail to be found. Then he turned back and met Greencoat at the top of the bend. "I hardly think there are any further up," he said. "If you don't mind I'll sit down here and rest a while."

"That's all right," boomed Greencoat. "I'll take a bit of exercise. A man gets quite stiff sitting in that truck." He went on searching, and Christian watched him furtively as he bent hastily to pick up something. Then Christian looked down into the valley where the truck stood, and the setting sun was shining over the dunes. Everything down there was thrown into sharper relief in the fading light, and the lengthening shadows made things stand out more than in the daytime. The stream of boulders emptied itself like a cascade into the stone basin, which overflowed and at one point took the form of two banks. On one stood the truck and on the other the trees, and there Christian saw a spiral of blue smoke rising steeply skyward. The long rays of the sun lit up two figures crouching near the fire.

Good Fortune and Big Tiger were discussing the best way of preparing rice, and incidentally Big Tiger was relating other things as well. "I found something," he began, delving in his pocket. "It looks like a cartridge, but I don't know to whom it belongs."

"Show me," said Good Fortune.

Big Tiger handed it to him, remarking that it was a very small caliber cartridge and perhaps might fit Good Fortune's pistol. He

should try it, because then he would have another shot if ever it came to a fight.

Good Fortune took out his pistol and found the magazine empty. He stared. Then he opened the holster, but there were no cartridges in it either.

"Ha!" he cried, and then again "Ha!" and then suddenly: "Some scoundrels have robbed me! My cartridges are all gone!"

"Of course one can't say who did it," said Big Tiger coolly. "But Greencoat has got quite a lot in his pants' pocket."

"I'll shoot him dead," cried Good Fortune, pushing the cartridge into the breech. "I'll do that as sure as I live! There's no greater scoundrel going than that foul fellow, and I'm only surprised that the rascal is still walking around alive! Heaven and earth are boundless, but his appointed end awaits every man! This is a good place for finishing him off."

"Perhaps if the honored gentleman would wait a bit," said Big Tiger.

"Why should I wait?" cried Good Fortune. "If you knew what I know, you wouldn't talk of waiting. I know my cartridges, and this is one of them. Now I've loaded my pistol, and when Greencoat comes he'll be surprised how quickly a man can be shot dead!"

"Wisdom forbids anger," Big Tiger objected.

"That's a saying of your grandfather," scoffed Good Fortune.

"My grandfather says you don't get any young tigers if you kill the old ones too soon. Greencoat may be useful to us in the end. You never know." Having said this he fell silent. Good Fortune, too, fell silent, and each had his own thoughts. Big Tiger perceived that Good Fortune was thinking of all the money he would like to get from Greencoat. Suddenly he shouted: "The rice is burning!"

Good Fortune jumped up horrified. "The wood fire was too hot," he lamented. "O woe, woe! That such a thing should happen to me! Haste brings misfortune. I shall lose face. What will Greencoat say when he tastes the burned rice?"

"He'll say nothing," countered Big Tiger. "He'll be a corpse lying around here somewhere."

Good Fortune frowned. He wanted to speak, but he couldn't. The sun floated fiery red over the sea of sand, and the shadows grew deep and purple.

"The honored gentleman," suggested Big Tiger, "has now got a cartridge. He can shoot Greencoat dead whenever it is urgent to do so. But Greencoat knows nothing of this and thinks nothing can happen to him. That's why he is becoming impertinent and indiscreet; and Mr. Good Fortune is at an advantage. I think that's as clear as the sand at the bottom of the water."

"You've got a wise head," said Good Fortune. "I'll put off the great act of justice for a while."

"Will the honored gentleman also please not show that he knows anything?"

"No, I won't let on to anything."

"Then Compass Mountain and I shall try to take the rest of the cartridges from Greencoat when we get a chance."

"How will you do that?" cried Good Fortune, and he shook his head. But then he said: "I believe you two will turn out a pair of regular devils!"

"We undertake the most difficult assignments," Big Tiger assured him. "Is the rice done?"

"Yes, it's done," sighed Good Fortune. "And it can be eaten, but it doesn't taste very nice."

"We two have a special liking for burned food," said Big Tiger, going over to the truck. He got up behind the steering wheel and sounded the horn four times.

Christian heard it, but Greencoat who had climbed up all the six twists of the road to the top, did not hear it.

"Tcho-fan! Food, food!" shouted Christian, but he got no answer.

Perhaps Greencoat has answered 'All right' thought Christian, but he did not bother to make sure and hopped joyfully from stone to stone down the slope.

"There's rice!" Big Tiger called up to him, laughing happily. This told Christian that their position was five times better than it had been half an hour ago.

25 CONTAINING THE STORY OF THE "VENERABLE CHIEF" AND AN ACCOUNT OF GREENCOAT'S INJURY

"Here I am!" said Greencoat, stumbling out of the darkness. "I hope you've had a nice meal. If mine is cold it doesn't matter in the least."

"I sounded the horn four times," said Big Tiger.

"And I shouted 'Dinner! Dinner!' very loud," said Christian.

"Sit down," said Good Fortune affably. "We've got a grand fire. And congratulations on unexpected riches! Did you find many silver pieces?"

"I didn't look for any," replied Greencoat with dignity, "so I didn't find any. I was only taking a bit of exercise. That's all."

"Help yourself," said Good Fortune. "You must be hungry."

"The rice is burned," remarked Greencoat, laying his chopsticks aside.

"I'll never get over that," lamented Big Tiger. "It's my fault. I let the fire get too hot. Please restrain your rightful anger."

"Of course," said Greencoat, making an effort to smile indulgently.

"Come, men," said Good Fortune. "We must fix our camp for the night." He stood up and went with Christian and Big Tiger toward the poplar trees. Two of them lay half buried in the sand, their split branches stretched upward. They pulled the dead branches free of the sand and dragged them to their campfire. Then Good Fortune set to work to make nice fire logs of the thick branches, while Big Tiger sawed off the forks. When they had a fine heap of firewood Good Fortune set it alight.

"Do you want to roast an ox," asked Greencoat, "or do you want to light robbers the way to us?"

"We needn't be afraid of robbers," said Big Tiger daringly. "Our respected elder has a pistol with lots of cartridges; so nothing can happen to us."

Greencoat made a contemptuous grimace and said he knew that, but just when they were most wanted pistols didn't go off.

"You're wrong there!" replied Good Fortune sharply. "Even an unloaded weapon can go off!" and he gripped the holster.

Big Tiger became terrified and hung on to Good Fortune's arm. "Don't shoot," he cried. "Please don't shoot! I can't bear shooting!"

"I can't either!" cried Christian. And he hung on to Good Fortune at the other side.

"Come, come," said Good Fortune, pacified. "I didn't know you were so scary."

"We have very delicate nerves," said Big Tiger.

"Pooh!" cried Greencoat, standing up. "No one could stand this heat. Why do you burn a whole heap of wood for nothing?"

"For your comfort," replied Good Fortune, sitting down at a little distance and watching the rustling flames shooting up into the night. When the fire had died down he fetched a shovel and spread out the glowing embers. Then he threw sand over them and flattened it out. Suddenly they were in darkness. The moon was a beautiful crescent poised coldly over the silent sea of sand, silvering the sharp edges of the rocks of Durben Mot.

"The *kang* is heated," cried Good Fortune. "May you sleep well."

"Am I to lie in the sand and be eaten by fleas?" asked Greencoat insolently.

"I don't care what you do," Good Fortune answered, and he took his coat, lay down on the warm sand, and covered himself up. "Come!" he invited Christian and Big Tiger. "Fetch your sleeping bags and lie down. We won't freeze tonight."

"This is a great idea," said Christian, as he lay down beside Good Fortune and felt the warmth under him. "We'll sleep like Prince Tchao."

"What about him?" asked Good Fortune.

"Just that," replied Big Tiger. "It's a poem we learned at school, and Kwi-Chan knows it too because I recited it to him."

"Say the poem to me," said Good Fortune. "I'd like to learn it too."

Then Big Tiger recited the poem of Prince Tchao who slept under a plum tree, and Good Fortune said he liked it and that Big Tiger should say it again tomorrow and the day after, and every day until he knew it too.

"Nonsense!" said Greencoat rudely. He had come after all and lain down beside Good Fortune on the warm sand. "Poems," he went on, "don't serve any useful purpose. What's the sense of saying 'The rain is falling' or 'The little wintry snowflakes flutter down.' We know already that it rains and it snows."

"A poem rhymes," Christian objected, "and that's what makes it beautiful."

"And it can be sung," said Good Fortune. "That's what matters."

"When a poem is written," said Big Tiger, "you can look at it, and it's like a picture and often more beautiful."

"Oh, rubbish!" growled Greencoat. "Tell me instead where we're going tomorrow."

"That depends on the sea of sand," said Good Fortune. "A man never knows how far it goes, or where there's a way through. Perhaps we shall get to Abder, perhaps we shall reach Yingen Ossu, or perhaps we shall get only as far as the Lonely Tree or perhaps get stuck somewhere and never get any place."

"You've got a lot of perhapses in your stock," muttered Greencoat, and he turned over and began to snore.

"Abder!" whispered Christian. "Is that the Box Mountain?"

"Hush!" said Good Fortune. "Don't speak to me of the Box Mountain; it's a dangerous mountain, and not far from here."

"I know that," said Christian. "Shall we see it?"

"We're driving by quite near it if . . ."

"If the spokes don't fall from the wheels," said Big Tiger dryly.

"Hush!" warned Good Fortune. "I'm not superstitious, but you never can tell. Good night!"

"We wish you rest and comfort," said Christian and Big Tiger, and then there was silence.

Night fell over the silent desert. So great was the vast loneliness that if Christian and Big Tiger had not been so tired they would have been frightened. Not a night bird called, and not a wolf prowled. It was lonelier than on Robinson Crusoe's island. For a while Good Fortune tossed about torn with ugly thoughts of vengeance, but then he said: "It can't be helped," turned over and fell asleep. He slept soundly until the cold breath of morning awoke him. Then he got up, gave the morning star a friendly nod, and set to work to get the fire going. He fetched water, and just as the flames shot up and the tea began to boil and he was about to call out, "Get up, men, the night is over!" he saw by the firelight a small gray snake peacefully coiled up on Greencoat's thigh. When Greencoat stirred a little in his sleep it raised its head, waved it to and fro, and hissed.

"That's fine," thought Good Fortune vengefully. But then he noticed that Big Tiger lay beside Greencoat, and that at any sudden movement he might just as easily be bitten.

There was no time to lose, as either of the sleepers might awake at any moment. Good Fortune went hot and cold with perplexity, and was actually thinking of trying to shoot the reptile, when a brilliant idea occurred to him. He dashed to the truck and got the whip. Then he crept noiselessly step by step up to Greencoat, until at last he stood beside him. The little gray snake was lying there quietly. He gripped the bamboo handle wrong way round in both hands, drew a deep breath, raised the whip, aimed, and then, not without some pleasure, delivered a fearful blow. The snake's head was smashed and its spine broken in several places. Greencoat awoke with a frightful roar, Christian sat up with a start, and Big Tiger slid hurriedly out of his sleeping bag.

"Help! Murder!" yelled Greencoat, trying to stand up, but falling back again with a groan.

"Has any sudden damage occurred?" asked Big Tiger soberly.

"He's smashing my bones!" yelled Greencoat.

"I've saved his life," said Good Fortune, lifting the dead snake on the whip and throwing it in front of Greencoat's nose. "There," he said. "The second half of your life hung on a thread."

"A sand viper!" cried Christian.

"Anyone bitten by it dies instantly," declared Big Tiger.

"There was no way out," declared Good Fortune. "A good hard blow had to be given, with the best intentions."

But Greencoat couldn't be convinced. He kept on whining.

"Let's see," Good Fortune asked good-naturedly, pulling down Greencoat's trousers. "The skin is broken," he said, "but the bleeding will stop as soon as it swells. You're getting on fine and should stop your bellowing. Come, tea is ready."

Greencoat sat up groaning. He dragged himself the few steps to the fire and then threw himself down again. "You have assaulted and injured me badly," he said in a feeble voice. "But wait awhile; there's a day for fishing and a day for drying the nets."

"Is that your thanks for help in mortal danger?" asked Good Fortune, furiously. "You should be saying: 'Thanks ten thousand times.' In fact, a *kowtow* wouldn't be out of place."

"Shut your mouth!" shouted Greencoat. "You could have removed the reptile with a shovel. Any child knows that."

"It was a poisonous viper, honored Sir," said Christian.

"It had been wakened from its winter sleep by the heat," Big Tiger explained. "Snakes are specially poisonous then."

"I was quite well," said Greencoat, "and now I'm seriously ill." He drank tea, but would have no millet. Christian ran to the truck and fetched the honey cakes.

"Thanks," groaned Greencoat, with a mean glance at Good Fortune; then he ate up a lot of the honey cakes. "I can't sit up in front today," he said, "because of this crime that has been perpetrated on me."

Good Fortune glanced up, blew his tea and said: "I know nothing about that." Then he finished his breakfast calmly and began to load the truck. Big Tiger brought along the shovel, Christian the cooking pot, and Good Fortune dragged the two thick branches which he also loaded in. "They're for this evening," he said. "And there's room enough for Greencoat beside them. You two can sit with me in front."

When everything had been stowed away Greencoat came limping over the stones. Again he said that a crime had been committed, but nobody answered him.

Big Tiger laid the two sleeping bags one on top of the other, saying: "Here's a soft place for you. I hope you'll be comfortable."

"Good," groaned Greencoat.

Good Fortune helped him up and he climbed in with a grimace of pain. Christian supported him behind, and Big Tiger, who was standing up on the truck, grasped him under the arm. When at last he was up Big Tiger pushed a blanket under his head and another under the injured leg, to raise it a little. He then hopped down from the truck, Good Fortune started up, and both boys sat down in the driver's cab in Greencoat's place.

"How was it about the cartridges?" asked Christian.

"At first," whispered Big Tiger, "he wanted to shoot Greencoat straight away. Then he thought to do it a little later on, and finally he postponed the great act of justice indefinitely." He could not say more, for Good Fortune got in and drove off.

The sky was calm and clear over the ravine of Durben Mot, which still lay in darkness, its edges sharply outlined in the morning light. But only Greencoat could see this. Big Tiger and Christian saw nothing but the sea of sand, toward which Good Fortune steered slowly. Nowhere was an outlet to be seen. At first they drove along by the gravel basin until it ceased and there was only sand. They could see the caravan road a little distance off, then it was no longer visible, for the sand became deeper, and Good Fortune looked worried. "There's no way out of this," he said. "We must drive through it until we get to the Soda Well."

The truck began to climb the low spur of the first dune. It bored its way through as well as it could, throwing up a lot of sand. Then it slid into the first of the furrows which separated the arch-shaped dunes. There was firm ground once more, the caravan track became visible, and Good Fortune whistled contentedly. But after little more than a hundred yards the second spur came to obstruct the route, and the truck had hard going.

"These accursed *barkhans,*" said Good Fortune, peevishly.

"What are they?" asked Big Tiger.

"When the dunes form semicircles," Good Fortune explained, "instead of running straight, as proper dunes should, they are called *barkhans.*"

Christian looked up, but the sun was still hidden behind the rocks of Durben Mot. The dome of heaven arched steely-gray in the hard light of morning, showing a little uncertain blue at the zenith. The dunes too were still colorless, but the further Good Fortune bored into their valleys, the higher they rose, and their curved spurs also grew higher. No longer did any firm ground break through. There was nothing anywhere but sand. The caravan road disappeared finally, and Good Fortune just had to drive on at random. He would have been quite content with this, and indeed would have thought nothing of driving blindly for a time if he could have made any headway. But he could not.

The semicircular dunes, the spurs of which had joined, formed a barrier of sand to defy the most expert driver. The front wheels dug deep into the sand, the back wheels did the same, and Good Fortune shut off the motor.

"It can't be helped," said Big Tiger. "We're stuck like the fox in the ice."

"Come on, men!" cried Good Fortune. "Take the shovels and planks. We must shift a big mountain." They set to work together, and the sand flew out on both sides.

"Now," said Good Fortune, when the passage through had been half cleared, "a little more shoveling and we shall be able to push the planks under the wheels. You boys shovel away and I shall go on ahead and see whether we shall be able to cross the sand or shall have to turn back."

A light morning breeze was sweeping clouds of sand from the ridges of the dunes. The sun was rising, the sky was turning a brilliant blue, and the sand was blowing from every *barkhan* like yellow smoke.

Good Fortune came back cheerful after half an hour's reconnoitering. "We must shovel a little more," he said, "and then we shall be rewarded for our perseverance."

"Hey," cried Greencoat from above, "have you got stuck?"

"We're shoveling," Good Fortune replied, "in order to drag your worthy person safely through the desert."

"I've been the victim of a malicious assault!"

"We shall have more to say about that later on," retorted Good Fortune angrily.

"All right," growled Greencoat. But he sounded more ill-humored than ever.

Good Fortune took no notice, but pushed two planks under the front wheels, thrust some of the branches under the rear wheels and ordered Christian and Big Tiger to hold the rest of the planks ready and keep laying them down in front of the truck until they got to firm ground.

Then Good Fortune started up the engine, and when it was running he once more went around the truck to see that everything was in order. Then he got in satisfied and drove very slowly from plank to plank. Big Tiger and Christian had to run to carry the planks from the back to the front. It was desperately hard work.

At last Good Fortune shouted "Enough!" and drove on to the next sand barrier, where the shoveling and plank-carrying was repeated. The sun climbed over the dunes and Greencoat complained that it was bothering him. But neither the boys nor Good Fortune made any reply; they were too busy shoveling and plank-carrying. The whole forenoon passed in this way. At last the crescents of the *barkhans* became lower and Good Fortune said he thought they might put back the planks and shovels on the truck.

"Bolna!" cried Christian and Big Tiger joyfully. And in fact they had hardly driven a *li* when a plain opened out in the midst of the dunes, and even though it was covered with sand, Christian and Big Tiger shouted with joy at the great deliverance. Good Fortune had to laugh, but they could see he was just as delighted as they were at the wide panorama and the firm ground under the wheels.

"Mountains and rivers are dangerous," said Good Fortune, "but sand is the most dangerous of all."

They saw the caravan track again, too. It ran towards the middle of the plain, where sedges grew sparsely over a shimmering whitish surface.

"Soda!" said Good Fortune. "The water which gives you stomach ache is here." He pointed to a well which was surrounded by a low, firmly trodden rampart. Everywhere there were traces of caravans—little heaps of camel dung in neat rows, deserted campfires, many bleached bones, and quite a number of animal skeletons. The warm air streamed into the open side window of the truck, and it smelled of dust, dried dung, rotten water, ashes, and all the other glorious things which rejoice the wanderer when the midnight hour is past and the tents are pitched. Good Fortune sniffed devoutly.

Suddenly he took his hand off the wheel, and waving it contemptuously, said: "These horseless cars are a foul invention. I'm ashamed to be driving in one of them." But after this self-accusation he drove on calmly, and Christian could not fathom his silent thoughts. Shortly afterwards he departed once more from the caravan track, which went on to the west, disappearing in the sea of sand.

"We have to make a big detour," said Good Fortune, and steered resolutely northward at a great speed. Around the plain stood the high dunes and *barkhans,* wave upon wave of them, but in the north their chains were interrupted, and he drove toward this break.

By the time he reached the breach the midday wind was sweeping over a great plateau bordered by dunes to the south and east. As far as the eye could reach westward the ground was gravelly, with here and there a few tamarisks. They were only storm-stripped, rigid sticks, with torn barks, and barely showed above the ground. Around their roots lay the drifts of sand which the wind had sent whistling over the desert. After two hours' journey the vista ceased to be bounded by dunes, and they got into a depression with an opening to the south.

"Why, yes!" cried Good Fortune. "This is the road we want. Have you got your map, Compass Mountain?"

"It's up near Greencoat."

"That's a pity," said Good Fortune, "because you could mark in a well which we shall reach soon. It's called Cheur Ampt. There we shall meet the caravan road again, and before long we shall arrive at the 'Lonely Tree' which is shown on the oldest maps. People say Genghis Khan slept in its shadow."

"And what comes after the Lonely Tree?" asked Christian.

"Then comes the mountain of which we've spoken, and if the spokes don't fall from the wheels we shall stop the night there. Are you hungry?"

"Yes, we're hungry, honored Sir."

"It can't be helped," said Good Fortune. "Rich people eat three times a day. But as we're not rich we eat only twice, so there's nothing before evening."

They soon reached Cheur Ampt Well, where the caravan road lay in the sun, waiting for Good Fortune to follow it to the Lonely Tree. But the route was bad. Again and again there were sandy belts, and it took more than three hours to cover the forty *li*. The Lonely Tree stood at the foot of a hill. It was a black poplar with a thick trunk and a miserable windswept crown. The once mighty branches were ragged and broken. Twenty paces off there was a well which Good Fortune said was half sanded up, because times had changed and the big caravans no longer used it. When Genghis Khan lived it was quite different. In those days the tree had leaves winter and summer, and the birds hopped through its branches and sang without ceasing.

"There was a beautiful meadow here with rare flowers," he continued, "and it was a miracle in the midst of the desert. But these are unworthy days, and that is why everything is dried up and the birds have flown away. Look at the Lonely Tree," he continued, slowing down, "so that you can tell them about it when you go home."

The three got out.

"May we take a little twig as a keepsake?" asked Christian respectfully.

"Nothing to stop you," said Good Fortune, and he lifted Christian onto his shoulders. Christian broke off three small twigs, and Good Fortune stuck one in his cap. Christian put the others away in the brief case which Greencoat handed down to him. He looked on the map for the Lonely Tree, but did not find it.

"That map is absolutely useless," said Good Fortune emphatically.

"Perhaps it's only a matter of looking long enough," Christian suggested. "Yesterday I found Durben Mot, and there's a lot of sand here, and if we've gone first west and then north and then south, we must be here, and the place is called Gantsen Mot, and there's a well near."

"That's wonderful!" cried Good Fortune, "and those who say a man should be sparing of his words are right. Gantsen Mot is the Mongolian for Lonely Tree, and I beg your pardon for my hasty speech."

"Pray don't mention it," said Christian, but he was very pleased. Christian now showed the compass to Good Fortune who said approvingly that it was a very useful instrument, but he didn't know why it was necessary since the sun shone in the day and at night the lord of the north* sat on his throne. So a compass in the long run only confirmed that the world went round just as it had always done, "even though we live in unworthy days," he added with emphasis.

* Shamg-ti, ruler of the cosmos, whose dwelling is on the polar star.

"But if the heavens are darkened by a storm," asked Big Tiger, "how do you manage then?"

"In that case you remain where you are," Good Fortune explained. "In the desert a storm blows up so much sand, and the sand thrashes about so terribly, that the camels lie down, and even a horseless car cannot go on because you can't see ten paces ahead. You would fall into a ravine or a well, and the flying stones would smash the windows of the car. The only thing to do is to stop and cover up the motor so the sand doesn't get into it."

"But if it rains?" asked Christian.

Good Fortune laughed. "Mist and rain, hail, thunder, lightning and dew are rare luxuries in the desert, and a man must submit to them. For that he needs no compass."

Thereupon Christian put away the compass, and they talked about other things; and when the sun was already going down, a gray, elongated table mountain appeared in the distance. In front of it rose a fiery red mass, square, and standing all alone. It was a tremendous size, though it towered but little over its surroundings.

Good Fortune sounded the horn loud and then soft, and this meant: "Danger! Look out!"

"Bator was born here," whispered Christian. Big Tiger nodded.

As they came nearer the road led downhill. A stony valley lay in a broad sweep around the gray table mountain and Mount Abder, and they could see the caravan road following the valley and coiling in the distance round a high plateau with a yellow shimmer.

"There's sand again there," said Good Fortune, "but I've had enough of it for today." He drove the truck away from the caravan camping grounds on to the level open space on the bed of the valley, opposite Mount Abder.

Christian and Big Tiger observed it. Four vertical, deeply riven red walls rose steeply from the windswept sand. It really does look like a box, thought Christian, but he did not dare to say it.

Good Fortune was more bustling than ever, and when one job was done, he ordered the next—filling the tank, pumping up the tires, making the fire. He was obviously afraid one of them might utter a thoughtless word about Abder, the Box.

Greencoat only came down from the truck for his meal. He was still limping, and remained silent apart from announcing that he wished to sleep on the truck so that another innocent snake would not get killed. Christian and Big Tiger willingly fetched their sleeping bags and left Greencoat their two fur coats. Good Fortune pulled up some dry tamarisks and lit a fire. Then he threw on top of it the branches he had brought from Durben Mot, raked out the embers and shoveled sand over them as the evening before. By this time night had fallen, the Box stood silent in the silvery moonlight, and Christian and Big Tiger lay down beside Good Fortune on the warm sand. The truck stood a good distance away, and so deep was the silence that they could hear Greencoat snoring.

Probably two or three hours had passed when Christian was awakened by the sound of hoofs, and raising his head he saw, a few paces away, a row of dark animals laden with little boxes. They were not camels—that he could see at once—but neither were they horses.

At this moment Big Tiger woke up. Right next to him a man leapt from the saddle and stood, a black silhouette, beside his dark mount. He wore a uniform like Good Fortune's. And the big animal, which looked like a horse, had long ears, so it was a mule. Good Fortune still slept on.

"Hey!" cried the soldier, tapping his padded trousers with his riding whip. "I want to say how pleased I am to see you!"

In a trice Good Fortune was on his feet. He looked over at the passing caravan of mules, and then at the soldier.

"Am I disturbing you?" asked the soldier. "I'm sorry to break your rest."

"A man's sleep is sacred," replied Good Fortune uncivilly. Had he not noticed that the other man also wore a pistol in his belt, he would probably have said "Scoundrel," or "I hear a lout speaking."

"One should not break old friendship," said the soldier, smiling.

"Neither should one be quarrelsome." Saying this he bowed and . . .

"Oh, Long Life!" cried Good Fortune. "I thought you were gathered to your fathers."

"I have escaped the sword," said Long Life simply. And they bowed very low and very joyfully to each other.

"How is it that you come riding this way?" asked Good Fortune.

"How is it that you come driving this way?" asked Long Life.

"It's good to meet," said Good Fortune. "Let us sit down and tell each other what is worth telling."

"I've nothing worth mentioning to relate," answered Long Life modestly.

Meanwhile the mules had passed by, one after the other. There were several soldiers with them, and one of them came up and wanted to dismount too, but Long Life shouted sternly: "Ride on! I'll follow you later. Wait for me at Cheur Ampt." The soldier rode on obediently and the quick clatter of hoofs faded away in the night.

"I see you've been promoted," said Good Fortune, "and I congratulate you."

"The little star is of no value," replied Long Life. He took a leather strap from his pocket and hobbled the mule's forelegs.

"It's warm here," said Good Fortune. "Let us lie on our stomachs and chat in comfort. It's many a day since I heard your voice."

"I've yearned for your company," replied Long Life. "A man who lives far from his native place rejoices when he meets a fellow townsman. Who are those two there?"

"Forgive me," said Good Fortune. "I forgot to tell you that these young princes are Compass Mountain and Big Tiger. You can tell me all your news without hesitation. We both know enough about old times. You need not touch on them."

"Will you please begin?" requested Long Life.

"How could I dare?" cried Good Fortune. "It is for you to speak first."

Long Life was silent for a while, and so deep was the silence all round that Greencoat's snores resounded like a two-handled saw, and Long Life asked: "Is there somebody else there?"

"There is somebody else, and you know him," said Good Fortune. "It's the honorable merchant."

"Shong-Ma is with you?" cried Long Life, horrified. "I heard he was dead."

"Hush!" said Good Fortune, and it was plain that the turn of the conversation embarrassed him. Christian and Big Tiger nudged each other.

"Shong-Ma is dead," said Good Fortune in a low voice, "but a certain Mr. Greencoat has taken his place."

"I've heard of him," said Long Life. "He carries on a lively trade."

"He's grown a long beard and nobody can recognize him."

"Then the Venerable Chief will seek him in vain," said Long Life, reassured.

Good Fortune shrugged his shoulders. That was none of his business, he said. It was the business of the Venerable Chief, and would Long Life please go on with his news.

"As you wish," began Long Life. "I was sorry when I heard you had become a soldier. I didn't want to be a soldier after the unfortunate events you know of, so I returned to Li-Yuan-Pei at Hami. 'How dare you hang your black face over my counter?' shouted Li. 'You have been incautious. Therefore bear your misfortune yourself.' So I left and became a soldier. First I was in the garrison of Sining-fu and later at Suchow. For six years all went well until the General in Hami got the fatal idea of making war on the Venerable Chief."

"I heard you didn't win the war," said Good Fortune.

"The Venerable Chief slaughtered us like lambs in spring," Long Life confessed.

"How was that?" asked Good Fortune sympathetically.

"We were a thousand strong," said Long Life, "and we had

everything necessary to win a war. We had even the latest automatic rifles and small portable machine guns which we carried on camels. Then we set out to march through the desert of stone and the sea of sand. When we arrived in front of the Venerable Chief's castle after a month we started shooting right away to show him what was up. He understood at once and shut the gates. He had only three hundred horsemen, but we were a thousand. There he was caught in a trap, and our General said: 'We need not hurry.' We were glad of that. 'When the bandits have nothing more to eat,' said our General, 'and have used all their fodder beans, they will come out. Then we shall shoot the Venerable Chief, and his three hundred men too.' So we made a deep trench around the castle, did a bit of shooting every day, and waited. The autumn passed by, and the weather got cold, and we froze miserably, especially at night. 'It doesn't matter,' said the General. He thought he had got up early, but he met people who hadn't slept at all; for when another night had passed and some of us lay there frozen, a mighty outburst of thunder and lightning rent the dawn. We thought the end of the world had come. Heaven and earth mingled in confusion, and the wall of the castle burst in several places and fell down. Then most of us imagined we had won, and we set up a great shout. But out of the breaches came the Venerable Chief's three hundred horsemen with nothing but their swords in their hands. The Venerable Chief himself was among them, and the barbarians were roaring like tigers. But we could not shoot them because of our frozen fingers. And our rifles and guns were frozen too, especially the automatic ones. So row after row of us were devoured by the sword. The bandits galloped through our trenches, and their horses stamped in blood.

"I ran to the few horses we had, for I saw the war was lost. And so I escaped with four others. But it was a retreat, neither voluntary, friendly, nor merry, for the enemy pursued us. Luckily we met a caravan which gave us beans for the horses. When we reached the Gashun Nor after ten days we were half dead. It was night, and we made a big fire of tamarisk. We shouldn't have done that, for suddenly we heard the clatter of hoofs and the tiger roar of two barbarians. I leaped into the darkness and fired many shots. One of the fellows fell from his horse and the other was thrown off too, for his horse took fright. We fell on him with sticks and swords, and I split his forehead open. There he lay, and I said: 'This dog and this son of a tortoise has met his deserts.' The firelight shone on his face, and suddenly I recognized Moonlight—the same Moonlight who had once spared the lives of us two. My comrades wanted to strip him of all he had, but I said: 'Leave him, I will not permit it.' Then we rode on, as the place was no longer safe for us."

"Did you kill Moonlight quite dead or only half?" asked Good Fortune.

"As dead as a corpse can be," Long Life assured him.

"That corpse," said Good Fortune, "goes wolf-hunting again. It must have been a very quick rebirth."

"How's that?" asked Long Life. "I'm lying here, and Moonlight's bones are lying by the Gashun Nor and are white from the winter's snows."

"No," replied Good Fortune. "It's not as you say. I saw Moonlight three days ago. He was merry and full of good will, and we made a pact of mutual friendship. He had a red sword scar from one temple to the other, but otherwise he was sound. When I met him he was in the act of killing a wolf with the lead bag."

"The order of the world must be disturbed," cried Long Life. "The dead rise up, and ride, and hunt."

"We live in queer times," said Good Fortune, "and such things may happen. But I advise you to avoid meeting Moonlight. As far as I can see, he's being met at Sunit by a man named Thunderbolt. He's probably already on his way to the Venerable Chief and you may meet the two redbeards in Cow Pond or even in the Valley of Dark Rushing Water. They are changing horses on the way. It seems to be a very urgent matter."

"I'm not afraid of Moonlight," said Long Life.

"Have you got a picked band of heroes with you?"

"No, but we're carrying precious goods on trust. That gives even a coward courage.

"How many cases?"

"Sixty. Each case is worth gold, since opium has become so dear."

"Where are you taking the stuff to?" asked Good Fortune contemptuously.

"We're to deliver it in Kwei-hwa. More than that I do not know."

"I'm not you," said Good Fortune. "Do as you think right."

"I shall follow your advice," said Long Life. "We will turn aside at Cheur Ampt and get on to the southern road near the monastery of the Rich Springs."

"There are two kinds of courage," said Good Fortune. "My heart rejoices that you choose the thoughtful kind."

"Experience has been my teacher," remarked Long Life, smiling. "But I'm still in the dark about you. It's now your turn to speak."

Then Good Fortune told how he had become a soldier of General Feng. "But you know," he said, "that was not what I wanted. I wanted to earn money to send to my old mother. One day our company was asked whether any of us could drive a horseless car. I stepped forward at once and ten others did the same—good-for-nothing louts most of them, who had never seen an automobile in their lives. But no more had I. A strange officer came and asked us about things of which we didn't even know the names. Then he realized that we were not motor drivers at all. When he came to me he asked me what I would do if the radiator steamed. I said: 'Where there's great heat, water is the thing.' This answer pleased him and he took me to Honan. I got a new uniform, for now I belonged to General Wu's army. The officer no doubt knew I couldn't drive a car, so he took me in hand for a week. When I could drive he presented me to the General. 'Here's the man,' he said, 'for whom I have been searching zealously. He's General Feng's best driver, and the General has only consented to release him to oblige Your Excellency.' Then he ordered me to drive backward and forward, and when General Wu saw I could do it, he made me his chauffeur. In time I learned everything without ever letting him see how little I had known in the beginning. When the war with Chang-Tso-ling broke out three years later I was able to take an automobile to pieces and put it together again. The General gave me a better wage, and I sent it to Suchow."

"I heard that," said Long Life, "when I came home from the war against the Venerable Chief. Your mother was telling everywhere that you had become a great gentleman and didn't forget your mother; and everyone was congratulating her on her worthy son. At home in Suchow you've got a big face. No one would be surprised if one day you bought your mother a palace with ten men servants and twenty maids."

"I haven't got that far yet," said Good Fortune gravely.

At this Big Tiger gave Christian a nudge and they both thought of what they had heard in White Stone under the *kang*.

"I've rested enough now," said Long Life, "and I must go and catch up on my men. Where are you traveling to now?"

"I'm driving to Sinkiang," said Good Fortune, standing up.

"How will you manage that," asked Long Life, "without falling into the hands of the Venerable Chief?"

"I've been thinking of that. As you have lost the war against him, I can't go straight through the desert. Is there still gasoline in Ollon Torre?"

"There is, but there's a military guard there."

"That doesn't worry me. I've an order from General Wu for the gasoline. Then I'll drive to Suchow, and from there by the Silk Road to Hami."

"All the same you must be very careful," Long Life advised. "Since the Venerable Chief captured our modern arms he's operating on the Silk Road too. From Anhsi to Hsing-hsing-hsia it is no longer safe. The Venerable Chief is as swift as a spirit."

"Thank you for your information," said Good Fortune, and he took Long Life aside and whispered a few words to him. Long Life then went to his saddle bag and gave Good Fortune a small package. "These will be sufficient," he said. "Take care nobody sees who's with you," he whispered as he mounted. "It might cost you all your lives!"

"No fear," Good Fortune replied in a low voice too. "You yourself would never recognize the honorable merchant."

"Anyone as cocksure as you are," said Long Life, "should be able to get through anywhere. Good-by, and may you have lucky stars for the whole of your journey."

Good Fortune bowed, and Christian and Big Tiger stood up and bowed too. They looked after Long Life as he rode off. When the quick beat of the mule's hoofs had died away, Big Tiger said: "Permit me to ask who is the Venerable Chief?"

"Oh, men!" cried Good Fortune. "The Venerable Chief should not be named by name any more than this mountain. I'm standing here, and the Venerable Chief knows it. Now I lie down, and he hears it. He is a man who fled into the wilderness where even a tamarisk cannot take root, and there his stronghold stands. He is the greatest robber within the four seas, and a murderer too. All the caravans which pass through the sea of sand have to pay him tribute. None can resist him, for success is on his side and failure is the lot of his enemies. The Mongols say he is a demigod. But he is a cruel devil."

"What's his name?" asked Big Tiger, softly.

"His name is Dampignak," whispered Good Fortune.

26 A CHAPTER FULL OF EVIL OMENS

THE NIGHT wore on. As the moon disappeared behind Mount Abder a big stone came loose on the summit and fell with a great bang into the valley. Good Fortune, who was still awake, took this for a warning sign, and decided to have two words with Greencoat. Then he fell asleep, but it was an uneasy sleep, and he awoke earlier than usual. He made a fire, put on the kettle, and then awoke Greencoat who was lying in the truck, snoring.

"What's up?" asked Greencoat, waking up with a sigh.

"I have to speak to you."

"Speak to me when it's day. I'm still sleeping, so it's not the right time."

"It is the right time," Good Fortune asserted. "I've to speak two words with you while the boys are asleep."

"I suppose you want to talk about money."

"I want to tell you this: Your company is a danger to us. The Venerable Chief is looking for you."

"He's been looking for me for twenty years. That's nothing new."

"The Venerable Chief is more powerful than ever. Long Life was here tonight."

"What's that? That incompetent little redbeard comes for a secret conference? How is the little no-good clown getting on? How is the little son of my heart?"

"The no-good clown has become a lieutenant. He tells me the Venerable Chief now rules the Silk Road, and no one is safe from the bandits between Anhsi and Hsing-hsing-hsia."

"Our truck travels faster than the fastest horse."

"*Our* truck? Who is speaking of *our* truck?"

"If you prefer it, I can say *my* truck."

"You conceited fool. The truck belongs to General Wu. It runs quickly, but a bullet can catch up with it."

"I see you're scared stiff," said Greencoat contemptuously.

"Better a bit of fear than a bellyful of arrogance," replied Good Fortune. "I'll drive to Sinkiang in spite of the Venerable Chief, but I'm just wondering whether I'll take you with me or leave you sitting in Suchow. You can think it over."

"What does that mean?" cried Greencoat, flaring up.

"It means," said Good Fortune, "that you give me five hundred silver batz in Suchow and the other seven hundred in Hsing-hsing-hsia. I don't wish to visit my mother with empty hands."

"Aha! The good son!" cried Greencoat. "The magnificent support of the parental mansion!"

"You'd better look out for your safety instead of scoffing at a man's natural affections. Answer me this: Are you sure of your agent in Hsing-hsing-hsia?"

"He's truly devoted to me."

"You once threatened to denounce me," said Good Fortune sharply. "My name isn't Greencoat, and it's not Shong-Ma either. Therefore it wouldn't occur to *me* to betray you to the Venerable Chief. But are you sure nobody else would do so? That's what I wanted to ask you."

"Aha," cried Greencoat, sitting up. "So that's it? I'm much obliged to you for bringing to my notice something I had never thought of. My agent in Hsing-hsing-hsia was with me twenty years ago when we played our little trick on the Venerable Chief. He's in the same boat with me now, and he can't get out."

"Then it's all right," said Good Fortune. "Come on now, the tea is ready."

"My leg!" groaned Greencoat, but he stood up and slid down from the truck.

"You must exercise it," Good Fortune advised him.

"I understand," said Greencoat with a grin, "that you're to get your five hundred batz in Suchow. I shall wire Li-Yuan-Pei."

"Beware!" warned Good Fortune. Then he asked casually: "Does Li-Yuan-Pei know your new name?"

"Yes," replied Greencoat, "but I don't use it in business. However, there's nothing to fear on that score. The Venerable Chief is mighty, it is true, and ghostlike in his methods, but he can't penetrate the secrecy of the post office."

Good Fortune scratched his head, and then he looked over with a puzzled frown at Christian and Big Tiger, who were lying quietly pretending to be asleep. If I only knew, he thought, how much of the truth these lads tell me, and where the lies begin. "Get up!" he shouted over crossly. "You must learn to tell the day from the night!"

They quickly rolled up their sleeping bags and carried them over to the truck.

"Hurry up!" cried Greencoat. "We're already taking breakfast."

"How is the esteemed gentleman's health?" asked Big Tiger.

"Can he move about better now?" asked Christian.

Greencoat gave a wry smile. "Very well," he said. "I had a severe injury, but I'm recovering."

"Mr. Greencoat is well again," said Good Fortune.

"Shall we make any big detours today?" asked Greencoat.

"No, the detours are over," replied Good Fortune. "We have to drive through the sandy desert of Yingen Ossu. There's no way of avoiding it. If all goes well we shall not be far from the Etzin Gol by tomorrow evening."

"Since that's so," declared Greencoat, "I will drive."

Good Fortune was not encouraging. "You have a road in front of you," he said, "but it will be hard going."

"It will be easy to follow it. As soon as we arrive at the Red Mountain . . ."

"Shut up!" cried Good Fortune angrily. He shouted so loudly that the words echoed back first from Mount Abder and then from the gray table mountain. Greencoat fell silent, startled.

A cold morning wind was blowing through the valley, the fire flickered restlessly, and Greencoat said: "It seems to me silly that you take the superstitions of the barbarians seriously. But that's your business. My business will be to drive to Kuku-tologoi."

"You're undertaking a lot," retorted Good Fortune. But he said no more, and when they had finished breakfast he started hustling them.

Christian and Big Tiger resumed their old places, and as it was cold they crept into their sleeping bags. They could hear Greencoat taking part in the preparations for departure. He started up the engine, crossly instructed by Good Fortune, and drove up the slope to the caravan track.

There was scarcely light enough to see the way, but that did not prevent Greencoat from getting up a high speed from the start. When he crossed the stony ground of the valley, the iron drums hopped. Christian and Big Tiger were bounced up, the cans slid to the middle of the truck, and Christian said: "It can't be helped. Ouch!"

Only when the car began to climb uphill the speed reduced. Soon the stones ceased, and the low sand dunes began to push their way right to the edge of the caravan track. The truck stopped jolting, and by the time the sun rose over the mountains Christian and Big Tiger had fallen asleep.

It was easy for Greencoat to drive. The fresh mule tracks pointed the way, and Good Fortune said appreciatively: "Here rode a man who is at home on the sea of sand." The dunes and their spurs had been cleverly circumvented, and the sand at no place lay as high as at Durben Mot. After only two hours Greencoat reached the well of Yingen Ossu, where the road bent sharply southward, and after another hour the region of dunes was left behind. Then the road bent westward again.

Greencoat was very proud of himself and looked challengingly at Good Fortune, who took no notice. When he still ignored him, Greencoat coughed and said: "I have crossed the sea of sand."

"That useless clown Long Life removed all difficulties by his skillful guidance," Good Fortune replied. "We should be thankful to him. Don't you think so too?"

Greencoat flushed angrily, but he kept his eyes fixed in front of him, and drove still faster. By midday they had passed two more wells, and Good Fortune realized that it would be possible to reach the Etzin Gol if they went on for two or three hours after dark. At the next well he said suddenly: "Stop! We'll have tea here!"

"What for?" asked Greencoat. "I was ill yesterday and you didn't think of stopping for tea."

"Yesterday wasn't today," said Good Fortune, reaching for the brake, and Greencoat had to give in.

"We're having tea," shouted Good Fortune. "Come down and bring a bit of sheep cheese with you!"

Christian and Big Tiger had fallen asleep, but they became alert at once. "We're coming!" they cried, and jumped down from the truck.

Good Fortune made a fire of *argal,* and while the kettle was boiling they all sat around the fire chewing cheese, and Good Fortune said: "This well is called Green Crevice."

Big Tiger and Christian looked around, but nowhere was any green to be seen. There was only a stony dry riverbed, waves and waves of sand, and a great expanse of gray stone desert with a few tamarisks. Two parched trees stood some distance away at the foot of a hill which was crowned by an *obo.*

"I've got a pistol here," said Good Fortune opening his holster. "And I had plenty of cartridges, but a shameless thief stole them."

"You didn't take care of them," said Greencoat coldly.

"I was very careless indeed," Good Fortune admitted. "I forgot the precautions which have to be taken against thieves."

"Then you are to be pitied," replied Greencoat contemptuously.

"Not really," said Good Fortune, putting his hand in his coat pocket. "Anyone who has friends is not alone in the world."

He opened the little carton which Long Life had given him, took out the cartridges one by one, and refilled the magazine before all eyes. "You don't mind, do you?" he asked Greencoat.

"Not at all. On the contrary, I congratulate you."

"I only ask," said Good Fortune, "because yesterday you thought a pistol wouldn't go off at the right moment—and look," he cried, pretending to be astonished, "there's one cartridge over. It must have escaped the thief's notice. It would have gone badly for you if I'd pressed the trigger in Durben Mot."

As he spoke Good Fortune kept his eyes fixed on Greencoat. But Greencoat turned neither pale nor red. "That was a long speech," he said. "Have you finished it?"

"I have," said Good Fortune, abashed, putting the pistol away.

"Then we shall drive on," suggested Greencoat. "It was an unnecessary stop."

Good Fortune sought in vain for an answer.

"Let us drive on," ordered Greencoat. And he went over to the truck and started up the engine, all with the utmost self-possession.

While they put away the things on the truck, Big Tiger said: "Will my respected elder permit me to ask him a question?"

"Ask it," said Good Fortune irritably.

"Why did the respected Mr. Good Fortune show Mr. Greencoat the new cartridges?"

"It just came into my mind," said Good Fortune. "I wanted to see the face he'd make."

"His face didn't change," remarked Big Tiger; "from now onward he will be careful instead of careless. That's the only result."

"I don't need your advice as to what's wise or unwise," Good Fortune replied angrily, "you're cheeky."

"I beg your generous forgiveness," murmured Big Tiger.

"Tut-tut-tut." Greencoat sounded the horn, and that did not improve Good Fortune's mood. He got in silently, and Big Tiger had barely time to clamber up with Christian's help. When they were sitting together again, comforting themselves with some honey cakes, Christian said: "Good Fortune is a blockhead."

"I told him so," replied Big Tiger.

"That was not wise," said Christian, "now we have two against us."

"I admit I was thoughtless, Kwi-Chan."

"It's not so bad," Christian quickly reassured him; "when we reach the Etzin Gol we will have half the journey behind us. We've now been six days on the way; six or seven days more and we're in Sinkiang."

"Don't forget that Good Fortune said he couldn't drive straight through the desert; so he'll make a big detour."

"Let's look," said Christian, taking out the map. But the Southern Sheet ceased just behind the Etzin Gol, so he had to take the Western Sheet. For a long time after that they were silent, for Christian was searching with the magnifying glass for the places he had heard Long Life mention, and especially the Silk Road. When he had found them all and measured the distances with the pencil, he said: "There are about six hundred *li* more; on the other hand the road may be better."

"But if the Silk Road is in the power of this Venerable Chief, what then?"

"Then Good Fortune will have to drive by night."

"The motor makes a frightful noise," Big Tiger objected; "traveling by night won't help."

"Then there's no way out," said Christian. "What do you know of the Venerable Chief?"

"I've never heard of him before. Good Fortune says his name is Dampignak."

"We'll ask Naidang about him," said Christian, folding up the map.

"Stop," said Big Tiger, "there's something else we should know. Can you find the Red Mountain that Greencoat is always speaking of, though it annoys Good Fortune?"

"Here it is," cried Christian. "If we continue as we're going now we'll see the Red Mountain before dark."

"I believe," said Big Tiger, "that Good Fortune was once a member of an honorable company which had its camp on the Red Mountain."

"And Long Life too," said Christian.

"And Greencoat?" asked Big Tiger.

Christian shrugged his shoulders. "Apparently he was something worse than a redbeard."

By this time Greencoat was driving like an old hand. The car often jolted over stones, but Greencoat paid no attention, and did not slow down. Then came flat gravelly ground alternating with long stretches where the car sank and rose, leaving deep wheel tracks in the crumbly *loess*. As far as the eye could reach there were hills and ranges of hills without name or number. Certainly many if not most of them had never been touched by human foot. And when one realized that this strange land continued indefinitely without a change of landscape, things such as railways and letter boxes simply faded from the mind. With nothing before one but the gray of the stones and the gleaming sand, even houses and trees seemed unimaginable.

Late in the afternoon a high pyramidlike mountain came into view. It was as red as Mount Abder, and the nearer they came the bigger it seemed, for the road descended into a broad valley, which formed a basin at the foot of the mountain. There was a well there with good water. Rocks and sloping spurs closed to form a semicircle in which the warm air seemed to stand still. The noise of the motor echoed back from the rocks as Greencoat drove slowly right through the basinlike valley. He need not have done this, for there was a convenient outlet to the south through a saddle gap in the mountains, which could be seen for a long way ahead.

Christian stood on tiptoe and peeped through the little window. He noticed that both men were staring grimly ahead, as if there was something frightfully interesting in front of them. "They're not talking at all," he whispered.

"That's fine," said Big Tiger, relieved. "We must drive the wedge deeper between them."

By the time it was nearing evening the Red Mountain had long since disappeared from view. Greencoat had driven well. The road ran southwestward over slight undulations, and the setting sun stood like a fiery gate right over the caravan track.

"If we had not stopped unnecessarily, we would be in Kukutologoi by now," remarked Greencoat. "Where do we spend the night?"

"At the Etzin Gol," said Good Fortune.

"Then you predict that we reach the Etzin Gol?"

"*You* won't, but I'll reach it before midnight," said Good Fortune rudely.

"Very well," growled Greencoat, "I've driven enough now—I think about six hundred *li*."

"Five hundred and eighty," said Good Fortune, glancing at the speedometer. "I congratulate you on the recovery of your leg."

"It's got bad again, I notice."

"Then give up the driving," said Good Fortune, reaching for the brake. When the car stopped he got out, and told Christian to fetch a can of water. Having filled the radiator he brought back the pail. "Put on your fur coats," he said, "we're driving on to the Etzin Gol. It will be freezing cold for a bit, for the moon looks frosty."

"We love driving at night," cried Christian.

"You'll soon have more of it than you bargain for," retorted Good Fortune. He thereupon climbed into the driver's cab and drove in the direction of the setting sun. Darkness fell quickly; the moon shone brighter and the road looked like a narrow silver ribbon. It was only when it disappeared between round hills that Good Fortune switched on the headlights. From then onward he drove more slowly.

"He's friendly again," said Christian.

"He's got something up his sleeve," said Big Tiger; "you'll see."

"Tut-tut-tut" sounded the horn, and when Christian and Big Tiger jumped up to see what was there, they could just perceive in the gleam from the headlights a blue travel tent and beside it five tethered camels which were pulling wildly on their nose cords and plunging up and down like young goats. Two men came running out of the tent. "We're terribly frightened!" they shouted.

Good Fortune drew up and one of the men took courage and came alongside, timidly avoiding the glare of the headlights. Good Fortune switched off the light and the general excitement eased off. "What's this place called?" he asked for an opening.

"You are in Kuku-tologoi, honored Sir."

"This is a car which goes of itself," Good Fortune declared, "but there's nothing to be frightened of."

"I have never before seen such a car; it looks terrifying."

"It takes getting used to," Good Fortune agreed. "Is your rest easy and good?"

"We rest easy and well."

"I hear," said Good Fortune, "that you are of the Torgut tribe. How is my friend Naidang and does he still live by the Narin Gol?"

When the Mongol heard this he became friendly and reported that Naidang still lived there and that he would certainly be delighted to receive such distinguished visitors.

Good Fortune waited a while until the two Mongols had taken the camels sufficiently far away, then he drove cautiously through the loose gravel and wind-blown deresen grass past the well of Kuku-tologoi.

It was not long before they came to a pass full of drifts, and Good Fortune, Big Tiger and Christian had to spend half an hour shoveling. "All clear!" cried Good Fortune joyfully, when the road was free. "In another hour we'll be at the Etzin Gol."

The night was calm; the twinkling stars were very near. Through them glided the moon, and if it had been a full moon they could have seen, after an hour's drive, the trees which line the

Etzin River as it winds through the desert. They stand close together and in places actually form little woods and thickets. But as it was more or less dark they only saw the trees when the truck halted and the moon seemed to be suspended in the branches of the high black poplars.

27 A CHAPTER THAT BEGINS BADLY AND ENDS WITH A GREAT SHOCK

"Hi!" called Good Fortune gently, "are you awake, you two sleepy-heads?"

"Yes, we're awake!" cried Christian.

"We're as lively as antelopes," cried Big Tiger.

"Be quiet," warned Good Fortune, "Greencoat is asleep, and I want two words with you quickly."

Big Tiger and Christian jumped down from the truck. The silence was absolute. Even the trees did not rustle; they stood like a dark wall, hiding what lay behind them, and seemed to form an endless chain from north to south, as if to shield some important secret. There was no river visible.

"We've arrived," whispered Good Fortune, "this is Ollon Torre. As soon as I've found those negligent sons of guns, I'll ask Greencoat something, and you must understand that you're to hold your tongues while I'm doing so. You mustn't even cough."

"We'll behave as if we weren't there," Big Tiger assured him.

"We'll neither cough nor speak," declared Christian.

"That's right," said Good Fortune, approvingly.

"Who are the honorable sons of guns?" inquired Big Tiger.

"You'll see them soon," Good Fortune promised; "get back to your places. I'll now make a tour of honor." Thereupon he went back to the driver's cab, slammed the door so that Greencoat woke up, and drove a stretch northward along the fringe of trees, honking continually. He then turned and came back to the same place. As he drew up a soldier emerged from the trees about a hundred paces away. The brass buttons of his uniform shone in the moonlight. He approached slowly, buttoning his tunic as he did so.

"This is a nice establishment!" cried Good Fortune; "you're sleeping while you should be on guard. Where is your rifle?"

The soldier stood still, but cautiously refrained from replying.

"It seems to me," said Good Fortune sternly, "that you haven't got a mouth or a tongue with which to say two words of excuse. Hurry up and make us a pot of tea!"

"I obey," cried the soldier, running off as fast as he could.

Good Fortune got out laughing, but Greencoat said: "You order people about as if you were an old and venerable general. It would become you better to be less forward."

This was too much for Good Fortune. To make matters worse, Christian had just come along, and heard it. "Other people," he cried indignantly, "have more reason to be humble. I have my joke when it pleases me and I'm serious too when it pleases me. Put that in your pipe and smoke it!"

There was an awkward silence.

"Hello, Kwi-Chan!" called Big Tiger from the truck, "I'll hand you down the sleeping bags."

"I'm coming," said Christian, but he took care to keep Good Fortune and especially Greencoat in view. First Good Fortune covered up the hood, and Greencoat remained standing alone at the door. Obviously he was undecided as to what he should do. After a while he sat down on the running board, put his head in his hands, and became absorbed in thought. At last he seemed to get an inspiration. He looked cautiously around at Good Fortune, but the latter was busy with the motor. He stood up, opened the truck door, and Christian heard him raising the seat and fumbling under it. Then he shut the door, cleared his throat to catch Good Fortune's attention, and said: "Owing to an accident which I do not wish to speak of again, I am in a severe state of suffering. My leg has swollen up from the long night journey. So I want to lie down. Have the people here got a tent?"

"Look around and see where the palace is," cried Good Fortune. "We'll be with you right away."

Greencoat limped along under the trees and disappeared into the thicket. Shortly afterwards Good Fortune came around the truck, took down the bag of rice and asked: "Are you ready?"

"Yes, we're ready, honored Sir," said Christian and Big Tiger, "is there anything else to see to?"

"No more for today," said Good Fortune. "But listen, boys: we're going to have a pleasant evening. I'd like to see what kind of a face Greencoat will make when I tell him to go to the devil."

He took the lantern from the truck and lit it, and then all three marched into the bushes from which the soldier had emerged. There a path led to an open space on which stood a tent. Not far from it, under the spreading branches of a tree, was a square dump covered with tent canvas.

"What's that?" asked Big Tiger.

"Those are gasoline drums," Good Fortune declared; "we'll fill up tomorrow."

In the open tent a fire was burning, the tea water was boiling, and in the background Greencoat was lying down attended by two soldiers, to whom he had already told his story in detail. "Push the blanket in better under my knee," he was saying, "I'm severely injured. Oh, woe! You're clumsy fellows. I won't be able to walk a step tomorrow. My leg is like a dead branch."

"Then you'd better remain here," said Good Fortune, entering. "Is the tea ready?"

The two soldiers nudged each other, and the one who at first had been too timid to utter a word said: "You speak high-sounding words like an old general. Don't you also find that he puts on airs, Springtime Snake?"

"Yes," said Springtime Snake brazenly, "I find that too."

"I'll soon make you think otherwise," declared Good Fortune, drawing a paper from his pocket. "I am the delegate of the great General Wu," he said with dignity, "and I shall inform him of how his seal has been respected." Saying this, he raised his lantern so that the light fell on the paper with the instructions and the great red seal of General Wu-Pei-Fu.

"You read it," said Springtime Snake timidly, "it has nothing to do with me."

The other soldier took the paper in both hands, and all of a sudden his whole tone changed. He bowed, as was fitting, before the red seal; then he said: "Pardon my ignorance, Venerable One. I see that your place is in the council of General Wu. Only give us your commands, that we may know how we are to serve you."

Good Fortune noticed that neither of them really knew how to read, and he said graciously: "You need not call me 'Lord of the Council' or 'Venerable Chariot,' but I wish you to know that I am to be supplied with gasoline on the instructions of His Excellency."

"May I look at the writing too?" Springtime Snake interjected.

"He can read figures," the second soldier explained.

"Yes, you may," Good Fortune agreed, "although you said just now that it had nothing to do with you."

"There's forty written here," said Springtime Snake proudly.

"It states here," said Good Fortune emphatically, "forty cans of gasoline or more. Please note that!"

"I do," said Springtime Snake. "Now please sit down, tea is ready."

"We've got bean noodles too," said the other soldier eagerly; "it's poor food and I hardly dare offer it to you."

"Bring it along all the same," said Good Fortune, "my younger brothers Big Tiger and Compass Mountain have a special liking for bean noodles."

"My name is Affliction," said the soldier. "Allow me to add some of the 'best vegetable' to the noodles." He took down a little bag which hung from the tent roof pole, and got a few onions out of it. While they were drinking the tea Affliction put the long gelatinous bean noodles on the fire and sliced onions into them; and Springtime Snake said: "That's a beautiful ring you've got, Big Tiger, and it would suit my name. Would you sell it?"

"The ring," began Big Tiger, and he was within an ace of adding "doesn't belong to me," but remembered in time. "The ring," he began again, falteringly . . .

"You see that he wouldn't sell it," Good Fortune interrupted. "His grandfather gave it to him to offset the splendor of his name."

"My parents had the same thought when naming me," said Springtime Snake complacently, "but that fellow there . . ."

"Hold your tongue!" cried Affliction, "it's silly to talk of that."

"To speak relieves the mind," said Good Fortune gravely.

"That may be," murmured Affliction, as he stirred the noodles with a stick. "So I'll tell you what Springtime Snake means. My father and my grandfather had magnificent names, but they didn't do them much good. My grandfather's name was Lord of Riches and his wretched hut stood not far from Labrang. He left my father nothing more than the beautiful name Autumn Joy. But Autumn Joy met with nothing but trouble at every season of the year. So he decided to name me Affliction. 'Perhaps this name will bring luck,' he said to my mother. But it hasn't done so up to now. For the past half year I've been sitting here with that fellow among the barbarians of the desert."

"So there are only two of you here?" asked Good Fortune.

"Yes, we're only two," Affliction said, "and it's downright miserable. Sometimes we chat together, but when we have quarreled we don't speak."

"You should be here with us," cried Springtime Snake. "I can be as silent as a carp, and I'm never the first to speak."

"Because you're a conceited idiot," scolded Affliction.

"Hush!" said Good Fortune. "You must keep the peace. We'd prefer you to tell us your news instead."

"That's just the trouble," sighed Affliction, "we've told each other ten times over all there is to tell, and we've talked twenty times over all there is to talk about. Now there's nothing more left to talk about, and so we often quarrel."

"You'll murder each other some day," Good Fortune predicted, "if the Venerable Chief doesn't get ahead of you."

"The Venerable Chief and our General Feng leave each other in peace because they are afraid of each other," said Affliction. "And that is also why two of us are sufficient guard here. We do not have to be very watchful, for the Mongols have no need of gasoline; and we sleep peacefully at night, as that's what the night is for."

"Do you know Long Life?" asked Good Fortune.

"Yes, we know him," answered Affliction.

"He's one of the Governor's soldiers," said Springtime Snake contemptuously; "the Venerable Chief gave them a fine beating."

"You should bless your lucky stars that you weren't there," said Good Fortune solemnly.

Springtime Snake fell silent, and Greencoat sighed loudly in the background. "My leg!" he wailed. "I believe it will be the end of me!"

"If the king of hell has ordained that someone is to die," Good Fortune consoled him, "he doesn't put him traveling in an automobile first. Tomorrow morning we'll fill our drums with gasoline, and we'll start out in the afternoon."

"Pray do not trouble yourself," Affliction requested, "Springtime Snake and I will do all the work. You have made a big journey and you should rest."

"How is the river?" asked Good Fortune.

"You needn't worry," Affliction replied; "the Etzin Gol is quite low at present."

"I heard that they're opening the dams in Maumu tomorrow or the day after," Springtime Snake interjected; "you'd better hurry."

"Nothing of the kind!" cried Affliction; "the spring sowing hasn't begun yet. It will be at least four weeks before the water rises. You could stay a day or two here; you're our honored guests."

"May I fetch my map?" asked Christian. "I would like to know where Maumu is."

"Yes, of course," said Good Fortune; "you can take the lantern."

As Christian left the bushes and walked calmly toward the waiting truck, he had no thought of either the map or the distant town of Maumu. How lucky, he thought, that Good Fortune has allowed me to take the lantern. He walked quickly, hopping merrily the last few steps, so cocksure did he feel of success. First he climbed on the running board and gently pressed the door latch of the driver's cab. Then he lifted Greencoat's seat and looked into the box. There were all sorts of wrenches, hammers and pliers in it, also some foodstuffs: onions, dried leeks, beans, two small bags of flour. Christian searched through them all, but he didn't find what he was looking for.

I thought he was stupid and I was clever, Christian reflected with shame. He set down the lantern and put the frame with its upholstery back into place. But Greencoat *must* have hidden something when he was nosing around here so cautiously. I must figure it out. And he sat down on the black leather seat. The springs creaked, and suddenly Christian had a brain wave. He lifted the seat again and this time looked under the springs. There, to his great excitement, he saw a small white canvas bag wedged into one of the spirals. He pulled it out and found in his hand a linen rag tied with a piece of string. There were cartridges in the bag—that he could feel at once. He put the little bag in his pocket, pushed the seat back and left the driver's cab, closing the door as quietly as he had opened it. Then he climbed into the truck and fetched the map.

As he returned to the tent Christian was so happy that he felt like singing and whistling. But he didn't dare, nor did he dare throw the canvas bag into Good Fortune's lap, saying, "unexpected riches have come our way," though that would have been fun. He had to be very discreet. As he hung up the lantern Big Tiger looked hard at him and perceiving that something had happened, blinked a bit more than necessary, which meant: Be careful! Say nothing foolish!

"You've left us sitting in the dark a good while," said Good Fortune, reproachfully.

"The noodles are ready," said Affliction.

"Greencoat," cried Good Fortune, "hi, Greencoat, are you asleep?"

"I'm not asleep," said Greencoat, "I'm hungry."

Affliction dished out the noodles, and all four ate until they had had enough; in fact, Christian and Big Tiger had several helpings each. Then Good Fortune told the soldiers Affliction and Springtime Snake how the cartridges had been stolen from him at White Stone. But the dastardly thief had forgotten one cartridge, and in Durben Mot . . ."

"You seem to be hinting that I'm the thief. That's an insult!" interrupted Greencoat indignantly.

"Can you be insulted?" asked Good Fortune.

"Did you hear him?" shouted Greencoat. "Now he is trying to blacken my name! I challenge him to search everything I'm wearing!"

"What's all this row for?" asked Good Fortune, suddenly shaken. "You know I didn't mean it that way."

"But I mean what I say," shouted Greencoat.

"Don't make a row," said Good Fortune, intimidated. "I can't stand shouting!"

"The soldiers are my witnesses that you have insulted me!"

"It sounded like it, certainly," said Springtime Snake, "offense has been given."

"I didn't notice that," Affliction declared. "Mr. Good Fortune spoke of some unknown thief and not of Mr. Greencoat. His name was not mentioned."

"That's right," said Good Fortune, "your name was not blackened."

"It got a bit tarnished," Springtime Snake interjected mischievously; "the matter is certainly not quite clear."

"Yes, indeed," cried Greencoat, "it is a dastardly slander. Why should I be suspected as a criminal? There!"—and he threw his coat at Good Fortune's feet—"search for your cartridges, you slanderer!"

"We must do as His Excellency wishes," said Springtime Snake, "he has the right to demand it."

Greencoat went on flinging one garment after the other at Good Fortune, who at last picked up courage and, muttering, "If I must, I must," began feeling each garment carefully.

Christian fidgeted restlessly in his seat. He looked at Big Tiger, but Big Tiger was sitting quietly scraping out his silver bowl, and looking as innocent as a babe. What shall I do? thought Christian. But then he remembered that Good Fortune had forbidden them to speak or even to cough. He tried to edge nearer to Big Tiger, but Big Tiger gave him a blank stare. This made Christian desperate, for he felt that everybody was pretending. So he decided to let matters take their course.

"I have found nothing," said Good Fortune.

"It was a case of unjust accusation," said Springtime Snake impudently, handing back the clothes with a bow to Greencoat, who received them haughtily. "My leg," he wailed, "I'll have to drag around this lame leg to the end of my days."

"Let's go to bed," said Good Fortune, grimly.

"Please take this place," said Affliction, spreading out some felt covers for Good Fortune on the left side of the tent.

"Thank you," muttered Good Fortune, covering himself with his coat and lying down. When Christian and Big Tiger had lain down in their sleeping bags, Affliction quenched the lamp. Greencoat groaned a few times and Springtime Snake asked sympathetically: "Does it hurt a lot, Excellency?"

"I'm used to suffering," sighed Greencoat. All the same it was not long before he began to snore.

Christian waited and waited for everyone to be asleep, but someone always began to stir. Then, while he was still waiting, his own eyes shut, and he didn't awake until the morning sun was shining.

While Affliction made breakfast and Good Fortune cleaned the motor, Big Tiger and Christian had a look around. The region was quite different from what they had pictured it. It was not magnificent, yet it was a pleasant place to wake up in. There were real trees, and round-backed hills fringed the horizon. Right behind the tent there was a little brook, and that was the Goitzin Gol, the eastern tributary of the great river Etzin. But it was only a miserable straggling little stream, and one step brought one to the other bank. There there were a few bushes, and behind them, rising as steeply as the sand permitted, an immense dune. A brilliant blue sky shone above.

"I didn't know that there was a bit of desert here too," said Christian.

"The sea of sand is mighty," said Big Tiger thoughtfully, as they began to climb the dune. Christian followed him; but wading deeply in the sand, and slipping back again and again, they only got half way up. From there they could see the slender ribbon of the Goitzin Gol wending its way northward along the edge of the dunes. On its banks stood a scattered army of black poplars and beam trees, like faithful and fearless guards. After the sun rose they could see the gray gravel desert which they had crossed during the night, as well as an endless number of distant hills.

"I have something to show you," began Christian slowly, "but don't get excited."

"Let's see it," said Big Tiger.

"I went to the truck in the night," Christian reported, "and had a look around. And what do you think? Under Greencoat's seat I found this canvas bag. We'll open it now."

"There are twenty-three cartridges in it. What do you bet, Kwi-Chan?"

"People can't bet when they think the same thing."

They sat down on the sand. Christian opened the bag and shook the cartridges out. There were twenty-three of them. "Should I have said two words?" he asked. "I felt sorry for Good Fortune."

"You needn't be sorry for him," said Big Tiger. "You were silent at the right time, and avoided misfortune and confusion."

"But if Good Fortune asks us," said Christian anxiously, "what should we answer?"

"Hammagua!" said Big Tiger, laughing. "Good Fortune won't ask us today, or tomorrow either. He's far too ashamed of having flaunted the new cartridges and spoiled everything by doing so. So a certain time will pass, and then when he asks us we'll say: 'Our revered elder told us to keep silent and not even to cough. So we were as silent as goldfishes in a bowl, because we're obedient boys.' You'll see," he added, "that all has happened for the best." Christian was not fully convinced.

They now saw Affliction coming out of the tent. He shouted loudly: *"Tsho-fan!* Food, food!"

"We're coming!" Big Tiger shouted down to him.

Affliction looked up astonished. When he saw Christian and Big Tiger sitting up on the sand hill, he gave a friendly laugh and called: "The elder gentlemen are earnestly requested to come to breakfast."

"We thank the most venerable gentleman," Christian called back merrily. Then he pressed the linen bag into Big Tiger's hand. "Tie them up," he said quietly, "and you keep them; you'll know the right time to show them."

"Thank you for your trust, Kwi-Chan. But if it goes wrong all the same?"

"Then it just can't be helped."

Big Tiger knotted up the bag and hid it away, and they slid down the sand hill. Before entering the tent they emptied the sand out of their shoes, and Big Tiger said: "Open your nostrils, Kwi-Chan!"

"Oh, that's fine!" cried Christian. "Affliction has been baking."

"Hurry," Big Tiger urged; "whenever there's anything good Greencoat has a ferocious appetite."

The rest were gathered in the tent, drinking tea and eating the good barley cakes which Affliction had fried in mutton fat. Greencoat was eating heartily. Good Fortune was sitting in dead silence hardly touching the food. Springtime Snake was watching the two antagonists with a look of malicious triumph. They were avoiding each other's eyes and there was little conversation.

"Eat," urged Affliction.

"Your generosity is great," said Good Fortune, but more he would not say.

"We smelled the delights of your frying pan a long way off," Christian announced.

"Your cakes smell as sweet as the catkins to hungry bees in spring," added Big Tiger.

"Then you must eat heartily," said Affliction, flattered, putting four cakes at once in the tea bowl of each boy. Greencoat cleared his throat with a tone of displeasure but Affliction took no notice, and asked: "What are the gentlemen's plans?"

"Mr. Greencoat wishes to rest for a day," Springtime Snake said. "The injured leg is very red and as thick as a temple pillar."

"We're setting out in an hour," Good Fortune announced, "when we've filled our drums."

"Springtime Snake and I ask you once more," said Affliction, "to favor us by allowing us to do all that for you. And the honored gentleman can rest meanwhile."

Good Fortune shook his head; but then he got an idea. "How far is it from here to the Narin Gol?" he asked.

"Not quite an hour," they answered.

"On foot or on horseback?"

"We have no horses," said Springtime Snake quickly.

"Or rather, we have horses, but they're not here," Affliction corrected. "We have given them in charge to a man named Naidang, who lives by the Narin Gol. There's grass there for the horses."

"This Naidang must be a trustworthy man?" said Good Fortune.

"Yes, he's a good man," declared Affliction.

"Is he, indeed?" interjected Springtime Snake, raising his forefinger. "He's said to be in league with the Venerable Chief."

"When the redbeards want a change of horses," Affliction admitted, "they go to him. But who would dare contradict them, anyway?"

"Well, well!" Greencoat now made himself audible, "the teacher won't speak up against the teacher, or the scoundrel against the scoundrel. All these lawbreakers should have their heads chopped off."

"His Excellency speaks like a wise judge of the old days," cried Springtime Snake.

Good Fortune felt like replying angrily that Greencoat was the last man who should advocate the beheading of other people, but at that moment Big Tiger approached him. "If our revered elder would kindly permit us," he said, "Compass Mountain and I would like to visit this man Naidang and speak two words with him. We have greetings to deliver to him."

Springtime Snake whistled through his teeth as much as to say: "Aha! So that's the kind you are!" but Affliction reproved him sharply. "Whistling is impolite," he said. "The young gentlemen can be back here in two hours at the most. Naidang lives half a *li* north of the caravan road. His *yurt* can be seen a long way off, because it stands near two trees."

"I'll go with you," said Good Fortune, "I want to make the acquaintance of this fellow Naidang."

"We'll fill the drums in the meantime," Affliction promised, "and please use our horses for the return journey. I'm sure Naidang will lend you a third one."

"Bolna!" cried Christian merrily.

"Have you got the book?" Big Tiger whispered.

Christian nodded, took the brief case under his arm, and then said: "We're ready, honored Sir."

"We're going," said Good Fortune. "I'll move the car up to the hedge, then you'll have only a few steps to it. Now, forty cans, mind! Or fifty, better still. We have a long run before us."

"We'll fill your drums and load up the rest," Affliction assured him.

"May I mount the truck with you?" Springtime Snake asked diffidently; "if you'll allow me, I should like to drive the car to the shrubs."

"Can you drive?" asked Good Fortune, astonished.

"I sat once before in a horseless car."

"Sitting is one thing, but driving is another," said Good Fortune laughing. "Eat your barley cakes and drink your tea!" Then the three set out.

At first Good Fortune was a bit glum, but his bad humor soon passed off, for the morning sun made walking a joy. The road was wide and well trodden, and led due west without windings. This was the result, Good Fortune said, of the centuries of experience passed down by the old caravan leaders. In the course of the ages they had found the most passable path.

The sand desert, which in the beginning came right up to the road, receded to the north after one *li*. After that there were bushes and pasture land on both sides of the road, with deresen grass growing in thick tussocks as high as a man, and here and there poplars and willows with extraordinarily thick trunks. With immobile dignity they bore the cries and the fluttering of long-tailed magpies.

"Wicked birds!" cried Good Fortune, throwing a stone at a flock of them.

"But they've done nothing," said Christian.

"They do great harm," said Good Fortune. "In the winter they sit coolly on the camels' backs and eat the fat camel lice."

Big Tiger remarked that that was a good work.

"I don't deny that," replied Good Fortune, "but those depraved magpies are not satisfied with lice. They peck the unfortunate camels' backs and humps and eat the living flesh, and the poor beasts can't defend themselves. The magpie is a wicked bird with nasty habits."

"Are there only magpies here?" asked Christian.

"No," replied Good Fortune, "there are many other kinds of birds. At this time the birds of the four zones and the ten thousand varieties are gathered together on the Etzin Gol. They come from the warm south and they fly to the north You will see them this evening."

"But won't we be far away from here this evening?"

"Dear me! I only said that to get a rise out of Greencoat. I promised you a day's rest here, and you'll have it."

"I'm very glad!" cried Christian.

In the deresen pastures stood thick clumps of trees which finally merged into a wood that, with its wild undergrowth, looked like a patch of primeval forest. At least Christian imagined that was what a primeval forest looked like. Snakelike tendrils, thick as ropes, hung from tree to tree, and ivy entwined the trunks. A swarm of magpies fluttered screeching into the parched branches of a great poplar which leaned, tired with age, over the path.

"There's something up there!" said Good Fortune. He stopped and looked at the excited magpies. They were hopping up to the top branches and down again, screeching loudly.

"What's going on, honored Sir?" asked Big Tiger. But Good Fortune did not answer, for at that moment there was a rustle of leaves and a magnificent cock pheasant, followed by two hens, flew across the caravan path.

"Partridges!" Big Tiger was going to shout, but he hadn't time, for at the same moment a dark spotted animal dropped from the lowest branch of the poplar and sprang on the cock pheasant's back with one leap. The bird screeched, but its screech was cut short, for the wildcat bit its neck through. It flapped helplessly a few times, the hens flew into the nearby thicket, and the wildcat stood erect.

"Help! Murder!" shouted Good Fortune, running as fast as he

could and waving his arms wildly. Christian and Big Tiger ran after him, waving too. The wildcat arched its back, spat and bristled when it saw them coming. But then it let its booty drop and scrambled up the poplar, where it perched in a fork and looked wickedly down at them. The magpies flew away with loud cries.

"You murderous wretch!" cried Good Fortune, shaking his fist at it. "I will execute you as a criminal." He took out the pistol and aimed. The cat did not stir. Either it had no idea what Good Fortune had in mind, or else it was prepared to die.

"I've warned you," cried Good Fortune, and pressed the trigger. There was a resounding bang, but still the wildcat did not fall from the tree. A dead branch came down instead. Christian ducked to hide his laughter, and Big Tiger said: "What about pardoning the criminal? He's had a terrible shock."

"Do you think so?" asked Good Fortune, looking dubiously up at the wildcat which was angrily beating its striped tail against the trunk of the tree. "The wicked beast must be punished," he said resolutely, picking up the dead pheasant. "Here is one for the pot."

After a few more steps the wood came to an end. A treeless plain with only scattered bushes here and there gave an open view for a short stretch. Camels could be seen, and as the three came nearer, sheep too; and some antelopes were grazing peacefully with them. When they saw the three wanderers the antelopes lifted their heads and fled.

By the roadside sat a girl with a big black poodle beside her. The dog snarled, but the girl held it back firmly and gave it a friendly slap. Good Fortune had never seen a dog like it before, and neither had Christian or Big Tiger. "Is that a dog?" asked Good Fortune.

"Yes, it's a dog," answered the girl, laughing and showing two rows of beautiful white teeth. "A Tibetan lama gave him to me. He was small then, but now he's big and clever."

"His great-grandfather must have been a lion," said Good Fortune, admiring the long black curls which hid the poodle's face and fell over its body, almost touching the ground. "Has he got eyes?"

"You can see them only when it's raining," answered the girl. "Have you had a good journey?" Saying this she looked roguishly and a little contemptuously at Good Fortune's shoes.

"Yes, we've had a good journey," Good Fortune declared proudly, "for we travel in a horseless car. It's now resting at the Goitzin Gol."

"I heard that car roaring last night. Does it travel on the ground or in the air?"

"It travels along the ground," said Good Fortune, taken aback.

"Then it's an ordinary car; I've seen one before. I wish you had brought one that travels through the clouds."

"You ask a lot," said Good Fortune, nettled.

"Forgive me," the girl asked; she looked innocently into Good Fortune's eyes and laughed again. "I am curious, and that is wicked of me, I know. Please don't tell my father I've been talking to you."

"How do you know I'm going to your father?" asked Good Fortune.

"Every stranger who comes to the Etzin Gol wants to see him. The soldiers go to him, and the redbeards honor his tent too."

"What's the name, then, of this father of yours?"

"People call him Picture Sheet, but I call him father."

"Then he's not the right man; I'm looking for a man named Naidang."

"That's he!" cried the girl, joyfully; "I was sure. Our tent is over there between the two big trees. You can follow the caravan track as far as the river, then you'll see the path which leads to it. But you'll get there faster if you cut straight across. You've already frightened my antelopes away. They won't come back any more today."

"But I wouldn't have harmed them," Good Fortune assured her.

"And the poor bird there, did it do you any harm?"

"A wildcat killed it," said Good Fortune; "I came too late to save its life."

"Then you killed the wildcat, no doubt," said the girl. "I heard your shot."

"I punished it," Good Fortune admitted, quickly changing the subject. "Please tell me your name."

"I'm called Sevenstars."

Good Fortune said that was a beautiful name; then he introduced Big Tiger, Christian and himself. And he did not omit to say that General Wu had sent him to the Etzin Gol; but he did not mention Greencoat.

"Do your young brothers also understand Mongolian?" asked Sevenstars.

"There are a few words which they do not know yet."

"I'll teach them those words," promised Sevenstars. "I'm a good teacher."

"Unfortunately we're in a hurry," said Good Fortune, "we will visit your father now, and tomorrow we continue our journey."

"Tinger metne!" said Sevenstars.

Then they said good-bye to Sevenstars and set out in the direction of the two high trees.

"What did she say?" asked Big Tiger.

"She said 'Heaven knows,'" Good Fortune replied; "that's what the Mongols always say when someone plans a journey. It has no importance."

Big Tiger felt like saying something about the inscrutable decrees of heaven but thought better of it.

Soon Good Fortune was well ahead of them and they could see only his round cap over the deresen grass, which was higher than a field of rye ripe for the harvest, for it grew in clumps on little hummocks which stood above the sandy ground. Good Fortune had to wend his way between them, his eyes fixed straight on the tree tops. When the deresen grass ceased the ground became firm, and they came to short steppe grass which was beginning to show a little timid green. There was now a clear view of the line of trees, above which towered the two thick rust-red trunks of the tall trees with Naidang's *yurt* between them. A few tethered horses were grazing nearby. Down the river there were still more horses, and Christian also saw two cows standing motionless in the shade of a willow.

Good Fortune waited for Christian and Big Tiger, so that they should all reach the *yurt* together. But Naidang was already coming to meet them. He was not nearly so impressive as Christian imagined a man should be whose name was known in a thousand tents. There was nothing at all remarkable either in his person or his modest attire. But if many Mongols acquire early in life the leathery wrinkled faces of old men, Naidang had done so to an exaggerated degree. His face was deeply scarred by smallpox, which left him not a single hair, even in his eyebrows. He was definitely no beauty. But he came forward to greet his visitors with a friendly smile as if they were old acquaintances, drawing his snuff bottle from his belt to greet them even before he reached them.

A lengthy exchange of courtesies took place, for Naidang had the polished manners of a man of the world. He inquired not only after their health and the health of their livestock, but he also asked: "Are you cold? Are you tired? Are you tremulous? Are you suffering from any other discomforts?"

When Good Fortune had given all the suitable denials, it was his turn to inquire Naidang's esteemed age. It was immediately noticeable that Naidang was at home in the correct forms of polite intercourse with Chinese people too, and knew what to say. "I have squandered fifty-three years of life uselessly," he answered sadly.

"How many honorable sons have you got?" asked Good Fortune amiably.

"I am burdened with two useless louts."

"I had a glimpse of your lily-fair daughter."

"That female is unfortunately not the only one; I have a second daughter whom I have married into a family now impoverished."

"I have heard wonderful things of the wealth of that family in White Stone," lied Good Fortune.

"You come from White Stone?" cried Naidang joyfully. "Please come in." He led his guests to the *yurt,* stopping before the door, and Good Fortune was persuaded, after some polite protests, to enter first.

"I am unworthy," murmured Christian, stumbling after him over the threshold. Big Tiger laid the dead pheasant by the door, and Naidang followed them in last.

Naidang's *yurt* was old, but very large and very clean. The chest opposite the doorway was of shining brown wood, trimmed with brass. On it stood a figure of the Buddha hung with blue *haddaks,* before which four little silver lamps burned. The fireplace was swept, the cushion seats lay ready, the iron kettle stood on the trivet, and a fire was already lit.

"I saw you coming," said Naidang. "Walking is a troublesome way of traveling."

"We usually travel in a horseless car," said Good Fortune casually. He then introduced Big Tiger and Christian to Naidang, who said: "I also speak some North Chinese. Formerly," he added modestly, "I used to go on long journeys; and one cannot go about without learning a little of everything."

"We are instructed," Christian began, "to give you greetings and wishes for a long life from Bator, from his father Dogolon, and from his mother. They have set out from White Stone, because they no longer like it there, and they have sold all the sheep, but they have not lost any of the camels."

"Was that a peaceful move," asked Naidang cautiously, "or did they have to pack up in a hurry?"

"Their decampment did not take long," Christian admitted.

"To be exact," said Big Tiger, "it took only two hours."

"Perhaps," Naidang suggested, "there were sheriff's men on the way from the *yamen* in Kalgan, or a merchant who disturbed their peace? There are such people."

"We know nothing about that," Good Fortune interjected quickly, "we are here today and gone tomorrow; we do not trouble about other people's affairs. We carry out our orders without either addition or omission."

Big Tiger and Christian bowed their heads, and Big Tiger said quietly: "We have another piece of news."

"We were traveling through the Valley of Dark Rushing Water," began Christian, "and there we met a man named Mateh. We spoke two words with him, and he gave us this." Christian opened the brief case and took out the little book. When Naidang saw it he gave a start, but his shock was only momentary. He sat quietly in his place as before, and Christian bowed. "This book," he said, "is sent to you by Mateh, who got it from Nowhere-at-all when he died."

While Christian was saying this Naidang put on his fur cap. Then he took the book from Christian's hands, touched it solemnly to his forehead, and laid it on the chest in front of the Buddha. "Tell me," he asked, "what you know of Nowhere-at-all's life and death."

"You shall hear it all," promised Good Fortune; and he proceeded to relate in the most minute detail, as if he had been present, how the storm broke out and how Nowhere-at-all threw the leaf of the sacred tree into the night wind, and how a leaf of the book flew away with it. "But," he added, "one should not sorrow after the written word." He also described his death and funeral.

When Good Fortune finished tears were rolling down the furrowed cheeks of Naidang. All were silent.

"We shall have tea," said Naidang, drying his tears. And he began with touching care to play the housewife. "My wife is gone with my eldest boy to take the camels to their spring pastures in the Nojen Bogdo Mountains. I have kept here only seven old camels, the sheep, and my talkative daughter. My second son is in the service of the *Wang*."

"Then you're alone?" asked Good Fortune.

"I beg you to be my guests all the same," cried Naidang, alarmed, "you will lack for nothing." He redoubled his efforts, threw a little lump of butter into each tea bowl, and promised to prepare a good meal. "If I only knew," he murmured, "ah, it's sad not to know." But he said no more, and Good Fortune carefully refrained from asking him the cause of his distress.

When they each had a steaming bowl of tea before them, Naidang said: "You have brought me the book of Nowhere-at-all which is also my book. Therefore I will explain all about it to you."

"We wait enlightenment," said Good Fortune eagerly.

"You know," began Naidang, "that the Etzin Gol formerly flowed elsewhere. The old riverbed is not far from here, but it is now silted up and hardly visible. Near it are the ruins of a great city, called Khara-khoto or the Black City. Many also call it the Dead City. Only the mighty walls are now to be seen, and the openings where the gates once stood. Inside there is nothing but sand and slates, and a few mounds of rubble."

"I saw Khara-khoto seven years ago," said Good Fortune; "the Black City is a sight to fill a man with fear."

"It is easy to learn fear there," Naidang agreed. "But Nowhere-at-all was a man without fear. He said to me: 'I want to learn the things of this world; come with me'—just as if it were a joy to look into the jaws of death. So we saddled our horses, and we reached the Black City late in the afternoon. We crept around everywhere, and in the center, where the *yamen* had probably stood, I stumbled against some bricks. They collapsed, and under them a hole opened. In the hole lay a heap of little rods with writing on them in some ancient script, which we could not read. 'Is there something here,' cried Nowhere-at-all aloud, 'which should not be touched?' He waited a while, listening to the right and to the left, but the stones and the slates gave no answer. Then Nowhere-at-all gave a satisfied nod. He bound the rods together and put them away; and I admired his fearlessness.

" 'One must know what the people of past ages thought,' said Nowhere-at-all. Later he tried to find out from learned lamas what was written on the rods, but the lamas said: 'We do not know; that is writing of the ancient wise men of China.' Nowhere-at-all thanked them for their trouble and went his way. He said to me: 'Those lamas are foolish men lacking in learning; their teachers forgot long ago to kick them in the face.' "

When Christian heard this he nudged Big Tiger and both laughed. Naidang laughed too; but then he said seriously: "Lazy pupils have to be spanked; otherwise they remain ignorant. It can't be helped."

"We know that," said Big Tiger.

"We have experience in this matter," said Christian.

"And then," asked Good Fortune, who was still thinking of the ancient writing, "what happened then?"

"Nowhere-at-all left the rods with me and rode away. When he came back to the Etzin Gol two years later to fetch my daughter he said: 'I have found a man who knows how to read the script of the old wise men. He is the cousin of the King of the Sunits, and he says that they are bamboo rods on which people wrote before there was paper, and I should bring them to him.' So Nowhere-at-all took the rods back with him together with my daughter, and I also gave him a book which I had. There were many blank pages in that book and . . ."

"What's that?" cried Good Fortune, jumping up.

"The drums of heaven are beating," cried Naidang in dismay, "someone has committed a great sin."

"Ha!" shouted Good Fortune, "there are scoundrels, and I know them!" Saying this he rushed out of the *yurt,* knocking his tea bowl over, and leaving a big splash on the freshly swept hearth.

28 CONCERNING WHAT HAPPENED AT OLLON TORRE

THERE WAS a sound of thunder. Yes, indeed, and that thundering sound came from quite near, and Christian and Big Tiger knew what it was. "Please forgive our bad manners," said Big Tiger hurriedly. But he was already half-way out the door, and in a trice both he and Christian were out under the trees. Naidang hurried after them, and they saw Good Fortune running down by the line of trees to the south.

"There," cried Christian, pointing to a cloud of dust which was rolling over the deresen pastures, "there he goes!"

"Is that your car?" asked Naidang.

"It was our car," said Big Tiger dryly, "but now there's someone else sitting in it, and it can't be helped."

Christian pulled Big Tiger by the coat and wanted to run after Good Fortune, but Big Tiger held him back. "The cow is gone from the barn," he said calmly.

"It can't be so," cried Christian. But he stood still when he saw the cloud of dust racing toward the belt of trees and reaching it. They heard the fierce barking of a dog, and at the same time two shots rang out. They sounded faint, and the noise of the motor drowned their echo completely. "That was Good Fortune," declared Big Tiger.

Then there was a slowly increasing roar, and Christian recognized the sound of the car coming to a difficult place, for there was a changing of gear. Thereupon two more shots rang out, this time answered by two others, which re-echoed like rolling thunder from tree to tree. "That was Springtime Snake," Big Tiger explained.

"The wretch!" raged Christian; and then all was quiet. The sound of the motor faded gradually away.

"We must find Good Fortune," cried Christian; and this time Big Tiger ran off with him at once.

A well-trodden path led from the *yurt* along the fringe of woodland. The branches of a tree hit Christian in the face, but he ran on, stumbled over a tree root, jumped up again, and Big Tiger overtook him. "It's nothing!" cried Christian, and they both ran on. At last they saw Good Fortune sitting near a willow by the edge of the caravan road, where it sloped steeply downhill. Below they could see water glistening. The black poodle was there too, barking and whining, and Sevenstars came running along in bare feet.

Christian forgot all conventional manners. "Are you wounded?" he shouted breathlessly from a long way off; but Good Fortune shook his head. He was staring alternately at the deep wheel marks down the slope, which became lost in the sand of the Narin Gol, and at the cloud of dust which still hung in the air on the other bank.

Then they all stood gasping for breath.

The Narin Gol was still a river. True, at the deepest part the water hardly reached to one's knees, and there was scarcely any current. But it was a good ten yards wide, and one could see from the steep banks that there might at times be high water. The ford of the caravan road was a bit wider still, and the slope of the banks seemed to have been artificially leveled at both sides. Nevertheless it was hard enough going for a loaded truck. There were deep tire marks on the moist ground, the morning sun shone brightly on them, and the sad little party looked helplessly at their herring-bone pattern in the sand.

There was silence until Naidang arrived. He tramped through the bushes, and when he saw that there was nobody dead or wounded he said sternly to Sevenstars: "Where did you leave your shoes?"

"I took them off, father," Sevenstars excused herself, "I was in such a hurry."

Good Fortune turned his head. "You might ask instead where I have left my car."

"If you like I will," said Naidang, squatting on his haunches beside Good Fortune. "Where did you leave your car?"

"It's gone," Good Fortune told him, "and there's no possible hope of getting it back. But there are rogues and scoundrels," he shouted suddenly, "there are swindlers and murderers, and I'll find *them* again all right!"

"Tinger metne!" said Naidang solemnly.

"You're right," cried Good Fortune, "heaven knows, but I know too. Hear me, you dogs and sons of dogs! Good Fortune will be on your tracks from now on!" And he jumped up and shook his clenched fists in the direction in which the car and its dust cloud had long since disappeared. At Good Fortune's shouting the poodle came bounding out of the water, growling, whereupon Good Fortune let his arms fall with a dejected smile. "Forgive me, all of you," he said, "for letting myself go like that and annoying you with useless words."

"Hammagua," replied Naidang, "we were pleased to hear it."

This made Good Fortune feel still more ashamed, and Big Tiger asked quickly: "Who was in the car in which we had the honor of traveling formerly?"

"Who else but the two redbeards, Affliction and Springtime Snake. Springtime Snake actually fired at me."

"Our revered elder also fired," Big Tiger reminded him.

"I was within my rights in shooting," Good Fortune defended himself, "and anyway the fellows were far away. But I saw Springtime Snake aiming at me. The side window of the car was broken; there must have been a struggle."

"I'll saddle four horses," suggested Naidang, "and we'll go and see what the fellows have left."

"They left a half-lame merchant," said Good Fortune glumly, "if they haven't killed him."

"You had someone with you?" inquired Naidang.

"He can't walk very well," said Good Fortune, "that is why he remained behind in Ollon Torre."

"We shall see how he's fared," said Naidang reassuringly. He walked off toward the *yurt*. Sevenstars disappeared with the poodle between the waving deresen grass, and Christian took Big Tiger aside: "I'd never have thought," he said, "that Affliction was a redbeard."

"You can only see people's skin, and not what's under it," said Big Tiger.

They followed Good Fortune and Naidang in silence. When they arrived at the *yurt* Naidang was already on horseback, and now he fetched three more horses. Christian wanted to help saddle them, but Naidang said: "Let them alone. They won't like your smell, for they are Mongolian horses. They'll kick you. Can you ride?"

"Yes, I can ride," said Christian, but his self-confidence vanished when he looked at the wild eyes of the horses, which had tufts of hair hanging over their foreheads. As soon as Christian came near them their tails lashed the ground and the most excited of them began to kick. We'd call those ponies in Peking, thought Christian, and he went and stood near Big Tiger who was looking on at a safer distance, while Naidang saddled. It was a lucky matter that Affliction and Springtime Snake had left all their riding equipment with Naidang, for he possessed only two saddles, one for himself and one for Sevenstars.

"*Yabonah!*" cried Naidang when he was ready.

"*Yabonah!*" answered Good Fortune gaily, and no one would have thought that he was a traveler who ten minutes ago had lost his automobile. "What'll we do with Compass Mountain?" asked Good Fortune. "He's got a foreign smell."

"He says he can ride," replied Naidang, but he did not sound very convinced. He handed out four whips, and Good Fortune said to Christian: "To fall from a camel isn't bad, to fall from a horse is worse, but the most dangerous thing is to fall from an ass. Therefore you have a good chance of remaining alive, for the horse stands midway between the dangers."

"Nevertheless," said Naidang, "one must be careful." He went into the *yurt,* brought back short reins, and then he chose an iron-gray piebald horse, which he led around in a circle a few times. He put the reins through the halter, held the horse's head down, and ordered Christian to put his foot in the enormous stirrup. "As soon as you're up keep a tight rein," he instructed him and . . . "now off you go!"

The gray pony snorted when Christian approached it. It pranced excitedly and wheeled around when he tried to grasp the saddle.

"It's no good," cried Good Fortune from a safe distance.

"Be brave and nimble," whispered Naidang, holding the stirrup firmly.

With one resolute leap Christian was in the saddle. He grasped the reins, Naidang let go, and the horse flung out its hind legs straight in the air. But Christian knew what to do. With all his strength he gripped the horn of the wooden Chinese saddle, and pressed his knees against the animal's sides. Meanwhile it was rearing and kicking at a pace which made Christian forget all the rules of horsemanship. When bucking and rearing proved useless, it tried leaping with all fours at once.

Naidang looked on, cursing the horse and all its ancestors; Good Fortune was proud of Christian's courage; but Big Tiger was getting really scared.

Suddenly the gray horse stretched out its neck, and Christian was just in time to catch the reins, which had slipped from his hand, before the animal went off in a wild gallop through the waving deresen grass. Big Tiger gave a loud yell, but Good Fortune laughed. Naidang raised his right thumb as a sign of the highest approval, for he saw that Christian was standing in the stirrups like a true Mongolian horseman and was letting the horse have its fling. As, in their wild dash, they neared the meadow in which the cows were grazing, Christian gradually shortened the reins and took his seat in the saddle, and that put an end to the dizzy ride. The horse continued to gallop a while longer, but then it fell into a trot, and by the time Christian circled back, horse and rider had agreed to put up with each other.

"Congratulations!" shouted Good Fortune, and Naidang raised both thumbs in a gesture of great respect.

Naidang then took the remaining horse and led it by the bridle to Big Tiger. "There's nothing to be afraid of," he said, "up with you!"

"But I've never been on a horse yet," said Big Tiger.

"You have to begin some time," Naidang explained. "This horse belongs to the soldier Affliction. It's a gaited horse and you will sit in the saddle as if you were in a horseless car."

Big Tiger looked at the brown horse with the white star on its forehead, and the brown horse sniffed the new rider and pawed the ground impatiently. It snorted when he mounted, but then was pleased to find its load light. The other three trotted on in the regular trot which Mongolian horses can keep up indefinitely, but the brown horse kept up a swinging gait. Naidang said that the animal would fetch a big price, and one could buy at least two ordinary horses for the money. "Now," he said, "the horses belong to you—the one on which Good Fortune is riding, and Big Tiger's brown one."

They rode at a walk through the wood on account of the many roots of trees, and finally came to the poplar which leaned across the road. "The murderous beast was sitting up there," said Good Fortune, pointing with his whip.

"What kind of . . ." Naidang began to ask, but he got no further, for Big Tiger shouted: "Here's someone coming!"

They all looked toward the clearing and saw a man running in their direction. Though he was still a long way off it was plain that he was exhausted, for he was stumbling and stopping for breath, and then staggering on.

"It's Affliction!" cried Christian.

"The redbeards are becoming good people," said Good Fortune, shaking his head. "How comes that?"

"We'll soon find out," said Naidang, urging his horse forward. It began to trot, then to gallop, and the other horses galloped after him. When they stopped in front of Affliction there was a big cloud of dust; pebbles were flying, hoofs were stamping, and Affliction fell on his knees.

"I am innocent," he wailed, "I did nothing wrong; but a crime has been committed."

"We know it," said Good Fortune sternly, "stand up!"

"I am sorry," cried Naidang dismounting and raising up the disconsolate soldier. "Don't be downhearted. We all know you are an honest man. But tell us what happened in Ollon Torre."

"You're wounded!" cried Good Fortune. "What happened?"

"It's nothing," replied Affliction, but he turned pale and faint and had to sit down by the side of the road. His right hand and arm were wrapped in rags through which blood was oozing.

Good Fortune jumped down from his horse, Christian and Big Tiger jumped down too, and Naidang tied the reins together. "It seems there's been some nasty work," said Good Fortune.

"Never in my life have I met such wickedness," said Affliction faintly. "All the misfortune came from that Greencoat whom you brought to us."

"Greencoat?" cried Naidang, shocked. "Was Greencoat here?"

"He was here, and now he's gone," said Affliction.

"Show me your arm," cried Good Fortune hurriedly, "we must first know what state you are in."

Affliction undid the rags. His five fingers were cut, and across the forearm was a gaping wound, which was still bleeding.

"Is the artery severed?" asked Christian.

"No, it's all right, or at least not much open," said Good Fortune. "Try if you can move your fingers, Affliction."

"I can," said Affliction, spreading them out.

"Then you're a long-lived man," Good Fortune said reassuringly. He bound the blood-stained rags around the wound again because there were no others, and then they all sat in a circle around Affliction.

"Tell us everything," Naidang requested.

"When you went away," Affliction began, "I opened the cans and filled the empty drums with gasoline, and Springtime Snake said: 'What's the good of hurrying? There's no need to.' So he remained sitting in the tent with Greencoat."

"And Greencoat," asked Naidang again, "what's happened to him?"

"I thought to myself," continued Affliction with difficulty, "now they're conversing about many things, and Springtime Snake will tell them to me afterwards and for a long while we won't need to quarrel. I had already filled two drums when

Springtime Snake came out of the tent; and Greencoat came too, and suddenly he was no longer lame but perfectly sound. 'Are you finished?' asked Springtime Snake, and when I said: 'No, I'm not,' Greencoat shouted, 'You're a lazy, good-for-nothing fellow!' 'He needs a helping hand, for he's not strong,' said Springtime Snake in my defense. Then they loaded up many cans and threw the two drums that were still empty off the truck. Greencoat brought the sleeping bags and the fur coats belonging to the two young gentlemen, and then Springtime Snake said: 'We'll go a bit of the way to meet them.' He fetched his gun and all his belongings out of the tent, and then I saw more or less what he had in mind. I said: 'No, that won't do; Mr. Good Fortune will be back here when it's time to come back. Stay where you are. You might miss him on the way.' 'All the better for him,' said Springtime Snake, 'otherwise I'll have to shoot a hole in his belly.' Thereupon Greencoat started up the engine, and I shouted to Springtime Snake, 'So that's what you're up to. Out with you!' But he slammed the door. Then I jumped on to the running board of the truck which was already moving, for Greencoat had got in behind the wheel. I smashed in the window and caught Springtime Snake by the collar, but Greencoat took up a whip and hit out at me. I fell into the bushes and remained lying there, and for a long time I knew nothing more. Then I started running, for I wanted to find you. More I do not know."

"But Greencoat," asked Naidang obstinately, "what about him?"

"I'll tell you," declared Good Fortune. "As I was coming out of Hwai-lai-hsien this man Greencoat was standing by the roadside. He *kowtowed* to me and said: 'Please, please, take me with you.' So I picked him up, as people must help each other. I thought he was an honorable person, but now I see he's a scoundrel."

"He always was one," said Naidang, "did Dogolon in White Stone not tell you about him?"

"Dogolon left in the night while I was asleep. Only these two young night-watchmen spoke to him."

"Did he not warn you against Greencoat?" asked Naidang.

"Yes, he warned us," Christian admitted, "and Bator also told us we should look out."

"And we did look out," Big Tiger continued, "and we found out that he stole a lot of cartridges from our respected elder."

"No doubt he did that," said Christian, "because even then he was planning to steal the truck, and he didn't want to get shot in doing so."

"But he hadn't any cartridges," cried Good Fortune. "I searched his clothing down to the seams."

"The cartridges were elsewhere," Big Tiger explained, diving into his pocket. "Compass Mountain found them last night when he went out to the truck with the lantern. I trust it will please our respected elder to identify his property."

"But why," cried Good Fortune, "did you not tell me that at once? At least I would have shot Greencoat before sunrise."

"We were forbidden even to cough," Big Tiger recalled.

"For that reason," continued Christian, "we were as silent as goldfishes in a bowl."

"Ah," shouted Good Fortune, "there's a time to speak up, and a time to be silent. You didn't know the right time. May the Venerable Chief cut off that scoundrel Greencoat's head if he catches him, and Springtime Snake's too!"

"Tinger metne," said Naidang solemnly.

"Yes indeed," sighed Good Fortune, "heaven knows. Yesterday evening I wanted to send Greencoat packing. If only I had done so!"

"Yabonah!" cried Naidang, standing up, "it's not good to sit in one place as long as you can ride."

"And what about this man?" asked Good Fortune.

"I'll walk slowly behind you," said Affliction.

"That won't do," cried Naidang, "you need care. My *yurt* is near, and Sevenstars is still nearer. Let her dress your wound, she knows how to."

"Thanks ten thousand times," murmured Affliction, standing up and beginning to walk. But he reeled alarmingly.

"Don't hurry," Good Fortune called back to him, "and don't move your arm."

Affliction nodded. Then Good Fortune mounted his horse. Big Tiger was already up, and Christian, merrily crying *"Yabonah!"* tapped the piebald on the neck and it neighed responsively.

When they arrived at Ollon Torre the place lay peacefully bathed in sunshine. The blue tent stood there, its entrance open, and the smoke of the dying fire curled like a thread to the roof. In front of the shrubs the empty tin cans lay about in confusion. The two iron drums had rolled away a little; near them were some pieces of broken glass and at one place there were drops of blood in the sand.

"The scoundrels," raged Good Fortune as he tied his horse to a little beam tree. Then he followed Naidang into the tent. It was pretty well cleared out. Big Tiger's and Christian's sleeping bags had disappeared, and so had the fur coats; the beautiful new paraffin lamp no longer hung from the tent beam, and Good Fortune searched in vain for his padded military coat. The little sack of precious rice was gone too.

"If only we'd taken the honey cakes," sighed Christian.

"And the sheep cheese too," said Big Tiger, "I got to like it."

"No use opening the umbrella after it has rained," said Good Fortune, seating himself on the few felt covers that were still left. "I'm not so depressed, really," he continued. "Is it not a burning shame to sit uneasily in a horseless car as long as one can ride?"

"You're right," agreed Naidang. "It is good to know these horseless cars, but it is better not to use them. They make a man restless of mind and uneasy of heart." He drew a long pipe out of his boot, poked in the fireplace until he found an ember, and began to smoke. "Let's take back Affliction's belongings," he said.

"Bolna!" cried Christian, "we'll tidy up a bit meantime." He went out with Big Tiger to collect the empty gasoline cans into a heap. Half of the full ones were still left. They spread the tent cloths over them, and when that was done, Naidang brought out Affliction's gun, coat, and a few other oddments. Then they all rode back the way they had come.

They found Affliction sitting on the threshold of Naidang's *yurt*. His arm was in a broad white sling, and he was still pale. The black poodle lay beside him, but when it saw the riders coming it jumped up and ran barking toward Naidang. Naidang let his reins drop, and the poodle took hold of them and led the horse to the front of the *yurt,* only letting go when Naidang had dismounted and said, "Good dog."

Sevenstars came out and greeted the guests. She had made a good fire, prepared noodles, and laid the cushions around the hearth. Naidang nodded with satisfaction, but still there seemed to be something missing, for he murmured again and again: "If I only knew, ah, it's sad not to know!" And he shook his head.

"I don't know either, father," Sevenstars assured him.

"Perhaps I might know," Good Fortune intervened.

But Naidang laughed and said he should not rack his brains, because what they were looking for was as lost for good as a day gone by. Then they all sat down. Good Fortune had to accept the place of honor, though he protested energetically and swore that he was a bad and worthless person who had been guilty of great negligence.

"Hammagua," Naidang cheered him, "there's no great harm in an undeserved change of possessions," and he began to serve the noodles.

After the meal Naidang said he was a bad host, for the drink of honor which he owed his guests was unfortunately not available. He was quite certain that there were several goatskins full of excellent milk brandy tucked away somewhere, but where these precious skins had got to, no one knew, and it was very sad.

"Have you had thieves here, too?" asked the unsuspecting Affliction.

"It's not that," replied Naidang, "but there are things which disappear without being stolen; on New Year's Night for instance."

"Why precisely then?" asked Good Fortune.

"Because I'm not at home at the New Year. I have to ride away."

"Of course," said Good Fortune, "one has to ride away at that time. Everyone knows that."

"When I come home, there's not a drop of *arrak* left, and my wife says: 'We had a lot of guests and they drank all the skin bags empty.' But that isn't true, for every time I'm away she buries one or two skins."

"She does that," Sevenstars explained, "so that we shall have a drink left for the Spring Festival."

"That may be," admitted Naidang, "and your mother is a splendid woman, but we've got a feast to celebrate right now."

"What feast?" inquired Good Fortune.

"In my opinion," said Affliction, "it's just an ordinary unlucky day and not a feast at all."

"For me," Naidang insisted, "it is a feast when such distinguished guests visit my wretched tent. And here we are sitting in the sea of sand, where a man gets thirsty. Ah, it is sad not to know!"

"Perhaps," Good Fortune suggested, "it would be a good thing to take a spade and dig a bit around where it looks as if a full goatskin would thrive."

But Naidang shook his head. "In the past," he said, "the spade helped, but that's over. My wife now hides the skins a long way off, and it is very sad."

"*Hammagua!*" cried Good Fortune, "we don't need any *arrak*. My car is gone. What's the loss of two goatskins of *arrak* compared with that!"

"They'll come back again," said Sevenstars reassuringly.

"And so will the car, in the end," said Naidang.

"There's no chance of that," Good Fortune explained. "We set out on an unlucky day on which the spokes fall from wheels. The inevitable was bound to happen. What else are calendars for?"

Naidang gave a few embarrassed coughs. "Let us continue where we were interrupted," he said.

"*Bolna!*" cried Good Fortune, "tell us about the bamboo rods with the ancient writing on them."

"We wait patiently for enlightenment," said Big Tiger.

"Did you get back the book?" asked Sevenstars, astonished.

"It has come home from its long journey," said Naidang. And reaching behind him to the chest, he picked up the thin book with the silken cover. "In this book," he declared, "there were many blank pages. I therefore gave it to Nowhere-at-all saying: 'Ask the old cousin of the King of the Sunits to write down in this book all that is written on the bamboo rods. Thus we shall both learn what the people in ages past have thought.' "

"The Mongolian script," said Good Fortune, deeply impressed, "is a high art which few understand."

"Does Mongolian writing look like Chinese?" asked Big Tiger.

"What a silly idea," cried Good Fortune. "If that were so, anyone could read it. The Mongols begin at the top on the east side, and when they get to the bottom they begin at the top again. When the page is finished it looks like a garden with graceful flowers and grasses in it, but only very few great professors know which way it goes and where the beginning or the end is. To know this one must be a scholar of high rank"; and saying this he laid his hands on his breast and bowed to Naidang who was visibly touched at being so honored.

"There is unfortunately no question of scholarship," protested Naidang. "I read what is written. Often I understand it, but more often I do not."

"Your modesty exceeds the permitted limits," Good Fortune dissented.

"We shall see," said Naidang, as he opened the book and began to read.

29 CONCERNING WHAT WAS WRITTEN ON THE LITTLE BAMBOO RODS

"To you, Naidang, I send greetings and tidings by the man known as Nowhere-at-all. I have read what is written on the bamboo rods, and I anxiously wonder whether the message from a past age will bring you good fortune or whether it will ruin you. If I knew you to be of the same mind as myself I would give you back the book with the pages still blank instead of filled with an account of what happened almost five hundred years ago. If you have courage to read what is terrible, and strength of mind to forget what you have read, then read and judge for yourself. Know too that the voice which speaks to you from the grave is that of a descendant of Khabutu-Khasar, the brother of Genghis Khan. This is told to you by Ubasha, Duke of the Western Sunits. Moreover, since nowadays people crane their necks and their eyes jump from their sockets when they see writing on old bamboo rods, I have burned the rods. Thus will confusion be avoided, and the great evils which arise from it."

Naidang paused, and Good Fortune, who was sitting beside him, said: "Read on, it seems to be a serious matter."

"I am wondering," replied Naidang, "whether I have got the will-power to forget, which the Duke asks of me. Consider, all of you, what I should do."

"There is nothing to consider," said Good Fortune; "until we know what happened in the Black City we cannot discuss it."

"But the Duke thinks this knowledge might bring misfortune," said Affliction dubiously. "And that is what will happen, most certainly. Wherever I am, a first-class misfortune is sure to happen. Hadn't I better go out?"

"Let us burn the book, father," pleaded Sevenstars. "Anyone who ever took anything out of the Black City had to die. Otherwise Nowhere-at-all would still be alive."

"The old wise men of past ages," said Big Tiger, "used to make knots in cords as a means of passing on information; later they wrote down what seemed important to them, so that it could be kept. Why, then, should there be harm in what is written?"

"Bravo!" cried Good Fortune, "and you, Naidang, may safely trust my younger brother Big Tiger. He has a grandfather who is a wise man. When Big Tiger says something, it is just as if his grandfather, who has the key of knowledge, were speaking. Therefore you may read the message without hesitation; no harm will come of it."

"If that is your opinion," said Naidang, "I see nothing against it. But promise me that you will keep secret what is now revealed concerning Etzina, and this promise must be binding as an oath."

"As an oath!" repeated Good Fortune and Affliction.

"As an oath!" said Big Tiger and Christian.

"As an oath!" whispered Sevenstars softly.

"What is Etzina?" asked Christian.

"The Black City," Naidang explained, "was called Etzina in the days when it was full of life and gaiety. You can still see traces of the woods which long ago surrounded the town like a ring a jewel. But the trunks fell from the roots and they lie there as the dead lay on the evening of the battle in which Etzina ceased to live."

Naidang took up the book again, and everyone tried to look less excited than he really was. Christian pretended to be as unconcerned as possible, but his eyes shone. Sevenstars was frightened and Affliction became a shade paler when Naidang began to read solemnly:

"We, Araptan, Prince of the Khoshut tribe, on the eve of our own destruction and that of our people, make known the following to the people who will come after us: Of all things that begin and end, nothing is more disastrous than war. We have not sought strife with the Emperor, yet neither have we avoided it when wisdom counseled that we should do so. Therefore we accuse ourselves, before the living and before those who shall follow us, of lack of wisdom, and we acknowledge ourselves guilty of the death of the thousands who shall die tomorrow. Etzina will no longer exist when we are gone, for the enemy stands before the gates in tenfold our strength, and the enemy is without pity. A victory will be announced to the Emperor.

"This is what happened: In a fight with a superior enemy retreat is no shame. After the battle of Maomu, when our auxiliary troops were failing us, we withdrew within the walls of our city of Etzina. The enemy pursued us, losing men and stores in many battles. We did not force our progress, yet success came to us uncalled for, because we persevered. Therefore we believed we would be saved from our great peril. The approaches to north, east and west were cleared of the enemy. Only to the south lay the Emperor's army, which withstood all attacks. We therefore sent out scouts to discover the cause of the enemy's invincibility, but it was too late. The Etzin Gol, which flowed under our walls, ceased to flow the following night, the riverbed dried up, and the wells of the city also became dry. At the same time the besieging army moved forward, now ten times stronger than before. By the work of a thousand times a thousand slaves and of prisoners of the great battles, the enemy had diverted the river into a new bed. Now the Etzin Gol flows far away from our city.

"Then the men and women of Etzina lamented loudly. Ten days have passed since then, and we are surrounded. We deepened our wells. At first they gave some water, but now they have dried up. The pitcher is broken, the well rope is torn, and the slime from the wells can no longer be drunk.

"Thus it happened and thus it will happen: Of all deaths there is none more shameful than death on the scaffold. Therefore, we shall open the gates at sunset and fight. The wall will fall into the moat. Fire will devour the city. When the sun has set not a single citizen of Etzina will live and breathe. A victory will be announced to the Emperor.

"Thus we have done, but our deed remains hidden: Into the deepest well that we dug in our despair we have today thrown all the precious things in Etzina. The silver fountain, which a foreigner wrought for us, we have commanded to be broken into pieces. It rests at the bottom of the shaft. Over it our merchants threw their silver and golden bars to the amount of a thousand times a thousand ounces. The women's jewels and the men's rings followed. Every man who had a ruby on his sword hilt tore it off. Pearls and precious stones disappeared into the well. Finally We, Araptan, threw in all our gold and the dagger which Khabutu-Khasar wore. We filled the well shaft with earth and leveled it down. Traders and strangers of future distant ages will pass by, but the treasures of Etzina rest forty feet beneath the ground, hidden as the thunder is hidden in the bowels of the earth."

Naidang stopped reading. He laid his hand on the book and looked around at his listeners, as if he wanted to search their hearts.

"And then?" asked Good Fortune, panting. "Is that all?"

"No, it is not all," answered Naidang calmly.

"Read on," urged Good Fortune, "it seems to be a serious matter."

"It's about a terrible misfortune," said Affliction, "I knew it would be."

"Affliction is right," said Naidang with a sigh. But then a sudden thought seemed to relieve his mind. He smiled, took his hand from the book and continued: "This it is which remains hidden until the day of discovery. We have resolved not to hinder that day. Therefore We are not entrusting our words to paper, which perishes. We are writing on the tough writing wood of ancient times, and burying it, that it may escape the fire. But you, unknown one of a later age, who will lift it from its grave, note this: No evil thought rests on the treasure of Etzina. Seek it beneath the mark "Great Treasure" which We are setting upon this spot. Now, there may be doubt in your heart, and you may think these are the words of a man writing with a distraught mind. We therefore show you the way and give you a sign of good omen, that your zeal may not fail. For you must delve forty feet into the earth until the uncertain light of the stars pales before the glitter of the jewels which shall dazzle your eyes.

"When you enter the city by the northern gate walk eighty paces ahead, and your foot will stumble against the remains of a stone wall. Bow there, if you will, for there stood Our palace. Follow the wall until it turns eastward. We cannot foresee whether you will still find the remains of the walls; therefore We say walk on until you find the big round stone which will lie undisturbed in its place, where the wall bends eastward. It was the base of the silver fountain, and no human hand can lift it. Do not seek the fountain shaft; it is filled up like all the others. From this point turn eastward. You will perceive the stairs in the city wall. Keep your eye fixed on them and take twenty paces toward them. Then stop and dig until you find a stone slab. It lies only two feet deep. On it are engraved the words: 'Great Treasure is near.' Lift the slab and dig two feet deeper, then you will find ten silver bars. They weigh a thousand ounces, and are a sign that you are on the right track, and an encouragement to persevere. Provide yourself with tools, and little baskets for drawing up the earth. But above all have with you tried and trusted men, who are with you at heart, for you cannot carry through the heavy task alone. Do not turn aside from the path which now leads northward. Walk on until you . . ."

"Read on," gasped Good Fortune, "this is a serious matter."

"There is nothing more to read," said Naidang, "there are only a few blank pages. The writing has ended." He laid down the book, and they could all see a tear in the thin rice paper, where a loose leaf had become detached. "Here," said Naidang, putting his finger on the binding thread, "hung the treasure of Etzina, for which a day of discovery will never dawn."

Good Fortune groaned. He was simply shattered. This second misfortune of the day seemed almost harder to bear than the first. They all stared in front of them in silence.

"You have lost a great deal, Naidang," said Good Fortune dejectedly.

"Not that I know of," replied Naidang, "one could not call it a loss."

"What," cried Good Fortune, beside himself, "you would not call a thousand times a thousand ounces of gold and silver any loss? And the pearls and precious stones? Think what you're saying!"

"I would not have moved a finger to get them," said Naidang.

"You lie!" shouted Good Fortune; but then he was horrified at his loss of self-control. "Forgive me," he begged; "my tongue ran away with me. But it simply cannot be as you say."

"But it is," said Naidang seriously. "No Torgut Mongol will ever disturb the peace of Khara-khoto."

"We would not have done anything wrong," said Good Fortune.

"Wisdom alone would counsel silence and inaction," replied Naidang.

"Why so?" asked Good Fortune, surprised.

"Nobody could dig out a treasure buried forty feet deep without its becoming known," said Naidang. "Ten thousand robbers would come rushing from all the eight zones of the earth. Not a Torgut Mongol would survive if that happened. Hence the wind which blew away the page in the Valley of Dark Rushing Water saved us from ruin."

"But the little treasure," asked Good Fortune obstinately, "I mean the ten silver bars? What about them?"

"Let us sleep on it," suggested Naidang.

Good Fortune was silent for a moment, but then he gave in and said, *"Bolna!"* for he hoped that Naidang would in time be persuaded at least to dig for the thousand ounces of silver.

"If the gentlemen will allow me," said Affliction timidly, "I mean . . . if I may say something too."

"Speak," urged Naidang, "we shall all have our say."

"We should leave well alone," said Affliction in a tone of conviction. "Surely somebody else was there ahead of us."

"How do you know that?" cried Good Fortune angrily.

"That's always the way," said Affliction, "either there was someone there already or someone will come."

"Who would come?"

"Someone who would take the silver from us."

"There's a remedy for that," cried Good Fortune, tapping his pistol holster.

"Those remedies don't always hit the mark," said Affliction, "or if they do hit, it's the wrong person who's hit, and nobody is to blame."

Good Fortune lapsed into sulky silence on hearing this, but Christian and Big Tiger found it hard to keep from laughing out loud.

Naidang closed the little silken book and laid it on the chest. "We shall discuss the matter tomorrow," he said.

30 ABOUT THE TREASURE SEEKERS' PLAN AND THE TERRIBLE STORY OF SHONG-MA

EVENING was falling and it was getting cool. Sevenstars had driven the camels and sheep nearer to the *yurt* and the poodle had watched to see that none of them straggled back to the deresen pastures. Naidang himself looked after the horses, for that was a man's job. As the sun sank behind the trees the poodle came running up to Sevenstars barking.

"He's marvelously intelligent," said Sevenstars, "he's telling me to tie up the camels and see to the sheep for the night."

"What's his name?" asked Christian.

"Just 'Dog'," said Sevenstars; "Mongolian dogs have no name of their own," and she ran after the poodle.

Christian and Big Tiger went with her. As they already knew how to tie up camels, they helped her to round them up one after the other and fasten them to the line. They undid the nose cord which was hanging around their necks, and led them up to the line which Naidang stretched between two poles, every evening at a different spot.

"Zook-zook!" cried Sevenstars. "Zook-zook!" cried Christian and Big Tiger too. Thereupon the camels knelt down, and Sevenstars counted them. When they got back to the *yurt,* Good Fortune said he would like to roast the pheasant but did not know how, as Naidang had no pan, since Mongols eat only boiled meat. If there was no objection, he would use the flat tea kettle as a pan. Then they sat down in front of the *yurt,* waiting for Naidang, who was still tying the horses. Christian wanted to go and help him, and get better acquainted with the piebald, but at that moment a flock of white swans flew with a swishing sound over the trees. Sevenstars, Christian and Big Tiger raced down to the river just in time to see them alight on the water not far from the ford. Having preened their feathers they swam silently down the dark river. Suddenly they began to utter excited cries, bent back their

necks, and expectantly swam around in a circle. Soon there was a swishing sound, and two small white objects dived into the water, came up again and swam through the circle of swans as if they were the chief personages there. But they were only two little ducks. At sight of them Sevenstars seemed overjoyed. She raised both thumbs as Naidang had done in approval of Christian's horsemanship, and whispered delightedly: "*Lam-shovo! Lam-shovo!*"

The ducks had the most magnificent plumage. Their breasts were golden, turning gradually to ivory, and their main feathers were pure white. Their wings were a light turquoise, like the evening sky. The drake had two golden shields on its head, and over them a tuft of dark feathers which hung down behind. It stretched out its red beak and began swimming upstream. The duck followed, and after them the swans swam in a straight line like obedient subjects. The procession disappeared under the dark foliage of overhanging branches. The water became still, green and dark again, and if an occasional twig had not sailed past, one would have imagined the Narin Gol to be a pond rather than a river.

Good Fortune, who had joined them unobserved, was just as childishly overjoyed as Sevenstars at the mere sight of the ducks. "These ducks are called lama birds," he explained, "because like the holy lamas they point the way to peace and happiness. Other birds like to follow them, and they thrive in their blessed company."

"Those two lama birds have not been long here," said Sevenstars. "We don't see them often, but I know they will nest on the little island a bit farther down the river. They will be safe there from the fox, which doesn't like the water, and the swans are wise and stay near them until they fly north."

Good Fortune confirmed what Sevenstars said, and added that it was a very lucky omen to catch a glimpse of lama birds. "You'll see," he said in a low voice to Christian and Big Tiger, "we'll find the silver that lies hidden in the Black City."

"But it belongs to Naidang," said Big Tiger.

"He'll give us some of it if we do the digging for him," asserted Good Fortune.

"I don't see any reason for that," Big Tiger dissented.

"Neither do I, really," Good Fortune admitted, and he stayed behind while Sevenstars returned to the *yurt;* "but it is so nevertheless. When I first got to know Mongols I thought they were like children and not sensible people at all, because they gave me food and wanted nothing in return. And I was a stranger to them, moreover, and no one knew me."

"That is what is called hospitality," said Christian. "Hospitality is a beautiful thing, but otherwise nothing special."

"But they themselves were not rich," said Good Fortune thoughtfully, "and gradually I learned that they are all like that. They are a strange people, quite different from us Chinese, and they give things away expecting no return beyond a *haddak* at most."

"Then," said Big Tiger, pensively, "they are better people than we are."

"Whether better or not," replied Good Fortune, shrugging his shoulders, "they are simply different. When they make a bargain they haggle just as we do, and there are lots of redbeards among them too."

"I have heard," said Big Tiger, "that there's nothing dishonorable in being a redbeard."

"Do you think that?" asked Good Fortune, giving Big Tiger a searching look.

"I think so, and Compass Mountain thinks the same."

"They say that being a redbeard is no disgrace as long as one is not found out," Christian agreed.

"That's just it," said Good Fortune, and he tramped back to the *yurt* lost in thought. "Not to be found out—that's just it."

Sevenstars sat in front of the *yurt,* scrubbing the tea kettle with sand. "Father says you want to roast and eat the bird?" she asked.

"Now that it's dead it must be eaten," said Good Fortune. Sevenstars shuddered at the thought, but went on bravely scrubbing. When the kettle was clean Good Fortune and Big Tiger went into the *yurt* and began roasting the pheasant in mutton fat, while Christian remained outside with Sevenstars. Soon the entrancing odor of roast fowl pervaded the air. At long last Good Fortune called out that dinner was ready. Sevenstars took Christian's hand and together they entered the *yurt,* where they found Good Fortune already carving up the bird.

Despite every persuasion Naidang refused to taste a bite of it, and Sevenstars held her hands before her face. The poodle stuck his big head expectantly into the tent but was shooed out.

"Why may he not come in?" asked Christian.

"A dog may not enter a tent," Good Fortune explained, "for the tent is only for human beings. Besides, he must keep watch outside, and how could he do that if he were pampered and allowed to lie about inside?"

Naidang nodded agreement. Then he watched attentively while his guests ate up the pheasant. Sevenstars collected the bones and brought them out to the poodle.

"I haven't had such a feast for many a long day," said Affliction. "I shall not be surprised if another misfortune happens."

But nothing happened. Naidang and Sevenstars drank milk and ate some cheese, and Christian wished he had some honey cakes to give them. Good Fortune tried to lead the conversation back to the Black City but gave up when he found that Naidang would not speak of it. Then Naidang distributed blankets and furs for the night, checked the flue, and shut the *yurt* door. "May you sleep well," he said when they were all lying in their places.

"It is not yet time to sleep," objected Sevenstars.

"I beg pardon for my ill-behaved child," said Naidang. "I am indeed very guilty for having brought up Sevenstars so badly. Please forgive me for it."

"That is far from true," cried Good Fortune. "I confess that we have most regrettably neglected our first duty as guests. But tomorrow Big Tiger will make amends for us. He knows many stories worthy of being told in every tent."

"I look forward to your stories," said Sevenstars to Big Tiger, but Big Tiger assured her that he was only a silly dunce. All disagreed vigorously. Finally, Big Tiger gave in. "I'll think over what's worth telling," he promised. Silence then fell on the tent. Christian lay beside Big Tiger, and they were both thinking hard.

"I know how it must be done," whispered Big Tiger.

"How what must be done?" asked Christian, surprised.

"How the silver must be got from the Black City," explained Big Tiger under his breath. Then he described in detail the plan which he had figured out, and asked Christian whether he thought it good.

"I couldn't think of a better one," said Christian admiringly.

"We'll dig by ourselves. Do you agree?" asked Big Tiger.

"If you could manage it," Christian admitted, "it would be splendid."

"Just leave it to me. Good night, Kwi-Chan."

"Good night, Big Tiger."

Then Big Tiger whispered into Christian's ear: "Naidang is as wise as the Yellow Emperor and as firm as a rock. Now I know why his name is spoken with respect in a thousand tents."

"Why?" Christian wanted to know.

"I'll tell you when we're quite alone," whispered Big Tiger.

It was a glorious night. A thousand times a thousand stars passed over the desert and over the Narin Gol. They were reflected in the water, and flooded the ruins of the tragic city of Etzina with a bluish light. The moon moved with them, and when it shone through the chimney hole of Naidang's tent Christian woke up.

To open one's eyes and look up at the drifting moon makes one feel sad without any reason. But Christian's sadness had a reason, for he was thinking of his home in Peking and imagining how everything was there. He saw his father pacing restlessly up and down on the porch, and his mother bending over his little sister's cot to hide her tears. And hidden away in some corner was the old amah who was being blamed, either with words or with looks, for his disappearance. His greatest fear was for her, for he was more at home in Chinese than in Western ways, and he knew what terrible things could happen. Indeed, if Big Tiger had not been sleeping so soundly he would have wakened him up merely to say: "I'm thinking of my amah." And Big Tiger would have understood. For often faithful servants who had been unjustly blamed took their lives on the thresholds of their employers' doors, and were found lying there the next morning. And the neighbors and passersby said: "It can't be helped; that family has committed a great sin, and has lost face." For all over the world it is the dead who are in the right.

Morning came, bringing much bustle, which was just what Good Fortune liked. First he sternly forbade Naidang to do any work, and Naidang then forbade him to as much as lift a finger. And so they became fast friends. "Don't you know," said Naidang indignantly, "that the Mongol *joss* bids us honor and serve our guests?"

"Please refrain from honoring miserable people of low origin," said Good Fortune.

"You are my guests," insisted Naidang, "more than that I do not know or wish to know."

Then Good Fortune tried pleading, and when he swore that

nothing gave him greater joy than cooking, Naidang gave in at last. He went to take the horses out to pasture, while Good Fortune looked after the household. Before sunrise Sevenstars had gone with the camels and sheep to the deresen pastures.

The few chores were soon done. Big Tiger and Christian shook and folded the blankets. Affliction tidied away the cushions. Good Fortune lit the fire. Then they had tea and millet. Sevenstars came riding back from the pastures on a camel, and when they were all sitting down together Naidang said: "I have decided to ride to the Black City with Good Fortune. What do you say to that?"

"Don't do it, father," cried Sevenstars. "Anyone who takes anything from the Black City dies."

"I will take nothing," replied Naidang, "so I won't die. But I would like to do my guests a service, if ten bars of silver do not seem too mean a thing to them."

"Never could we accept such a gift!" protested Good Fortune. "The silver is your property, for you are the finder."

"For that very reason," asserted Naidang, "I can do what I please with my property. You have suffered a great loss; permit me to give you a trifle instead." He drew a *haddak* from his belt and, kneeling, offered it to Good Fortune. "Do not disdain my poor gift," he pleaded, "for yourself and for your friends. True, I am worried about how it will begin and how it will end, for you may also be endangered. But I have thought out everything and there are ways and means," he added slyly, "which we shall discuss later."

Good Fortune hesitated. Dearly though he would have loved to have the silver from the Black City, the death of Nowhere-at-all intimidated him, and Sevenstar's fears made him uneasy too. "This is an uncanny business," he admitted.

"Hammagua!" cried Naidang. "Haven't you heard: No evil thought rests on the treasure of Etzina."

"You need not fear," Affliction suddenly made himself heard, "you may accept the gift without hesitation. For surely somebody was there already."

"If it should turn out that way," said Naidang calmly, "then you must accept four of my camels. Why should I have many camels when you have none and need some?"

"Your goodness is without end or measure," said Good Fortune and, bowing profoundly, he accepted the *haddak*. Then he drew another one from his belt and offered it to Naidang.

"We shall set out tomorrow morning," said Naidang, and thanked him for the return gift.

"Bolna!" answered Good Fortune resolutely.

"But if you have no one with you," Big Tiger broke in, "you may be attacked."

"What do you mean?" asked Good Fortune.

"I am thinking of the four high walls of the city," Big Tiger explained. "If someone is digging inside a city, he cannot see what is going on outside. People might come the way, and say: 'Let us look at the Black City,' and then they would enter the gateway and see our respected elder lifting the silver bars out of the hole, and that would be bad."

"Hm!" muttered Good Fortune, "we certainly don't want people walking round Khara-khoto while we're there."

"There are many things to be thought of," Christian interjected; "Big Tiger has a plan. It might be well to say: 'Speak that we may know it.'"

"Bolna!" cried Naidang, "let Big Tiger speak!"

"If I don't have to be there," said Affliction, "it will certainly be a splendid plan."

"It can't be done without Affliction," Big Tiger objected, "and Sevenstars must help with it too."

"Oh, woe!" cried Sevenstars, "I would be no good for that."

"I see already," said Affliction, "that it is not a good plan."

"Be quiet," ordered Naidang, "let us hear what it is."

"I find that with Sevenstars we are six," said Big Tiger, "and that is exactly the necessary number for the undertaking. For Khara-khoto has four walls, one in each direction. That is in the account which we heard."

"That is so," affirmed Naidang.

"If we have a sentry posted on each wall," continued Big Tiger, "then we are safe from all sides. If someone comes on foot he can be seen from a long way off; a rider can be seen still sooner; and a caravan is heard long before it is seen. Someone need only call 'Hello' and the two who are digging cover up the hole with the stone slab turned upside down. Then nobody can read 'The great treasure is near' and if people ask any questions, we can say: 'We're resting for a bit, because there were ghosts here just now who frightened us, but our faintness will pass off.' "

"Great praise is due to you, Big Tiger," cried Naidang, "and we shall follow your plan."

"But who shall keep guard and who shall dig?" asked Good Fortune.

"Our respected elder is right," said Big Tiger. "It must be decided in advance what we're to do. Since the Black City is such a terrifying place, it is best if Compass Mountain and I do the digging. We both come from a long way off, and therefore the spirits, if there are any there, do not know us, and before they get to know us, we will pack up the silver and be gone."

"You have courage," said Naidang, "but will you still have it when you stand among the ruins?"

"We hope we shall endure the sight," said Christian.

"Agreed!" cried Good Fortune, "but let us hear again how we are to find the stone and the silver."

Thereupon Naidang put on his cap, took down the book from the chest, and read out Prince Araptan's description until he came to the place where he said: "Provide yourself with tools, ropes and small baskets." "We do not need those," he said, closing the book. "Now we shall burn these written words as is the custom."

"I would not do that," objected Good Fortune. "The holy men of the old times set down words so that they should last. Why will you go against their command?"

"It might happen," said Naidang, "that a word would take wing, and nothing could ever bring it back again. It is better to destroy all."

He took the book, loosened the binding threads, and threw the pages one after another into the fire. They blazed up, then crinkled and turned black. The writing still stood out in white and gray until Sevenstars took tongs and beat down the fluttering black pages as if they were enemies. "Now you can do nobody any harm!" she cried with relief. Then she went out lightheartedly and immediately afterwards could be heard trotting away on her camel.

"I must go too," said Naidang, "I shall be back in the evening."

"Where are you going?" asked Good Fortune.

"Ride with me," Naidang invited him, "we have a lot of work to do."

"But who will do the cooking?" asked Good Fortune.

"I shall do it," Big Tiger offered. "Our elder need not worry."

As Naidang and Good Fortune rode away Christian and Big Tiger cried: *"Yabonah! Sä Yabonah!"* They would have liked to know what Naidang was up to, but neither dared to ask.

"Perhaps Sevenstars knows," said Christian.

"We'll ask her," Big Tiger decided.

Sevenstars was sitting, as the day before, by the side of the caravan track with the black poodle beside her.

"We met a man named Thunderbolt," said Christian casually. "He had a gun; perhaps you know him?"

"Yes, I know him," replied Sevenstars, "he's a lama."

"Do lamas also carry guns?"

"Usually they don't, but sometimes they have one."

"I thought," began Christian again, "that lamas stayed in monasteries and prayed."

"Not all of them," Sevenstars informed him. "Some leave the monastery, but they still remain lamas. Perhaps they haven't learned to read well, or they were not obedient, or perhaps they wanted to live in a tent again and in the saddle—above all in the saddle, for that's where we Mongols are at home."

"And what about the Venerable Chief?" Christian asked straight out.

"What do you know about him?" cried Sevenstars.

"I've heard that he's a robber and that he's got a strong castle made all of stone somewhere in the middle of the desert."

"He's a prince," said Sevenstars softly, "and a great warrior. It is said, too, that he is a lama, but whether he has a gun or not I do not know."

"He must have one," Christian surmised, "for he has enemies."

"We hear there's a certain Shong-Ma whom the Venerable Chief hates very much," said Big Tiger courageously.

"Shong-Ma is a devil!" cried Sevenstars in a horrified tone.

"People have spoken of him as if he were a human being," said Big Tiger, "for there are certain men looking for him, for instance the lama Thunderbolt."

"I hope he'll find him," cried Sevenstars, her eyes blazing angrily. "Unfortunately it's not known for certain if he's alive. For a long time he was said to be dead, and now there's a rumor going round that he's still alive and hiding under another name."

"Do people know the other name?" asked Christian.

"No, they don't," said Sevenstars, "but the sharp eyes of the Venerable Chief are searching everywhere, and they'll find Shong-Ma if he's alive."

"What has he done?" Christian sounded her.

"I'll tell you, and when I've told it, you'll be frightened."

"Of whom?" asked Big Tiger.

"Of Shong-Ma, of course," cried Sevenstars. "You should count yourselves lucky that you only hear about such monsters and don't meet them."

"You never know," said Christian thoughtfully. "You may go for a walk, and sit on the edge of a wash tub because you're tired and want to watch the pigeons. And suddenly you're scared, because someone is standing behind you with eyes like a wolf, and he spits into the washtub and his black beard trembles."

"That's not he," said Sevenstars, "Shong-Ma has no beard, and he looks like an ordinary man; that's why it's so hard to find him."

Big Tiger signed to Christian to keep quiet. "Go on, tell us about Shong-Ma," he said.

"He's from the Sining-Fu district," began Sevenstars, "but what can you do with a man who lives like a great gentleman and runs up big debts which he cannot pay on New Year's Day?"

"You can put him in jail," said Christian.

"Shong-Ma couldn't be put in jail," continued Sevenstars; "he fled through the three kingdoms as far as Manchuria. There he began trading with the Chinese settlers at the other side of the Hsingan Mountains and with the impoverished Tchachar and Naiman Mongol tribes. But he also found a prince who had great riches in cattle and old family treasures. When the prince rode to Urga with his men twenty years ago for the *Koorultai,** this Shong-Ma gathered a gang of ruffians. They attacked the prince's *yurts,* stole the cattle, and carried away the contents of the chests from the tents. And they murdered all the women and children."

"What are you saying?" cried Christian.

"Why are you so shocked?" asked Sevenstars. "Didn't I tell you he's a devil?"

"Compass Mountain never knew until now," said Big Tiger calmly, "that there are men more wicked than wolves or tigers."

"Since the attack on the prince," continued Sevenstars, "Shong-Ma has remained invisible. There was a rumor that he had been seen in Lanchow, but that's a long time ago. The prince forsook the pastures of his ancestors and swore to kill every Chinaman whom he would meet in the steppes. Twenty men of his tribe

* *Koorultai:* Assembly of Mongol princes.

swore that oath with him, and many joined him when he began his campaign of vengeance."

"Did he do what he intended?" asked Christian, horrified.

"He did what he had to do," declared Sevenstars, "for an oath cannot be broken. He conquered villages and whole towns, and not a single Chinese person was left alive in them. When he had spilled enough blood he released his men from the oath and built himself a castle in the middle of the desert. Now he is looking only for Shong-Ma. His men are on the road at all times, especially in Sining-Fu and Lanchow. His spies sit at the campfires of the caravans listening, in the hope of hearing something. When Thunderbolt was with us twenty days ago he was in a particular hurry. The Prince, he said, had got news that a man named Moonlight, whom they had mourned as dead, was living at the court of the Sunit *Wang*."

"Many people call Moonlight Little Paw," said Big Tiger.

"How do you know that?" asked Sevenstars, astounded.

"We hunted the wolf with him," reported Christian, "and that's how we became friends."

"I am glad," cried Sevenstars; "for we shall see Moonlight soon again."

"Do you know," asked Big Tiger, "why the lama Thunderbolt went to fetch Moonlight in such haste?"

"He didn't tell us," said Sevenstars, "but it must be on some important matter, for Moonlight sits at the Prince's left hand, and he's always the first in the saddle for important undertakings."

Big Tiger meditatively turned the ring on his thumb. "So the Prince is the Venerable Chief, and the Venerable Chief is Dampignak, and Dampignak is . . ."

"Don't say he's a robber," cried Sevenstars, "he's a noble man. Many fear him, but there are also many who love him."

"Nobody who kills the innocent is a noble person," said Big Tiger. "We came across the holy Abbot Yolros Lama, whom Dampignak met many years ago. The Abbot said to Dampignak: 'You darken the light. No noble man lives thus!' And Dampignak threw himself on the ground and wept."

"He didn't do that," cried Sevenstars, excitedly.

"The holy man Yolros Lama," replied Big Tiger firmly, "told us so himself, and Yolros Lama speaks no lie. Remember, he's a Living Buddha."

"But," said Sevenstars, speaking with deep emotion, "how else is a person to live who has suffered such a calamity?"

"Perhaps," said Big Tiger, "Dampignak is a man who considers it right to be stubborn, and is proud of it. But he shouldn't be. My grandfather says: 'A noble person sees the good and imitates it. If he has faults, he gives them up.' "

"Is your grandfather a learned man?"

"No, he's not a learned man, he's only my grandfather."

"And what do *you* think?" Sevenstars said, turning to Christian.

"I think," said Christian, "that Big Tiger's grandfather is right."

Then Sevenstars became silent, knit her brows and looked straight out at the caravan road, on which the wheelmarks of the truck could be seen. She was drawing figures with a reed in the sand and blotting them out again with an air of reluctance.

Christian's heart grew heavy. For the first time he had an inkling of the dark powers which make people insensitive to the sufferings of others. Big Tiger had stopped twisting the ring. He was looking thoughtfully at the silver snake, and did not raise his eyes until the poodle began sniffing and pricking up his ears.

"Sit still," Sevenstars commanded in a low voice. "And you two also please keep quiet. If you wait a bit my antelopes will come."

"Do they belong to you?" asked Christian.

Sevenstars had to laugh although she was sad. "They only belong to themselves," she said, "but all the same they're mine."

The poodle grew restless. He wanted to dash off, but Sevenstars held him firmly by the collar. "He will never understand that he's not to chase them. He frightened away all our hares, and they never came back. It's sad."

"Did you have hares too?" asked Big Tiger.

"Yes, we had lots of hares," said Sevenstars; "they lived quite near our *yurt,* and when foxes or strange dogs hunted them they came running to us for protection. I used to stroke their long ears and their necks and feel their hearts beating, and they wouldn't go out until I looked round and told them the way was clear."

"With us hares run away as soon as they see people," said Big Tiger.

"Hush!" said Sevenstars, and all three kept dead quiet, for the curved antlers of an antelope buck had appeared above the high deresen grass, as the animal gazed over cautiously. In their joy and excitement Christian and Big Tiger forgot Shong-Ma and the Venerable Chief. They thought they had never seen anything more beautiful than the proud and graceful animal with its trusting brown eyes. The buck came slowly nearer, then stood carefully observing the poodle, while the does, unperturbed, dispersed over the pasture, nibbling at the leaves and gazing without fear at the group by the wayside. Gradually they moved off and mixed with the sheep and the camels, whom they seemed to have long known as good friends.

"They know we don't harm them," said Sevenstars.

"They walk as if they were stepping on air," said Big Tiger; "that's what makes them so beautiful."

"Don't you hunt antelopes here?" asked Christian.

"Yes, we hunt them," Sevenstars admitted, "but only if meat is scarce."

"And the hares?" asked Big Tiger.

Sevenstars was horrified. "One mustn't hunt the hare," she said, "he's such a small animal; and besides, there's a hare in the moon. What would *he* think?"

"Excuse me," said Big Tiger, "I had forgotten the hare in the moon."

"He was in great danger last year," said Sevenstars.

"How was that?" asked Christian.

"The moon was round and beautiful," recounted Sevenstars. "We were already asleep, when suddenly the camels got restless. They jumped up, and the dog whimpered as if in pain. That woke me up. I roused my father and mother and my brothers, and we went out. We got a terrible fright. The beautiful moon had turned blood-red, and half of it was no longer there. 'Hurry,' cried father, 'the hungry wolves of the heavens want to eat the hare in the moon! We must drive them off.' So we snatched anything that was to hand, and father got his gun and fired several shots. We all shouted and made a lot of noise, and in the end it helped. The moon became bright again, the wolves had to let go their prey, and the hare sat on its haunches as before and looked down at the world. We were all very glad."

"That's called an eclipse of the moon," said Christian, "I learned at school what causes it, but I've forgotten."

"You should have been more attentive," said Sevenstars reproachfully.

By this time it was midday, and the sun was at its hottest. The poodle ran down to the river for a drink and Sevenstars went out to the deresen pasture and came back with three camels. "We must water the animals," she said, giving Christian and Big Tiger each a leading cord. *"Jirr!"* they cried, and led the camels behind them.

"Stop! That's not the way to do it," said Sevenstars. "People were not made to go on foot through the world. They have two legs so they can ride."

"But it's only a short way to the river," Big Tiger objected.

"We Mongols think," Sevenstars held forth, "that people should ride whether the journey is long or short. *Bolvo?"*

"Bolna!" said Christian.

"But the camels have no saddles," said Big Tiger. "How are we to ride them?"

"I'll show you how," said Sevenstars, calling "zook, zook!" The camels plopped down obediently on their knees and slid forward until their hind legs dropped and the heavy body sank. Then they tucked in their hind legs and looked wonderingly around to see what was coming.

"You must jump on to their backs quickly," said Sevenstars, "because most camels stand up as soon as they notice you're going to ride them. We've no saddle or stirrups, but just watch me!" She drew up the nose cord lightly, gripped the animal's shoulder, and in spite of her heavy boots, swung with incredible agility on to the camel's back just as it stood up.

"Don't pull so hard," warned Sevenstars when she saw that Big Tiger had drawn his camel's nose cord taut. The camel stretched out its neck, roared angrily, and would have spat at Big Tiger if he hadn't loosened his hold. But mounting was not so difficult as it looked. Only one had to be quick and, once up, grip the animal hard with one's knees. Christian and Big Tiger were quick and nimble and before one could count one-two-three they were perched up, proudly conscious that they had become camel riders.

"Drive the sheep together," ordered Sevenstars. "Each of you must ride out in a wide semicircle, to see that no sheep remain behind. Meanwhile I'll fetch the camels and wait for you."

Christian and Big Tiger shouted *"Bolna!"* Then Big Tiger rode out through the deresen pasture until it ceased and the horses pasture began. Christian rode to the edge of the wood and plucked a good big branch with which to drive the sheep before him. The antelopes had long since disappeared. At first it seemed easy to round up the sheep, but some straggled, and while Christian rode after them the whole flock had dispersed again in a trice.

Sevenstars called the poodle, and once he arrived on the scene the work went smoothly. He held the flock together and Christian and Big Tiger only needed to round up the stragglers. When Christian caught up with Sevenstars she handed him the ropes of the four camels, while she counted the sheep as they went down to the water. They wagged their thick tails and stirred up a great

cloud of dust. Many were staggering under the weight of their enormous tails as they scrambled over the rough ground.

"Sixty-four," said Sevenstars. "That's right."

The riders dismounted at the riverbank. Sevenstars tied the camels' guide ropes around their necks and they began to drink. One could see their bellies filling out and stretching. At intervals they shook their upper lips, looked around them haughtily, and squirted water all over in sheer high spirits. The sheep drank much more politely, quickly left to make room for the camels, and went off to nibble at the bushes. They were left the whole afternoon on the pasture which was usually reserved to the horses and the two cows.

"Don't forget you have to tell us a story when father comes back tonight," said Sevenstars.

"My knowledge is poor," replied Big Tiger.

"Where did your father go to?" asked Christian.

"He's gone to fetch my cousin Turakina," replied Sevenstars. "Someone must stay with the sheep when I go with you. But don't say anything to Turakina about Etzina and the silver."

"We are used to keeping silent," said Christian proudly.

31 CONCERNING THE FIRST FIND, AND CONTAINING THE STORY OF YU-SAN AND YU-LAN

"NAIDANG is late," said Big Tiger; "the sun will set soon."

"Something must have happened to him," said Affliction gloomily.

"What could happen to him?" asked Big Tiger.

"It needn't be very bad," replied Affliction; "a cramp in the leg would be enough."

Big Tiger was kneeling before the pastry board cutting dough strips. Affliction sat opposite him, rolling noodles as thin as knitting needles and throwing them into the saucepan. Sevenstars was sitting in front of the tent, hacking a brick of tea into small pieces, and pounding the pieces to crumbs in a stone mortar. She gave Christian the pestle. "The tea must be like coarse dust," she said, and went off to pen the sheep. While she was away Big Tiger came to see what the pounding was.

"I'm pounding the tea into coarse dust," explained Christian.

"Stop!" said Big Tiger. "You've pounded it far too fine already, and Affliction has made the noodles much too thin. Good Fortune won't be a bit pleased. Come and look at the swans instead."

They crept along under the trees as far as the ford. There wasn't a stir or a sound there. The water was like a dark mirror, and little lumps of ice were floating on it like water lilies. It seemed, too, that the Narin Gol had risen.

"Let's see what it's like further up," suggested Big Tiger. "We know our way as far as this already."

"Bolna!" cried Christian eagerly. They forced their way through the thicket, but there was no longer any path, only thorn bushes and old dead branches entwined with liana and ivy. A mighty uprooted poplar lay across their path, its crown touching the ground.

"The expedition has to stop here," said Christian. "We'd need an axe to get further."

"There's something up there," cried Big Tiger, pointing to the poplar trunk.

Christian tapped it. "It's hollow," he said. "An owl or a wildcat or a lynx lives in here."

"No," Big Tiger disagreed. "Thorns and brushwood have been stuffed into it. An animal doesn't do that."

"Perhaps it's a bird's nest."

"Let's see," said Big Tiger.

Christian clasped his hands, Big Tiger stepped on them, got hold of a branch and swung himself up to a fork which came out from the trunk. "Come up," he cried; "there's something here which I can't make out. You must see it for yourself."

Christian hesitated, but when Big Tiger assured him that the branch would hold them both, up he came and sat astride it. "You can't know just by looking," said Christian. "We'd need a rag or a glove." And he pulled at the thorns.

"We must get them away," Big Tiger decided.

"But if something jumps out suddenly?"

"We'll work slowly. If some hidden creature wants to come out, we'll have time to get away."

"Bolna!" said Christian, and he looked uneasily at the sky, thinking it would soon be dark. The mysterious bundle of thorns was stuck fast in the hole, and they both had to pull hard and long before it moved. At last they drew it out.

"There's nothing stirring," said Christian, peeping cautiously into the dark hole.

"I can't see anything," said Big Tiger, looking in too.

"The smell would knock you over," said Christian. "Something is rotting here."

"We must get to the bottom of this," decided Big Tiger, breaking a twig and poking it into the hole.

"What's wrong with you?" asked Christian alarmed, when he saw Big Tiger turning pale. "Is there something in there?"

"There's some soft thing that sighs when I poke it. You try!"

Christian took the stick timidly, and found with horror that there was something wobbly which sighed and gurgled in the hollow of the tree. It made him feel quite sick too, and he had to sit down on the branch.

"Hello!" cried Big Tiger, to show he had regained his courage. "Hello!" Christian replied feebly. Then they looked at each other and tried to laugh, but they felt they were in a bad fix, and it was getting very dark.

Meanwhile Big Tiger had thought up something desperately daring. "We must count one, two, and at two we'll reach into the hole together and pull out whatever is in there," he said.

"But if it struggles?"

"Even if it struggles," declared Big Tiger resolutely.

"And if it bites?"

"Then we'll let go quickly."

"*Bolna!*" said Christian, resignedly. "I'm with you!"

"One!" counted Big Tiger, laying his hand on the edge of the hollow. Christian admired him and followed his example. Then Big Tiger cried "Two" and as quick as lightning they both stretched their arms into the dark hole and grabbed the object, and Big Tiger shouted "Hold tight!"

"But it's wriggling!" cried Christian.

"Not much," said Big Tiger gasping, "it's an animal, but it's got no hair, or very little. Pull quickly before it wakes up. It's hibernating."

"You pull," said Christian, who wanted to let go. But he was immediately ashamed of himself, and they both pulled out the animal whose skin they had been gripping so desperately.

Christian felt faint with horror but kept his eyes bravely open. Big Tiger didn't feel too brave either. "It's a sleeping animal," he said faintly, looking at the booty.

"But it hasn't got a head, and very little legs either."

"That's because it's dark," said Big Tiger. "Oh, Kwi-Chan!" he shouted suddenly, "it's not an animal at all, but it was one once.

Now it's a goatskin full of *arrak*. And that's why the smell is knocking us over!"

"If that's what it is, there's a second one!"

"Yes, there is," said Big Tiger, poking again; "but we couldn't pull it out. It's too far in."

"We'll leave it where it is," said Christian. "Then Naidang's wife won't be too angry with us when she goes to look for it."

They pushed back the bundle of thorns into the mouth of the hole, and climbed down. The moon had risen, and they could see the distant glow of the fire through the open door of the *yurt,* and could hear Sevenstars calling alternately "Kwi-Chan" and "Hu-Ta," and the poodle barking.

"We're coming!" Christian called back.

"What'll we say to them? Quick!" whispered Big Tiger.

"Will we have to tell a lie again?" asked Christian anxiously.

"It can't be helped," said Big Tiger; "but it must be a splendid one, and still not really a lie. For we mustn't betray Mother Naidang's hiding hole."

"You're late," said Affliction. "Dinner is ready and Mr. Naidang has been waiting a long time."

"Please forgive us," cried Christian, while Big Tiger ducked down and laid the goatskin behind one of the rust-red trees in the shadowy moonlight.

In the *yurt* they were all sitting round the big pot of noodles. Beside Sevenstars sat a strange girl, laughing and whispering.

"I have brought Turakina back," said Naidang, "to mind the *yurt* and the sheep while we're visiting the old märin."

"I have been anxious to make the acquaintance of that worthy man," said Good Fortune. "He doesn't live far from here, and we'll be there and back in a day's ride."

"May we go with you?" asked Big Tiger politely.

"Of course," said Naidang. "You honor me."

"Same here!" muttered Good Fortune, completing the silent understanding between the treasure hunters.

After dinner they had tea. Sevenstars, who sat near the door with Turakina, shut the two wings. "I do not want one of Big Tiger's words to get lost," she said.

"Would it be possible for you to tell us all that your wise grandfather knows of the things of this world?" asked Affliction eagerly.

"I have not got the ability to impart his wisdom," said Big Tiger modestly, but Naidang countered: "We pray you to do so."

"First," began Big Tiger, "may I tell you something that I think worth mentioning."

"Certainly," said Naidang amiably.

"Compass Mountain and I practice the art of silence," confessed Big Tiger. "For this reason, as evening was falling we went up by the river in silence. We sat down at the ford, and because it is difficult to make a beginning in the practice of the ten thousand rules of wisdom, we decided to act like the three apes."

"What did they do?" asked Affliction, eager for knowledge.

"The first shut his ears," declared Big Tiger, "the second his eyes, and the third his mouth. And so they learned mutually not to hear, not to see and not to speak. For this they became renowned. Many people carved them in wood or put them into music, and many, who were serious-minded, took the three apes as models. We did so too, thinking it a good beginning. But when I wanted to shut my ears I heard a rustling in the air; and when I wanted to shut my eyes I saw two lama birds falling from the sky; luckily I was just able to keep my mouth shut, or I would have shouted out my delight. The lama birds were not swimming downstream like yesterday; they were saying *'yurr, yurr!'* and swimming over to the other bank. Compass Mountain whispered: 'They're calling come, come!' 'I hear them,' I said, 'and I believe we must do what they want us to do.' So we took off our shoes and stockings and waded into the river. But it was very cold.

"And now the lama birds were no longer saying *'yurr, yurr,'* but *'yama, yama,'* and flapping their wings. 'What do they mean?' I asked, and Kwi-Chan answered: 'They're calling goat, goat, and

I don't understand why.' But we soon knew why, for there was a dead goat lying on the bank; it had been washed in and its body was swollen up. It must have been lying in the water a long time, because the head and horns were gone and it had no legs any more, and we brought it back with us."

"Would you like to see it?" asked Christian eagerly, standing up.

"We'll bring it in," said Big Tiger, opening the door.

"Phew! A dead goat!" cried Sevenstars. "Phew!" echoed Turakina indignantly.

"Leave it outside!" cried Good Fortune. "Dead goats stink."

"We only want the gentlemen to see that we're accustomed to telling the truth," replied Big Tiger.

"Just show it," said Affliction, "but don't bring it in. It would make me sick."

Big Tiger and Christian went out to the trees, lifted the goatskin out of the moonlit shadows, and carried it to the *yurt* door. Big Tiger lifted it up and said: "This is the goat without head, horns or legs. And it smells of *arrak*."

"Ha!" cried Good Fortune, "what a pair of proper little rascals, first-class scamps! There's no limit to what the young get into nowadays."

Naidang jumped up, but then bethought himself and, approaching Big Tiger with dignity, he bowed with deep emotion. "You have brought me what my heart yearned for," he said. "Where have you been so long?" he asked, stroking the goatskin affectionately. "Ah, I know, you were lying in the water, but you have remained dry." He grinned. "I don't want to hear where you were, or to see where you lay hidden, but I wish to do honor to your two finders. Come, fetch glasses for the two sons of princes, Big Tiger and Compass Mountain!" he cried.

Sevenstars brought the brass can, and Turakina distributed graceful china beakers not much bigger than thimbles.

Naidang put on his fur hat which made him look as dignified as a king in the midst of his subjects; and Affliction and Good

Fortune too put on their military caps with the five-colored star. Christian and Big Tiger made haste to follow suit; then all sat down with covered heads.

"Dsha, dsha, dsha," murmured Naidang, raising the first beaker to his forehead and handing it to Big Tiger in both hands, with great solemnity.

"I do not dare," replied Big Tiger politely, nevertheless accepting the beaker.

"You must drink it all," whispered Good Fortune.

Big Tiger did so, but he coughed, for the *arrak* burned like fire and took his breath away. Good Fortune slapped him energetically on the back. "Well, well!" he said. "Did you never drink a drop of spirits before?"

"I didn't either," said Christian apologetically, seeing that Naidang was giving the next beaker to him.

"Courage!" whispered Good Fortune.

Christian tried his luck and emptied the beaker at a gulp. "I . . . I . . . do not da . . . dare," he gasped, and like Big Tiger he began to cough.

After the second round of drinks Naidang beamed joyfully. "Now is the time," he said, "to rejoice our warmed-up spirits with a story."

"It need not be quite so true as the one about the speaking lama birds," chaffed Good Fortune.

"The story I'll tell you," said Big Tiger, "is about a man named Yu-San. His wife was called Yu-Lan, and their little son was called Yu. All three had much in common. In the daytime Yu-Lan lay on the *kang,* while Yu-San stood at the door waiting for rain. In doing so he forgot to water his fields in time. 'Have you been working?' asked Yu-Lan in the evening, and Yu-San replied: 'I have been working.' 'That is good,' said Yu-Lan, but it was not good at all. It was bad. However, by the time Yu-Lan noticed that, it was too late. The spring sowing dried up, and Yu-San said: 'That is because there was no rain.' 'Good-for-nothing fellow!' cried Yu-Lan.

'Go dig the ground up again, and we shall make a second sowing.'

"So Yu-San went out to the fields with his hoe, and the old grandfather sat in the corner and said: 'Will you buy me a coffin, beloved daughter, since my son forgets this filial duty?' But Yu-Lan shouted: 'Time enough for that, old fool!' She lay down on the *kang,* and the little son Yu amused himself pulling the white hairs one by one out of the grandfather's beard."

"Oh, that was terrible," sighed Affliction; "but go on with it. It's a sad story. I like it."

"When Yu-San looked at the field," continued Big Tiger, "he began sweating. He looked at his hoe, and his sweat flowed in streams, and he fell exhausted into a furrow. 'I shall remain lying here,' he said to himself, 'and by evening I shall have picked up plenty of courage, and when Yu-Lan comes to the field I shall say to her: "You lazy creature, do you not know that digging and hoeing are women's work?"' This idea pleased Yu-San greatly, and he slept soundly until he was wakened by footsteps. 'You tramp!' shouted Yu-Lan, kicking him. 'Why aren't you hoeing?' 'You lazy creature,' whimpered Yu-San; 'don't you know that digging and hoeing are women's work?'

"When Yu-Lan heard Yu-San's impertinent words she was horrified. He has suddenly become brave, she thought; I shall have to fear him. She took the hoe, but she had only hoed three or four strokes when she hit against something hard. 'Is there something there?' sneered Yu-San. 'Yes,' stammered Yu-Lan, 'and it's hard.' 'I'll help you,' said Yu-San graciously, and the two began digging together. The sun went down, and at long last they unearthed an old cask.

" 'It seems usable,' said Yu-San, tapping the staves. 'We could sell it,' suggested Yu-Lan, 'for we've really got nothing to put into it.' 'Good,' said Yu-San. 'Now we'll roll the cask home. Grandfather can scrub it in the night; he can't sleep in any case. And in the morning, when it's clean, we will sell it in the town.'

"So they gave the poor grandfather a brush, and while Yu-San and Yu-Lan slept he scrubbed the cask, until the night turned to pale morning. But the grandfather turned pale too; he fell down in a faint, and the brush fell into the cask. It had scarcely reached the bottom when there was a rustling noise, and the whole cask filled up with brushes. When the sun rose Yu-San and Yu-Lan woke from their deep sleep, and the grandfather woke from his deep swoon. All three stood around the cask and wondered, and little Yu was there too.

" 'Unexpected riches have come our way,' said Yu-San. 'Fetch a basket and fill the brushes into it, and I'll sell them in town.' Yu-Lan did as he bade her, and as quickly as she took the brushes out of the cask, it filled up again. Yu-San and Yu-Lan then realized that it was a magic cask.

"A prosperous life now began for Yu-San and Yu-Lan. Each morning they went into town and sold the brushes which the grandfather had to pick out of the cask. When they came home well fed Yu-Lan scolded the old grandfather: 'You old fool, you have been lazy!' And Yu-San said: 'The barn should be full of brushes long ago. You must bend down faster. In these circumstances there's no question of buying a coffin.'

"Little Yu hopped to and fro and piped: 'I've been kicking him all the time, but still he hasn't worked any faster. He's lazy.' 'Don't bother, my darling,' Yu-Lan said. 'Here's a silver batz for your trouble.'

"Little Yu took the silver batz and aimed it at the head of his grandfather, who was bending down with a groan to pick up a brush. The poor grandfather immediately got a bump as big as a hen's egg, but the batz fell into the cask. In no time the brushes had disappeared, and the cask filled up with silver batzes."

"What a wonderful cask," cried Good Fortune; "a really useful cask!"

"Wait," said Affliction. "This story will end badly. You can see that already."

"Go on," said Sevenstars. "What happened then?"

"A first-class misfortune," prophesied Affliction.

"No," said Big Tiger. "Now Yu-San and Yu-Lan became really prosperous. The old grandfather with the big bump on his head was given a shovel. 'Shovel, you old fool!' they told him. Yu-San removed the brushes from the barn, and the grandfather was told to fill it up to the roof with silver. 'If you've finished in four days,' said Yu-San, 'I'll buy you a beautiful coffin.' 'Leave it to me, Papa,' cried little Yu, 'I'll beat him with my whip if he's lazy.'

"Yu-San and Yu-Lan now no longer went on foot. They bought a donkey, and as they did not have to barter as before, but only had to hand out money, they did their shopping very happily. They ate expensive foods and drank the best wines, and of course they bought themselves silk garments, sternly insisting that the vendors call Yu-San 'Your Excellency' and Yu-Lan 'Gracious Lady.'

"Meanwhile the grandfather stood beside the cask shoveling silver. His knees trembled, but when he wanted to rest little Yu came with his little whip and lashed his ankles. The grandfather sighed, and because it was his last sigh, he fell head over into the cask, and his legs stuck out.

"In the evening Yu-San and Yu-Lan came home on their donkey. A mountain of silver batzes lay piled in the barn, and in the cask lay the dead grandfather. Little Yu held his little whip in his hand and piped: 'I did my best, but he died for spite.'

"Yu-San took hold of the grandfather, pulled him out of the cask and laid him on the threshing floor. 'It can't be helped,' he said; 'now we'll have to buy a coffin.' 'You're wrong,' cried Yu-Lan. 'You must buy two coffins; there's another grandfather in there.' 'Oh, woe!' exclaimed Yu-San, taking the second grandfather by the collar and pulling him out.

"But the cask kept filling up again and again with dead grandfathers as quickly as Yu-San pulled them out. In the end there was a whole crowd of them, and Yu-San cried out in desepration: 'I'll pull out this one, but not another.' He had just pulled him out with a gasp when the cask broke into a thousand pieces.

"There was fearful lamentation, for Yu-San and Yu-Lan had to mourn more than a hundred dead grandfathers, and to buy more than a hundred coffins, and to find money for more than a hundred burials. Not a single silver batz was left; in fact, they had to borrow money for which their little son Yu is still earning the interest by hard labor."

"Serves him right," said Affliction joyfully.

"There was no blessing on that business," said Good Fortune. "And small wonder," he added, "when the laws of heaven and reverence for old age are disregarded."

"We'll drink one more glass and then go to sleep," said Naidang. "We must be in the saddle before sunrise."

32 OF GREAT DANGERS, AND OF NAIDANG'S WISDOM

"*Yabonah!*" cried Naidang, rising joyfully in the stirrups.

"*Sä Yabonah!*" cried Turakina. With one hand she waved good-by to the party riding off, and with the other she held back the poodle who was barking and struggling on his leash.

"I'll be back soon," Sevenstars, who was the last to leave, called to him. "Mind the sheep and the camels, don't frighten my antelopes, and watch the *yurt*. Do you hear me?"

The dog probably didn't hear everything, for by the time Sevenstars had finished her instructions Naidang was already fording the Narin Gol. The water splashed against the horses' bellies, and as it was cold they rode at a gallop up the other bank. Then they took the caravan road. The wide tire marks of the truck ran along it, and Good Fortune glanced at them from time to time, uttering a curse. Naidang cursed to keep him company, and if curses came to roost, Greencoat and Springtime Snake, wherever they were, should have dropped dead on the spot. Affliction rode silently, lost in thought. He was able to move his arm again, but Good Fortune warned him to keep his hand between the buttons of his tunic as if in a sling. Christian and Big Tiger followed, and behind them came Sevenstars.

After about a *li* a narrow path bent southward. Good Fortune spat into the last tire track, muttering more maledictions. From then onward they rode in Indian file. It was cold, and Christian and Big Tiger were freezing and missing their fur coats.

There had been frost overnight and the grass was white. A blue strip of fog lay over the ground, and the few trees showing above it looked as if floating on thin clouds. The ribbon grass, which fringed the path here and there, shone like silver, and Christian, who kept his eyes open, said to Big Tiger: "Do you notice anything?"

"What is there to notice, Kwi-Chan?"

"That our horses have got no shoes."

Big Tiger looked first at the hoof marks in the soft ground and then at the horses' hoofs, and when he saw that Christian was right, he asked Sevenstars, who was riding behind him: "Have your horses got no iron shoes?"

Sevenstars wanted to know what such things were. When told she said: "Our horses don't need such things. When they kick they can kill a person just as quickly as if they wore iron shoes."

At this answer Christian rode on ahead to call Good Fortune to explain to Sevenstars what horseshoes were for. "With us," said Good Fortune, "horses have to go over stones which would wear off their hoofs if they hadn't iron shoes to protect them, whereas with you there is only the steppe or the soft ground of the desert, and very few stones. So the horses' hoofs grow tough and don't need irons."

"Our horses need nothing at all," said Sevenstars proudly.

"And you give them nothing either," retorted Good Fortune reproachfully, "not even a stable. Your horses stay out in the heat of summer and the snowstorms of winter. The icicles hang from their manes and bellies, and jingle like caravan bells. What amazes me is that your horses survive the winter at all."

"They don't all survive it," replied Sevenstars. "Half the foals die every year."

"Are you surprised at that, considering the treatment they get?" cried Good Fortune.

"But we don't treat them at all," said Sevenstars, offended; "they die because the weaker must die. That's all there is to it."

"And when there's snow," asked Christian, "how do they get food?"

"Our horses are smart," said Sevenstars; "they paw the snow away until they find something to eat."

Christian continued his questioning: "But if the snow is very deep?"

"Well, then they have to wait until it melts. But there aren't any heavy snowfalls. I've never yet seen deep snow on the Narin Gol," said Sevenstars.

"But I've seen many starved horses," muttered Good Fortune, riding on ahead again.

Shortly afterwards they halted at a copse by a little pond. A cloud of small brown birds whirled up, circled once more over the trees, and flew northwards.

"Woodcocks," said Good Fortune. "Yesterday they hadn't arrived yet. Spring has come!"

Naidang dismounted and disappeared into the bushes, returning with two spades. "You'll pardon us," he said to Affliction. "Good Fortune and I went to Ollon Torre yesterday to pack up and hide away the blue tent in case someone should think it belonged to nobody. For there are people," he continued, "who get such ideas."

"Ten thousand thanks," said Affliction.

"We took the two spades and hid them here, for we need them today. You'll have them back tomorrow." Wrapping the two spades in a piece of blue canvas, Naidang tied them to the front of his saddle, and they rode on.

After an hour the sun got warm and Christian and Big Tiger no longer felt frozen with cold. Sevenstars pointed westward with her whip. "The Dondur Gol," she said, indicating a second row of trees, which formed a sharp angle where they joined those fringing the Narin Gol.

Shortly afterwards Naidang left the caravan road and turned again toward the Narin Gol. He insisted they should now all ride in single file. "For no one is to know," he explained, "how many riders passed this way."

The trees by the river's brink became fewer, and presently there were bushes instead, and sand too, and little undulations of the ground. The distant Narin Gol could be seen glittering in the morning sun. Nobody thought the fording would offer any difficulty; you just rode through the water and were across—or that's what it looked like until they came to the bank. Then they noticed that there was a strong current, and that the earth of the steep, corroded banks gave way under the horses' hoofs.

Naidang had to use his whip to force his unwilling horse on to the other bank, and no sooner were its forefeet on the crumbling slope than there was a frightful commotion. A wild black beast with hanging tongue shot past the waiting riders and sprang with a joyful howl half on to Naidang's crupper, and then with one leap into the water.

"Dog!" shouted Sevenstars fiercely, but it was too late. Naidang's roan horse bucked, throwing its unsuspecting rider into the Narin Gol. Sevenstars screamed. Good Fortune leaped from his saddle and ran to the bank as Naidang stood up, dripping like an angry sea-god, up to his waist in water. The poodle scrambled out, shaking himself, and celebrated the reunion with much barking and tail-wagging.

"Dog!" shouted Naidang angrily, reaching for his whip about to float downstream, together with his fur hat. "And you're a dog too!" he cried to his roan steed, which had followed him out of the water.

"Father!" wailed Sevenstars. "Are you alive?"

"I'm alive all right," answered Naidang, "but I've got a shaking. Come on," he said, and grasped the reins of Good Fortune's horse.

"Let me mount first," said Good Fortune. He jumped on quickly and Naidang led the horse across the river. The others followed without incident.

"I knew," sighed Affliction, "that I should have stayed at home." But nobody listened to him. They all dismounted and Good Fortune got busy. "Take off your coat," he said to Sevenstars.

"No, I'll take mine off," cried Affliction.

"Very well, both of you," said Good Fortune. He helped Naidang, who was chilled through, out of his wet clothes, and wrapped him in the two dry coats. Christian and Big Tiger ran to fetch wood, and when they got back Good Fortune had already got a fire going on the narrow riverbank. "More wood," he ordered. "I must have good big logs."

Christian and Big Tiger dragged over big branches; Affliction helped them, and Sevenstars stood with the horses. The poodle sat beside her looking on. For the first time the round black eyes, which never left Sevenstars, could be seen under the long wet locks. "Dog!" she scolded him. "I ordered you to mind the sheep, but you have disobeyed me. You are a bad dog!"

The poodle bent his head guiltily, but not for long. He was far too pleased to have found Sevenstars again, wagged his tail joyfully, and even tried to bark, though somewhat awed by Naidang's presence.

Meantime Naidang sat on the ground, icy cold. Good Fortune emptied the water out of his boots, hung his wet clothes on branches around the fire to dry, taking care not to let them singe. He was in excellent spirits. After a while, however, he felt that something was missing, and tried hard to remember what it was. Naidang's clothes will be dry in an hour, he thought, and then we can ride on to the Black City, and then . . . Suddenly the missing object came to his mind. He felt dazed with shock and had to sit down.

"What's wrong with you?" asked Naidang, his teeth chattering.

"The spades," groaned Good Fortune. "The spades are gone!"

"And my fur hat too," said Naidang. "It sank where the water is deepest. And it wasn't old at all; in fact, it was almost new."

But Good Fortune had no ears for either comfort or sympathy. He put his head in his hands and almost wept. Christian and Big Tiger, who were dragging another branch out of the bushes, stood and stared in astonishment, and so did Affliction. "Has something else happened?" asked Affliction gasping.

"Nothing new," said Naidang. "The spades are gone, but we've only noticed it now."

"If that's all that's wrong . . ." cried Christian.

"Nothing except my fur hat—that's gone too," said Naidang.

"The hat sank," said Christian. "It can't be helped. But I'll fetch the spades." Saying this, he pulled off his jacket and shirt.

"What are you doing?" cried Naidang in alarm. "I tell you the spades are lying under the water."

"That's just it," said Christian, taking off his shoes.

Good Fortune raised his head, but already Christian had taken off his pants and everything else, and gone into the river.

"The poor boy!" cried Affliction. "He's lost his senses!"

"He's all right," said Big Tiger. "He can swim; you needn't be a bit frightened about him."

"Kwi-Chan!" cried Sevenstars entreatingly, "you'll die; you're not a fish!"

Good Fortune jumped up, but Big Tiger held him back. The honored gentleman, he said, need not be in the least uneasy. There are people who can swim, he assured him, and Compass Mountain was one of these.

Meanwhile Christian made straight for the scene of the accident. The water was bitterly cold and muddy. The bottom of the river couldn't be seen, and Christian had to search with his feet for the spades. As he drew near to the western bank the current became stronger. The water came up to his waist, and was terribly cold. He had great trouble to keep from being swept away. I'll have to turn back, he thought, I must certainly turn back. I can't feel any longer what I'm stepping on. But at that moment his big toe caught in a string, and the string belonged to the blue canvas in which the spades were wrapped.

Christian dived immediately. It all happened so quickly that he didn't hear the yell that rose from the other bank. They all cried out—Naidang, Good Fortune and Big Tiger, and loudest of all Affliction, who in his excitement pulled his injured arm out of his tunic. Sevenstars held her hands before her face and broke into heartrending sobs. The poodle, who had followed Christian to the riverbank, stood still and began to bark.

He was still barking when Christian surfaced, several yards downstream, for the current had carried both himself and the bundle of spades quite a bit on. When he got back to the middle of the river, half stumbling and half swimming, he stood up. He staggered with exhaustion, took one step, a second one, then no more. . . . Suddenly he felt himself dragged up. As though in a dream he could hear the joyous barking of the poodle, but he only really came to when he was lying by the campfire and felt Good Fortune's strong hands rubbing him vigorously with a shirt. He soon recovered fully. Sevenstars was there too. She had simply left the horses to themselves when she saw Good Fortune rushing to Christian's assistance as he collapsed.

"You gave me a terrible fright," said Sevenstars. "You did something one should not do." She knelt by Christian feeling if there was still life in him, her frightened eyes full of tears.

"Go get my saddle bag!" ordered Naidang. "I've just thought of something."

"Quick, quick!" cried Good Fortune. He had noticed Naidang filling a bottle from the goatskin before they started.

When Sevenstars came back with the saddle bag, Naidang took out the bottle. Then he looked around for his hat, forgetting he had lost it. "Oh, woe!" he cried, scratching his bald pate, "a man can't drink bare-headed!"

But there was Big Tiger kneeling before him, with a *haddak* spread out on his hands, and on the *haddak* lay his own fur cap.

"Do me the honor," said Big Tiger politely, "to accept this poor worn fur cap, for I have no better." Naidang protested to the extent prescribed by good manners, but then accepted the gift with thanks. The cap fitted him splendidly, and now he was able to hand out the drinks. The *arrak* revived their drooping spirits, the sun got warmer, and the fire dried Naidang's clothes and Good Fortune's pants.

"That dog is a rascal," scolded Naidang. "Where is he now?"

"It seems to me he's a real unlucky dog," remarked Affliction.

"It's all been his fault," agreed Naidang. "He's only a trouble-maker."

Sevenstars wanted to contradict them, and Christian was about to say: "He's a most well-bred dog," but he hadn't time. There was the sound of fierce barking, of a man's voice, and the crack of a whip. They could hear a crunching as of bones being splintered, and then the poodle's raging attack again.

"Dog!" cried Sevenstars, running in the direction from which came the sounds of strife. "Dog! Come here!" But this time the poodle didn't come.

Big Tiger followed Sevenstars, while Christian hurriedly pulled on his clothes.

Immediately beyond the thicket which bordered the riverbank

there was a depression, which was probably flooded at times of high water. Reeds and sedges grew in it, and the horses had dispersed over it and were eating what they could find. Behind this hollow there was a longish hill with a clump of trees on top. It was from there that the noise of battle resounded.

When Sevenstars arrived panting at the foot of the hill, still calling "Dog, dog, come here!" she saw a man in the red robe of a lama. He leaned against a tree for support, defending himself with kicks against the poodle's attack. Some ten yards off stood a saddled horse with a light-colored tail and mane. It was tied to a tree and was pulling excitedly at its rope.

"Dog! Come here!" cried Sevenstars once more. At last the poodle left his enemy and came, exhausted and bleeding, to her feet. "Poor, silly dog!" she said. She looked up at the tree against which the man had been standing, but he was there no longer. He had run to his horse, untied it, mounted, and was riding away full tilt, beating the animal with his fist.

"Hey, you!" cried Sevenstars. "Why are you riding away?" But she got no answer. The man rode down the other side of the hill, the trot turned into a gallop, and it was all Sevenstars could do to hold back the poodle, who wanted to rush after his enemy. "Be good," she warned him, "you have done enough mischief."

Sevenstars and Big Tiger climbed to the top of the hill. Under the tree against which the man had leaned to protect his back lay a broken whip. The poodle had bitten it right through. When Big Tiger picked it up, he saw that the handle was finished with a silver disk. At first sight it looked like a coin, but it had no date and no written characters, nor was there a dragon on it. Instead there was a snake with open jaws, its forked tongue sticking out. In the bared upper jaw the poisonous teeth showed like needle points.

"What's wrong with you?" asked Sevenstars.

"I want to get off the leather loop, but I can't."

"You look pale—let me try."

"I'll manage," replied Big Tiger, hiding the handle in his hand. Then, when Sevenstars turned away, he took out General Wu's penknife, cut off a bit of the bamboo handle together with the silver-trimmed end and the thong, and hid them away.

"There's something strange here," cried Sevenstars. "Something to think about. Come and see!"

"I'm coming. What have we to think about?"

"That man. He's not a Torgut Mongol."

"How do you know that," asked Big Tiger.

"I know, for I know all the Torgut Mongols, at least all of them around these parts. Look here!"

"What am I to look at?" asked Big Tiger, and he looked down at the ground, because Sevenstars also was looking at the ground.

"He's ridden back to where he came from," Sevenstars explained.

"Then he's gone home again," decided Big Tiger, "and he didn't want to make our acquaintance first."

"Haven't I told you already he doesn't come from here," cried Sevenstars impatiently, "so he can't have ridden home! You must think hard about this man."

"I shall," agreed Big Tiger, seating himself on the root of a tree. He wondered whether it would be wise to tell Sevenstars about the snake, but it struck him that he himself was wearing a snake ring on his thumb. So that wouldn't do, he thought. Then he reflected it might be best to say straight out that he thought the man was a redbeard.

"Have you finished thinking?" inquired Sevenstars.

"Yes," replied Big Tiger, but before he could say more, he was interrupted by the barking of the poodle. This time the barking was welcoming, and immediately afterwards Christian appeared between the trees. The poodle sprang up at him joyfully, and Christian pitied him for his bleeding nose and other injuries.

"I'm glad you've come," cried Sevenstars. "Big Tiger won't believe me that the man who was here just now is a bad man."

"You think he's a redbeard?" asked Christian.

"He's quite definitely a redbeard," declared Big Tiger suddenly, "but we haven't discussed that yet."

"We've said everything possible about the matter," Sevenstars protested, "but you can't say right off, 'There's been a redbeard here,' without first discussing it."

"Oh, I see," said Big Tiger, feeling the silver snake coin in his pocket. "Perhaps the man is one of those who sit at the campfires of caravans now and again, listening to hear if anyone knows anything about Shong-Ma."

"But we're not a caravan," said Sevenstars.

"May be that's why he rode away," reflected Christian.

But Sevenstars wanted no further discussion. "We've finished thinking now," she said; "let's fetch the horses."

They went down to the hollow, collected the horses, and led them to the camping place. The poodle licked his bleeding nose.

"Were there many casualties?" asked Affliction.

Sevenstars reported everything, and when she had finished Naidang wanted to know if the stranger had a gun.

"No, he didn't," said Big Tiger.

"We'll make a detour all the same," said Naidang. "For there are people who watch others, though nobody asks them to. Mount your horses, men!"

He put on his coat, though it was still quite damp, and his boots, which were even more damp. Good Fortune took the bundle of spades in front of him on his saddle.

At first they rode along the riverbank downstream for a while.

When the brushwood on the banks ceased and they had reached a strip of scant trees, Naidang said resignedly: "We are in the hands of heaven." Saying this he left the Narin Gol and the others rode after him in single file. There was no road or path anywhere.

For over an hour they rode eastward through a continuously changing landscape. But one thing was always there, and that was the sand. At one spot it would be strewn as if shaken by hand over the plain, then again it formed dunes, or lay in drifts at the foot of the yellow clay hills. There were tamarisks, and just when one thought the desert had begun and would never cease, a pair of antelopes ran through the valleys between the dunes, or a group of trees stood in a hollow between parched reeds and deresen grass.

When they saw in the distance a row of ancient poplars, spaced wide apart, Naidang turned off to the southeast. "There the Etzin Gol flowed," he said, "in the days when heaven and earth were still in harmony."

Not a word more was said, and each looked ahead eagerly, anxious to be the first to catch a glimpse of the walls of the Black City. They were no longer riding in single file. In the smoothly rising clay ground, which was furrowed in many places, the horses' hoofs left only faint marks.

Big Tiger made a sign to Christian to drop back a bit. Then he said: "I've something to show you. It belongs to the man who we think is a redbeard." He dipped into his pocket and handed Christian the silver coin with the snake on it.

"I'm frightened too," said Big Tiger when he saw that Christian bit his lips, and that his hand, which he had stretched out so confidently, was trembling. "This thing was on the handle of the whip which the poodle bit through."

"Certainly the man will come back to look for it," said Christian.

"He'll waste his time," replied Big Tiger, coolly. "Why was he so excited, and why did he ride off without greeting us? I'd have given him back the coin."

"He'll follow us," said Christian, but Big Tiger merely shrugged his shoulders as if the confederates of the Venerable Chief were nothing to worry about. "One shouldn't be frightened," he said after a while, "if darkness falls and the light fades away. We've resolved to be brave, like the old men of the mountain."

"Ah!" sighed Christian, "there are people who escape misfortune by prudence. But are we such people?"

"Naidang is one of them," asserted Big Tiger. "We must follow his example."

"Naidang? Why Naidang?"

"Didn't you notice how he acted and how he withstood temptation? He was firmer than a rock."

"I didn't notice any temptation. Was there one?"

Big Tiger urged his horse nearer to Christian's. "Is a treasure of gold and jewels, such as Prince Araptan describes, no temptation?"

"It is a temptation," Christian admitted, "but . . ." Here words failed him to express his bewilderment. So he only said: "What on earth do you mean?"

"I watched closely," explained Big Tiger. "From the moment that Good Fortune began to breathe heavily and Naidang smiled, I kept my eyes fixed on him. Naidang read only half the last page. I watched his eyes traveling along the lines, and when he stopped reading there were at least seven or eight lines left, which he didn't read. Apparently there was nothing very important on the page which the wind blew away."

"And the rest," asked Christian, "I mean the part concerning the treasure of Etzina—did Naidang throw that into the fire?"

Big Tiger nodded. "Naidang withstood temptation," he said. "He deserves the greatest respect."

Big Tiger was silent, and without a word Christian handed him back the coin with the snake. They trotted along side by side; then the horses slowed down to a walk, for the dead forest of which Naidang had spoken began. Innumerable trunks of trees lay on the ground half buried in sand, and one could scarcely make out where the roots had been and where the crowns, which had once

been full of green leaves and the twitter of birds. The naked trunks remained, their gray bark looking like stone, and they lay as they had fallen, singly or one over the other, when the parched soil no longer held them.

When the dead forest came to an end the hard clay soil became still harder, the horses' hoofs clattered, and the walls of the Black City rose before them, for all to see. The midday sun was shining warmly.

Naidang raised his whip like a lance, the horses began to gallop, and the ground quaked under their hoofs.

33 OF THE FINDING OF THE LITTLE TREASURE AND THE RETURN BY A DIFFERENT ROUTE

At a time when other races were still shooting with bows and arrows, the Chinese had discovered gunpowder. But they only used it to make fireworks and set off firecrackers with a big bang during the New Year Festival, so that the evil spirits which are everywhere would take fright and remove themselves to some other place. But there were also other means of keeping them away. For instance, it had been found out that the wicked spirits, though they are full of cunning and malice, can only walk straight ahead. Nobody had ever yet seen one of them slipping round a corner. That is why a wall used to be erected behind each gateway, at a little distance away from it, and somewhat wider than the gateway. Thus people or carts could walk or drive to the right or the left past the wall, but the evil spirits couldn't. When they wanted to enter a town they banged their noses against the wall and had to withdraw without entering. These walls were called spirit walls, and they proved quite effective. And everyone who built a house with a wall around it also made sure to build a spirit wall behind the entrance.

In Khara-khoto too the people had built spirit walls. Nobody going through the hole in the city wall where the gate once had been could see right in, for the spirit wall had remained standing. Only when one went round it did one see the great expanse of ruins. This, Good Fortune had said, was a sight to inspire terror, and Christian and Big Tiger, who had never seen a ruined town before, shivered with horror although the sun was shining. There was really nothing much to see, but it was just that which was terrifying. There was scarcely a trace of any house left. Only where the *yamen* had stood a few fragments of stone rose above the square of rubble, around which the high walls stood, desolate and solemn. Naidang dismounted. He looked at Christian and Big Tiger, but did not speak of what they were about to do. He simply said: "Let's tie the horses."

Taking a heavy stone, he tied a rope crosswise about it, and to this he fastened the horses' reins. The poodle lay down exhausted in the shade near the horses.

"Here are the spades," said Good Fortune. He too seemed afraid to speak. All had the feeling that they were about to do something wrong.

Affliction hung back with drooping head, leaning against the spirit wall. "Is that someone coming?" he asked suddenly. "Oh, it's only you," he said as Naidang slouched along in his heavy boots.

"Wouldn't it be better for us to go back home?" asked Sevenstars timidly.

"Especially since I'm with you," said Affliction.

"Silence!" said Naidang. "I won't hear of such a thing. You," he went on to Affliction, "go to the east wall, Sevenstars to the west wall, I'll remain here, and Good Fortune will go to the south wall. Get behind the parapet and watch through the loopholes. You two," he said to Christian and Big Tiger, "start work when all the guards are posted on the walls. But then be as quick as you can."

Christian took the bundle of spades under his arm. "Come," he said to Big Tiger.

"Right!" said Naidang approvingly. "Now good luck to you, and unexpected wealth!" He turned to the slope which led up to the city wall, and Sevenstars and Affliction followed him. The poodle lifted his head, but at Sevenstars' order remained with the horses.

Good Fortune turned toward the south gate. "Let me go with you," he shouted after Christian and Big Tiger, who had gone on ahead.

"Fifty-five, sixty-five," counted Big Tiger out loud, pacing with even steps. Christian counted softly with him, and Good Fortune's lips moved too. "Eighty!" Big Tiger announced, stopping and looking around him.

"That's it!" cried Good Fortune. He went down on his knees in a *kowtow,* touching the ground with his forehead three times.

"Where?" asked Christian.

"Where you're standing," answered Good Fortune.

Christian and Big Tiger bowed too, for they were standing on the remnants of a brick wall which rose two fingers high above the rubble.

"Here's where Araptan's palace stood," whispered Christian. He looked around, but the desolation was the same everywhere. At every step they came on pieces of earthenware or china. The citizens of Etzina must have had an immense lot of crockery. It looked almost as if they had had nothing but earthenware pots and china bowls. There were brown, green and painted fragments, some only baked and others beautifully glazed. But not a single pot or bowl had remained whole.

"I see the round stone," cried Big Tiger suddenly. He pointed before him, but did not wait to know if Christian and Good Fortune saw it too. He went straight up to a circle which looked as if it had been drawn with a compass in the rubble, and when he reached it he pushed aside the covering stones with his foot. Underneath was a yellow sandstone, with something engraved on it. One could see the sun horses and the tree of the universe with a stone blossom on every twig. Where the branches bent down they touched the wheel of the seasons and the raised hammers of the smiths. One saw that much and no more. But when Big Tiger bent down and brushed away the brick dust and the broken pottery, the wagoners also came into view. They carried spokes in their hands, and the frame of a wheel, which they were assembling.

"Leave that alone," said Good Fortune to Big Tiger. "This isn't the right time for looking at old stones." He glanced back. Naidang was standing high on the wall near the north gate, Sevenstars was just rounding the corner to the west wall, and Affliction was already half way to the east wall. He seemed in a hurry. Good Fortune decided to move off as well.

"We must step toward the east," said Christian.

"Twenty paces," said Big Tiger.

"Go on, you," said Christian; "you are better in pacing off."

Big Tiger stepped forward with even paces, and while doing so he kept looking up at the ramp of the east gate and counting aloud.

"Twenty!" he cried. "This is where the Little Treasure is hidden."

"I can't see anything," said Christian.

"Let's start," said Big Tiger.

"Wait," objected Christian. "First Good Fortune must be at his post."

So they waited a while longer. The sky was blue and cloudless. The broken pottery of the Black City glistened in the sun, and Good Fortune's quick footstep faded away. When he got to the south wall he waved to them, and Affliction and Sevenstars waved too. Naidang only nodded, for he was staring attentively over the dead forest as if there was something to see. Because of this Christian was not quite sure if his nod was the signal to proceed.

"Are you afraid?" asked Big Tiger.

"I'm not afraid," said Christian; "but Naidang didn't wave like the rest."

"That doesn't matter," said Big Tiger reassuringly, beginning to push the earth and the rubble aside. Then each took a spade and began prodding and digging to see if he could hit on something solid which might be a stone.

"Nothing here," said Christian.

"There must be," said Big Tiger.

"Perhaps someone has been here before us," Christian replied, throwing a swift glance toward the east gate, where Affliction stood near the loophole on the wall. But his back was turned and he didn't stir.

"Hello!" cried Big Tiger suddenly.

"Hello!" said Christian. "Have you struck something hard?"

"Yes, here it is," replied Big Tiger, and put his finger to his nose knowingly. Then both dug busily. They took off their coats, and that made things easier. At every stroke of their spades they could see a bit more of the stone slab which was as yellow as the base on which the silver fountain had once stood.

"I'd like to have seen the silver fountain," said Christian.

Big Tiger stuck his spade in the ground beside him, and Christian did the same, for now the stone slab was free. It was somewhat bigger than a large chess board, and divided into a number of squares. Eight eights, counted Christian; but before he had time to say that apparently the people of Etzina had played chess, a whistle was heard from the north wall.

"What's that?" cried Big Tiger, alarmed.

"Naidang's noticed something," said Christian.

They looked over to the north gate, where the horses stood near the spirit wall, and where Naidang stood up above, leaning against the rampart. He was looking intently toward the dead forest, and at the same time with his hand making signs to them that they should hurry.

"Perhaps someone's coming," guessed Big Tiger.

"I know who's coming," replied Christian, "and you know, too."

"Well, it can't be helped," said Big Tiger, bending down. "The fellow wants his snake coin back."

"If that's what it is, we'd better hurry," said Christian.

They raised the slab together, and then took to their spades again. On the other side of the slab there were letters engraved, but Big Tiger scarcely glanced at them, and Christian not at all. They dug as fast as they could. At first they had been careful not to scatter the earth about, but now they no longer minded. Quick, before it's too late! thought Christian. The earth flew up; it was a little damp, and here and there a bit of charcoal sparkled. Suddenly Christian's spade grated against something and glanced off a piece of gray metal. The scratched spot shone brightly.

"Number one," cried Christian, lifting a silver shoe out of the hole.

"A hundred ounces," said Big Tiger, with an expert air, weighing the lump of silver in his hand. It was shaped like a little boat, and a square sign was stamped on its center.

"Come on!" urged Christian.

One silver shoe after another came to light. When all ten were lying in a row on the edge, the hole was empty.

There was another whistle, and this time Naidang made urgent signs that they should hurry up. Christian and Big Tiger threw the earth back into the hole, covered it with the slab inscribed "The Great Treasure is near" upside down, and then, as quickly as possible, shoveled sand and rubble over it.

"Would you notice anything?" asked Christian.

Big Tiger knit his brows critically: "You'd notice that someone had been digging here," he said, "because of the fresh earth. But tomorrow it will be hardly visible, and the day after it will look like everything else."

"The day after tomorrow is far off," said Christian.

He knelt down and packed the silver bars into the blue canvas in which the spades had been wrapped before, and Big Tiger knelt beside him and tied the cord. "We can't undo what's done," he said. "Now we've to get away as fast as we can."

Christian then secured the knots as an American Marine in Peking had taught him. They hung the bundle on their spades and carried it between them.

"Hello!" shouted Christian.

"We've made it!" cried Big Tiger.

Good Fortune forthwith left his post at the south gate. He came down the ramp in big leaps, and Affliction came from the east gate. All met near the horses. The poodle leaped up, barking joyfully.

Only Naidang remained at his post on the north wall. Hidden behind a parapet, he was watching carefully, and when he saw that all were assembled he called down: "Come up to me, but don't be seen from outside."

"Is someone there?" asked Good Fortune.

Naidang frowned in perplexity. "I don't see anyone, but I notice there's someone there."

"I understand," said Good Fortune, but he had no idea what Naidang meant. While he led the way up the ramp, which formerly had steps but was now only a sandy, sloping channel, he gave directions: "Up there, creep on all fours until each of you is behind a breastwork. Then stand up. Do exactly as I do."

"Bolna!" cried Christian.

"Stay down there, dog!" Sevenstars told the poodle.

When they got up on the wall they crept along one after the

other behind the rampart like a family of bears, until each was screened by a high parapet and could stand up. Christian and Big Tiger looked out cautiously.

"Do you see anything?" asked Naidang.

"I see the hard clay ground with cracks in it, but there's nobody there. Behind it I see the dead forest with the trees lying about. But there's no one there, either."

"And you?" asked Naidang.

"I see what Compass Mountain sees, and nothing more."

"Look closely," said Naidang. "Behind the dead forest there's a hill to the east, which reaches down to the poplars, where the Etzin Gol used to flow. Can you see that?"

"I see the hill," said Big Tiger, "but it's very far away."

"There's an *obo* on the hill," said Christian.

"It's not an *obo,*" Naidang pointed out; "it's an old wall which, like everything belonging to the Black City, is a ruin. There's only a little bit of it left. It's the height of a man and twenty feet long. Keep your eyes on that wall."

"Aha!" said Good Fortune.

"I'd rather not," said Affliction.

"Is there something there?" asked Christian.

"There is, sometimes," answered Naidang, "but you have to watch very closely. There it is again," he cried, "did you see it?"

"It's a branch waving in the wind," said Good Fortune. "That's quite plain. Behind the wall there's a little tree or bush, and when a gust of wind comes . . ."

"But there isn't any wind," said Sevenstars.

"I've got it!" cried Christian.

"It's not a matter of what you've got," said Good Fortune, irritably; "it's a matter of the tree that's behind that wall."

"There's a horse behind the wall," said Christian, "and because he's impatient he's swishing his tail. And that's the thing that looks like a branch blowing in the wind."

"Compass Mountain is right," said Naidang. "There's a horse

behind the wall, and where there's a horse there must be a rider. He can't be seen, but he's there. And so we must make plans that we don't fall into the tiger's jaws."

"The horse has a light-colored tail," cried Sevenstars. "The man who hit my dog on the nose had a horse like that."

"I thought so," said Naidang, gloomily.

Good Fortune tapped his holster significantly. "The human body," he said, "has seven openings. I'll make an eighth one in that scoundrel's body!"

"No," cried Affliction, in alarm. "That won't do. We have to think of something better."

"What does Big Tiger think?" asked Naidang.

"A voluntary retreat is the saving of the noble and the confusion of the wicked."

"This time," said Good Fortune, "your grandfather's counsel isn't good enough. How can we withdraw when that bird out there has his neck stretched out toward us?"

Big Tiger pointed to the heaps of big round stones which lay at intervals behind the parapet. These were intended for the defenders of Etzina to throw down on the heads of their enemies. "Here's a stone as big as a man's head," said Big Tiger. "We'll push it into the loophole. Then it will look as if someone was watching here. And it will be a long time before the rider to whom the horse belongs notices that he's been fooled. When at last he ventures into the town we'll be gone long ago, for we'll ride out by the south gate. No one can see behind the spirit wall, and we'll withdraw peacefully and unnoticed."

"Big Tiger knows more than how to draw his breath," cried Naidang enthusiastically. "Some day his voice will be heard in the assembly of sages and his word will carry!"

"I'm only a poor ignorant boy," protested Big Tiger modestly. "It is my grandfather's knowledge which I pass on."

"You're a fine rascal," said Good Fortune benevolently, "and your grandfather's another."

"Come and mount your horses, men!" cried Naidang.

Good Fortune pushed a great stone into one of the loopholes, and one after the other they crawled along on all fours until they got to the ramp. When they got to their horses, suddenly all felt in splendid spirits. Even Affliction managed to smile.

Naidang alone stood with knit brows, glancing from the blue cloth bundle to the spades, and back again. "This won't do," he said. "We must pack up the spades and take out the silver."

"Bolna!" said Christian, and began to undo the knots. "The silver is a little gray, but that doesn't matter." And he opened up the cloth. There lay the ten silver shoes. Good Fortune took one of them and scratched it with his nail until the bright metal showed. He gave a nod of satisfaction.

"Let each of us five men hide away two silver shoes," said Naidang.

"I too?" asked Affliction.

"You're one of us," replied Naidang amiably. "Stick them into your pocket. Hurry up, hurry up!"

Thereupon each took two silver shoes, and Naidang packed the spades in the blue canvas. They then set out, Naidang leading. The horses' hoofs beat sharply on the rubble which crackled and crumbled; and the round base of the fountain, upon which smiths had wrought the wheel of the seasons, lay in its place in the sun.

"It's a pity," said Big Tiger to Christian. "I'd have liked to see the other pictures."

"So would I," said Christian, putting a hand in his pocket. "Look what I found on the city wall when we were creeping on all fours." It was a black bronze arrowhead, completely corroded like the instruments of the observatory in Peking. "Take it as a keepsake," he said.

"You give me a valuable present, and I've nothing to give in return," said Big Tiger. "But wait a moment," he added, remembering the silver coin with the snake on it. "I have this, but it's not a real present, as it doesn't belong to me."

"Never mind," Christian comforted him. "Now each of us has a snake which doesn't belong to him; and I'm curious to know what will come of it."

During this conversation they had got to the former center of the city, where there was a high hill of rubble and some remains of walls. The *yamen* had stood here, Naidang said, but even that wasn't certain. They were nearing the south gate, and as they rounded the spirit wall Christian cast a last glance back at the tragic Black City which was no longer a city. The horses trotted out the gateway and for a time not a hoof beat could be heard, for the sand stood high in drifts and the horses had difficulty wading through it.

Scarcely twenty paces from the city gate a camel path led from east to west or west to east, depending on which way one wished to go. Naidang took the path going west, which ran alongside the city walls. Here the storms of centuries had piled up vast masses of sand against the walls. The projecting bastions were buried in sand up to their pinnacles, and only the battlement showed. At the southwest corner, perched high on the round tower, stood a Mongol *chorten*.* This was the last distinguishable feature of the dead city.

The hard, yellow, cracked clay soil spread before them, and it was impossible to imagine that luxurious gardens surrounded by bamboo hedges and flowering shrubs had once stood here. Instead of blooming apricot trees there were now tamarisks with gnawed barks, and deep sand covered the fertile soil. The path led through a labyrinth of hills, which to Naidang's satisfaction completely hid the group of riders. Naidang urged his horse to a smart trot. It was evident that he was anxious to get away from the Black City as quickly as possible. The sun was warm, Naidang's wet coat was steaming, and the poodle's tongue was hanging out.

* *Chorten:* A Mongolian or Tibetan shrine, usually built over the bones of a holy man.

After two hours the route led them over a brook. There were trees again, and grass, and wooded hills. One might have imagined that they were real woods if the sea of sand behind them had not been so yellow and so endless.

Between the hills a river glistened. The horses slowed to a walk, their hoofs clattering over round stones or pounding on moist sand. And then the party found themselves before the broad bed of the Ikhe Gol. The horses immediately pressed forward toward the water, but Naidang called out: "Ride on! They must not drink yet."

Holding a tight rein he urged his own roan into the water, which was rushing northward with a strong current, scarcely a foot deep. From the middle onward it got deeper, but it was not until they neared the other bank that the water reached to the animals' bellies. The riders drew up their knees, the poodle swam, and the river was crossed. Once more smooth round stones and sand covered the ground, and the camel track, which Naidang had been following previously, ran westward, well trodden out.

"That's the way to Sinkiang," said Naidang, lifting his right arm like a signpost.

"I know," muttered Good Fortune. "If you'll excuse me, I'd like to examine it a bit."

"That's not necessary," cried Naidang; "the old märin will be able to tell us."

He turned his horse and rode northward down-river without waiting for an answer from Good Fortune. Their path led through high deresen grass and scrub. The Ikhe Gol curved round at this point and disappeared from view, but its farther course could be traced by the fringe of trees. A pleasant stretch of low flat country opened up between two ranges of hills, and in the middle of it stood a new white felt tent. A faint curl of smoke rose from the smoke vent and circled in the warm air.

"The old man is at home," murmured Naidang, well pleased.

He halted under a stout poplar, took the empty bottle from the saddle bag and stuck it in his belt. "Give me the silver bars," he said; "we'll put them into the saddle bag now. It is for the sake of the truth," he added smiling, "which I must make pleasant for the old märin. But please do not think me a liar for that reason."

They all protested they would not, and Good Fortune asked Naidang how he could think such a thing of them. "The truth needs to be helped on to its feet; everyone knows that," he added.

"But there are people," warned Affliction, "who notice when you're helping it."

"I would have you know," said Good Fortune sternly, "that our respected elder, Naidang, is an unrivaled master of the ten thousand rules in this respect."

Affliction apologized, and Naidang packed the silver shoes into the leather bag. Then, standing up in the stirrups, he pushed the blue bundle of spades into the lower branches of the poplar. Having done these things he became gay.

"Yabonah!" he cried, and they rode at a headlong gallop up to the *yurt*. As they dismounted a thin naked arm raised the entrance curtain. Then a dark red Tibetan wool vest appeared. Fine gold lace trimmed the upright collar from which a long neck emerged. It sat firmly on bony shoulders, supporting a face whose eyes were keen and bright. The old man wore a black Chinese cap and an equally black shining pigtail. Long white sheepskin trousers and plaited straw shoes completed the old märin's attire.

"The pigtail is false," whispered Naidang with a confidential grin. He threw the reins to Sevenstars and went forward with a smile to meet the old märin. "Is your rest easy and good?" he called out.

"Oh, Picture Sheet!" said the märin, his face alight with joy. "Have you had an easy journey?"

"Easy and good," lied Naidang. "We come direct from home."

"Indeed?" said the märin skeptically. "It doesn't look much like it." And he pointed to the poodle which was shaking the water out of its long coat.

"That dog is different from others," Naidang explained. "His thick coat holds water half a day."

"That is unhealthy," said the märin, observing the poodle sharply.

"That's true," admitted Naidang. "He often coughs, especially at night."

They then exchanged snuff bottles, after which Naidang introduced his guests one by one. "You may speak to the märin in your native language," said Naidang to Christian and Big Tiger. "He comes from the land of the Tchachar Mongols. In the old days, when the Empress sat on the Dragon's throne, he was responsible for five hundred horses of the imperial herds. In those days he often went to Peking."

"We have just come from Peking," said Big Tiger, bowing.

"But we're here now," said Christian, also bowing.

The märin seemed pleased. His wrinkled face was like old leather, and he had a roguish twinkle in his eyes. His aquiline nose was in striking contrast to his high Mongolian cheekbones. But for them he would have looked like an old Red Indian chieftain. "Come in!" he cried encouragingly. "It's warm in here."

He helped Sevenstars to tie up the horses, and was the last to enter the *yurt*. A bright wood fire was blazing, the tea kettle was singing, and the right number of cushion seats lay ready, as if the märin had expected the visitors.

"Did you see us coming?" Naidang asked uneasily.

"I heard the horses and then I saw you," the märin admitted, filling the tea bowls.

"Naidang has told me about you," began Good Fortune, "and about the wide and varied experience which adorns your great age. I begged him to make us acquainted."

"Picture Sheet exaggerates," murmured the märin politely; "I am only an ignorant clown."

"As for me," said Affliction, "I was only riding along with the others; please excuse my presence."

"I welcome every honorable man," cried the märin.

"Speaking of honorable men," began Naidang, "I want to ask you something."

"If you wish to ask me about Greencoat, he was with me the day before yesterday."

"It is not without reason that all marvel at your wisdom," cried Naidang. "That's the very man we're looking for."

"He was attacked by a murderous gang," reported the märin darkly.

"How terrible!" said Naidang, grinning.

"Oh, the scoundrel!" roared Good Fortune. "He's a ruffian, and his father was one before him!"

"See these two young princes," said Naidang. "Do they look like members of a murder gang?"

"We were speaking of honorable people," said the märin seriously. "Let us therefore investigate how the matter really stands."

"The matter stands this way," cried Good Fortune angrily, "namely, that Greencoat is a criminal who should be brought before the magistrate."

"He's on his way to the magistrate," answered the märin, "to lodge a complaint as quickly as possible." Saying this, he gave

Good Fortune a searching look, and Good Fortune immediately began fidgeting on his seat.

"Is your seat not comfortable?" asked the märin.

"It is perfect," muttered Good Fortune.

"Speak!" requested Naidang, taking his pipe from his boot. "Tell us what you know. Then we will tell you our story."

"The day before yesterday, toward midday," began the märin, "I heard a thunder without beginning or end. It quickly came nearer, and then I knew it was one of those roaring horseless cars. The thunder stopped suddenly behind the hill and soon afterwards Greencoat came running. "I've come to warn you," he said, "that a notorious robber and murderer has arrived at Ollon Torre. His name is Good Fortune."

The märin paused and everyone looked at Good Fortune. He had pulled himself together, however, and was sitting quietly on his cushion, and the battery of eyes did not upset him. "It is the way of criminals," he said, contemptuously, "to accuse other people of their own crimes."

"Well said," cried Naidang. "That's just so." And he lit his pipe contentedly.

"I asked Greencoat," continued the märin, "whether something had happened, and he said: 'Yes, something *has* happened. I bought myself a horseless car with which I intend going on the Silk Road to liven up my trade. I had been traveling many days and came at night to the Goitzin Gol. There was a tent there, and in the tent were two of General Feng's soldiers, and the deserted soldier Good Fortune, who is a notorious redbeard. Two boys, one of them a foreign devil from beyond the seas, were also there. The whole thing looked very suspicious to me, but Good Fortune told me he had rescued the youngsters from a robber band and was now taking them home to their parents. I accepted his story,' said Greencoat, 'though I didn't believe a word of it. I then asked the soldiers to sell me some gasoline.' 'We can't do that,' said one of them, whose name was Springtime Snake. 'The General has forbidden us.' 'Come now,' said the other. 'Our General won't miss a few cans.' He demanded an outrageous price, but I paid it.

"The rascals knew then that I had money with me and decided to kill me. The honest soldier Springtime Snake was horrified, but what could he do? While I was asleep the children, who are practiced thieves, stole my pistol and all the cartridges I had. Then the criminals wanted to murder me, but as Springtime Snake wouldn't have any traffic with them, they began quarreling among themselves, and I woke up. There was a fearful struggle. I fought my way out like a tiger. The accursed kids bit me, and if Springtime Snake hadn't taken sides with me, I would have come to a frightful end. But I just managed to escape, and now I'm on my way to Suchow to notify the magistrate, so that he'll send police and soldiers to liquidate that nest of robbers.'

"Greencoat then bade me good-by, saying: 'I'd advise you, old märin, to leave at once and hide until the rascals are shot. As your friend I warn you.' 'Thank you for the news,' I said. 'I'll follow your advice.' "

"And you've stayed here all the same?" asked Naidang. "How's that?"

"I wanted to make the acquaintance of the robbers and murderers," replied the märin smiling.

"They're all here," Naidang assured him. "You should really be trembling."

"I am indeed trembling," asserted the märin. "Permit me to strengthen myself."

He put a little copper can of *arrak* to warm on the hot embers, and while the glasses went round, Naidang told what had happened in Ollon Torre.

The märin wagged his head thoughtfully and his pigtail swung to and fro. "This is a pressing matter," he said. "Let me think. In seven days"—and he ticked them off on his fingers—"the soldiers from the *yamen* may be here."

"And two days have passed already," Naidang reminded him.

"So only five are left," said the märin. "Probably the soldiers will need longer, but we can't count on that. Greencoat is a friend of the chief magistrate in Suchow, so it will be easy for him to get his story accepted and have soldiers sent out at once."

"Will they really shoot us?" asked Christian.

"Heaven only knows," replied the märin. "We're living in queer times, and the good old days are gone. I'd advise you to get away quickly."

"I've been thinking that too," said Naidang. "My friends have no mounts and no provisions. So I searched some old chests, and found ten silver shoes which I had completely forgotten about."

"It's easy to forget such things," said the märin seriously. He carefully scrutinized the silver which Naidang was unpacking, scratching and biting it here and there. "It is good," he said. "I can't read the stamp, but it is pure silver. I'll give you its weight in current silver coinage. Isn't that what you want?"

"That's rather little for it," said Naidang. "Don't you think so yourself?"

"I'm a poor man," sighed the märin, locking up the silver shoes in his chest. "I confess that if we had more time a higher price could be obtained, but the matter is urgent. The Chinese money-changer on the Morin Gol won't give me one batz more than the usual rate of exchange. Haven't you said yourself that you must hurry? So accept it."

"I won't bargain with you," said Naidang magnanimously. "Have you got scales?"

"What on earth are you saying? I've never used scales in all my life. I'm not one of the people who forget the silver bars they've got in their chests, and then don't even know their weight."

"There are a thousand ounces in all," muttered Naidang. "I only wanted you to make sure for yourself."

"Your word is enough for me," said the märin solemnly. "I'll bring you the batzes tomorrow."

"There's another trifling matter," said Naidang.

"The trifling matter is silence. Don't worry about that."

"*Bolna!*" cried Naidang, relieved. "Then there's nothing more to discuss. Our business is done, and we're off."

"Why hurry?" cried the märin. "Let's drink another glass in peace." He filled the glasses, and when he came to Big Tiger the märin lent him his black cap; "for," said he, "wine must be approached with reverence. What have you done with your cap?"

"Big Tiger gave me his cap because my hat fell into the Dondur Gol and sank," explained Naidang.

"Things," said the märin, "cannot always remain where they should. I have a hat which never fitted me properly, because my plait is so thick. Perhaps it would suit you?"

He opened the chest again and took out a magnificent Mongolian fur hat, which he offered to Big Tiger on a *haddak*.

"Ten thousand thanks," said Big Tiger. "I am unworthy of your generous gift. But the hat *does* fit me."

"Bravo!" cried the märin. "You are a master of correct behavior." He gleefully filled a glass for himself, then reached down nimbly behind the chest and produced a stringed instrument. It looked like a small wooden drum with a long bridge, over which two strings were stretched.

"Oh, märin," begged Naidang, who had quite forgotten that it was time to go, "please sing us the song about Chussera."

The märin screwed up his eyes. "But that's a sorrowful song, old Picture Sheet," he said. He took up the bow; he himself was the first whose eyes filled with tears when the melancholy cadences had barely begun. In spite of this he sang very loudly. Christian and Big Tiger could only understand an occasional word about the beautiful grass and the *yurt,* but when the song came to an end they said: "It was as beautiful as the violin playing of the Yellow Emperor, and more so."

The märin nodded, pleased with the flattery, but suddenly he stood up. "It seems to me there's somebody around the tent who shouldn't be," he said. "Will you excuse me?" He slipped out of

the tent so quickly that even Naidang did not at once grasp what he meant. But then a nasty suspicion occurred to him, and he ran quickly after the märin. The others followed on his heels.

"No trace of anything," said the märin, emerging from behind the *yurt*, "though I could have sworn . . . but of course it's easy to be mistaken."

"What could you have sworn?" asked Good Fortune.

"That someone was creeping about. Just as I picked up the violin I heard a noise, but I thought it was your dog."

"Our dog would have torn any stranger to shreds," Naidang assured him. "He's a dog of the highest breeding and worth a whole pack."

"Dog," cried Sevenstars, "come here!"

"He's gone," said Christian; "there's no sign of him."

"Perhaps he suddenly got thirsty and ran down to the river," said Big Tiger.

"He never does that," Sevenstars objected. "It must be something else. Dog! Come here!" But she called in vain.

Naidang went and untied the horses. "We must go," he said angrily, "whatever becomes of that confounded dog. Didn't I say he was no good?"

"He's a real unlucky dog," agreed Affliction.

"Father," pleaded Sevenstars, "let me stay here and wait for the dog."

"You may remain two hours," said Naidang, "but you must set out then to be home before dark."

"Please, may we stay too?" asked Christian and Big Tiger.

"Very well," said Naidang. Then, while the old märin was looking around once more behind the *yurt,* he took them aside. "From here we ride straight down-river," he whispered; "otherwise the old man will suspect something. And you must pick up the spades, but don't be seen doing it."

"We're accustomed to doing things without being seen," said Christian.

"Don't worry," said Big Tiger. "We'll think of a good explanation."

"*Yabonah!*" cried Naidang. "Hi, märin! We're off! I have to go home to the herds."

"May your road be easy and good!" cried the märin, slouching quickly along in his straw shoes. "All the same," he said to Naidang under his breath, "I think there's been someone here. There's a spot behind the *yurt* which looks as if someone had been kneeling there."

"Watch the silver," warned Naidang as he mounted. "There are some queer birds knocking around these times."

Good Fortune and Affliction mounted too, and Good Fortune said: "We live in an unworthy age, and there are people who go prowling about."

"Don't be uneasy about me," said the märin. "No one has ever harmed me yet."

"*Sä Yabonah!*" cried Big Tiger, Christian and Sevenstars.

The märin looked hard after the riders. "Simple old Picture Sheet!" he murmured. "Come on, children," he added aloud, sitting down in the sun in front of the *yurt*. "Let's find out where your dog can be. Sit down."

"How could we venture to seat ourselves in your presence?" asked Big Tiger.

"We would not dare," murmured Christian.

Saying these polite words, they bowed and sat down beside the märin. Sevenstars sat opposite them.

"Your good manners warm a man's heart," said the märin. "They remind me of the good old days, before the order of the world was disturbed. But I notice something which I don't like." He pointed to the ring on Big Tiger's thumb, and Big Tiger got red, for he had a foreboding that the wily old märin knew the snake and its meaning. While he was seeking in vain for an explanation, Christian came to his aid.

"That ring—" said Christian very slowly. "Do you mean the ring on Big Tiger's thumb, or is it something else?"

"His grandfather gave it to him," put in the unsuspecting Sevenstars. "Good Fortune said so, and he also said it's a lucky ring."

"Oh, indeed?" said the märin, with the suspicion of a wink. "If Good Fortune said so it must be true. But come, children, let us not forget the dog." Saying this, he took from his belt pouch nine old copper coins of the Ming dynasty.

Sevenstars was highly delighted. "He's going to throw the nine coins," she whispered. "He's consulting the oracle. Then we'll find the dog."

"*Tinger metne,*" said the märin, thoughtfully polishing one of the coins on the stone of the threshold. Then he shook the coins in his cupped hands, breathed on them, and shook again. He seemed to be murmuring an incantation. He shook once more, then spread the coins out on his right palm, one after another, where they lay black or white, as the märin said, on the right or wrong side. The polished coin came second.

Sevenstars was greatly excited. She didn't venture a question, however, but looked timidly up at the märin, as if she could read good or bad news from his face. But that was quite impossible, for the old man, being an experienced reader of omens, was utterly impassive. "Your dog has gone over the mountain," he said, casually, "for he smelled a wolf; but nothing has happened to him. You'll find him again at the hour of the ape.*"

Sevenstars bowed profoundly. "That's splendid! Many, many thanks!" she cried. She looked up at the sun and immediately wanted to dash off. "It's the hour of the ape already," she said.

"Stay a bit longer," said the märin. "There's no hurry. The dog is waiting for you."

But Sevenstars begged the märin to permit her to go. She ran straight to the horses and untied them. Big Tiger and Christian wanted to help her, but the märin held them back. "My child," he said in a low voice to Big Tiger, "I've never seen your ring before, but I know the snake and I know what it means. Allow me to ask where you got the ring?"

"The holy man Yolros Lama gave it to me, saying that it would bring me help in time of need."

The märin breathed a sigh of relief. "I was in great anxiety," he said, "but now I know all is well. Go your way in peace, my child, and you too." Then, to their great surprise, he embraced Big Tiger and Christian. This had never happened to them before. When they had mounted Christian said casually: "We'll ride around by the hill to look for the dog."

"That's right," replied the märin amiably; "and don't forget to take down the long thing that friend Picture Sheet stuck up in the poplar."

"We won't forget," said Christian, thoroughly flabbergasted. "Good-by!"

"*Sä Yabonah!*" cried the märin. He seemed to want to say something else, but instead turned back to the *yurt*. It was new and white, showing the comfortable circumstances of its owner.

When they were out of hearing and the horses were trotting along briskly after their long rest, Big Tiger said, shaking his head: "It can't be helped. Secret things are open to that old märin."

* 3-5 P.M.

They halted under the poplars, and Christian stood up in his stirrups and pulled the bundle of spades out of the branches. He then tied them to his saddle.

The märin's white *yurt* disappeared from view, and the horses trotted through the high deresen grass. Not far from the ford through which they had come Sevenstars turned to the west. Soon the grass ceased, the scrub receded, and a long succession of dunes, with overhanging ridges, spread out along the route. Suddenly right before them they saw what Sevenstars had been looking for. Along by the verge of grass, just where the last traces of herbage struggled with the sand, and green spikes of reed stood out of the ground as if they had been stuck in there, ran two wheel tracks. They were wide, and in places the tread of the tires could be seen.

"This is the shortest way to Ollon Torre," said Sevenstars, pointing.

"Greencoat drove this way," said Christian.

"Where's the dog?" asked Big Tiger.

"There's the hill we could see from the märin's *yurt*," cried Sevenstars. "My dog is there."

"*Tinger metne,*" said Christian doubtfully.

"No!" cried Sevenstars indignantly. "The old märin said, 'The dog is there,' so it *is* there."

"I didn't mean to make you mad," said Christian apologetically. Then they followed the wheel tracks at a smart trot. When, well ahead, the trees fringing the Ikhe Gol reappeared, Christian detected a dark spot between the wheel treads. Big Tiger saw it too, and Sevenstars began calling: "Dog! Dog! Come here!"

But the black dot didn't move. Instead it began to bark.

"There he is!" cried Sevenstars joyfully. "He must have killed the wolf!"

"Then it must have been a very young wolf," said Big Tiger.

Sevenstars threw him an angry glance and rode faster. As they got nearer they saw that the poodle was standing over a gray heap of fur, and they could hear him barking. At last he grasped the lifeless thing in his teeth and dragged it busily toward the riders.

"He's killed the wolf," cried Sevenstars proudly, "and now he's bringing it along."

"The wolf has a string round its body," said Big Tiger.

"It's a sheepskin he's carrying," said Christian.

Sevenstars didn't answer, for the heap of fur was lying there, and they could see now what it was. The poodle stood beside it, barking joyfully. Then he tugged again at the rolled-up sheepskin which was tied around with a string. Someone must have lost the fur.

"It's my coat," said Christian, dismounting.

"Greencoat lost it," said Big Tiger. "The string broke, so the bundle fell from the truck."

"The dog knew by the smell that it was your coat," said Sevenstars to Christian, "that's why he waited here. He's no ordinary dog. He looks for things even before one says, 'Lost—seek!'"

"Nothing escapes him," applauded Christian.

"But what about the wolf?" asked Big Tiger.

Sevenstars thought a little and then said: "Come!" She followed the tracks of the poodle for about a hundred paces, until a second trail of pad marks, scarcely visible, branched off from it. "The wolf went this way," Sevenstars explained, "and from here the dog saw the coat, so he ran to it, because the traces of the wolf are old. My dog is clever."

"He's an extraordinary dog," admitted Big Tiger; and Sevenstars was pleased.

As the moon rose in the east pouring a gentle light over the grass and bushes and all the foliage, the tardy travelers reached the Narin Gol. Naidang was waiting for them on the riverbank.

"There's news," he said.

"Good or bad?" Sevenstars asked him.

"It's not good," said Naidang. The poodle barked joyfully on seeing him again.

34 WHAT HAD HAPPENED TO TURAKINA, AND GOOD FORTUNE'S LONG SPEECH

GOOD FORTUNE and Affliction sat in the *yurt* eating the food which Turakina had prepared for them, and Christian, Big Tiger and Sevenstars were there too. They were waiting for Naidang to tell the news, but he was silent.

Turakina was crouched in the half-dark near the door, and she didn't even ask: "Have you had a good journey?" She hung her head as if she had done something wrong. Yet everything was in order. The sheep were in the fold, the camels and the cows were tied up, the fire was burning, and the food had not been burnt.

But there was a strange brown horse, with a light-colored tail and mane, tied to the line between the rust-red trees. Christian and Big Tiger had noticed it at once, and Sevenstars was quite alarmed. And Turakina's horse, on which she had come, was missing. "It's always like that," said Affliction gloomily. "Wherever I am something bad happens. Either the pole star is seen at midday or the sun shines at midnight."

"Nothing bad has happened," Naidang reported. "It's true, I fell into the water because the dog ran away from Turakina, but on the other hand she has got a splendid horse in place of an inferior one."

"How did that happen?" asked Sevenstars, looking at Turakina, who began to cry.

"Oh, please don't cry," murmured Good Fortune. "It can't be as bad as that."

"Tell us, so that we may know just as if we had been here ourselves," ordered Naidang.

"It wasn't my fault," sobbed Turakina.

"Nobody said it was," said Naidang. But this didn't comfort Turakina.

"This is—is," she began to stammer, "how it was. If you had come a few minutes sooner you would have seen the lama, too.

Although his horse was almost exhausted, he rode up at a gallop. When he leaped from the saddle he threw the reins in my face, shouting, 'There!' I wanted to run away, but I couldn't, for he gave me such a look that I could only stop where I was. He was like a dried-up tree with a brown bark, and his beard was waving in the wind. His eyes were restless and glittered queerly. He took the bridle and saddle off his stallion and ordered me to put them on my horse. While I was doing this he talked to his horse as if it were a human being. Then he tied him to the line. 'Are you ready?' he shouted, and I answered: 'Yes, Sir!' 'Your horse is no good,' he shouted, 'I don't think you'll see it alive again. Give me a whip!' I fetched my own, for he didn't have one. 'Does the man who is called Picture Sheet live here?' he asked, and when I nodded he said: 'You can tell him I don't take a stone for a man's head even if it's pushed into a loophole. And tell him to take care of my stallion as if he were Bosafabo, until Moonlight comes. He's to ride him.' As he said this he gave my horse such a blow that she reared and galloped off. But he turned back and threw me two gold pieces. 'This is for your mare,' he shouted. 'You may keep it even if you get her back.' And he rode off. Then you came, and you could have seen him if he hadn't been gone."

"Very likely," said Affliction. "But it's all the better for us we haven't seen him."

"I'd have given him a piece of my mind," cried Good Fortune, "on good and bad manners. I'd have asked him whether he knew how to salute a person, and I'd have recited the rules of the Mongol *joss* to him. Show me the two gold pieces," he asked Turakina.

Turakina passed them, and he turned them over and over. "I don't know this sort of money," said he, "so it can't be worth much."

"Those two pieces are imperials,"* declared Naidang. "In olden days you could get a horse for one of them."

"The old days are not today," said Good Fortune scornfully.

* *Imperial:* A Russian coin of the Czarist regime.

"Today," retorted Naidang, "many people give two horses for a gold piece like one of those."

"Then that fellow is crazy," cried Good Fortune. "He knows nothing of the rules of life, he is unacquainted with the Mongol *joss,* and he is ignorant of the value of money."

Naidang shook his head. "That man," he said, "ignores the conventions—that is his pride. He thinks no more of gold and silver than of the stones by the wayside—that is his security. He prefers to speak with horses and dogs than with human beings—that is because he is full of grief."

"Father!" cried Sevenstars, horrified. "You are speaking of the Venerable Chief!"

"Yes," said Naidang, "that's the man I'm speaking of, for that's the man who was here."

When Naidang said this, absolute silence fell on the gathering. Each one was wondering whether danger threatened now, and if so, what it was.

After a silence which seemed very long, Naidang said: "Forget that I spoke of Dampignak. What is good for him is not good for all, and whether or not it is good for him, only heaven knows."

"My word!" said Good Fortune gruffly. "You make as much fuss about the Venerable Chief as if he were the Yellow Emperor, whereas he's just an ordinary redbeard."

"He's an unhappy man," said Naidang solemnly.

Sevenstars went out to bring the poodle a few bones and bits of meat she had secretly been saving for him. The stallion was standing in the moonlight, trembling from head to foot. His thick head was held in the halter, the halter was tied to the line, and the line was pulled taut. Although she was frightened, Sevenstars went up to him and loosened the reins. The stallion looked up and snorted, but as soon as he found that he could do so, he lay down.

What a monster that man is, thought Sevenstars. He rides a fine horse nearly to death, he beats my dog with a whip—and he's a prince. Then she turned back to the *yurt,* where they had all lain down to sleep.

Next morning Naidang and Sevenstars were up before sunrise.

"Do you get up as early as this every morning?" asked Christian.

"The night is over," answered Sevenstars, surprised, "so one must get up."

"One could remain in bed," said Christian.

Sevenstars shook her head. "That wouldn't do," she said firmly. "What's the sun for?"

"It's still behind the mountains."

"That's just why," said Sevenstars. And she pounded the brick tea in the mortar.

When they were all sitting round the kettle drinking their hot tea and chewing millet, Good Fortune made a long speech. It began: "We have resolved . . ." (meaning Naidang and himself) and ended with: "and that, then, is our decision." Between these statements he told them what to do with the money which the old märin was to bring. "Put it away in the chest," Good Fortune said, "until Naidang and I come back again. It's no longer the silver it was before. It has been changed into just ordinary money, for which Naidang is to sell us five camels. For we can't wait until someone is daring enough to venture through the desert again in a horseless car to look for us. We might have to wait ten years for that, and we've got only five days."

"Four," said Naidang.

"Counting today it's five," said Good Fortune, "but four days will be enough time to fetch the five camels we need. Then we shall set out for Sinkiang, and Affliction will come with us."

"Wherever I am . . ." Affliction began. But Good Fortune cut him short. "Would you prefer to remain here until Springtime Snake or a soldier from the *yamen* shoots you dead before you have time to open your mouth and say: 'I'm innocent'? That would be a sticky end, I may tell you. So we'll set out four days from now. And we'll travel in comfort this time, for of course we'll take your blue tent. I'm looking forward to the journey even if we have to watch out to keep from being caught by the Venerable Chief. Then in fifty days," he concluded cheerfully, "we'll be in Urumchi."

Naidang tucked a big bottle away in his saddle bag and warned Sevenstars to beware of the stallion. "Don't try to hobble him," he said, "or he'll trample you to death."

"I'll be careful," promised Sevenstars. "Big Tiger and Christian will mind the sheep and the camels, Affliction will do the cooking, and we'll all be all right."

"Bolna!" said Naidang. Then he rode off with Good Fortune to fetch five good camels from the spring pastures on the Nojen Bogdo.

35 AN OLD ACQUAINTANCE TURNS UP

EACH DAY the sun shone warmer, and bigger flights of migrating birds flew northward. Christian and Big Tiger herded the sheep and the camels, and the black poodle kept them company, for by now they were very good friends. In the beginning he had tried to go to the horses' pasture with Sevenstars, but the stallion chased him off the moment he sighted him.

The best time was evening, when all their day's duties were done and Affliction called them to supper. Afterwards Affliction told them stories from his sorrowful life, and Sevenstars told about what she knew, or sang to them. And they were all quite merry, because they had no money to mind. For the old märin had come the very next day as he had promised, but without the cash.

"Tell your father," he had said to Sevenstars, "now, what should you tell him? Let me think." And for a long time he had sat at the fire wondering. At last he said: "You must tell Picture Sheet

that the Chinaman had no money, but another man has money, only I can't get it for eight weeks, and he must wait until then. Can you remember my words without mixing them up?"

"I hear your words," said Sevenstars, "and none of them will be lost."

"That's good," said the märin. He rode off, taking with him Turakina, to whom Sevenstars had lent a horse. "I've a hundred silver batzes for you," he said to her benevolently. "That's the exact value of your two gold pieces."

Turakina had never hoped to get such a lot of money, but she said promptly: "I won't give the gold pieces for less than a hundred and twenty batzes. Do you understand me, märin?"

"Badly," said the märin gruffly. "But all the same, I agree. You'll get a hundred and twenty silver batzes, but no more."

"I should have said a hundred and fifty," thought Turakina sadly. And the two rode on.

On the second evening there was a full moon. Big Tiger, Christian and Sevenstars were sitting in front of the *yurt* while Affliction, who took his household duties seriously, was bustling about inside.

"Today is the sixteenth day of the second moon," said Christian. "We've been traveling thirteen days."

"If we're here much longer we shall see Bator again," said Big Tiger.

"That would be lovely," cried Sevenstars; "but it's impossible, for you have to be gone before the soldiers arrive."

"When Bator comes," said Christian, "you must tell him everything that has happened. The rest—I mean what's still to happen —I'll write him in a letter as soon as I get home. Can one write a letter to Ollon Torre?"

"Yes, you can," answered Sevenstars, "but it stays in Maomu until someone fetches it. As we ride to Maomu at least every two or three years, we'd be sure to get it."

"Is there no faster way?" asked Christian.

"Why should it go faster? We learn what's in the letter as soon as we come across someone who can read Chinese."

"Would that be in another two years?" asked Big Tiger.

"No," said Sevenstars. "We pay a visit to the King of the Torguts on New Year's Day. There's a scribe at his court who can read Chinese letters. So we hear everything very quickly."

"Then I'd best write straight to the King," said Christian.

"Oh, if you do that," cried Sevenstars joyfully, "we'll have your letter very, very quickly. The King sends a messenger to Maomu every three months for the mail and the government paper. Listen now, and I'll tell you how to address the King."

Christian took out his notebook and wrote on the last page what Sevenstars dictated:

To the Venerable King of the Torguts
Dola Bilay-Kung-Wang-Dashi,
Etzina (Kansu Province)

"His scribe will read the letter and tell us what's in it," said Sevenstars.

"But if there's something secret?"

"Then you must write the secret things in such a way that only we can understand. Can you do that?"

"That's just in our line," Big Tiger assured her.

"There's sometimes a muddle," said Christian, "but it can be straightened out."

Big Tiger looked up at the moon. He thought of the ring on his thumb, and then he thought of General Wu's letter, which Christian was carrying in his pocket. Finally he sighed, and Christian, who was thinking again of the old amah in Peking, sighed loudly too.

"Do you have some trouble?" asked Sevenstars.

"We have, but we must swallow it," confessed Christian. "We're thinking of the fifty days' journey. It's a very long time."

"*Hammagua!*" cried Sevenstars. "The lovely time in which all trouble disappears is beginning now. Next full moon we'll celebrate the Spring Festival, *Kaush-orova.* Mother will come, and my second brother will be home too. His name is Gontshuk."

"Where is Gontshuk now?" asked Christian.

"Hasn't father told you?" inquired Sevenstars, cautiously.

"He said he was in the service of the prince."

"So he is," said Sevenstars ardently. She stood up and went into the tent, as if she had suddenly remembered something which was to be done. Christian and Big Tiger looked at each other. Both thought "there's something fishy here." But neither spoke.

The third day passed like the first and second, and Sevenstars said: "Tomorrow evening father and Good Fortune will be back with the camels, and the day after you'll ride off. I shall cry: *Sä Yabonah,* but I know that I'll weep afterwards, because we will be parted forever."

"Don't be unhappy," begged Christian.

"We're not worth weeping about," said Big Tiger.

"If you like," suggested Christian, "I'll weep with you, and then you won't be alone weeping, and it will be quite easy."

"But you can't do that," said Sevenstars, trying to smile, "for you're a man."

"The young people of today are a poor lot," said Affliction. "If one were to weep at every little parting, one's eyes would never be dry. But there are other things to cry about, and doubtless you'll meet them in good time."

"Especially if you're about," said Big Tiger impudently.

"Yes, indeed," answered Affliction, with a sigh.

On the fourth day after breakfast Christian produced a piece of soap from the brief case.

"Are you going to wash?" asked Big Tiger, alarmed.

"No," replied Christian. "Take off your shirt."

"Why should I?" asked Big Tiger, horrified.

"Because I'm going to do the laundry today."

At this Big Tiger became cheerful again. "I was afraid you were going to have us wash ourselves," said he.

"No fear," said Christian. "I think it's best to put off washing until we arrive in Urumchi. It's not worth while before then."

"Let me do your laundry," said Affliction. "I'm expert at it."

"Bolna!" cried Christian, but Big Tiger said: "How could we dare to trouble you?"

"What I mean," stammered Affliction, "is that a valuable piece of soap is something one doesn't often find. So I'd like, if I may, to wash my shirt a little—naturally only a little."

"Wash it well," said Christian.

"Don't skimp with the soap," said Big Tiger. "We won't need it any more."

Affliction thanked them and went down to the river with the shirts. Christian and Big Tiger went out to the pastures with the sheep and camels. In the afternoon, as they were sitting by the caravan road, the poodle suddenly cocked his ears and sat up. The distant sound of caravan bells became audible.

"There's a caravan coming," said Christian.

"You'll find it's the one we got the rice from," said Big Tiger.

"Then we'd better clear out."

"Yes, it would be wiser," said Big Tiger, "but where to?"

"Let's hide in the *yurt* with Affliction," suggested Christian. "No one could see us there."

"Yes," Big Tiger agreed. "Come, dog, let's go."

The poodle followed unwillingly. He would have liked a good fight with the caravan dogs. Instead he had to help to drive the camels and sheep into the deresen pasture. When they knew by the sound of the bells that the head of the caravan had reached the wood, Christian and Big Tiger strolled into the *yurt*.

"What's wrong?" asked Affliction.

"A caravan is coming," Christian explained, "and perhaps also a man with whom we exchanged two unfriendly words on the way."

"That's why we think it's wiser to stay in the tent," added Big Tiger, "until these people have passed by."

Affliction was full of approval. "Come right in," he said. "It's well to keep out of trouble. Better retreat than be attacked. You're a wise pair."

He sat outside in the sun with the poodle, while Christian and Big Tiger squatted in the semidarkness of the *yurt,* listening to the caravan bells and to the shouts of the drivers as they urged the beasts across the Narin Gol. There was a great sound of splashing and trampling, and when they were all across and Christian was just about to raise the door curtain, the sound of a trotting horse became audible. The poodle immediately rushed toward the rider, but Affliction called out: "Dog! Come back!"

The poodle obeyed, but was still snarling when a voice they recognized said: "Have you eaten already?"

Affliction returned the greeting, and the voice said: "Does Naidang the Picture Sheet live here?"

"Yes, he lives here," said Affliction, "but he's not at home."

"All the same, can't I have a cup of tea?"

"Yes, you may, but you must drink it outside. There's a sick man in the *yurt*."

"But I see no sign of that."

"You don't see him," explained Affliction, "because the *yurt* isn't a cricket cage."

"I know that, but where's the sickness rope?"

"What are you saying?" asked Affliction. "Ah, yes—but we haven't got a sickness rope."

They could now hear the stranger dismounting. "That's nonsense," he said angrily.

"Hush!" said Affliction. "The sick man is asleep, and if he's not asleep, he's awake."

"You're lying. When there's anyone sick in a Mongol *yurt* a rope hangs by the left side of the door—the sickness rope. Everyone knows it and passes by the tent. But there's no rope hanging here, so you're lying."

"Watch your speech," said Affliction. "All our ropes are out in use, including the sickness rope."

"But you've got a clothes' line."

"That's a horse line."

"There are pants and shirts hanging on it, including two very small shirts."

"Aren't they nice?" said Affliction. "I've washed them with real soap and they're white as the clouds in spring."

"Enough of that!" shouted the man. "Where are the two little monsters?"

"Sit down beside me," said Affliction to him, invitingly. "I love to hear about monsters of past ages. Have you ever seen a dog like this one?"

"Who are you," cried the man, "that you dare to mock me? I met two little bandits on the road, and I see by those shirts that they're here."

"Did I tell you about our dog?" asked Affliction. "He's different from all other dogs. He can tear a man or beast into shreds. Sit down. It's very pleasant here."

"You're making a fool of me," cried the man, moving toward the door of the *yurt*.

Affliction stood up and placed himself in front of it. "Your talk isn't pleasant to hear," he said. "Let's talk about dogs instead."

"Shut up!" shouted the man. He raised the entrance curtain and Affliction, trying to stop him, nearly fell over. But the dog had already got his teeth into the man's leather pants and was pulling him back. Meantime Affliction tripped him up with his foot. He fell. "I warned you," cried Affliction. "Now I must hold back the dog or he'll devour you!"

"Hold him or I'll strike you dead!"

"I'm not afraid of that," said Affliction gently; "but try if you like."

"I'm not asking your permission," cried the man furiously. But suddenly he was struck silent. In the doorway stood Christian and Big Tiger, holding Affliction's gun between them.

"Shall we press the trigger?" asked Big Tiger.

"Stop!" shouted the man. "Help! Murder!"

"Wait a moment," said Affliction. He knew well that the gun wasn't loaded, for Springtime Snake had taken all the cartridges except the ten he had in his pocket. He now took out one of these, saying: "There are lots more in the gun. I'm just telling you, not that it matters."

"Put away the gun!" panted the man. "What do you want?"

"I'd like to talk to you about dogs," said Affliction. "I hadn't finished. Please sit down. Dog! Be quiet!"

The poodle lay down, still growling, beside the door, but he never took his eyes off the stranger. Affliction sat down beside him, and Christian and Big Tiger disappeared into the *yurt*.

"Look at this savage dog," began Affliction. "I pacified him with two words; I'd like to pacify you also, for we're not murderers."

"And we're not bandits," said Big Tiger, coming out with a bowl of tea and bending his knee politely before the stranger. "I'm Big Tiger," he said, "and this is my friend, Compass Mountain."

"We met you under an unlucky star, old uncle," said Christian. He put a lump of butter into the tea and watched it melt.

"You extorted twenty pounds of rice from me," growled the man. But he accepted the bowl of tea.

"We only forgot to pay for it," explained Christian.

"You rode off in a great hurry," said Big Tiger, "just as we were about to ask you what it cost."

"Perhaps you still remember the price?" inquired Affliction.

"A silver batz," growled the man.

Taking two of General Wu's silver batzes out of his pocket Big Tiger said: "Your little servants are much distressed because they are late in paying. Please forgive the low rate of interest."

"Right!" said the man, looking dubiously from one to the other. Then he pocketed the money.

Seeing that matters were now miles better than they had been, Affliction said: "Permit me to ask your worthy name?"

"What for? My name is Ma, like that of most Kansu men. There's nothing remarkable about that."

"Old Mr. Ma," said Big Tiger, "if you meet the respected Mr. Greencoat on the road, will you be so good as to give him our regards and sincere good wishes?"

"How do you know that I'll meet him?" asked Ma, startled.

"That's quite simple," replied Big Tiger. "When two trading gentlemen meet in the desert, they don't just say, 'It's very hot,' or 'It's snowing!' They discuss important business matters. One needn't tax one's brain to know that."

"You're quite right," said Ma, flattered. "Before you came along with the truck I had concluded a good business deal with Mr. Greencoat. The stuff in question is old jewelry."

"I'd like to meet this Mr. Greencoat . . ." exclaimed Affliction. He got no further, for Big Tiger gave him a dig in the ribs and Christian pinched his leg.

"What's the matter?" asked Ma, taken aback.

"This soldier Affliction," said Big Tiger casually, "has been wanting for a long time past to meet Mr. Greencoat, having heard of the fame of that merchant. But of course he has no chance of meeting such a distinguished gentleman."

"I am unworthy," said Affliction, beginning to understand.

"I wouldn't say that," cried Ma benevolently. "I could manage an introduction where others might fail."

"May I ask," said Big Tiger, "whether Mr. Greencoat would have any use for a capable man?"

"Hm!" said Ma, looking dubiously at Affliction.

"You may not realize it by looking at him," broke in Christian, "but he knows how to drive a horseless car, and that's an unusual art."

"Oh!" cried Ma. "At that rate there might be something in it. Mr. Greencoat told me he wants to buy such a car."

"He's already bought it," said Big Tiger.

"Splendid!" cried Ma. "Then I'll be glad to act as go-between."

"We thought so," said Christian.

"It's only a question," replied Ma, "of how to manage a meeting."

"Yes, that's it," said Christian.

"Perhaps in Hsing-hsing-hsia?" Big Tiger beat about the bush.

"No," replied Ma. "I don't touch Hsing-hsing-hsia. It's a long way off my route. My caravan is traveling under a contract in a ninety days' journey to Kucheng. So I'm meeting Mr. Greencoat in Ming-shui. We've an appointment there for the fourth day of the third moon, early in the morning."

"I've heard of Ming-shui or Mighty Water," Big Tiger lied boldly.

"It must be a wonderful place," said Christian.

Ma smiled. "I wouldn't exactly say that," he replied indulgently. "There hasn't been water there for many a day. There's nothing but an abandoned frontier fortress with ruins inside it and a high wall around it. It's there I'm meeting Mr. Greencoat."

"Is it very far to Ming-shui?" asked Big Tiger.

"You see," said Christian, "we're continuing our journey tomorrow. Unfortunately Mr. Greencoat couldn't take us with him because he had business in Suchow."

"I know," replied Ma, smiling meaningly. "He had a lot of

bother from you two little scamps. So this is the result. But if you've good camels you can overtake us," he continued reassuringly. "Then we can talk about Mr. Affliction's wishes."

"Your kindness is boundless," said Affliction humbly, with a deep bow. "Thanks ten thousand times."

Ma stood up and took his horse by the bridle. "I must be off now," he said. "I can't leave my people longer. Good-by, you two young rascals. I'll see you again in Ming-shui."

"May your road be peaceful," replied Christian and Big Tiger.

"I wish you many lucky stars," murmured Affliction.

"Dog, stop here!" cried Christian. But the poodle ran barking behind Ma until he crossed the ford.

Affliction looked after him puzzled. "The fellow's a numbskull," he said, "but he can't help it. There should be a sign BEWARE hung up in front of you two. You made him talk of things he should have kept under his hat. How do you manage it?"

"It's quite easy," said Big Tiger.

"When a man is a caravan leader," explained Christian, "that doesn't mean he's an honorable merchant."

"But if you put it into his head that he *is* one," continued Big Tiger, "it gives him such joy and pride that he's hardly able to distinguish an ox from a horse."

"Forgive my dullness of wit," said Affliction. "I very nearly spoiled everything."

"*Hammagua!*" cried Christian merrily. "It has all turned out for the best." And he took out the notebook in which he had made a calendar. "Today is the eighteenth day of the second moon," he said, and he wrote in all the days up to the fourth day of the third moon. There he made a cross, and beside the cross he wrote "Ming-shui," and beside Ming-shui he wrote in brackets [Mighty Water—Frontier Fortress—Meeting with Greencoat]. Then he counted the days. "Fifteen," he said.

"Only heaven knows what will happen between now and then," said Big Tiger.

"A lot," said Affliction.

"We must ask you not to breathe a word of what we've learned to Good Fortune or anyone else."

"I'll fetter my thoughts and bind my tongue," promised Affliction.

And they went to the pasture to take the camels and sheep to the water. The poodle ran along beside them.

"Tomorrow we leave the Narin Gol," said Big Tiger.

"Yes," sighed Christian.

"It can't be helped," said Big Tiger, by way of comfort, but this didn't cheer Christian up, and they finished their evening tasks in silence.

Sevenstars came in from the pasture with the horses, and they ate the meal which Affliction had prepared. Then they got out the blankets for the night, and Sevenstars laid by some dry wood to have ready for kindling a quick fire when Naidang and Good Fortune would come back.

"Sleep well!" said Sevenstars.

36 HOW CHRISTIAN AND BIG TIGER NEARLY BECOME REDBEARDS

THE STARS twinkled over the steppe and the moon rose over the wood. Absolute silence reigned, but the poodle, who was lying awake, cocked his ears, for he thought he heard the noise of hoofs. When he was quite sure, he jumped up and ran out barking furiously to meet the unknown enemy. Sevenstars, Christian and Big Tiger woke up. "Father is coming!" cried Sevenstars joyfully.

"Don't be frightened," said Affliction, "if it turns out to be someone else."

"It can't be," cried Sevenstars indignantly. And she stirred up the embers, laid dry sticks on them, and opened the smoke vent.

"But the dog is barking," said Affliction, "and he's not stopping either."

"He does that," declared Sevenstars, "to show his great joy."

"He's very angry," said Affliction. "That's quite plain."

Christian and Big Tiger pulled on their jackets and ran out. They heard a smart trot, the poodle's loud barking, and in between a thundering voice shouting: "Get away! Dog of a dog!" followed by a volley of abuse.

"That man . . ." whispered Big Tiger.

"Is Thunderbolt," said Christian.

"Dog, come here!" they both cried together. At the second call there was a rustle in the bushes, and the poodle came rushing toward them panting. Christian caught him firmly by the ruff. Immediately afterwards the silhouette of two riders emerged. Their heavy stirrups clanked with a bell-like sound. Then the riders dismounted. One of them came up to Christian and Big Tiger with a rapid swinging stride.

"I heard right!" he thundered. "Hey, Little Paw, aren't you a blockhead! But Thunderbolt knew the voices of his dear little friends at once!"

Christian and Big Tiger bowed politely. "May your road be easy and good," they said in Mongolian.

Thunderbolt was speechless. He pulled his carbine from his shoulder and struck it on the ground. "Did you hear that, Little Paw?" he thundered. "Hi, Little Paw! Where are you hiding?"

But Moonlight was standing by the stallion, patting his neck and talking to him. He didn't hear Thunderbolt or see what was going on. Only when Thunderbolt went up to him and tapped him on the shoulder did he say: "Do you see who's been here?"

"Aha!" roared Thunderbolt, and then was silent. But he pulled himself together quickly and ran to the *yurt*. Sevenstars, who had just got to the door, he pushed rudely aside. Thrusting his carbine into her hand in his haste, he gathered up his cloak and prepared to *kowtow*.

"Don't do that," cried Affliction, flabbergasted, from inside. "I'm not the man you're looking for!"

Thunderbolt took a step backwards. "You soldier Affliction," he cried. "I see now. You sit before me, good friend."

"It only looks that way," said Affliction modestly.

"He means," cried Big Tiger, "that you shouldn't pay attention to him. He hates being made a fuss of. Please sit down." And he led Thunderbolt to the seat of honor.

"Tea will be ready right away," said Christian. "Have you had a good journey?"

"Are you cold?" asked Big Tiger. "Or are you tired?"

"How is your esteemed health?" inquired Christian.

But when Thunderbolt tried to answer he didn't get time. For Big Tiger went on to ask how the horses were and whether either of them had gone lame. It was many a day since Thunderbolt had encountered such politeness. When Moonlight at last appeared in the doorway he called out to him, his voice full of emotion: "These two honorable younger brothers of ours have become real Mongols!"

"Is that so?" asked Moonlight, smiling.

"Not quite as much as the honored Mr. Thunderbolt thinks," confessed Christian.

"Don't mister me!" cried the lama. "Didn't I say you're my younger brothers?"

"We salute our elder brother with a *kowtow* of obedience," said Big Tiger and Christian. But Thunderbolt raised them to their feet and placed them on his left.

"Unfortunately we lack the slightest understanding of the language," said Big Tiger. "So we beg you to speak Chinese with us."

"We have only a few minutes," said Moonlight. "Tell us your news."

"Sevenstars will tell you," said Big Tiger.

She had just come in, and because she was a girl, had sat down in the lowliest place, near the entrance. She was just about to ladle the tea into the bowls, and she shook her head. "It is unbecoming for a girl to speak where there are five men," she said. "How could I dare to say two words?"

"*Hammagua!*" cried Moonlight. "You hear how these lads talk. They have no useful words. Unless"—and he looked at Affliction—"what about you?"

"No good," cried Affliction. "I'm only the poor soldier Affliction, and my father . . ."

"I know," said Moonlight. "Thunderbolt told me about you and the other rascal who guards the gasoline depot in Ollon Torre."

"Who used to guard it," said Affliction gloomily.

"It appears," said Moonlight, "that something's happened there."

"Yes, something did happen," agreed Affliction. "A terrible disaster."

"Then Sevenstars must tell us," Moonlight decided. "Women don't exaggerate half as much as men."

Sevenstars told them that Greencoat and Springtime Snake had stolen the truck, and how it all happened. Then she added: "We all visited the old märin, and when we came home there was a strange stallion standing at the line, and Turakina said there had been a lama here who had told her: 'Moonlight is to ride the stallion when he comes!'" But she said nothing about the Black City.

"The old märin," added Big Tiger, "gave us more news. For Greencoat had visited him and told him he was going to lodge a complaint against us with the magistrate at Suchow. Naidang has gone off with Good Fortune to fetch camels for us, so that we can escape in time."

"Nonsense!" shouted Thunderbolt. "Much easier shoot all soldiers. You, Little Paw, ride ahead alone. I stay here with gun. Give five, six, eight, nine soldiers hearty greeting."

"No, that wouldn't do," replied Moonlight seriously. "Now I have heard what has happened, so we'll ride on."

"The tea is boiling," said Sevenstars. "Please wait two minutes."

She filled the tea bowls, and then beckoned Christian and whispered something to him. But Christian whispered back: "I am too unimportant. Big Tiger is the elder of us. He should do it, or what about Affliction?"

"No," Sevenstars interrupted him. "Affliction won't do. He's a soldier, and these two are gentlemen of the mountains. That makes a difference."

"Bolna!" said Christian, and then he whispered to Big Tiger, and Big Tiger put on the magnificent fur hat which the old märin had given him. Meanwhile Sevenstars filled the little brass can with *arrak*, and when Big Tiger solemnly ordered, "Hand me the can!" she knelt down meekly and held the brass can up to him. Big Tiger took it. He filled the first beaker in silence, and Moonlight was almost beside himself with enthusiasm over the dignity with which he did it. But Thunderbolt snorted so hard that his beard trembled in the wind from his nostrils.

"The unworthy little fellow begs you, in the name of the master of the house, not to disdain two beakers of watery wine." Bowing before Moonlight he said: *"Dsha, dsha, dsha!"* just as he had heard Naidang doing.

Moonlight first raised the beaker to his forehead and then drank. Thunderbolt's turn came next, and after him Affliction's and Christian's. When the first round had been drunk Thunderbolt slapped his thigh. "Aha," he cried in a voice of thunder, this time in Mongolian, "you son and grandson of good custom, my tent is your tent! It would be wrong of you to absent yourself longer from it."

"He's inviting you to visit him," said Moonlight, when he noticed that Big Tiger didn't quite understand.

"My elder brother squanders his heart," replied Big Tiger politely.

But Moonlight was already standing up, muttering something about great haste and many thanks.

Big Tiger immediately left everything and ran out of the tent.

He was Naidang's deputy, and Christian, who was his ally, ran after him. Behind him ran Affliction and Sevenstars, so that the rules of correct behavior should be fully observed.

"It's a pity," muttered Thunderbolt as he shouldered his carbine. "I regret the spoiled ambush." He turned to Sevenstars: "Which horse?" he asked.

"This one," said Sevenstars, pointing to the gray piebald which Christian had ridden the first day.

While Thunderbolt changed saddles Moonlight went up to Sevenstars. He was wearing a new sheepskin coat with the white skin outside, and over it a blue silk sash which also was new, with his silver-handled dagger stuck in it.

"Is Gontshuk where he should be?" he asked her.

"Yes, he's there," she replied.

"How many horses?" asked Moonlight.

"Four," said Sevenstars. "Choose them."

Moonlight pushed his fur hat thoughtfully back off his forehead, and his sword scar looked like a dark ribbon. "Four are too many and too few," he said. Sevenstars didn't understand what he meant, nor did Christian and Big Tiger. Affliction disappeared, for these cryptic utterances seemed to him to bode no good.

"Mount, Little Paw! Mount!" roared Thunderbolt. "*Yabonah!*"

"Ride on," ordered Moonlight. "I've not finished thinking."

"Oh, my young brothers!" boomed Thunderbolt. "My heart is heavy at parting from you!"

Christian and Big Tiger bowed profoundly. "May your road be peaceful," they said, respectfully. Thunderbolt bowed too, and crying *"Yabonah!"* in a sorrowful boom, he swung into the saddle.

"Sä Yabonah!" cried Christian and Big Tiger.

"Lie down, dog!" cried Sevenstars, and the poodle remained lying, but growled and barked until the hoof beats died away. The stars were twinkling, the moon was shining brightly, and it was cold. Moonlight was standing by the *yurt* with Sevenstars, still thinking hard. The stallion pawed the ground impatiently, and suddenly whinnied loudly.

"I'm coming," cried Moonlight, loosening the reins from the line.

"Good-by, Sevenstars," he said. "Greet your father Picture Sheet and tell Good Fortune he need not fear."

Sevenstars bowed in silence.

"You two come as far as the river with me," ordered Moonlight. "I have two words to say to you."

"We hear you and obey," said Christian and Big Tiger.

"I'll be back in a minute," said Christian. He ran to the *yurt* and returned with the sheepskin coat which the poodle had found. Then he walked along beside Moonlight, who let the stallion free. The horse went down to the river to drink, and Moonlight sat down on the bank. Christian and Big Tiger sat opposite him, with the sheepskin coat spread over them like a tent.

"Have you got only one coat?" asked Moonlight.

"Greencoat has got the other one," said Big Tiger.

"He had this one too," said Christian, "but it fell off the truck and the dog found it."

"Indeed?" said Moonlight. But he said no more, for he was busy thinking again. "What do you know about Good Fortune?" he asked suddenly.

"We know he's a soldier," said Christian.

"He belongs to General Wu's army," said Big Tiger.

"And Greencoat?" "What do you know of him?"

"Greencoat is a merchant," answered Christian, "but now he's a . . ." He stopped and went hot and cold, and nudged Big Tiger to say something quickly.

"Compass Mountain means," stammered Big Tiger, "that Greencoat is no longer a merchant."

Moonlight laughed good-humoredly. "That's true," he said, "but you needn't hesitate to say that now Greencoat has become a redbeard. It's true that I'm one too, but there's a certain difference."

"There's a distinct difference," agreed Christian.

"A tremendous difference," added Big Tiger, warmly.

"Speaking of redbeards," continued Moonlight, "I consider it my duty—please understand what I want to tell you, my children," he interjected almost affectionately. "You've had your first bad experience and I wouldn't like you to have another. There's something you should know. I don't mean it's that way now, but it was once and it might be again, so . . ." he went on awkwardly. "Do you understand, sons of heroes?"

"Perhaps Mr. Moonlight means . . ." began Christian.

"That Good Fortune also was a redbeard once," continued Big Tiger.

"We know that already," said Christian.

Moonlight gazed at them dumfounded. "I think I've told you before that you seem born for the steppes. Now I see that you seem born for the desert as well. How did you extract that from Good Fortune?"

"We didn't have to extract it exactly," said Big Tiger modestly. "We just happened to listen when Greencoat and Good Fortune were quarreling."

"Tell me what you know," said Moonlight.

"Good Fortune was a robber on the Red Mountain," said Big Tiger, "and Greencoat was the receiver of stolen goods."

"Now we've told you everything," said Christian. "More we do not know. Besides, all this happened seven years ago, for Good Fortune said that whenever they quarreled."

"I've learned something from you which I did not know. Now I'll tell you something you do not know," said Moonlight.

"Please do," said Christian.

"Our elder is very kind," said Big Tiger.

"You know who my chief is?" began Moonlight.

"Yes, we know," said Christian.

"Men call him the Venerable Chief, but he is my prince. Seven years ago, when our rule over the desert began and we built the castle, there were ten thousand robber bands menacing the caravan routes. The robbers were mostly deserted soldiers. We wiped them all out. From the Etzin Gol to the frontier of Sinkiang not a single bandit was left. We alone remained. We exacted a tribute of one silver batz from the caravans for each laden camel. In return we gave them safe convoy, which pleased the merchants. Thus we helped trade, and preserved the security of the five human relationships.

"But one day we heard that a new band had appeared in the Red Mountain, east of the Etzin Gol. My prince ordered me to destroy it, for its members were said to be dangerous men. So I took twenty camels, seven men, and my horse. We disguised ourselves as merchants and went our way peacefully, and our caravan bells resounded far and wide. We camped at the well near the Red Mountain. Thunderbolt was with us too. I shaved off his black beard, and when night fell I bade him remain in the camp with two men. I hid with the others half-way up the valley behind some big crags, and we loaded our rifles. Do you know the Valley of the Red Mountain?"

"Yes, we know it," said Big Tiger and Christian.

"Thunderbolt made a fine big fire which lit up the whole camp," continued Moonlight. "If the redbeards had been clever they would have seen at once that there was something afoot. For there is no wood anywhere around the Red Mountain for a fire like that. But they behaved like real blockheads. They were eleven men strong, but only nine came, and they set upon poor Thunderbolt. He and his two comrades fell on their knees and surrendered, begging for mercy. Then we opened fire, and it was easy for us to pick the redbeards off, for they stood in the full glare of the campfire, kicking Thunderbolt in the face as he lay on the ground roaring. But soon they were roaring themselves, and we finished the last three off with our butt ends. It was all as easy as fun. After a while, however, I remembered that we should have killed eleven, and there were only nine dead men lying around us. So I mounted my horse while Thunderbolt got the caravan ready for the road. But it was night, and I couldn't find the trail. So I told Thunderbolt to go on ahead, and I remained behind alone on the Red Mountain. We left the robbers' arms and all their possessions lying there to make doubly sure that the two remaining redbeards would come back. I hid my horse in a ravine and settled down behind a rock to await the dawn and the coming of the two surviving sons of the mountain. Before long two young fellows came, and by heaven's decree there they were within aim of my gun. When they saw the dead men they trembled as a wick trembles when you light it. Their days were near being numbered, for I had my finger on the trigger. They began to weep and lament over their dead comrades and then they carried the bodies out and laid them in a heap. In the dawn of the morning two vultures came circling round above us. Their dark shadows glided over the rocky walls of the valley, and a third one sat on an *obo* with its head tucked into its feathers. It was waiting like myself.

"'Oh, Long Life,' cried one of the men, 'who ordered these unhappy ones to do what they did and to be what they were?'

"'Do not lament so loudly,' said the other. 'He is a scoundrel; but we will be scoundrels too if we do not bury these dead men, but leave their wandering spirits to seek a resting place in vain.'

"'You can spare yourselves the trouble,' I said, stepping out with my gun. 'Lay down your arms!'

"They fell on their knees and begged for mercy.

"'There's no use wasting words,' I said. 'I've come to finish you off.' They were silent, and the shadows of the vultures crossed to and fro over them. It was an uncanny sight and an ill-omened place. 'Stand up,' I said. 'We are alone together here, and so I can do what I could not do otherwise.'

"They thanked me, striking their foreheads on the ground three times, but still remained on their knees before me. 'My name is Good Fortune,' said one. 'I am yours to command.' 'My name is Long Life,' said the other. 'I am your obedient servant.'

" 'I command you to stand up,' I said, and they did so. 'I will take your horses and guns,' I said, 'but I want nothing else.' They led me to where their horses stood, and helped me to tie the guns into a bundle and pack the cartridges into a bag. 'Go back to where you came from,' I told them. 'The Etzin Gol is not far off. You can reach it on foot. And if ever we meet in this life again, do not forget that you owe me obedience.'

"Then they swore a sacred oath that they would be at my service until I should release them from their vow. And so we parted. Afterwards it struck me that I had forgotten to question them about the man they called a scoundrel. But it was too late. I rode on with the horses and guns until I overtook Thunderbolt. 'We need say no more about this matter,' I said to him, and he laughed triumphantly when he saw the eleven horses and eleven guns.

"And now," ended Moonlight, "I have met Good Fortune again and I recognized him at once. From you I know that Greencoat was the man they called a scoundrel. But I have never seen Long Life since."

"The honorable Mr. Moonlight is mistaken there," said Christian.

"Yes, our revered elder has indeed seen him since," Big Tiger confirmed; "he merely failed to recognize Lieutenant Long Life."

"Because it was night," said Christian.

"You know more than I do," cried Moonlight. "Are you *gurtums,* who call up spirits and learn from them what no mortal knows?"

"Oh, no, we are not magicians," said Big Tiger modestly.

"It was not Long Life's fault that your second meeting with him was a sad one," Christian assured him.

"At least he could have greeted me and said: 'Have you eaten yet?' Every decent person does that."

"He couldn't do so," explained Big Tiger, "for our honorable elder was lying on the ground at the time, and did not want food."

"Because his skull was split open," explained Christian.

Moonlight drew his hand across his forehead. "This," he said, touching the scar, "is a deformity of the face."

"It is a scar from a sword," said Christian dryly.

"Well, yes, it must be something of the sort," Moonlight admitted. "It's true, I was there when it happened, but I'm not certain if it was from a sword."

"Yes, it was," Christian assured him.

"And the sword was in Long Life's hand," Big Tiger added.

"What?" groaned Moonlight. "The treacherous dog broke his trust!"

"He was not a treacherous dog who broke his trust," contradicted Christian. "Long Life merely did not recognize you at first."

"Because it was so dark," said Big Tiger.

"And because you had fallen from your horse," said Christian, "and had lost consciousness."

"But *he* hadn't lost consciousness," cried Moonlight.

"He had his senses," Christian admitted, "and when he saw what he had done, he was sorrow-stricken."

"His sorrow was very great," Big Tiger affirmed, "for he thought you were dead."

"And he ordered his soldiers to leave the place," Christian continued; "for he was an officer."

"And the soldiers had to obey," said Big Tiger. "And when they wanted to strip you of all you had, Long Life said: 'I won't permit it'."

"Did he really?" asked Moonlight doubtfully.

"Why? Did you lose anything?" asked Big Tiger. "I mean, apart from your consciousness?"

"No," Moonlight admitted. "That was all I lost."

"Your clothing and your sheepskin coat saved you," said Christian, "and that you owe to Long Life."

"The good boy!" said Moonlight. "Where on earth did you meet him?"

"Near Mount Abder," replied Christian.

"Hush!" said Moonlight. "That is a dangerous mountain, and not one to name carelessly—even here, where it is far from us. You might lose a second truck."

"But we haven't got a second one," said Big Tiger.

"We'll do our best to get back the first one," said Christian.

At this Moonlight became all attention. "Pray, how will you set about that?" he asked slowly. "Anyone who listens to you two should pay careful heed, because you say nothing that hasn't got something behind it. You're a quick-witted pair of rascals. Never have I come across smarter."

Big Tiger and Christian drew the coat over their heads the better to be able to say a private word to each other in case of need, and Christian nudged Big Tiger to begin.

Big Tiger said: "We have an appointment to meet Greencoat, but he doesn't know anything about it. It's very secret."

Moonlight was dumfounded. He pushed his fur hat back off his ears. "Children," he cried, "your wits astound me. Won't you enter our brotherhood? We search within the four seas for fellows of your sort, but like the Four-not-alike, they are never to be found."

"We would like very much indeed to join you," said Big Tiger politely. "It would be an honor which our poor talent does not deserve. But we've got to go home."

"My old amah is waiting for me," said Christian.

"May I ask where you are meeting Greencoat?" Moonlight inquired, moving closer.

"We have arranged to meet Greencoat," said Big Tiger slowly, "on the fourth day of the third moon."

"The place is called Ming-shui," said Christian, "and he will be waiting there for a certain Mr. Ma. We found this out, and decided we must be there too."

Moonlight let his hands drop, but he clenched his fists so tightly that the fingers cracked. He seemed shaken by some violent emotion, and Big Tiger and Christian shrank back in alarm when he suddenly bent his knee before them and touched his forehead to the ground. "Thanks ten thousand times!" he murmured. "Thanks ten thousand times!"

Big Tiger dropped the coat and pulled at Moonlight to stand up.

"We are only boys, unworthy of such respect," said Christian.

"Young fools should be treated with mildness and tolerance," said Big Tiger, "but not with honor."

"Oh, sons of heroes and grandsons of sages!" cried Moonlight. "You have opened my eyes. How am I to thank you? Now I know who is coming to Ming-shui."

He looked from one to the other, gradually calming down as he did so. "We must get down to work," he said resolutely, "but only we three. Promise this by the ring on your thumb."

"No," cried Big Tiger, horrified, "not by this ring!"

"Forgive me," begged Moonlight. "I did not mean to frighten you. It will be enough if you just promise me not to speak of this to anyone."

"We promise," said Christian.

"We are experienced in keeping secrets," said Big Tiger.

Moonlight smiled. "You will hear from me soon," he said, standing up. "May your road be easy and safe!"

"Sä Yabonah!" cried Big Tiger and Christian. They drew the coat over their shoulders and watched Moonlight tramping with heavy strides over the wet sand. The stallion came toward them, and Moonlight swung into the saddle. He was scarcely in the saddle before the animal plunged through the water.

"We've forgotten something," said Big Tiger. "We should have asked Moonlight why four horses are too few and too many."

"It doesn't matter," Christian replied. "We'll ask Sevenstars. After all, Gontshuk is her brother."

They went back to the tent, but Sevenstars did not know either.

"I don't at all like this way of saying yes and no all in one," said Affliction. "You'll see nothing good comes of it."

"And father isn't coming home either," sighed Sevenstars.

"Haste makes for mistakes," said Big Tiger, to comfort her. "And Naidang will avoid that."

"He will if he can," said Affliction, yawning, "but many people can't."

Sevenstars closed the smoke vent. "Come to bed and sleep well," she said, and Christian and Big Tiger were glad to obey her.

37 LEAVE-TAKING OF SEVENSTARS AND NAIDANG

THE MORNING STAR was twinkling all alone in the heavens. The pastures were covered with hoar frost, and the tall poplars by the Narin Gol pointed upward to the sky, which was just turning blue. A fog floated over the river.

So this is the day of parting, thought Sevenstars sadly, when she came out of the *yurt*. The poodle looked up but did not stir. It was too early. He waited until Sevenstars came and sat down with the mortar and pestle, to pound up the brick tea. This awoke Christian, Big Tiger and Affliction. The sheep and camels had long since been lying with their eyes open, and the horses—it was impossible to know whether they ever slept—were standing at the line. The coats of Moonlight's and Thunderbolt's over-ridden stallions were rough and pasted with dried sweat, and the hoar frost glistened on their fetlocks and manes.

"Oh, you poor creatures!" cried Sevenstars, laying aside the mortar. "I forgot you last evening!" She ran to the line and loosened their reins. Before lying down the horses rolled on their backs, all fours in the air, beating up a cloud of dust, snorting with pleasure, and making their rough coats look even shaggier.

"Why do they do that?" asked Christian.

"Because they're itching," said Sevenstars.

"Oh, I see!" said Christian, and he thought of the glacis in Peking where horses didn't roll on the ground but were rubbed down and covered with a blanket when they had sweated. He went to open the sheep pen, Big Tiger untied the camels, and in the *yurt* Affliction made the tea.

They were at breakfast when Naidang and Good Fortune arrived. "Have you had a good journey?" asked Sevenstars, and her father replied, "Yes!"

Christian and Big Tiger looked at the camels, which were walking along with stately tread, their heads high. They were young and strong. Their humps were fat and large, and their protruding upper lips gave them a haughty, insolent expression. One of them carried on a pack saddle the blue tent in which Affliction and Springtime Snake had lived. The poles swung up and down as the animal walked.

"Don't unload," cried Good Fortune. "We have to start at once."

Christian and Big Tiger felt a stab through their hearts. And Sevenstars, who also heard these words, turned away. Suddenly all joy had gone out of life, the camels roared angrily when made to kneel down, and even the rising sun failed to cheer; it only warned

them to hurry. Christian and Big Tiger became sadder and sadder, and Good Fortune said: "We have to be at the Morin Gol by evening, and we'll travel through the night."

"Go in and drink your tea, Good Fortune," cried Naidang. "We'll be saddling."

"It's always like this," sighed Affliction. "When you're merry and comfortable somewhere you're suddenly told: 'Pack up; there's a carload of devils coming!' "

He brought out his own saddle and Springtime Snake's, and lengthened the cinches to go round the camels' bellies. Naidang produced two old wooden saddles with quilted covers for Christian and Big Tiger. Besides the nose cords, the camels had plaited goats' hair halters. "In case of emergency," said Naidang, "for a nose cord can break."

"But . . ." said Christian.

"Unfortunately," said Naidang, "there's no 'but'. It's high time to be off."

"We know that well," said Christian, "but . . ."

"Hammagua!" cried Naidang. "What's the trouble?"

"It's this," insisted Christian. "The old märin brought no money."

Naidang laughed. "The rain often falls late," he said. "I'll be able to give you some for your journey."

"It's not that," said Christian. "Big Tiger and I have enough for an emergency. But the camels?"

"They're yours," said Naidang solemnly. "There's nothing more to be said."

"Thanks ten thousand times," said Christian and Big Tiger. But Naidang shut his ears.

"How much money have you got?" he asked quietly.

"About forty-five silver batzes between us."

"That's sufficient," declared Naidang. Then he asked Sevenstars if there was any news, and she told him about the visit of Moonlight and Thunderbolt. She also said something about Gontshuk and the horses, but she whispered this, and her father muttered, "Good!"

"Come on, men! Mount!" he cried aloud. *"Yabonah!"*

Good Fortune and Affliction came out of the *yurt,* the latter carrying his gun. "I've still got ten cartridges," he said, "so the thunder may roll and the night may fall. We're ready for anything!"

Everyone looked at him, astonished at these brave words. "Forgive my unseemly bragging," he said, suddenly abashed. "But it's true. I hit the mark whenever I fire. Therefore ten cartridges are plenty."

"I'll go part of the way with you," said Naidang.

Christian and Big Tiger bowed to Sevenstars. "We wish you joy," they said. "May your days be long and happy."

"Come here, Compass Mountain," said Sevenstars. They entered the *yurt*. There was little light in it, and Sevenstars shut the door behind them. Two big tears were rolling down her cheeks, but she was smiling. Holding his two ears she kissed Christian right in the middle of his mouth. Then she pushed back the door, and they stepped out into the sunshine, where Big Tiger was waiting.

"I'm of no importance and I possess nothing," said Sevenstars sobbing, as she drew a *haddak* from her belt. "Therefore I have no present to give you except the dog. He is to go with you."

"That's quite impossible," cried Christian. "He's a dog in a hundred. Never could we accept so great a gift."

"He's a night watcher and a carrier of express news," said Big Tiger. "You can't possibly do without him!"

Sevenstars knelt down and laid the *haddak* on the ground in front of her, saying simply: "The dog no longer belongs to me."

Christian picked up the *haddak* and raised it to his forehead, while Big Tiger bowed in silence. Then Christian took the Duke of Hanta's sky-blue *haddak* out of the brief case. On it he laid General Wu's comb, which had never been used, and said: "It is with our hearts we thank you; this is only a trifling keepsake."

"The very stones and cliffs bow before your generosity," said Big Tiger.

Sevenstars took the *haddak,* lifted up her arms, and ran weeping into the *yurt.*

"Yabonah!" cried Naidang. "It's time to be off!"

"Why are you standing there like lost chickens," Good Fortune chided them. "Hurry up!"

Sevenstars came out of the tent again. "Father!" she called, "the dog is no longer mine. He's to go with Compass Mountain and Big Tiger."

"That's a grand idea!" cried Naidang. "Dog! Come with us!" At this the poodle sprang up on him, barking joyfully.

Naidang was the only one on horseback. "I'll be home tonight," he called back to Sevenstars. Then he took his place at the head of the procession. Good Fortune rode behind him on a stately camel. He had no saddle bag, but his pistol holster looked splendid and warlike, with its red silk tassel hanging over his gray quilted coat. Next came Affliction, who was far better equipped. In front of him lay his military coat with the gold buttons, and his big gun, with which he could shoot so surely, hung from his shoulder. He leaned back a little in his saddle, for he was leading the pack camel behind him, laden with the blue tent, the spades, and Christian's fur coat. Christian and Big Tiger, sitting lightly in their saddles like experienced camel riders, each with a whip hung on his wrist, brought up the procession.

"May your road be easy and good!" cried Sevenstars.

"We wish you peace!" cried Big Tiger.

Christian wanted to call out too, but he couldn't, for he had to bite his lips to keep from crying. But he waved to her with both hands, and she called out: *"Sä Yabonah!"*

She kept calling *"Sä Yabonah!"* until the riders were far away. Then she threw herself weeping on the ground. There was no one to see her, and not even the poodle was there to comfort her. He was running merrily ahead, and was first to cross the Narin Gol. As he shook the water from his coat his eyes shone like black buttons. Then he ran up the slope and down again, barking loudly.

They were traveling faster than ordinary caravans, for the camels had no heavy loads. As they passed the point where the wheel tracks turned south, Good Fortune tapped his pistol.

"Let it be," said Naidang. "Sevenstars tells me there are other people too on the lookout for Greencoat."

"How's that?" asked Good Fortune brusquely. "Who do you mean?"

"Moonlight was in my tent last night. Didn't you notice that?"

"He didn't leave any visiting card," said Good Fortune irritably. "It must have been an informal visit."

"He was in a hurry," admitted Naidang. "But he took the stallion, so you could have seen he had been there."

"He left a message for our revered elder," cried Big Tiger.

"Then tell it to me. Perhaps it's urgent."

"We were to tell our revered elder," reported Big Tiger, "that he need have nothing to fear."

"Is that all?"

"That's all."

"The message," Good Fortune remarked scornfully, "is not very urgent."

"But it's good news," said Naidang. "On the road you have before you such words are precious."

"I know what you mean," muttered Good Fortune. "And I also know who you mean. But words of that kind are like a drawer that you open and find empty."

Naidang said nothing more. He would have expected Good Fortune to be pleased, but he wasn't. He muttered in a tone of vexation, "We'll just see," and after a while, "there's something behind this!"

"Ah!" sighed Affliction. "There are many things you can't know and many things you can't see, perhaps even behind those trees." He meant the poplars by the Dondur Gol, which fringed the horizon. They were stately trees, and the Dondur Gol was a real river. The slope which led down to the ford was trodden with fresh camel tracks. Good Fortune knit his brows as he observed them.

"A caravan must have passed here yesterday or the day before," he said. "Didn't you see it?"

"We heard the bells," said Big Tiger.

"But only in the distance," said Affliction. "In fact, hardly at all."

"The dog was barking so loudly," said Christian.

"It wouldn't surprise me if that scoundrel is just ahead of us," muttered Good Fortune.

"Who do you mean?" asked Naidang, all unsuspecting.

"Ah, I was just thinking of a mean fellow we met on the way. It was hard to persuade the miserly creature to sell us a bag of rice." Saying this, he urged his camel into the river, which flowed more slowly than the Narin Gol but was deeper. Naidang had to draw up his knees, the poodle had to swim, and only the two young camel riders were completely at ease.

"It's not far from the lake," said Naidang. "That's why the water flows slowly."

As they rode on Christian took out the map and opened the Western Sheet. "Here are the twin lakes," he said. "One is called the Gashun Nor and the other the Sokho Nor. All the tributaries of the Etzin Gol flow into them, and they don't all flow out again."

"Is all that written on your map?" asked Naidang, astonished.

"Yes, it's all there," said Good Fortune, loftily, "and a lot more."

"Am I on it too?" asked Naidang.

"Not yet," Good Fortune explained. "But when Compass Mountain goes home to where they make the maps, he'll say to the map makers, 'There's something missing here,' and they'll say, 'Please forgive our ignorance.' Then they'll insert what is lacking and write in, 'Here dwells Naidang, the Picture Sheet.' "

Naidang asked to have the map passed to him and examined it with due respect.

"Here's where we are now," said Christian, bending down from his camel. "We have still forty *li* to the Morin Gol."

"This map is a precious thing," said Naidang politely.

"It's a priceless document," said Good Fortune. "I realized that the minute I saw it."

"What is it like at the Sokho Nor?" asked Christian.

"Like everywhere else in the world," answered Naidang, "there's land and water."

"A sad place, probably," said Affliction.

"Well, yes, it is a bit melancholy," Naidang agreed. "The Sokho Nor is as big as the sea, but the Gashun Nor is still bigger. Around it there is a white fringe. It is not the winter's snow, but salt, and beyond that is nothing but yellow desert. The water of the lake is blue, and more beautiful than the sky. It is beautiful beyond all telling. And above it stands the Nojen Bogdo, the Mountain of the Gods. But you can't drink a drop of that blue water, for by heaven's decree it tastes of salt and is not for man."

"And isn't that sad enough?" asked Affliction. "Even here it's none too cheerful." And he pointed all round with his whip.

They were traversing a great plain, and the ground was hard and covered with sand and little stones. The caravan track went through it like a furrow, westward. It was barely visible, but still, it was there, and it was the only thing to hold on to. The sun was climbing higher, the day was warm, and the poodle was running quietly beside the camels. They walked at a steady pace, one behind the other. Naidang began to sing, and Christian said to Big Tiger, "I'm hungry."

"So am I," said Big Tiger.

"There are two standards of living," Affliction held forth. "We have now reached the 'thirteen-grains-of-millet' stage, where often you eat little, but more often nothing. That's the one I know best."

"We don't like it at all," said Christian.

They rode on, and Naidang continued singing. It was only in the late afternoon that the landscape began to change. Little sandhills appeared, each with its scraggy tamarisks. Gradually the tamarisks became bigger, scrub showed up, and finally isolated poplars and little strips of woodland. But there were no continuous rows of trees here such as fringed the two other rivers. Even the grass grew only in patches and the blades were thinner than on the Narin Gol. The twigs were thinner too, and even the poplars looked frail and threatened rather than firmly and permanently rooted. Between the trees one could see far out over the desert to the distant blue mountains.

The Morin Gol flowed through a wide bed of gravel and the sandbanks were larger than the narrow rivulets. These were really only little brooks across which one could jump easily, but the water was as clear as a mountain spring. On the opposite bank stood the Chinese money-changer's *yurt,* and Mr. Ping's wares lay under a gray tent canvas beside it. The poodle barked and Mr. Ping came out, but it was already too late. His vicious watchdog rushed to meet the poodle, and right in the middle of the Morin Gol, on a sandbank, the battle started.

The two dogs fought savagely, while the owners, the one party on camels, the other on foot, stood on either bank calling "Dog! Come back!" Naidang looked on unconcerned, and let his horse drink. The camels pressed forward to the water, and Good Fortune said calmly: "It can't be helped. The dogs are going to eat each other up."

"No," cried Christian desperately, raising his whip. He wanted to drive his camel out to the scene of the battle, but Affliction held him back. "That's not necessary," he cried. "Just wait a moment."

He slipped down from his camel and picked up two stones. Then, very calmly and carefully, he took aim. Mr. Ping's yellow dog, which had just got on top, gave a leap and a howl, and ran off with the poodle after him. Affliction aimed and let fly again. "There!" he said. "That fight is decided."

They could actually see the stone bouncing on the poodle's hindquarters. He doubled up, and ran back to the sandbank whimpering.

Christian, Big Tiger and Good Fortune were astounded, and Naidang turned round in his saddle, raised his two thumbs skywards, and shouted: "A magnificent shot!"

On the other bank stood Mr. Ping. "You've hit my dog nine-tenths dead," he shouted. "You'll have to pay for him."

Affliction mounted, and while the camels were slowly drinking and squirting water around, he said apologetically: "I didn't mean to really hurt them, and I beg pardon of the owners."

"That's all right," said Big Tiger. "You're a master marksman."

"Could you teach me stone-throwing?" asked Christian.

"Is there a way of learning that art?" asked Big Tiger.

"There's a way," said Affliction, "but it's a long one. My grandfather taught me about stones, and my father trained me in marksmanship. People who live in the mountains of Labrang and have no guns, have to learn to throw stones. As a boy I practiced every day while I herded the goats. When I could hit a tree at fifty paces my grandfather died. After another three years I seldom missed a pole even at a hundred paces. By the time I never missed at all my father died. I had no fear of wild dogs or stray wolves by then. Later I became a soldier and learned to shoot. But shooting is no art. It has only spoiled my stone-throwing. You saw how badly I threw right now." They all gazed in amazement at Affliction, who added sadly: "I meant just to graze your dogs. Please excuse my lack of skill."

Meanwhile the camels and the horse had drunk their fill, and Naidang led the way across the Morin Gol. The hoofs clattered over the gravel and the camels' pads crunched it. The poodle lay waiting on the sandbank. He tried to wag his tail, but it hurt. Then he trotted along beside Christian and Big Tiger, lapping water now and then, and glowering at the other bank where his enemy had withdrawn.

Mr. Ping, who now recognized Naidang, was completely appeased. "Oh!" he cried, with joyful emotion. "Greetings to the esteemed Mr. Picture Sheet. Have you had a good journey, old uncle?"

"How is your dog?" asked Naidang.

"Splendid! Couldn't be better," said Mr. Ping, giving Affliction an angry look. But then he noticed the red silk tassle of Good Fortune's pistol, and its owner's elegant military bearing, and his tone changed. "What distinguished visitors!" he sighed. "Ah, please do come into my miserable hut."

Christian, Big Tiger and Affliction tied up the camels. When they entered the tent Mr. Ping was already serving bean noodles. Naidang was sitting on the seat of honor, smoking. Good Fortune, who noticed that his identity puzzled Mr. Ping, left him guessing.

"Was the old märin with you?" inquired Naidang, after Mr. Ping had handed out some warmed barley brandy.

"My heart has long been depressed by the absence of his visit," confessed Mr. Ping. "Had he some matter to discuss with me?"

"Not that I know of," replied Naidang. "It only just occurred to me to ask you."

"The venerable old märin is tough in business," Mr. Ping remarked cautiously.

"So am I," said Naidang.

At this Mr. Ping gave up any attempt at investigation. Plainly he had lost some deal, and not a small one either, for the old märin did not trade just in saucepans and reels of cotton. He dealt in horses and camels, and in complicated money transactions where one can either gain or lose. But the märin never lost, for he accepted no paper notes, and dealt only in gold or silver. In fact, wicked tongues whispered that he was the banker of the Venerable Chief.

When they had finished the bean noodles Naidang beckoned Mr. Ping to his side. "I need various articles," he said. "First of all an iron cooking grate."

Mr. Ping remarked sadly that the price of iron had risen terribly, then he timidly took Naidang's hand. The men's long sleeves fell over their joined hands, and no one could see what they were doing. While they sat solemnly opposite each other, Naidang kept his eyes fixed on Mr. Ping watching for any possible shiftiness, and Mr. Ping watched Naidang equally closely in order to exploit to the full the least sign of yielding.

Unfortunately, both were so well versed in the game that neither could catch the other out. Their business was done mainly by a silent and very secret play of the fingers. Mr. Ping pressed Naidang's hand twice with the thumb and once with the little finger. He was asking a shameless price. Naidang's face remained impassive. With a single pressure of the thumb he indicated his counter offer. This was as expected, but Mr. Ping made a grimace of pain, to show how deeply the offer had offended him. He let go Naidang's hand indignantly, but when that didn't work, his hand returned penitently to Naidang's. Eventually they agreed on one and a half silver batzes and the bargain was clinched. They let go hands, and a sigh of relief went through the tent.

"I also need forty pounds of the best flour," said Naidang boldly.

"Oh, Picture Sheet," sighed Mr. Ping. "I advise you to have the second best. It is blossom-white like the best, and even if it's a bit more gray, that's no harm."

"Your hand," said Naidang. "I must have the best."

When their hands joined, and the sleeves hid them, Naidang pinched the ball of Mr. Ping's thumb as a greeting. Mr. Ping remained very friendly. He knew that Naidang dared not lose face either before him or before his guests, once he had been so rash as to demand the best flour.

"Well, if you must have it, you must," mumbled Mr. Ping, shrugging his shoulders and by a firm pressure of the hand naming an outrageous price, from which he came down little by little. When their hands separated, Mr. Ping took down his calculating board, and by pushing about some balls, noted the prices agreed. But he did it all so quickly, hiding it the while with his coat, that even Big Tiger could not read the prices. Mr. Ping owed this discretion to his customers.

In this way Naidang bought a kettle, a brick of tea, some salt, a few pounds of bean noodles, garlic, mutton fat and a small water cask which Christian and Big Tiger filled. The goods were weighed and packed, and loaded on the pack camel in two even packs, one on each side.

"We're off!" said Good Fortune.

Naidang nodded, and while Good Fortune tightened the cinches, Naidang drew Affliction aside. "I have got two horses from you," he said.

"I know nothing of that," declared Affliction. "The horses didn't belong to me."

"We must look at this matter correctly," Naidang explained. "The *amban* of Suchow wants to shoot you dead. Am I to give him two horses as a reward, one of them moreover an ambler? It would be contrary to all custom, and a great injustice."

Affliction stepped timidly back, and said he didn't want to commit any injustice.

"Nor do I," declared Naidang. "It would sadden me for the rest of my life. Therefore I sold the horses yesterday to a man who is taking them to Ningshia today. That's a long way off."

"But they're not my horses," Affliction reminded him.

"*Hammagua!*" said Naidang. "The horses are sold and paid for, and I have bought your provisions with the money. But there was a balance, and here it is. Quick!" And he pressed a heavy little package into Affliction's hand. Affliction put it away with a sting of conscience, but Naidang didn't worry. Then he went up to Mr. Ping, who was standing by the *yurt* door, and said: "I'll stay with you a little."

Mr. Ping smiled sourly. Then Good Fortune came up with Big Tiger, Christian and Affliction in a row behind him. They all bowed and raised their hands to their foreheads, and Good Fortune said: "Fate bids us depart. We do not know where it will lead us, but wherever we go we shall remember your noble kindness. May your days be joyful and peaceful!" And with this Mongolian greeting he offered Naidang a perfectly new, especially fine *haddak,* woven with lucky symbols. He had extorted it from Mr. Ping on the strength of the big purchase while Naidang was talking to Affliction.

Naidang accepted the *haddak,* and Mr. Ping exclaimed: "Oh, what a rarely beautiful piece!"

When all were mounted Good Fortune rode off in front.

"*Sä Yabonah!*" cried Naidang and Mr. Ping.

"*Sä Sotyenah!*" cried Christian and Big Tiger.

The poodle didn't know what to do. First he went with the riders, but then turned back and stood barking in front of Naidang.

"Dog, come here!" cried Big Tiger.

"Off with you!" cried Naidang, but the poodle jumped around and would not leave Naidang.

"It can't be helped," said the latter, seizing his whip. But this did not help. At last Mr. Ping produced the leather collar with which he tied up his own shaggy dog at night beside his stack of wares. "It costs a silver batz," he said.

"We'll discuss that later," growled Naidang. "Give it to me."

Thus the poodle got a collar. Naidang put a rope on it and

Christian and Big Tiger turned back once more. As Naidang came up to them, the three found themselves alone together, Good Fortune and Affliction having gone on ahead, and Mr. Ping having returned to his *yurt*. "When you meet the Venerable Chief," said Naidang, "say to him: 'The Mongol Naidang of the Torgut tribe, called Picture Sheet, greets the Venerable Chief and asks him please to send the silver batzes direct to Naidang who lives at the Narin Gol, instead of by the old märin.' Do you understand?"

"Yes, we understand everything," said Christian.

"We will give your message," said Big Tiger.

"Farewell, my children," cried Naidang cheerfully.

He handed Christian the leash and stroked the poodle's black coat. For a long time he stood there looking after the riders and the poodle until they became smaller and smaller, and the sun went down.

I put one over on the old märin this time, he thought with satisfaction.

38 ABOUT THE TERRIBLE THINGS WHICH HAPPENED IN THE BEAUTIFUL VALLEY CALLED "NAMELESS"

It seemed to Christian and Big Tiger as if they had always lived in the desert. They felt at home quickly, because there life is reduced to its very simplest. There was nothing at all but the hard ground to ride on and the sky to look at. In the sky the stars were twinkling, and as the moon had not yet risen, Good Fortune had to be careful not to lose his way. Once more he had no other guide than the narrow camel track, to which he had to keep. But Good Fortune was happy and satisfied. He knew this route from other people's account of it just as well as if he had already traveled it himself. Of course he knew the Silk Road in the south better. It was a better road too, and one met somebody on it almost every day. But Greencoat was traveling there with the truck; indeed he might be in Hsing-hsing-hsia already.

There is really no reason why I should care, thought Good Fortune. But then it seemed to him that there might be one, and he decided he would turn into the Silk Road as soon as he should reach the Sinkiang frontier; perhaps at Ming-shui, he thought. Then he turned round to Affliction, who was riding behind him.

"Do you know Ming-shui?" he asked.

Affliction gave a start, but quickly pulled himself together. "I've never heard of the place," he lied bravely.

"Where is it?" asked Big Tiger.

"Just where the province of Kansu ends and Sinkiang begins," explained Good Fortune, "there's an old frontier fortress out in the middle of the desert."

"Is there anything special about that old fortress?" asked Christian anxiously.

"Not exactly," replied Good Fortune. "It's fallen into ruins, but you get to Hsing-hsing-hsia in a good two days' ride from there. I think it would be a good place for us to stop and look around a bit."

"We think so too," said Christian and Big Tiger.

Then they fell silent, and because it was night and none of them had a watch, the time began to drag, and Christian wished they would strike camp here and make a fire, for he was freezing. True, he had a coat, but he wouldn't wear it, for Big Tiger had none. So they both froze, the stars glittered, and their feet got colder and colder in the stirrups.

An hour passed, and then another, and Christian began to think caravan life was a hard one. He felt he couldn't sit in the saddle any longer, and was just going to ask Big Tiger whether he thought it permissible to walk for a while, or whether walking was totally against the rules for caravans, when Affliction slipped down from his camel, took it by the reins, and led it behind them. Thereupon Christian and Big Tiger leaped from their saddles as if at a word

of command, and the poodle was overjoyed to have company again, especially as it was still on a leash.

"I was afraid," confessed Big Tiger, "that it might not be honorable to go on foot when you're a caravan."

"I also thought that one could only ride," said Christian.

Affliction was very much astonished. "You don't ask a traveler how he's covered a thousand *li*," he said, "as long as he gets there."

"Sevenstars taught us," said Christian, "that our legs are meant only for riding, not for walking."

"That may well be true of Mongols," said Affliction. "They have themselves tied to their horses when they're tired."

"What's that you're saying?" cried Good Fortune, dismounting too. "Moonlight wouldn't be called Little Paw if he too hadn't walked one time."

Affliction, who did not know the story, asked Good Fortune to tell it to him. But just then Good Fortune stood still, and the poodle began to growl. "There's someone around," said Good Fortune, lowering his voice.

"He's got a horse with him," whispered Affliction.

"Then he's a redbeard," Good Fortune concluded. But he remained quite calm.

"Why do you stop?" cried a voice out of the darkness. But then the poodle began to bark loudly, and Christian had to hold him. They could no longer hear each other, so loud was the barking, and by the time it had ceased, and the dog was only gnashing his teeth, the stranger had galloped up to them. He stopped his horse right in front of Good Fortune. "Is your journey easy and good?" he asked. While saying this his eyes traveled from one to the other, until they came back to Good Fortune.

"Easy and good," replied Good Fortune. "Who are you?"

The man shook his head over such an improper question, and his pigtail swung round. This apparently meant disapproval, but they could not see clearly. "I have two words to say to you," announced the man. "When I have said them I must ride on."

"Speak!" said Good Fortune.

Sitting upright in his saddle, the man continued in a singing drawl: "Moonlight sends greetings to Good Fortune, Compass Mountain, Big Tiger and another, whose name I forget."

"That other is quite unimportant," interjected Affliction.

"Moonlight says: 'A son must go whence his father sends him—that is past. A friend shall go whence his friend bids him go—that is now.' Where I have been sitting just now waiting for you a fresh track leads northward. Moonlight bids Good Fortune follow that track." He stopped speaking and turned his horse. "*Bolvo?*" he asked brusquely.

"Bolna," replied Good Fortune resignedly.

"That being so," said the man, in a more friendly tone, "may I give you a bit of advice? Pitch your tent here and wait for daylight. The trail is faint, and you might lose it in the night. But ride on early, for there's neither food nor water here for the camels. You'll find both by midday, however."

"Is that all?" asked Good Fortune.

"What more do you expect?"

"The name of the well," said Good Fortune.

"It is called Nameless."

"Oh, I see!" said Good Fortune, bowing farewell. For the man was haughty, and he had a gun.

"Sleep well!" cried the stranger, urging his horse on and riding back the way he had come.

Good Fortune turned round diffidently to Big Tiger and Christian. All of a sudden he was no longer the leader who decided about the road to be taken and the camping place for the night. Someone else had taken over command.

It was different from taking orders under General Wu. The General would say: "Good Fortune, drive me to Hwai-lai-hsien." Good Fortune would drive to Hwai-lai-hsien, and the General would say: "Stop! I'm getting out here." That was all clear and simple, and it was natural for Good Fortune to obey, for behind the orders of General Wu there was nothing personal—only the map with the little flags, and the abacus. But here someone spoke to him from afar out of the darkness of the night, and requested a service as a friend. But behind the request stood a threat. Nothing had been said of what would happen if Good Fortune refused. But refusal was out of the question.

"Unload," ordered Good Fortune angrily. And Affliction proceeded to set up the tent. The ground was hard and smooth. He swept the stones aside, drove in the pegs, pushed the roof pole through the rings and fastened the stays. It was quick work.

Meanwhile Christian and Big Tiger laid a line on the ground, fastened it with tent pegs, and led the five camels up to it, placing them at the correct distance apart. When they cried "zook-zook," and the camels lay down, they tied them for the night.

Good Fortune disappeared and came back with an armful of tamarisk branches, just enough for a fire.

The moon rose like a ball of fire over the horizon. Then it turned yellow, and finally shone pale and still over the dead landscape.

"I was happy riding to my heart's content between the four seas," said Good Fortune. "I wanted to strike camp where I thought fit and where it pleased me to do so. Must someone always come to order a fellow about?"

Affliction stirred a pinch of salt into the boiling tea. "That has always been my lot. I've never known anything else but to be ordered about," he said.

"And what does your grandfather say?" inquired Good Fortune.

"When superior power oppresses," declared Big Tiger, "the time has come to be silent, and the straight road would not be the shortest."

"If that's so," said Good Fortune, "we must take the crooked road. Your grandfather has proved himself a sterling source of good counsel."

They drank tea and warmed their hands at the little fire. When Good Fortune said, "We have only six hours to sleep," they gathered together all the covers they had. The felt floor coverings from Ollon Torre they laid over the ground. Christian and Big Tiger got under the one fur coat, and Affliction and Good Fortune shared Affliction's topcoat.

"If only our dog doesn't bite his leash through," said Big Tiger.

"He'll eat it up," said Affliction. "The 'thirteen-grains-of-millet feeding' doesn't suit everybody."

"He's no ordinary dog," Christian objected. "He knows he has to guard the camels and ourselves."

"*Tinger metne,*" said Good Fortune. The poodle yawned loudly. He was much too tired to gnaw his leash.

Before sunrise next morning Good Fortune was already out searching for tamarisk wood. While Affliction made the breakfast Christian and Big Tiger saddled. The poodle got a bowl of lukewarm water, and by the time the sun was up all were in the saddle.

The region looked different by daylight. The hills, which the darkness had hidden, were all visible, and the tamarisks looked as if a child had stuck them here and there on a sand castle. To the north were blue mountains, their jagged peaks floating on the morning mist.

"Where is the trail?" asked Christian, as Good Fortune turned aside from the caravan track.

"Watch out for it," muttered Good Fortune.

Affliction halted his camel, and the pack camel stopped too. "As the bad business has begun," he said, "we must watch out and let nothing escape us."

"I've noticed nothing," said Big Tiger.

"Is there something?" asked Christian.

Affliction looked after Good Fortune, but Good Fortune was riding on, and one could see that he was watching out as hard as he could.

"There are horses' tracks here as well as camel tracks," said Affliction. "Two of them are going northward, and Good Fortune is following them. The others accompany the caravan track westward, and those no longer concern us, at least not for the present."

They rode on together and could see the hoof marks of two horses wherever Good Fortune's camel had not trodden on them. One hoof mark was heavier than the other.

"That's the stallion," said Christian.

"Moonlight and Thunderbolt rode along here," said Affliction in a low voice, "but before they turned northward they met Mr. Ma and the other man who is accompanying the caravan. Perhaps there was a second or even a third redbeard there too. Over there, where there are a lot of hoof marks, they stopped and talked. And they didn't dismount, for there are no footprints. Then Moonlight and Thunderbolt rode north, the caravan went on, and the fellow who wouldn't tell us his name waited for us."

"We admit we were unobservant," said Big Tiger.

"From now on," promised Christian, "we'll use our brains better."

"May I ask what you two think of the situation?" inquired Affliction. "You see, we three are now in the same boat, and the wind is beginning to rise."

"You mean," said Big Tiger, "what the men had to say to each other, and why Thunderbolt and Moonlight left the caravan road?"

"That's just it," said Affliction uneasily. "When it comes to guess hidden reasons, few are clever and many are stupid."

"One person couldn't get to the bottom of that alone," Big Tiger admitted modestly. "I think Moonlight and Thunderbolt did not want to go by the caravan road at all, but when they saw the fresh camel tracks they rode after them to see who they had in front of them."

"I knew," cried Affliction, "that you could guess hidden things."

"After they had spoken to Ma," said Christian, "they rode north to reach the place where Gontshuk is waiting for them with fresh horses. You know—four horses—'too few and too many.'"

"That's just what I don't like," sighed Affliction; "that yes and no in one."

"No great harm in that," said Big Tiger reassuringly. "But why have we got to ride after the two of them now?"

"Because Moonlight doesn't want us to travel with Mr. Ma's caravan. He has something special in mind for us."

"Probably some first-class misfortune," said Affliction. "Ah, we four are indeed to be pitied."

The morning passed. A wind had risen, and little white clouds were scurrying across the sky from west to east. It was all Good Fortune could do to keep the trail in sight, not because of the wind but because the ground was becoming stonier. They were reaching the foothills of the mountains which had looked blue and hazy in the dawn. Between the ranges of hills the lake beds were dried-up clay with deep cracks. As long as the trail led across them the hoof marks were distinctly visible. But once past them, the trail was lost in a stony slope and Good Fortune sought for it in vain. Suddenly he halted. "It can't be helped," he said.

"Here's a hoof mark," cried Christian, pointing to a little spot of earth between the stones.

"Wild asses," said Good Fortune scornfully.

"Where there are wild asses," declared Affliction, "the world is at an end. And there's an end of hope too, of course."

"There must be grass around here," said Good Fortune. "Grass means water, and water means . . . well, it doesn't matter what it means. Anyway, we must turn back. We've lost the trail."

He turned his camel and they all rode down the stony slope again, to the dried-up lake bed. When they came back to the spot where Moonlight's and Thunderbolt's tracks could been seen, Good Fortune dismounted and walked, watching the ground step by step. At times he thought he saw a track, but then he would come to a spot where there wasn't a speck of earth or sand. The wretched stones covered everything. Through them some scrub and heathlike plants and a few thistles had pierced their way. Mounting his camel again he said to Christian: "Let the dog free. We shall ride back to the caravan track and he won't run away from us then."

"Bolna!" cried Christian, jumping down from his camel. "The dog will be glad."

"He'll be the ruin of us," prophesied Affliction.

The poodle jumped with joy when Christian took off the leash. Then the retreat began. Good Fortune rode on in front, and the poodle ran far ahead. The ground was smooth and stoneless, and when the poodle turned round and barked to tell everyone how happy he was, he swept the brown, fissured ground with his tail but no dust swirled up. Nothing swirled up but a thin red ribbon, and this the poodle grabbed. It fell at his feet, and when he'd picked it up and turned it round a few times with his paws, he sniffed it earnestly. Then he stood up and barked proudly, as he had done when he found Christian's fur coat.

"What have you there, dog?" asked Good Fortune.

"It's sad," said Affliction. "It's the remains of some dead person."

"Rather small remains," said Good Fortune, ironically.

"It's nothing of the kind," said Christian. "The little ribbon belonged to the stallion. It was plaited into his mane."

"He had two ribbons," said Big Tiger.

"Take it with you," advised Good Fortune. "A horse gets those ribbons when he wins a race. Take it to the Venerable Chief as a present, and he'll be very pleased."

"Dog!" said Christian. "You're no ordinary dog." He stroked

the thick head, and then he said again, but in a commanding tone, holding the ribbon under the poodle's nose: "Dog! Seek—find!"

The poodle seemed to have been waiting for just that word. He ran on, his nose close to the ground, until he came to the spot where the trail ceased among the stones.

"He's lost the scent," said Good Fortune.

"No, he hasn't," cried Christian. "He's only waiting for us."

"Is there anything wrong?" asked Affliction, who did not understand.

"The dog is showing us the way," Christian explained.

"A bit late," said Good Fortune dubiously. But he turned his camel and rode back.

They had not yet reached the edge of the dry lake bed when the poodle resumed his trot. Instead of running up the mountainside in the direction of the trail, he turned east and ran across the gravel which was piled up at the foot of the slope. The camels had to walk slowly, for the stones were slippery and the path was slightly uphill. Presently the gravelly slope dropped gently into a broad valley, with another brown, basinlike clay bed. But no hoof marks were to be seen in this one. The poodle ran on ahead. Where the valley narrowed and drifts of sand covered the ground, the tracks could be seen again. The little caravan proceeded uphill for half an hour and was already approaching a plateau and a great clear space, when suddenly the poodle disappeared into a side valley. Boulders barred the way.

Good Fortune was the first to dismount. The others followed suit. They led their camels between two walls of rock until the gorge widened and they had a clear view into a depression which looked like an abandoned stone quarry. But here a sight which they never expected met their eyes—high deresen grass filled the bottom of the basin, and around its edges, between patches of scrub, a few beam trees struggled for life. The wall of rock had collapsed in the middle and its ruins were spread far around. The landslide which had followed its fall hid the back part of the basinlike de-

pression. There they heard the poodle barking loudly, and he sounded as if he were hopping with joy. The barking came nearer, and as Good Fortune rounded the rubbly slope, where the ground was soft, a horseman trotted toward him. He was riding a gray piebald, and Christian recognized the horse at once.

"Did you have a good journey?" he asked, bowing to Good Fortune.

"Is your rest peaceful, Gontshuk?" Good Fortune replied.

"I have neglected my duty by being late," confessed Gontshuk. "Moonlight ordered me to come as far as the dried lake to meet you. You must have started very early."

"We were very nearly not getting here," said Affliction, "but the dog led us to you."

"May I beg you not to mention this to Moonlight," cried Gontshuk, alarmed.

"Why should we?" said Good Fortune laughing, "since we're here now. Are you alone?"

"Yes," answered Gontshuk; "and I meant to go home as soon as I had met you. But now I can't."

"Why can't you?" asked Good Fortune.

"Has something happened?" inquired Affliction.

"Something is going to happen," declared Gontshuk, pointing to the sky. They all looked up. The sun was stinging and the little white clouds were no longer scurrying. Two eagles were soaring at a great height, and watching their calm flight, one would think that the air was motionless. The vault of the sky was clear and blue over the walls of rock, except for two transparent white strips which were coming, the one from the north, the other from the south, to meet like the arch of a bridge which still lacked the keystone. But that was just the point.

Gontshuk raised his arms over his head, and when his hands touched he said significantly: "It will be three hours from now."

"I hadn't noticed it," said Affliction, "but now I do."

Good Fortune merely nodded and said: "We must stir ourselves." He took his camel by the reins and stepped smartly forward. Gontshuk showed the way, but in fact it was visible, for the depression was at an end. The cliffs rose straight over a sandbank and a watery swamp, from which a little stream flowed, in places forming pools and then losing itself in the deresen pastures. When they came nearer they could hear the dripping of water.

On the sandbank lay Gontshuk's few belongings—a kettle, a bag, a few blankets and some harness.

"It's safest under the rocks," said Gontshuk; "that is, if a rock doesn't fall, or if the mountainside doesn't collapse."

"We're in heaven's hands," replied Good Fortune, and they began to unload. There was firm ground near the sandbank, and Affliction set up the tent. Good Fortune told Big Tiger to water the camels, while Christian went to fetch fresh water. The water was clear and cold, but very shallow. The camels had dispersed along the waterhole and it looked as if they would drink it dry.

"Hold them back," cried Christian, and Big Tiger held back the camels until the cask was full. "Why are you hurrying so much?" he asked Big Tiger. "Don't you know we have three hours yet?"

"Three hours until what?" asked Big Tiger.

"I don't know," confessed Christian, "but something frightful is on the way."

"It can't be helped," said Big Tiger, looking at the sky where the white arches of clouds were imperceptibly approaching each other. The eagles were still circling noiselessly overhead.

"It's very hot," said Christian, as he set down the water cask in front of Affliction. "Will there be a thunderstorm?"

Affliction looked up. He was busy making a dung fire, and that was no easy matter, for he had no wood. When he had put on the kettle and begun to prepare the bean noodles, he asked: "What's that you're saying?"

"I expect there's a thunderstorm coming," said Christian; "the sun is so hot."

"The best weather is in the autumn," declared Affliction, "not now."

"Are thunderstorms good weather?" asked Christian.

"They bring rain," said Affliction.

"And what's going to come down now?" asked Christian.

"Sand," said Affliction, pointing to the two arches of cloud. "My hearty good wishes for two or three days sound sleep. I hope you'll enjoy it."

"Thanks ten thousand times," said Christian. He went to Big Tiger who was fastening the camels' reins loosely around their necks as Sevenstars had taught him. "There's a sandstorm coming," he said. "Affliction says it will last two or three days."

"What's all the excitement for?" asked Big Tiger, thinking of the dust storms which swept over Peking in the spring. They came from the Gobi Desert, people said. And everyone went home and mended the holes in the paper windows, and that was all. But then Big Tiger recalled what Good Fortune had said about sandstorms, and he was frightened.

"If we're held up here for three days," he said, "how shall we be in Ming-shui on the fourth day of the third month?"

"Mr. Ma will also be held up," Christian reminded him.

"He can make up for lost time," said Big Tiger, "but we can't say to Good Fortune: 'We must march three hours longer every day from now on, because we have an appointment.'"

Christian scratched his head and said quietly: "We shall have to think hard over this."

"*Kwai, kwai!*" shouted Good Fortune. "If you're finished watering the beasts and drawing water, go gather *argal*. The heavens will grant us only a short time more."

Christian and Big Tiger went to and fro gathering all the dung they could find, breaking dried branches from the beam trees, and bringing them to Affliction to stow near the fireplace. Gontshuk rode through the pasture driving the horses before him, but the stallion was not among them.

"Should we corral the camels too?" asked Christian.

"It's not necessary," said Gontshuk. "Camels are more sensible than horses. They don't run away. They just lie down."

"Food, food!" called Affliction. "Hi, Good Fortune, *kwai, kwai!*"

Good Fortune did not come until everything was in order. He threw back a flap of the tent, to have an open view of the pasture. One could see the camels grazing, and the boulders of rock between which the stream trickled. One could also see the blue sky with the arches of cloud and, high in the air, the eagles soaring. While they were all eating their bean noodles, Gontshuk took a piece of dried mutton from his bag and passed it around. "It's better to eat it now without sand," he said.

Afterwards they drank tea, and the poodle got a piece of meat.

It might have been toward four when the arches of cloud met. The sun was still shining gaily, and Good Fortune was just about to give Gontshuk greetings from his father Naidang which he hadn't been told to give. But he hoped to start a lengthy conversation this way. Suddenly, however, Affliction stuck out his head, pointed to the sky and said, "The bad business is beginning."

All but Gontshuk looked out to where Affliction's finger was pointing. Christian and Big Tiger were just in time to see two dark objects fall from the sky. Just over the rocks the eagles spread their wings and disappeared. They had taken shelter.

Immediately afterwards the tent became as dark as a cellar. No one noticed the howling of the storm, or the tumult with which it broke into the gorge. For a torrent of stones big and small came pelting down on the tent. Evidently they had been lying on the edge of the rocky plateau. Now they fell straight down and Good Fortune, who was sitting at the back of the tent on the seat of honor, got the biggest share and the biggest stones. He screamed.

Gontshuk murmured prayers, and his beads slipped through his fingers. Affliction drew his military coat over his head, and Christian and Big Tiger took refuge under the sheepskin coat. Nobody knew how it happened, but suddenly the poodle was in the tent too, seeking shelter beside Christian. "Good dog!" whispered Christian, fondling his wet muzzle. "Don't be frightened," whispered Big Tiger, holding his trembling paw.

"Don't be frightened," repeated Affliction bravely, as he fell with the kettle over Good Fortune. The earth trembled, and the tent poles were pulled up at least a hand's breadth by the pressure of the air. It lasted only a second, but Good Fortune's thumb was caught under a pole and when the gust passed he could not pull it out.

There was a frightful thunder clap, a sizzle and a stink. Fortunately the stink was only the burning camel dung which had been soaked by the tea kettle. But the ashes were so hot that they burned the poodle's paws, and he jumped up on Affliction's back. There he lay. Affliction lay too, and Good Fortune couldn't stand up either, for his thumb was still under the pole.

Christian and Big Tiger were the first to get on their feet. It was still dark, but the ground no longer trembled, the thunder had ceased, and only a few little stones were whizzing over the tent roof, and falling in the grass some distance off. But one could still hear the roaring of the storm and see the clouds of sand whirling about in the rocky basin. The sun hung above like a distant red lamp. The poodle slunk guiltily out of the tent.

Gontshuk wound his prayer beads round his wrist and looked

around at the survivors. "Has anyone been badly hurt?" he asked.

"I haven't," said Christian, proceeding to shake Affliction.

"I haven't either," said Affliction, "or not much." He tried to stand up, and succeeded. He was pale but relieved. "Accept my condolences," he said, "Good Fortune is done for. I beg the young princes to curb their grief."

"What?" screamed Big Tiger. "What are you saying?"

"I can't do anything about it," sighed Affliction. "We'd need a lantern."

"One can see that without light," said Gontshuk, exerting all his strength to raise the tent pole and get Good Fortune's thumb free. But the thumb, though free, didn't move.

"Good Fortune!" cried Christian sorrowfully, pushing aside the hand with the thick swollen thumb. But Good Fortune made no answer, and Gontshuk let the tent pole drop again with a heavy thud. "We must call back his spirits. They can't be gone far yet," he advised.

Christian filled his silver bowl with water and splashed it in Good Fortune's face. Good Fortune opened his eyes, but his color did not come back for a long time. "My head," he moaned, "my ears, my neck! I'm hurt all over."

Affliction rolled up a felt rug, pushed it under Good Fortune's head, and covered him up with his coat. "Lie on your side," he advised. "Then the lump on the back of your head won't hurt. What's that? Your shoulder is hurting too? Wait now. I'll look and see if any of the horses are dead. Horse fat makes a grand ointment."

He peeped out of the tent, and saw Gontshuk like a shadow through the reddish clouds of sand. Near him stood four horses at the line. None of them was missing or lying down, for Gontshuk had cautiously set up the line a good distance from the rocky wall. Now that no more stones were falling from the rock face, he moved the line into the shelter of the rock.

"I thought," said Gontshuk when he came back, "that the tent would stand the rain of stones better. I must note that for the future."

"The future is uncertain," said Good Fortune. "The present is all that is certain." And he felt the back of his head, to see if the lump was still there.

"It will get bigger," Affliction consoled him. "We have time to wait." He tidied up the tent. Big Tiger swept away the ashes, and Christian hammered back the pegs which had been loosened when the air pressure had lifted the tent.

"What happened to me?" asked Good Fortune.

"You've got a misshapen thumb," Affliction informed him.

Good Fortune looked at his purple swollen thumb but remained heroically silent. Outside the storm was raging over the cliffs and howling in the clefts, and the sand was falling on the tent like fine rain. Farther off stones were still dropping on the grass.

"See to the camels," ordered Good Fortune. He was already recovering.

Christian and Big Tiger jumped up and Gontshuk went with them. As they left the shelter of the cliffs the strong wind nearly blew away Big Tiger's beautiful fur hat.

"Number one," cried Gontshuk, pointing to the pack camel which was lying in the deresen grass with its back to the wind. Its long neck was stretched on the ground, its eyes were half-shut, but the nostrils were moving.

"There are no more of them here," muttered Gontshuk, and Christian wondered how he knew. In the semidarkness, through which the clouds of sand swept like veils, they couldn't see ten yards before them. But just before the storm broke Gontshuk had looked, not at the eagles, but at the camels, and had noted exactly where they were. So now, like a sleepwalker, he made straight for the spot where he had last seen the second camel. But he found none.

Before them rose the outlines of mighty blocks of stone which had not lain there before, and they stumbled over boulders and sharp-edged rocks and had to make a big detour, for a fresh avalanche of rocks had brought a further large area of ground into motion, and the landslide was still going on.

"Watch out," Gontshuk warned. "It's very easy to die."

Big Tiger and Christian groped after Gontshuk, who himself was groping blindly, and was only able to find an outlet to the upper part of the valley when the outlines of the southern cliffs emerged before them. They didn't meet a single camel, but the poodle suddenly appeared, running along before them, wagging his tail confidently.

"Camels also die easily," Gontshuk roared above the storm. "They seem in fact to like dying." For he wanted to prepare Christian and Big Tiger for the possibility that they might never again find them.

"But there are some here," cried Christian.

"At least two," shouted Big Tiger, pointing to tracks in the loosened earth.

Gontshuk knit his brows and raised his thumbs in sign of approbation. "Dog!" he shouted. "Seek—find, if you're any good." He pressed the dog's nose down on the camel tracks, but it was no longer necessary. A few steps farther on they found the four camels huddled close together.

39 HOW THE CARAVAN TRAVELED ALONG THE PATH OF MEDITATION

For two days and three nights the black storm howled. The food was full of sand. They all had to blow their noses continually, and Christian's and Big Tiger's skin now looked exactly alike. Even brown-skinned Gontshuk looked like a yellow sandman.

"How much longer will it last?" asked Christian on the morning of the third day, as they drank their tea and chewed their millet, crunching the sand between their teeth.

"Why should things change?" asked Affliction. "Heaven and earth are united. It is the image of peace. As for me—I'm having a very good time." And he wiped a collection of sand from the corners of his eyes.

"It couldn't be better," agreed Good Fortune ironically. He was able to sit up straight again, and with care could even put on his hat.

"All the same," said Gontshuk, "I'll ride home today."

"Don't be rash," Good Fortune warned, for he noticed Gontshuk shaking the last fodder beans out of the sack. "Only heaven knows how it's going to turn out."

"The sun will be shining by midday," asserted Gontshuk. "I'll go."

"That's fine," cried Christian. "Then we'll be able to ride on."

"Are you in such a hurry?" asked Good Fortune.

"Yes, we are," said Christian. "Because the amah is waiting for me, and Big Tiger has to go back to school."

"And what about your school?"

"My teachers are all right," explained Christian, "but when I asked only one day off for Big Tiger his teacher said he was sorry for him."

Good Fortune stood up and looked out. He came back highly excited. "Come on," he cried. "The storm is abating and the sun is coming out."

"I see no end of the storm," said Affliction. He had just turned back to the tent when with one stroke everything changed. It was as if an ugly curtain had suddenly been drawn back, or the conductor of a brass band had laid down his baton in the middle of a piece. The horns and trumpets were silent, the fanfares no longer blared, and the big drum ceased to roll. From the rim of the rocky basin beamed a blue, windless, sunny sky. Only in the distance a sinister grayish-yellow wall rolled eastward.

At the bottom of the valley the camels were grazing as if storm and sunshine made no difference. With them were four brown animals with white bellies and curious long ears, which they pricked up as they looked over fearlessly.

"What are those?" asked Christian.

"Wild asses," said Affliction, "the last creatures in the world."

"We shall ride at midday," said Good Fortune. While they all took off their clothes and shook out the sand, Good Fortune asked Gontshuk casually: "Have you got a message for me?"

"I have," said Gontshuk, as he emptied his boots. "Moonlight sends you greetings and Thunderbolt begs his younger brothers to think kindly of him."

"Does he mean you two?" asked Good Fortune.

"He must," admitted Christian, embarrassed.

"A certain relationship has arisen," explained Big Tiger.

"My! won't your worthy parents be pleased," said Good Fortune. "Your grandfather will be particularly charmed."

"I hope for grandfather's approval," said Big Tiger. "He loves both the usual and the unusual virtues."

"There are some very unusual virtues there," Good Fortune assured him, "but as I'm no judge of the virtues I reserve judgment. Speak on, Gontshuk."

"You have a good road before you now," continued Gontshuk. "Ten *li* north of here there is a path which is little used. You will hardly meet a soul on it, and so you will travel pleasantly. There is even a well here and there."

"A magnificent route," muttered Good Fortune.

"It is a road of fasting and meditation," Gontshuk explained. "The pilgrims who go to Lhasa use it. After five days you will reach a magnificent place. It is called Ikhe Gol, the Big River. There are real trees and grass there, and good water; and a man who speaks little."

"What's his name?" asked Good Fortune.

"He is called Toeless," answered Gontshuk. "More I do not know."

"He must be a criminal," said Good Fortune.

"He was unwise," admitted Gontshuk, "and so something happened to him."

"Better still," muttered Good Fortune. "It's not often one meets such fine company. Take care now you don't acquire a new relation," he said, turning to Christian and Big Tiger.

"We will be very reserved," promised Christian.

They set out at the hour of the sheep.* The sun was shining brightly and warmly. The air was absolutely still, and the boulders lay about the valley called Nameless as if they had always lain there. Only the newly broken parts glistened, and the little stream formed pools here and there which trickled away.

"Yabonah!" cried Gontshuk gaily. He was mounted on the gray piebald and was driving the other three horses before him.

"Yabonah!" cried Christian and Big Tiger.

They rode together through the narrow pass, until they reached the valley which led to the height. There they parted. "You'll get to the Path of Meditation in a good hour," said Gontshuk.

"Words are poor things," said Big Tiger. "All the same I beg you to give our greetings to your father Naidang and Sevenstars."

And Christian said: "You're not me, but I wish I were you, for then I could see Sevenstars again."

"I'll give them all your greetings," promised Gontshuk.

"May old Picture Sheet live a thousand years!" cried Good Fortune.

Then they parted.

On the high plateau which they now crossed, the trail had been wiped out by the storm. The tips of a few tamarisks showed above the waves of sand, and the cracks in the ground were filled with sand like plowed furrows after a snowfall. In the blue sky the

* 1-3 P.M.

eagles were soaring again, the camels were treading the first tracks in the sand, and everything was as fresh as if life were beginning anew.

Christian and Big Tiger were very happy. Now they were a real caravan traveling through the desert without even a track before it. True, Good Fortune was turning north to find the Path of Meditation, but in spite of this they were venturing into the unknown like the great adventurers of past ages. Moreover, they were sitting on real camels, and the water was gurgling in the water cask. They rode thus for more than an hour. The landscape remained the same, for the plateau was large; only at the edges rose sharp mountain peaks.

Suddenly Good Fortune headed westward. Turning round in the saddle he said: "Every highroad leads to Peking. Every narrow path leads to Lhasa."*

So they were now on the Path of Meditation. Apparently it was also a path of concealment, for Christian, who was last in the file, only saw it when he turned his camel. It was a mere shadow, a wavering thread, which ran toward a distant mountain ridge. And they rode along following this thin shadow of a path. The mountain ridge, which seemed at the end of the world, and so far away it could not be reached before the next day at the earliest, changed color after only three hours. It loomed higher, and they could see that it was not blue, but yellow and gray like the desert. But the streams of stones which tumbled from its ravines were light, almost white, and the path went up the biggest of these boulder-strewn slopes. There it was lost, and one could only hope that it would appear again later.

"Halt!" ordered Good Fortune. "We'll make camp."

"Bolna!" cried Christian joyfully. But then he realized that they had only marched a short stretch. He quickly counted up on his fingers the days which remained until the fourth day of the third moon.

* The capital of Tibet, and a renowned place of pilgrimage.

"We've still got nine days," he whispered to Big Tiger, and Big Tiger replied softly: "It can't be helped."

"It looks as if there might be water here," remarked Good Fortune.

"Let the unlucky dog loose," Affliction advised. "He's not without talents."

The poodle, when freed, did not understand what was required of him, so he just ran to and fro barking joyfully.

Good Fortune had meantime climbed the stony slope to see if the path continued above it. Affliction remained with the camels, and Christian and Big Tiger said: "Dog! Come with us!" They walked along the edge of the stream of stones until they came to a round open space overshadowed by a high rock. This space was as smooth as a floor, and fringed with tamarisks. It was cold and dark in the shadow of the rock, but Big Tiger realized at once that a heavy stone which stood in the middle had not just rolled there by itself. Christian too noticed this and said: "Let's uncover the well."

They rolled the stone aside, and as they were by now experienced old caravan men, they brushed away the sand before lifting the plank. Then they called Affliction. He came with the camels, and Good Fortune came too, for he had found the Path of Meditation again above the white stream of stones.

"You've found an excellent place," said Good Fortune. "We'll pitch the tent here."

"There's water here too," said Big Tiger. "Our dog is full of wisdom."

"He's no ordinary dog," asserted Christian.

They stood proudly beside the poodle, and as they had not exactly lied, they didn't blush.

Then the blue tent was erected for the first time merrily and without haste. In the west the sun was standing over endless jagged mountain peaks, or perhaps they were not mountains at all, but only hills or sand dunes looking like mountains because there was nothing high with which to compare them. They were glittering magnificently, and the rim of the horizon was purple like that evening in Durben Mot. The fiery orb of the sun glided slowly earthward. Then darkness fell suddenly.

Christian and Big Tiger went to collect the camels, which were nibbling the tamarisks, and the poodle went with them. They all worked like a well-trained team in which each man has his allotted task and does it without fuss. Good Fortune collected tamarisk wood and drew water, Affliction cooked noodles again, and Christian and Big Tiger watered the camels and tied them to the line. After they had eaten, and the fire was still flickering softly, Good Fortune started to hold forth.

"Well, the time has come . . ." he began.

"Excuse me," Affliction interrupted him. "Health comes first, and garlic is the best vegetable." He distributed cloves of garlic, and when they had all nibbled them, Good Fortune resumed: "The time has come for the moon to wane. Dim though its light is, it suffices to find the Path of Meditation. So we must get up soon after midnight and keep on the march till the forenoon. For the camels have to find their food on the road. It's not the pleasantest way to travel, but what does that matter?"

"It doesn't matter a bit," cried Christian and Big Tiger eagerly.

And they all lay down to sleep.

40 CONCERNING TOELESS, A CRIMINAL, WHO DWELT IN THE MIDDLE OF THE GOBI DESERT

"QUICK! Get up!" shouted Good Fortune. "The moon is rising!" But the moon didn't come out, and the camels stood saddled.

"The moon is late," said Good Fortune, taking his camel by the reins and leading the way up the stony slope. The others followed. They all walked, for it was very cold. The stones slipped under the camels' feet and rolled down into the valley. The black walls of cliff echoed back each question, and an icy breeze blew down the gorges. Affliction buttoned up his coat.

Further on the ground was firmer and when the moon rose and the gorges of the stony mountains changed to gentle valleys, they all mounted their camels. The going was slow and continuously uphill. The stars came nearer and nearer, and then one after the other disappeared, and the mighty sun rose over the parched earth. Toward ten o'clock they put up the tent and let the camels loose to find what food they could. But there was nothing but tamarisks.

Christian and Big Tiger went to sleep. Good Fortune slept too, and Affliction just dozed until it was time to prepare the food. Then Christian and Big Tiger collected the camels, and the poodle helped them.

Once again the camels were allowed to try their luck and nibble the tamarisks down to the wood. They were only rounded up when they strayed too far from the camp, but as soon as darkness fell they were tied to the line. Affliction served noodles, garlic and tea. The poodle had a bowl of water and left-overs.

They marched in this way four nights and five days, and each night was colder than the last. Christian and Big Tiger froze at night. By day they were hungry. They came on wells several times, as Gontshuk had said they would, but the water was stale and the tea tasted like yesterday's. They didn't meet one single person. There were no animals either, and when they passed a dead camel by the wayside the sunken skin was still on the skeleton, and they could see the dried-up contents of the belly, for there weren't even wolves or vultures around.

"It's time we reached the Ikhe Gol," said Affliction sullenly.

"We're almost there," said Christian.

"You astound me," said Affliction.

"How?" asked Big Tiger.

"The knowledge of you two," interjected Good Fortune. He stopped to mount, and they all did the same, for it was late morning and the sun had warmed up.

"Since yesterday," declared Christian, "we have the trails of Moonlight and Thunderbolt in front of us again."

"I've noticed them," said Good Fortune sleepily.

"They're still there," said Affliction. "Anyone can see them."

"That proves we're on the right road," said Big Tiger.

"We know it," said Good Fortune.

"As we promised Affliction we'd be more observant," said Christian, "we noticed that for the past half-hour the hoof prints show more speed."

"The horses galloped along here," said Big Tiger, pointing to the Path of Meditation.

"Oh, you young rascals," cried Good Fortune, "you're like real redbeards and better. I wouldn't be surprised if the gentlemen of the mountains came to beg you, on their knees, to be their chiefs."

"It would be too much of an honor," said Big Tiger.

"We'd have to grow up first," said Christian.

They rode between round sandhills on which thorny shrubs grew, and Good Fortune was no longer sleepy. Affliction too looked eagerly ahead. The camels sniffed expectantly and stepped out more briskly.

When the sandhills flattened out, a fertile plain with bushes and trees suddenly lay before their eyes. In summer it would be green and magnificent as an island in the midst of the sea. They looked down between the branches of the trees, and though the trees were many, they could see the roof of a hut, with a curl of smoke from it. The grass was yellow. Where it ceased a merry little brook came out as if hurrying to meet the world. But the world all round was desert, and the little brook could not turn back. It ran just a little way, then divided, like the end of a rope, into several ragged fringes. There were tussocks of grass here and there. A few blades of reeds stuck like daggers through the sand, but nothing more could be seen of the stream. The path led through a thicket of little beam trees and thorny scrub. In a small clearing two sheep were grazing, the hoof marks of horses were to be seen, and then, suddenly, there was a square field, a genuine tilled piece of land with furrows, in which broken brown stalks and seed capsules lay.

"*Ene yu beino?*" asked Christian and Big Tiger, who did not recognize the crop.

Good Fortune and Affliction exchanged significant glances, and Good Fortune said slowly: "This is a burning shame. It's opium poppy."

At the end of the field stood a clay hut. It had a window and a door, and four discolored white walls. The window was decently papered, and there was only one little peephole in the lower pane. The door was made of old blackish boards, and the poodle pushed it open with his muzzle. A burning ember flew out at him, and he withdrew his thick head in haste and barked furiously, then fled for refuge to Christian and Big Tiger, who had leaped from their saddles, shouting, "Dog! Come here!"

Good Fortune went ahead and stopped ten paces from the door, which had closed again mysteriously and as if of itself. Christian as he stood near him thought of the ginger-bread house and the witch who had come out of it.

"If there's anyone here," shouted Good Fortune, "let him show himself."

"Don't waste words," cried a deep male voice. "Come in and drink tea."

Good Fortune looked at Affliction, and Affliction took down the gun from his shoulder. "It seems," he said joyfully, "that we're invited in. That's what it sounded like, anyhow."

"By a criminal," muttered Good Fortune, "and an opium grower."

Affliction was not so narrow-minded. "Venerable old uncle," he called out, "have patience for two seconds! Be quick!" he ordered in a low voice. "We'll unload here and set up the tent. You," he said to Good Fortune, "have not got the right approach to people who bury themselves in the wilderness like the saints of past ages. Let me speak with him."

"All right," growled Good Fortune. "You'll quickly establish a kind of relationship. My congratulations in advance."

Near the hut there was a clear space, where two stakes had been rammed into the ground and a line stretched between them.

"We mustn't camp here," said Affliction. "It's the place for the horses."

"Horses?" asked Big Tiger.

"Yes, horses," said Affliction, and he pointed to the heaps of dung here and there.

"What about here?" asked Christian.

"All right," said Good Fortune indifferently.

The place was like a fairytale. There was a meadow surrounded by bushes, and a little slope on one side, also covered with trees, the roots of which sprang out of the ground like bent bows, but turned back again to seek the brook which ran along the boundary of the meadow.

And to all these splendors Good Fortune merely said a sulky "All right." But Good Fortune's mood did not depress Christian and Big Tiger. They were glad to note that Affliction was happy. As soon as the tent was up they let the camels loose. The poodle drank at the stream and ran around, joyfully wagging his tail. But he seemed afraid to venture near the hut.

"Come," said Affliction. "We'll go in now."

"Perhaps there'll be something to eat," said Christian to cheer up Good Fortune, who was sitting in a black mood on a saddle before the tent.

"It's the same every day," sighed Good Fortune. "Wherever I go I happen on rogues and swindlers. I'd like to meet honest people for a change."

"Our respected elder need only look at us," said Big Tiger.

"You?" cried Good Fortune. "I see robber chiefs in front of me." But then he had to laugh, and Christian and Big Tiger took him under the armpits and helped him to his feet. They entered the hut together, behind Affliction.

The black board door opened noiselessly and closed automatically behind them, for it was fitted with a rope-and-pulley contraption, worked by an iron ball which hung from the middle of the roof. The ceiling was unplastered and one could see the smoky rafters. The fireplace was in the corner opposite the door. It had a portable grate like the fireplaces in every tent, but here there was a real chimney. By the fireplace was an open space with a smooth clay floor. A chest stood in the center, and behind it a *kang,* covered with straw matting. And on the *kang* lay a man dressed in blue trousers and jacket. He had a grayish pigtail, a powerful nose, and a thin drooping moustache. He might have been about fifty years old, and looked like an honest farmer.

"We wish you good rest," said Affliction.

"We wish you comfort," said Christian and Big Tiger.

Good Fortune bowed silently.

The man climbed down from the *kang*. It was immediately obvious that he could not walk well. Grabbing a stick, he hurried over to the fire, turning around on the way to invite his guests, with a bow and a wave of arms, to sit down on the *kang*.

"After you," said Good Fortune.

"How could we dare," said Affliction.

"Don't talk nonsense," cried the man. "Sit down." Without waiting for them to obey his invitation, he picked up the tea kettle from the hot embers. When he came back with it Christian and Big Tiger had obediently climbed up on the *kang*, and Good Fortune was sitting beside Affliction on the edge of it, his feet resting against the chest.

The man took out of the chest painted porcelain cups and little dishes of melon- and sunflower-seeds, all in the style of the best inns.

Affliction gave a satisfied wink. He seemed to have expected all this.

"Please speak," said the man. "I like listening."

Affliction began the introductions. "My unworthy name is Affliction," he said, "but it's not worth mentioning. Please, honored uncle, regard it as unsaid. And here are the useless rascals Compass Mountain and Big Tiger, who are best forgotten at once. And beside me is Good Fortune, a man constantly dogged by misfortune."

"From Suchow?" asked the man, turning round so quickly that his pigtail swung too.

"Yes, from Suchow," said Good Fortune. "Does that surprise you?"

"It doesn't surprise me," answered the man, taking down a cylindrical copper boiler from the wall and filling the cavity with burning charcoal.

"Is it permissible to ask your worthy name?" asked Affliction.

"No," replied the man rudely. "Call me Toeless as everyone else does. It's all the same to me."

"And to us also," said Affliction cheerfully. "Names are worth nothing, one might say. That has been proved during a thousand times a thousand years. My grandfather, for example, was called Lord of Riches. Do you notice anything, Toeless?"

"I notice nothing," said Toeless, "but speak on. Your talk pleases me."

So Affliction told the sad story of his grandfather, Lord of Riches, and of his father, Autumn Joy, who had nothing but ill luck at all seasons. Meantime the copper kettle began to steam. When the water was bubbling Toeless brought the kettle along.

"Eat," he said, laying a plateful of cut-up raw meat beside the cauldron, and handing round bone chopsticks.

Christian watched to see what Affliction would do, and Affliction looked to see if Good Fortune knew how to proceed, and all three looked at Big Tiger who, with the air of a polished man of the world, spiked a piece of meat on his chopstick and held it in the boiling water until it was cooked. Christian took note of how it was done, and Good Fortune and Affliction also took their lesson. When in the course of time the water had become a meat soup, Toeless fetched soup plates, and on each plate he laid a rolled chrysanthemum leaf as a flavoring for the soup, all in the manner of the best inns. He then took a bowl full of bones, and laid a fine piece of meat on top of them. "Give this to your dog," he said. "He doesn't know me."

Christian opened the door and the iron ball came down a bit lower. The poodle was standing expectantly outside. He swallowed the meat in one snap, then sat down in the sun crunching the bones.

"You and you," said Toeless suddenly to Christian and Big Tiger, "are you full?"

"Thanks ten thousand times, great old man," said Christian.

"The gentleman is generous beyond reason," said Big Tiger.

"Nonsense!" snapped Toeless. "I'm not a gentleman. Understand that!"

Big Tiger climbed quickly down from the *kang* and stood beside Christian. They both bowed, and Christian said: "We obey your wish."

"It is sad not to be permitted to do you honor," added Big Tiger.

Toeless stood leaning on his stick, looking from one to the other. "You and you," he said as before, tipping each of them on the chest, "and I—we ride in an hour, on horses."

"Halt there!" cried Good Fortune, jumping up from the *kang*. "I'll wash your ears for you, old *Hung-hu-tse,* and then you'll hear distinctly what's permissible and what's not. These two sons of princes are in my charge, and I'd like to see the man who dares to come and say: 'Go here or go there' to them."

"Don't get worked up, Good Fortune," said Toeless calmly. "What I say will be done."

"Ha!" shouted Good Fortune. "There are scoundrels who think they possess the golden roll of command, but they've only got confounded cheek. You're one of them. Who are you, you old coxcomb, horse thief and liar, that you should talk as if you were the Yellow Emperor?"

"I'm your uncle," said Toeless dryly. "You should be ashamed to abuse your father's brother."

Absolute silence fell. They could hear the dog cracking the bones outside and, farther off, the camels trampling through the long desert grass. A ray of sunshine came through the peephole in the paper window, and the dust which Good Fortune had raised danced in it.

Affliction sat on the *kang* smiling. "It's not often," he said, "that one sees such a joyful family reunion."

"You my uncle!" exclaimed Good Fortune, stepping backward three paces. "I don't know you."

"That's only right," said Affliction. "Every genuine family reunion begins with failure to recognize."

"Shut your mouth!" cried Good Fortune indignantly. "This man. . . ."

"This uncle," Affliction corrected gently.

"Does your mother still live in Lion Lane?" asked Toeless.

Good Fortune leaned against the wall, staring at Toeless, but Toeless only smiled.

"No, she's gone from there," muttered Good Fortune dully.

Toeless went and opened the chest. When he had found what he wanted he closed the lid and sat on it. "Excuse me, dear nephew," he said, "I find it hard to stand. Take this trifle. It is for your mother." Saying this, he laid two gleaming silver bars beside him on the chest. "You need not hesitate," he said. "They date from the days when I owned the inn The Hundred Sides of Truth in Anhsi."

"I heard of it," Good Fortune admitted unwillingly, coming nearer and observing Toeless even more closely than he observed the silver. "Pardon me, old uncle," he said finally. "I do not wish to be unjust to anybody, but . . ." and he stood irresolutely and with bowed head before Toeless. At last he gave him a slight bow.

Toeless accepted it in good part. He uttered no word of complaint over the lack of filial respect, in fact he tapped Good Fortune familiarly on the stomach with his stick, saying: "Sit down beside me. I have just experienced the first joy in seven years. I knew you the minute you came in the door, you're so like your father, particularly when you are angry. Unfortunately there's no time now for lengthy explanations. Matters are urgent. The Venerable Chief wishes to see Compass Mountain and Big Tiger on the second day of the third moon before sunrise."

"The Venerable Chief?" shouted Good Fortune indignantly. "So you're one of those now?"

"Yes," said Toeless. "I'm one of them now, and we ride in half an hour. Everything is ready."

"Come over here, you two," cried Good Fortune, mastering his anger with difficulty. "What do you think of this?"

Christian and Big Tiger had already exchanged several winks. They were ready to go with Toeless, and Christian was just about to say so when he met a warning look from Big Tiger. It came just as Good Fortune was asking angrily, "What do you think of this?" and he understood that he could not say now what he had wanted to say. Something else would have to be said—something which would restore Good Fortune's dignity. Therefore Christian kept silent and Big Tiger stepped forward a pace.

"My friend Compass Mountain and I," he said, "have no opinion of our own in this matter."

Christian also stepped forward a pace. "Up to the present," he said, "our respected elder has given all instructions, and they have proved absolutely right. As obedient children we beg him to say what he thinks best, and we shall do it."

Those were beautiful words, and Good Fortune sat upright. He was proud of Christian and Big Tiger, but his anger was still seething. Affliction now put in his oar. "I too," he said to Toeless, "have been under the orders of your worthy nephew for many days, and it pleases me well."

These were also beautiful words, but now it was Good Fortune's turn to speak, and he just couldn't. His heart began pounding most frightfully, and he could think of nothing else but this: "My face has become black, quite black, and everyone can see it." Good Fortune despised his uncle. He'd have liked nothing better than to spit at him.

Toeless raised his stick and tapped the earthen floor, and they all noticed that he and not Good Fortune wished to speak. "Moonlight was here three days ago," he began, "and I know from him who you are. Moonlight said: 'We have lost three days by the sandstorm. If Good Fortune knows the way to Tsaghan-burgussun and thence to the castle, give him three horses and tell him he must be there with Compass Mountain and Big Tiger in two nights and three days. It is important for him and for all of us. If he does not know the way, you must ride with them, and I rely on you.' "

"And Affliction?" asked Christian.

"It doesn't concern me," cried Affliction. "It has nothing to do with me."

"Yes, indeed it has," said Toeless. "You will ride slowly after them with the camels. A guide will be waiting for you at Tsaghan-burgussun, and in a few days you will be all together again."

"It can't be helped," cried Good Fortune in a tone of desperation. He put his head in his hands. His self-command seemed suddenly to forsake him, and he wept and shouted: "Ah, you are one of those who are ruining my life. Where are you sending me now? Where are you sending these boys, my young brothers? To the castle? Ha! You're a lot of scoundrels and we're in your hands. But I curse you and all who are in league with the Venerable Chief!" He stood up. "I do not know the way to Tsaghan-burgussun," he said.

"Then I must go," said Toeless, "though I am old, and . . . you know, dear nephew, why it is hard for me to ride?"

"Yes, I know," replied Good Fortune, laughing scornfully. His cruel laughter seemed to give him satisfaction. He could now at last show this man what he thought of him; this uncle whose toes had been cut off, and whom nobody at home ever spoke of because he was a criminal and had lost face. Good Fortune sat down heavily on the chest and his glance fell on the two silver bars. He would push them from the chest on to the ground, and in two minutes he would stand up and go.

"Rest for a while," said Toeless; "but you"—and he turned to Affliction—"come with me."

He put on a sheepskin coat, reached for his stick, took down a little brass horn which hung on the door, and went out. Affliction followed him willingly. They walked side by side like brothers, and when they had gone ten paces they reached the top of the poppy field, and walked together to the end. Where the thicket began there was a kind of bench made of bricks, and from this bench they could view the whole place: the poppy field, the hut and the horse line.

"I've been here three years," said Toeless, "and now I am leaving, never to return."

"But what happens to your property?" cried Affliction.

"That's just what I want to speak to you about. You are a sorrowful man, and such people are reliable, for they expect little or nothing. As soon as I've gone with the boys, you two make yourselves at home in my hut. Remain here tonight and ride on tomorrow morning. You will have two unloaded camels. Load up the chest and all my things. There are not many. Can you slaughter sheep?"

"No," cried Affliction, alarmed. "I can't do that."

"You've got a gun. Can you shoot?"

"Yes, I can shoot," said Affliction.

"Then shoot my two sheep. Good Fortune will cut them up, and you'll have meat for a long time. Follow the Path of Meditation. If you do fifty *li* every day you'll come on the third day to a valley where there's water and grass and high cliffs. The valley is called Tsaghan-burgussun, and a guide will be waiting for you there to take you to us."

"And what then?" asked Affliction.

"A new beginning always follows the end," said Toeless. "Be comforted. I have learned to know the miseries of the world."

"And so have I," said Affliction sympathetically.

"Nevertheless, I am not a criminal."

"No more am I," declared Affliction.

"Now," explained Toeless, "I am going to settle an old account. But I wanted to look over my home once more. I have done so now, and I'm ready."

He stood up and Affliction stood up too. When they reached the end of the field Toeless took out the brass horn and blew. It made a long wavering sound, and Toeless waited.

"Go in," he said to Affliction, "and fetch me the sack which is on the floor near the *kang*. There are real oats in it, Russian oats from Uliassutai."

When Affliction opened the door, he found Good Fortune still sitting on the chest and the boys standing timidly by the fireplace exactly as he had left them. The two silver bars were lying glittering beside Good Fortune on the chest. "Your uncle," said Affliction casually, "is a man deserving much honor."

Good Fortune raised his head and opened his mouth as if to speak, but shut it again without saying anything. Then he gave his cap a push, but that was all.

"Have I told you before," inquired Affliction, "that your uncle is a man toward whom my heart turns?"

"Be silent," cried Good Fortune. "Consider what you're saying."

"I have considered it," replied Affliction with dignity. He took the sack, and as he went out again he winked at Christian and Big Tiger. While they opened the door for him he whispered: "There's nothing to fear. That uncle is a pillar of virtue."

The door closed noiselessly. They could hear the tramping of hoofs outside, and the soft *lai, lai, lai* of Toeless, who sounded as if he were speaking horse language with the horses.

"You say something," whispered Big Tiger.

"You can do it better," whispered Christian.

"We'll both speak," said Big Tiger, taking Christian's hand. They walked up to Good Fortune in silence. For a few seconds all were still. Then Good Fortune pushed the silver bars aside, as if by doing so he could hide the tormenting proof of kinship. He pushed them until they dropped over the edge of the chest and fell with a thud on the ground. Then, at long last Good Fortune lifted his head, but because he had wept, he hid his face in his hands. "Go away!" he said. "A man such as I am has no right to give orders here."

"We have to go," said Big Tiger. "Previously our respected elder has had secrets which he kept from us. Will he please excuse us if we now have a secret which we keep from him."

"But it's not a bad secret," said Christian quickly. "It's a good one. In fact," he added, "it's not a secret at all, but an appointment."

"With whom?" cried Good Fortune. He took his hands from his face and laid them expectantly on his knees. "Tell me, so that I shall be easier in my mind letting you go from me."

"We shall be with our respected elder again in Ming-shui," replied Big Tiger.

Good Fortune smiled sadly. "You're a pair of rascals," he said. "And you talk as if I were someone who didn't know your tricks. Well, I don't care. But I have to tell you, for you must know, the kind of man you're going riding with. This uncle of mine"—he paused involuntarily—"is a murderer."

Again there was silence, and Christian and Big Tiger felt deeply shaken.

"One can't say worse than that about one's father's brother, can one?" said Good Fortune. "Perhaps you think it can't be true, because when a man is a murderer his head falls into the hangman's basket. Did you notice his beautiful hands, the long even fingers with the stubby tips? Those hands once killed a man. Afterwards it came out that the dead man was a common robber, a Mongol, and one of Dampignak's band—a gentleman of the mountains. You see, my father's brother was lucky. Instead of cutting off his head they only cut off his toes, and he has walked on his heels since. His home was burned down by Dampignak's men in revenge, and he himself disappeared. We were very glad when he did. But what's the good? My family is shamed and disgraced."

"Undeserved misfortune brings no blame," cried Big Tiger. "We are sorry for our respected elder."

"But," said Christian, "your worthy uncle is now himself one of the company of the Venerable Chief. How is that?"

"I can't make that out," said Good Fortune. "There's something queer there, a real mystery."

"We'll try to unravel it," promised Big Tiger.

"Are you taking on assignments of that kind again?" asked Good Fortune. "You'd better mind your own business."

"Your worthy uncle doesn't look like a murderer," Christian assured him.

"Affliction called him a pillar of virtue," said Big Tiger.

"Oh, holy saints of past ages!" cried Good Fortune, "Affliction should be eating thistles and braying. I know what I know, and you shall know it too. He did it with a kitchen knife. So look out whenever he takes a knife in his hand."

"We shall," promised Big Tiger.

"I'll give you something which will make the old man sit up," said Good Fortune, tapping his pistol. "But will you be able to handle it?"

"No," cried Big Tiger, alarmed. "Please don't give it to me."

"And what about you?" asked Good Fortune.

"I couldn't manage it very well either," confessed Christian. "You have to press the trigger. That's all I know."

"That's enough," said Good Fortune. "See this lever. You must push it to the side; otherwise nothing happens. But only use it in an emergency."

"I shall not touch it otherwise," promised Christian.

"And you must watch out," said Good Fortune. "It's best if only one of you sleeps at a time, and the other keeps watch. You're clever lads. Now you must learn endurance." While continuing his fatherly warnings, he shortened the strap of the holster and hung it on Christian's shoulder. The pistol was heavy, and the red silk tassel dangled down almost to Christian's knees. "Do you think, Compass Mountain, that you really know how to shoot?" he asked, suddenly doubtful.

"I know," Christian interrupted him politely, "that one doesn't shoot. Shooting is unfair."

"What is that?" asked Good Fortune.

"Compass Mountain thinks," Big Tiger explained, "that one doesn't shoot as long as one has a mouth to speak with."

"I see you understand me," Good Fortune concluded, well pleased. "Of course there are exceptions, for instance my uncle; you could without hesitation . . . I mean, a man like that isn't much loss. But with other people there might be unpleasant consequences." He stood up. "I'm not one for ceremony," he said, "but you must promise me you'll take good care of yourselves and act just as if I were with you."

"We beg our respected elder to stand above us and receive our promise," said Big Tiger.

"You are like a father and mother to us," said Christian. "Therefore it is fitting you should do so."

"Since you wish it," said Good Fortune, standing up on the chest. Then Christian and Big Tiger went on their knees in token of filial obedience, and it was all very solemn.

As they stood up and Good Fortune was about to get down from the chest, the door suddenly opened, the iron ball slid and there was a dull thud.

"Are you ready?" cried Affliction.

"Ha!" shouted Good Fortune. But he went white and had to sit down. It was lucky that he had his hat on, and that the *kang* was just behind the chest, for he was on the point of fainting. "There are scoundrels," he groaned, "but I didn't know you were one of them."

Affliction was much distressed. "You'll be all right presently," he said, reassuringly. "Don't faint, for we need you."

"What for?" asked Good Fortune weakly.

"Your uncle wants to say good-by to you. He's already mounted."

"Let him ride to the devil!" shouted Good Fortune.

"He will presently," promised Affliction. "There's just one trifling matter." And he took a white sheepskin coat off the *kang*. "Please excuse me," he said, and as there was nothing else to hand, he took off his own coat and pushed it under Good Fortune's sinking head. "Come," he whispered to the boys. "We have to hurry."

"We're going," said Big Tiger, "and we wish our revered elder a speedy recovery from illness."

"I'm not ill," sighed Good Fortune, "but I'm not particularly well. When shall heaven permit us to be together again?"

"In ten days," answered Big Tiger, at random.

"It might be eleven," said Christian.

"Or twelve," added Affliction. "Take this coat, Big Tiger. It's yours. It may be a bit big for you, but it will do." He looked at Good Fortune who was getting back his color. Then he pushed Christian and Big Tiger toward the door.

The stamping of hoofs could be heard outside, and the joyful barking of the poodle. Then Good Fortune heard Affliction say: "Your nephew cannot come, unfortunately. When he stood up to come out, your door ball caught him on the head. With his dying breath he wished you many happy stars."

"I heard it distinctly," said Toeless.

"Dog! Come with us!" cried Christian and Big Tiger.

Then the dog began barking. Affliction cried: *"Sa Yabonah!"* The sound of the trotting hoofs grew fainter and then faded away.

In the hut all was silent, and Good Fortune sat upright and looked around him. The room was empty and very tidy. "Like a first-class inn," thought Good Fortune.

41 THE TRUE STORY OF UNCLE TOELESS

As THEY left the Ikhe Gol behind Christian looked up at the sun. It seemed to be about four o'clock. The horses were well rested and would have galloped with the least encouragement. But Toeless did not allow galloping. He rode on ahead, and when, after they had gone a *li,* he slackened his reins, this was the signal for the cavalcade to drop into the short regular trot which is the natural gait of Mongolian horses. In the beginning Christian's horse was restive and tried to break away, until he got used to the strange rider with the foreign smell. Then his hoofs took the same rhythm as the others', soft and even as a rapid timepiece.

Toeless sang gently to himself.

The Path of Meditation was more distinct now, and looked almost like an ordinary caravan track. But it seemed to have been trodden more by hasty hoof beats than by the thoughtful tread of camels, for it remained narrow. It had grown firm and a bit deeper, and the horses followed it as if running for their lives. The poodle trotted behind them, panting.

After three hours the sun went down. They had reached a high plateau, flat as a roof, with a wide panoramic view. A maze of dunes lay to the south, and to the north rose quiet old stone mountains. Between them ran the Path of Meditation, visible for miles ahead.

"We shall rest," said Toeless, dismounting carefully. "I'll tie the horses myself. They don't know you well enough."

The poodle lay down panting and exhausted.

"Are you tired too?" asked Toeless.

"We're not very fresh," Christian admitted.

"It can't be helped," said Toeless sympathetically.

"Don't let that trouble you," said Big Tiger. "Your nephew Good Fortune commanded us to stick it out, and we're obedient boys."

"Did he command you to do that? Now I'll command you," said Toeless. "When people have to endure hardship an empty stomach won't do. Take down the bags from the saddles."

He watched their reaction with pleasure. He had forgotten nothing. Not only had they got double sheepskins over the hard saddles, but behind each saddle was a leather bag containing dried meat, wheat bread baked in fat, Mongolian cheese, garlic and honey cakes. They settled down to a glorious feast.

"There's a good well a hundred paces further on," said Toeless. "But we shall eat first. We have done the day's march of a caravan, and we've twice as long before us yet."

Christian and Big Tiger sampled everything. Wheat bread, which they had not tasted for so long, seemed even more fragrant to their nostrils than the wild smell of the red meat which Toeless cut into slices with a sharp knife.

"This is antelope meat," said Toeless, passing the knife to Christian and Big Tiger, who had quite forgotten their promise to beware if the old man took a knife in his hand.

Half an hour passed and the stars came out. Christian and Big Tiger were well fed and somewhat rested, and so was the poodle. Toeless unhobbled the horses, and the three mounted and rode to the well, which was really only a round hole in the ground. It was full to the brim, in fact overflowing a little, and the stars were mirrored in it, but no movement of a spring could be seen.

"Human beings first," said Toeless, pushing the poodle away. He held the horses while Christian and Big Tiger drank from their silver bowls. The water was very cold, and they could only drink it slowly.

The horses sneezed when Toeless let them loose. "Let them do as they please," he said to Christian. "They are Mongolian horses of the highest breeding, Kerulen horses, and they know themselves what is good for them and what is bad. Watch how little they drink and how cautiously. They are not ordinary horses. You'll get to know them." Toeless blew a gentle blast on his horn. The horses raised their heads, left the well instantly, and came back to him. He gave each of them one or two honey cakes.

"Beware of falling asleep," Toeless warned them as they mounted. "We shall be seven hours in the saddle."

"The poor dog," said Christian.

"He'll be able to stick it out," said Toeless, "for the horses have to slow down in the dark."

This was not noticeable in the beginning. The horses trotted along as in broad daylight, but when the plateau came to an end and the Path of Meditation led through sandhills and stony valleys, the trot slowed down and the horses often walked. Toeless gave them full freedom, neither urging nor restraining them. The night was pitch-dark. One could only guess where the earth began, for there were no stars. There seemed, moreover, to be a mist in the air. When they had been in the saddle a couple of hours a subtle change came. Nobody noticed it coming, but there it was. Sharp outlines seemed to divide sky and earth. There was the silent desert below, and the sky above, and all was clear and solemn.

Christian and Big Tiger, who had nearly fallen asleep several times, became all alert. It must have been long past midnight. The poodle was keeping up with them bravely.

Toeless had not exaggerated the qualities of his horses in the least. When either of the boys was overcome by sleep, and the pressure of his legs on the horse's sides slackened, the horse immediately ceased to trot. When the boy began to sway dangerously in the saddle, the horse stood still. Then Toeless would turn round and call out kindly: "Oho! Little son!" At this Christian and Big Tiger would feel ashamed, but as it happened to both of them, it wasn't so bad.

Once they passed through a stony gorge where three trees stood in a line. A well, thought Christian, but Toeless passed by, and the horses' trot began to quicken. They rode through a broad valley between hills to the east and mountains to the west, and the ground was level. The ground rose again, the rocks had smooth, round edges, and the path ran into a deep ravine. The horses picked their way cautiously downhill, holding back with their hindquarters' spread.

"Tsaghan-burgussun!" cried Toeless, and again there were trees. Tall desert grass reached up to their stirrups, and when a little stream crossed the path, Toeless halted.

"A hundred and fifty *li,*" he said. "Little sons, you've ridden bravely."

"Please sit down," pleaded Big Tiger, when he saw how Toeless staggered. "Compass Mountain and I know what's to be done." Their own legs were stiff, but they limbered up when they moved about. They unsaddled the horses, but left the saddle pads on them. Then they went to collect firewood, and brought it to a nice smooth place on the sand.

"What are you doing?" asked Toeless.

"We're making a heated *kang* of sand," explained Christian.

Toeless said he did not know such a thing and was curious to see how it was done.

"And we don't know your fire-lighter and are curious to see how it works," said Big Tiger.

"Matches go out, or you don't have them when you want them," said Toeless. "But there's always stone and steel, and some kindling to be found." He struck fire. The tinder caught the spark. Toeless blew on it. Then he took a bundle of dry deresen grass, and soon the fire was blazing brightly and evenly. The high flames shot into the darkness, lighting up the silent trees which stood like the wings of a stage around an exciting play.

"Is so much wood necessary for what you want to make?" asked Toeless.

"Yes, it is," said Christian.

"You'll soon see what it's for," said Big Tiger.

As they had no shovels they used their hands to cover the glowing embers with sand, so it took much longer to make the sandbed than that night in Durben Mot.

"Sleep well," said Christian and Big Tiger, as they invited Toeless to lie down on the warm sand.

"Little sons, this is a splendid thing," said Toeless. He covered himself up with his coat, and as Big Tiger now had a coat too, which reached to his toes, they were all comfortable. Christian put the pistol under his fur cap, intending to sleep on it, but found it too uncomfortable.

"I believe," whispered Big Tiger, "that neither of us need stay awake."

"There's nothing to fear," whispered Christian, and he laid the pistol down between himself and Big Tiger. "Toeless is a good uncle."

They both fell asleep with easy minds. The moon rose, but it was a dim little crescent. That did not matter, however, as the dawn came immediately afterwards. But it didn't awaken Christian and Big Tiger. Only when Christian felt someone blowing on his face and tapping him gently on the shoulder, did he open his eyes. It was full day, the sun was shining, and the poodle was lying beside him.

"Are you finished sleeping?" inquired Toeless kindly.

"Yes, we're finished," said Christian, standing up promptly.

"How is your worthy health?" inquired Big Tiger.

Toeless frowned. "Didn't I tell you to drop that nonsense?" he said irritably. "Come and take tea."

"Tea?" exclaimed Big Tiger.

"Yes, tea," said Toeless. "There's not much, but there's some." He sat down beside a little fire. He had stuck two forked sticks in the ground and laid a green branch across them. On this branch hung a little copper flask, in which Toeless had carried an iron ration of water. It was already boiling. Each of the boys was able to fill his bowl twice, for Toeless had already breakfasted. He had also let the horses loose. Now he sat smoking on a saddle pad.

"That's a fine big pistol you've got," he remarked.

Christian slowly chewed a mouthful of meat before answering:

"Your nephew, the esteemed Mr. Good Fortune, lent it to me."

"No doubt he's very anxious about you."

"He's anxious about all of us," asserted Big Tiger.

"As regards me," said Toeless, "I heard him saying something different."

"He only said that," explained Big Tiger, "because his mind was confused. Your iron door ball fell on his head and hurt him."

"His pride caused that," said Toeless. "Why did he stand up on the chest?"

"Because we asked him to," said Christian.

"What nonsense!" snorted Toeless. "Letting you pay him homage as if he were a chief." He puffed vigorously at his pipe. "Served him right," he added.

Christian and Big Tiger did not dare to contradict. Toeless was opposed to all politeness and convention, and that was that. So they went on eating in silence.

"Do you know how to use that thing?" asked Toeless, looking intently at the pistol. Christian went on chewing, but Big Tiger hurriedly swallowed his bite and said: "My friend Compass Mountain is a celebrated pistol shot."

"If that's so," said Toeless, "you must show me how you do it."

"Showing is much too dangerous," replied Big Tiger.

"Are you afraid?" asked Toeless.

"Not very often, but we are sometimes," Christian admitted.

"We're a bit afraid now, for instance," said Big Tiger.

"Of whom?" asked Toeless, straight out.

"Of the pistol," replied Big Tiger, smiling politely.

"That's a pity," said Toeless; "for I was going to ask Compass Mountain to do me a favor. He's a foreigner from beyond the seas, and I thought it would be easier for him to do what I want, especially as we're alone in the desert."

Christian and Big Tiger looked around apprehensively, but there was no stir in the deresen grass, and nobody was hiding behind a tree.

"We'd like very much to oblige you," said Christian.

"We take on difficult commissions, too," asserted Big Tiger.

"I have one for you," said Toeless. "Listen now. If we come to a certain place and meet someone who looks like a wicked man, and if I say: 'Aim at that man, Compass Mountain,' will he fall down dead?"

"If he's a long-lived man he mightn't at once," said Big Tiger solemnly.

"Shooting is a bad business," declared Christian. "Good Fortune says there might be unpleasant consequences."

"Not with this man," Toeless assured him. "You could shoot him without hesitation; I mean, a man like that isn't much loss anyway."

"We have already got a similar commission," Big Tiger confessed. "Two at the same time would be too much. Besides, we haven't many cartridges."

Toeless shook his head with an air of displeasure. "My commission deserves priority," he said. "I'll explain it to you. Did Good Fortune tell you who I am?"

Christian and Big Tiger nodded solemnly. Then Big Tiger said cautiously: "Your nephew told us that once on seeing a kitchen knife you lost the prudence which is necessary in handling kitchen knives."

"That's right," replied Toeless. "But people generally know only half a story, and they give it out as the whole."

"Please tell us the missing half," said Christian.

"Don't leave us longer in ignorance," said Big Tiger.

"Well, it can't be helped," said Toeless indifferently. He filled his pipe with green tobacco, stroked his beard, and drew his hand across his forehead.

"I once had an inn in Anhsi," he began. "And I had a wife and two sons. I stood all day cooking in the kitchen, for I was a good cook and had many customers. My wealth increased, and I was a happy man until seven years ago. Then came misfortune, and almost overnight all that was beautiful and peaceful was torn from me. Misfortune took the form of a man with a black moustache hanging over the corners of his mouth, and domineering eyes. The moment he entered I noticed there was something which did not please him. A lot of people were there, eating and drinking. But he went haughtily up to the center table and said: 'Make way. I want a meal,' and pushed aside the glass of a Mongol who was sitting there. Well, that's all right. That's what happens. The Mongol is a barbarian, and he's a fine gentleman.

"I brought him what he wanted—bamboo shoots, eggs with fir-blossom, gammon of ham, and partridge. The Mongol watches him eating, his eyes nearly popping out of his head. But it wasn't with envy; it was something else. The fine gentleman goes on eating, and notices nothing. After a while he stands up and comes into the kitchen to me. 'Are you alone?' he asks. And I say: 'We're alone. What do you want of me?' 'I hear,' he says very insinuatingly, 'that your eldest son is getting married. I've got a gift for a bride, just a chance purchase, a wonderfully beautiful hair ornament.' 'Let me see it,' I said, laying down my meat knife.

"The gentleman takes a package from his pocket. He unwraps it and lays before me on the table two golden hair clasps, the like of which I had never seen. 'They could be reworked,' says he casually. 'It's Mongolian jewelry and perhaps not to your taste. But it's pure gold. I think about two thousand silver batzes would be the price.'

"As he says this the door opens and the Mongol comes in. He sees the jewelry on the table and he turns pale. The fine gentleman turns round angrily. The two look at each other and the Mongol's face becomes distorted with fury. 'Now I know you,' he snarls, and wants to lunge at him. But the fine gentleman snatches the knife from the meat bench and drives it into the Mongol. Then he snatches up the jewelry and rushes out the door. 'Murder! Murder!' he shouts. 'Hold the man! Catch him! I'm going for the police.' And he's gone.

"After a while he comes back with the police officer and a posse of soldiers. The officer crossexamines me and, knowing me, he says: 'That's all right.' They arrest the stranger. But he's no longer got any gold on him—nothing but a few silver batzes, just enough to pay his bill.

"So I was brought before the chief magistrate in Suchow. When I got there the fine gentleman had disappeared, and on the chief magistrate's table lay a long elaborate indictment, which read: 'Conspiring with robber bands. Murder for the purpose of eliminating witness of unlawful actions.'

"The chief magistrate at once closed the public hearing, and ordered a secret trial. My friends and the police officer of Anhsi were sent away. I was alone, and I was lucky not to be executed. It was stated in the accusation that the murdered Mongol was one of the Venerable Chief's band. 'Strike that out,' said the chief magistrate scornfully. 'Dampignak avenges murder himself. Read on,' he ordered, and the court scribe read: 'Leaving aside the murder, the crime of conspiring with thieves and murderers must be expiated.' So they cut off my toes, and when I returned home a few weeks afterwards, I found my inn burned down and my wife and two sons murdered. My friends no longer knew me, and the district magistrate closed the door of the *yamen* against me. Those who owed me money brought it unasked, and I left Anhsi as an outcast. I rode out of the city gate on an ass, intending to go to Sinkiang.

"The town was hardly out of sight when a Mongol came up to me, but as there were travelers within sight he took his hand off his dagger and said: 'Follow me.' I rode with him, and when the Silk Road was out of sight I said: 'I'm not the man you're looking for.' 'Do not try to save your life,' cried the Mongol. 'We know that you have stabbed one of our men to death. All the world knows it.' 'The world knows only half,' I said. And then I told him the missing half, and now you also know it."

"We thank you for your trust," said Big Tiger.

"But what happened then?" asked Christian.

"Nothing more happened," said Toeless. "The Mongol—his name was Moonlight—brought me to the stronghold of the Venerable Chief, and every morning on our journey there he went on his knees and begged my forgiveness for what had happened at Anhsi, for he had been the ringleader. The Venerable Chief made me tell him everything. I had to describe the ornaments exactly. He wanted to know how many turquoises were in the hair clasps. When I answered, 'There were four in each of them, and a big one in the middle,' he pressed his lips together till they went white, and he looked like a dying man. 'Would you know that man again?' he asked me. 'Yes, I would,' I said, 'even if he had become as old as a ghost.' 'Unfortunately I can't send you to the Silk Road,' said the Venerable Chief, 'for everyone knows you there, and Shong Ma would keep out of your way.' "

"Shong-Ma?" cried Christian and Big Tiger.

"Yes, that's his name," said Toeless. "Do you know him?"

"We've heard of him," said Big Tiger cautiously.

"Sevenstars told us he murdered the Venerable Chief's family," said Christian.

"Yes, that's the man," cried Toeless. "And I've been waiting all these years for him to come along the Path of Meditation one day. For that was my task. Often the Mongols caught a man who had a beard and dark sinister eyes. Then they'd call me to the castle, and when I'd say, 'No, that's not he,' they'd let the man go. But four days ago when Moonlight and Thunderbolt were with me, Moonlight said: 'Give up your post, for we'll catch him in a few days.' I asked Moonlight to tell me what he intended doing, but he made a secret of it. 'You'll see Shong-Ma,' he said, 'before the new moon is full, but whether dead or alive I do not know.' "

"Honored old father . . ." began Big Tiger.

"Drop that!" cried Toeless angrily.

"Permit me to insist this time," said Big Tiger. "My friend Compass Mountain and I can no longer bear not being allowed to honor you as you deserve."

"I am what I am," cried Toeless, "a criminal, whose toes have been cut off."

"He who does not praise himself and does not boast of his merits," said Big Tiger, "is a truly modest man. But he who takes on himself crimes which he has not committed, commits an outrage against himself."

"Who says that?" growled Toeless.

"My grandfather says it," replied Big Tiger, "and you may believe him, for he knows the things of this world. Please tell us your worthy surname."

"I have relinquished it, because my family cast me out. You must call me by the same name as before."

Christian and Big Tiger stood up and bowed very deeply. Raising their clenched fists to their foreheads they said: "Worthy old Toeless, we beg you to accept the promise of our filial obedience in all things."

"Enough, enough!" cried Toeless. But he stood up and returned the bow.

Christian and Big Tiger finished their breakfast in much happier spirits. Toeless looked on and said benignly, "You've wormed it out of me," and he even smiled. "We must ride on," he continued, "to get to the meeting place by evening."

"Whom are we meeting," asked Christian, "if it's in order to inquire?"

"I do not know who's coming," declared Toeless. "Someone is to bring us fresh horses at the Hidden Well. You know, one can't keep riding the same horses."

"We understand," said Big Tiger, "and now we'll fetch the horses."

"You needn't," said Toeless, and he blew on his little brass horn. The horses came one after the other. "Douse the fire," he said. "There's another grassy valley not far from here. There was a fire there last year, and since then I haven't seen any more animals around."

Christian fetched water and doused the fire. Then he put the copper flask, freshly filled, into Toeless's saddle bag.

Toeless rode ahead, as the day before. The morning sun was shining, the horses' coats glistened, and the whole world seemed warm and friendly. As they left the valley of Tsaghan-burgussun, where there was no grass and no water, they passed a solitary black poplar. Big Tiger wrote on a piece of paper from Christian's notebook: "The mystery has been cleared up. Your uncle is a pillar of virtue. We wish you a happy journey." Then Christian wrote his beautiful name Compass Mountain underneath, and Big Tiger signed it too.

"What are you doing?" Toeless called back, noticing the halt.

"We're leaving greetings for Good Fortune," said Big Tiger. Christian made a cut in the trunk of the poplar and fastened the paper in such a way into it that Good Fortune couldn't miss it when he would ride by.

Toeless muttered something about an unnecessary nuisance, but when they caught up with him he said kindly: "Thank you, little sons, for greeting my unworthy nephew, though he does not deserve such devotion."

Christian and Big Tiger protested, but Toeless said: "There is something which you do not know."

"If you mean," began Big Tiger cautiously, "that Good Fortune was once a redbeard . . ."

"We know it," said Christian.

Toeless stopped his horse and let Christian and Big Tiger come up to him. For quite a while nothing could be heard but the clinking of the bridles and the snorting and stamping of the horses. The poodle looked on from a safe distance. When Toeless still remained silent, Christian said apologetically: "We found that out in the course of time."

"Being a redbeard is an honorable profession," added Big Tiger. "Your worthy nephew deserves little blame."

Toeless laughed. "Little sons!" he cried, and laughed again.

"You seem to be a proper pair of young scamps. You know all sorts of things. But tell me this," he added seriously. "Do you know why the Venerable Chief wants to see you? Has it got anything to do with Shong-Ma?"

Christian started. Now that Toeless had asked, they had to say yes or no, for there wasn't any other answer. It can't be helped, thought Christian desperately. We shall have to tell a lie. He looked at Big Tiger, but Big Tiger was looking surprised and saying: "We haven't got an appointment with Shong-Ma, but with a certain Mr. Ma, and as it's urgent, Moonlight is lending us his help. Perhaps you know Mr. Ma? He's a caravan leader."

"Yes, I know Ma," said Toeless. "He's a petty, stingy fellow. Whenever he travels on the Silk Road he stops off at my hut. He should have been a merchant on his own account long since, but he lacks firmness in the cheekbones for that. What does he want with you?"

"We want something of him," said Big Tiger. "The soldier Affliction doesn't want to be a soldier any more, so Ma has promised to help him to become something else."

"Ah," said Toeless, disappointed. "That's a business of no great consequence. But the Venerable Chief, what does he want with you?"

"Perhaps," said Christian, with a breath of relief, "he wants to know how things are doing with General Wu, and how matters stand in the world. We've just come from the war, and we were present when General Wu conquered the Nan-ku Pass. And that is probably of interest to the Venerable Chief."

"That may be," said Toeless thoughtfully. But he wanted to know everything. "Moonlight told me that a horseless car was stolen from you," he said. "What about that?"

"We just lent it out," asserted Big Tiger. "We're to get it back in Hsing-hsing-hsia or perhaps even before we get there. And then you must come and ride with us, honored old uncle, for you want to go to Sinkiang, don't you?"

Toeless looked annoyed. "There's no question of that yet," he said. "We shall ride on now."

"May I venture to ask what road we're taking?" asked Christian.

"There isn't any road," Toeless explained. "The Hidden Well should be reached exactly at midday from here. The Mongols ride through the pathless desert as if they were on the Silk Road. I once tried to do it too, but I got lost, and was lucky to find myself back in Tsaghan-burgussun. Since then I make a detour. Do you see the mountain over there in the west?"

"It's very far away," said Big Tiger, "but we see it."

"We shall have to go over there," explained Toeless, "because from the foot of that mountain one can see a saddle gap in the line of hills. Then I shall know which way to turn. For one must have a landmark."

"I've got a compass," said Christian shyly.

"Ah!" cried Toeless joyfully. "But do you know how to use it?" he asked dubiously.

"My friend is called Compass Mountain," Big Tiger explained proudly, "because he possesses the highest understanding of compasses."

"How could I forget that," cried Toeless, and he begged Christian to take over the lead. "Your knowledge will spare us three painful hours wading through deep shifting sand."

Christian said nothing but took out the compass and glanced at the map. He was relieved to find Tsaghan-burgussun on it. There was a blue ripple there, indicating water. One could see the brown shaded cutting of the valley, and even the Path of Meditation, though it was a very thin line. To the north were mountains, and in the west there were also mountains. But in the south the map showed nothing but white and yellow. There was no blue ripple, only a few mountains, and sprawled over them the words "Boro Ola." Quite far off—more than two hundred *li,* Christian estimated—two crossed hammers marked the words "Old Gold Region." But that was all. That's going to be difficult, thought Christian, folding away the Western Sheet and taking the compass in his hand.

"*Yabonah!*" he cried as confidently as he could, and then he rode on ahead. Toeless kept up with him for a while, to observe what he did, and he noticed that it was difficult.

Before them lay a desolate, dead desert land covered with stones and fine sand. The sand was yellow, the stones were yellow, and the ground which they covered was yellow too. One looked into endless space, as on the ocean.

The horses started to trot, but their hoofs were hardly audible. Christian watched the compass anxiously. The needle pointed northward, where there were sufficient landmarks anyhow. To the south, where the end of the needle pointed and where the figure 180 was written, there was nothing but bare desert. Here and there lay a fairly large rock, on which Christian took his bearings, but it was soon past, and another landmark had to be found. It was good that the horses kept of themselves to the direction one had set on. So Christian could let his reins hang, hold the compass in both hands, and watch the wavering needle. When it stood still and its end showed somewhere midway between the horse's ears, he needed only a bit of luck to find a rock or a sand drift ahead. When he found nothing, he just had to wait and watch the needle.

"It's strenuous," said Toeless. "I see that from your face."

"One must concentrate," replied Christian. "That makes all the difference."

At this Toeless let him ride on undisturbed, for he did not want to break in on anyone's thoughts. A few times he turned round and looked back at Tsaghan-burgussun, but the mountains were becoming smaller, the valley cutting was growing indistinct, and Toeless again looked straight in front of him, watching out for the saddle gap which he knew. When four hours had passed in this way, he became uneasy. The smooth ground had changed to rough, there were many big stones, and Christian was glad of these. They were going downhill, too, and to the right, where the sun was, a faint ridge of hills was emerging—just a shadowy suggestion.

"Halt!" cried Toeless. "We're somewhere where we shouldn't be."

Christian made no reply. He looked at the compass, and then looked back. The track of the horses was as if drawn with a ruler, and quite far away there was a dark speck. Poor dog, thought Christian, and he was glad that Toeless had called "Halt!"

"Where should we be?" inquired Big Tiger. "Please give us your opinion."

"Somewhere else," answered Toeless, "where there's a saddle gap which can be seen a long way off."

"Perhaps it will still come," said Big Tiger, trying to be reassuring.

"No, it won't," replied Toeless. "On my roundabout route I took seven hours to get to the Hidden Well. The Mongols say they need only four. Four hours have passed."

"We're approaching from another side," Christian suggested. "That's why we can't see the saddle gap which you're looking for."

"It has to be seen," insisted Toeless, "for there isn't any other landmark."

"Dog!" cried Big Tiger. "Poor dog, are you tired?"

The poodle came trotting slowly along. His red tongue was hanging out of his black mouth, and his breath was coming in short jerks. Toeless shook his head regretfully. "Dogs are all right for camel caravans," he said, "but they can't keep up with horses."

"He'll recover if we wait a few minutes," said Christian.

"All right," muttered Toeless unwillingly, and he looked at the poodle which was standing by undecided.

"Lie down," said Christian.

"Rest," said Big Tiger. But the poodle didn't heed this well-meant advice. He wagged his tail, then ran on, his tongue hanging out, sniffing. He was no ordinary dog.

"*Yabonah!*" cried Christian joyfully. "We'll be there at once. The dog smells water."

Toeless shook his head, and his gray pigtail swung round. "Impossible!" he cried. "The Hidden Well is covered with planks, and there's a lot of sand over the planks. It's a secret well, and only the gentlemen of the mountains know it, for it was they who dug it."

"All the same," said Christian, "we should ride on."

"Very well," said Toeless indifferently. "One mistake more won't make much difference."

The poodle ran on ahead, the route continued downward, and the ridge of hills to the right grew higher. At their feet lay deep sand. Finally the horses had to slow down to a walk, but the poodle ran faster and faster. He disappeared when the ridge of hills bent westward, and suddenly they heard barking.

"Blind enthusiasm," muttered Toeless.

"No!" cried Christian, but then he gripped his reins and pulled his horse back. For behind the bend were two blue tents before which the dog stood barking. There were horses there, and men going to and fro, and one of them stood and stared astonished at the dog who, torn between flight and aggression, was trying to frighten him with his barking. Out of the bigger of the two tents, which was decorated with lucky symbols in white, a man emerged dressed in a white sheepskin coat with a blue sash. "Dog! Come here!" he shouted.

"That man . . ." said Big Tiger, bending over his saddle, "is Moonlight," continued Christian, in a tone of relief.

42 THE RING FINDS ITS OWNER

"WE EXPECTED you to come from over there," said Moonlight when the greetings were over. He pointed to a saddle gap in the ridge of hills, the only interruption in the even run of crests, which reached their highest point here, and dropped away to the south just as gradually as they had risen.

"We came from another direction," Big Tiger explained, "because we followed our compass, and then the dog smelled water."

"A wonderful dog," said Moonlight, looking around. But the poodle was standing by the well, from which two men were drawing water for the horses. "Come and have tea," he continued. "Sembilik will look after the horses."

They entered the smaller, undecorated tent. A young fellow was sitting at the fire.

"Go see to the horses and camels, Sembilik," said Moonlight.

The tent housed four men. One could see this from the coats that lay rolled up, and the guns which lay beside the coats. The ground was covered with felt rugs. Otherwise the tent was bare, apart from a kettle and a copper can, which Moonlight now picked up. "Drink," he said pleasantly, and when the bowls were filled he continued with an artful smile: "I've brought three fellows with me who don't understand a word of Chinese. So we can talk about everything that's happened and that's going to happen. How's Good Fortune?"

"He was not well when we left him," said Christian.

"The iron door ball caught him on the head," said Big Tiger. "He was a bit stunned."

"Good Fortune wished me to the devil," said Toeless dryly.

"Why?" asked Moonlight. "Did you quarrel?"

"There are more often differences of opinion between relatives than between strangers," Big Tiger explained.

"Relatives?" asked Moonlight with a puzzled air. He pushed

his fur hat back off his forehead. The dreadful injustice of Anhsi oppressed his mind. "Relatives?" he asked once more, for nobody said anything.

"We do not wish to anticipate the worthy Mr. Toeless," explained Big Tiger.

"The matter is best not spoken of," cried Toeless. "And what is he, anyway? A wretched nephew, an adventuring nobody of a soldier—what does he matter?"

"All the same," countered Christian gently, "the old uncle was overjoyed to meet him. That was plain to see."

"Seeing him again knocked me over," explained Toeless. "He's so like his father, who was my brother."

"Reunion is a good thing," cried Big Tiger. "My grandfather often said that."

"You may take it Big Tiger is right there," Moonlight asserted. "For it's the function of grandfathers to interpret the meaning of heaven and earth. I rejoice to say that you have found a splendid nephew."

Toeless bent over his steaming tea bowl. His face got hot and red, and he tried to ignore Moonlight's words. As long as Shong-Ma still lived, there would be no joy in life for him. That had been so for many years now.

"Will Good Fortune come?" asked Moonlight.

"He has good camels," replied Toeless. "He will be in Tsaghanburgussun the day after tomorrow, and Affliction will be traveling with him. They're bringing my goods and chattels."

"Good," said Moonlight, well pleased. "The guide will set out tomorrow." Turning to Christian and Big Tiger he added: "Come! The Prince wants to meet you."

The pleasant tent with the lucky signs in white was only ten paces away. In front of the entrance a lance was stuck in the ground, with a horse tail, dyed red, hanging from it. So still and warm was the air that not a hair stirred. Big Tiger and Christian took off their coats.

"I'd stumble and fall in mine," said Big Tiger apologetically.

"Is it too long for you?" asked Moonlight, smiling. "Well, well, you'll grow into it."

"I have to ask you something," whispered Big Tiger.

"Don't mention it," Moonlight anticipated him. "I've got another coat long ago."

"Forgive me for being so late in thanking you," said Big Tiger. "I didn't know who the generous donor of the coat was. You've risked freezing to death for my sake."

"You see I'm alive," replied Moonlight, laughing. "Come now."

But Big Tiger remained standing and said: "I've another question. Does the Venerable Chief know about the ring which I have on my thumb?"

"He knows nothing about it," whispered Moonlight. "It's up to him to claim the ring as his property, or not. Now, we'll go in."

The beautiful big tent had a triangular entrance curtain decorated with a white butterfly. The horses were stamping at the well nearby, the sky was blue, and one could see far out into the vast desert. To the west was the range of hills which looked like a smooth wall with only one single gap in it. But even this was filled with blue sky, and all was peaceful around. Nevertheless Christian and Big Tiger felt their legs shaky and heavy. It's the long ride, thought Christian, but he perceived that it was not only his legs that were heavy, but his heart was heavy too.

The poodle came running and barking around their legs. "You must stay outside," said Christian sternly.

"Take off the pistol," whispered Moonlight, and Christian obeyed. Moonlight pulled aside the entrance curtain, pushed the boys in before him, and closed the tent.

It was half dark inside, a little fire was burning, and at the back sat the man of whom Turakina had said that he looked like a dried-up tree with a brown bark. He had the waving beard too, but it hung down and did not wave any more than did the horse tail outside the tent. The man's black eyes fastened on Christian and Big Tiger.

"We bow in reverence," they said with a graceful *kowtow*. The man bowed to them and raised his hands to his forehead in salutation. "Have you had a good journey?" he asked.

"We traveled in peace. Does the Prince sit lightly and well?"

"Please sit down," said Dampignak. "Here," he cried imperiously when he saw that Christian and Big Tiger wanted to sit at the right-hand side and as far away and near the exit as possible.

"We do not dare," said Big Tiger.

"We are unworthy," said Christian.

They resisted as hard as they could, but Moonlight, with gentle force, obliged them to sit down on two ordinary felt covers, rolled to make seat cushions. So there they were sitting to the left of the dreaded warrior Dampignak, otherwise known as the Venerable Chief, who was a prince, and who was also, men said, a notorious robber. He wore the red robe of a lama, his bare arms lay under the folds of the scapular, his hands rested on his crossed legs, and his whole body was completely motionless apart from his left thumb, which kept pushing the beads of a prayer chaplet over the forefinger. His head was uncovered, and the front half shaved bare in the manner of Tibetan and Mongol dignitaries. The long hair began just in front of the crown. It was black like his beard, but was plaited into a stiff pigtail, which was very thick at the top and thin at the end, like a whipcord.

Aside from the portable grate, on which no kettle stood, there was nothing in the tent except some felt rugs and a coat.

"Sit down," said Dampignak.

Only then did Christian and Big Tiger notice that Moonlight was still standing at the entrance. He now sat down to the right of Dampignak, and looked at the fire in silence. Some moments passed, and when nobody spoke Moonlight took his pipe out of his boot, filled it, lit it at the fire, and began puffing. Dampignak still remained silent.

In front of the tent the poodle, who lay beside the pistol, stretched himself and yawned loudly. Suddenly Dampignak turned toward Christian, who was sitting next to him. His monk's robe exuded a smell of campfires and horses. "Have you brought me something?" he asked.

Christian took the little red ribbon from his pocket, and offered it to Dampignak with both hands. He remembered what Good Fortune had said, and Good Fortune proved right. Dampignak relaxed, his sunken eyes lit up, and his twitching lips took on an expression of great joy. Smiling as happily as a child the Venerable Chief took the ribbon from Christian's hands and showed it to Moonlight, who was grinning.

"Now, was my account of them exaggerated?" cried Moonlight. "The like of these lads are not to be found between the four seas."

"It wasn't we who found it," said Christian. "It was the dog."

"The dog?" asked Dampignak. "Do you mean that black devil?"

"That's he," said Christian. "He's no ordinary dog."

"I've noticed that," replied Dampignak. "But I wasn't asking for the red ribbon. I was asking about something else."

"I've got that too," said Christian, again dipping into his pocket. It was the silver disk with the snake on it, which was like a coin and was made to fit the handle of a bamboo stick. Dampignak took it and pocketed it as if it were a copper coin. Then he looked into the fire again and the joy was gone from his face.

"You dug up ten silver bars in the Black City," he said. "Why did you leave the Great Treasure untouched? It was quite near." He stopped speaking, and there was dead silence. They could hear the poodle panting. Yet Dampignak had said all this in quite an ordinary voice, as if he were talking about the weather. Christian became confused and Big Tiger felt as if he had been found out. Neither of them could conceive how Dampignak had come by the secret of the Black City, and Big Tiger slowly drew his left hand over his right, to hide the ring. It isn't yet the right time for Dampignak to see it, he thought. Aloud he said: "The directions to the Great Treasure got lost."

"How was that?" asked Dampignak impatiently.

"It happened through the prudence of Naidang, who is called Picture Sheet," Christian explained. "The treasure of Etzina was at his disposal, but wishing to prevent disaster, he burned the description of its hiding place."

"It was completely destroyed," confirmed Big Tiger. "I watched its destruction very carefully."

"And you remained silent?" cried Dampignak. "How could you dare look on in silence while a vast treasure was being burned?"

"It was not our place to speak," said Big Tiger simply.

"Report!" ordered Dampignak, as if he were speaking to his robbers. He leaned back his head, closed his eyes, shut his lips tightly, and his thumb continued to propel the beads of the chaplet over his forefinger. Christian and Big Tiger nudged one another, each wanting the other to speak.

"Let each of you say what he knows," said Dampignak, without raising his eyelids.

Then Christian began to tell about Naidang and Nowhere-at-all, and how they had found the bamboo rods, and how Nowhere-at-all had journeyed far and wide and asked learned lamas to interpret to him what was written on the rods. 'We do not know,' said the lamas. 'That is ancient writing of past ages, which we do not understand.' Nowhere-at-all had thanked them for their trouble, but later he had said to Naidang: 'Those lamas are foolish ignorant men; their teachers forgot to kick them in the face.' "

"Enough," cried Dampignak, compressing his lips harder than ever. He was about to say something, but Moonlight broke into loud guffaws of laughter. He positively bawled with delight.

"Little Paw! Stupid Little Paw!" said Dampignak admonishingly. But even he couldn't keep a straight face. He actually smiled. Then he said: "That's enough. Now we know your story. For Thunderbolt and I were the learned lamas, and Moonlight was with us in the tent.

"Many years ago," he continued, "the three of us made a journey, and we were camping at Kuku-tologoi when Nowhere-at-all came the way. 'I know that man,' I said, and we hid our guns. Thunderbolt and I were wearing lamas' robes, and I said to Moonlight: 'You're our servant.' Nowhere-at-all came into our tent, and he didn't recognize me, for it was ten years since he had seen me. At that time I was a prince and not a lama, and I had no beard. After a while Nowhere-at-all showed us a bundle of bamboo rods and asked us what was written on them. Thunderbolt, who can neither read nor write, knit his brows learnedly. Then he passed the rods to me, and I saw what they were. I put them in their order, and read the story of Etzina, and when I had taken it all in I said to Nowhere-at-all: 'That is ancient writing of past ages, and I do not understand it.' At this Nowhere-at-all thanked us and went his way. But I immediately wrote down the account of how to find the Little Treasure and the Great Treasure, so that I should not forget it in case I should ever need riches."

"But what if someone else had carried them off?" asked Christian.

The Venerable Chief smiled again. "Nobody could have done that," he said. "My people are everywhere. I often rode alone to Etzina and tried the stone with the chessboard on it, and it always lay untouched under its covering of rubble until you came. I have also stood on the shaft of the well in which the Great Treasure lies hidden until the day of recovery, and I have thought of the mighty bulk and the mighty weight of the gold. But I did not in fact know that there was any living being who shared the secret with me since the death of Nowhere-at-all."

It's queer, thought Christian, that, since he was a robber, he didn't simply take the rods from Nowhere-at-all.

"Perhaps," continued Dampignak, "one of you thinks that I might have spared myself the trouble, and simply robbed Nowhere-at-all of the rods. That would have been simpler, wouldn't it, Compass Mountain?"

Christian got red. They must all have seen that, though there wasn't much light in the tent, and Christian was ashamed.

"It can't be helped," said Big Tiger bravely. "I also think it would have been simpler just to take them."

Dampignak glanced at Moonlight, and Moonlight murmured something like "Bravo." At any rate it expressed approval.

"You're honest," said Dampignak. "I'd have taken the rods without hesitation from any other man, for a robber's principles are not those of a provincial governor's. But gratitude is a virtue which is taken for granted even among robbers. When I first met Nowhere-at-all I was no lama, neither was I a robber. I was young and beardless, but I was in despair. I was sitting in the tent of a holy man at Yellow Hill Gap, and I wanted to go away, for the world was dark for me. 'Wait one hour,' said the holy man. 'I do not wish you to go away without a gift. But as I possess nothing I must wait until someone comes the way and makes me a gift.' An hour passed, and a merry fellow came along on a camel. It was Nowhere-at-all. He brought three leaves from the sacred tree which grows at the Monastery of the Hundred Thousand Pictures in Kumbum, and I was given one of the leaves as a gift. That is why I did not grasp the treasure of Etzina though it was mine to take. When the hour comes I shall give Naidang as much as he will have, for the memory of Nowhere-at-all is dear to me. I still possess that leaf to this day." From the folds of his robe he took a thin volume which was pressed between two little plates of wood and tied with a red silk twine.

"Don't open it," cried Big Tiger, frightened. "Nowhere-at-all died when he threw the leaf into the night wind and . . ."

"And what?" asked Dampignak.

"Don't open it," begged Big Tiger again, raising his hands beseechingly.

A silence deeper than ever fell on the tent as Big Tiger raised his hands and let them fall slowly again. The ring on his thumb shone—a dull silver. Everyone stared at him, and nobody dared to look anywhere else, above all at the Venerable Chief. Now he'll roar or do something mad, thought Big Tiger, but he let his hand lie on his knee. Christian fixed his eyes on the silver snake, and Moonlight too looked down at it. The long shaft of his pipe trembled in his hand. It hurt him to see his master grieved. He had not imagined it would be like that. The little flames in the fireplace flickered and the smoke climbed up to the ceiling of the tent. Outside the sun was shining.

"Yolros Lama is dead," said Dampignak hoarsely.

"That happened," said Big Tiger, "because the leaf of the sacred tree fell on the ground and got trodden on." He tried to take the ring from his thumb, but Dampignak raised his hand.

"Not now," he said. "I have squandered twenty years of my life worthlessly. Leave me alone."

"We shall go," said Moonlight.

He gathered up his cloak, stuck his pipe into his boot, and then rushed out of the tent before Christian and Big Tiger, so that custom might not be disregarded.

43 A CHAPTER IN WHICH WE LEARN MANY IMPORTANT THINGS

CHRISTIAN and Big Tiger sat the whole afternoon in front of the small blue tent, and when the sun sank behind the hills they helped Sembilik to feed the horses and water the camels.

"Are you Mongols?" asked Sembilik.

"Not yet," said Christian, "but we will be soon."

Sembilik laughed. "You can manage camels already," he said approvingly. But there were only two camels, which, Sembilik explained, were for carrying the tents and the few things needed for a desert journey. "We ride on horses," he said proudly, "and we've got plenty of them."

Besides Sembilik there were only two silent elderly men who seemed rather hostile to the boys. Their occasional words sounded like the rumble of distant thunder. "Put the pot on," "Fetch water," or "Put that thing away," they said to Christian. The latter words referred to the pistol, which Christian had donned again.

Despite the sunshine it was a dreary afternoon. Toeless lay sleeping in the tent; Moonlight had gone to Dampignak for orders and only came back in time for supper. The men sat round the fire and from the open door one could see into the vast night landscape.

"A new moon," said one of the men.

"How many more are to pass?" asked another petulantly.

"Now, Yuchi!" replied Moonlight. "Don't meddle in matters which are for the Prince to decide."

"We want to see him made King at last," said Yuchi. "On the eve of the battle of Kobdo he promised us we would. That's a long time ago."

"In those days," Moonlight recalled, "we were in league with many princes who today are against us."

"Why does he not force them to acknowledge him?" cried Yuchi. "He's more powerful than they all, and he's a Khoshut."

"Be quiet!" commanded Moonlight. "This has lasted for years, so what do a few more days matter?"

"A few more days?" asked Yuchi distrustfully.

"We are leaving the castle before the moon is full," said Moonlight. "The time is near."

"*Yabonah!*" cried Sembilik joyfully.

"Hush!" said Moonlight. "You know what has to happen before then."

"That old story," growled Yuchi.

"I won't tolerate such talk," said Moonlight sternly. "Look at Toeless. He's been made a cripple; and something still worse befell the Prince."

"When shall we set out?" asked Toeless.

"The Prince's orders are that we set out before sunrise," answered Moonlight. "Sembilik shall ride to Tsaghan-burgussun to await Good Fortune and Affliction. Yuchi and Sanienbayer are to pack up the tents and follow with the camels and horses. You,

Toeless, are to ride with them and wait in the castle until Good Fortune arrives."

"Never!" said Toeless, beside himself.

"It can't be otherwise," said Moonlight.

"It must be otherwise," shouted Toeless.

"No, it cannot," said Moonlight.

The eyes of Toeless filled with angry tears. "Shong-Ma will escape you," he wailed. "You have never been able to catch him. You've always caught the wrong man. Only I can recognize him. I'll seize him and I won't let him go. I must be there."

"It can't be," said Moonlight again.

At this point Toeless resorted to pleading. "You know, Moonlight," he said, "that I seek no gain. I seek only vengeance. For years I've been sitting alone in the silent desert. If you go without me you'll get into trouble."

Toeless had been too long alone, and had spent too many nights with fierce thoughts of vengeance to be able to relinquish them now. They grew pale in the daytime while he tended the sheep or hoed the poppy field. But as soon as darkness fell they were with him again. They crouched beside him at the fire, and went to bed with him on the *kang*. They never left him.

"He's right," said the rebellious Yuchi. "You must take him with you."

At this Moonlight stood up with a growl and went over with Toeless to the Venerable Chief. Yuchi closed the tent and lay down to sleep with the silent Sanienbayer. Young Sembilik sat at the fire and shook his head. "If he has his way it will be the first time the Prince's wishes are set aside," he said.

"Shut up!" cried Yuchi fiercely. But at that moment Moonlight came back, followed by Toeless, who was pale and bowed down with disappointment. Nobody said another word, the fire went out, and Big Tiger lay down beside Christian.

"Oh, Kwi-Chan," whispered Big Tiger, "do you understand what that means?"

"It can't be helped," whispered Christian. "What does your grandfather say to it?"

"He says the cry for vengeance is like the crow of a cock. It tries to reach to heaven, but it can't."

"And we're to be there," whispered Christian, unhappily.

"We'll have to stick it out."

"You're as brave as the old men of the mountain. I admire you."

It was a calm and glorious night. The stars pursued their silent courses. Everyone except Toeless slept, and when Sembilik got up and made a fire, Toeless stared into the flames with crazed eyes. He was pale and silent, and when Moonlight stood up and took his gun, he still did not stir.

"The time has come," said Moonlight to Christian and Big Tiger. "We're leaving."

"Worthy old uncle Toeless," said Big Tiger. "We have to go, but we shall count the hours until we can rejoice in your presence again."

"We hope it will be soon," said Christian.

And they both bowed deeply. Toeless nodded but did not look up, and they left the tent on tiptoe.

Sembilik was holding four horses ready. And then the Venerable Chief came. His red robe looked black, for it was still night, and the stars were twinkling coldly. The poodle ran from one to the other. He did not bark, but as Dampignak went by he growled softly.

"Where's Yuchi?" asked Dampignak. "Tell him and Sanienbayer to come." They both came out of the tent, and Dampignak said: "We heard your talk yesterday evening, Yuchi. How long have you been with us?"

"I have served you for sixteen years."

"Hand your gun to Sanienbayer, take a camel and your share of meat, and leave us. We do not wish ever to see you again, Yuchi."

"It would not be good for you," added Moonlight.

Yuchi remained silent, and so did Sanienbayer. As the Venerable Chief mounted they saluted him with a *kowtow*. Moonlight then mounted, and after him Christian and Big Tiger. Their saddle bags hung behind them and their sheepskins were folded double on the saddles as before. Nothing had been forgotten. Only the horses were different ones. They were somewhat bigger, and they tossed their heads, but none of them got excited, even when Christian mounted.

Sembilik cried *"Sä Yabonah!"* but it was a joyless farewell.

The Venerable Chief rode ahead. Moonlight began to sing, and Christian and Big Tiger recognized the tune.

"The old märin also sang the song about Chussera to us," said Christian, when Moonlight finished.

"I wish the old märin was here," sighed Moonlight. "He's a clever old man, and he has the Prince's ear because he's his friend."

"Is there something wrong?" asked Big Tiger.

"Can it be spoken of?" asked Christian.

"Yuchi spoke of it," replied Moonlight. "Didn't you hear him?"

"It seems a difficult matter," said Big Tiger. "It was not the right time to speak."

"The Prince is harsh in his judgments," said Christian.

"No, he's lenient," said Moonlight. "When a servant rebels, the reasons are many and deep. Yuchi was not bad, but now he will become bad. For he lacks patience, and patience is the first virtue which a robber needs. A robber without patience should have his head chopped off."

"Does a robber need virtues?" asked Christian, surprised.

"He needs them more than other people," explained Moonlight. "He will never be a great robber unless he knows where something is to be gotten—that's his instinct. He must be the first in a fight—that's his courage. He must be the last to retreat—that's his sense of duty. He must share the booty justly—that's his goodness. But the most difficult requirement in a robber is that he should never attempt the impossible—that is his wisdom. I do wish we still had the old märin with us."

"Was he with you once?" asked Christian.

"You are asking a question which must not be answered," replied Moonlight.

"But we're not traitors," said Christian.

"Nor are we inquisitive," said Big Tiger, proudly.

"Forgive me," said Moonlight. "But, you know, a robber's life is a dangerous one. The old märin was not a redbeard, but he was with us in the castle for two years. During that time he only went out at night, and so nobody ever saw him in our company, and therefore he has been able to live peacefully on the Etzin Gol. It was through him we first got word that an army was coming to besiege us, and he watched the treasure of Etzina, of which he and I alone know anything. It is true, of course, that only the Prince knows the place where the gold and jewels lie buried and could find the Great Treasure. So you see the richest man in the world riding out there ahead of you."

The sun rose. Its rays wakened the blue of the heavens, and the earth became yellow like the day before, when Christian had to ride by the compass. Dampignak's red robe floated in the breeze like a flag. The richest man in the world, thought Christian, and it all seemed very uncanny.

"The treasure of Etzina," said Moonlight, "is his rightful heritage. For Dampignak is a Khoshut, a direct descendant of Araptan."

They rode on the whole afternoon. Dampignak never looked round. He needed no compass. In the south lay dunes, and Dampignak rode round them. The route led through chains of hills, and he led the way without hesitation into one of a hundred valleys, all of which looked exactly alike. They didn't meet a single cairn or *obo,* for there were no travelers to need a landmark. Mortals had no business whatever there.

But whenever Christian peeped at his compass, it always pointed the same way. They were riding south-westward, without the slightest deviation. The heading was 135 degrees, Christian noted.

They halted at midday and Moonlight hobbled the horses. Dampignak sat down ten paces away. He closed his eyes and the beads of his chaplet began to glide through his fingers. He looked almost as if he were asleep, but his lips moved slightly, his thumb pushed the next bead forward, and one could see that he was awake and praying.

Christian and Big Tiger took down their saddle bags, and the poodle watched them expectantly. His tongue was trembling in his open mouth, and he was panting hard.

"There's no water here," said Big Tiger. They sat down beside Moonlight and opened their bag.

"I'm not in the habit of eating on a journey," said Moonlight; but he took a cake of wheat bread out of politeness. They themselves shared one between them. When they opened the bag again to get some meat for the poodle, they found Toeless's copper water flask in it.

"Toeless is kind beyond measure," said Moonlight. "I know that well. I'm very sorry he had to stay behind."

"May we ask the reason?" said Big Tiger.

"The reason is simple," said Moonlight. "His hate is so boundless that it would make him rash. We can't risk having such people with us on our undertakings. For that reason only four of us are riding to Ming-shui. And if we meet Shong-Ma, even the Prince will stay behind until we've got what we've been searching for twenty years."

"Ene yu beino?" asked Christian.

"We're looking for the Prince's family jewels," said Moonlight in a low voice. "Since Shong-Ma offered to sell two hair clasps to poor Toeless, we've heard nothing more of the treasure. The hair ornaments of the Princess alone were worth five thousand horses. But it's not for that reason we're looking for them."

"We understand," said Big Tiger. "But where would Shong-Ma have the jewels?"

"Tinger metne," said Moonlight.

Christian took his courage in both hands. "And what then?" he asked.

"Then Shong-Ma must die," said Moonlight. "He won't escape this time."

Christian turned pale. He knew that was the only answer, but hearing it spoken instead of just thinking it made a frightful difference. When Good Fortune had shouted: "I'll shoot Greencoat dead," it was quite certain that he wouldn't do so. It was only necessary to plead with him and pretend to think him a terrible war god, and all was well again. For Good Fortune was a human being like themselves. But Dampignak was a pitiless avenger.

Christian looked at Big Tiger, but Big Tiger was hanging his head. Without raising it he said: "Worthy Mr. Moonlight, we'd rather not ride to Ming-shui."

"But don't you want to get your truck back?" Moonlight reminded him.

"We'd like to," Christian admitted, "and we know now that this Greencoat or Shong-Ma is a very wicked man. But we've betrayed him, and that's wicked too."

"The house of the wicked collapses without mortal help," replied Moonlight. "When I got back to the castle with Thunderbolt, the Prince already knew that Greencoat was Shong-Ma. So you didn't betray him. But how did he come to know? Well, he came to know because it had to come out at last, and because we've got friends. You know that we went to war with the Governor of Kansu and he lost the war. He is our neighbor in the south. But to the west lies Sinkiang, and the old Governor in Urumchi is our friend."

"Is that Marshal Yang-Tseng-hsin?" inquired Christian.

"Yes, that's he," said Moonlight, "and he's friendly to us because we guard the trade routes. The caravans can travel in safety and trade is flourishing. Therefore Marshal Yang's frontier guards often do us a good turn, and when we meet them at Ming-shui we get all the news. They told us that the great merchant Greencoat had requested an audience of the old Governor three months ago on the subject of the robber Dampignak. The Prince thereupon resolved to keep an eye out for this gentleman.

"We soon found out that Greencoat had a branch office at Hsing-hsing-hsia and that his caravans were traveling only by the Silk Road. Since then our people have been roaming southward as far as the Silk Road. From time to time we cut the telegraph wires, so the mail people had to send a messenger with the telegrams to the next station until the wire was mended. We caught this messenger, and just took the written telegrams from him. But first we allowed him to copy them, so that the old Governor would not be annoyed with us and trade would not suffer. A horseman brought these telegrams quickly to the castle and the Prince read them, but only two of them seemed to him to be important. The first one came nearly a month ago, and was addressed to Governor Yang in Urumchi. But I don't know exactly what was in it, as I was still with the King of the Sunits at that time."

"Little Paw!" cried Dampignak admonishingly. He stood up and came toward them slowly. Moonlight grinned embarrassed.

"You should not tell a lie," said Dampignak seriously.

Moonlight defended himself. "I know only half or less," he said. "I was not there."

Dampignak sat down between Big Tiger and Christian. "The first lightning letter ran: 'To His Excellency Yang-Tseng-hsin, Marshal of China, Tihwa-fu. Sending Compass Mountain and Big Tiger to you today. Arrive about ten days. Wu-Pei-Fu.' That lightning letter came from Hwai-lai-hsien," said Dampignak, smiling. But his smile lasted only a moment; then he continued as if he hadn't seen the frightened look on Christian's face and Big Tiger's wink. Probably he didn't see either how Christian grasped his breast pocket, for he was looking straight ahead. "At that time," continued Dampignak, "I didn't know who Compass Mountain and Big Tiger were, but now I do."

He paused again, as if he were waiting for one of them to say something. But Christian did not stir, and Big Tiger remained silent. They waited anxiously to see if Dampignak would touch on the secret of the sealed letter or whether the danger would pass over.

"The second lightning letter which I intercepted," continued Dampignak, "read: 'To Li-Yuan-Pei, Hami. Send forty cans of gasoline to Hsing-hsing-hsia urgent. Shong-Ma.' An hour later I set out for the Etzin Gol. I rode day and night, for I hoped to catch Shong-Ma. The telegram came from Ashan, and I thought he would come by the southern road past the Black City. I looked up the old märin, who told me about Greencoat. Thus I learned what I did not know, but I arrived too late. Instead of Shong-Ma I saw you, and now I know all."

"Now we understand what was not clear," said Christian.

"We thank you for your esteemed confidence," said Big Tiger.

"Give your dog a drink," said Dampignak. "We have to set out, for you're twenty days behind. The old Governor in Urumchi will be anxiously watching out for you."

Christian picked up the water bottle and Big Tiger went to get an eating bowl, for there was nothing else for the dog to drink out of. They were so busily occupied that they did not see how the Venerable Chief smiled meaningly at Moonlight and how Moonlight, grinning broadly, tapped his chest on the spot where he thought General Wu's letter was reposing on Christian's breast.

"Yabonah!" cried Dampignak, hanging his prayer chaplet round his neck and going to his horse. Moonlight was already there, holding the horses, and they all mounted. They moved south toward a mountain range which rose from the stony plain. There was sand too, but it lay no higher than a hand's breadth. One could feel the hard ground beneath, and the poodle trotted along contentedly when the horses slowed down to a walk. But as soon as the sand ended the horses began to trot, and seemed to want to make up for lost time. The mountains were not high. One of the

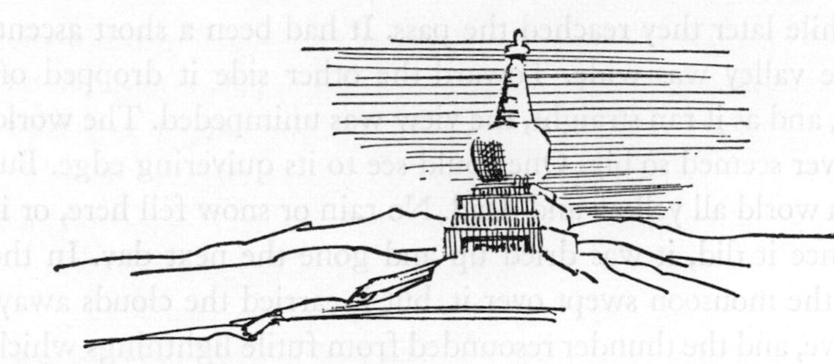

many peaks was crowned by an *obo,* and Dampignak was obviously steering his course by this.

Shortly before the ascent began they met a caravan track which led from the north, and Christian took out the map. The party were riding side by side with slack reins.

"Show me your map," said Dampignak. He looked at it for a long time, and then gave it back. "Where are we now?" he asked. "I can't read that writing."

"It's English," said Christian. "I believe we're coming into the mountains called Boro Ola now."

"We're already in them," said Dampignak. "The Hidden Well is also in the Boro Ola Mountains."

"Then," said Christian, "this is the caravan road which leads to Suchow."

"Good," said Dampignak. "But what's written here?" and he pointed to the little crossed hammers.

"The words 'Old Gold Region' are written near the hammers, and I really don't know . . ."

"Quite right," Dampignak interrupted him. "The map makers know more than the traders who pass the way, water their camels at the well, and have no idea that gold was once dug there."

"Is there a well there too?" asked Christian.

"Only recently," said Dampignak. "It was sanded up, but I got it cleaned out. That's why the people across the seas don't know about it yet. You can tell them when you get back."

"I'll remember that," promised Christian.

A while later they reached the pass. It had been a short ascent, and the valley was wide. Toward the other side it dropped off steeply, and as it ran straight, the view was unimpeded. The world had never seemed so big. One could see to its quivering edge. But it was a world all yellow and dead. No rain or snow fell here, or if perchance it did, it was dried up and gone the next day. In the spring the monsoon swept over it, but it carried the clouds away, far above, and the thunder resounded from futile lightnings which struck angrily upon the sand. Where on earth the water for the well came from was a puzzle.

But it was certainly there, and as the riders trotted down the mountainside, the poodle ran on ahead. At the foot of the last hill, which was scarcely a hill at all, he stopped and whimpered with joy. He was impatient for Moonlight to lift the planks and remove the sacking from the well hole. The shaft was lined with willow rods, and one could see to the bottom. Christian and Big Tiger looked down, and each knew that the other was thinking of Bator and his story of the well which Nowhere-at-all had dug with such toil at White Stone.

When they had watered the horses, and the poodle lay peacefully blinking at the sun, Christian told the story of the well at White Stone, and the Venerable Chief listened attentively. "Nowhere-at-all was a strange man," he said. "He spoke to the beasts and the stones, and they all answered him gladly. He wouldn't have stopped here for one moment," and he hit the ground with his whip.

Christian and Big Tiger did not venture to ask why not, but it was unnecessary, for Dampignak continued: "The treasure of Etzina came out of these mountains, my children. All the gold which the Khoshut Mongols possessed was dug here. A devil found it, and Araptan took it because he wanted to become powerful as Dagan. He assembled warriors, but they were too few. And he heaped up gold, but it was too much. When he needed workmen he invaded the provinces of the Emperor and depopulated whole villages. They lie here buried under the stones. The Emperor warned Araptan, but he warned him as brother warns brother, with mild reproof. For the Emperor was well pleased with Araptan for heaping up so much gold for him and taking upon himself a blood guilt which offered the Emperor a welcome excuse for war.

"When Araptan began to win the Mongol princes with gifts, and when his warriors became numerous, the Emperor, who was cunning, knew it was time to check him. He thought he would carry away the treasure of Etzina as a strong thief takes a chest on his shoulders and runs. But his soldiers stormed a burning city, and found ruins and rubble instead of gold. It was here"—and again he tapped the ground—"that Araptan's downfall began, and it is an ill-omened place. Let us ride on." And he stood up.

Moonlight covered the well and Christian and Big Tiger helped him. They looked around for any sign of an old shaft or mine hole. But the hills and the mountains seemed as untouched and unchanged as at the beginning of the world, and the caravan road ran straight up through the broad valley. It led from Suchow to Barkul, and none of those who passed thought or knew of the gold so near them. Only the map makers in Europe knew about it, and for the first time Christian looked at his Western Sheet with a shudder of awe at the thought of so much secret tradition.

From now onward the way led southwest again. The great plain rose and sank, but the difference in level was scarcely noticeable, so gradual was it, and so measureless the space. When the first foothills from the west obstructed the view, Dampignak turned round and, pointing ahead, said: "Another hour."

They were already two hours in the saddle. The poodle was trotting along panting, and the sun had long since shown the approach of evening. Soon after they saw a caravan track that ran parallel with the route they were following.

"This is the road to Hami," said the Venerable Chief, as Christian got out the map.

"Ma rode along here," said Moonlight, pointing to the fresh camel tracks. "So he's in front of us."

The mountain ridge to the south came no nearer. In fact, it receded, the terrain grew more level, and in the end looked like sea waves when the sun plays on the water. And it went on and on like that. The hour Dampignak mentioned had long since passed. It must have been a Mongolian hour, which means that it was as long as two others.

When it had passed, the waves in the sea of sand ended too. Suddenly a gray expanse of gravel lay before them, as flat as the bed of a stream or as the glacis around a fortress. In the middle were three hills. They were not high, or in any way remarkable. On the middle one, which was the largest, stood a fortress surrounded by walls of hewn stone. It consisted of square buildings and a watchtower with windows opening on all sides. One could see the sentry from far away.

A bugle call resounded through the clear air.

It was still bright day, and the sun stood high over the horizon, but evening was falling rapidly. The shadow of the watchtower lay over the flat roofs of the nearby buildings. Then it fell over a wall of the inner courtyard into the interior.

The horses slowed down to a walk, one could hear the poodle panting alongside, and a rider galloped out of the gateway in a cloud of dust, slapping his horse with his boots on breast and belly, his yellow cloak flapping in the wind. While still a long way off he roared: "Oh, my young brothers, my heart is full of joy!"

Dampignak turned to Christian and Big Tiger with a smile. "I didn't know you were related to Thunderbolt," he said.

"It turned out that way in the course of time," said Big Tiger.

"It is an honor for us," said Christian.

44 HOW CHRISTIAN AND BIG TIGER WERE HONORED IN THE ROBBERS' STRONGHOLD

When they rode through the gateway Big Tiger and Christian thought they would only have to stand up in their stirrups to be able to look over the castle wall, so low did it seem. Two men were standing at the gate, one on each side, and they saluted Dampignak with a *kowtow*. He returned the greeting, raising his clenched fists only to his breast. For he was not an ordinary robber chief, but a Khoshut, a prince of the line of Araptan.

The gate, which was made of stout planks, stood open. Inside the low wall was a watchman's house, and a round tower of the same height stood beside it. On the platform Christian noticed two machine guns covered with canvas. One flight of steps led up the hill, and the low walls ran along both sides of it. Grinning confidently Thunderbolt told how the caravan leaders had to pay their tribute in the watchman's house. But they were glad to do it, he affirmed, in return for safe conduct and guidance, and Mr. Ma had been there yesterday. Saying this, he looked sideways at Christian and Big Tiger, but their faces betrayed nothing.

"This is a magnificent castle," said Christian, to change the subject.

"This fine palace exceeds all expectations," said Big Tiger.

Up above the real fortress wall, made of roughly plastered stone, began. It was higher than the little wall of the outworks, and there were narrow loopholes in it—a tremendous lot of them, right around.

Here, too, the gate stood open, but the sentries carried naked swords, with which they saluted. Behind the gateway the ground was paved, and the clatter of the horses' hoofs resounded from the opposite wall. But it was not a spirit wall with open exit to both sides as in Etzina. In Dampignak's fortress they were more concerned with defense than with spirits. The gateway turned sharply to the left; they rode through a narrow tunnel, which opened on broad ramps leading to the walls. A bastion, on top of which stood more machine guns and a light field piece, was rising close to the gateway. The space where they stood was separated from the inner courtyard of the castle by yet another wall. A narrow passageway appeared to lead to it, but once more a rectangular space was separated off. This one was large and full of life. In the fortress wall were iron rings, at which stood rows of horses—probably a hundred. Above their heads ran the defense passage, but there was only one man on guard up there. He saluted Dampignak and nodded to Christian and Big Tiger as if they were old acquaintances. "That's Mendo," said Thunderbolt. "He waited for you behind the Etzin Gol, but as it was night you didn't know what he looked like."

Almost the whole of the north side of the square was occupied by a house even more solid in construction than the fortress wall itself. The walls were thick, as one could see from the few window openings and from the battlement which was pierced with numerous loopholes. Young men and old emerged from the doorway, all wearing heavy riding boots and brightly colored Mongolian clothes. They surrounded the party, greeting them with loud exclamations.

Dampignak dismounted.

"Come!" cried Moonlight.

"But our saddle bags," Christian reminded him.

"Leave everything be," said Moonlight. He took Christian and Big Tiger each by a hand and led them through the ever-increasing circle of men, who came running from all sides; they popped up on the battlement of the casemate, and many crowded the narrow edge of the *loess* cliff on which the fortress and the square watchtower stood.

"Look at the dog," cried some.

"Never was a dog so black," cried others.

"He must be a devil," said others again.

Their way continued upward between windowless walls. It was cold and dark in the narrow passages and there was a strong odor of horses. Then a square opened before them. It was completely level, and right in the middle of it stood three snow-white *yurts* on round foundations of clay bricks. Two steps led up to the entrances. Without looking to right or left Dampignak went straight up to the middle tent, which had a blue felt top. He disappeared into it, and the sentries shut the wings with their left hands. Like the sentries at the gate they carried heavy cavalry swords in their right hands.

Moonlight stopped in front of the first tent. "This is the guest tent," he said. "The Prince lives in the next one, and the third is for Thunderbolt, Damiensuren, and myself."

"Who is Damiensuren?" asked Christian.

"He commands the fortress when the Prince and I are away. You will make his acquaintance." He opened the little door wings. The twelve animals representing the twelve months were carved on them, six on each, beginning with the tiger, the hare and the dragon. Then came the snake. "Go ahead," urged Moonlight, pushing the boys before him.

The last beams of daylight were pouring through the open smoke vent in broad streaks which were broken by the roof stays, giving the impression of the railings of a cage. The whole interior could be taken in at a glance. Dark Kashgar rugs lay on the floor. The fireplace in the center, as in all *yurts,* was swept clean, and a small fire was burning. Two sheepskins spread opposite the entrance indicated the sleeping places. And that was all the furnishing.

Christian and Big Tiger hardly dared to step on the beautiful rugs, and after the first step they stopped, for they saw that on each of the sheepskins lay a blue Mongolian coat, a dark-red silk scarf, an embroidered pouch with something in it, a pair of riding boots, and a magnificent new silk hat trimmed with gray fox fur.

Behind Christian and Big Tiger stood Moonlight, enjoying it all. He was grinning from ear to ear, but when Christian turned round he looked solemn and knelt down before him, holding a blue silk *haddak* in his hands. "Accept these worthless gifts from your friend Moonlight," he begged.

Then Christian too knelt down, took the *haddak,* and raised it to his forehead. Murmuring "Thanks ten thousand times for measureless kindness," he felt about anxiously in his pocket, and to his intense relief found Sevenstars' beautiful sky-blue silk *haddak,* which he offered to Moonlight. "It is for both of us," he said, quickly laying it over Big Tiger's hands too; "for we have got only one."

Moonlight smiled and said: "I am unworthy of so great a gift; you embarrass me, sons of heroes." Then Big Tiger too received a *haddak* from him, as custom demanded.

"I must go now," said Moonlight, "and I wish you a good night."

As soon as Moonlight had left the tent Christian and Big Tiger tried on the boots first of all.

"Much too big," said Christian.

"No, they're right," said Big Tiger. "You must wear the stockings with them."

"What stockings?"

"Those there," said Big Tiger, pointing to two thick felt stockings which looked like another pair of boots. They had to be pushed into the boots, and then the boots fitted perfectly and were beautifully warm. The red-edged tops of the felt stockings stuck out a bit over the decorated uppers. This kept the legs comfortable and protected them from getting chafed.

Christian then wanted to try on the coat, but quickly desisted when a savage growling started outside.

"Dog!" cried Big Tiger.

"Be quiet!" cried Christian, running to the door. The poodle was standing on the brick threshold gnashing his teeth and looking as if he wanted to spring on two men who were standing some distance off, looking frightened. Christian seized him firmly by his black locks and then called out to the men: "You needn't be afraid."

The two men entered carrying the leather saddle bags, the saddles, the brief case with the compass, and the horse blankets.

"Do you think we'll soon get some food?" asked Christian when the men were gone. "The dog is hungry too."

"He's all right," said Big Tiger, opening a saddle bag. "We'll keep the cheese for traveling, but we'll give him the meat." And they gave him two big pieces of dried meat. The Mongols, who were watching them from the roof of the casemate opposite and from the battlements around, were laughing, but some of them shook their heads angrily. "That's not necessary," they shouted over.

"I'm afraid we've done something wrong," said Christian.

"It can't be helped," Big Tiger replied. "Now let's try on the coats."

The coats were blue outside and seemed to be made of silk, for they had a dull shimmer. They were lined with white lambswool, and trimmed with gold braid. The high collars were yellow. The coats reached down to the boots, but when Christian and Big Tiger wound the red sashes round their waists, this raised them to just the right length.

"Now for the pouches," said Christian, pushing his own into his sash. It was made of green silk with red edges, and embroidered with lucky symbols. There was a slit in the center, and when Christian put his hand in he found a silver snuff bottle.

They tried the snuff. "This snuff . . ." began Big Tiger, but he could say no more, for his eyes filled with tears. He could not even tell Christian how funny he looked. They both had to just sneeze and sneeze, so much so that the poodle started barking. "What on earth is this stuff good for?" asked Big Tiger, sitting down exhausted.

"It will be grand in school," said Christian. "I'll save mine up for the arithmetic class."

When they had recovered they put on their fur hats, and suddenly found themselves complete Mongols. As a final touch they tucked their silver food bowls away in their coats.

"You look like Bator," cried Christian.

"Your amah would be flabbergasted," said Big Tiger. And he looked at the last rays of the sun, which shone on the roof poles, and the soot which hung from the roof in long threads. "Today is the first day of the new moon," he continued. "Just think, we only wanted to fly our kite."

"Instead of being in school, here we are in a robber's fortress," said Christian, "and I didn't believe that there were still such things in the world."

"Why didn't he want the ring?" asked Big Tiger thoughtfully. "After all, it belongs to him."

"We must think that out," said Christian. But they hadn't time, for the door opened and two men entered. They wore round hats with a coral knob on top, from which hung a red silk cord. They held silver plates on their outstretched hands, and bending one knee, said: "Please eat in peace."

Christian and Big Tiger took the plates, but several more were brought, and Big Tiger at last protested: "We can't eat a whole lamb each."

"You're our Prince's honored guests," said the men. "Eat as much as you can. We shall be back again."

Christian and Big Tiger ate heartily, but they saw at once that they could never finish the many courses, or even the lamb and the antelope meat. They took only a little of the fritters, and just broke the top off the mountain of cheese. But they drank all the milk, which tasted both sour and sweet at the same time. After a while one of the men came back and gave them more.

"Ene yu beino?" asked Christian.

"Mare's milk," replied the man, and the red string of his ceremonial hat fell forward as he bowed. "But now you must begin to eat," he admonished them.

Big Tiger and Christian looked at each other in wonder, but the man had disappeared.

"I can't eat any more," said Christian.

"We're like ants in front of the Wu-Chan Mountains," said Big Tiger.

"It's getting dark," said Christian. "They won't see how much we leave."

Evening had come on and the *yurt* was darkening imperceptibly. A little bit of evening sky could be seen through the smoke vent, but it soon grew dim. The stars came out, and the two servants came back to the tent.

"Thanks ten thousand times for a glorious meal," said Christian.

"You lavish too much kindness on us," said Big Tiger.

The men bowed in silence, and kneeling took the plates which Christian and Big Tiger handed to them. "Sleep well," they said, and one of them shut the smoke vent, leaving only a little peep of sky visible, as thin as the crescent moon. Before lying down to sleep Christian and Big Tiger went out of the tent once more. The poodle lay at the foot of the steps, a water dish and a bowl beside him. He jumped up joyfully.

"How are you?" asked Christian.

"Are you an honored guest too?" asked Big Tiger, stroking his head. Then they looked up at the darkening battlements, where a man was leaning against the breastwork. Down in the courtyard the horses were pawing and champing, the steps of the sentinels could be heard, and, in the distance, the howling of wolves.

"They must have lost their way," said Christian.

"Like ourselves," said Big Tiger.

Christian sighed and waited for Big Tiger to say, "It can't be helped," but Big Tiger only stroked the poodle. "Do you think, Kwi-Chan," he asked, "that they're all like this?"

"I wouldn't like to be the Prince," replied Christian evasively.

"Perhaps Naidang is right," said Big Tiger, "and he is only an unhappy man."

They went back to the tent, and when they had covered themselves with the old coats, for the new ones seemed far too new and precious, they fell asleep. They were too tired to worry any more about being in a robber's castle. They had eaten and drunk, and now they slept.

Moonlight, who opened the door a little later, shut it softly again. "They're asleep already," he reported to Dampignak.

Next morning the two men with the red silk hats appeared while it was still dark. They lit the fire and brought breakfast, which this time included a big can of milk. They also brought a can of hot water, two wet hot cloths, and two towels. Christian and Big Tiger realized what they were meant to do, but they didn't take out their cake of soap. They just wiped their faces and hands with the wet cloths, dried them, and said, "*Bolna.*" The men nodded comprehendingly.

Just as Christian and Big Tiger were winding their sashes around their waists, in came Moonlight. "That's not the way to do it," he said.

"Lend us your light in this difficult matter," Big Tiger requested.

"Better two together," explained Moonlight, and he told Christian to press an end of the scarf against his body. "Now wheel round," he said, and while Christian revolved, he held the broad silk sash taut, letting it glide gradually through his hands. It ran in neat folds, and finally Moonlight tucked in the end. "That will hold," he said, with an air of satisfaction. Then he fixed Big Tiger's sash. When they both had on their new hats, Moonlight said: "I will now show you the castle. It was built to last for ages, but what of it? We may abandon it soon."

They left the tent. The pale morning light promised a beautiful day. The watchtower was still in darkness, but the outlines of the fortress walls could be seen, and the light was coming through the loopholes from the east. They climbed up a ramp to the highest defense point of the fortress, which stood on a plateau of *loess* cliffs that had been cut away to form steep walls. Above there were more walls with loopholes, surrounding a completely empty quadrangle. On the east side stood the watchtower, but it too was surrounded by walls, which were intended as the last place of retreat.

Then they crossed the little inner courtyard and mounted a wooden staircase leading to the first floor of the watchtower. It was dark and there were no windows. The only light came from a square opening above. A steep shaky ladder led to the platform of the tower. Before mounting Christian and Big Tiger slipped off their boots. They found themselves in the turret, which had four empty window openings. The guard greeted them. On the wall hung a gun and a brass horn.

They were just in time to see the sun rising over the edge of the desert. Its fiery orb climbed out of the blue haze, bathing the desert, the gravelly plain, and the three hills in flaming radiance.

The guard blew a long blast of his horn out of each window hole, to north, south, east and west. A new day had come.

Looking down from the breastwork Christian and Big Tiger could see the whole fortress below them, with its courtyards and fortification, which reached down into the valley. Water was being drawn from many wells, and horses were standing all round the walls. Men were going to and fro with pails and nose bags, and camels and horses were being driven out through the open gateways.

"They're going to the big deresen pasture which is not far from here," Moonlight explained.

They could also see, far below them, the big square where the three white *yurts* stood. The two men with the red silk hats were coming out of the one in which they had slept, carrying saddles, and heavy, freshly filled saddle bags.

"It's nearly time to start," said Moonlight solemnly. And while the boys slipped into their big Mongolian boots he said: "I have to hurt you, I'm afraid. The dog must stay here and wait for Good Fortune."

They were not prepared for this. "He's no ordinary dog," said Big Tiger sorrowfully.

"Even extraordinary dogs bark when they should be quiet," Moonlight explained. "You must understand that."

"It's hard to understand," said Christian, stroking the poodle. "He'll have a good time here," Moonlight assured them, taking each by a hand. The guards in front of Dampignak's tent dipped their swords in salute, opened the door wings, and Dampignak came forward to meet his guests. He was no longer clad as a monk; he had left off his red lama's cloak. When he saw the astonished faces of Christian and Big Tiger he smiled.

"Pray be seated," said Dampignak, but Christian and Big Tiger refused, murmuring "After you," and "We do not dare," and Dampignak listened to them seriously. "My children," he said, "you are the first guests of this fortress who have come to me without fear. It is my wish to honor you."

Christian and Big Tiger did not know what to do. They knelt down and said: "We are unworthy boys. Please forgive our disobedience."

But Dampignak raised them to their feet, and made them sit on two white panther skins, and as they had no alternative, they had to allow the Venerable Chief to bow the knee before them. "My friend Moonlight," he said, "who accompanies me everywhere, begged me to allow him to give you Mongolian clothes. So there's little for me to give. But please accept a small token of my friendship."

While Dampignak said this Moonlight laid two *haddaks,* thin as gossamer, over his hands, and on them he placed two silver-handled daggers with silver chain fastenings.

"We do not dare," murmured Christian. "Accept our thanks ten thousand times."

"You squander your heart," said Big Tiger. "You are like the midday sun."

The Venerable Chief sat down. "Before we go," he said, "please tell me how matters looked in Peking when you came away."

"We really didn't notice there was a war on," answered Big Tiger. "We went out to fly our kite, and everything was as usual."

"No one knew anything," said Christian. "Only when we came to Chi-chi-men station there were suddenly cannons and soldiers there. But the soldiers were in no humor for war."

"They simply ran away at the Nan-ku Pass," said Big Tiger.

"And General Wu didn't have to fire any shots," said Christian. "He simply occupied the Great Wall because there was no enemy there."

"He's taken Peking, and he got Tientsin with one bold stroke," the Venerable Chief informed them. "I heard that from the telegraph people in Anhsi."

"General Wu-Pei-Fu will end the civil war and there will be a beautiful peace," cried Big Tiger.

The Venerable Chief said: "It is for that reason you are on this journey. You are messengers of peace. Do you know that?"

"We did not know it," said Big Tiger.

"We know it now," said Christian.

The Venerable Chief groped slowly in the folds of his gray cloak, and took out the thin volume pressed between two wooden boards. "You needn't be afraid," he said, smiling at Big Tiger. "The leaf of the sacred tree will not be destroyed." He untied the silken cord. On top lay a sealed envelope, and Big Tiger read the bold painted inscription: "To the Most Venerable Governor Yang-Tseng-hsin, Marshal of China, Governor of the Western Province Sinkiang, Tihwa-fu."

Christian also began to read, and when he came to 'The Most Venerable Governor,' Dampignak said to him: "As you, Compass Mountain, are the secret courier of General Wu, please take my letter also, and bend your knee on my behalf as you hand it to the Venerable Excellency. Be careful, my children, for a letter belonging to the robber chief Dampignak would bring danger on its bearers, if it fell into wrong hands."

"I shall never again put my hand on my breast pocket," Christian vowed.

"We shall be so secretive," said Big Tiger, "that we ourselves shall no longer know what others are not to know."

Christian took the letter in both hands, raised it to his forehead, and then put it away where General Wu's letter had lain for the past month.

"I admire my elder brother Wu," said Dampignak. "He is courageous and resourceful. The people cling to him as children to their father and mother, but he knows his limitations. He hates pomp and he loves modesty. He is sending you to the great ruler whom I also would wish to serve. My elder brother Wu could have found no more gifted messengers than you two."

"We are of no account," objected Christian.

"We deserve no consideration," said Big Tiger.

"It does not often happen," continued Dampignak, "that the will of heaven is made so manifest."

He opened the thin volume, which contained many blank pages, and two in the middle which were closely written on. A silken binding thread held them together. Between them lay a brown, dried sandalwood leaf. Dampignak lifted it out carefully, laid it aside, and tore the written pages out of the little book. It was then quite blank, and Dampignak laid the sacred leaf carefully back in the middle. Then he pressed the little book between the wooden plates, tied the red cord, and put the volume away in the folds of his cloak.

"Through you," said the Venerable Chief, "I learned of the wisdom of Naidang, whom men call Picture Sheet. He withstood temptation, in order to avoid evil. For me there is no temptation. I know the place, and I know that gold and jewels put the world into confusion. You have reminded me of that fact while there was still time. Behold, for a second time you will see an immeasurable treasure burned."

He crumpled up the thin paper and threw it into the fire. It flared up, the black sheets curled, and as they fell to pieces Dampignak stood up. "We must ride now," he said.

He stuck an old silver-handled dagger in his sash, and Moonlight showed Christian and Big Tiger how to do the same.

"We three now wear the same daggers," said Dampignak. "I got mine copied for you when Moonlight told me how bravely you had conquered the wolf." Without waiting for an answer he walked rapidly out of the tent, and Moonlight followed him. As they passed the guest tent Moonlight stopped and said: "You need not be a bit uneasy about your dog. Nothing will happen to him. But you must tie him up now."

"Dog! Come here!" cried Christian. He put on the leather leash, and fastened it to a ring in the foundation of the tent.

"Good Fortune and Affliction will be here in four days," said Moonlight.

"And Toeless," added Christian.

"Tell your dog to guard your belongings well."

"And the pistol?" asked Christian.

"The pistol too," said Moonlight. "It's enough for me to have one."

"Dog," said Big Tiger, "we're going now, and you mustn't be lonely for us." But the poodle didn't want to be left behind. He pulled on his leash, barked and whined.

Down in the courtyard all the horses had disappeared except four which stood saddled. A tough-looking thickset man with a black moustache was holding three of them, and Thunderbolt was holding the brown stallion with light mane and tail.

Dampignak mounted forthwith and Moonlight had just time to introduce the boys to the stranger, who proved to be Damiensuren, warden of the fortress. "Mount," said Damiensuren. "I've picked the best horses for you. You needn't be frightened of them; they'll keep step with him." He meant Dampignak's stallion.

"Sä Yabonah!" Thunderbolt called after the Venerable Chief. Then he came running with outstretched arms. "Oh, my young brothers," he roared, embracing them in turn. "Shall we ever meet again in this life?" There were tears in his eyes, and he began suddenly pulling at his thick fingers as if he wanted to wrench them off. "Excuse great lack of manners. *Haddak* in haste forgotten," he blurted in his bad Chinese, "but here's a souvenir of poor lama Thunderbolt." Saying this, he pushed on Christian's thumb the ring he had had on his little finger. To Big Tiger he gave the one from his middle finger, but it would not fit even his thumb. "No good fit," moaned Thunderbolt. But Moonlight trotted off, and Big Tiger and Christian had to follow.

"Sä Yabonah!" roared Thunderbolt mournfully. *"Sä Yabonah!"* cried Damiensuren without emotion; and the cry was taken up on the watchtower and all the battlements.

45 CONTAINING FRESH NEWS OF MR. GREENCOAT

THE HORSES, which were fresh and swift, followed the caravan road. It ran westward and was level, although the southern mountains were now near. Again and again it looked as if their foothills would encroach on the caravan track, but that was not so. There was no gradient.

Not until afternoon, when the shadows were growing longer, did the horses slow down to a walk, for they were mounting a slope. From the north, too, the foothills of mountains jutted out into the caravan road, and finally the plain merged into a broad valley, and the surrounding mountains were capped with blackish-green stone. Teeth of rock pressed through the *loess,* sand and gravel, as if to show what the Black Gobi hid beneath its surface. The valley was strewn with a thin layer of sand on which the trail of Ma's caravan was sharply imprinted.

"Ma is not far ahead of us," said Moonlight. "He's camping tonight at Steep Rock Well and tomorrow night in Ming-shui. He's keeping his appointment."

"So are we," said Christian.

The Venerable Chief turned aside from the caravan track and rode south into the mountains. After half an hour the black cones came nearer, and spikes of rock could be seen rising from the primeval desert here, there and everywhere. It seemed a world apart. Dampignak threaded his way between the rocks, then turned into a valley bounded by round conelike hills, with a stream running through it, and near the stream were two blue tents.

Here too everything was prepared. The red horse-tail pennant was flying, but the tents were plain blue and both alike. Two men were waiting outside and they greeted Dampignak. "Nothing has happened," they said. "Everything is going well. Tangat is coming to report at midnight." And they took the horses.

"Be my guests and share my tent," said Dampignak to Christian and Big Tiger. "Let us stay together as long as we may."

When they were at tea the men brought Christian and Big Tiger their saddle bags and the brief case, and Moonlight said to the men: "Take down the horse-tail pennant. You never can tell."

The Venerable Chief sat motionless, with bowed head, staring into the fire. His prayer beads were gliding through his fingers, his lips moved silently, and his eyes were half closed.

Christian and Big Tiger went out to look around and see where the water came from and where it went to. "It's well the dog wasn't with us," said Christian.

"He'd never have kept up," admitted Big Tiger. "We rode very fast."

"And he'd have barked where he shouldn't."

"It seems no one is to know we're here," said Big Tiger. "Moonlight has got the horse's tail taken away."

"The gentlemen are very cautious," said Christian, with a backward glance at the tent. It was open and a man was sitting at the fire, cooking.

They came to the horses which were standing at a line with nose bags on. The second man appeared over the hills riding a camel and driving three others in front of him toward the encampment. Suddenly he stopped short and at the same time they heard a distant call, but could see nobody, for the valley was surrounded by hills and mountains. On the southern side some scrub and yellow-wood was growing, but farther up it was completely barren and nothing was to be seen but the black teeth of rock. The cry was repeated, this time a little nearer, but it was quite a while before the rider came into view. His camel was stumbling along and threatening to fall, obviously completely exhausted. When the rider caught sight of the tents he dismounted, and walked along beside the camel man, who had dismounted too.

"A stranger," said Big Tiger.

"We must tell Moonlight," said Christian.

They went back to the tent and announced that a stranger was coming along on a camel which could hardly walk another step. "Bring him to me," ordered Dampignak, "but do not say who I am."

"Perhaps he knows already."

"No fear of that," replied Dampignak. "My men are silent."

Christian and Big Tiger went to meet the stranger. He was a Mongol, tall, weatherbeaten and beardless, and the deep lines in his face were almost like black strokes of a pen. His cheeks were hollow, and he looked undernourished. His camel was even more emaciated than he. Its humps were shrunken and the skin hung loosely like an empty bag over the protruding ribs. The man wore on his breast a finely engraved silver case hanging on a silken cord.

Christian and Big Tiger saluted, and when the man took his snuff bottle from his sash they were glad that they had snuff bottles too. Then they ran forward and opened the tent, begging the stranger to enter. At the sight of Dampignak he bent his knee and saluted politely, and they exchanged snuff bottles.

"You see before you an officer of the old Governor in Urumchi," Moonlight lied valiantly. "He has charge of the frontier post."

"I thought I had already passed Ming-shui," said the stranger. "Please forgive my ignorance."

"Yes, Ming-shui lies behind you. But we've come a little way over the frontier to keep an eye on Dampignak's people. Now and then we have to remind those redbeards who they are and where they belong."

The stranger hesitated to reply. One could see that he would have preferred to remain silent. At last he said cautiously: "You're right. There are people who complain of the redbeards."

"Is that possible?" cried Moonlight.

"Where do you come from?" asked Dampignak casually.

"My name is Dambit," said the stranger, "and I'm a pilgrim on my way from Lhasa, but heaven only knows if I'll ever see my home again, for my camel is nearly finished and it's a long way to Djun-Sunit."

"How long have you been traveling, Dambit?"

"Nearly three years. I hoped to be home by the beginning of the fourth year."

"I see your hardships have not been in vain," said Dampignak, bowing before the little silver casket which Dambit carried on his breast.

"I received the blessing of the Dalai Lama," said Dambit simply.

"You're a lucky man," cried Dampignak, "and it is a joy to have you with us."

For a moment there was silence, but at last Moonlight could contain himself no longer. "Where do you want to go from here, friend Dambit?" he asked.

"I'm trying to reach the Path of Meditation, but I've lost my way. How many days' ride northward is it?"

"It's not good riding straight to the north from here. You would find no water. Ride as far as the caravan road that comes from Hami. You'll reach it in an hour. Follow it eastward and in two days you'll reach the Venerable Chief's stronghold. Ask there for the Path of Meditation; the fellows will show you the way. They are said to be friendly to pilgrims and poor travelers."

"I'd be afraid all the same," said Dambit. "I've been urgently warned."

"That's right," said Moonlight. "We've instructed our frontier soldiers to warn everyone. I note they do their duty. Solitary travelers at any rate. . . . What do you think, Captain?"

Dampignak did not reply. He looked past Moonlight, and it was obvious that he did not wish to answer.

"It wasn't the frontier soldiers who warned me," said Dambit. "It was someone else. As a matter of fact the soldiers said: 'Don't be afraid. The redbeards will give you a gift if they meet you.' And they asked me to give their greetings and congratulations to one of them who was dead and is now alive again."

"I call that dereliction of duty," cried Moonlight. "What do you say, Captain?"

Christian and Big Tiger bowed their heads. They realized why Moonlight was talking so loudly, and they found it hard to keep from laughing. Big Tiger clenched his fists, Christian bit his tongue, but the Venerable Chief said quite coolly: "That's the strange thing about people. They take the worst bandit to their heart rather than the authorities who protect them. What was the name of the man to whom you were to give congratulations on the restoration of his life?"

"His name is Moonlight," answered Dambit, "and the sword, so the soldiers said, went clean through his temples. And he died. But in the night Kalatchakra came and restored him to life. That was the soldiers' story, and Moonlight must be a great warrior and a good man, for such miracles are rare in our days."

"Look at me," said Moonlight. "My skull was also cleft open by a sword, but nobody makes any fuss about it."

Dambit started back when Moonlight pushed his hat off his forehead. The fiery red scar ran from one temple to the other, and Moonlight said with a laugh: "It's not exactly ornamental, but you needn't be all that scared."

"It's not that," stammered Dambit. "It's the likeness. A man who had seen Moonlight described him to me."

"I venture to hope," said Moonlight, "that I'm not like *him*."

"But that's just what scared me," said Dambit. "The day before yesterday I met two men with a horseless car, and one of them described Moonlight to me in every detail. He said: 'He and the Venerable Chief are the worst criminals in the ten thousand states. But I'll see to it that the executioner's sword gets them in the end.' "

"So much the better," said Moonlight gaily. "The gentleman will spare us a lot of trouble. What's his name, by the way?"

"The man with him called him Mr. Greencoat."

"Oh, indeed?" cried Moonlight. "I must tell you, Dambit, that Mr. Greencoat is an old friend of mine, a man whose fame fills the valleys. What a joy it would be to meet this long-lost friend in the wilderness! Where did you meet the dear delightful fellow?"

"I just came along when his car was stuck in a gravel bank between Hsing-hsing-hsia and the place called Falling Wall."

"I hope you helped him."

"Yes, I helped him because people should help each other. He told me to shovel, and I shoveled. He told me to carry planks, and I dragged them along. Then he was able to drive on."

"And the good fellow surely gave you a princely reward?"

"I asked no reward."

"But surely, if I know him aright, he helped you as you had helped him."

Again Dambit hesitated to reply. At last he said: "Since Mr. Greencoat is your friend we need not speak of that."

"I understand," said Moonlight. "In his hurry friend Greencoat forgot to thank you."

"It wasn't that," said Dambit.

"What was it then? Did he embarrass you with his generosity?"

Dambit shook his head. "Since you want to know," he said, "I'll tell you. This Mr. Greencoat shouted at me: 'What are you standing there for, you lousy fellow! I have no riches to bestow on you. Go and get your reward from Moonlight, who has robbed me. No doubt you're also an old redbeard.'"

"Now, now," said Moonlight, appeasingly. "Friend Greencoat is a trifle hard. He's a Tungan and he knows nothing of the Mongol *joss*. And perhaps driving a horseless car has gone to his head. It disagrees very much with many people."

"Enough," cried Dampignak. "Your Greencoat doesn't seem to deserve great praise. Let's have tea."

"May the little boys also venture to ask a question?" said Christian modestly.

"Certainly," said Dampignak.

Christian turned to Dambit. "My friend Big Tiger and I," said he, "saw Mr. Greencoat as he passed us by at the Etzin Gol. At that time he had nothing on the truck except iron drums and cans.

May I ask what load he was carrying when you met him?"

"The car was full of empty cans," replied Dambit, "except for one big iron drum which stood in the front, in a corner."

"Was his companion a soldier?" asked Big Tiger.

"No, he was not a soldier," replied Dambit. "He was a small, thickset, short-winded man. He called Greencoat 'Honored Sir,' and he wore a faded black merchant's coat."

"In which direction did Greencoat drive off?" asked Christian.

"He drove northward."

"Was he armed?" Big Tiger inquired.

Dambit laughed. "You're asking a lot of questions," he said. "But I remember seeing a gun lying in the driver's cab, in which they were both sitting."

"One more question," said Christian. "I'd very much like to know at what hour you met Greencoat?"

"The midday sun was shining," replied Dambit, surprised. "Why do you want to know that?"

"It's just the way of my friend Compass Mountain," replied Big Tiger coolly, "to ask questions which have no meaning."

"Drink your tea," cried Moonlight, filling Dambit a bowl and putting a piece of sheep butter into it.

Christian picked up the brief case with the compass, and Big Tiger stood up too. "We're going to have a look around," said Big Tiger. They climbed the first hill behind the tent and went down the other side where nobody could see them. Christian took out the map and compass. "Here's Ming-shui," he said, "and here's Hsing-hsing-hsia. We're here, and the day before yesterday Greencoat was between Hsing-hsing-hsia and Falling Wall."

"Where's Falling Wall?"

"I don't know, but it must be here where the mountains begin. Do you see these pointed things that look like a toothbrush? The toothbrush is the sign for rocks, and Falling Wall must be there, and when I get home I'll write to the map makers about it."

"But what's there now?" asked Big Tiger.

"It's all quite clear now," Christian assured him. "It was in this valley"—and he put his finger on the spot—"midway between Hsing-hsing-hsia and the cliff region, that Dambit met Greencoat."

"Where's the valley?" asked Big Tiger, for he wanted to know exactly.

"It can't be seen," admitted Christian, "but it must be there since Dambit spoke of a gravel bank in which the car got stuck. It's only in valleys that there are gravel banks."

"Aha," said Big Tiger, silently admiring Christian's familiarity with valleys.

"Dambit could ride only slowly," continued Christian, "because his camel was done in. So it took him three days to get here. Greencoat was in Falling Wall one or two hours later, that's to say by the afternoon."

"That was the day before yesterday," said Big Tiger.

"Yes," replied Christian, "but what's he doing there for so long? His appointment with Ma is for the day after tomorrow. That means he's there five days. What's he doing at Falling Wall?"

"I don't know. And since neither of us knows," said Big Tiger, "it's not at all clear. How far is Falling Wall from Ming-shui?"

"About seventy *li,*" Christian estimated, "or it might be eighty. That's a day's journey with a camel, half a day on horseback, or two hours by car. But of course that depends on the road."

"It can't be helped," said Big Tiger. "There's always something we don't know."

"Perhaps we'll find out," said Christian reassuringly, but though he thought hard and though Big Tiger said, "Greencoat is just resting a bit," it seemed to them improbable that he would need five days to do so.

When Moonlight shouted "Food, food!" and "Where are the sons of heroes hiding?" they gave up their reflections and went back to the tent, but on the way a new question occurred to Christian, and he found it hard to wait for the meal to be over. Dambit, who had been fasting so long that he could not eat much, told of

his pilgrimage. He had spent more than half a year in the sacred city of Lhasa, and he described with great ardor and enthusiasm the glories he had seen, and the wild inaccessible mountain region in which the walled-up hermits lived. But he said no word about his own hardships; they were written on his face. All listened with rapt attention. But before Moonlight had time to say "Good night and sleep well," Christian burst out, "May I ask what Falling Wall looks like?" and when he noticed that everyone was speechless with astonishment, he added, "Please forgive my ignorance."

"I've never been there," said Dambit, "but the Captain will know, for it's in the frontier region."

"We've only come here recently," Moonlight explained promptly. "We really belong to the life guard of the old Governor in Urumchi, as I mentioned before. And I think we should go to sleep now."

"Sleep well," said Dampignak, and this put an end to all conversation.

Christian awoke when the camel man came to make the fire. Dampignak was sitting wrapped in meditation, his prayer beads gliding through his fingers. He had probably been sitting like that half the night. Christian did not dare to get up and say: "Have you slept well?" He waited until Moonlight awoke and in his brusque, cheerful way roused the sleepers and gathered them round the tea kettle.

There was little talk. Dambit the pilgrim went out to offer a water sacrifice for the souls of the departed before sunrise. When he came back Moonlight served tea and millet with butter. They could hear the camel men breaking up their tent and saddling the camels.

"We're starting out presently," said Dampignak. "You, Dambit, go with the two camel men. They will show you the way. But first please take your rightful share of our provisions." He stood up, and Dambit and the others followed him out of the tent. Dampignak's men had spread out all the provisions on a blanket, including the contents of Christian's and Big Tiger's saddle bags. They had divided them into seven heaps of flour, millet, dried meat and cheese, and seven small portions of tea and salt.

Dambit bowed to Dampignak. "May your way be peaceful," was all he said. Then he went to his camel, took down his empty saddle bag, and filled in his portion of flour. The tea and cheese went into his sash pouch; he put the salt in a little wooden box, and he tied the dried meat behind on his saddle.

Christian and Big Tiger looked on in surprise. Dampignak's men put away their own portions and Christian's and Big Tiger's. "That's a rule of the Mongol *joss,*" Moonlight explained aside. "Genghis Khan's law prescribes that the traveler share honorably with the man who has nothing, and no thanks must be either asked or given."

"And do all Mongols follow this law?" asked Christian.

"Yes, all of them," said Moonlight.

Dampignak remained standing beside Dambit, watching the preparations for departure. Christian and Big Tiger helped to dismantle the tents, but when they were about to load the camels, Dampignak cried, "Wait a minute," and walked over with Dambit to the place where the camels were lying. "These four camels are mine, Dambit," he said. "I should like to exchange one of them with you for yours, because yours is young and I like it. Will you therefore kindly choose which of these four you'd like best."

"How can that be?" asked Dambit. "My camel is thin and weak."

"What I say holds," replied Dampignak.

At this Dambit bowed shyly. "Many thanks; it has all turned out wonderfully," he murmured, and chose the worst of the camels.

"Not that one," said Dampignak, and taking the strongest camel by the reins, he led it up to Dambit. "Thank you, Dambit, for granting my wishes," he added. "May your journey be peaceful." With a slight bow he turned and went up to his horse. Dambit looked after him.

"Don't let it worry you," said Moonlight, tapping Dambit on the shoulder. "That's the sort he is, you see. He's a chief."

"May your journey be easy and peaceful," said Christian and Big Tiger, and they followed Moonlight to where a man was holding the horses.

"Tangat hasn't come," said Dampignak.

"I'll give him a piece of my mind," cried Moonlight, furious. "Is nobody to be relied on nowadays?" And he felt his pistol holster.

"*Yabonah!*" cried Dampignak.

They all mounted. Dampignak bent over and spoke to his horse. The stallion shot forward and bounded up the hill, making the sand and stones fly.

"*Sä Yabonah!*" cried Dambit. He was standing waving, but suddenly he stopped short and went down on his knees in a *kowtow*. "That's the horse of the Red Lama," he gasped. And he was still kneeling as Moonlight, Christian and Big Tiger rode past him, their whips raised aloft in a salute. The horses broke into a gallop, and the camels and the three men were soon left far behind.

The early morning gave way to a radiant day. The sunlight gleamed on the black rocks, it was already getting warm, and the horses slowed down to a walk of their own accord. But when they reached the caravan road again the stallion began to trot.

Moonlight was in a bad humor. From time to time he looked up at the sun, then down at the tracks of Ma's caravan, and each time he muttered something menacing about Tangat's non-appearance.

When the northern range of hills receded, giving way to a broad plain, Moonlight rode beside the Venerable Chief and exchanged a few words with him, ending with, "It can't be helped. I shall break his bones." Again he meant Tangat.

Very soon afterwards they turned aside and dismounted. Moonlight hobbled the horses at the foot of a hill, and then they all climbed the hill, from which they had a fine view. The Venerable Chief withdrew, Moonlight sat down, and Christian and Big Tiger lay on their backs and looked up at the blue sky, thinking that they might perhaps spot some eagles or some little white clouds, but the sky remained blue and soon they were both asleep. An hour passed, and the midday sun had reached its zenith when Moonlight espied a distant rider galloping over the plain. It was Tangat. Moonlight wanted to slip down to the caravan road unseen, but the Venerable Chief held him back.

"No breach of the peace, Little Paw," said Dampignak. "Bring him to me. He must be heard first."

"As you wish," muttered Moonlight; but one could see he found obedience difficult.

When Tangat saw Moonlight's angry face he felt like laughing. Obviously he had no sense of guilt about his lateness. Then his glance fell on Christian and Big Tiger, whom he had noticed before, but had not taken for foreigners, because they were wearing Mongolian clothes and riding boots, decorated in brown and green, with white-edged soles. But now Tangat stood staring from one to the other as if thunderstruck. Then he grasped his head to make sure he was not dreaming.

"I suppose you've never seen a foreigner before, little brother?" asked Moonlight in a friendly tone. Then he shouted: "Out with your report, good-for-nothing fellow!"

So absorbed was Tangat in observing the boys that he was thoroughly startled. He bent the knee before the Venerable Chief, saying: "I beg for forgiveness for coming late, but I couldn't help it.

I did as my commander Mr. Moonlight ordered: Together with Bank I accompanied Ma's caravan as far as Steep Rock Wall. We pitched camp there shortly before midnight. When everyone was asleep I meant to ride off to report that the journey had been without incident. I had already got to my horse when the dogs began barking and immediately afterwards six strange horsemen with guns and a packhorse arrived. At first I thought they were some of our people . . ."

"Numbskull!" cried Moonlight. "I told you none of our men were on the frontier."

"Go on, Tangat," said Dampignak quietly.

"It was the frontier captain, Kao-Cheng, who had arrived with five men," said Tangat. "He saluted me and asked me where were the Prince and the Commander Mr. Moonlight. He asked to be excused for crossing the frontier but said that the great old Governor in Urumchi had ordered him to go and search for two young sons of princes whom he had been expecting for a long time. Their names are Compass Mountain and Big Tiger."

"You see them here," said Dampignak.

"At that rate," replied Tangat, "it's no longer necessary to relay the frontier captain's request to oblige the old Governor by joining in the search for the two young gentlemen. I begged the Captain not to mention the matter to Ma for I thought to myself it was more than likely that there was something behind it all."

"Your first sensible thought," growled Moonlight.

"Captain Kao-Cheng remained in camp, so I had to remain too, for they had all wakened up, and I wanted to be sure that Kao-Cheng would keep quiet about his assignment. At last, an hour ago, he rode back to the frontier with his men, and Ma will also set out soon for Ming-shui. I told him: 'I have lost my whip and must go look for it. I shall be back soon.' "

"You have done right all along," said Dampignak.

Tangat beamed. "May I inform Captain Kao-Cheng," he asked,

"that the two young sons of princes have been found? He's camping tonight at Stony Stream as usual."

"Numbskull!" cried Moonlight again. "Don't you realize that the matter is very secret?"

"Where will Ma camp?" asked the Venerable Chief quietly.

"Ma says Stony Stream is not a good place for the camels. He's going to put up the tents near the old fortress. He says it's nice and level there, and that the ground is soft and without stones."

Moonlight nodded approvingly. He gave Christian and Big Tiger a sly wink, and the Venerable Chief said: "You may go over to Stony Stream tonight. Greet Captain Kao-Cheng and say to him: 'The Prince sends greetings to the Captain. He himself will come three hours before sunrise and present Compass Mountain and Big Tiger to the Captain. And will the Captain kindly keep a good watch on everything that happens until then. The Prince will be grateful to him for this.' Now go."

Tangat *kowtowed* to the Prince. "I have heard your instructions," he said, "and no word will go unheeded." He saluted Moonlight, Big Tiger and Christian, and hurried down the hill to his horse.

"Sä Yabonah!" cried Moonlight, mollified. *"Sä Yabonah!"* repeated Christian and Big Tiger.

Tangat flourished his gun in salute and galloped off.

For three hours Dampignak remained where he was behind the hill. The caravan road lay bathed in sunshine, but nobody came the way, and Christian and Big Tiger felt the time dragging. They nibbled a bit of cheese, but as there was nothing to drink they soon stopped. At the foot of the hill the horses stood, their heads hanging. Moonlight had gone to sleep. At last the Venerable Chief stood up. "The time has come, Little Paw," he said.

They rode back to the caravan road at a leisurely pace. It was only when the terrain rose to the north, that Dampignak gave the signal to trot.

The space in front of the cliff was empty. Ma had gone on with his caravan, but the campfires were still smoldering. Around the well the ground was wet with spilled water, and camel dung lay at even intervals in a neat row. An hour after their arrival Moonlight watered the horses. "What a pity," he said, "the water isn't good and we have no tea kettle."

"I've got something that will do," said Christian, taking out Toeless's copper flask.

"It can be put straight into the embers," said Big Tiger. "We've boiled tea in it before."

Moonlight was very pleased, for it was their last chance of eating before the next morning, he said.

Christian and Big Tiger collected camel dung, and Moonlight revived one of the deserted campfires. As there were no sticks to make a tripod he built up a little square with stones, and placed the copper flask on top of it. They drank tea and ate dried meat and cheese, but when evening fell the Venerable Chief said: "You would have done better to have slept."

"We have slept and we're fit as a fiddle," said Christian and Big Tiger.

"So am I," said Moonlight.

"Then," said Dampignak, "let the night's journey begin."

46 HOW MA AND GREENCOAT SHOUTED FOR HELP IN MING-SHUI FORTRESS

THE NEW moon ran its brief but radiant course. By the time it turned red and was about to disappear, Christian and Big Tiger were already an hour in the saddle. They rode westward along the caravan track at a trot. Since they had left Steep Rock Well, they rode below a continuous wall of cliffs. They felt as if they were alongside a town wall and could not see beyond. They only knew that it was the great, seemingly endless sea of boulders which stretched from north to south, farther and farther, faintly illuminated by the stars.

When the Pleiades came out, Dampignak turned aside from the caravan road. Passing through a gap in the steep rocky walls, he emerged on to the high plateau. Up there he rode for a short way northward, then turned west again. He kept an eye on the rim of cliffs, in order to keep the same distance from the caravan trail. They rode at a walk.

Shortly before midnight Dampignak dismounted. The plain had suddenly come to an end. They could hear the caravan bells and see far over the plain. Right in the middle on a small hill stood a square pile. From its square shape they could guess that this was the old frontier fort of Ming-shui, with its high outer walls still intact. What lay behind them could not be seen. In the west dimly lighted hills were visible, forming a boundary to the plain.

Moonlight took the horses by the reins and gave them to Christian. "Hold them a moment," he said in a low voice. Then he slung the stirrups across the saddles so they would not clank. "I'm going now," he said.

Dampignak nodded. "Greet Captain Kao-Cheng," he said, "and tell him I'll be there at the appointed time."

Moonlight went off with the horses.

Christian and Big Tiger were feeling rather unhappy, and each of them was thinking the same thing: The bad business is beginning now. When the sound of the hoofs had died away, Dampignak beckoned them, and they went up to the edge of the cliffs and lay down on the ground. Below them ran the caravan road. A medley of noise came from the direction of Ming-shui—the roaring of camels, the shouts of the drivers, and in between the hammering down of the tent pegs. Then the camp fires flared up, but one could only see the reflections flickering up and down the hill and the fortress walls, for the three tents of Ma's caravan were facing south.

The camp was not lively for long. The camels were unloaded and tied up, the men drank tea, and the fires went out one after another. When Moonlight came back an hour later all was quiet, and only the faint light of the stars illumined the fort.

"What have you found out?" asked Dampignak.

"Captain Kao-Cheng sends you his respectful greetings, and he begs you, my Prince, to honor him with a visit as soon as possible. The poor fellow is positively on thorns," said Moonlight, with a laugh. "And do you two know why he's so impatient?" he asked, turning to Christian and Big Tiger.

"We can't think why," said Big Tiger. "Please enlighten us."

"Why, you lads seem to know everything else," said Moonlight. "And this is quite simple. Captain Kao-Cheng hopes to get a promotion when he is able to notify the old Governor that he's found the two golden pheasants."

"If that's so," said Dampignak, "we must hurry. In any case it's best, for the man who's out early catches the tiger."

They walked across the gravelly space, on Moonlight's cautious direction one behind the other. The dark ravine continued to their left, and it was only after a quarter of an hour's walk that Dampignak turned into it. A cool breeze blew up from it, and the darkness was no longer impenetrable. They could see rocks and stones, and finally a boulder-strewn slope down which they wended their way cautiously to the valley. Despite all their care stones loosened under their feet and noisily bounced downhill.

The noise rejoiced the heart of Kao-Cheng who came running eagerly to meet them, bending his knee in greeting when only half way. He was wearing a black uniform with brass buttons. "Only ten steps more," he called, and then, "Only five," and finally, "Here we are." The encampment consisted merely of a few felt rugs on which Kao-Cheng's men squatted or lay in their sheepskins. They had no uniforms. The horses stood a little higher up, where it was wider and there was a little desert grass. A guard was standing with them.

After the salutations Kao-Cheng said: "I have forbidden my men to light a fire because your presence, my Prince, leads me to conclude that there's something special afoot."

"Your prudence is praiseworthy, Captain," Dampignak replied. "It will not be forgotten, and your men will be duly rewarded. How much longer will you be here?"

"Another full week," said Kao-Cheng.

"On the sixth evening my messenger will bring you a small reward for your trouble."

"You are much too kind, noble benefactor," cried Kao-Cheng, and his men added their approbation when told. They immediately became more cheerful and affable, gave up the best places and fetched saddle covers as seats for the guests.

"Behold the sons of princes, Compass Mountain and Big Tiger," began Moonlight. "Their arrival will put you into favor with the old Governor."

Kao-Cheng was waiting for this. "May I send my messenger with the telegram to Hsing-hsing-hsia?" he asked. "He's waiting."

"Have patience," said Moonlight. "It's time enough tomorrow."

Kao-Cheng's face dropped. "As you wish," he said.

"The fact is," continued Moonlight, "that the lads have business here."

"I thought as much," said Kao-Cheng. "People don't make a journey as long as that just to be able to say 'I've been here and there.' What do the young gentlemen want?"

"We would like to visit the merchant Greencoat," said Christian. "We heard he had arrived in Hsing-hsing-hsia."

"Oh, what a shame!" cried Kao-Cheng. "Greencoat drove on to Hami four days ago in a magnificent horseless car. He's doing great business."

"To Hami?" asked Moonlight, taken aback.

"Yes, definitely to Hami. The soldier Hu met him just beyond Hsing-hsing-hsia, tearing along in his horseless car. The heavens darkened but Hu raised his gun, for he's a brave soldier, and he wanted to show Greencoat we were watching the frontier. Greencoat stopped the car, and his Hsing-hsing-hsia manager was sitting beside him. 'Don't you see that we're in a hurry?' shouted the manager. 'Hold your tongue,' said Greencoat. 'I'm very glad to see the frontier guards are keeping their eyes open.' 'Where are you going?' asked Hu, and Mr. Greencoat said: 'To Hami.' Hu was very much surprised and said: 'I venture to ask why the gentlemen are not going by the Silk Road which is a good road, instead of through the middle of the desert, where the going is rough, and it's a big detour besides?' 'I'll explain that,' said Mr. Greencoat affably. 'We're driving this way as we want to try out the northern route, and because there's much to learn. Besides, I've business in Tashbulak.' Then the gentlemen drove on, and the heavens darkened again. The horseless car made a kind of earthquake, so to speak. Hu said the clatter was like the devil's bone mill."

Moonlight began to curse, but the Venerable Chief stopped him.

"Now, now," said Kao-Cheng, returning to the point. "Perhaps something can be done about it. If the young gentlemen would like to send a telegram to Hsing-hsing-hsia, that would be possible."

"How does one get from here to Hsing-hsing-hsia?" asked Christian.

"It's not far at all," Kao-Cheng assured him cheerfully. "Two days' ride, and you're there. Formerly it was much quicker."

"How was that?" asked Big Tiger.

"In those days there was a direct route by Falling Wall," said Kao-Cheng, "and a fine route it was. All the caravans going north used it, and the ones coming down from the north rested there. It has a real stream, at least three hundred feet or longer. And there's grass and trees, and a wall of rock as high as the heavens, with caves in it. You needed no tents at Falling Wall—you just went into the caves, and it was fine and warm. That's what Falling Wall used to be like."

"And what is it like now?" asked Christian. "Did something happen at Falling Wall?"

"Yes, something happened, but it's a long time ago, and we needn't speak about it," said Kao-Cheng.

"Speak, Captain," said Dampignak. "We've got time."

"It's an honor to tell the story, though I was not there," said Kao-Cheng, bowing. "If I'd been there, I wouldn't be here now. Ten winters ago a caravan was camping at Falling Wall. An east wind was blowing the smoke into the caves, so the men made a big fire in the open and sat around it eating their meal. Probably a fine meal too, for the caravan was on government business. Whether it was day or night, nobody knows. But suddenly there was a frightful peal of thunder, and the wall of rock caved in. Up till then the place was called Blessed Shelter but that was soon over. The caravan lay crushed flat as rice paper. All the dogs and the ten soldiers lay dead, and the six camel drivers were killed too."

"Except one," interrupted Moonlight.

"How do you know that?" asked Kao-Cheng.

"There must have been one to tell the story. Otherwise you wouldn't know it."

"That's true," said Kao-Cheng, abashed. "But it's better not to mention the survivor at once. Anyhow he was only a boy. He was at the stream when it happened, and he fell into the water, and the clothes froze on his body. The poor creature lost his mind, all but a glimmer. He caught a camel that was running away, and he rode, nobody knows how, as far as Hsing-hsing-hsia. There he told that the heavens had fallen on Blessed Shelter and that all the men and dogs were dead, and most of the camels.

"There had been some snow too," continued Kao-Cheng, "and when people came to the place five days later they found only the caved-in rock, and here and there a bit of an arm, or a crushed dog. The frontier captain—it was another man in those days—noticed at once that it had been a rich caravan. 'What a pity,' he cried. At that moment more rocks fell, and it was just plain luck they escaped. They ran without stopping, north, south, east and west, and when they'd assembled again they rode home. Since then the place has been called Falling Wall."

"And the camels?" asked Christian.

"And the loads?" asked Big Tiger. "What happened to them?"

"That's just it," replied Kao-Cheng. "They found nothing. But later a few brave fellows, real tigers of courage, went to Falling Wall, and as it was known that the caravans were carrying silver bars to the mint in Peking, they thought they'd pick up something. Naturally there were officials among them, grand gentlemen from Peking. They sighed over the many dead whom they couldn't see, and the silver which they couldn't find. Their few sighs brought the stones, big and little, tumbling down again, and they ran for their lives. Now the place lies deserted and no more caravans come from the north road to Hsing-hsing-hsia, for the new road is difficult and takes two days instead of one and a half. With horses I mean. By camel it's longer."

"Aha," said Moonlight. "So that was before our time."

"Yes, it was before you gentlemen honored our neighborhood," Kao-Cheng admitted politely. "Such a thing would hardly have happened otherwise."

"Would you permit us to view Falling Wall tomorrow, Captain?" asked Dampignak.

"In my company, of course," replied Kao-Cheng eagerly. "It is, so to speak, a necessary honor for me."

"A good idea, that, Captain," said Moonlight, giving him a friendly slap on the shoulder.

"Is it?" asked Kao-Cheng, dubious but cheerful.

"You'll soon be a colonel," said Moonlight, "and all these fellows will be non-commissioned officers."

When Kao-Cheng repeated this to his men they forgot they were freezing cold. One of them stood up and fetched a big brass can, and as they could not warm it, the men drank the brandy cold. Moonlight also drank some, for politeness' sake, but he said: "The young gentlemen are unused to drinking. They want to sleep."

Christian began to yawn and Big Tiger helped him. Moonlight took them behind a jutting rock. "Let's sleep," he said. But Tangat suddenly appeared again, and wanted to pass his news to Kao-Cheng.

"You see, we're here already," said Moonlight. "When Ma goes on tomorrow, you shall remain with Bank until we fetch you."

"I shall do as you command," replied Tangat, and disappeared.

It was a good hour before Kao-Cheng and his five men were asleep. The man who was guarding the horses was the first to drop off. But Dampignak remained awake. He signaled to Moonlight, whereupon Moonlight pulled off his boots, and Christian and Big Tiger did the same. They all tied the boots to their whips and carried them over their shoulders. Step by step they crept down the valley with its rocky stream, until they were sufficiently far away.

"Have you noticed anything?" whispered Moonlight, as they put on their boots again.

"Yes, we have noticed something, honored Sir."

They went a few steps farther over the gravelly streambed, until Moonlight, despite the darkness, made out where they were. The valley bent sharply southward, and now they were on a good straight road alongside the wall of rock on the right. There were no more stones either.

"We're on the caravan road," said Moonlight; and Christian and Big Tiger noticed that too. The valley grew wider and suddenly ended. They stood at the foot of the stony slope on which they had lain with the Venerable Chief looking toward Ming-shui when Ma's caravan came and struck camp there.

"Listen to me, sons of heroes," said Moonlight. "What shall we do now? We must do something."

"What about looking around a bit?" suggested Christian.

"Yes, we'll do that," said Moonlight.

"Compass Mountain thinks we should examine the fortress,"

said Big Tiger. "We could look down into the camp from up there, and see whether anyone is coming."

"Ma is to meet Greencoat there on business early tomorrow morning," Christian recalled.

"The business concerns old jewelry," added Big Tiger.

"What's that you're saying?" shouted Moonlight excitedly.

"Not so loud," begged Christian. "Mr. Ma only mentioned that by chance, and more we do not know."

"But I know more," said Moonlight, gnashing his teeth. He looked wild and distraught in the darkness. After a moment's thought he continued: "I know the fortress, and it has only one entrance, only one real one, and that's the gateway in the south. If you go in there you see everything that's going on. There are heaps of clay bricks which once were houses, and around the lot there's a wall with battlements, and that's all. You can sit down anywhere, and from any point you can see the whole place, for the fortress is small."

"You think," said Big Tiger, "that it would not be wise to go in the gateway, as there might be someone inside sitting on a heap of ruins, who would be surprised to see us?"

"Yes, that's what I thought," Moonlight admitted. "But there's no other way. We must wait for daylight."

"What about the entrance that's not a real one?" asked Christian.

"Oh, yes," said Moonlight. "You mean the water gate?"

"If there's a water gate," said Christian, "that's what we mean."

"There is a water gate," explained Moonlight, "but it's half choked with earth and sand. It was never big, and now it's probably a mere mouse hole, or shut up altogether. That happens quickly in the desert."

"We'd like to look at it," said Christian.

"At which side is it?" asked Big Tiger, who was all for exactitude.

"*Yabonah!*" Moonlight replied by way of answer, stepping out resolutely.

The hills which formed a boundary to the plain in the west were small. They looked like round mole hills. Farther on they got bigger and higher and finally became mountains. But one could not see the mountains for it was night, and Moonlight merely slipped along behind the first row of mole hills. When he arrived opposite the fort of Ming-shui he stopped, and then stepped cautiously out to the edge of the level space. Between it and the chain of hills ran a broad strip of water-worn stones—the empty bed of the little river which once flowed from the Valley of the Stony Stream. Into it ran a deep, dry ditch, which came in a straight line from the dark fortress. Moonlight crossed the riverbed with rapid strides and when he reached the ditch he beckoned Christian and Big Tiger.

"This ditch leads directly to the water gate," he whispered. At first he was able to walk upright, and Christian and Big Tiger couldn't see over the sides, though they were crumbled in many places. But soon Moonlight had to bend down in order not to be seen by anyone coming the way. Finally bending down was not enough and they had to crawl on all fours up to the fortress wall. The old ditch had become a silted-up channel here, and it ran steeply up the hill on which the fort stood.

The walls of the fort were made of clay bricks like the walls of Etzina. They were plastered, high as a tower, and very thick. Christian and Big Tiger noticed this when they got to the water gate. It was a dark hole, and they saw that by bending down they could get into it. Inside it was like a sentry box. Big Tiger ran his hand along the roof and at once felt the holes in which the iron bars of a grating had once been. They must have been nearly as thick as a man's arm, and have stood quite close together. An enemy could hardly have got his hand through. But iron bars are precious things, and for this reason they were gone long ago.

"I'm very sorry," said Moonlight. "You'll have to go through alone. I might go a little way, but then I'd get stuck. I'm too big."

Christian and Big Tiger looked at the dark hole in the back wall.

They felt the crumbling clay bricks of the ceiling and side walls. On the bottom lay blown-in sand.

"Let's try if we can get through this passage into the fort," said Christian.

"Yes, let's try," said Big Tiger.

They took off their beautiful Mongolian coats and hats. Moonlight sat down under the water gate and looked out into the night. Over there was a labyrinth of little hills, behind them the bigger ones, but the mountains were still invisible. They were far away and shrouded in darkness. Between the hilly region and the fortress lay the narrow strip of level ground shimmering in the starlight. The sanded-up ditch through which they had crawled ran like a rope across it.

Moonlight could hear the work starting behind his back. Christian was the first to creep into the dark passage, which slanted upward. With both hands he threw the sand behind him between his legs, and Big Tiger in turn threw it behind him.

"Can you make it or not?" asked Moonlight.

"Up to now it's possible," Christian's muffled voice replied, "but the passage is getting narrower and I see nothing but darkness in front of me."

"Hi, Compass Mountain!" cried Moonlight suddenly. "If that's the case you had better take the whip and poke along in front of you in case there's anything ahead."

"What would there be?" asked Big Tiger.

"There might be a fox, for instance," said Moonlight.

Big Tiger crawled quickly after Christian and passed him the whip. "Moonlight sends you this," he said, "in case you meet a fox."

"No fear of that," said Christian. "Wherever there's a fox hole there's a stink, and it doesn't stink here."

"What did he say?" asked Moonlight when Big Tiger came back with another load of sand.

"There's no stink of foxes," Big Tiger explained.

"All the same he should watch out," said Moonlight, and Big Tiger crawled back and warned Christian.

"There's something in the way," said Christian, "and it won't move."

"Perhaps it's a stone," said Big Tiger.

"It's not a stone," replied Christian. "Or perhaps it is." He took the bamboo-handled whip and poked with all his strength against the obstacle. Suddenly there was a dull rumbling sound. Clay bricks fell from the roof, and a thick cloud of dust filled the passage.

"What is it?" cried Moonlight in alarm, when the cloud of dust welled forth from the hole.

Big Tiger couldn't answer, much less could Christian, who could only wag his legs, for he lay under a heap of clay bricks and couldn't get a breath of air. Big Tiger grabbed the wriggling legs, but only Christian's boots remained in his hands. He went hot and cold with terror. Throwing the boots aside he once again grabbed the legs and pulled with all his might. His heart was in his mouth, and he propped himself against the wall of the shaft. He was at the end of his tether and couldn't get his breath. In two minutes, he thought despairingly, we two shall have to die together, far from our homes. But then he suddenly felt someone pulling off his boots.

"Hold on!" shouted Moonlight, but his voice seemed only a whisper, so thick was the air. He gripped Big Tiger's ankles grimly and immediately he felt himself being pulled along. The pulling hurt. Suddenly there was a jerk, then another, and then he was dragged through the hole, with Christian after him, for he hadn't let go of him. To his joy he felt a breeze of fresh air. Moonlight was kneeling beside him.

"Let go," said Moonlight roughly, and Big Tiger opened his clutching fingers. For a while he just lay there. Then he realized what had happened, and he felt his way through the darkness to the exit. There sat Moonlight, holding Christian on his lap. He was wiping the dust from his mouth, and Christian was breathing and opening his eyes.

"Don't be cross," begged Big Tiger.

"Who says I'm cross," snapped Moonlight. "I'd like to hug you both." He drew Big Tiger up to the edge of the watergate, and there they sat until their hearts quieted down, and Moonlight said: "That happens because man is a poor mortal thing. No more creeping under the earth!"

"I believe," Big Tiger objected timidly, "that the passage is now free. I felt a draft of air."

"Draft of air or not," said Moonlight solemnly, "you'll stay here now."

For a while no one said anything, then Big Tiger began again. "Perseverance brings success," he murmured to himself, and then, "By marching forward the right place is reached."

"What's he mumbling?" asked Moonlight.

"It's his grandfather who's mumbling," declared Christian. "He's got a grandfather who deserves to be heeded, for he's a wise man."

"Would your grandfather want you to crawl under the ground and lose your breath?"

"I don't mean that," explained Big Tiger. "But one should leave nothing untried, because there's such a thing as sticking it out."

"I see," said Moonlight, "that you're quite incorrigible. But this time," he said, "I'll creep in as far as I can go."

Christian and Big Tiger wouldn't hear of that. Someone might come at any moment, they said, and it was necessary to keep watch. Moonlight gave way. "You're right," he said. "That's what we're here for."

He took his stand at the water gate again, and Big Tiger said softly: "Until now we two have done everything together, Kwi-Chan."

"And we'll go on doing so," replied Christian, and because he knew what Big Tiger meant, he let him take the lead without opposition.

First Big Tiger got their boots out of the passage and Christian put them out where Moonlight was sitting.

"How are you feeling?" inquired Moonlight anxiously.

"I'll be careful," promised Christian, and he quickly crawled back into the passage in which Big Tiger was stuck like a prop, busily scratching. Christian waited for Big Tiger to push out sand and rubble, but Big Tiger did nothing of the kind.

"Is there a stoppage?" cried Christian, alarmed. Instead of an answer he got a kick in the face, for Big Tiger had slid forward. From this Christian perceived that they were making headway—Big Tiger was moving ahead.

Where he had broken through there was a heap of loose clay, sand and rubble, but Big Tiger noticed a draft, and high above him he could see a little bit of sky and a star. It's a long way back, thought Big Tiger, and he began to push away the obstruction in front of him. It was easier than he had expected. He dug his feet into the ground for a final effort and was getting through. He crawled over the rubble and found himself in a kind of cave, like the one in which Moonlight was sitting, only that it was half filled with rubble at the farther end and had no free exit. There was just the little bit of sky and the star.

"Hello!" Christian called gently.

"Hello!" Big Tiger called back, and made room for Christian, who had just crept in through the passage.

"Where are you?" asked Christian. "Have you found that out?"

"Not quite yet, but we've got through under the wall. I'll tell Moonlight."

Together they cleared the entrance to the passage and then Big Tiger disappeared to tell Moonlight they had got through.

Christian looked around him. There was not much to see. The cave was just like the other one. In the roof there were holes for iron bars which had disappeared, and apparently one could have walked out of it on the level if the exit had not been blocked with a heap of rubble. Christian climbed up on this loose pile of broken clay bricks, slate and wood, and stuck his head into the open. He craned his neck but could see nothing more than a high heap of ruins to the right, of which this pile of rubble, on which he was sitting, was the lowest spur, so to speak; and to the left the dark wall of the fortress. The sky was full of stars, and it was still night.

Christian strained his ears, but all was silent. At first he thought of pushing the rubble aside and creeping on all fours into the open, but he was doubtful whether Big Tiger would approve. So he drew in his head, slid down the heap of rubble until he reached the entry to the underground passage again, and waited there. It was a weary wait. Sometimes he imagined he heard Big Tiger speaking, or an excited whisper from Moonlight. But then all was silent again. Some minutes passed and Christian wondered whether he should crawl through the passage again to find out what was up, but he realized in time that Big Tiger would probably be crawling along too and their heads would bang together in the middle of the passage, and neither would be able to move forward and would find it very hard to crawl backward.

Suddenly the waiting came to an end. Christian could hear the boots being pushed aside. He could also hear Moonlight cursing and Big Tiger pleading in an earnest whisper: "Please, please, not now!" Moonlight growled, and then Big Tiger left him and came crawling back.

Christian had no need to ask: "What's up?" for Big Tiger's head had scarcely emerged from the subterranean passage than he said: "It's frightful, Kwi-Chan. He's there!"

"Greencoat?" asked Christian.

"Yes, on a donkey, carrying something behind him." He crawled out of the narrow passage and sat down beside Christian on the floor of the cave. "Were you outside?" he whispered.

"No," said Christian. "I wanted to wait for you."

Big Tiger gave a sigh of relief. "That means there are no traces of us outside," he said.

"Nowhere," said Christian. "But you must peep out and see what's there, and we must think what to do next."

Big Tiger climbed up on the heap of rubble, and craned out. When he came back he whispered: "It can't be helped. We can't make any move."

"Tell me about Greencoat," said Christian.

"When I got back to Moonlight he was listening hard and put his finger on his mouth. Then I listened too, and I heard the trot of an ass. First it was far away, then it came nearer, and then suddenly there was someone crossing the open space just near the ditch through which we crawled. Down there, where the fortress hill begins, he turned the donkey, and Moonlight began to tremble because it was Greencoat. Greencoat rode round the fort, and it seems he must have come into it by the gateway to the south because if he'd gone down to Ma's camp we'd hear the dogs barking by now."

"Did Moonlight want to shoot?" asked Christian.

"He was dying to shoot," replied Big Tiger. He said no more, but put his hand over Christian's mouth, for small stones and bits of clay brick began rolling down the mound of ruins outside, and a little sand came like a spray of dust into the cave.

"You or I?" whispered Christian into Big Tiger's ear.

"You," Big Tiger answered.

"No, you're cleverer," whispered Christian.

At this Big Tiger crawled up the slope of rubble once more, but this time so slowly and cautiously that Christian lost patience and began crawling after him. At last Big Tiger was up, and Christian watched him pushing his head inch by inch through the opening. That lasted a frightful time, but scarcely had Big Tiger peeped out than he withdrew his head quick as lightning. Again some stones rolled down the slope of rubble, and a cloud of dust shut out the view.

When the dust cleared Christian saw that Big Tiger had his finger to his lips, and then he held his clenched fist to his nose. It was hard to understand what he meant, but suddenly it became clear. Big Tiger put out first his thumb, then his first finger. Two, thought Christian. That means Ma's arrived, and now they're sitting on the mound of ruins and if we're lucky . . .

"So there you are," they heard Greencoat say without any formal greeting. His voice was gruff as usual, and though he was a good way off and speaking in an undertone, they could understand most of what he was saying, and imagine the rest.

"I've been waiting here on the wall half an hour," replied Ma in an injured tone. "And it wasn't very pleasant."

"Nonsense," growled Greencoat.

"Things keep falling down all the time," said Ma, "and it's quite unnerving. This is an uncanny place."

"I know that," snarled Greencoat. "But let's get down to brass tacks. Here's the jewel casket."

"I've considered the matter," said Ma, "and four thousand is too much."

"Four thousand is too little, you mangy pickpocket."

"Three thousand five hundred, and no more."

"Four thousand."

"Impossible," wailed Ma. "What if I can't dispose of the stuff?"

"Your own stupidity would be to blame. I tell you how you'll do it. Kucheng is naturally no place for such goods. You must take them to Peking with you. If you're clever you'll get double the money from a foreigner there."

"Why don't you do this business yourself then?" asked Ma, eying him slyly.

"Stupid devil," cried Greencoat louder than he meant to. He stood up, as Big Tiger noted from the dribble of sand. "I wanted to throw a good deal your way," he continued hoarsely, "but I see my kindness is wasted on one who is unworthy of it."

"Don't be excitable, old gentleman. Now, let's say three thousand five hundred, and here's my note. Li-Yuan-Pei can cash it right away."

"You mangy tramp!" snarled Greencoat. "You seem to think I'm a half-wit. I've given you the list of the stuff and the weight. It's all pure gold."

"May I have a look?" asked Ma politely. For a minute there was silence. Then they thought they heard the sliding cover of a wooden casket creaking, and a gasp of admiration escaped Ma.

"Now you see, little friend. So out with the other five hundred."

"Why that?" asked Ma insolently. The sliding cover creaked again and Christian and Big Tiger heard Greencoat saying angrily: "You old scoundrel, you won't get away like that!"

"All right," replied Ma, scornfully. "But first I must convey to you ten thousand greetings and sincere wishes for your welfare."

"From some bandits like yourself?"

"No, from the two young gentlemen, Compass Mountain and Big Tiger."

"Son of a dog!" shouted Greencoat. "Give me back that casket!"

"You have my note and I've got the casket. Our business is concluded . . ." Ma had not finished speaking when the blow of a fist right in the face sent him reeling. He rolled down the pile of rubble and the casket with him.

Christian and Big Tiger could hear the stones tumbling down and the dull thuds of Mr. Ma rolling over and over. The peephole of their cave darkened, and Big Tiger slid down the rubble to the ground, to where the subterranean passage began.

"Ooh!" he wailed. "My shoulder!"

Christian was just about to slide down after him when he saw before him the object which had fallen through the peephole and hit Big Tiger. It was a wooden box, about the size of a box of a hundred cigars. Christian picked it up. It was heavy. "Let's go!" he whispered to Big Tiger. "We must get out as fast as we can. I've got the box!"

"What box?" asked Big Tiger, still slightly stunned. But then he understood quick as lightning, for outside a piercing yell resounded: "Help! Murder! Help!"

It was Mr. Ma.

Once more sand and stones dropped through the peephole. As Big Tiger crept into the passageway, the hole closed up completely and it became pitch-dark. Christian could see nothing at all. Where the hole had been someone was stamping and struggling, and that was Greencoat, who had run after Ma and was at the same time looking for the casket. But although he had fallen through the hole only up to his knees, and was apparently uninjured, he was roaring just as loudly as Ma. He was thoroughly terrified, perhaps also because Christian had given him a fierce bite in the bare calf before fleeing into the passage after Big Tiger. He pushed the casket carefully before him.

Moonlight was waiting for them outside. He had heard Ma and then Greencoat shouting for help, but now all was silent as before. Big Tiger put his finger to his lips imploringly. "Have patience for two minutes," he whispered to Moonlight, and then he asked him to sit down in his old place. He and Christian pulled on their boots, put their coats round their shoulders, and sat down beside him.

"Your two minutes are very long," muttered Moonlight. "Hush!" said Christian, and "Hush!" said Big Tiger whenever he wanted to speak. They knew well why it took so long. Apparently Greencoat was still crawling around in the rubble looking for the casket and raging because he couldn't find it anywhere and because he dared not venture into the cave full of wild beasts that bit.

Only when the edge of the night sky was touched with the gray of dawn, and the stars were fading, but it was still so dark that a rider could cross the plain without being really visible, Christian and Big Tiger heard the trot of an ass. They quickly held Moonlight's arms as he tried to grab his pistol. But their precaution was unnecessary, for this time Greencoat did not ride past the water gate. No sooner had he emerged from behind the fortress wall than he made straight for the hills in the west, and disappeared.

"There goes the beast!" said Moonlight grimly. "Come, let's mount our horses!"

"In hurry there is error!" said Big Tiger thoughtfully, rubbing his sore shoulder.

"Have you got something to say?" inquired Moonlight impatiently.

"We should speak of Big Tiger's grandfather," said Christian.

"Is that the one who said: 'By marching forward the right place is reached?' " asked Moonlight.

"Yes, that's the one," said Christian.

"We did in fact find the right place," said Big Tiger, "and something fell down on my shoulder and hurt me."

"It's made of wood," said Christian, "and we've brought it back with us, because it's wrong to despise anything."

He laid the casket with its slide cover in Moonlight's lap. Moonlight's arms dropped, and his hands trembled.

"Perhaps," said Big Tiger, "you should look and see what's in it."

"I do not dare," said Moonlight.

"Permit me," said Christian, and he slid back the cover. It crunched, but that was because of the sand, which now fell on the gold and the pearl necklaces which filled the box. On top lay a coronet with a circle of small turquoises and a big one in the middle. Beside it were two little lockets like the one Dambit wore on his breast, but they were made of pure gold studded with pearls. Underneath were bracelets, rings, and chains, all of pure gold. Christian and Big Tiger gazed at the treasure, and they felt like Ma who could not suppress his breathless admiration seeing them even in the dark. But now there was a little pale shimmer of dawn.

Christian looked up at Moonlight to see what he would say. But Moonlight had tears in his eyes. They ran down his furrowed cheeks and dropped into the casket on to the gold and the turquoises. He slid back the cover. "Twenty years ago," he said, "the young Princess wore that circlet, and she was lovely and gentle."

He drew his hand across his eyes. Then suddenly his eyes hardened and he cried: "Up, up, to our horses!"

Christian and Big Tiger pulled on their coats. Then they left the water gate and ran down the hill and into the ditch, where this time they walked boldly upright. It was bright in the east, but the square fort of Ming-shui, where once there had been so much water that they needed a water gate and a conduit, was still shrouded in darkness.

Moonlight carried the jewel casket under his arm. As they went up the valley of the Stony Stream the Venerable Chief came toward them all alone.

Moonlight knelt down and raised the casket to his forehead, but one could see from his twitching shoulders that he was unable to speak because tears had overcome him again. He held the casket up for a long time, until Dampignak took it from his hands. The eyes of the Venerable Chief grew dark and troubled. They wandered from the casket to Moonlight and from Moonlight to Christian and Big Tiger, who also saluted him with a *kowtow*.

"It was not I," cried Moonlight, sobbing. "It was they. They crawled under the earth, and their breath left them."

"Little Paw," said Dampignak solemnly, handing him back the casket, "the turning point has come." He lifted Christian and Big Tiger up and embraced them in silence.

Afterwards, as they walked down the valley and could already see Kao-Cheng and his men, who had lit a fire at break of day and were drinking tea, the Venerable Chief said quietly to Christian and Big Tiger: "Forgive me, but I cannot thank you. Words are such poor, empty sounds."

47 A CHAPTER IN WHICH THE CRISIS IS GRADUALLY APPROACHING

"MY WORD! I see the gentlemen have been taking a morning walk," Kao-Cheng called out from quite a long way off.

"We have been presenting the water sacrifice," lied Moonlight, putting the casket into Big Tiger's saddle bag before all eyes. "The vessels of sacrifice have to be purified before sunrise," he explained, with a glance at the casket.

"I understand," said Kao-Cheng politely. "It is a good act for the spirits of the departed. May I invite the gentlemen to have tea?"

Christian and Big Tiger were hungry. They emptied out Christian's saddle bag for everyone to have a share, and when the soldiers saw that there was not only millet, but dried meat and cheese too, they became quite talkative. Four of them were Tungans and one was a Sart with a big black beard. Christian and Big Tiger could not understand the Tungans although they spoke Chinese, and the Sart remained silent. Kao-Cheng had to act as interpreter.

"Will the noble benefactors"—and he bowed to Christian and Big Tiger—"please forgive the ignorance of my men. They give thanks for a royal breakfast, but unfortunately the speech of the educated is a closed book to them."

Despite this difficulty there was plenty of talk until Moonlight said it was time to set out. But it was not so easy to get started. The horses had to be fed and watered, and the pack horse had to be loaded.

"What's the hurry for, honored Sir?" asked Kao-Cheng. "In hurry is error."

"Listen to me," said Moonlight. "You would like to be made a colonel, wouldn't you?"

"I have no objection to promotion," Kao-Cheng admitted.

"There are various ways of achieving promotion," Moonlight continued. "There's bribery, but that's expensive and uncertain. There are exceptional mental gifts, but how is a man to show that he has them? The surest way to earn promotion is to catch a criminal."

"But there are none here," said Kao-Cheng regretfully. "And if there were, they would not say they are criminals. They are silent, so to speak."

Moonlight held Kao-Cheng fast by one of his brass buttons. "You're right," he said. "It is very difficult to catch criminals, because you can't see from the fellows' faces that they're criminals. But we have found out, nevertheless, that the greatest criminal within the four seas is around here."

Kao-Cheng was horrified. "Here?" he cried. "Then I must know him."

"Yes, you certainly do," said Moonlight, "and his name is Greencoat."

"What?" screeched Kao-Cheng. "The honorable merchant Mr. Greencoat?"

"Tell me how you came to get the order to search for the two sons of heroes, Compass Mountain and Big Tiger?" asked Moonlight.

Kao-Cheng sighed. "Actually, it's a state secret, but as you already know most of it, I'll tell you the whole story. One day a telegram came from the old Governor in Urumchi ordering all frontier officers but particularly myself to search for the young gentlemen. They had left Hwai-lai-hsien, it said, on the sixth day of last month, and they were expected in the capital on the sixteenth day, but they hadn't arrived."

"Have you thought this matter out?"

"I have spent countless sleepless nights thinking it out, and days too."

"But you didn't go about it right," said Moonlight. "Tell me, how long does it take to travel from Kalgan to Urumchi?"

"Ninety days by camel."

"Right," said Moonlight. "And from Hwai-lai-hsien it's two days longer. How, then, could the journey be made in ten days?"

"Perhaps with one of those new horseless cars," said Kao-Cheng.

"Bravo!" cried Moonlight. "I see you're a proper captain and not a numbskull. The two young sons of princes were traveling in such a car; for remember they're young Excellencies. But this accursed Greencoat stole the car from them at the Etzin Gol. And now he's driving around in it himself, and I shouldn't be surprised if we catch him at the place called Falling Wall."

"Ha!" shouted Kao-Cheng, leaping to his feet. "Have you saddled, you lazybones? Are you ready, you five sleepy-heads?"

"Don't be too hasty," said Moonlight. And he called Christian and Big Tiger to give the Captain an account of what had happened at the Etzin Gol.

"The wretch!" shouted Kao-Cheng. "I thought he was an honorable merchant traveling to Hami. And now he's a stinking car thief hiding at Falling Wall. And we'll catch him. But it's a dangerous region."

"Catching criminals is always dangerous," said Moonlight. "You can't do it in a melon garden. Go now and tell your men that we're going to catch Greencoat. Let them load their guns and take the horse hair out of the barrels. And you can promise them a generous reward into the bargain."

Kao-Cheng gathered his five soldiers around him and spoke to them. Then they all talked excitedly together, and finally they roared "Bravo!" on account of the reward. After that everything went very quickly, and in a few minutes the men were in the saddle. Kao-Cheng rode ahead. The sun had risen, but it was cold in the Valley of the Stony Stream. Moonlight would have preferred to ride back to Ming-shui in order to follow the ass tracks from there, but Dampignak said: "Leave this to Kao-Cheng. He knows the shortest way."

They remained a bit behind the Captain and his five men, and Dampignak asked the boys to tell him what it was like in the passage under the fortress wall and how they had come by the casket. Christian told what he knew, and Big Tiger helped him, and when they'd finished their story Moonlight said: "In the end Greencoat killed Ma too; I heard him shouting for help."

"We don't believe he killed him," replied Christian. "Ma had time to run away while Greencoat was struggling with his legs caught in the hole."

"Oh, I remember," said Moonlight. "That was why he also shouted for help, the ruffian."

"He shouted because he was frightened," said Big Tiger, "and he was frightened because Christian bit him in the leg to make him afraid of the hole. Otherwise he'd have found us."

"He wouldn't be alive if he had," said Moonlight savagely.

"It's better as it is, Little Paw," said Dampignak.

They had reached the pass leading out of Stony Stream Valley, and the horses began to trot. The hills had become mountains which, though not high, blocked the view completely. In many places a groove could be detected in the ground. That was the former caravan road, now obliterated. After two hours the riders reached a high plateau, which gave an open view at least to the north. Suddenly Kao-Cheng pulled up, and the whole cavalcade halted. The track of an ass appeared from a side valley to the left and followed the old silted-up caravan road as far as the eye could reach.

"What's up?" asked Moonlight innocently.

"There's been a donkey here," replied Kao-Cheng. "Perhaps it strayed."

"There was someone riding it," asserted Moonlight. "Otherwise it wouldn't have followed the old road."

"You're right, Sir," said Kao-Cheng. "We must think this out."

"Well said," said Moonlight, dismounting. "Let us hold a war council." He led the horses aside to hobble them, and beckoned Christian and Big Tiger to follow him.

"Greencoat is just in front of us," he whispered exultantly. "We'll ride on now and get him."

"But what about our truck?" Big Tiger objected timidly.

"No fear about that," said Moonlight. "I'll trample Shong-Ma's ribs in until he confesses where he left it."

"I'll have none of that," said Dampignak sternly. He had come unobserved and was standing beside Moonlight. He was the same Venerable Chief that Christian and Big Tiger had been presented to when they saw him for the first time sitting in the tent at the Hidden Well, and yet he was another man. His hand lay calmly on his belt and his eyes no longer flashed, although he was looking straight ahead. His anger has left him, thought Big Tiger.

"I shall take over command from now on," said Dampignak, and he went over to where Kao-Cheng was sitting with his men. They made room for him respectfully. When Moonlight, Christian and Big Tiger had also joined the circle, Dampignak said: "I find myself on strange ground here, Captain, and your commander is the great old chief in Urumchi. His authority has been greatly harmed by the car thief Greencoat. In this matter you and I are allies, but as it is difficult for two helmsmen to steer a ship into port at the same time, I beg you to permit me to take over command."

"Most willingly," said Kao-Cheng, who really did not know what to do, "provided only that my men don't notice anything."

"Your face will be saved," promised Dampignak. "I shall tell you what's to be done, and you shall pass on my orders as if they came from yourself."

"Agreed!" cried Kao-Cheng. "Those are words which I am happy to hear and orders which I shall carry out."

"How can Falling Wall be reached in a horseless car?" asked Dampignak.

"Only from the south," replied Kao-Cheng, "where the valley is open and broad. Toward the north it gets narrow. There, it's a defile, so to speak. But Your Highness will see for yourself what it's like, for we're on the road which leads through the narrow defile into Falling Wall. We shall be there in two hours, and then the danger of death from falling rocks awaits us."

"I should like to spare you that danger," said Dampignak.

"Your servants will obey you all the more willingly because of it," Kao-Cheng assured him.

"Would you find Falling Wall even without a road?" inquired Dampignak.

"I'd find it by day or by night," asserted Kao-Cheng, "but more easily by day."

"Then ride on without delay," ordered Dampignak. "Occupy the exit to the south, but instruct your men to be very cautious. None of them must be seen, for Greencoat will reach Falling Wall from the north shortly after you. His business manager is there already, and apparently there's a third man too, whom we do not know. If Greencoat tries to leave Falling Wall today, stop him and arrest him. If he refuses to halt, fire, and hit him."

"Fine!" cried Kao-Cheng eagerly. "Hitting the mark is our strong point, our specialty, so to speak. I've got a Sart here"—and he pointed to the bearded man—"who's as swift as a spirit. If camel lice could fly he'd bring them down like snowflakes in winter. He's yours to command. Do you want him to shoot one man, or two at a time?"

"As he's such a good shot," said Dampignak, "let him hit the tires of the car and leave the men alive."

"What's the good of shooting wheels?" asked Kao-Cheng, astonished.

"To make a frightful bang," said Moonlight, "and then the car can't run any more."

"Falling Wall will fall again," said Kao-Cheng, much troubled.

"So much the better," said Moonlight. "If the thunder of its fall confuses the criminals, they will be all the easier to catch."

"Post yourselves where there are no rocks," ordered Dampignak.

"That's a good plan," cried Kao-Cheng joyfully. "Permit me to instruct my soldiers and pass on your orders." Dampignak nodded, and Kao-Cheng explained the matter to his men.

Before they set out, he ordered the Sart to *kowtow* to Dampignak. "This is the magic marksman," he said by way of introduction. "His name is Kasim. Now we're off."

"Remain at your posts until sunrise tomorrow morning," ordered Dampignak. "We shall be with you then, and we shall enter Falling Wall together. If anything happens in the meantime we're near you, and shall stand by you."

"We shall win the siege," cried Kao-Cheng proudly. "The criminals will tremble at the sight of us." He mounted his horse and followed his men, who were already riding on. They waved their rifles, and Big Tiger and Christian cried: *"Sä Yabonah!"*

"Wait two minutes," said Dampignak to Moonlight. He asked Christian for the map and studied it carefully. Then he pointed to the shaded rock region and asked whether Falling Wall was there.

Christian said, "Big Tiger and I think it is," then suddenly he cried, "Yes, it is for certain!" because he had discovered the brackets that indicate a narrow defile, and they were at the northern end of the valley.

Dampignak nodded. "But it's a pity we don't know which side of Falling Wall is the higher," he said, "the one with the rocks or the other."

"But we *do* know," cried Christian eagerly, "and it's the east side, where there are no rocks, or only small ones."

"How do you know that?" asked Dampignak.

Christian took out the magnifying glass and pointed to the figure written on the mountains to the east of Falling Wall. It was 7073.

"This figure tells the height of the mountains in feet," he explained. "When there are a lot of peaks together, the figure is always on the highest one. So the rocky side is the lower."

"Is 7073 feet very high?" asked Big Tiger.

"Yes, it's high," said Christian. "But as the place where we're standing now is 6560 feet high, the difference is only 513 feet."

"Bolna!" cried Dampignak, standing up and patting them on the back, as much as to say, "You're bright lads to work with."

Then they all mounted. The Venerable Chief rode ahead as before, watching everything. He kept the donkey's tracks constantly in view, and would have spotted Greencoat a long way off, for the disused caravan road led steadily uphill by the edge of a range of mountains, though the ascent was scarcely noticeable. To the north stretched a completely inaccessible high plateau, furrowed with a thousand fissures.

It was past midday before the slope leveled out. Dampignak rode more cautiously than ever. For about two *li* the donkey's trail ran dead straight, then the route went downhill. The high plateau to the right broke off in steep walls of rock. To the left the slope was creased with numerous recesses which further down merged into a black rock. The valley became a gorge, and one could see where it led to.

Dampignak stopped, and they all dismounted.

"Little Paw," said Dampignak solemnly, "I am not used to giving you orders, but I must do so now." He pointed with his whip to the edge of a brown wall of rock, which stood opposite the deep rents in the mountainside and the dark gorge. "Falling Wall begins over there," he said. "Go into the gorge. Find yourself a suitable place, and take a look down into the valley to see what's going on. Then creep back to the gorge, and stay there until sunrise; I forbid you to do anything on your own, but I authorize you to fire on anyone who attempts to get out through the defile."

"Even on the third man?" asked Moonlight. "You spoke of a third one."

"Even on him," said Dampignak.

"Where does this third man come from all of a sudden?" inquired Moonlight.

"Little Paw!" cried Dampignak. "Stupid Little Paw! Do you think a donkey would go all on its own to Falling Wall merely to enable Shong-Ma to ride?"

"You're right," said Moonlight, abashed. "But if it's some innocent person who brought the ass?"

"He is not quite innocent," said Big Tiger.

"Aha!" cried Moonlight. "There you are again, knowing something nobody else knows."

"We just think something," explained Christian, "and it often turns out to be right."

"And what have you thought?" inquired Dampignak.

"We generally think the same," said Big Tiger. "Compass Mountain thinks the third man is a soldier."

"And Big Tiger thinks his name is Springtime Snake," declared Christian.

Moonlight whistled through his teeth. "I remember," he said. "That's the scoundrel who fired at Good Fortune at the Etzin Gol. It would be fun to have him in front of my gun!"

"Take some food with you and go," said Dampignak.

Big Tiger opened his saddle bag, which also contained the jewel casket, and each of them took what they needed for the night. Moonlight then took his pistol out of its holster and stuck it in his belt. "It's quicker this way," he said, "if there isn't much time."

"I rely on you, Little Paw," said Dampignak.

"I hear and obey," replied Moonlight. Then he took a solemn farewell of Christian and Big Tiger. "Beware of the deadly falling rocks, sons of heroes," he warned them. "Under a rock you'd get no breath at all, and I couldn't pull you out, or perhaps only half." Christian and Big Tiger wanted to shout *"Sä Yabonah!"* but Dampignak forbade them. So they only waved as Moonlight disappeared downhill behind projecting rocks.

"Come on," said Dampignak, turning his horse and taking Moonlight's horse by the reins. They rode back the way they had come. Big Tiger and Christian did not know what to make of it all until, after a *li,* Dampignak dismounted. The brown rocks of Falling Wall had disappeared from view, and so had the gorge. To the right lay the high plateau with its many fissures and clefts, and to the left the mountains. They were as gray as if a rain of stones had fallen and then gathered in great channels. The creeks, which ran from the broad crests to the valley below, showed light and shade but no speck of green, not even a thistle.

"Is it 7073 feet high there?" asked Dampignak.

"It must be," said Christian. "The mountains are all low, but that's the highest of them."

Christian and Big Tiger took off their coats and laid them over their saddles, while the Venerable Chief looked for a spot from which they could start the climb. His eyes wandered over the stony gorges, the rocks, and all the creeks to the summit. "We can't do it with horses," he said. "How long would it take you two to get up there?"

"We'll take off our boots, then we can climb faster," said Big Tiger.

"An hour," said Christian, "or perhaps only half an hour."

"Good," said Dampignak. "Put on your coats again and take the whip."

"But what about the jewel casket?" asked Big Tiger.

"If it's not too heavy, take it with you," said Dampignak. "I'll take the horses over to Kao-Cheng. Wait for me on the mountain."

"And what if something happens?" asked Christian.

"Do what you think fit, but on no account go into the valley."

"We hear and obey," they said.

They started to climb, carrying the casket in turns. After a while they stopped to wave back at Dampignak, but they could only hear the trot of the horses, for the creeks proved to be narrow defiles which ascended steeply. One could see the edges but nothing beyond. Big Tiger and Christian hurried up on to the nearest terrace of rock. But still they could not see Dampignak. He must have turned into a side valley, and they were not yet high enough to have a view over the whole mountain range. After climbing up a long stony ravine they noticed that going barefoot was not such a simple matter.

"It needs practice," said Christian, when the stones started rolling down on their toes. Eventually they got to the last terrace, and from then on it was not too bad. A soft layer of desert dust lay in the flat trough which led to the top. Christian had almost completely forgotten the need for caution, and felt like shouting "Hello!", for everything could be seen from up there.

"Lie down flat!" cried Big Tiger, for standing they could be seen from everywhere.

The view was magnificent. They could see the many mountains round which they had ridden, the hills which grew smaller and smaller, the valley of the Stony Stream, the little plain, behind it the big endless one, and in the foreground the squat fortress of Ming-shui, which looked like a die that someone had lost. All this was spread before them, but Christian and Big Tiger scarcely glanced at it. For there was something far more exciting at the other side. The real summit of their mountain was still a good bit higher up, but they saw quite enough from their vantage point.

"They're cooking," said Christian.

"That means they're leaving today," said Big Tiger, who always drew conclusions.

"But where's the truck?"

"I don't see it either. Only the ass is there."

"And Springtime Snake," said Christian. "But where have they put the truck?"

"Do you think they can see us?" asked Big Tiger.

"Better take off our hats," suggested Christian.

They crawled back a bit, took off their hats, and laid them near the casket with their boots. Again they looked down into the valley which had once been called Blessed Shelter. Opposite them rose a steep wall of brownish-red rock. Backing it was a precipitous mountain slope which, they could see, trailed off into empty stone valleys. Down below they saw caves, to which led a sandbank which extended over the bottom of the valley. Deresen grass grew there, and great blocks of rock lay about all over the place.

In the north the walls of rock were quite close to the steep mountainside, forming the gorge in which Moonlight was sitting, hoping for someone to come along to get shot.

To the south the valley lay open. The walls of rock ceased suddenly, and sand and dust-covered hills took their place. In between

them an empty strip of gravel lay glistening in the sun. Only a glimpse could be seen of the stream which flowed into it.

"Perhaps the truck is at our side of the valley," said Christian.

"It may be," said Big Tiger, leaning over. "It's no use trying to see. There are rocks on our side too."

"We must watch what they do," said Christian.

The three were at their meal—Greencoat, the stout agent, and Springtime Snake. There was a kettle on the fire, and they did not seem to be talking much, but obviously they had no fear of Falling Wall for they had made the fire right beside the biggest cave, under the overhanging rock, and near a great mound of fallen rocks.

Suddenly Big Tiger nudged Christian. "Look over there," he said excitedly.

"Perhaps that's Kasim," said Christian.

"And there's another, and over there another."

They had only now noticed Kao-Cheng's soldiers, who were

posted on the hills at the exit of the valley. They looked mere specks, for only their heads could be seen.

"Greencoat is encircled," said Big Tiger. "It can't be helped." His eyes still searched the hills. "Where are the horses?" he asked.

"Kao-Cheng has hidden them," said Christian.

Down below they had finished their meal. Greencoat, whom they recognized easily despite the distance, stood up and went into the cave. He soon came out and spoke to Springtime Snake. He was obviously giving him something, for Springtime Snake made a *kowtow* of thanks.

"Now he's saying 'Thanks ten thousand times,'" remarked Big Tiger.

"What for?" asked Christian.

"We must find that out," replied Big Tiger, who was beginning to enjoy the game thoroughly.

"But what if someone shoots him first?" Christian objected.

"Then we'll find out afterwards," said Big Tiger coolly.

Down in the valley Springtime Snake had stood up after his *kowtow*. He saluted the agent with a curt bow and went over to the ass. But the ass didn't want him. He was nibbling greedily at the deresen grass, and when Springtime Snake approached he lifted his tail and ran away, kicking with his hind legs several times. The stout agent, who was sitting at the fire, slapped his stomach with pleasure at the spectacle, but Greencoat gave him a resounding blow in the face.

"The gentlemen are not very nice to each other," remarked Christian.

"A man can't quarrel with his boss," said Big Tiger. "Look how the fat man is running." The agent had jumped up and was running quick as a weasel to catch the ass which the clumsy Springtime Snake was approaching from the rear. The ass kicked again and Springtime Snake fell down, though he was too far away to be hit.

"The coward," said Christian.

Meantime the agent arrived on the scene and with incredible agility caught the ass by the ears and led him to the fire. Springtime Snake limped behind.

"Did he get hurt after all?" asked Christian, surprised.

"No, he's only pretending," said Big Tiger.

Springtime Snake went on with his play-acting. He threw himself on the ground and rubbed his leg as if it were injured. When the agent had saddled the ass there seemed to be an argument. Springtime Snake gesticulated vehemently and did not want to stand up. In the end the agent helped him into the saddle and he rode off toward the southern exit of the valley.

Christian and Big Tiger were frightfully excited. They watched fascinated as Springtime Snake trotted cheerfully along by the brook. Just where the water trickled away and the last tussocks of deresen grass stood like lost sentries, Springtime Snake turned round in the saddle and waved. Perhaps Greencoat waved back, but they could only see Springtime Snake. Nor did they notice the black speck on the first hill rising a little. It was only for an instant and they saw nothing more, except that the ass suddenly collapsed under Springtime Snake. The crack of the shot came much later. By this time Springtime Snake had struggled clear of the ass and was running as hard as he could back to Falling Wall, his hurt leg completely forgotten. And that was only natural, for more shots resounded all round and echoed between the rocks, but the rocks did not move.

"Why are they all shooting?" asked Christian indignantly.

"I don't know," replied Big Tiger. "It seems shooting is contagious."

Greencoat had thrown himself on the ground where he was, but the nimble agent had disappeared into the cave. The last shots resounded as Springtime Snake reached the sandbank. Without stopping to think he flung himself down beside Greencoat and both of them stuck their heads in the sand as if they imagined that would help.

"We must get back," said Christian hurriedly. "When they lift their heads they'll look round to see what's wrong."

"If we lie still, they'll take us for stones," said Big Tiger.

"Remember how the Venerable Chief spotted us in the Black City," said Christian.

At this Big Tiger gave in, and they crawled back to where their boots and hats lay beside the jewel casket.

"What now?" asked Big Tiger, looking round him.

Christian looked around too and both noticed that they weren't near the top of the mountain. They also saw that a spiky crest ran along the ridge which would make a much better hiding place and lookout than the domed summit on which they had been lying. So they took their things and continued their climb, crawling the last lap.

There was not much room up there, but they could move freely, at least on all fours. Big rough stones formed a crude parapet, with several narrow peepholes. Lying behind them, they could watch what was going on down at Falling Wall.

48 FATE MARCHES ON

At first nothing happened. The agent had re-emerged; Greencoat was looking up at the sky, though the sun was no longer visible. It had just glided over the edge of Falling Wall and the first shadows were darkening the valley. Springtime Snake was looking around him, very frightened.

"What a pity we can't hear what they're saying," said Christian.

"But we can see it," replied Big Tiger. "Look at Greencoat."

Apparently he was ordering Springtime Snake and his agent to do something, but both were refusing. So he began to rain blows and kicks on them, and when this did not help he picked up the whip which Springtime Snake had brought back from his unlucky trip, and gave the little agent a terrible beating. Springtime Snake would have liked to run away, but he was afraid; blows were a trifling matter compared with being shot at, and so he too got his share. When Greencoat had finished he went off, smart and upright, as if he were just taking a walk across the valley between the blocks of rock. He jumped across the brook and disappeared.

"He's going to the truck now," said Big Tiger.

"Perhaps he'll try to drive off," said Christian. "Listen!"

But they heard nothing. Greencoat came back after a while carrying Springtime Snake's gun in one hand and a gasoline can in the other. The agent hurried to take the can from him. He carried it into the cave, and Springtime Snake laid the gun against the wall of rock. Then he came back, the agent reappeared too, and they both stood beside Greencoat.

Greencoat seemed to be expounding a plan to them. He pointed ahead, then behind, he raised both hands above his head, then clenched his fists. Down came his fists, and Springtime Snake stepped aside in alarm. After this Greencoat stood like a general whose orders permit of no objection. He looked first at one, then at the other, and both nodded submissively.

"Perhaps," said Christian suddenly, "one of us should cross over to the other side."

"But it's only two hours to sundown," warned Big Tiger.

"That will be enough."

"Then go, Kwi-Chan. It's the first time I can't be with you."

"Let fate decide," suggested Christian picking up a stone. "You must say right or left, and whoever has the stone goes."

"Remain together," said Dampignak, who was lying behind them, smiling. They wheeled around staring in astonishment.

"And we've been listening so hard," exclaimed Christian.

"You're as silent as a ghost," said Big Tiger.

"Where did you want to go?" asked Dampignak.

"We'd like to see where the car is," said Christian.

"They have some plan of action," said Big Tiger. "Perhaps we could see from the other side what it is."

"Then go," said Dampignak, "and follow in my tracks. I didn't go over stones anywhere. You'll be with Kao-Cheng in half an hour. Take horses, for you can ride up the slope behind Falling Wall, until you're over the wall of rock. But remain at a safe distance from the edge."

"We hear and obey," cried Christian and Big Tiger.

They slipped quickly into their boots and put on their hats. Then they noticed that Dampignak wore felt shoes. "I borrowed them from Kao-Cheng," he explained. "Otherwise I could hardly have surprised you. Felt shoes are better for mountain climbing."

"The casket is over there," Christian mentioned hurriedly, and then they ran down the mountainside.

Dampignak's tracks came from the south. He had picked his way carefully, avoiding the slopes of gravel which flowed down from the summit on to a mountain ridge, where the gravel collected into a lake of loose stone. Here the going ceased to be difficult. Instead of the numerous gorges and defiles, as on the north side, there was only the mountain ridge, which led in a broad sweep down to the valley. Dampignak's trail went right through the middle of it, and far below they could see the horses, and Kao-Cheng sitting at a fire with one of his men. The blue smoke climbed straight up into the blue sky.

"Kao-Cheng knows his way all right," said Christian.

"That's why he's a frontier captain," said Big Tiger.

The stream, which trickled behind Falling Wall, seemed to emerge here again. Little pools glittered in the sun, and yellow deresen grass stood in straggling tussocks around the water. The horses were finding some sparse grazing.

"Come and have tea!" cried Kao-Cheng, stamping heavily toward Christian and Big Tiger in Dampignak's riding boots.

"We have something to do first," said Big Tiger, and he explained why they had come. But Kao-Cheng was adamant.

"Drinking tea is also an important matter," he said. "In doing the one we shall not neglect the other." He sent his man to fetch and saddle the horses while they drank tea.

"Did Kasim kill the ass?" asked Big Tiger.

"Wasn't that a master shot?" cried Kao-Cheng eagerly. "Kasim is like Yu-Tsu the Archer, and his shots come like lightning from the clouds."

"But why did the others fire too?" asked Big Tiger.

"To frighten the enemy," said Kao-Cheng. "That is laid down in the Six Rules for Warriors, and also in the Golden Code of War." And he marched impressively as a god of war up to the horses. "My gun," he commanded imperiously. The man brought it in haste. One could see how impressed he was by events. Things like this did not happen on the frontier every day.

They galloped as far as the winding gravel bed which came from Falling Wall. Just before reaching it Kao-Cheng pointed to the firm ground which distinctly showed the wheel tracks of the truck. "The criminals drove along here," he said.

Big Tiger thought of Dambit, who had shoveled gravel for Greencoat. "If we had a spade we could dig a ditch for the car to get stuck in," he said.

"I see," said Kao-Cheng. "You mean a kind of car trap. Don't worry; we have Kasim. He'll fire at the tires and they'll go bang."

He moved cautiously a little to the south, and they could see his four men in the distance. They were lying on the hills within calling distance of each other, but Kasim was well to the front. Kao-Cheng waved encouragement, and the horses slowed down to a walk. They had crossed the valley and were now going up the mountain slope which formed the back of Falling Wall. The high ground was bathed in sunshine, but when they got to the top the shadow of the wall of rock was already climbing up the other side of the valley.

"May we request the esteemed Captain to wait here with the horses?" asked Big Tiger.

"Certainly," replied Kao-Cheng. "These heavy boots unfortunately prevent me from taking part in the reconnaissance. But take care the scoundrels don't spot you."

Christian and Big Tiger walked upright as long as they saw their shadows before them. Then they lay down and crawled to the edge of the wall of rock. Beneath them they saw the fire glowing, and the little fat man sitting beside it. Springtime Snake and Greencoat were not visible. But the truck was standing at the other side of the stream under a steep wall of rock. Christian and Big Tiger were overjoyed at the sight of it; it seemed like seeing an old friend again. It was packed full with cans, the gate boards were up, the hood was closed, and it was ready for the road.

"Perhaps Greencoat is in the cave?" asked Christian.

"What did he fetch the can of gasoline for?" asked Big Tiger.

They were silent, for there was no answer to either question. But suddenly the door of the driver's cab opened and Greencoat got out. Springtime Snake followed, pulling out a shovel and pickaxe. Greencoat took some tools out of the tool box. Then he climbed up on the truck. Springtime Snake ran to help but at a sign from Greencoat remained standing below.

The gasoline cans from Ollon Torre were standing higher than usual and showed almost halfway over the sides. The iron drum which Dambit had mentioned was also in its place behind the driver's cab. Greencoat tried the weight of several cans until he found the right one. He handed it down to Springtime Snake, who started to fill the tank. But it took only a little more gasoline, and he soon handed back the can.

Springtime Snake opened the radiator, dipped in his finger, and held it up to Greencoat. This seemed to satisfy Greencoat, who now took up the tools, shut the door, and crossed the stream. He threaded his way through the boulders and rocks just as coolly as if not a single shot had been fired, but he failed to inspire courage in Springtime Snake, who followed with the pick and shovel, casting frightened glances down the valley.

"Are you ready?" the agent called out to them, but Greencoat did not deign to answer.

"What do you think of it?" whispered Christian.

"Wait two minutes," replied Big Tiger. "Perhaps we'll find out something more."

They looked down, but the fat man was again sitting alone at the fire. Greencoat and Springtime Snake had gone into the cave. A few moments later, however, Springtime Snake emerged with an armful of cotton, threw it down before the agent, and disappeared into the cave again. Soon he came back with more cotton. The fat man began to twist it, and Springtime Snake watched him for a moment. Then he took the pickaxe and began to hack out a narrow ditch in the direction of the stream. He had not progressed far with this work when Greencoat came out of the cave and took the pick from him. With only a shovel, Springtime Snake's work slowed down. But on the other hand, muffled blows of the pick came from the cave, succeeded by the sharp metallic sound of a chisel being driven into stone.

"Kwi-Chan," whispered Big Tiger, "I'd like to know what they're up to."

"They're going to blow up Falling Wall," replied Christian.

"Yes," said Big Tiger. "But what for?"

"If we say to Kao-Cheng now 'Falling Wall is going to collapse again tonight,' what do you think he'll do?" asked Christian.

"He'll ride off with his five men, and it can't be helped."

"That's why Greencoat wants to blow it up," said Christian. "An explosion makes confusion, and in the confusion he'll drive off. The truck is standing ready. You see how far the lumps of rock fell last time. There are none on the edge of the stream."

"Now it's all clear," said Big Tiger, "and we'll go."

"We'd better hurry," said Christian.

They looked down once more. The fat man had stood up. He was carrying a pack of cotton under his arm, busily twisting it as he walked, and laying the rope along the bottom of the ditch.

"They'll pour gasoline over it afterwards," said Christian, "and when they're safely in the truck and the engine is started, they'll light it."

Big Tiger looked very worried. "What shall we do?" he asked. "Can we do anything?"

"Let's tell Dampignak," suggested Christian. "He's in command, and it would be cheeky to forestall him."

"Bolna!" said Big Tiger, beginning to creep back. Christian also crept backwards, but soon they stood up and ran as quickly as they could back to the horses. When they reached Kao-Cheng they were quite out of breath.

"What's the hurry for?" asked Kao-Cheng, surprised. "In hurry is error."

"Greencoat wants to break through," Christian informed him.

"Is he preparing to attack?" inquired Kao-Cheng uneasily.

"We don't think so," Big Tiger reassured him; "but they want to get away."

"Ha! Ha! Ha!" laughed Kao-Cheng. "The poor devils haven't got a team of flying dragons, nor can they ride on the clouds. How can they escape us?"

"In the horseless car," said Big Tiger.

"They won't try that," Kao-Cheng assured them. "I've ordered my soldiers to start firing every hour or oftener as soon as it's dark. That will frighten the enemy and prevent my men from falling asleep. They're as wary as antelopes, but what good is that? They have to be kept awake. The life of a frontier guard is a hard one."

"All the same," said Christian, "we do not wish to lose a minute."

"As the young gentlemen wish," said Kao-Cheng. He emphasized the words "young gentlemen" rather more than necessary, indeed almost offensively.

But Christian and Big Tiger were in a hurry and Kao-Cheng gave in. He wanted to show them that he was ready to go out of his way to oblige them, and they rode at a gallop as soon as they got down into the valley.

"One of us should remain with the horses," said Big Tiger.

"We'll toss for it," suggested Christian.

"No," said Big Tiger. "I'll stay and you'll go."

The sun was going down when they reached Kao-Cheng's camp. "Report to the Prince," said Kao-Cheng, "that we're impatiently awaiting a fight with the criminals."

"I shall report your words faithfully," promised Christian.

"What?" cried Kao-Cheng. "Does that mean you're going to climb up into the rocky wilderness alone?"

"It means," said Big Tiger, "that my feet are tired, and I can't climb any more. If the esteemed Captain will permit me, I should like to rest here for a while. I shall help to tie the horses."

"Tie them?" exclaimed Kao-Cheng. "Why tie them since we're spending the night watching?"

"Our horses are used to being tied. If they're not standing quietly together at night they're unhappy."

Kao-Cheng laughed uproariously. He had never heard that horses could be either happy or unhappy. He was still limp with laughter when Christian said: "I'll be back soon."

At this he pulled himself together. "Stop!" he said. "We must have a password as it may be night by then. What about 'Old Governor'?"

"That's good," said Christian. "I'll shout 'Old' and you'll reply 'Governor.' That's how we've learned this business." And off he went.

He climbed the mountain ridge, and as he stood under the summit the sun sank. But Christian had no eyes for the wild beauty of the radiant gold and red plain, the flaming hills, and the steep black wall opposite, which descended to a bottomless abyss. He raced along, again following Dampignak's trail, and reached the jagged crest of the summit as night fell.

"Where's Big Tiger?" asked Dampignak immediately.

"He remained with the horses," replied Christian, "as we didn't know what Kao-Cheng would do if Falling Wall collapses."

"Good," said Dampignak, and Christian continued his report. Dampignak knew almost everything already. He had seen the fat man twisting the cotton and Springtime Snake shoveling; and he had heard Greencoat hammering and tapping in the cave. When Christian told him, however, that the truck was standing ready to rush through the southern exit, Dampignak gave a violent start and seemed to want to dash off immediately. But he thought better of it. He looked up at the evening star, then at the crescent moon; then his glance dropped to the bottom of Falling Wall. The fire was still burning, the agent was sitting beside it, the night was completely still, and a cool breeze was blowing up from the gorge.

"They're ready," he said. "We must hurry."

At that moment Springtime Snake emerged from the cave carrying Good Fortune's beautiful storm lantern. He said a few words to the agent, then the two went into the cave.

"Too late," murmured Dampignak. "Kasim is our only hope now." And he stared down at the speck of light.

For the first time Christian saw how roomy the cave was. The two men walked upright into the vault, but stopped after a few paces. Springtime Snake held up the lantern. Then they were lost to view. Only the friendly yellow glow could be seen reflected on the fissured walls. For a few seconds the tall frame of Springtime Snake and the small one of the fat man were sharply silhouetted as they stood motionless together. Suddenly they drew apart and made way for a third who emerged from somewhere, handed something to the fat man and disappeared again. After that they noticed that the agent had a pickaxe in his hand, and when Greencoat came back he handed him more tools. Thus loaded the agent turned back to the truck, with Springtime Snake behind him carrying the lantern. He was holding it lower now, and it was plain that he was lighting the way for Greencoat too, who was pouring gasoline over the white cotton rope as he went.

They had got to the exit of the cave and were just stepping into the open when a shot rang out. It was the first of the nocturnal terror shots which Kao-Cheng had ordered his men to fire; but it was also the last. The sharp report shook Greencoat and terrified Springtime Snake so completely that his knees gave under him and he simply slumped down. Greencoat snatched the lantern from him and held it high, but the glass was shattered, and a ribbon of flame shot through the cave. For the fraction of a minute it was lit up and bright as noonday. Then a flash of lightning shot out from it, blinding and sharp as the stab of a dagger, a pale glow swept over the quaking rock, and then all went down in the thundering explosion which rent Falling Wall from top to bottom.

Even on the summit of the mountain the earth shook under the momentous force of the collapsing cliffs. Christian felt the blast, and the breath of hot wind which rose above the thundering roll of the masses of rock. When it ceased a great rain of stones came rolling down from all sides into the gorge. A cloud of dust rose right up to the summit on which Christian had lain with Big Tiger, and hovered there for a long time.

"Is it over?" asked Christian, sniffing.

The air smelled of dry dust, of hot stone, a little bit of gasoline, and of something that Christian didn't know. Perhaps it's gunpowder, he thought, or perhaps it's something worse.

Dampignak stood up. "Come," he said quietly.

Christian picked up the jewel casket which lay where Big Tiger had put it. His heart beat fiercely as he followed Dampignak, who was walking down the mountainside in Kao-Cheng's felt shoes. The night gleamed clear and cool over the stony slopes, and soon they saw the shimmering mountain ridge which led down to the valley. When they got near Kao-Cheng's camp they could hear the snorting of horses and the agitated voices of men. Kao-Cheng was shouting excitedly and in between they could hear Big Tiger's voice saying again and again: "Wait just two minutes. Please wait."

"No," cried Kao-Cheng. "When the heavens fall it is a sure sign that this is no place for us. We have ventured too far forward."

He had one foot already in the stirrup when Dampignak stepped into view. "Captain," he said, "I hear that you are in a hurry to get away. May I ask you to please let us change shoes before you go?"

"Oh, I see," said Kao-Cheng, abashed. "But then . . ."

"We shall sit down," suggested Dampignak.

"Your Highness," objected Kao-Cheng, "my men are all here but one. They have narrowly escaped death. Nobody is in the mood for sitting down in such circumstances."

"Where's Kasim?" asked Dampignak.

"That's just it," replied Kao-Cheng. "He's nine-tenths dead; or perhaps altogether."

Dampignak began to pull off the felt shoes. "Order your men to unsaddle and prepare a meal," he said. "Meanwhile the boys and I will go look for Kasim. Where are our horses?"

"They're here," said Big Tiger. He was standing apart holding the stallion. Christian was holding the others.

Kao-Cheng had no more to say. He was petrified with astonishment at Dampignak's utter indifference to earthquakes and collapsing cliffs, but he was relieved to know what was to be done. He himself would have just ridden off at random into the night, unable to tell his men where they were going. So he sat down and pulled off Dampignak's boots, growing calmer as he did so.

"That's right," said Dampignak. "You must set your men an example." At these words Kao-Cheng's breast swelled with pride. He began giving orders, and his soldiers, who at first had grumbled, soon stopped and unsaddled quite eagerly.

When Dampignak mounted, Kao-Cheng stood up and wished the party good luck and long life; he nearly added riches, but it didn't seem in place just then. Meantime Christian had fastened the saddle bag containing the jewel casket to his saddle. Then they rode off behind Dampignak.

By the time they reached the gravelly slope which ran from Falling Wall, Christian had told Big Tiger all there was to tell: Greencoat was dead, so were Springtime Snake and the agent.

Big Tiger nodded. "We've been suffering a hundred useless worries," he said, "and in the end heaven has passed the death sentence." Christian knew well what Big Tiger meant. All three had died far from their homeland. They were uncoffined and unmourned, with no one to offer prayer and sacrifice for their souls. They were nobody's ancestors. They were dead.

They rode in silence along the gravel slope, and when they got near the hill on which Kasim lay, they heard him calling and saw him waving, and they waved back. He came down toward them, and then stood still. *"Salaam!"* he cried, stretching out both arms.

Christian and Big Tiger leaped from their horses and ran to meet him. The bearded Turki* greeted them like brothers in his own language, yet they knew what he meant. Big Tiger replied in Chinese, and Christian told him in Mongolian how glad they were

* Turkis, originally from Turkistan, are one of the races inhabiting Sinkiang. They are Mohammedans.

to see him alive. Together they walked over to where Dampignak had dismounted. Before Kasim had time to speak the Venerable Chief greeted him, and Kasim thanked him with much emotion, then pointed down into the gorge. Dampignak shook his head. "At break of day we shall go and see what's there," he said.

"*Inshallah!*"* replied the pious Moslem.

Christian offered Kasim his horse. With a grateful smile he accepted, lifting Christian up in front of him. And so they rode back to Kao-Cheng. While still far off they could see the faint glow of the campfire.

Suddenly someone stood before them roaring: "Halt! Who goes there?"

"Old," answered Big Tiger.

"I guessed it was you," replied Kao-Cheng.

"You have to say something else, Captain," Christian reminded him. "You might be a stranger or even an enemy."

"By night only the password will do," added Big Tiger.

"You're right," cried Kao-Cheng. "I was only putting you to the test. Did you find Kasim? Ah, I see you've come back without him. Alas, we must mourn him!"

"I'm Compass Mountain," cried Christian, jumping down from the saddle, "but behind me rides another."

"*Salaam!*" cried Kasim solemnly.

He was immediately surrounded by the Tungans, who had fled when the rocks collapsed. Later Kao-Cheng told them that to save the faces of the Tungans, Kasim had said he had lost consciousness when the earth quaked, and only that had made him stay behind.

As they all sat around the fire Dampignak told what had happened at Falling Wall. "Thus it is when fate takes its course," said Kao-Cheng wisely. "There are a thousand ways of losing one's life. When the thunder roared and the earth heaved up and down like a scale beam, we only smiled and sat tight!" He looked around the circle triumphantly, and those of his hearers who understood his

* *Inshallah:* "As God wills."

language cast down their eyes, abashed by his shameless talk.

Dampignak smiled, Big Tiger felt like answering, and Christian was tempted to ask where Kao-Cheng wanted to ride off to an hour ago. But they were all too tired to say anything. They were thankful for the warm fire, and fell asleep without taking tea. Kao-Cheng sat proud and upright beside them.

49 A CHAPTER IN WHICH MANY TEARS FLOW

CHRISTIAN and Big Tiger had to be shaken before they awoke. Dawn was breaking, the stars were growing pale, and Kao-Cheng was shouting: "Get up, men!" His brow was clouded and his step was heavy.

Christian and Big Tiger looked around. Dampignak was sitting beside them. The fire had burned down, but a can of hot tea was standing in the embers.

"Drink," said the Venerable Chief. "There'll be nothing to eat until we get to Falling Wall." Then he bowed to Big Tiger. "Now," he said, "you may give me the ring."

Big Tiger drew it from his thumb, raised it to his forehead, and bent his knee: "The holy man Yolros Lama ordered me to give the ring to him who desires it with a great desire."

"I have that desire," said Dampignak. He knelt down before Big Tiger and received the simple silver ring as if it were a great treasure.

Kao-Cheng, who was bringing the horses, was so alarmed at the sight that he stood stock-still. Here was a man whom one had to address as "Your Excellency" or "Your Highness" kneeling before a mere boy. Kao-Cheng's astonishment grew greater and greater, but he groped in vain for an explanation. Finally he thought it must be a ceremony foretelling great dangers to be faced. He could hear Big Tiger saying: "Yolros Lama bade you think of him in this hour as of one who has departed from the world."

"I am thinking of him," said Dampignak.

At this Kao-Cheng could no longer contain himself. The whole business was too uncanny. He cleared his throat noisily and took a pace forward. "Is it allowed to ask what is to happen next?" he began timidly.

"I told you yesterday, Captain," replied Dampignak, "that we would enter Falling Wall at sunrise together. The hour has now come."

Kao-Cheng was gripped with cold fear. "The sun is still behind the mountains," he said.

"It will be shining by the time we ride into the gorge."

"Ride into it?" cried Kao-Cheng, petrified. But he pulled himself together and said: "May I ask in what order you wish us to ride, so that I can give my men the necessary instructions."

"That's up to you," replied Dampignak solemnly. "The first to enter Falling Wall wins the right to the booty, with the exception of the car, which belongs to General Wu."

"Is *he* around here too?" cried Kao-Cheng, dismayed.

"General Wu is not here," Dampignak explained, "but his delegates are." And he pointed to Christian and Big Tiger.

Kao-Cheng was too bewildered to understand. "As Your Highness is our guest," he said, "the right of entering Falling Wall first is yours."

"Thank you, Captain," said Dampignak.

When Christian and Big Tiger had drunk a bowl of tea the party mounted. Kao-Cheng rode beside Dampignak, the others followed, and a soldier led the pack horse behind.

The dull gray of early morning lay over the desert. The stones were not yet glittering and the sand was colorless. When they came to the hill on which Kasim had lain, the gorge opened before them. They could see the brown walls and, as it had got brighter by then, the fresh breaks in the stone face. They also saw the dead donkey. But that was all, for the sloping spurs of Kasim's hill obstructed the view. The party halted and Kao-Cheng and several of his men dismounted. The first rays of the sun were touching the steep cliffs of Falling Wall, and the sky was turning a delicate blue. It was a peaceful scene.

All waited in silence. At last Kao-Cheng suggested it might be time to make their triumphal entry, as he called it. "Wait a minute," said Dampignak, pointing to Kasim, who had climbed the hill and was kneeling up there, with his feet to the west, saying his morning prayers. When he had finished he came and asked Dampignak whether he might have the honor of entering Falling Wall with him. Kao-Cheng began to interpret the Turki's words, but Dampignak had grasped what he wanted and answered with a friendly nod, saying, "*Bolna!*"

"Please, do not talk so loud, Your Highness," begged Kao-Cheng, "or something may happen; but if something does happen," he added proudly, "I shall hasten to your aid."

"Thank you, Captain," said Dampignak, raising his whip, and the stallion shot off like an arrow. Christian and Big Tiger galloped after, with Kasim between them. The clattering hoofs threw up the stone dust which had gathered in the night. At first they traversed nothing but slopes covered with shattered rock and boulders which had rolled down the mountainside. Then they met the stream which emerged from the valley and trickled through the gravel. There a wall of rock began. It was not quite as high as the walls of Ming-shui but apparently it was of the same black stone as the mountains in which they had met Dambit. Close to this wall of rock stood the truck.

Dampignak held his reins tighter. Kasim, who had his rifle lying across the saddle, slung it over his shoulder, smiled, and pointed down to the driver's cab, in which someone was sitting. When the riders stopped a few yards from the truck the fellow sounded the horn. The horses rose on their hind legs as if at a word of command, and Moonlight hastily let go of the horn.

"Little Paw!" cried Dampignak. "Stupid old Little Paw! So you're here already!"

"Your orders were to remain in the gorge until sunrise," replied Moonlight, "and I did so, though I found it hard." He looked inquiringly at Dampignak.

"They're dead," said Dampignak, dismounting. "Such was the will of heaven."

"I know," said Moonlight, "and I rejoiced in my heart. How is it that I'm sad now?"

"Little Paw," said Dampignak, "for twenty years we have been under stress. Time softens hatred. Do not bewail its loss. Now let us look at the truck before Kao-Cheng arrives."

"It stinks," said Moonlight.

"All horseless cars stink," said Christian.

"Especially when they're full of cans of gasoline," added Big Tiger.

"Dambit said the cans were empty when he met Greencoat," Christian recalled.

"We'll see," said Big Tiger. He climbed into the truck and tried to lift one can after the other, but they were all too heavy except the one out of which Springtime Snake had filled the tank.

"It's not gasoline that's in them," said Big Tiger. "It must be something else."

"And the drum?" asked Christian.

"It's full," said Big Tiger, "and I believe it's gasoline." He could not open it, for it was standing in the corner.

Christian and Big Tiger found a hammer in the tool box and hammered the bolts out of the rings. The gate board fell down, and then all stood around and gaped, too astonished to say a word. On the floor lay row after row of silver bars, one against the other. Over the first layer boards had been laid, and on the boards lay more silver bars. It looked like a cargo of small gray bricks. On top of them were more boards, and on the boards stood the cans. Anyone looking at the truck from the outside would have thought Greencoat had only a load of gasoline and nothing else.

Kasim drew one of the slender bars from under the boards and examined the stamp. Then he passed it to Dampignak saying: "There is no God but Allah, the Almighty, the Great!" At this Christian and Big Tiger realized there was something special about the silver, and not understanding Kasim's words, they looked inquiringly at Dampignak.

"This is the stamp of the old Governor in Urumchi," he said. "The silver belongs to him."

He pushed the bar back in its place, and Moonlight lifted down one of the cans. When he opened it there was a slight smell of gasoline, and some liquid ran out—it was only water. But at the bottom of the can lay eight silver bars. It was the same with all the others, and that was why they were so heavy.

All of a sudden Big Tiger and Christian realized why Greencoat had spent five days in Falling Wall, and various other things became clear to them too.

"We shall call Kao-Cheng," said Dampignak.

Kasim rode off to fetch him, and when they were alone Moonlight said: "Shong-Ma murdered a whole caravan to get this silver, but I can't understand why he didn't move it away from here sooner. Ten years is a long time."

"It is easy to understand," Big Tiger explained. "It couldn't be done with a camel caravan. There'd be too many other people knowing about it. So he left the silver lying in the cave, possibly in a side passage covered over with sand and stones. It was safe lying there, and the jewel casket too, because naturally everybody was afraid to go near Falling Wall any more."

"Greencoat took his time," said Christian. "He waited for an opportunity, and when he met Good Fortune in Hwai-lai-hsien, he thought this was his chance. From the outset he wanted to get the truck from Good Fortune."

"But Good Fortune withstood the temptation," asserted Big Tiger.

"I don't believe it," said Moonlight.

Christian and Big Tiger contradicted him vehemently. They wanted to help Good Fortune to recover face, and they praised his honesty. "It couldn't be helped," they said. "If Greencoat wanted the truck he had to steal it. So that's what he did. Good Fortune is a model of honesty."

"I see the time coming," said Moonlight with a grin, "when redbeards will die out. It can't be far off when they're becoming converted to virtue at this rate."

He glanced at Dampignak to see what he would say, but Dampignak was looking at the wall of rock, where the new rubble had fallen on the old, blocking the cave with a whole mountain of boulders.

"Kao-Cheng is coming," said Christian.

The frontier captain and his men were riding cautiously into the valley, in single file, all eyes on the newly collapsed wall, where the falls had left big bright yellow patches. They were expecting a fresh landslide at any moment.

Kao-Cheng put his best foot forward. "Peace and order are restored," he cried, "and I hear there is vast booty. How fortunate," he continued with a smile, "that the thieves have spared us the trouble of loading. Never was there such a victory!"

"We must discuss the matter," replied Dampignak. And he asked Kao-Cheng and his men to sit down in a circle around him. "As we were the first," he began, "to enter Falling Wall . . ."

"And Kasim," Kao-Cheng reminded him.

"And Kasim," Dampignak agreed, "we have won the right to distribute the booty. The criminals lie dead under the rocks, and there's nothing of theirs left but the saddle and bridle of the ass. These we award to Kasim."

"But all the silver?" asked Kao-Cheng, taken aback. "What about it?"

"It will be returned to its lawful owner," replied Dampignak. "For we are in his province, in which the laws of the wise old men prevail. It is your responsibility, Captain, to see that not one silver bar goes astray. As for us, Moonlight and I come from the country in which our laws are valid. One of these laws says: 'What a gentleman of the mountains lays his hand on is his.' Therefore the can containing the eight silver bars which Moonlight took down from the truck is our property and at our disposal. Does this division seem just to you, Captain?"

"It is just," said Kao-Cheng, deeply disappointed.

"Your deeds will bring you recognition and renown," said Dampignak reassuringly. "But for the present be content with a trifle. We command that the eight silver bars be distributed. Each of your men shall receive one. You, as their leader, shall receive two, and you shall send one of your men to Hsing-hsing-hsia with the pack horse to buy with the last one all the food and drink for a merry feast."

At these words Kao-Cheng's dejected face brightened instantly. "Thanks ten thousand times for your vast generosity," he cried enthusiastically. "In all our miserable life we have never had such luck." He bowed deeply, then each of his men came and *kowtowed* before Dampignak, giving thanks for the gifts which Moonlight handed out.

"Now let us eat what we've got," said Dampignak.

Kao-Cheng's men unloaded the pack horse and made a fire by the side of the stream. Christian and Big Tiger went to gather wood. Behind the sandbank, where the dead ass lay, there was lots of fire wood and Moonlight went with them to show the way. "Tell me how it all went in the night," he asked the boys eagerly. "I saw a lot, but not all, for I was far away."

So Christian told him all he knew, and Big Tiger added what Christian forgot.

"But the thing which Shong-Ma gave Springtime Snake?" asked Moonlight. "What was it?"

"Unfortunately," said Big Tiger, "we know nothing about that."

"Springtime Snake is dead," said Christian, "so we can't ask him what he said 'Thanks ten thousand times' for."

They collected the fire wood and on their way back, as they passed the spot where the dead ass lay, Christian saw a round object shining in the gray gravel. He picked it up. It was a silver box with a beautifully engraved cover. "Here's the thing," he said, "and it's silver."

They all looked at the little box, and Christian tried to lift the cover, but it would not come off.

"That's not a box you can open," said Moonlight in a melancholy voice.

Then Christian and Big Tiger noticed that the sides were divided into six compartments, and between them were six other divisions which moved to and fro, but only a little way. The animals representing the months were engraved on the twelve divisions.

"It's a toy," said Moonlight, "to teach Mongol children the cycle of the year, and it belonged to the Venerable Chief. When he was a little child, I was a little child too, and we played with it, naming the months of the year. When his little son was four years old he gave it to him. And then came the murderer, Shong-Ma."

Christian stood holding the silver toy, and Big Tiger stood beside him. Both looked up at Moonlight, their eyes asking what they were to do with it. But Moonlight was at a loss too. "Give it to Dampignak," he said at last, turning away.

"Let's put it into the casket when no one is looking," suggested Big Tiger.

"You must do it soon," said Moonlight, "for the Prince and I are going back after breakfast."

"And what about us?" asked Big Tiger, dismayed.

"You shall remain with the truck until Good Fortune comes. He'll be with you in three days."

"Will you permit us the joy of seeing you again?" asked Big Tiger.

"We beg you to do so," said Christian.

"My children, don't make it too hard for me," Moonlight begged them, looking a picture of grief.

They found the whole company gathered round the fire, everyone talking at the same time. The kettle was boiling, the tea was bubbling, and Big Tiger fetched his saddle bag and turned out the contents. Christian also opened his, and when nobody was looking he pushed back the slide cover of the casket and laid the silver toy in between the golden bracelets and hair ornaments.

Kao-Cheng's provisions included *zamba,* salted vegetables, and bean noodles. Breakfast was hardly over when he began talking about supper. But then something suddenly occurred to him. "Hu!" he shouted. "Saddle your horse!"

"What is he to do?" asked Moonlight.

"He's to ride off at once," said Kao-Cheng. "It's very urgent."

"In hurry there is error," said Moonlight. "The horses must be fed."

"But the telegram," cried Kao-Cheng. "I must send a telegram."

"What do you want to write in the telegram?" inquired Moonlight.

Kao-Cheng made a sweeping gesture. "Everything," he said loftily.

"You can't do that," said Moonlight. "A telegram should have only ten words. Do you have paper?"

"What for?" asked Kao-Cheng, discomfited.

"For writing," said Moonlight.

"I'm not keen on writing; it's a slow business," replied Kao-Cheng. "I tell Hu what is to be written, and he memorizes it. The clerks in Hsing-hsing-hsia do the rest. That's their business."

Christian fetched his brief case. "Captain," he said, "words can get lost, and then suddenly half the telegram is missing. Big Tiger is a scribe of distinction. From all the words that there are, he'll pick out ten which will tell the old Governor all he must know."

"But you must not forget anything," warned Kao-Cheng.

"No fear," said Christian. "Don't you see Big Tiger is thinking it up already?"

"Be quiet, men!" ordered Kao-Cheng, and all looked on as Big Tiger wrote, and they marveled at the speed with which he could complete such a difficult thing as a telegram. "Exactly ten words," said Big Tiger.

"Please read it aloud," said Kao-Cheng. "You know I've got weak eyes."

Big Tiger cleared his throat a little and read: "Compassmountain, Bigtiger, and lost silver treasure found. Arrival midmonth. KAOCHENG."

"I've counted with him," cried Moonlight. "Never have I heard of a telegram which embraced the hundred scenes of an event in ten words as this one does."

"But what if you arrive before that time?" Kao-Cheng objected.

"All the better," said Moonlight. "Then the old Governor will have a pleasant surprise."

"I doubt if he likes surprises," said Kao-Cheng dubiously. "Remember, he's an old man. The banquet wouldn't be ready and the flags wouldn't be out."

"Don't you worry about that," Dampignak broke in. "The old Governor won't be taken by surprise. He'll instruct all the stations on the way to notify him when Compass Mountain and Big Tiger arrive and when they leave. In his province the front wheel of a car never gets loose without the back one knowing it."

"The Prince is right," cried Kao-Cheng enthusiastically. "The old Governor's domain is a model, so to speak." At that moment a lump of rock broke loose from the rock face opposite and crashed down. Kao-Cheng jumped with terror.

"Did I speak too loudly?" he whispered.

"You roared like an ox," said Moonlight. "Beware! Last night I listened to bones cracking."

"How ghastly!" said Kao-Cheng.

"You saw and heard little of last night's doings," continued Moonlight. "Let me tell you, so you'll know. First came a wind which singed the mountains and blew my hat off." Then—" thinking he was well launched, he took his pipe out of his boot, but Dampignak interrupted him. "Little Paw," he said, "this isn't the right time for your story. We're leaving."

"Already?" cried Kao-Cheng, taken aback. "I had hoped Your Highness would grace our feast with your presence."

Moonlight put back his pipe. "Captain Kao-Cheng," he said, "the next time we meet on the frontier I'll tell you the rest. It does not have to be now. For such stories become more varied in their incidents and more magnificent in their events as time goes on."

"They become continually better worth telling, so to speak," agreed Kao-Cheng.

"Well said," cried Moonlight. "We understand one another." He stood up and went to the horses. Kao-Cheng and his men helped him to saddle, and Christian and Big Tiger went up to Dampignak.

"Please may we accompany you a bit of the way," said Christian.

"We beg you to grant us this honor," pleaded Big Tiger.

"Ride with us to the place where we began the ascent of the mountain yesterday," said Dampignak. "There we shall say farewell."

"We thank you," said Christian and Big Tiger, hurrying to the horses.

"The story of our deed will be told in every tent," cried Kao-Cheng as Dampignak mounted his horse. The men gathered round and each expressed his modest wish for a good journey. "I forgot to tell Your Highness," cried Kao-Cheng, "that there is a government paper printed in the capital. In a few weeks the educated people of all nations will learn of the magnificent victory of justice over crime at Falling Wall."

"Send us a copy," said Moonlight, laughing.

"Farewell, Captain," cried Dampignak. Then they trotted down toward the narrow defile in which Moonlight had spent the night. Here too were old willow trees, and their shoots surrounded the place at which the stream broke with a slight ripple through the gravel. The smell of damp earth and wet stone brought a waft of memory of the distant world in which there were animals and plants.

They dismounted and led the horses over the loose stones into the gorge. It was as Kao-Cheng had said. One could touch the opposite walls with one's outstretched arms, and the path led abruptly upward. It was difficult going, the horses stumbled, and one could see that it could not have been easy even for a camel caravan to get through here. But camels walk calmly and carefully, and the path promised safety. It led northward to where the desert comes to an end, heaven knows where. There would be grass again, and trees, tents and white monasteries, and, at the end of the path, big towns, Uliassutai and, still farther on, Kobdo. One had but to follow the trail to get there.

It took only about ten minutes to squeeze through the narrow bottleneck, and the blue sky grew nearer. The path turned sharply eastward and they were able to mount again. Soon they reached the place where Moonlight had dismounted the previous afternoon, and from there to the place of parting was only another *li*.

Dampignak pulled up and they all dismounted. "Heaven only knows," said the Venerable Chief, "if our ways shall ever meet again. If heaven is kind to me, you shall one day see the robber prince Dampignak again, but in another role." He embraced Christian and Big Tiger. When Moonlight bent down to them his face was wet with tears.

"Please, please, do not weep," begged Christian. "If you do, I shall have to howl out loud." He looked at Big Tiger and saw that his eyes too were full of tears; Big Tiger had become very fond of Moonlight. For a while the Venerable Chief looked out over the deeply fissured plateau as if there was something to see there.

Then he mounted. Moonlight took Christian's and Big Tiger's horses, tied the reins together, and lifted down the leather bag in which the casket was. "This bag will come back to you refilled in three days," he promised.

Christian went up to Dampignak and said: "We have forgotten something and I must say it before it is too late. The Mongol Naidang of the Torgut tribe, who is called Picture Sheet, salutes on bended knee. 'Will the Venerable Chief,' he said, 'kindly send the silver batzes direct to Naidang who lives at the Narin Gol instead of by the old märin.' "

"That has been done," replied Dampignak, smiling. "Naidang has got his money."

He raised his whip in greeting, Big Tiger and Christian shouted *"Sä Yabonah!"* and they kept on shouting it until they could see nothing but a cloud of dust. Then they were alone in the vast stony desert, under the blue, cloudless sky. Christian wanted to say something, but as he had wept more than Big Tiger, he resolved not to be the first to speak. So they sat in silence by the wayside.

"I wish Good Fortune was here," said Big Tiger finally.

"Or at least the dog," said Christian.

They stood up and began to walk back. At each step they had to lift their heavy riding boots with conscious effort, otherwise they would have only slouched along. Down the defile the going was

easier. The boots slid almost of themselves over the round loose stones. When the rocks separated and the air, cooled by water, was wafted toward them, they could see the truck through the branches of the willows. But the horses were gone, and there was only one man sitting by the dying fire.

"Kasim," said Christian.

"But where are the others, and the horses?" asked Big Tiger.

"Kao-Cheng was frightened of this uncanny place," Christian surmised. "He's gone back to his old camp."

"Kao-Cheng is afraid he'd see the pole star at midday," said Big Tiger. "He lacks courage."

"You can't blame him," said Christian. "Falling Wall is no good place."

Kasim came to meet them. He was cheery and spoke gentle, kindly-sounding words in his own language, but it was only when he tried the language of signs that they understood him. Their guess proved right. Kao-Cheng had returned to his old camp behind the mountain. But Kasim remained with them.

50 ABOUT MANY FORESEEN AND UNFORESEEN EVENTS

THE THREE days mentioned by Moonlight passed by. Christian and Big Tiger cleaned the truck and emptied the water out of the cans. They looked into the drum and found it contained gasoline. Kasim helped them to pump up the tires, and twice a day he rode over to Kao-Cheng to get food. Sometimes Christian or Big Tiger relieved him of this duty, and each time Kao-Cheng asked whether Good Fortune had arrived. But actually Kao-Cheng was in no hurry. Hu had come back from Hsing-hsing-hsia on the third day with a lot of good things, so these inquiries were a mere formality.

The fourth day passed and Good Fortune had not come. Christian got out his thickest notebook and began writing.

"What are you doing?" asked Big Tiger.

"I'm writing a diary," said Christian. "I should have started it long ago. Now I have to make up for lost time, and it's a lot of work."

"Why have you got to do that?" asked Big Tiger.

"So that I shall know later what has happened, where we were, and whether the sun was shining, or whether there was storm or snow."

"There were all those things and I never thought of them again."

"That's just it," said Christian. "That's just why it's necessary to write them down."

Big Tiger remained unconvinced. He sat in the sun, and as there was no more work to do, Kasim collected black and white stones, swept a place clean near the truck, and drew a square on the ground with a wrench. He divided the square into many squares, and he and Big Tiger played checkers until evening. But still Good Fortune did not come.

The evening of the fifth day came. Christian had finished writing, and Kasim had just ridden off to fetch the food when the clatter of hoofs resounded from the gorge. Something black swept along under the willows, and a seemingly endless splashing of water became audible.

"Dog, come here!" shouted Christian and Big Tiger and the poodle jumped up on them. He jumped up first on one and then the other, ran round in circles and barked continuously, and so frightfully loudly that if the gallant Captain had heard him he would certainly have been terrified.

But Falling Wall did not stir.

Christian and Big Tiger ran to meet Good Fortune, who was the first to come down through the defile. He was sitting proudly on the haughty camel which was projecting its upper lip, slipping with its front legs, and braking with its hindquarters. Good Fortune was wearing the pistol with the red tassel, looking very impressive. After him came Affliction, on foot, leading the pack camel, and Toeless, riding Christian's camel, brought up the rear.

"So there you are!" said Good Fortune, dismounting. He had meant to show that he was hurt because he had missed everything both at Ming-shui and at Falling Wall. And Moonlight had told him some glorious tales when they had met at the Venerable Chief's stronghold.

Christian and Big Tiger bowed politely. They said: "We have taken care of ourselves as our esteemed elder desired, and we have acted as if he were there. We are immeasurably glad to see him again."

This salutation broke the ice in Good Fortune's heart. "Oh, you young rascals! It gladdens my heart to see you! I have long missed the sight of you," he cried.

Affliction left the three camels standing, and Toeless slipped down carefully from his saddle. For a time everyone talked at once and nobody could hear anything. In between, the poodle barked; but the camels went silently and thoughtfully down to the water. When the noise had quieted down a little Affliction said: "I hear there's been a first-class catastrophe."

"Over there," said Christian, pointing to the masses of rock which lay at the foot of the wall, and at all the rubble which lay for a wide radius around.

Toeless stared at the mountain of broken rock which covered the mouth of the cave, but he said nothing. Having lived in Anhsi, he knew the story of Falling Wall. Nor was he in the least surprised that Shong-Ma had turned out to be behind the disaster. But he was not at all pleased with how things had turned out.

"I knew they'd never catch him," he growled, knitting his brows. "And they didn't!"

"It was heaven's decree," declared Affliction quietly, "that he should be crushed to death. What can mortals do against that?" Toeless did not reply, but it was plain that he did not share Affliction's opinion.

Together they led the camels up near the truck and Christian and Big Tiger helped to unload. The blue tent was set up, and when Kasim returned there was a fire burning. There was plenty to eat, and plenty to talk about, for Kasim could converse with Toeless, who spoke Turki like a Sart. Good Fortune got busy with the truck. "You've cleaned it up wonderfully," he said. "Now let's see if the motor will work." He pulled up his sleeves and turned the crank a few times. The engine began to hum, and the camels, which luckily were already tied, jumped up.

"We shall start tomorrow," said Good Fortune joyfully. "The next day we shall be in Hami and I shall have the pleasure of paying my respects to Mr. Li-Yuan-Pei. He won't be too pleased to see me."

"Food, food!" cried Affliction, and as there were spiced meat dumplings for supper he did not have to call twice.

Afterwards Christian wrote in his diary: "Today is the tenth day of the third moon. Good Fortune, Affliction, and Uncle Toeless arrived. It was as in the story books: our dog was the first to greet us. He barked very loud and licked our faces. It was fine. Good Fortune says he has brought us something, but he won't give it to us until the morning. He behaves as if tomorrow was New Year's Day instead of being April. He's going to visit Li-Yuan-Pei in Hami, and I believe we shall have to stop him from shooting again, or at least pretend to. Toeless told us that they're packing up at the castle and that Moonlight said Dampignak is going to be a great king, and that all the silver we have on the truck is only chicken feed and they don't need it. But Good Fortune looked quite perturbed when he saw it, and Affliction said something would definitely happen, but that he'd prefer not to be there when it does. Good Fortune has ridden over to Kao-Cheng on Kasim's horse to make a plan. It will be late when he gets back. We're sleeping in the tent again and our dog is guarding us."

Good Fortune came back in the night. The waxing moon was shining down on the silent valley, the stream glittered and the cans shone. The snores of the sleepers resounded from the dark tent and the dog gave a few loud barks. Good Fortune would have liked to shout: "Get up, men! We're starting!" But with only one headlight and the battery out of action, he had to let it be. Before dawn, however, he got up, made a fire, put the kettle on, and roused everyone relentlessly.

"Men!" he cried, eager for action. "This is what Kao-Cheng and I have agreed. You, old uncle, shall come with us to Hsing-hsing-hsia, and Kao-Cheng shall come with us also, because he is responsible for the silver. Affliction shall follow with the camels. And then you can plan what you want to do."

"We've already decided," said Affliction, "and we've also found a name."

"What have you done?" asked Good Fortune.

"The main thing," said Affliction, "is to find a good name, a really meaningful name, so that people won't dream of stopping anywhere but at our inn."

"You mean to open a saloon?" cried Good Fortune.

"A first-class inn," Affliction corrected him tactfully, "with at least three or four rooms, and in each room a *kang* which won't smoke. Nobody need ever again ask in Hsing-hsing-hsia: 'Where is Your Excellency staying?' for naturally His Excellency will put up at the inn Contented Cheerfulness, where Uncle Toeless shall look after the kitchen and I shall be porter and head waiter."

"What?" asked Good Fortune; and then, "Do I understand you aright?" and, "Why exactly in Hsing-hsing-hsia?"

"Dear nephew," said Toeless, "you need not be very bright to know that. Hsing-hsing-hsia is the first town inside the old Governor's province. All who travel on the Silk Road have to put up there. Up till now there are only miserable low dives in Hsing-hsing-hsia, but we shall change all this."

"Ha!" cried Good Fortune. "There are rogues, and there are people who think of tomorrow instead of yesterday and the day before. I congratulate you."

"Please accept our heartiest congratulations," said Big Tiger.

"May the inn Contented Cheerfulness prosper," said Christian.

Good Fortune went to the luggage and opened a parcel which was firmly tied up in blue cloth. "This is the right time," he said. "Gain follows loss. See what the Venerable Chief sends you!" He opened the cloth. There lay the ten silver bars from the Black City, six heavily loaded bags, and a whole lot of *haddaks*.

"Now I shall have to think hard to remember the words the Venerable Chief commissioned me to say," said Good Fortune. He laid the silver shoes in twos; that made five presents, and over each he spread a *haddak*. "Come here, you two," he said to Christian and Big Tiger, who knelt down politely. "That's right—reverence is called for now, because you have acquired another relative. The Venerable Chief said: 'Give my brothers Compass Mountain and Big Tiger two silver bars each as a souvenir of the Little Treasure and of their brother Dampignak, who embraces them.' "

Big Tiger and Christian stood up. "And now you," said Good Fortune.

"Me?" cried Affliction, alarmed.

"Don't be frightened," said Good Fortune. "You're not the brother of a prince, but you also are to have two silver bars because you were in the Black City too. 'Give them to the man,' said Dampignak, 'who stood on the east wall keeping a lookout.' "

"And you're to get two also, old uncle," continued Good Fortune. " 'Present them to old Toeless,' said Dampignak. 'We have done worse things to him than a man can bear. Pray him to forgive me and Moonlight, that our remorse may be lessened.' "

Toeless looked sorrowfully at the silver bars and at the blue *haddak* which half covered them, but Affliction said: "The present is given with a good intention. You should accept it."

"I too," said Good Fortune, "beg your forgiveness for my bad behavior, old uncle. Moonlight told me of your misfortune, and it has made my heart heavy." He threw himself on his knees before Toeless and touched the ground with his forehead four times.

"Stand up," said Toeless. "I have nothing to forgive you."

Good Fortune took the two remaining silver bars which belonged to himself, and then he pointed to the six bags. "These silver batzes are for Kao-Cheng and his soldiers. Will you please inform Kasim of this, honored uncle, and tell him to take them to Kao-Cheng, who is waiting for us at the end of the valley."

When Kasim was informed he beamed with joy. There were fifty silver batzes in each bag, and that was a great deal of money. He packed them up and mounted his horse at once.

The tent was then broken up and packed away. Affliction led the camels out of the valley of Falling Wall to behind the hill on which Kasim had lain. That was the meeting place with Kao-Cheng.

Uncle Toeless took his seat in the driver's cab, and Christian and Big Tiger jumped up on the running boards as Good Fortune started up. The motor hummed, and through sheer habit Good Fortune sounded the horn again and again as he drove along with a thundering noise under the barrier of rocks. The poodle ran behind barking. The din echoed back from Falling Wall, but the rocks did not move.

At the exit from the valley Kao-Cheng was awaiting them with his soldiers. "Unhoped-for riches have come our way," he said with a smile. "In the name of all I salute the envoy of the Prince whose generosity has lightened our wretched lot."

"It was a pleasant duty," replied Good Fortune. "And now get in, please."

"Where?" asked Kao-Cheng uneasily, looking at the strange vehicle on which the cans left no room for anyone.

"Let us throw off the cans; they're unnecessary," suggested Good Fortune.

"But there's something in them," Kao-Cheng reminded him.

"That's just why I waited for you to be present," Good Fortune explained. "You have to be here to count the silver bars as we take them out of the cans."

"That's not necessary," cried Kao-Cheng loftily. But then he remembered he was an important officer, so while Christian and Big Tiger emptied the cans, he watched the silver bars being piled up, and counted them. "Good," he said finally with dignity. But he did not betray how many there were.

While Christian and Big Tiger were making a pile of the empty cans in the bed of the stream, Affliction came running toward them, carrying some things he had forgotten: the freshly filled saddle bag and Christian's and Big Tiger's sheepskin coats and felt shoes. They at once took off their magnificent new Mongolian costumes and folded them neatly away. Then they climbed into the truck, taking the poodle with them.

"Hold him tight!" said Good Fortune. "He has to get used to driving in an automobile."

"I'll sit with you two," cried Uncle Toeless. "There's fresh air and entertainment up there. You must tell me everything."

"We welcome you, old uncle," said Christian.

Kao-Cheng and Good Fortune clasped hands for him, and Uncle Toeless climbed up. Big Tiger and Christian took him each by an arm and made a comfortable place for him. He sat down, nodding happily.

"Is Affliction traveling alone?" asked Christian anxiously.

"Don't you worry," replied Toeless. "Kasim is going with him and he will probably stay with us and take charge of the stables."

"At that rate," said Big Tiger, "you will have two master marksmen to entertain the guests of the inn Contented Cheerfulness with stone-throwing and sharpshooting."

"I wish you a pleasant journey, old uncle," said Affliction, walking alongside. "Ah! The unlucky dog is up there too. May many lucky stars shine on you all the same!"

They couldn't hear any more, for just then Good Fortune started up. The Tungans had all they could do to hold their horses. Affliction stepped back a few paces, but Kao-Cheng sat proudly in the driver's cab and waved out of the now glassless window. Christian and Big Tiger roared *Sä Yabonah,* the Tungans also

shouted something, and Affliction wished a lucky journey, though he thought it most unlikely they would have it.

It was early in the morning, and Affliction would have been extremely surprised if anyone had told him that the truck had thundered through the only street of Hsing-hsing-hsia two hours later, raising a cloud of dust, and had stopped before the biggest house in it. "The criminal lived here," said Kao-Cheng, getting out.

Two soldiers were standing before the hall door, which was pasted up with broad strips of paper. To left and right shone two fresh red seals.

"Open!" ordered Captain Kao-Cheng.

"No!" said the soldiers, crossing their guns. "The orders of the old Governor are that the hall door is only to be opened to Colonel Kao-Cheng. Forgive us, Captain, but we cannot obey your orders."

Christian and Big Tiger jumped down from the truck, and the poodle jumped down after them and started barking furiously because everything was strange and new to him—the dust, the houses, the people, and above all the soldiers who were making angry faces.

"We congratulate you on your promotion," cried Big Tiger.

"The Captain," said Christian, "has attained a very high rank We congratulate him."

Then the Mayor came running. He knew Kao-Cheng and tore down the paper seals, the soldiers presented arms, and before he went to sleep Christian wrote in his diary:

"We are in Hsing-hsing-hsia and it is the eleventh day of the third moon. The poodle is lying in the truck because he knows he has to watch it. He is no ordinary dog. Greencoat's house is big. There are four rooms in it and two big storerooms full of bales of cotton. There are forty cans of gasoline in the yard and they belong to us. The name Li-Yuan-Pei is stamped on them, but the Mayor says that's to be disregarded. The house and everything in it belongs to nobody, because the caretaker and the servants were frightened when they heard what had happened at Falling Wall. And now the Mayor is frightened too because he should have arrested them, but he couldn't for they weren't there when he tried to. But Good Fortune calmed him down and said it doesn't matter, and Kao-Cheng said though he's a colonel now he'll shut his eyes in the case of people who are not so brainy or so watchful as himself. This made the Mayor very much ashamed and he thanked the gallant colonel for his tolerance, and Kao-Cheng said he was surprised other people hadn't noticed it, but he had suspected all along that Greencoat was not a merchant but a criminal.

"The house and the yard are to be sold by auction tomorrow but the Mayor says he'll manage things so that it will go to Toeless; they will just begin the auction a bit early and it will be quite simple. Kao-Cheng is very pleased about this and very gracious, and he has promised the Mayor he'll allow him to remain in office, as he's the right man for it, and he's promised Toeless he'll honor him whenever he comes to Hsing-hsing-hsia. We know what that means and Uncle Toeless knows too. We're going to Hami tomorrow and Kao-Cheng is coming with us to make a report to the old Governor and tell him how to catch criminals. The manager of the telegraph station came out and inquired after our health. He has to send a telegram about it and another one as soon as we go out the gate. Kao-Cheng says the province is well ruled."

The following evening Christian wrote:

"Today is the twelfth day of the third moon and we are in Hami. We drove more than a hundred and twenty miles along the Silk Road through the desert, and if Kao-Cheng hadn't got sick on the way we'd have been here an hour sooner.

"We said good-by to Uncle Toeless early this morning. He was very sad and said: 'Little sons, in four years you will be grown-up men and you must visit me then, if the world is still in existence.' We promised him we would, and asked him to give our greetings to Kasim and Affliction and to tell Affliction we'd look out for a good place in Peking to practice stone-throwing, and we'd be experts when we'd see him again. The telegraph man came too and then we drove off and he ran into his house where the telegraph wires are.

"I believe he sent a telegram because when we came through the town gate of Hami we had to drive very slowly there was such a crowd there, soldiers with drums and trumpets too, and they blew and drummed and Kao-Cheng said it was in honor of him. Afterwards we had to drive to the *yamen,* and there was a general to receive us who put his hand to his cap. He was very thin and sick looking. Big Tiger says that's from smoking opium and that it's a wicked shame. We drank tea with him; when it's a formal invitation you drink nothing or only a sip at the most. We showed the general we knew how to behave, and when he tried to make us drink the tea we handed back the cups three times, and then the visit ended. Hami is a magnificent town. Up till now it has been desert everywhere but here it's one melon garden after another, and there are trees and streets and lots of shops. Far up in the north there are high snowy mountains. They speak Turki in Hami and there's a castle as high as a tower with a Mohammedan King in it. The King sent us a red visiting card inviting us to visit him. Good Fortune said he'd rather visit Li-Yuan-Pei. We took his pistol from him before he went. But we had only just eaten ten poppy cakes and some candied apples and dates and salted almonds and nougat that the thin general sent us, when Good Fortune came back. He said 'That son of a dog has run away too and his shop is sealed up.' After that we visited the King who lives outside the gate where only Mohammedans live. We went through a big gate and it was dark inside and there were two men with big gray beards. They held halberds in their hands. My teacher says that's medieval and it's past, but it's not past in Hami. A very friendly man came and led us into the courtyard. Five frightful animals were chained there. They snarled and showed their teeth. I thought they were white tigers, but Big Tiger says they're snow leopards, his uncle knows them. At the end of the courtyard there was a wooden staircase and an old man was standing on it. He smiled and came to meet us, and we guessed he was the King. There was a pavilion at the top of the stairs where we had to drink tea. We handed back our cups three times to show how polite we were, and each time the King put another lump of sugar in them. We thought he should know one doesn't take sugar in tea. Luckily someone spoke Chinese, and he said we should drink the tea as we were guests of a Mohammedan Turki and not of a Chinaman, and the customs were different everywhere. Then we had a question and answer game. The King asked the questions, the interpreter asked them again, and we answered. And when we got home a big parcel of sweets had already arrived with the greetings of the Turki King."

When Christian had finished writing, he and Big Tiger went into the courtyard where the poodle was lying beside the truck. They took some dried meat out of their bag and fetched some water from the kitchen, for here it was not as in Dampignak's castle. In Hami a dog had to fend for himself. Then they prepared a sleeping place for him up on the truck, and told him to watch carefully.

"That's not necessary," said two soldiers, who had come to guard the truck and the silver during the night. But Big Tiger said: "He's used to doing that. He's no ordinary dog."

When they returned to the guest room Kao-Cheng and Good Fortune were already lying on the *kang*. Kao-Cheng could not sleep for a long time. He could hear the night watchmen beating wooden clappers to warn thieves of their presence. Then the poodle growled, and Kao-Cheng heard him gnashing his teeth. "The accursed dog," said one of the soldiers under his breath.

"There's nothing we can do," whispered the second soldier.

Rogues, thought Kao-Cheng, amused. He smiled, for he could feel for poor soldiers who seldom got paid. But he could not get to sleep all the same. It was morning before he fell into an uneasy slumber. But then Good Fortune got up, filled the tank and the radiator, and as the sun rose the truck drove out the western gate.

The desert began again right away after Hami, but it no longer reigned supreme. Here and there were isolated farms and little hamlets, and fertile *loess* soil could be seen forcing its way through the sand. Only water was lacking. It had to be led laboriously through underground canals from the foot of the nearby mountains to the fields. The cart track which connected the villages was bad, and there were only two settlements some sixty miles apart which had more than five houses. One was Lo-tung, where the road to Turfan through the Devil's Valley branched off, and the other was Tsikioking, which they reached late in the afternoon.

Men and children stood in the road staring at the unusual guests. There was an inn of a kind, but one look at the guest room was enough for Good Fortune. When he came back he said: "We shall sleep on the truck. We didn't get lice up till now, and we'll keep clear of them."

Christian gave Big Tiger the diary, and Big Tiger wrote carefully in his beautiful Chinese ideographs:

"We are in Tsikioking. It is the thirteenth day of the third moon. The inhabitants of this village are Sarts. The men wear big beards and the women are never seen. There are high bare mountains all around. Kao-Cheng speaks perfect Turki, and we admire him for that. He got a splendid supper for us, a dish called *palao,* made of rice with a lot of mutton and raisins and slices of quince. Good Fortune is very well, so is Compass Mountain, and so am I. The dog is guarding us, so we can sleep in peace. It was a lucky day with good omens."

Nobody thought of disturbing the nocturnal peace of Tsikioking, and they all slept well. When the *mullah's** call to morning prayer rang through the air, Good Fortune got up, yet they did not reach the high pass of Ta-chi-tu, which leads over the Barkul mountains, until past midday. From there onward the route was downhill, and they arrived at Kucheng in the evening, an hour before the gate closed. It was quite late when Christian took out the diary and wrote:

"Today is the fourteenth day of the third moon. The moon is shining into the courtyard where our truck is standing beside another one belonging to the Governor. There's an oil lamp in our room and lots of things to eat. There was an express letter waiting for us with hearty greetings from the Marshal. He's glad he will see us soon.

"We left Tsikioking and went up high snowy mountains. All the same the water boiled in the radiator and we had to get out and push the brake shoes under, and it was fun to watch Kao-Cheng's face when the truck wouldn't go. But it went on a bit, and then another bit, and then we came to Tashi-tu which looks just the same as Tsikioking, only there are no telegraph poles.

"We took tea out in the street, and we saw a man on a horse coming from Barkul. He looked thin and miserable. Good Fortune shouted 'Son of a dog,' and 'Lousy ruffian,' and made a grab at his whip, but Kao-Cheng held his arm and said: 'Why do you want to beat the honorable gentleman?' Then all of a sudden a big crowd gathered and they said: 'There must be a mistake.' Big Tiger and I went up to the man on the horse and greeted him politely. It was Mr. Ma and he looked quite done in. Good Fortune raged on, but we said Mr. Ma wasn't a stingy fellow and if he

* *Mullah:* Religious teacher of Mohammedanism.

had his camels with him he'd give us a fine present for old times' sake. 'Where are your camels?' Good Fortune asked him, and Ma said he had left the caravan long ago. He had ridden on ahead day and night and had spent a fortune on fodder, but it was no use, his horse was half dead. Good Fortune said: 'You're an irresponsible wretch,' and Ma cried and said he was ruined. Then we invited him to have tea and when he saw all the lovely food from the Turki King, he cheered up. Good Fortune asked him: 'Why did you ride on ahead?' and Ma said it was because he had to send an urgent telegram in Tsikioking. Good Fortune said: 'Even if you get a fresh horse you won't be there before tomorrow evening.' Then Big Tiger said very slowly: 'If the esteemed Mr. Ma wishes to telegraph to Li-Yuan-Pei that he's not to pay Greencoat any money, that's not necessary.' You would not think it should frighten people when you try to help them. But Ma went dead white and Kao-Cheng had to hold him up, and the men of Tashi-tu stepped back two paces because they thought Big Tiger must be a prophet. Then I said: 'There's nothing to be frightened about. The check for three thousand five hundred batzes is lying under a mountain of stones where no one can find it, and Greencoat can't cash it because he's lying under the stones too. And Li-Yuan-Pei isn't in Hami any more. His hall door is sealed up and soldiers are guarding it.'

"Then the men of Tashi-tu shouted *Allah akbar!** and it took Mr. Ma a long time to understand that there are boys who crawl about in passages under old forts and happen to hear two men quarreling about a jewel casket and a check. In the end Mr. Ma smiled feebly and said: 'So you *are* little bandits after all!' But Good Fortune said: 'Ride back to your caravan, you negligent fellow,' and he gave him lots of good advice: 'Don't get mixed up in shady business again, you numbskull,' and 'If you go near rotten fish you soon stink yourself!' As we had learned from Moonlight the proper thing to do, we divided the gifts of the King

* *Allah akbar:* "Allah is great."

of Hami into three parts and laid a *haddak* over Mr. Ma's share which we presented to him kneeling. We got so many blessings that we arrived in Kucheng safely. We are now honored guests in the *yamen* and the old Governor has sent us another truck so that the heavy load of silver can be divided. Kao-Cheng watched and counted, and now he knows how many silver bars there are, but he doesn't say, because it's a state secret.

We are driving tomorrow to the capital which has two names. The Chinese call it Tihwa and the Turkis call it Urumchi, and the Bogdo Ola can be seen from there, though it's very far away. That's a Mongolian name meaning Mountain of the Gods. It's so high no one has ever got to the top of it yet. It says on the map that it's 21,000 feet high. People can't breathe so high up. But how can someone sitting on a chair in London know that? The Bogdo Ola is full of snow and ice, and where the snow stops there are woods, and there live the Kirghiz, who speak Turki. Big Tiger says Sinkiang is a puzzling country. I find that too, but we're going to sleep now, and Kao-Cheng is snoring already because he has to stay awake and watch out so much."

51 WHAT GOES ON AT A STATE RECEPTION

"GET UP, MEN! Up you rascals!" shouted Good Fortune. "Oh, forgive me, Colonel. But the engine is running already, there's a lovely moon, and we shall have breakfast on the way."

Kao-Cheng got up with a sigh. "I'm used to being cheated of my sleep," he said. "The life of a frontier guard is a hard one." And he took Good Fortune aside. "My office obliges me to watch everything," he whispered. "I shall have to go in the other truck today. True, the driver doesn't look like a rogue, but he might become one on the way."

Good Fortune was highly pleased. "I understand," he wailed, raising his hand with a gesture of regret. "You must deprive me of your valued company."

"There's no way out," Kao-Cheng excused himself. "I must exercise supervision."

"I agree with you entirely," Good Fortune assured him. "I shall drive in front, so that you can supervise both cars."

"What are you saying?" cried Kao-Cheng indignantly. "I did not mean it that way." But he was very pleased.

"You can sit in front with me," said Good Fortune to Christian and Big Tiger.

"We'd like to very much," replied Christian, "but we can't."

"The dog might get lost," said Big Tiger.

"Hold him tight," whispered Good Fortune, "if I drive a little faster than usual."

The courtyard of the *yamen* lay silent and cold in the moonlight. One of the military guards stood up and opened the gate, and Good Fortune drove very slowly and carefully through it into the empty main street of Kucheng. The town gate also opened before him without his having to get out, and Christian and Big Tiger saw by the headlights of the second truck that Kao-Cheng was following. But it was not for long. As soon as they drove through the gate Good Fortune tapped on the pane, winked and grinned. Then he stepped on the gas. A cloud of dust rose, the town gate disappeared, the lights of Kao-Cheng's car grew dim, and Christian and Big Tiger held the poodle tight. An hour later they and the dog were fast asleep.

It was still night. Good Fortune had started out at the hour of the tiger* for his own good reasons. He wanted to drive into Urumchi when the midday gun would be going off, and people would be lying on their *kangs* for their midday rest. He did not want trumpets and drums to meet him, as in Hami, and above all he wanted to leave Kao-Cheng well behind. For Good Fortune

* 3-5 A.M.

had become thoroughly tired of publicity. Unfortunately things turned out differently.

At dawn they drove through Tsinushwan. The houses were shut up and the men were working in the fields. A blue fog floated over the ground and Good Fortune was obliged to drive slowly. But that was not for long. The few tilled fields soon gave way to desert, and by the time the sun rose the cart track led over an endless expanse of gravel. It made no difference whether one drove on the side or followed the road. In the south, rising ever higher and higher from insignificant spurs, towered the wild, snowcapped peak of Bogdo Ola, its summit veiled in cloud.

"Heaven and earth are colliding," said Christian when he awoke.

"Heaven and earth are uniting," said Big Tiger.

They gazed in silence at this marvel which they had never seen before—a mountain which reaches into the clouds even on a bright clear morning. Then they looked around for Kao-Cheng, but the second truck was nowhere to be seen.

When the gravel desert came to an end and fine sand took its place, Good Fortune returned to the cart track. To right and left spread a dense growth of tamarisks, with reeds between. Startled pheasants flew across the road. Soon the roofs of a village appeared, surmounted by a minaret.* A new wooden bridge spanned the river which flowed down from the mountains, and the short bazaar street was swept clean. In the middle of it stood a table covered with a white cloth, and three dignified-looking men with gray beards came forward and bowed. Good Fortune had either to stop or run them over. So he stopped the car and got out. Neither party could understand the other's language, but obviously they were being welcomed with many respectful words. Christian and Big Tiger crossed their arms and said "*Salaam*" as they had learned from Kasim.

* *Minaret:* A high, slender tower attached to a mosque, from which the summons to prayer is called.

"You are to take breakfast now," said Good Fortune. "Show the Mussulmans you are hungry, else they will be offended."

"We hear and obey," said Christian and Big Tiger, getting busy on a piled-up plate of hot meat patties. Good Fortune did likewise. He had been told in confidence by the driver of the second truck that a breakfast would await them in Fu-kan. Apparently this was the village, and Good Fortune asked Christian to find it on the map. "This is Fu-kan," said Christian, and the three old men nodded.

"How many more *li* are there to Urumchi?" asked Good Fortune.

"Not much more than a hundred," replied Christian. "But we go up the mountain."

Good Fortune was astonished. "If that's so," he said, "we'll arrive in Urumchi at midday when nobody will expect us."

"Will our respected elder please look at those," said Big Tiger, pointing to the new telegraph poles which towered above the houses.

After leaving Fu-kan the cart track ran for a long stretch between large fields of reeds on one side and the foothills of the high mountain range on the other. It curved imperceptibly southward and equally imperceptibly climbed from the flat country of the marshlands to the height of Urumchi, which is really a valley between two mountain walls, each of them rising to nearly twenty thousand feet.

Like everything in that vast country, the town had a quality of openness. As soon as Good Fortune saw its outlying vegetable and melon gardens, he drove more slowly. His courage was ebbing, and he wished he could wait for Kao-Cheng. I shall go only as far as the first houses, he thought. But they lay back from the road behind irrigation canals, surrounded by trees and hedges. The trees were still leafless. One could only guess that the town lay beyond the veil of mist which hovered over an avenue that began suddenly and ended in an open, sunny square.

A crescent of strange low new buildings surrounded this square. They had unusually high gates, two of which stood wide open. When Good Fortune reached this square he saw that there was no way out. He couldn't understand why a military band should be standing there, the men wearing red and white feather rosettes on their caps, and why the worthy gentlemen who were waiting in rows should have such solemn faces. But then the big drum boomed three times like a roll of distant thunder, the bandmaster raised his baton, the trumpets blared, the kettledrums rumbled, the dignified gentlemen smiled and bowed, Good Fortune pulled the brake, and the poodle jumped down and barked. The state reception was in full swing.

At first Christian and Big Tiger did not know what to do. Then, as the music continued, they picked up courage and jumped out after the dog. Standing side by side in the square they raised their fists to their foreheads and bowed very low. The music ceased, the midday gun went bang, and Christian and Big Tiger said as loudly as they could: "This is too great an honor. We are unworthy boys."

Everyone could hear them. The bandmaster flung his arms in the air—the signal for a flourish of trumpets. A gentleman in a beautiful black silk robe and formal hat came forward, took Christian and Big Tiger by the hand and invited Good Fortune to get down. This gentleman, who, as they found out later, was a Minister of State, introduced Big Tiger and Christian to the others, including a stout jolly general with a moustache like the poodle. When the formal greetings were over the General took Christian and Big Tiger by the hair and shook them, saying they were proper young scamps and that he was their friend Wui-Hung-Wen.

At last the reception ended. Good Fortune drove the truck through one of the open gateways into the new garage. They all had a cleaning, for the private car of the Governor was waiting for them in the courtyard. The General was waiting too, and he pasted up the garage door with wide strips, wrote his name on them, and posted two guards in front of it.

"Tell me," he said to Christian and Big Tiger, "where did you get those magnificent clothes and the silver daggers?"

Christian and Big Tiger got red again, but Good Fortune said coolly: "They are a gift from their brother Dampignak."

Wui-Hung-Wen knit his brows and said nothing but sat down heavily beside the driver. His good humor was gone. "To the *yamen!*" he ordered the chauffeur.

Christian and Big Tiger, who were sitting with Good Fortune on the back seat, became very uneasy. Even the poodle seemed intimidated, and the journey through the town was anything but a joyride. The car drove slowly and the drive was long, for the Governor's *yamen* was outside the town in a square enclosed by high walls. It was more like a fortress than a government headquarters. Guards stood at the gateway and presented arms. In the courtyard, which was as big as an arena, the car drew up.

Wui-Hung-Wen jumped out and acted as guide. He walked through many corridors and passed many doors until he stopped in a pleasure garden which looked like that of a wealthy Peking house. Opening a door under the projecting roof, he invited them to enter. The room contained a round table and several low seats. But the remarkable thing was that there were two big shining glass windows through which they could look out on the garden. To the south it was open and merged into a park with a stream which formed an artificial waterfall that ran into a pond. The pond shimmered, a white camel-hump bridge led over it, and beautiful old trees towered over the distant red walls of the *yamen.*

"Please sit down," said Wui-Hung-Wen formally. Then he hurried off, but turned round at the door, raised his white-gloved right hand and let it drop again. "Oh, my poor friends," he said, and disappeared.

Good Fortune remained standing, completely dumfounded. Taking off his cap he threw it on the table. "I've made a pretty mess of things," he said. "We're in a bad fix. Only General Wu can save us."

Christian and Big Tiger could not understand the turn of events at all. Had not Dampignak said that the Marshal was his friend—had all this suddenly changed?

"Be big-hearted and forgive me," said Good Fortune. "I confess I have been guilty of thoughtless words."

"Don't mention it," said Big Tiger.

"I have a letter from Dampignak in my pocket," said Christian. "Even if our respected elder had said nothing, what the fat general has heard would have come out. It is just an undeserved misfortune."

"May heaven preserve us from the arm of the law," cried Good Fortune, horrified. "We must get rid of that letter! Give it to me and I'll swallow it."

"Thoughtless action brings evil," warned Big Tiger.

"No!" cried Good Fortune. "You don't know these people, and your grandfather doesn't know them either. Give me the letter. Quick!"

He had not finished speaking when there were loud footsteps outside and Christian drew his hand back from his breast pocket as General Wui-Hung-Wen opened the door and saluted. In the doorway stood a very calm, very erect old gentleman with a snow-white beard. He was dressed with the simplicity which in China is considered correct for scholars and statesmen and all men of dignity. He wore a plain gray *ishang** and a black silk jacket, and his bald head was covered with a round velvet skull cap. The eyes under the bushy white eyebrows looked searchingly and almost pityingly at Christian and Big Tiger, who raised their fists to their foreheads and bent the knee in salutation. Good Fortune *kowtowed*.

Yang replied with a slight bow. He tipped Christian and Big Tiger on the shoulder. "Sit down, children; you have done a great

* *Ishang:* A man's coat.

deal for me," he said. "And you too"—he turned to Good Fortune—"please sit down. I have to speak to you all."

All three said: "We do not dare," but Wui-Hung-Wen showed them to their seats with a grim face. As soon as the Marshal sat down the General seated himself beside him. Christian and Big Tiger looked down at their white-edged boots, but when the Marshal began to speak they looked up. He spoke in a low voice which sounded far away: "I wished to greet you joyfully, but to my sorrow I cannot do so. Do not grieve too much, my children; fate will run an uneven course. He who realizes this does not overvalue life nor despair about death. Your brother Dampignak has left the world."

Christian and Big Tiger were silent. They bent their heads and stared again at the tips of their boots. They struggled against tears and against the frightening silence of the beautiful white room. Suddenly a wild sigh broke forth from the depths of Wui-Hung-Wen's ample breast. All eyes turned on him. He was sitting motionless, staring into the garden and looking angry. But tears were rolling down his shaggy moustache and dropping on the gray trousers with the red stripe.

"The General knew and loved him," said Yang, by way of explanation. "Dampignak," he continued, seeking to distract attention from Wui-Hung-Wen, "must have been a man for whom neither right nor wrong existed. He was as indifferent to ignominy as to worldly honors. When first I took up office in Sinkiang I heard that he was just a murderer. I had nothing to do with him, for his bands operated in Mongolia and not in my territory. Some few years ago, however, he built a stronghold in the desert, and as it was not far from the frontiers of my province, I had to concern myself with him. I proceeded cautiously and he proceeded likewise with me. One day he asked for a mediator to be sent to him, and I sent General Wui-Hung-Wen. In less than half an hour the gentlemen had come to an agreement, and General Wui-Hung-

Wen came back with a report that he had met the wisest and most just of men."

"He was a man of his word," muttered the General. "There is no need to say more."

"Nobody denies it," admitted Yang, with a smile. "Dampignak wiped out all the robber bands which were operating as far as the Etzin Gol and farther. In return he levied a reasonable tribute on travelers. This had been agreed between us, and this was done, and we lived in mutual peace and understanding. Last winter, it is true, someone came and complained of Dampignak, but General Wui-Hung-Wen showed him the door.

"I advised beheading him at once," the General recalled, and blew his nose.

"Greencoat is dead," said Yang, "and as I know no more than that as yet, please give me your report."

"But it's a long story," warned Christian.

"Out with it," snapped Wui-Hung-Wen; "and don't skip any of it."

"If His Excellency permits," began Christian, "we shall tell everything."

Yang smiled, and Big Tiger and Christian began their story. Good Fortune was a little uneasy when they first came to speak of him and Greencoat. But he soon noticed there was no need, for Christian praised Good Fortune's honesty, and Big Tiger said he was a driver so capable that it would be difficult to find his equal anywhere. It was a good hour before they came to the end of their story, and Big Tiger had just said: "That is all, and more we do not know," when a great hubbub was heard in the hallway. Someone was shouting: "Let me through, you ass! I have to tell His Excellency how I liquidated the criminals. His Excellency is waiting impatiently for me. Be off, you greenhorn! Out of my way, you fool!"

Wui-Hung-Wen stood up eagerly.

"Let him in," said Yang, "and be nice to him. He has deserved it."

The General went out, and they could hear him saying: "What's all this row about? Who is disturbing the old chief's midday rest? Whoever it is will lose his head without delay. Ah, so it's you, Kao-Cheng? You should be ashamed of yourself, but I'll let you off once more if you keep absolutely quiet and don't speak another word."

"But my report?"

"You can make it to me. But now be silent if you value your life." He pushed Kao-Cheng in the door, and the newly promoted colonel threw himself on his knees, although he was not sure whether it was really the Marshal who was sitting before him.

"Stand up, Colonel," said Yang. "Here is your seat." Saying this, he drew a vacant chair to his left side. Kao-Cheng threw a triumphant glance at Wui-Hung-Wen, and murmuring a perfunctory "I am unworthy," sat down beaming on the seat of honor.

"Your Excellency . . ." he began, with a deep bow.

"So you insist?" interrupted Wui-Hung-Wen.

"Let the Colonel have his say, General," said Yang. "He wants to explain to me how to catch criminals."

"There are various ways of doing it," began Kao-Cheng, "but it can't be done in a melon garden. . . ."

"Friend," Wui-Hung-Wen interrupted him again, "you're inclined to be wordy. It will shorten proceedings if I put questions and you reply. I have but one question to put to you: Will you have tea with us?"

"It is too great an honor," murmured Kao-Cheng, taken aback.

But Wui-Hung-Wen clapped his hands and a servant dressed in sky-blue silk appeared with tea and a pile of confectionery, salted almonds, and red raspberry sweets.

"This is not a formal tea," explained Wui-Hung-Wen. "You have had a long journey, so you must really eat."

At first Big Tiger and Christian were rather timid, but Wui-

Hung-Wen would not tolerate this. He filled their plates, poured out more tea, and in between tried to stem Kao-Cheng's talk.

After a while the Marshal stood up. "Stay here," he said to Kao-Cheng and Good Fortune. "The General has something to say to you. But you two come into the garden with me."

He walked out calm and erect and Christian and Big Tiger followed him. As they stepped into the open they could hear Wui-Hung-Wen saying: "Come on, speak up! How many silver bars are there altogether, old redbeard?" They did not hear what Kao-Cheng replied, and as it was a state secret they did not want to know.

"Dog, stop there!" ordered Christian.

"Is he yours?" asked the Marshal.

"Yes, we got him as a present from Sevenstars," said Christian.

"He's different from other dogs," remarked Big Tiger.

"Let him come with us then," decided the Marshal.

They walked along together under the willows. "I have been waiting a long time for you," said Yang, "and when I got word from Hsing-hsing-hsia that Big Tiger and Compass Mountain were boys, I could hardly believe it. Now I see that General Wu could not have sent better messengers."

"We just chanced to cross his path," said Christian apologetically.

"We are unworthy of his confidence," said Big Tiger. "We arrived late."

"No need to mention that," said Yang. "What have you got to tell me?"

"We have a letter," Christian informed him. "Forgive us; it's a bit crushed." He took General Wu's letter out of his pocket and raised it to his forehead.

"He also gave us two words to pass on to you," Big Tiger recalled. "They are: 'Ask my elder brother Yang to think kindly of me.' "

Yang unfolded the letter carefully and his eyes flew over the contents. But one could not see whether the letter contained good or bad news. The Marshal's face remained unmoved. He looked down toward the willows by the water's edge but seemed to be looking past them.

"We have another letter too," said Christian timidly, and remembering Dampignak's words, he motioned to Big Tiger, and they both went down on their knees. "Our big brother Dampignak," said Christian softly, "bade us hand this letter on our knees to the aged and venerable Excellency."

This time Yang raised the letter to his forehead before opening it, and when he had read it, he said: "You have brought me news which would have been of some importance ten days ago. But times have changed since then, and it would be useless to be saddened by that."

He stuck the letters into the cuff of his *ishang,* and they walked back over the camel-hump bridge into the garden and past the room from which Wui-Hung-Wen's voice sounded. They could hear something about "magnificent deeds of heroism" and "reward," and Yang smiled. He walked a little faster, and beckoned Christian and Big Tiger to follow him.

Behind the buildings which surrounded the garden ran a covered passageway which led into a wider and more beautiful garden. In its center stood a high reception hall with a tiled roof resting on red pillars. On each side were bright rooms with glass windows.

Yang walked past the reception hall and into the second room. It contained a large rosewood table covered with stacks of papers and letters. Piles of books lay on a lacquered table at the side. Yang pointed to another table with low seats around it, and when Christian and Big Tiger, obeying his wish, sat down beside him, the Marshal took the letters out of his cuff.

"You have rendered excellent service as couriers," he said, "but fate was against you. General Wu-Pei-Fu offered me the vacant post of President of China. He knew that haste was necessary, but he dared not send this message by telegram. Therefore he merely announced your coming to me, and hoped you would arrive in time. But you arrived too late. Li-Yuan-Hung became President for a second term, because my consent did not arrive."

"We confess we are tardy messengers," said Big Tiger.

"We did not take the necessary precautions against car thieves," said Christian.

Yang shook his head. "That is not so," he said. "Accidents are nobody's fault. What seems good or bad to our eyes today may change to just the opposite tomorrow."

"But Dampignak?" asked Christian. "May we ask what happened to him?"

"Dampignak," replied Yang, "put two and two together when he intercepted the telegram announcing your coming. Perhaps," he continued smiling, "he tried to sound you out a bit?"

"Moonlight did," replied Christian.

"Indeed?" said Yang. "However, heaven decreed otherwise. Dampignak wished to proclaim himself King of all the Mongols south of the new frontiers. He assured me of his obedience and of his loyalty to the Chinese Republic, if I as President should consent to his plan. I would have done so," said Yang, "for he was a man of his word. But now his light has sunk into the depths of the earth, and we mourn him."

"How did it happen?" asked Big Tiger.

"Dampignak fell by the hand of a murderer," replied Yang. He went over to his desk and came back with a big book in which he turned several pages. When he had found what he was looking for he read: "On the thirteenth day of the third moon telegram from Hsing-hsing-hsia: 'Dampignak was shot three days ago by an expelled member of his band named Yuchi. Dampignak's organization is becoming disunited and is breaking up.'"

The Marshal looked up. He closed the book, and Christian said: "Permit me to ask if that . . ." But then he flushed and stopped, horrified at his forwardness. "I beg ten thousand times for pardon," he said, penitently.

"It's my diary," said Yang. "Is that what you wanted to know?"

"Pardon, Your Excellency," Big Tiger interjected. "You see, it's because my friend Compass Mountain also writes a diary."

"He does well," replied Yang. "In everything there is something worth noting. I began writing a diary when I came from the narrow life of Yunnan into the vastness of Sinkiang. At the end of the thirty-two volumes which you see here, I realized that the narrowness remained. It could not be escaped. I had merely exchanged one narrowness for another. For even the Middle Kingdom, between the four seas, is like a grain of rice in a barn."

Christian and Big Tiger gazed at the Marshal's diaries, which were all bound alike, and they thought of their names being in them. So they were down in the history of Sinkiang, and that was a very great honor.

"We should like to send your parents a telegram," said Yang.

"Please do," said Christian.

"It would be a comfort to our people," said Big Tiger.

Yang took a sheet of paper, wetted a brush with India ink, and wrote with a firm hand and without a moment's reflection: "Compass Mountain and Big Tiger arrived here in good health to my inexpressible joy. Leaving day after tomorrow. Arriving Peking end of month. Yang-Tseng-hsin, Marshal of China."

"I regret," said Yang, "that I can only keep you with me one day, but in consideration for your parents I must be content with that. Now take the telegram to the station. I shall give you a guide."

In the evening Christian wrote in his diary:

"Today is the fifteenth day of the third moon, and we are in Tihwa which is called Urumchi. The high snowy mountains are quite near and that is why it is colder here than elsewhere. But that doesn't matter much, as there's coal which costs nothing. People don't even have to crawl underground. They just take a wheelbarrow and pickaxe and have only to go out far enough, until they come to a place where they can hack out the coal. Then they carry home the lumps and it's nice and warm.

"Marshal Yang is called the Tupan here, and as he likes us he's sorry we can't stay longer. We are sad that our brother Dampignak is no longer alive, and Moonlight was right when he said a robber without patience is a bad fellow.

"We sent a telegram in the afternoon to say they needn't worry about us at home. We rode to the station on two ponies and the clerk pushed all the other telegrams aside when he saw the signature of the old Governor. 'This is a government telegram,' he said, 'so it will go very quickly and be in Peking in a few hours.' The clerk was very friendly and he asked sweet as sugar whether we were the young Excellencies, and Big Tiger replied that he saw two useless little urchins before him. So we left behind us a good reputation for modesty.

"Then we rode back to the *yamen* where we live in a room two doors from the Marshal's, and the light is still burning in his room because he also is a man who writes a diary. Good Fortune is with us today but tomorrow he's going to live where the new garages are, as he's been made chief inspector of all the Governor's automobiles. General Wui-Hung-Wen said it doesn't matter if Good Fortune doesn't go back to General Wu, because he'll write to General Wu explaining everything to him and telling him they need Good Fortune in Urumchi.

"Kao-Cheng has left, and twenty soldiers rode off with him. The Marshal ordered them to hurry back to the frontier, as no one knows what the robbers may be up to now that Dampignak is gone, and perhaps the caravan roads are no longer safe. Kao-Cheng has got a decoration because he's a soldier of the Marshal. He says one can see the province is well governed."

When Christian had written that much he sat down for a while with Big Tiger and Good Fortune outside the door under the projecting roof. The full moon was floating over the tall trees in the park, the noise of the town had died down, and nothing could be heard but the occasional barking of a dog. This made the poodle growl each time, but Christian stroked his thick head saying: "Dog, be quiet! The Tupan is writing his diary."

"Last full moon we were at the Etzin Gol," said Big Tiger thoughtfully.

Good Fortune sighed. "It's the same always and everywhere," he said. "As soon as a man is happy and contented somewhere, he hears, 'You must go.' "

"Affliction said that," Big Tiger recalled.

"But he also said," continued Christian bravely, "that we'd never be finished weeping if we cried at every little parting."

"But we're not weeping," snapped Good Fortune, wiping his eyes.

They went back to the room and all had a long night's sleep. When Christian and Big Tiger woke up the sun was shining, but the place beside them on the *kang* was empty. Good Fortune had slipped away at dawn.

52 A CHAPTER IN WHICH THE OLD GRANDFATHER HAS THE LAST WORD

"TODAY is the sixteenth day of the third moon, and we woke up sad because Good Fortune had gone. For who can help being sad if you always have to say good-by to friends and don't know if you will ever see them again. Big Tiger and I sat on the *kang* and cried a bit because we were alone, and you may cry when you're alone. We really didn't want any breakfast, but a servant dressed in blue silk came and led us into the Marshal's room. He was sitting there with Wui-Hung-Wen, and they were waiting for us to drink tea with them and eat fritters and chestnuts and sweet yam roots and other things we didn't know. There were also pigeons' eggs.

"After that we went into the town to buy things to take home. We found a candy shop where they make everything you want quick as lightning out of sugar syrup, and you look on while they're making it. I ordered a fan for mother, a pipe for father, a doll for my little sister, and the three wise apes for the amah. Big Tiger bought the Yellow Emperor for his grandfather, and the candymaker made them all and said we had made a good choice.

"There was a big crowd gathered in the bazaar and there was music. Then a man began to sing; he said first that his song was quite new and had never been heard before, and it was called 'The Song of the Brave Colonel Kao-Cheng.' So we listened and heard how to catch criminals and that it can't be done in a melon garden but in a valley where the rocks fall down and an immense treasure of silver lies hidden in a cave until Kao-Cheng found it. And he had got promoted for that and had got a decoration besides for rescuing two helpless little boys. We went away quickly as we didn't want to cause excitement or get congratulations on being rescued.

"The main street of Urumchi is like a canal. When the children run across it they try whether the mud goes only up to their knees or up to their waists. They do it barefoot and pull up their pants. It's a lovely game but it can only be played in the spring when it's very hot in the daytime. The snow melts in the mountains and the water runs down everywhere and into the main street too, and the horses trample it into mud. In the summer the street is dry again and the children have to think up another game.

"In the afternoon we visited Good Fortune. He has noticed already that the Governor's cars are not well kept. The people who have charge of them haven't had as thorough a training as Good Fortune. He's going to call for us early in the morning and we have to be up before dawn. We know by now that when Good Fortune says tomorrow morning he means shortly after midnight. Then we drive for two days to the Russian frontier. There's to be a farewell party this evening in the big reception hall near the Marshal's room and all the gentlemen who were at the reception when we arrived are to be there."

"Why didn't you go on writing your diary?" asked Christian's father, as he sat with the diary open before him on his knees.

"Because nothing more happened," said Christian. "We just went on and on traveling by car and truck, and by steamer on the Irtish, but we were alone all the time because the people talked in Russian and we had no acquaintances."

"It's just when nothing is happening that you should write a diary," said his father. "The Marshal does that too. Now you've begun you shouldn't stop at once."

So Christian wrote on the last page of his notebook:

"Yesterday evening we arrived in Peking. There was a new moon. Father and mother were at the station and the amah was there too with my sister in the baby carriage. The amah hadn't been so frightfully frightened as I had always imagined she was, because General Wu came at once when he conquered Peking and he told her not to be a bit afraid and that nothing would happen to us. Big Tiger's father and mother came too, and also his grandfather, and all his uncles and aunts and cousins were standing behind the barrier. That was because we had sent a telegram from Mukden. We were all terribly excited. Mother cried and so did the amah. The poodle barked and people were frightened and asked if he was really a dog. Now he's sleeping on a mat which has been put under the roof specially for him, and tomorrow we're going for a walk with him as we want to find a place to practice stone-throwing. I know a place already under the wall at the Ha-ta-men Gate where the soldiers practicc their brass instruments, but they're not there in the afternoon and we can throw stones then. There are flags out in the streets because we have a new President, but his name isn't Yang-Tseng-hsin. That's a pity because if it was Yang we could visit him often, and General Wui-Hung-Wen too. I have laid out an exhibition on my bookshelf. The silver bars from the Black City are at one side, and the King of the Sunits' silver eating bowl on the other side, and the dagger of my brother Dampignak lies in the middle on the *haddak* which he gave me. I am wearing Thunderbolt's ring on my thumb, because Thunderbolt is also a brother of mine and I hope he's still alive. We're going to buy notepaper tomorrow and then we'll write a long letter to Bator and Sevenstars. Perhaps I shall also buy a new diary.

"Big Tiger's grandfather is an old man and I wish I had a grandfather too because he patted our heads and said it was a good thing for boys to start being brave and enterprising in their early years. Big Tiger and I think he's right there."